BEST
SHORT
NOVELS
2005

Edited by
Jonathan Strahan

SCIENCE
FICTION

For Stephen, fellow adventurer, brother, best friend,
who was there when I spoke my first words,
and hopefully will be there when I say my last.

Each year the list grows longer. Any book like this one is as much the product of a small community of friends, family, and colleagues as it is the work of one person. This year I'd particularly like to thank: my new agent, Howard Morhaim, who made it abundantly clear why I need him and has quickly become indispensable; my editor, Andrew Wheeler, who has been generous and supportive well above and beyond the call; Bill Schafer of Subterranean Press and Marty Halpern and Gary Turner of Golden Gryphon Press, who were kind, gracious, and generous when they didn't have to be; Justin Ackroyd, who was instrumental in making sure one story made the final book and who has been a constant supporter of my work and this anthology series; Jack Dann, anthology guru, pal, and confidante; and my *Locus* colleagues Nick Gevers and Rich Horton, who have always been there to discuss the best short fiction of the year when I needed it most. Thanks also to the following good friends and colleagues without whom this book would have been much poorer, and much less fun to do: Lou Anders, Simon Brown, Pete Crowther, Ellen Datlow, Terry Dowling, Gardner Dozois, David Hartwell, Jay Lake, Deborah Layne, Kelly Link, Gavin Grant, Sean Wallace, Sean Williams, the various posters to the Night Shade Message Boards, and all of the book's contributors.

And, last but not least, the big ones. Extra special thanks to my three angels, Marianne, Jessica, and Sophie (aka Christy), who make every day an adventure and fill it with joy, and to Charles, friend, mentor, and inspiration, who has given me so much.

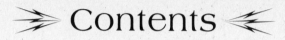 Contents

Introduction

by Jonathan Strahan

When I sat down to work on the first book in the *Best Short Novels* series in November of 2003 it was in the belief that we are in the middle of a second great Golden Age in short genre fiction, a Golden Age that is producing an extraordinary crop of longer stories. It seemed to me then, and still does now, that it would be a valuable service to readers to gather the best of those stories in a continuing series of books. It was something that had been attempted unsuccessfully before (Terry Carr edited two excellent volumes of the *The Best Science Fiction Novellas of the Year* in 1979 and 1980), but given more space—Carr was restricted to just four or five stories—I was confident it could work, and work well. That confidence was borne out by the very generous response of readers and critics to *Best Short Novels: 2004*, which in turn has led to the book you now hold in your hands.

Before we go too much further, though, it might be useful to clarify what I mean by a "short novel" and what kind of stories I've looked to gather here. While the good folk at the Science Fiction and Fantasy Writers of America define a novella as being a work of fiction between 17,500 and 40,000 words in length, I've taken a somewhat more relaxed approach, considering stories that are over 15,000 words to be short novels. Why? The novella, originally defined as a "short narrative tale, especially a popular story having a moral or satirical point," or as "a small new thing" when translated from the Italian, should give a writer enough room to build a world, create believable characters, and examine a single idea in some depth. As long as a writer did those things, I didn't really want to quibble over word count. I also felt that it would be a better service to you, the reader, to bring together the best stories I could find, rather than worry too much about the details of definition. And what kind of stories? Well, I was looking for new, challenging, and interesting science fiction and fantasy that would entertain, provoke, and reward. I think the ten stories in this year's book do all of those things, and more.

As I mentioned last year, short novels are being published in ever increasing numbers, and in an ever increasing variety of places. The trade journal *Locus* estimated that somewhere in the vicinity of 2,130 new short genre stories were published during 2004. By even a conservative estimate, that's well over ten million words of new fiction, a veritable tsunami of novellas, novelettes, and short stories. More than any single reader could hope to read, and more than any single reader would likely have time to find. Those stories appeared in anthologies, collections, magazines, and chapbooks, on websites and in webzines, on just about any sliver of paper or screen you could imagine. They were, literally, everywhere. And a lot of those stories were short novels, and they were good.

The best and most reliable place to find short novels remains the four major genre magazines, *Asimov's, Fantasy & Science Fiction, Analog,* and *SciFiction. SciFiction,* under the astute editorship of Ellen Datlow, had an extraordinary year in 2004, publishing a string of outstanding stories, including short novels by Paul Witcover, Severna Park, and Suzy McKee Charnas. The best, though, was the collaboration between Gardner Dozois, George R. R. Martin, and Daniel Abrahams that appears here. *Asimov's,* in its last year under long-time editor Gardner Dozois, had a good year, publishing nine novellas, four of which I'm reprinting here. In addition to those fine stories by Gregory Feeley, Ian McDowell, James Patrick Kelly, and Judith Berman, *Asimov's* published good long works by Charles Stross, R. Garcia y Robertson, and Allen Steele. *F&SF* also had a very good year, publishing five novellas and a number of other excellent longer stories. In addition to the powerful story by Bradley Denton reprinted here (one of my personal favourites of 2004), *F&SF* published excellent long work by Matthew Jarpe and Jonathan Andrew Sheen, Alex Irvine, and others. The longest-running and, arguably, most traditional magazine in the field, *Analog*, seemed to me to have a pretty good year, publishing five novellas, easily the best of which was Michael Flynn's "The Clapping Hands of God," which was a very strong contender for this book.

Those stories, though, only represent the tip of the iceberg. A welcome trend in recent years has been the proliferation of novella-length chapbooks, mostly from the small presses. The most productive of these presses, and one of the best, is Peter Crowther's U.K.-based PS Publishing, which published four such chapbooks by Paul Park, Lisa Tuttle, Gary Greenwood, and Stephen Baxter. The Baxter tale, *Mayflower II*, is a fine generation-ship story set in his Xeelee universe that stands amongst his best work and is reprinted here. Established North American small presses Golden Gryphon and Subterranean Press both published solid stories, Robert Reed's *Mere* and Caitlin Kiernan's *The Dry Salvages* respectively, while newcomer Aqueduct produced an interesting piece, Nancy Jane Moore's *Changeling*. A handful of short novels also appeared as original stories in short story collections. The best of these, Charles Stross's "The Concrete Jungle," appeared in his short collection *The Atrocity Archives* from Golden Gryphon, but I was also impressed by Adam Roberts' Swiftian "Eleanor," the alternate America of Jay Lake's "Our Lady of American Sorrows," Kage Baker's "Company" yarn "Mother Aegypt" and L. Timmel Duchamp's alternate history, "The Héloïse Archive."

Finally, anthologies. The best single anthology for science fiction novellas, and a contender for the best original SF anthology of the year, was Robert Silverberg's impressive *Between Worlds*, which featured strong stories by James Patrick Kelly, Stephen Baxter, Nancy Kress, Walter Jon Williams, and others. Other anthologies featured the occasional strong short novel: Eleanor Arnason's "The Garden" was the highlight of *Synergy SF*, Patricia McKillip's "The Gorgon in the Cupboard" was best in the romantic fantasy anthology *To Weave a Web of Magic*, and Gregory

Feeley's "Gilead" in *The First Heroes* and Gene Wolfe's *"Golden City Far"* in Al Sarrantonio's *Flights* also deserve to stand amongst the best short novels of the year.

All of which brings us to the end of a possibly too brief roundup of the year in short novels. If I could have squeezed another story or two in here I might have added James Patrick Kelly's "The Wreck of the *Godspeed*," L. Timmel Duchamp's "The Héloïse Archive," Gregory Feeley's "Gilead," and maybe Gene Wolfe's "Golden City Far." But, as large as this book is, no book is infinite, so let those stand as something for the intrepid reader to seek out later. For the moment, I'd like to close by sincerely thanking the Science Fiction Book Club for its confidence in this series and this book, and by thanking you, the reader, for your support as well. I hope you enjoy reading this book as much as I enjoyed assembling it, and that we get to meet again next year to resume our journey.

Jonathan Strahan
February 2005
Perth, Western Australia

BEST
SHORT
NOVELS
2005

MEN ARE TROUBLE

by James Patrick Kelly

James Patrick Kelly graduated from Notre Dame in 1972 and has been a full-time writer since 1977. He attended Clarion in 1974 and 1976, and his first story, "Death Therapy," appeared in 1978. He has published four novels, Planet of Whispers, Freedom Beach *(with John Kessel),* Look into the Sun, *and* Wildlife, *but is best known for his more than fifty published short stories, which have been collected in* Heroines, Think Like a Dinosaur *and* Strange But Not a Stranger, *and include classics like "Mr. Boy," "Think Like a Dinosaur," "Itsy Bitsy Spider," "10^{16} to 1," and "Undone."*

Kelly has won the Hugo Award twice, the Locus Award, and has been nominated for the Nebula Award eight times. He lives in New Hampshire with his wife and children, is chairman of the New Hampshire Council on the Arts, and writes a regular column for Asimov's Science Fiction.

1

I STARED AT my sidekick, willing it to chirp. I'd already tried watching the door, but no one had even breathed on it. I could've been writing up the Rashmi Jones case, but then I could've been dusting the office. It needed dusting. Or having a consult with Johnnie Walker, who had just that morning opened an office in the bottom drawer of my desk. Instead, I decided to open the window. Maybe a new case would arrive by carrier pigeon. Or wrapped around a brick.

Three stories below me, Market Street was as empty as the rest of the city. Just a couple of plain janes in walking shoes and a granny in a blanket and sandals. She was sitting on the curb in front of a dead Starbucks, strumming street guitar for pocket change, hoping to find a philanthropist in hell. Her singing was faint but sweet as peach ice cream. *My guy, talking 'bout my guy.* Poor old bitch, I thought. There are no guys—not yours, not anyone's. She stopped singing as a devil flapped over us, swooping for a landing on the next block. It had been a beautiful June morning until then, the moist promise of spring not yet broken by summer in our withered city. The granny struggled up, leaning on her guitar. She wrapped the blanket tight around her and trudged downtown.

My sidekick did chirp then, but it was Sharifa, my about-to-be ex-lover. She must have been calling from the hospital; she was wearing her light blue scrubs. Even on the little screen, I could see that she had been crying. "Hi Fay."

I bit my lip.

"Come home tonight," she said. "Please."

"I don't know where home is."

"I'm sorry about what I said." She folded her arms tight across her chest. "It's your body. Your life."

I loved her. I was sick about being seeded, the abortion, everything that had happened between us in the last week. I said nothing.

Her voice was sandpaper on glass. "Have you had it done yet?" That made me angry all over again. She was wound so tight she couldn't even say the word.

"Let me guess, Doctor," I said, "Are we talking about me getting scrubbed?"

Her face twisted. "Don't."

"If you want the dirt," I said, "you could always hire me to shadow myself. I need the work."

"Make it a joke, why don't you?"

"Okey-doke, Doc," I said and clicked off.

So my life was cocked—not exactly main menu news. Still, even with the window open, Sharifa's call had sucked all the air out of my office. I told myself that all I needed was coffee, although what I really wanted was a rich aunt, a vacation in Fiji and a new girlfriend. I locked the door behind me, slogged down the hall and was about to press the down button when the elevator chimed. The doors slid open to reveal George, the bot in charge of our building, and a devil—no doubt the same one that had just flown by. I told myself this probably had nothing to do with me. I told myself that the devil was seeing crazy Martha down the hall about a tax rebate or taking piano lessons from Abby upstairs. Sure, and drunks go to bars for the peanuts.

"Hello, Fay," said George. "This one had true hopes of finding you in your office."

I goggled, slack-jawed and stupefied, at the devil. Of course, I'd seen them on vids and in the sky and once I watched one waddle into City Hall but I'd never been close enough to slap one before. I hated the devils. The elevator doors shivered and began to close. George stuck an arm out to stop them.

"May this one borrow some of your time?" George said.

The devil was just over a meter tall. Its face was the color of an old bloodstain and its maw seemed to kiss the air as it breathed with a wet, sucking sound. The wings were wrapped tight around it; the membranes had a rusty translucence that only hinted at the sleek bullet of a body beneath. I could see my reflection in its flat compound eyes. I looked like I had just been hit in the head with a lighthouse.

"Something is regrettable, Fay?" said George.

That was my cue for a wisecrack to show them that no invincible mass-murdering alien was going to intimidate Fay Hardaway.

"No," I said. "This way."

If they could've sat in chairs, there would've been plenty of room for us in my office. But George announced that the devil needed to make itself comfortable before we began. I nodded as I settled behind my desk, grateful to have something between the two of them and me. George dragged both chairs out into the little reception room. The devil spread its wings and swooped up onto my file cabinet, ruffling the hardcopy on my desk. It filled the back wall of my office as it perched there, a span of almost twenty feet. George wedged himself into a corner and absorbed his legs and arms until he was just a head and a slab of gleaming blue bot stuff. The devil gazed at me as if it were wondering what kind of rug I would make. I brought up three new icons on my desktop. *New Case. Searchlet. Panic button.*

"Indulge this one to speak for Seeren?" said George. "Seeren has a bright desire to task you to an investigation."

The devils never spoke to us, never explained what they were doing. No one knew exactly how they communicated with the army of bots they had built to prop us up.

I opened the *New Case* folder and the green light blinked. "I'm recording this. If I decide to accept your case, I will record my entire investigation."

"A thoughtful gesture, Fay. This one needs to remark on your client Rashmi Jones."

"She's not my client." It took everything I had not to fall off my chair. "What about her?"

"Seeren conveys vast regret. All deaths diminish all."

I didn't like it that this devil knew anything at all about Rashmi, but especially that she was dead. I'd found the body in Room 103 of the Comfort Inn just twelve hours ago. "The cops already have the case." I didn't mind that there was a snarl in my voice. "Or what's left of it. There's nothing I can do for you."

"A permission, Fay?"

The icon was already flashing on my desktop. I opened it and saw a pix of Rashmi in the sleeveless taupe dress that she had died in. She had the blue ribbon in her hair. She was smiling, as carefree as a kid on the last day of school. The last thing she was thinking about was sucking on an inhaler filled with hydrogen cyanide. Holding her hand was some brunette dressed in a mannish chalk-stripe suit and a matching pillbox hat with a veil as fine as smoke. The couple preened under a garden arch that dripped with pink roses. They faced left, in the direction of the hand of some third party standing just off camera. It was an elegant hand, a hand that had never been in dishwater or changed a diaper. There was a wide silver ring on the fourth finger, engraved with a pattern or maybe some kind of fancy writing. I zoomed on the ring and briefly tormented pixels but couldn't get the pattern resolved.

I looked up at the devil and then at George. "So?"

"This one notices especially the digimark," said George. "Date-stamped June 12, 2:52."

"You're saying it was taken yesterday afternoon?"

That didn't fit—except that it did. I had Rashmi downtown shopping for shoes late yesterday morning. At 11:46 she bought a thirteen-dollar pair of this season's Donya Durands and they were missing. At 1:23 she charged eighty-nine cents for a Waldorf salad and an iced tea at Maison Diana. She checked into the Comfort Inn at 6:40. She didn't have a reservation, so maybe this was a spur of the moment decision. The desk clerk remembered her as distraught. That was the word she used. A precise word, although a bit highbrow for the Comfort Inn. Who buys expensive shoes the day before she intends to kill herself? Somebody who is distraught. I glanced again at my desktop. Distraught was precisely what Rashmi Jones was not in this pix. Then I noticed the shoes: ice and taupe Donya Durands.

"Where did you get this?" I said to the devil.

It stared through me like I was a dirty window.

I tried the bot. I wouldn't say that I liked George exactly, but he'd always been straight with me. "What's this about, George? Finding the tommy?"

"The tommy?"

"The woman holding Rashmi's hand."

"Seeren has made this one well aware of Kate Vermeil," said George. "Such Kate Vermeil takes work at 44 East Washington Avenue and takes home at 465 12th Avenue, Second Floor Left."

I liked that, I liked it a lot. Rashmi's mom had told me that her daughter had a Christer friend called Kate, but I didn't even have a last name, much less an address. I turned to the devil again. "You know this how?"

All that got me was another empty stare.

"Seeren," I said, pushing back out of my chair, "I'm afraid George has led you astray. I'm the private investigator." I stood to show them out. "The mind reader's office is across the street."

This time George didn't ask permission. My desktop chirped. I waved open a new icon. A certified bank transfer in the amount of a thousand dollars dragged me back onto my chair.

"A cordial inducement," said George. "With a like amount offered after the success of your investigation."

I thought of a thousand dinners in restaurants with linen tablecloths. "Tell me already." A thousand bottles of smoky scotch.

"This one draws attention to the hand of the unseen person," said the bot. "Seeren has the brightest desire to meeting such person for fruitful business discussions."

The job smelled like the dumpster at Fran's Fish Fry. Precious little money changed hands in the pretend economy. The bots kept everything running, but they did nothing to create wealth. That was supposed to be up to us, I guess, only we'd been kind of discouraged. In some parts of town, that kind of change could hire a Felony 1, with a handful of Misdemeanors thrown in for good luck.

"That's more than I'm worth," I said. "A hundred times more. If Seeren expects me to break the arm attached to that hand, it's talking to the wrong jane."

"Violence is to be deplored," said George. "However, Seeren tasks Fay to discretion throughout. Never police, never news, never even rumor if possible."

"Oh, discretion." I accepted the transfer. "For two large, I can be as discreet as the Queen's butler."

2

I could've taken a cab, but they're almost all driven by bots now, and bots keep nobody's secrets. Besides, even though I had a thousand dollars in the bank, I thought I'd let it settle in for a while. Make itself at home. So I bicycled over to 12th Avenue. I started having doubts as I hit the 400 block. This part of the city had been kicked in the head and left bleeding on the sidewalk. Dark bars leaned against pawnshops. Board-ups turned their blank plywood faces to the street. There would be more bots than women in this neighborhood and more rats than bots.

The Adagio Spa squatted at 465 12th Avenue. It was a brick building with a reinforced luxar display window that was so scratched it looked like a thin slice of rainstorm. There were dusty plants behind it. The second-floor windows were bricked over. I chained my bike to a dead car, set my sidekick to record and went in.

The rear wall of the little reception area was bright with pix of some Mediterranean seaside town. A clump of bad pixels made the empty beach flicker. A bot stepped through the door that led to the spa and took up a position at the front desk. "Good afternoon, Madam," he said. "It's most gratifying to welcome you. This one is called . . ."

"I'm looking for Kate Vermeil." I don't waste time on chitchat with bots. "Is she in?"

"It's regrettable that she no longer takes work here."

"She worked here?" I said. "I was told she lived here."

"You was told wrong." A granny filled the door, and then hobbled through, leaning on a metal cane. She was wearing a yellow flowered dress that was not quite as big as a circus tent and over it a blue smock with *Noreen* embroidered over the left breast. Her face was wide and pale as a hardboiled egg, her hair a ferment of tight gray curls. She had the biggest hands I had ever seen. "I'll take care of this, Barry. Go see to Helen Ritzi. She gets another needle at twelve, then turn down the heat to 101."

The bot bowed politely and left us.

"What's this about then?" The cane wobbled and she put a hand on the desk to steady herself.

I dug the sidekick out of my slacks, opened the PI license folder and showed it to her. She read it slowly, sniffed and handed it back. "Young fluffs working at play jobs. Do something useful, why don't you?"

"Like what," I said. "Giving perms? Face peels?"

She was the woman of steel; sarcasm bounced off her. "If nobody does a real job, pretty soon the damn bots will replace us all."

"Might be an improvement." It was something to say, but as soon as I said it I wished I hadn't. My generation was doing better than the grannies ever had. Maybe someday our kids wouldn't need bots to survive.

Our kids. I swallowed a mouthful of ashes and called the pix Seeren had given me onto the sidekick's screen. "I'm looking for Kate Vermeil." I aimed it at her.

She peered at the pix and then at me. "You need a manicure."

"The hell I do."

"I work for a living, fluff. And my hip hurts if I stand up too long." She pointed her cane at the doorway behind the desk. "What did you say your name was?"

The battered manicure table was in an alcove decorated with fake grapevines that didn't quite hide the water stains in the drop ceiling. Dust covered the leaves, turning the plastic fruit from purple to gray.

Noreen rubbed a thumb over the tips of my fingers. "You bite your nails, or do you just cut them with a chainsaw?"

She wanted a laugh so I gave her one.

"So, nails square, round or oval?" Her skin was dry and mottled with liver spots.

"Haven't a clue." I shrugged. "This was your idea."

Noreen perched on an adjustable stool that was cranked low so that her face was only a foot above my hands. There were a stack of stainless steel bowls, a jar of Vaseline, a round box of salt, a bowl filled with packets of sugar stolen from McDonald's and a liquid soap dispenser on the table beside her. She started filing each nail from the corner to the center, going from left to right and then back. At first she worked in silence. I decided not to push her.

"Kate was my masseuse up until last week," she said finally. "Gave her notice all of a sudden and left me in the lurch. I've had to pick up all her appointments and me with the bum hip. Some days I can't hardly get out of bed. Something happen to her?"

"Not as far as I know."

"But she's missing."

I shook my head. "I don't know where she is, but that doesn't mean she's missing."

Noreen poured hot water from an electric kettle into one of the stainless steel bowls, added cool water from a pitcher, squirted soap and swirled the mixture around. "You soak for five minutes." She gestured for me to dip my hands into the bowl. "I'll be back. I got to make sure that Barry doesn't burn Helen Ritzi's face off." She stood with a grunt.

"Wait," I said. "Did she say why she was quitting?"

Noreen reached for her cane. "Couldn't stop talking about it. You'd think she was the first ever."

"The first to what?"

The granny laughed. "You're one hell of a detective, fluff. She was supposed to get married yesterday. Tell me that pix you're flashing ain't her doing the deed."

She shuffled off, her white nursemate shoes scuffing against dirty linoleum. From deeper in the spa, I heard her kettle drum voice and then the bot's snare. I was itching to take my sidekick out of my pocket, but I kept my hands in the soak. Besides, I'd looked at the pix enough times to know that she was right. A wedding. The hand with the ring would probably belong to a Christer priest. There would have been a witness and then the photographer, although maybe the photographer was the witness. Of course, I had tumbled to none of this in the two days I'd worked Rashmi Jones's disappearance. I was one hell of a detective, all right. And Rashmi's mom must not have known either. It didn't make sense that she would hire me to find her daughter and hold something like that back.

"I swear," said Noreen, leaning heavily on the cane as she creaked back to me, "that bot is scary. I sent down to City Hall for it just last week and already it knows my business left, right, up and down. The thing is, if they're so smart, how come they talk funny?"

"The devils designed them to drive us crazy."

"They didn't need no bots to do that, fluff."

She settled back onto her stool, tore open five sugar packets and emptied their contents onto her palm. Then she reached for the salt box and poured salt onto the sugar. She squirted soap onto the pile and then rubbed her hands together. "I could buy some fancy exfoliating cream but this works just as good." She pointed with her chin at my hands. "Give them a shake and bring them here."

I wanted to ask her about Kate's marriage plans, but when she took my hands in hers, I forgot the question. I'd never felt anything quite like it; the irritating scratch of the grit was offset by the sensual slide of our soapy fingers. Pleasure with just the right touch of pain—something I'd certainly be telling Sharifa about, if Sharifa and I were talking. My hands tingled for almost an hour afterward.

Noreen poured another bowl of water and I rinsed. "Why would getting married make Kate want to quit?" I asked.

"I don't know. Something to do with her church?" Noreen patted me dry with a threadbare towel. "She went over to the Christers last year. Maybe Jesus don't like married women giving backrubs. Or maybe she got seeded." She gave a bitter laugh. "Everybody does eventually."

I let that pass. "Tell me about Kate. What was she like to work with?"

"Average for the kind of help you get these sorry days." Noreen pushed at my cuticles with an orangewood stick. "Showed up on time mostly; I could only afford to bring her in two days a week. No go-getter, but she could follow directions. Problem was she never really got close to the customers, always acting like this was just a pitstop. Kept to herself mostly, which was how I could tell she was excited about getting married. It wasn't like her to babble."

"And the bride?"

"Some Indian fluff—Rashy or something."

"Rashmi Jones."

She nodded. "Her I never met."

"Did she go to school?"

"Must have done high school, but damned if I know where. Didn't make much of an impression, I'd say. College, no way." She opened a drawer where a flock of colored vials was nesting. "You want polish or clear coat on the nails?"

"No color. It's bad for business."

She leered at me. "Business is good?"

"You say she did massage for you?" I said. "Where did she pick that up?"

"Hold still now." Noreen uncapped the vial; the milky liquid that clung to the brush smelled like super glue's evil twin. "This is fast dry." She painted the stuff onto my nails with short, confident strokes. "Kate claimed her mom taught her. Said she used to work at the health club at the Radisson before it closed down."

"Did the mom have a name?"

"Yeah." Noreen chewed her lower lip as she worked. "Mom. Give the other hand."

I extended my arm. "So if Kate didn't live here, where did she live?"

"Someplace. Was on her application." She kept her head down until she'd finished. "You're done. Wave them around a little—that's it."

After a moment, I let my arms drop to my side. We stared at each other. Then Noreen heaved herself off the stool and led me back out to the reception room.

"That'll be eighty cents for the manicure, fluff." She waved her desktop on. "You planning on leaving a tip?"

I pulled out the sidekick and beamed two dollars at the desk. Noreen opened the payment icon, grunted her approval and then opened another folder. "Says here she lives at 44 East Washington Avenue."

I groaned.

"Something wrong?"

"I already have that address."

"Got her call too? Kate@Washington.03284."

"No, that's good. Thanks." I went to the door and paused. I don't know why I needed to say anything else to her, but I did. "I help people, Noreen. Or at least I try. It's a real job, something bots can't do."

She just stood there, kneading the bad hip with a big, dry hand.

I unchained my bike, pedaled around the block and then pulled over. I read Kate Vermeil's call into my sidekick. Her sidekick picked up on the sixth chirp. There was no pix.

"You haven't reached Kate yet, but your luck might change if you leave a message at the beep." She put on the kind of low, smoky voice that doesn't come out to play until dark. It was a nice act.

"Hi Kate," I said. "My name is Fay Hardaway and I'm a friend of Rashmi Jones. She asked me to give you a message about yesterday so please give me a call at Fay@Market.03284." I wasn't really expecting her to respond, but it didn't hurt to try.

I was on my way to 44 East Washington Avenue when my sidekick chirped in the pocket of my slacks. I picked up. Rashmi Jones's mom, Najma, stared at me from the screen with eyes as deep as wells.

"The police came," she said. "They said you were supposed to notify them first. They want to speak to you again."

They would. So I'd called the law after I called the mom—they'd get over it. You don't tell a mother that her daughter is dead and then ask her to act surprised when the cops come knocking. "I was working for you, not them."

"I want to see you."

"I understand."

"I hired you to find my daughter."

"I did," I said. "Twice." I was sorry as soon as I said it.

She glanced away; I could hear squeaky voices in the background. "I want to know everything," she said. "I want to know how close you came."

"I've started a report. Let me finish it and I'll bring it by later . . ."

"Now," she said. "I'm at school. My lunch starts at eleven-fifty and I have recess duty at twelve-fifteen." She clicked off.

I had nothing to feel guilty about, so why was I tempted to wriggle down a storm drain and find the deepest sewer in town? Because a mom believed that I hadn't worked fast enough or smart enough to save her daughter? Someone needed to remind these people that I didn't fix lost things, I just found them. But that someone wouldn't be me. My play now was simply to stroll into her school and let her beat me about the head with her grief. I could take it. I ate old Bogart movies for breakfast and spit out bullets. And at the end of this cocked day, I could just forget about Najma Jones, because there would be no Sharifa reminding me how it cost me to do my job. I took out my sidekick, linked to my desktop and downloaded everything I had in the Jones file. Then I swung back onto my bike.

The mom had left a message three days ago, asking that I come out to her place on Ashbury. She and her daughter rattled around in an old Victorian with gingerbread gables and a front porch the size of Cuba. The place had been in the family for four generations. Theirs had been a big family—once. The mom said that Rashmi hadn't come home the previous night. She hadn't called and didn't answer messages. The mom had contacted the cops, but they weren't all that interested. Not enough time would have passed for them. Too much time had passed for the mom.

The mom taught fifth grade at Reagan Elementary. Rashmi was a twenty-six-year-old grad student, six credits away from an MFA in Creative Writing. The mom trusted her to draw money from the family account, so at first I thought I might be able to find her by chasing debits. But there was no activity in the account we could attribute to the missing girl. When I suggested that she might be hiding out with friends, the mom went prickly on me. Turned out that Rashmi's choice of friends was a cause of contention between them. Rashmi had dropped her old pals in the last few months and taken up with a new, religious crowd. Gratiana and Elaine and Kate—the mom didn't know their last names—were members of the Church of Christ the Man. I'd had trouble with Christers before and wasn't all that eager to go up against them again, so instead I biked over to campus to see Rashmi's advisor. Zelda Manotti was a dithering old granny who would have loved to help except she had all the focus of paint spatter. She did let me copy Rashmi's novel-in-progress. And she did let me tag along to her advanced writing seminar, in case Rashmi showed up for it. She didn't. I talked to the three other students after class, but they either didn't know where she was or wouldn't say. None of them was Gratiana, Alix or Elaine.

That night I skimmed *The Lost Heart*, Rashmi's novel. It was a nostalgic and sentimental weeper set back before the devils disappeared all the men. Young Brigit Bird was searching for her father, a famous architect who had been kidnapped by Colombian drug lords. If I was just a fluff doing a fantasy job in the pretend economy, then old Noreen would have crowned Rashmi Jones queen of fluffs.

I started day two back at the Joneses' home. The mom watched as I went through Rashmi's room. I think she was as worried about what I might find as she was that I would find nothing. Rashmi listened to the Creeps, had three different pairs of Kat sandals, owned everything Denise Pepper had ever written, preferred underwire bras and subscribed to *News for the Confused.* She had kicked about a week's worth of dirty clothes under her bed. Her wallpaper mix cycled through koalas, the World's Greatest Beaches, ruined castles and Playgirl Centerfolds 2000–2010. She'd kept a handwritten diary starting in the sixth grade and ending in the eighth in which she often complained that her mother was strict and that school was boring. The only thing I found that rattled the mom was a Christer Bible tucked into the back of the bottom drawer of the nightstand. When I pulled it out, she flushed and stalked out of the room.

I found my lead on the Joneses' home network. Rashmi was not particularly diligent about backing up her sidekick files, and the last one I found was almost six months old, which was just about when she'd gotten religion. She'd used simple encryption, which wouldn't withstand a serious hack, but which would discourage the mom from snooping. I doglegged a key and opened the file. She had multiple calls. Her mother had been trying her at Rashmi@Ashbury.03284. But she also had an alternate: Brigitbird@Vincent.03284. I did a reverse lookup and that turned an address: The Church of Christ the Man, 348 Vincent Avenue. I wasn't keen for a personal visit to the church, so I tried her call.

"Hello," said a voice.

"Is this Rashmi Jones?"

The voice hesitated. "My name is Brigit. Leave me alone."

"Your mother is worried about you, Rashmi. She hired me to find you."

"I don't want to be found."

"I'm reading your novel, Rashmi." It was just something to say; I wanted to keep her on the line. "I was wondering, does she find her father at the end?"

"No." I could hear her breath caressing the microphone. "The devils come. That's the whole point."

Someone said something to her and she muted the speaker. But I knew she could still hear me. "That's sad, Rashmi. But I guess that's the way it had to be."

Then she hung up.

The mom was relieved that Rashmi was all right, furious that she was with Christers. So what? I'd found the girl: case closed. Only Najma Jones begged me to help her connect with her daughter. She was already into me for twenty bucks plus expenses, but for another five I said I'd try to get her away from the church long enough for them to talk. I was on my way over when the searchlet I'd attached to the Jones account turned up the hit at Grayle's Shoes. I was grateful for the reprieve, even more pleased when the salesbot identified Rashmi from her pix. As did the waitress at Maison Diana.

And the clerk at the Comfort Inn.

3

Ronald Reagan Elementary had been recently renovated, no doubt by a squad of janitor bots. The brick façade had been cleaned and repointed; the long row of windows gleamed like teeth. The asphalt playground had been ripped up and resurfaced with safe-t-mat, the metal swingsets swapped for gaudy towers and crawl tubes and slides and balance beams and decks. The chain link fences had been replaced by redwood lattice through which twined honeysuckle and clematis. There was a boxwood maze next to the swimming pool that shimmered, blue as a dream. Nothing was too good for the little girls—our hope for the future.

There was no room in the rack jammed with bikes and scooters and goboards, so I leaned my bike against a nearby cherry tree. The very youngest girls had come out for first recess. I paused behind the tree for a moment to let their whoops and shrieks and laughter bubble over me. My business didn't take me to schools very often; I couldn't remember when I had last seen so many girls in one place. They were black and white and yellow and brown, mostly dressed like janes you might see anywhere. But there were more than a few whose clothes proclaimed their mothers' lifestyles. Tommys in hunter camo and chaste Christers, twists in chains and spray-on, clumps of sisters wearing the uniforms of a group marriage, a couple of furries and one girl wearing a body suit that looked just like bot skin. As I lingered there, I felt a chill that had nothing to do with the shade of a tree. I had no idea who these tiny creatures were. They went to this well-kept school, led more or less normal lives. I grew up in the wild times, when everything was falling apart. At that moment, I realized that they were as far removed from me as I was from the grannies. I would always watch them from a distance.

Just inside the fence, two sisters in green-striped shirtwaists and green knee socks were turning a rope for a pony-tailed jumper who was executing nimble criss-crosses. The turners chanted,

> Down in the valley where the green grass grows,
> There sits Stacy pretty as a rose!
> She sings, she sings, she sings so sweet,
> Then along comes Chantall to kiss her on the cheek!

Another jumper joined her in the middle, matching her step for step, her dark hair flying. The chant continued,

> How many kisses does she get?
> One, two, three, four, five . . .

The two jumpers pecked at each other in the air to the count of ten without missing a beat. Then Ponytail skipped out and the turners began the chant over again for the dark-haired girl. Ponytail bent over for a moment to catch her breath; when she straightened, she noticed me.

"Hey you, behind the tree." She shaded her eyes with a hand. "You hiding?"

I stepped into the open. "No."

"This is our school, you know." The girl set one foot behind the other and then spun a hundred and eighty degrees to point at the door to the school. "You supposed to sign in at the office."

"I'd better take care of that then."

As I passed through the gate into the playground, a few of the girls stopped playing and stared. This was all the audience Ponytail needed. "You someone's mom?"

"No."

"Don't you have a job?" She fell into step beside me.

"I do."

"What is it?"

"I can't tell you."

She dashed ahead to block my path. "Probably because it's a pretend job."

Two of her sisters in green-striped shirtwaists scrambled to back her up.

"When we grow up," one of them announced, "we're going to have real jobs."

"Like a doctor," the other said. "Or a lion tamer."

Other girls were joining us. "I want to drive a truck," said a tommy. "Big, big truck." She specified the size of her rig with outstretched arms.

"That's not a real job. Any bot could do that."

"I want to be a teacher," said the dark-haired sister who had been jumping rope.

"Chantall loves school," said a furry. "She'd marry school if she could." Apparently this passed for brilliant wit in the third grade; some girls laughed so hard they had to cover their mouths with the back of their hands. Me, I was flummoxed. Give me a spurned lover or a mean drunk or a hardcase cop and I could figure out some play, but just then I was trapped by this giggling mob of children.

"So why you here?" Ponytail put her fists on her hips.

A jane in khakis and a baggy plum sweater emerged from behind a blue tunnel that looked like a centipede. She pinned me with that penetrating but not unkind stare that teachers are born with, and began to trudge across the playground toward me. "I've come to see Ms. Jones," I said.

"Oh." A shadow passed over Ponytail's face and she rubbed her hands against the sides of her legs. "You better go then."

Someone called, "Are you the undertaker?"

A voice that squeaked with innocence asked, "What's an undertaker?"

I didn't hear the answer. The teacher in the plum sweater rescued me and we passed through the crowd.

➤ ➤ ➤

I didn't understand why Najma Jones had come to school. She was either the most dedicated teacher on the planet or she was too numb to accept her daughter's death. I couldn't tell which. She had been reserved when we met the first time; now she was locked down and welded shut. She was a bird of a woman with a narrow face and thin lips. Her gray hair had a few lingering strands of black. She wore a long-sleeved white kameez tunic over shalwar trousers. I leaned against the door of her classroom and told her everything I had done the day before. She sat listening at her desk with a sandwich that she wasn't going to eat and a carton of milk that she wasn't going to drink and a napkin that she didn't need.

When I had finished, she asked me about cyanide inhalers.

"Hydrogen cyanide isn't hard to get in bulk," I said. "They use it for making plastic, engraving, tempering steel. The inhaler came from one of the underground suicide groups, probably Our Choice. The cops could tell you for sure."

She unfolded the napkin and spread it out on top of her desk. "I've heard it's a painful death."

"Not at all," I said. "They used to use hydrogen cyanide gas to execute criminals, back in the bad old days. It all depends on the first breath. Get it deep into your lungs and you're unconscious before you hit the floor. Dead in less than a minute."

"And if you don't get a large enough dose?"

"Ms. Jones . . ."

She cut me off hard. "If you don't?"

"Then it takes longer, but you still die. There are convulsions. The skin flushes and turns purple. Eyes bulge. They say it's something like having a heart attack."

"Rashmi?" She laid her daughter's name down gently, as if she were tucking it into bed. "How did she die?"

Had the cops shown her the crime-scene pictures? I decided they hadn't. "I don't think she suffered," I said.

She tore a long strip off the napkin. "You don't think I'm a very good mother, do you?"

I don't know exactly what I expected her to say, but this wasn't it. "Ms. Jones, I don't know much about you and your daughter. But I do know that you cared enough about her to hire me. I'm sorry I let you down."

She shook her head wearily, as if I had just flunked the pop quiz. One third does not equal .033 and Los Angeles has never been the capital of California. "Is there anything else I should know?" she said.

"There is." I had to tell her what I'd found out that morning, but I wasn't going to tell her that I was working for a devil. "You mentioned before that Rashmi had a friend named Kate."

"The Christer?" She tore another strip off the napkin.

I nodded. "Her name is Kate Vermeil. I don't know this for sure yet, but there's reason to believe that Rashmi and Kate were married yesterday. Does that make any sense to you?"

"Maybe yesterday it might have." Her voice was flat. "It doesn't anymore."

I could hear stirring in the next classroom. Chairs scraped against linoleum. Girls were jabbering at each other.

"I know Rashmi became a Christer," she said. "It's a broken religion. But then everything is broken, isn't it? My daughter and I . . . I don't think we ever understood each other. We were strangers at the end." The napkin was in shreds. "How old were you when it happened?"

"I wasn't born yet." She didn't have to explain what *it* was. "I'm not as old as I look."

"I was nineteen. I remember men, my father, my uncles. And the boys. I actually slept with one." She gave me a bleak smile. "Does that shock you, Ms. Hardaway?"

I hated it when grannies talked about having sex, but I just shook my head.

"I didn't love Sunil, but I said I'd marry him just so I could get out of my mother's house. Maybe that was what was happening with Rashmi and this Kate person?"

"I wouldn't know."

The school bell rang.

"I'm wearing white today, Ms. Hardaway, to honor my darling daughter." She gathered up the strips of napkin and the sandwich and the carton of milk and dropped them in the trash-can. "White is the Hindu color of mourning. But it's also the color of knowledge. The goddess of learning, Saraswati, is always shown wearing a white dress, sitting on a white lotus. There is something here I must learn." She fingered the gold embroidery at the neckline of her kameez. "But it's time for recess."

We walked to the door. "What will you do now?" She opened it. The fifth grade swarmed the hall, girls rummaging through their lockers.

"Find Kate Vermeil," I said.

She nodded. "Tell her I'm sorry."

4

I tried Kate's call again, but when all I got was the sidekick I biked across town to 44 East Washington Avenue. The Poison Society turned out to be a jump joint; the sign said it opened at 9:00 P.M. There was no bell on the front door, but I knocked hard enough to wake Marilyn Monroe. No answer. I went around to the back and tried again. If Kate was in there, she wasn't entertaining visitors.

A sidekick search turned up an open McDonald's on Wallingford, a ten-minute ride. The only other customers were a couple of twists with bound breasts and identical acid-green vinyl masks. One of them crouched on the floor beside the other, begging for chicken nuggets. A bot took my order for the twenty-nine cent combo meal—it was all bots behind the counter. By law, there was supposed to be a human running the place, but if she was on the premises, she was nowhere to be seen. I thought about calling City Hall to complain, but the egg rolls arrived crispy and the McLatte was nicely scalded. Besides, I didn't need to watch the cops haul the poor jane in charge out of whatever hole she had fallen into.

A couple of hardcase tommys in army-surplus fatigues strutted in just after me. They ate with their heads bowed over their plastic trays so the fries didn't have too far to travel. Their collapsible titanium nightsticks lay on the table in plain sight. One of them was not quite as wide as a bus. The other was nothing special, except that when I glanced up from my sidekick, she was giving me a freeze-dried stare. I waggled my shiny fingernails at her and screwed my cutest smile onto my face. She scowled, said something to her partner and went back to the trough.

My sidekick chirped. It was my pal Julie Epstein, who worked Self-Endangerment/Missing Persons out of the second precinct.

"You busy, Fay?"

"Yeah, the Queen of Cleveland just lost her glass slipper and I'm on the case."

"Well, I'm about to roll through your neighborhood. Want to do lunch?"

I aimed the sidekick at the empties on my table. "Just finishing."

"Where are you?"

"McD's on Wallingford."

"Yeah? How are the ribs?"

"Couldn't say. But the egg rolls are triple dee."

"That the place where the owner is a junkliner? We've had complaints. Bots run everything?"

"No, I can see her now. She's shortchanging some beat cop."

She gave me the laugh. "Got the coroner's on the Rashmi Jones. Cyanide-induced hypoxia."

"You didn't by any chance show the mom pix of the scene?"

"Hell no. Talk about cruel and unusual." She frowned. "Why?"

"I was just with her. She seemed like maybe she suspected her kid wrestled with the reaper."

"We didn't tell her. By the way, we don't really care if you call your client, but next time how about trying us first?"

"That's cop law. Me, I follow PI law."

"Where did you steal that line from, *Chinatown*?"

"It's got better dialogue than *Dragnet*." I swirled the last of my latte in the cup. "You calling a motive on the Rashmi Jones?"

"Not yet. What do you like?" She ticked off the fingers of her left hand. "Family? School? Money? Broke a fingernail? Cloudy day?"

"Pregnancy? Just a hunch."

"You think she was seeded? We'll check that. But that's no reason to kill yourself."

"They've all got reasons. Only none of them makes sense."

She frowned. "Hey, don't get all invested on me here."

"Tell me, Julie, do you think I'm doing a pretend job?"

"Whoa, Fay." Her chuckle had a sharp edge. "Maybe it's time you and Sharifa took a vacation."

"Yeah." I let that pass. "It's just that some granny called me a fluff."

"Grannies." She snorted in disgust. "Well, you're no cop, that's for sure. But we do appreciate the help. Yeah, I'd say what you do is real. As real as anything in this cocked world."

"Thanks, flatfoot. Now that you've made things all better, I'll just click off. My latte is getting cold and you're missing so damn many persons."

"Think about that vacation, shamus. Bye."

As I put my sidekick away, I realized that the tommys were waiting for me. They'd been rattling ice in their cups and folding McWrappers for the past ten minutes. I probably didn't need their brand of trouble. The smart move would be to bolt for the door and leave my bike for now; I could lose them on foot. But then I hadn't made a smart move since April. The big one was talking into her sidekick when I sauntered over to them.

"What can I do for you ladies?" I said.

The big one pocketed the sidekick. Her partner started to come out of her seat but the big one stretched an arm like a telephone pole to restrain her.

"Do we know you?" The partner had close-set eyes and a beak nose; her black hair was short and stiff as a brush. She was wearing a black tee under her fatigue jacket and black leather combat boots. Probably had steel toes. "No," she continued, "I don't think we do."

"Then let's get introductions out of the way," I said. "I'm Fay Hardaway. And you are . . . ?"

They gave me less than nothing.

I sat down. "Thanks," I said. "Don't mind if I do."

The big one leaned back in her chair and eyed me as if I was dessert. "Sure you're not making a mistake, missy?"

"Why, because you're rough, tough and take no guff?"

"You're funny." She smirked. "I like that. Usually the people we meet are so very sad. My name is Alix." She held out her hand and we shook. "Pleased to know you."

The customary way to shake hands is to hold on for four, maybe five seconds, squeeze goodbye, then loosen the grip. Maybe big Alix wasn't familiar with our customs—she wasn't letting go.

I wasn't going to let a little thing like a missing hand intimidate me. "Oh, then I do know you," I said. We were in the McDonald's on Wallingford Street—a public place. I'd just been talking to my pal the cop. I was so damn sure that I was safe, I decided to take my shot. "That would make the girlfriend here Elaine. Or is it Gratiana?"

"Alix." The beak panicked. "Now we've got to take her."

Alix sighed, then yanked on my arm. She might have been pulling a tissue from a box for all the effort she expended. I slid halfway across the table as the beak whipped her nightstick to full extension. I lunged away from her and she caught me just a glancing blow above the ear but then Alix stuck a popper into my face and spattered me with knockout spray. I saw a billion stars and breathed the vacuum of deep space for maybe two seconds before everything went black.

Big Ben chimed between my ears. I could feel it deep in my molars, in the jelly of my eyes. It was the first thing I had felt since World War II. Wait a minute, was I alive during World War II? No, but I had seen the movie. When I wiggled my toes, Big Ben chimed again. I realized that the reason it hurt so much was that the human head didn't really contain enough space to hang a bell of that size. As I took inventory of body parts, the chiming became less intense. By the time I knew I was all there, it was just the sting of blood in my veins.

I was laid out on a surface that was hard but not cold. Wood. A bench. The place I was in was huge and dim but not dark. The high ceiling was in shadow. There was a hint of smoke in the air. Lights flickered. Candles. That was a clue, but I was still too groggy to understand what the mystery was. I knew I needed to remember something, but there was a hole where the memory was supposed to be. I reached back and touched just above my ear. The tip of my finger came away dark and sticky.

A voice solved the mystery for me. "I'm sorry that my people overreacted. If you want to press charges, I've instructed Gratiana and Alix to surrender to the police."

It came back to me then. It always does. McDonald's. Big Alix. A long handshake. That would make this a church. I sat up. When the world stopped spinning, I saw a vast marble altar awash in light with a crucifix the size of a Cessna hanging behind it.

"I hope you're not in too much pain, Miss Hardaway." The voice came from the pew behind me. A fortyish woman in a black suit and a roman collar was on the kneeler. She was wearing a large silver ring on the fourth finger of her left hand.

"I've felt worse."

"That's too bad. Do you make a habit of getting into trouble?" She looked concerned that I might be making some bad life choices. She had soft eyes and a kindly face. Her short hair was the color of ashes. She was someone I could tell my guilty secrets to, so I could sleep at night. She would speak to Christ the Man himself on my behalf, book me into the penthouse suite in heaven.

"Am I in trouble?"

She nodded gravely. "We all are. The devils are destroying us, Miss Hardaway. They plant their seed not only in our bodies, but our minds and our souls."

"Please, call me Fay. I'm sure we're going to be just the very best of friends." I leaned toward her. "I'm sorry, I can't read your name tag."

"I'm not wearing one." She smiled. "I'm Father Elaine Horváth."

We looked at each other.

"Have you ever considered suicide, Fay?" said Father Elaine.

"Not really. It's usually a bad career move."

"Very good. But you must know that since the devils came and changed everything, almost a billion women have despaired and taken their lives."

"You know, I think I did hear something about that. Come on, lady, what's this about?"

"It is the tragedy of our times that there are any number of good reasons to kill oneself. It takes courage to go on living with the world the way it is. Rashmi Jones was a troubled young woman. She lacked that courage. That doesn't make her a bad person, just a dead one."

I patted my pocket, looking for my sidekick. Still there. I pulled it out and pressed *record.* I didn't ask for permission. "So I should mind my own business?"

"That would be a bad career move in your profession. How old are you, Fay?"

"Thirty-three."

"Then you were born of a virgin." She leaned back, slid off the kneeler and onto the pew. "Seeded by the devils. I'm old enough to have had a father, Fay. I actually remember him a little. A very little."

"Don't start." I spun out of the pew into the aisle. I hated cock nostalgia. This granny had me chewing aluminum foil; I would have spat it at Christ himself if he had dared come down off his cross. "You want to know one reason why my generation jumps out of windows and sucks on cyanide? It's because twists like you make us feel guilty about how we came to be. You want to call me devil's spawn, go ahead. Enjoy yourself. Live it up. Because we're just waiting for you old bitches to die off. Someday this foolish church is going to dry up and blow away and you know what? We'll go dancing that night, because we'll be a hell of a lot happier without you to remind us of what you lost and who we can never be."

She seemed perversely pleased by my show of emotion. "You're an angry woman, Fay."

"Yeah," I said, "but I'm kind to children and small animals."

"What is that anger doing to your soul? Many young people find solace in Christ."

"Like Alix and Gratiana?"

She folded her hands; the silver ring shone dully. "As I said, they have offered to turn themselves. . . ."

"Keep them. I'm done with them." I was cooling off fast. I

paused, considering my next move. Then I sat down on the pew next to Father Elaine, showed her my sidekick and made sure she saw me pause the recording. Our eyes met. We understood each other. "Did you marry Kate Vermeil and Rashmi Jones yesterday?"

She didn't hesitate. "I performed the ceremony. I never filed the documents."

"Do you know why Rashmi killed herself?"

"Not exactly." She held my gaze. "I understand she left a note."

"Yeah, the note. I found it on her sidekick. She wrote, 'Life is too hard to handle and I can't handle it so I've got to go now. I love you mom sorry.' A little generic for a would-be writer, wouldn't you say? And the thing is, there's nothing in the note about Kate. I didn't even know she existed until this morning. Now I have a problem with that. The cops would have the same problem if I gave it to them."

"But you haven't."

"Not yet."

She thought about that for a while.

"My understanding," said Father Elaine at last, "is that Kate and Rashmi had a disagreement shortly after the ceremony." She was tiptoeing around words as if one of them might wake up and start screaming. "I don't know exactly what it was about. Rashmi left, Kate stayed here. Someone was with her all yesterday afternoon and all last night."

"Because you thought she might need an alibi?"

She let that pass. "Kate was upset when she heard the news. She blames herself, although I am certain she is without blame."

"She's here now?"

"No." Father Elaine shrugged. "I sent her away when I learned you were looking for her."

"And you want me to stop."

"You are being needlessly cruel, you know. The poor girl is grieving."

"Another poor girl is dead." I reached into my pocket for my penlight. "Can I see your ring?"

That puzzled her. She extended her left hand and I shone the light on it. Her skin was freckled but soft, the nails flawless. She would not be getting them done at a dump like the Adagio Spa.

"What do these letters mean?" I asked. "IHS?"

"*In hoc signo vinces.* 'In this sign you will conquer.' The emperor Constantine had a vision of a cross in the sky with those words written in fire on it. This was just before a major battle. He had his soldiers paint the cross on their shields and then he won the day against a superior force."

"Cute." I snapped the light off. "What's it mean to you?"

"The Bride of God herself gave this to me." Her face lit up, as if she were listening to an angelic chorus chant her name. "In recognition of my special vocation. You see, Fay, our Church has no intention of drying up and blowing away. Long after my generation is gone, believers will continue to gather in Christ's name. And someday they'll finish the work we have begun. Someday they will exorcise the devils."

If she knew how loopy that sounded, she didn't show it. "Okay, here's the way it is," I said. "Forget Kate Vermeil. I only wanted to find her so she could lead me to you. A devil named Seeren hired me to look for you. It wants a meeting."

"With me?" Father Elaine went pale. "What for?"

"I just find them." I enjoyed watching her squirm. "I don't ask why."

She folded her hands as if to pray, then leaned her head against them and closed her eyes. She sat like that for almost a minute. I decided to let her brood, not that I had much choice. The fiery pit of hell could've opened up and she wouldn't have noticed.

Finally, she shivered and sat up. "I have to find out how much they know." She gazed up at the enormous crucifix. "I'll see this devil, but on one condition: you guarantee my safety."

"Sure." I couldn't help myself; I laughed. The sound echoed, profaning the silence. "Just how am I supposed to do that? They disappeared half the population of Earth without breaking a sweat."

"You have their confidence," she said. "And mine."

A vast and absurd peace had settled over her; she was seeing the world through the gauze of faith. She was a fool if she thought

I could go up against the devils. Maybe she believed Christ the Man would swoop down from heaven to protect her, but then he hadn't been seen around the old neighborhood much of late. Or maybe she had projected herself into the mind of the martyrs who would embrace the sword, kiss the ax that would take their heads. I reminded myself that her delusions were none of my business.

Besides, I needed the money. And suddenly I just had to get out of that big, empty church.

"My office is at 35 Market," I said. "Third floor. I'll try to set something up for six tonight." I stood. "Look, if they want to take you, you're probably gone. But I'll record everything and squawk as loud as I can."

"I believe you will," she said, her face aglow.

5

I didn't go to my office after I locked my bike to the rack on Market Street. Instead I went to find George. He was stripping varnish from the beadboard wainscoting in Donna Belasco's old office on the fifth floor. Donna's office had been vacant since last fall, when she had closed her law practice and gone south to count waves at Daytona Beach. At least, that's what I hoped she was doing; the last I'd heard from her was a Christmas card. I missed Donna; she was one of the few grannies who tried to understand what it was like to grow up the way we did. And she had been generous about steering work my way.

"Hey George," I said. "You can tell your boss that I found the ring."

"This one offers the congratulations." The arm holding the brush froze over the can of stripper as he swiveled his head to face me. "You have proved true superiority, Fay." George had done a good job maintaining our building since coming to us a year ago, although he had something against wood grain. We had to stop him from painting over the mahogany paneling in the foyer.

"So I've set up a meeting." I hated to close the door; the stink of the varnish stripper was barbed wire up my nose. "Father Elaine will be here at six."

George said nothing. Trying to read a bot is like trying to read a refrigerator. I assumed that he was relaying this information to Seeren. Would the devil be displeased that I had booked its meeting into my office?

"Seeren is impressed by your speedy accomplishment," George said at last. "Credit has been allotted to this one for suggesting it task you."

"Great, take ten bucks a month off my rent. Just so you know, I promised Father Elaine she'd be safe here. Seeren is not going to make a liar out of me, is it?"

"Seeren rejects violence. It's a regrettable technique."

"Yeah, but if Seeren disappears her to wherever, does that count?"

George's head swiveled back toward the wainscoting. "Father Elaine Horváth will be invited to leave freely, if such is her intention." The brush dipped into the can. "Was Kate Vermeil also found?"

"No," I said. "I looked, but then Father Elaine found me. By the way, she didn't live at 465 12th Avenue."

"Seeren had otherwise information." The old varnish bubbled and sagged where George had applied stripper. "Such error makes a curiosity."

It was a little thing, but it pricked at me as I walked down to the third floor. Was I pleased to discover that the devils were neither omnipotent nor infallible? Not particularly. For all their crimes against humanity, the devils and their bots were pretty much running our world now. It had been a small if bitter comfort to imagine that they knew exactly what they were doing.

I passed crazy Martha's door, which was open, on the way to my office. "Yaga combany wading," she called.

I backtracked. My neighbor was at her desk, wearing her Technopro gas mask, which she claimed protected her from chlorine, hydrogen sulfide, sulfur dioxide, ammonia, bacteria, viruses, dust, pollen, cat dander, mold spores, nuclear fallout and sexual harassment. Unfortunately, it also made her almost unintelligible.

"Try that again," I said.

"You've. Got. Company. Waiting."

"Who is it?"

She shook the mask and shrugged. The light of her desktop was reflected in the faceplate. I could see numbers swarming like black ants across the rows and columns of a spreadsheet.

"What's with the mask?"

"We. Had. A. Devil. In. The. Building."

"Really?" I said. "When?"

"Morning."

There was no reason why a devil shouldn't come into our building, no law against having one for a client. But there was an accusation in Martha's look that I couldn't deny. Had I betrayed us all by taking the case? She said, "Hate. Devils."

"Yeah," I said. "Me too."

I opened my door and saw that it was Sharifa who was waiting for me. She was trying on a smile that didn't fit. "Hi Fay," she said. She looked as elegant as always and as weary as I had ever seen her. She was wearing a peppered black linen dress and black dress sandals with thin crossover straps. Those weren't doctor shoes—they were pull down the shades and turn up the music shoes. They made me very sad.

As I turned to close the door, she must have spotted the patch of blood that had dried in my hair. "You're hurt!" I had almost forgotten about it—there was no percentage in remembering that I was in pain. She shot out of her chair. "What happened?"

"I slipped in the shower," I said.

"Let me look."

I tilted my head toward her and she probed the lump gently. "You could have a concussion."

"PI's don't get concussions. It says so right on the license."

"Sit," she said. "Let me clean this up. I'll just run to the bathroom for some water."

I sat and watched her go. I thought about locking the door behind her but I deserved whatever I had coming. I opened the bottom drawer of the desk, slipped two plastic cups off the stack and brought Johnnie Walker in for a consultation.

Sharifa bustled through the doorway with a cup of water in one hand and a fistful of paper towels in the other but caught herself when she saw the bottle. "When did this start?"

"Just now." I picked up my cup and slugged two fingers of Black Label Scotch. "Want some?"

"I don't know," she said. "Are we having fun or are we self-medicating?"

I let that pass. She dabbed at the lump with a damp paper towel. I could smell her perfume, lemon blossoms on a summer breeze and just the smallest bead of sweat. Her scent got along nicely with the liquid smoke of the scotch. She brushed against me and I could feel her body beneath her dress. At that moment I wanted her more than I wanted to breathe.

"Sit down," I said.

"I'm not done yet," she said.

I pointed at a chair. "Sit, damn it."

She dropped the paper towel in my trash as she went by.

"You asked me a question this morning," I said. "I should've given you the answer. I had the abortion last week."

She studied her hands. I don't know why; they weren't doing anything. They were just sitting in her lap, minding their own business.

"I told you when we first got together, that's what I'd do when I got seeded," I said.

"I know."

"I just didn't see any good choices," I said. "I know the world needs children, but I have a life to lead. Maybe it's a rude, pointless, dirty life but it's what I have. Being a mother . . . that's someone else's life."

"I understand," said Sharifa. Her voice was so small it could have crawled under a thimble. "It's just . . . it was all so sudden. You told me and then we were fighting and I didn't have time to think things through."

"I got tested in the morning. I told you that afternoon. I wasn't keeping anything a secret."

She folded her arms against her chest as if she were cold. "And when I get seeded, what then?"

"You'll do what's best for you."

She sighed. "Pour me some medication, would you?"

I poured scotch into both cups, came around the desk and handed Sharifa hers. She drank, held the whiskey in her mouth for a moment and then swallowed.

"Fay, I . . ." The corners of her mouth were twitchy and she bit her lip. "Your mother told me once that when she realized she was pregnant with you, she was so happy. So happy. It was when everything was crashing around everyone. She said you were the gift she needed to . . . not to. . . ."

"I got the gift lecture, Sharifa. Too many times. She made the devils sound like Santa Claus. Or the stork."

She glanced down as if surprised to discover that she was still holding the cup. She drained it at a gulp and set it on my desk. "I'm a doctor. I know they do this to us; I just wish I knew how. But it isn't a bad thing. Having you in the world can't be a bad thing."

I wasn't sure about that, but I kept my opinion to myself.

"Sometimes I feel like I'm trying to carry water in my hands but it's all leaking out and there's nothing I can do to stop it." She started rubbing her right hand up and down her left forearm. "People keep killing themselves. Maybe it's not as bad as it used to be, but still. The birthrate is barely at replacement levels. Maybe we're doomed. Did you ever think that? That we might go extinct?"

"No."

Sharifa was silent for a long time. She kept rubbing her arm. "It should've been me doing your abortion," she said at last. "Then we'd both have to live with it."

I was one tough PI. I kept a bottle of scotch in the bottom drawer and had a devil for a client. Tommys whacked me with nightsticks and pumped knockout spray into my face. But even I had a breaking point, and Dr. Sharifa Ramirez was pushing me up against it hard. I wanted to pull her into my arms and kiss her forehead, her cheeks, her graceful neck. But I couldn't give in to her that way—not now anyway. Maybe never again. I had a case, and I needed to hold the best part of myself in reserve until it was finished. "I'll be in charge of the guilt, Sharifa." I said. "You be in charge of saving lives." I came around the desk. "I've got work to

do, so you go home now, sweetheart." I kissed her on the forehead. "I'll see you there."

Easier to say than to believe.

6

Sharifa was long gone by the time Father Elaine arrived at about
ten minutes to six. She brought muscle with her; Gratiana loi-
tered in the hallway surveying my office with sullen calculation,
as if estimating how long it would take to break down the door,
leap over the desk and wring somebody's neck. I shouldn't have
been surprised that Father Elaine's faith in me had wavered—
hell, I didn't have much faith in me. However, I thought she
showed poor judgment in bringing this particular thug along. I
invited Gratiana to remove herself from my building. Perhaps
she might perform an auto-erotic act in front of a speeding bus?
Father Elaine dismissed her, and she slunk off.

Father Elaine appeared calm, but I could tell that she was as
nervous as two mice and a gerbil. I hadn't really had a good look
at her in the dim church, but now I studied her in case I had to
write her up for the Missing Persons Index. She was a tallish
woman with round shoulders and a bit of a stoop. Her eyes were
the brown of wet sand; her cheeks were bloodless. Her smile was
not quite as convincing in good light as it had been in gloom. She
made some trifling small talk, which I did nothing to help with.
Then she stood at the window, watching. A wingtip loafer tapped
against bare floor.

It was about ten after when my desktop chirped. I waved
open the icon and accepted the transfer of a thousand dollars.
Seeren had a hell of a calling card. "I think they're coming," I
said. I opened the door and stepped into the hall to wait for them.

"It gives Seeren the bright pleasure to meet you, Father
Elaine Horváth," said George as they shuffled into the office.

She focused everything she had on the devil. "Just Father, if
you don't mind." The bot was nothing but furniture to her.

"It's kind of crowded in here," I said. "If you want, I can wait
outside . . ."

Father Elaine's façade cracked for an instant, but she patched it up nicely. "I'm sure we can manage," she said.

"This one implores Fay to remain," said George.

We sorted ourselves out. Seeren assumed its perch on top of the file cabinet and George came around and compacted himself next to me. Father Elaine pushed her chair next to the door. I think she was content to be stationed nearest the exit. George looked at Father Elaine. She looked at Seeren. Seeren looked out the window. I watched them all.

"Seeren offers sorrow over the regrettable death of Rashmi Jones," said George. "Such Rashmi was of your church?"

"She was a member, yes."

"According to Fay Hardaway, a fact is that Father married Kate Vermeil and Rashmi Jones."

I didn't like that. I didn't like it at all.

Father Elaine hesitated only a beat. "Yes."

"Would Father permit Seeren to locate Kate Vermeil?"

"I know where she is, Seeren," said Father Elaine. "I don't think she needs to be brought into this."

"Indulge this one and reconsider, Father. Is such person pregnant?"

Her manner had been cool, but now it dropped forty degrees. "Why would you say that?"

"Perhaps such person is soon to become pregnant?"

"How would I know? If she is, it would be your doing, Seeren."

"Father well understands in vitro fertilization?"

"I've heard of it, yes." Father Elaine's shrug was far too elaborate. "I can't say I understand it."

"Father has heard then of transvaginal oocyte retrieval?"

She thrust out her chin. "No."

"Haploidisation of somatic cells?"

She froze.

"Has Father considered then growing artificial sperm from embryonic stem cells?"

"I'm a priest, Seeren." Only her lips moved. "Not a biologist."

"Does the Christer Church make further intentions to induce pregnancies in certain members? Such as Kate Vermeil?"

Father Elaine rose painfully from the chair. I thought she might try to run, but now martyr's fire burned through the shell of ice that had encased her. "We're doing Christ's work, Seeren. We reject your obscene seeding. We are saving ourselves from you and you can't stop us."

Seeren beat its wings, once, twice and crowed. It was a dense, jarring sound, like steel scraping steel. I hadn't known that devils could make any sound at all, but hearing that hellish scream made me want to dive under my desk and curl up in a ball. I took it though, and so did Father Elaine. I gave her credit for that.

"Seeren makes no argument with the Christer Church," said George. "Seeren upholds only the brightest encouragement for such pregnancies."

Father Elaine's face twitched in disbelief and then a flicker of disappointment passed over her. Maybe she was upset to have been cheated of her glorious death. She was a granny after all, of the generation that had embraced the suicide culture. For the first time, she turned to the bot. "What?"

"Seeren tasks Father to help numerous Christers become pregnant. Christers who do such choosing will then give birth."

She sank back onto her chair.

"Too many humans now refuse the seeding," said the bot. "Not all then give birth. This was not forseen. It is regrettable."

Without my noticing, my hands had become fists. My knuckles were white.

"Seeren will announce its true satisfaction with the accomplishment of the Christer Church. It offers a single caution. Christers must assure all to make no XY chromosome."

Father Elaine was impassive. "Will you continue to seed all non-believers?"

"It is prudent for the survival of humans."

She nodded and faced Seeren. "How will you know if we do try to bring men back into the world?"

The bot said nothing. The silence thickened as we waited. Maybe the devil thought it didn't need to make threats.

"Well, then." Father Elaine rose once again. Some of the stoop had gone out of her shoulders. She was trying to play it calm, but I knew she'd be skipping by the time she hit the sidewalk. Probably she thought she had won a great victory. Maybe. In any event, she was done with this little party.

But it was my little party, and I wasn't about to let it break up with the devils holding hands with the Christers. "Wait," I said. "Father, you better get Gratiana up here. And if you've got any other muscle in the neighborhood, call them right now. You need backup fast."

Seeren glanced away from the window and at me.

"Why?" Father Elaine already had her sidekick out. "What is this?"

"There's a problem."

"Fay Hardaway," said George sharply. "Indulge this one and recall your task. Your employment has been accomplished."

"Then I'm on my own time now, George." I thought maybe Seeren would try to leave, but it remained on its perch. Maybe the devil didn't care what I did. Maybe it found me amusing. I could be an amusing girl, in my own obtuse way.

Gratiana tore the door open. She held her nightstick high, as if expecting to dive into a bloodbath. When she saw our cool tableau, she let it drop to her side.

"Scooch over, Father," I said, "and let her in. Gratiana, you can leave the door open but keep that toothpick handy. I'm pretty sure you're going to be using it before long."

"The others are right behind me, Father," said Gratiana as she crowded into the room. "Two, maybe three minutes."

"Just enough time." I let my hand fall to the middle drawer of my desk. "I have a question for you, Father." I slid the drawer open. "How did Seeren know all that stuff about haploid this and in vitro that?"

"It's a devil." She watched me thoughtfully. "They come from two hundred light years away. How do they do anything?"

"Fair enough. But they also knew that you married Kate and Rashmi. George here just said that I told them, except I never did. That was a mistake. It made me wonder whether they knew who you were all along. It's funny, I used to be convinced that the devils were infallible, but now I'm thinking that they can screw up any day of the week, just like the rest of us. They're almost human that way."

"A regrettable misstatement was made." The bot's neck extended until his head was level with mine. "Indulge this one and refrain from further humiliation."

"I've refrained for too long, George. I've had a bellyful of refraining." I was pretty sure that George could see the open drawer, which meant that the devil would know what was in it as well. I wondered how far they'd let me go. "The question is, Father, if the devils already knew who you were, why would Seeren hire me to find you?"

"Go on," she said.

My chest was tight. I took a deep breath. Nobody tried to stop me, so I went ahead and stuck my head into the lion's mouth. Like that little girl at school, I'd always wanted to have a real job when I grew up. "You've got a leak, Father. Your problem isn't devil super-science. It's the good old-fashioned Judas kiss. Seeren has an inside source, a mole among your congregation. When it decided the time had come to meet with you, it wanted to be sure that none of you would suspect where its information was actually coming from. It decided that the way to give the mole cover was to hire some gullible PI to pretend to find stuff out. I may be a little slow and a lot greedy but I do have a few shreds of pride. I can't let myself be played for an idiot." I thought I heard footsteps on the stairs, but maybe it was just my own blood pounding. "You see, Father, I don't think that Seeren really trusts you. I sure didn't hear you promise just now not to be making little boys. And yes, if they find out about the boy babies, the devils could just disappear them, but you and the Bride of God and all your batty friends would find ways to make that very public, very messy. I'm guessing that's part of your plan, isn't it? To remind us who the devils are, what they did? Maybe get people into the streets again. Since the devils still need to know what you're up to, the mole had to be protected."

Father Elaine flushed with anger. "Do you know who she is?"

"No," I said. "But you could probably narrow it down to a very few. You said you married Rashmi and Kate, but that you never filed the documents. But you needed someone to witness the ceremony. Someone who was taking pix and would send one to Seeren . . ."

Actually, my timing was a little off. Gratiana launched herself at me just as big Alix hurtled through the doorway. I had the air taser out of the drawer, but my plan had been for the Christers to clean up their own mess. I came out of my chair and raised the taser but even 50,000 volts wasn't going to keep that snarling bitch off me.

I heard a huge wet pop, not so much an explosion but an implosion. There was a rush of air through the doorway but the room was preternaturally quiet, as if someone had just stopped screaming. We humans gaped at the void that had formerly been occupied by Gratiana. The familiar surroundings of my office seemed to warp and stretch to accommodate that vacancy. If she could vanish so completely, then maybe chairs could waltz on the ceiling and trashcans could sing *Carmen.* For the first time in my life I had a rough sense of what the grannies had felt when the devils disappeared their men. It would be one thing if Gratiana were merely dead, if there were blood, and bone and flesh left behind. A body to be buried. But this was an offense against reality itself. It undermined our common belief that the world is indeed a fact, that we exist at all. I could understand how it could unhinge a billion minds. I was standing next to Father Elaine beside the open door to my office holding the taser and I couldn't remember how I had gotten there.

Seeren hopped down off the bookcase as if nothing important had happened and wrapped its translucent wings around its body. The devil didn't seem surprised at all that a woman had just disappeared. Maybe there was no surprising a devil.

And then it occurred to me that this probably wasn't the first time since they took all the men that the devils had disappeared someone. Maybe they did it all the time. I thought of all the missing persons whom I had never found. I could see the files in Julie Epstein's office bulging with unsolved cases. Had Seeren done this thing to teach us the fragility of being? Or had it just been a clumsy attempt to cover up its regrettable mistakes?

As the devil waddled toward the door, Alix made a move as if to block its exit. After what she had just seen, I thought that was probably the most boneheaded, brave move I had ever seen.

"Let them go." Father Elaine's voice quavered. Her eyes were like wounds.

Alix stepped aside and the devil and the bot left us. We listened to the devil scrabble down the hall. I heard the elevator doors open and then close.

Then Father Elaine staggered and put a hand on my shoulder. She looked like a granny now.

"There are no boy babies," she said. "Not yet. You have to believe me."

"You know what?" I shook free of her. "I don't care." I wanted them gone. I wanted to sit alone at my desk and watch the room fill with night.

"You don't understand."

"And I don't want to." I had to set the taser on the desk or I might have used it on her.

"Kate Vermeil is pregnant with one of our babies," said Father Elaine. "It's a little girl, I swear it."

"So you've made Seeren proud. What's the problem?"

Alix spoke for the first time. "Gratiana was in charge of Kate."

7

The Poison Society was lit brightly enough to give a camel a headache. If you forgot your sunglasses, there was a rack of freebies at the door. Set into the walls were terrariums where diamondback rattlers coiled in the sand, black neck cobras dangled from dead branches and brown scorpions basked on ceramic rocks. The hemlock was in bloom; clusters of small, white flowers opened like umbrellas. Upright stems of monkshood were interplanted with death cap mushrooms in wine casks cut in half. Curare vines climbed the pergola over the alcohol bar.

I counted maybe fifty customers in the main room, which was probably a good crowd for a Wednesday night. I had no idea yet how many might be lurking in the specialty shops that opened off this space, where a nice girl might arrange for a guaranteed-safe session of sexual asphyxia either by hanging or drowning, or else get her cerebrum toasted by various brain lightning generators. I was hoping Kate was out in the open with the relatively sane folks. I didn't really want to poke around in the shops, but I would if I had to. I thought I owed it to Rashmi Jones.

I strolled around, pretending to look at various animals and plants, carrying a tumbler filled with a little Johnnie Walker Black Label and a lot of water. I knew Kate would be disguised but if I could narrow the field of marks down to three or four, I might actually snoop her. Of course, she might be on the other side of town, but this was my only play. My guess was that she'd switch styles, so I wasn't necessarily looking for a tommy. Her hair wouldn't be brunette, and her skin would probably be darker, and contacts could give her cat's eyes or zebra eyes or American flags, if she wanted. But even with padding and lifts she couldn't change her body type enough to fool a good scan. And I had her data from the Christer medical files loaded into my sidekick.

Father Elaine had tried Kate's call, but she wouldn't pick up. That made perfect sense since just about anyone could put their hands on software that could replicate voices. There were bots that could sing enough like Velma Stone to fool her own mother. Kate and Gratiana would have agreed on a safe word. Our problem was that Gratiana had taken it with her to hell, or wherever the devil had consigned her.

The first mark my sidekick picked out was a redhead in silk pajamas and lime green bunny slippers. A scan matched her to Kate's numbers to within 5 percent. I bumped into her just enough to plant the snoop, a sticky homing device the size of a baby tooth.

"Scuse me, sorry." I said. "S-so sorry." I slopped some of my drink onto the floor.

She gave me a glare that would have withered a cactus and I noodled off. As soon as I was out of her sight, I hit the button on my sidekick to which I'd assigned Kate's call. When Kate picked up, the snoop would know if the call had come from me and signal my sidekick that I had found her. The redhead wasn't Kate. Neither was the bald jane in distressed leather.

The problem with trying to locate her this way was that if I kept calling her, she'd get suspicious and lose the sidekick.

I lingered by a pufferfish aquarium. Next to it was a safe, and in front of that a tootsie fiddled with the combination lock. I scanned her and got a match to within 2 percent. She was wearing a spangle wig and a stretch lace dress with a ruffle front. When she opened the door of the safe, I saw that it was made of clear luxar. She reached in, then slammed the door and then trotted off as if she were late for the last train of the night.

I peeked through the door of the safe. Inside was a stack of squat blue inhalers like the one Rashmi had used to kill herself. On the wall above the safe, the management of The Poison Society had spray-painted a mock graffiti. *21L 4R 11L.* There was no time to plant a snoop. I pressed the call button as I tailed her.

With a strangled cry, the tootsie yanked a sidekick from her clutch purse, dropped it to the floor and stamped on it. She was wearing Donya Durand ice and taupe flat slingbacks.

As I moved toward her, Kate Vermeil saw me and ducked into one of the shops. She dodged past fifty-five-gallon drums of carbon tetrachloride and dimethyl sulfate and burst through the rear door of the shop into an alley. I saw her fumbling with the cap of the inhaler. I hurled myself at her and caught at her legs. Her right shoe came off in my hand, but I grabbed her left ankle and she went down. She still had the inhaler and was trying to bring it to her mouth. I leapt on top of her and wrenched it away.

"Do you really want to kill yourself?" I aimed the inhaler at her face and screamed at her. "Do you, Kate? Do you?" The air in the alley was thick with despair and I was choking on it. "Come on, Kate. Let's do it!"

"No." Her head thrashed back and forth. "No, please. Stop."

Her terror fed mine. "Then what the hell are you doing with this thing?" I was shaking so badly that when I tried to pitch the inhaler into the dumpster, it hit the pavement only six feet away. I had come so close to screwing up. I climbed off her and rolled on my back and soaked myself in the night sky. When I screwed up, people died. "Cyanide is awful bad for the baby," I said.

"How do you know about my baby?" Her face was rigid with fear. "Who are you?"

I could breathe again, although I wasn't sure I wanted to.

"Fay Hardaway." I gasped. "I'm a PI; I left you a message this morning. Najma Jones hired me to find her daughter."

"Rashmi is dead."

"I know," I said. "So is Gratiana." I sat up and looked at her. "Father Elaine will be glad to see you."

Kate's eyes were wide, but I don't think she was seeing the alley. "Gratiana said the devils would come after me." She was still seeing the business end of the inhaler. "She said that if I didn't hear from her by tomorrow then we had lost everything and I should . . . do it. You know, to protect the church. And just now my sidekick picked up three times in ten minutes only there was nobody there and so I knew it was time."

"That was me, Kate. Sorry." I picked up the Donya Durand slingback I'd stripped off her foot and gave it back to her. "Tell me where you got this?"

"It was Rashmi's. We bought them together at Grayles. Actually I picked them out. That was before . . . I loved her, you know, but she was crazy. I can see that now, although it's kind of too late. I mean, she was okay when she was taking her meds, but she would stop every so often. She called it taking a vacation from herself. Only it was no vacation for anyone else, especially not for me. She decided to go off on the day we got married and didn't tell me and all of a sudden after the ceremony we got into this huge fight about the baby and who loved who more and she started throwing things at me—these shoes—and then ran out of the church barefoot. I don't think she ever really understood about . . . you know, what we were trying to do. I mean, I've talked to the Bride of God herself . . . but Rashmi." Kate rubbed her eye and her hand came away wet.

I sat her up and put my arm around her. "That's all right. Not really your fault. I think poor Rashmi must have been hanging by a thread. We all are. The whole human race, or what's left of it."

We sat there for a moment.

"I saw her mom this morning," I said. "She said to tell you she was sorry."

Kate sniffed. "Sorry? What for?"

I shrugged.

"I know she didn't have much use for me," said Kate. "At

least that's what Rashmi always said. But as far as I'm concerned the woman was a saint to put up with Rashmi and her mood swings and all the acting out. She was always there for her. And the thing is, Rashmi hated her for it."

I got to my knees, then to my feet. I helped Kate up. The alley was dark, but that wasn't really the problem. Even in the light of day, I hadn't seen anything.

8

I had no trouble finding space at the bike rack in front of Ronald Reagan Elementary. The building seemed to be drowsing in the heavy morning air, its brick wings enfolding the empty playground. A janitor bot was vacuuming the swimming pool, another was plucking spent blossoms from the clematis fence. The bots were headache yellow; the letters RRE in puffy orange slanted across their torsos. The gardening bot informed me that school wouldn't start for an hour. That was fine with me. This was just a courtesy call, part of the total service commitment I made to all the clients whom I had failed. I asked if I could see Najma Jones and he said he doubted that any of the teachers were in quite this early but he walked me to the office. He paged her; I signed the visitors' log. When her voice crackled over the intercom, I told the bot that I knew the way to her classroom.

I paused at the open door. Rashmi's mom had her back to me. She was wearing a sleeveless navy dress with cream-colored dupatta scarf draped over her shoulders. She passed down a row of empty desks, perching origami animals at the center of each. There were three kinds of elephants, ducks and ducklings, a blue giraffe, a pink cat that might have been a lion.

"Please come in, Ms. Hardaway," she said without turning around. She had teacher radar; she could see behind her back and around a corner.

"I stopped by your house." I slouched into the room like a kid who had lost her civics homework. "I thought I might catch you before you left for school." I leaned against a desk in the front row and picked up the purple crocodile on it. "You fold these yourself?"

"I did," she said. "I couldn't sleep last night, so finally I gave up and went for a walk. I ended up here. I like coming to school early, especially when no one else is around. There is so much time." She had one origami swan left over which she set on her own desk. "Staying after is different. If you're always the last one out at night, you're admitting that you haven't got anything to rush home to. It's pathetic, actually." She settled behind her desk and began opening windows on her desktop. "I've been teaching the girls to fold the ducks. They seem to like it. It's a challenging grade, the fifth. They come to me as bright and happy children and I am supposed to teach them fractions and pack them off to middle school. I shudder to think what happens to them there."

"How old are they?"

"Ten when they started. Most of them have turned eleven already. They graduate next week." She peered at the files she had opened. "Some of them."

"I take it on faith that I was eleven once," I said, "but I just don't remember."

"Your generation grew up in unhappy times." Her face glowed in the phosphors. "You haven't had a daughter yet, have you, Ms. Hardaway?"

"No."

We contemplated my childlessness for a moment.

"Did Rashmi like origami?" I didn't mean anything by it. I just didn't want to listen to the silence anymore.

"Rashmi?" She frowned, as if her daughter were a not-very-interesting kid she had taught years ago. "No. Rashmi was a difficult child."

"I found Kate Vermeil last night," I said. "I told her what you said, that you were sorry. She wanted to know what for."

"What for?"

"She said that Rashmi was crazy. And that she hated you for having her."

"She never hated me," said Najma quickly. "Yes, Rashmi was a sad girl. Anxious. What is this about, Ms. Hardaway?"

"I think you were at the Comfort Inn that night. If you want to talk about that, I would like to hear what you have to say. If not, I'll leave now."

She stared at me for a moment, her expression unreadable. "You know, I actually wanted to have many children." She got up from the desk, crossed the room and shut the door as if it were made of handblown glass. "When the seeding first began, I went down to City Hall and actually volunteered. That just wasn't done. Most women were horrified to find themselves pregnant. I talked to a bot, who took my name and address and then told me to go home and wait. If I wanted more children after my first, I was certainly encouraged to make a request. It felt like I was joining one of those mail order music clubs." She smiled and tugged at her dupatta. "But when Rashmi was born, everything changed. Sometimes she was such a needy baby, fussing to be picked up, but then she would lie in her crib for hours, listless and withdrawn. She started antidepressants when she was five and they helped. And the Department of Youth Services issued me a full-time bot helper when I started teaching. But Rashmi was always a handful. And since I was all by myself, I didn't feel like I had enough to give to another child."

"You never married?" I asked. "Found a partner?"

"Married who?" Her voice rose sharply. "Another woman?" Her cheeks colored. "No. I wasn't interested in that."

Najma returned to her desk but did not sit down. "The girls will be coming soon." She leaned towards me, fists on the desktop. "What is it that you want to hear, Ms. Hardaway?"

"You found Rashmi before I did. How?"

"She called me. She said that she had had a fight with her girl-friend who was involved in some secret experiment that she couldn't tell me about and they were splitting up and everything was shit, the world was shit. She was off her meds, crying, not making a whole lot of sense. But that was nothing new. She always called me when she broke up with someone. I'm her mother."

"And when you got there?"

"She was sitting on the bed." Najma eyes focused on something I couldn't see. "She put the inhaler to her mouth when I opened the door." She was looking into Room 103 of the

Comfort Inn. "And I thought to myself, what does this poor girl want? Does she want me to witness her death or stop it? I tried to talk to her, you know. She seemed to listen. But when I asked her to put the inhaler down, she wouldn't. I moved toward her, slowly. Slowly. I told her that she didn't have to do anything. That we could just go home. And then I was this close." She reached a hand across the desk. "And I couldn't help myself. I tried to swat it out of her mouth. Either she pressed the button or I set it off." She sat down abruptly and put her head in her hands. "She didn't get the full dose. It took forever before it was over. She was in agony."

"I think she'd made up her mind, Ms. Jones." I was only trying to comfort her. "She wrote the note."

"I wrote the note." She glared at me. "I did."

There was nothing I could say. All the words in all the languages that had ever been spoken wouldn't come close to expressing this mother's grief. I thought the weight of it must surely crush her.

Through the open windows, I heard the snort of the first bus pulling into the turnaround in front of the school. Najma Jones glanced out at it, gathered herself and smiled. "Do you know what Rashmi means in Sanskrit?"

"No, ma'am."

"Ray of sunlight," she said. "The girls are here, Ms. Hardaway." She picked up the origami on her desk. "We have to be ready for them." She held it out to me. "Would you like a swan?"

By the time I came through the door of the school, the turn-around was filled with buses. Girls poured off them and swirled onto the playground: giggling girls, whispering girls, skipping girls, girls holding hands. And in the warm June sun, I could almost believe they were happy girls.

They paid no attention to me.

I tried Sharifa's call. "Hello?" Her voice was husky with sleep.

"Sorry I didn't make it home last night, sweetheart," I said. "Just wanted to let you know that I'm on my way."

MAYFLOWER II

by Stephen Baxter

Stephen Baxter lives in Buckinghamshire in the British Midlands and has been a full-time writer since 1995. His first stories appeared in Interzone *in the late '80s and he has subsequently published twenty novels (two in collaboration with Sir Arthur C. Clarke and five for younger readers), three collections of short fiction, and three nonfiction books. He has won the Philip K Dick, John W. Campbell Memorial, British Science Fiction Association, Kurd Lasswitz, Seiun, Locus, and Sidewise awards. His latest novel,* Exultant, *moves his new "Destiny's Children" series decisively into the far future of his sprawling "Xeelee" future history. Upcoming is the final "Destiny's Children" novel,* Transcendent, *and* Sunstorm, *a new collaboration with Sir Arthur C. Clarke.*

The story that follows, a generation starship tale set in the early days of the "Xeelee" sequence, is a powerful and moving tale of the impact of the passage of time and what happens when a group of people step outside of human history.

TWENTY DAYS BEFORE the end of his world, Rusel heard that he was to be saved.

"Rusel. Rusel . . ." The whispered voice was insistent. Rusel rolled over, trying to shake off the effects of his usual mild sedative. His pillow was soaked with sweat. The room responded to his movement, and soft light coalesced around him.

His brother's face was hovering in the air at the side of his bed. Diluc was grinning widely.

"Lethe," Rusel said hoarsely. "You ugly bastard."

"You're just jealous," Diluc said. The Virtual made his face look even wider than usual, his nose more prominent. "I'm sorry to wake you. But I just heard—you need to know—"

"Know what?"

"Blen showed up in the infirmary." Blen was the nanochemist assigned to Ship Three. "Get this: he has a heart murmur." Diluc's grin returned.

Rusel frowned. "For that you woke me up? Poor Blen."

"It's not that serious. But, Rus—it's congenital."

The sedative dulled Rusel's thinking, and it took him a moment to figure it out.

The five Ships were to evacuate the last, brightest hopes of Port Sol from the path of the incoming peril. But they were slower-than-light transports, and would take many centuries to reach their destinations. Only the healthiest, in body and genome, could be allowed aboard a generation starship. And if Blen had a hereditary heart condition—

"He's off the Ship," Rusel breathed.

"And that means you're aboard, brother. You're the second-best nanochemist on this lump of ice. You won't be here when the Coalition arrives. You're going to live!"

Rusel lay back on his crushed pillow. He felt numb.

Diluc kept talking. "Did you know that families are *illegal* under the Coalition? Their citizens are born in tanks. Just the fact of our relationship would doom us, Rus! I'm trying to fix a transfer from Five to Three. If we're together, that's something, isn't it? I know it's going to be hard, Rus. But we can help each other. We can get through this . . ."

All Rusel could think about was Lora, whom he would have to leave behind.

➤ ➤ ➤

The next morning Rusel arranged to meet Lora in the Forest of Ancestors. He took a bubble-wheel surface transport, and set out early.

Port Sol was a ball of friable ice and rock a couple of hundred kilometres across. It was actually a planetesimal, an unfinished remnant of the formation of Sol system. Inhabited for millennia, its surface was heavily worked, quarried and pitted, and littered with abandoned towns. But throughout Port Sol's long human usage some areas had been kept undamaged, and as he drove

Rusel kept to the marked track, to avoid crushing the delicate sculptures of frost that had coalesced here over four billion years.

This was the very edge of Sol system. The sky was a dome of stars, with the ragged glow of the Galaxy hurled casually across its equator. Set in that diffuse glow was the sun, the brightest star, bright enough to cast shadows, but so remote it was a mere pinpoint. Around the sun Rusel could make out a tiny puddle of light: that was the inner system, the disc of worlds, moons, asteroids, dust and other debris that had been the arena of all human history before the first interstellar voyages some three thousand years earlier, and still the home of all but an invisible fraction of the human race. This was a time of turmoil, and today humans were fighting and dying, their triumphs and terror invisible. Even now, from out of that pale glow, a punitive fleet was ploughing towards Port Sol.

And visible beyond the close horizon of the ice moon was a squat cylinder, a misty sketch in the faint rectilinear sunlight. That was Ship Three, preparing for its leap into the greater dark.

The whole situation was an unwelcome consequence of the liberation of Earth from the alien Qax.

The Coalition of Interim Governance was the new, ideologically pure and viciously determined authority that had emerged from the chaos of a newly freed Earth. Relentless, intolerant, unforgiving, the Coalition was already burning its way out through the worlds and moons of Sol system. When the Coalition ships came, the best you could hope for was that your community would be broken up, your equipment impounded, and that you would be hauled back to a prison camp on Earth or its Moon for "reconditioning."

But if you were found to be harbouring anyone who had collaborated with the hated Qax, the penalties were much more extreme. The word Rusel had heard was "resurfacing."

Now the Coalition had turned its attention to Port Sol. This ice moon was governed by five Pharaohs, who had indeed collaborated with the Qax—though they described it as "mediating the effects of the occupation for the benefit of mankind"—and they had received anti-ageing treatments as a reward. So Port Sol was a "nest of illegal immortals and collaborators," the Coalition said, which its troops had been dispatched to "clean out." They seemed indifferent to the fact that in addition to the Pharaohs, some fifty thousand people called Port Sol home.

The Pharaohs had a deep network of spies on Earth, and they had had some warning. As the colonists had only the lightest battery of antiquated weaponry—indeed the whole moon, a refuge from the occupation, was somewhat low tech—nobody expected to be able to resist. But there was a way out.

Five mighty Ships were hastily thrown together. On each Ship, captained by a Pharaoh, a couple of hundred people, selected for their health and skill sets, would be taken away: a total of a thousand, perhaps, out of a population of fifty thousand, saved from the incoming disaster. There was no faster-than-light technology on Port Sol; these would be generation starships. But perhaps that was well: between the stars there would be room to hide.

All of these mighty historical forces had now focused down on Rusel's life, and they threatened to tear him away from his lover.

Rusel was an able nanochemist, he was the right age, and his health and pedigree were immaculate. But unlike his brother he hadn't been good enough to win the one-in-fifty lottery and make the cut to get a place on the Ships. He was twenty-eight years old: not a good age to die. But he had accepted his fate, so he believed—for Lora, his lover, had no hope of a place. At twenty she was a student, a promising Virtual idealist but without the mature skills to have a chance of competing. So at least he would die with her, which seemed to him some consolation. He was honest with himself; he had never been sure that this serenity would survive the appearance of the Coalition ships in Port Sol's dark sky—and now, it seemed, he was never going to find out.

Lora was waiting for him at the Forest of Ancestors. They met on the surface, embracing stiffly through their skinsuits. Then they set up a dome-tent and crawled through its collapsible airlock.

In the Forest's long shadows, Rusel and Lora made love: at first urgently, and then again, more slowly, thoughtfully. In the habs, inertial generators kept the gravity at one-sixth standard, about the same as Earth's Moon. But there was no gravity control out here in the Forest, and as they clung to each other they drifted in the tent's cool air, light as dreams.

Rusel told Lora his news.

Lora was slim, delicate. The population of this low-gravity moon tended to tallness and thin bones, but Lora seemed to him more elfin than most, and she had large, dark eyes that always seemed a little unfocussed, as if her attention was somewhere else. It was that sense of other-world fragility that had first attracted Rusel to her, and now he watched her fearfully.

With blankets bundled over her legs, she took his hand and smiled. "Don't be afraid."

"I'm the one who's going to live. Why should I be afraid?"

"You'd accepted dying. Now you've got to get used to the idea of living." She sighed. "It's just as hard."

"And living without you." He squeezed her hand. "Maybe that's what scares me most. I'm frightened of losing you."

"I'm not going anywhere."

He gazed out at the silent, watchful shapes of the Ancestors. These "trees," some three or four metres high, were stumps with "roots" that dug into the icy ground. They were living things, the most advanced members of Port Sol's low-temperature aboriginal ecology. This was their sessile stage. In their youth, these creatures, called "Toolmakers," were mobile, and were actually intelligent. They would haul themselves across Port Sol's broken ground, seeking a suitable crater slope or ridge face. There they would set down their roots and allow their nervous systems, and their minds, to dissolve, their purposes fulfilled. Rusel wondered what icy dreams might be coursing slowly through their residual minds. They were beyond decisions now; in a way he envied them.

"Maybe the Coalition will spare the Ancestors."

She snorted. "I doubt it. The Coalition only care about humans—and their sort of humans at that."

"My family have lived here a long time," he said. "There's a story that says we rode out with the first colonising wave." It was a legendary time, when the great engineer Michael Poole had come barnstorming all the way to Port Sol to build his great starships.

She smiled. "Most families have stories like that. After thousands of years, who can tell?"

"This is my home," he blurted. "This isn't just the destruction of us, but of our culture, our heritage. Everything we've worked for."

"But that's why you're so important." She sat up, letting the blanket fall away, and wrapped her arms around his neck. In Sol's dim light her eyes were pools of liquid darkness. "You're the future. The Pharaohs say that in the long run the Coalition will be the death of mankind, not just of *us*. Somebody has to save our knowledge, our values, for the future."

"But you—" *You will be alone, when the Coalition ships descend.* Decision sparked. "I'm not going anywhere."

She pulled back. "What?"

"I've decided. I'll tell Andres . . . and my brother. I can't leave here, not without you."

"You must," she said firmly. "You're the best for the job; believe me, if not, the Pharaohs wouldn't have selected you. So you have to go. It's your duty."

"What human being would run out on those he loved?"

Her face was set, and she sounded much older than her twenty years. "It would be easier to die. But you must live, live on and on, live on like a machine, until the job is done, and the race is saved."

Before her he felt weak, immature. He clung to her, burying his face in the soft warmth of her neck.

Nineteen days, he thought. *We still have nineteen days.* He determined to cherish every minute.

But as it turned out, they had much less time than that.

❧ ❧ ❧

Once again he was woken in the dark. But this time his room lights were snapped full on, dazzling him. And it was the face of Pharaoh Andres that hovered in the air beside his bed. He sat up, baffled, his system heavy with sedative.

"—thirty minutes. You have thirty minutes to get to Ship Three. Wear your skinsuit. Bring nothing else. If you aren't there we leave without you."

At first he couldn't take in what she said. He found himself staring at her face. Her head was hairless, her scalp bald, her eyebrows and even her eyelashes gone. Her skin was oddly smooth, her features small; she didn't look young, but as if her face had sublimed with time, like Port Sol's ice landscapes, leaving this palimpsest. She was rumoured to be two hundred years old.

Suddenly her words snapped into focus. "Don't acknowledge this message, just move. We lift in twenty-nine minutes. If you are Ship Three crew, you have twenty-nine minutes to get to—"

She had made a mistake: that was his first thought. Had she forgotten that there were still sixteen days to go before the Coalition ships were due? But he could see from her face there was no mistake.

Twenty-nine minutes. He reached down to his bedside cabinet, pulled out a nano pill, and gulped it down dry. Reality bleached, becoming cold and stark.

He dragged on his skinsuit and sealed it roughly. He glanced around his room, at his bed, his few pieces of furniture, the Virtual unit on the dresser with its images of Lora. *Bring nothing*. Andres wasn't a woman you disobeyed in the slightest particular.

Without looking back he left the room.

The corridor outside was bedlam. A thousand people shared this under-the-ice habitat, and all of them seemed to be out tonight. They ran this way and that, many in skinsuits, some hauling bundles of gear. He pushed his way through the throng. The sense of panic was tangible—and, carried on the recycled air, he thought he could smell burning.

His heart sank. It was obviously a scramble to escape—but the only way off the moon was the Ships, which could take no more than a thousand.

He couldn't believe what he was seeing. Had the sudden curtailing of the time left triggered this panic? But these were citizens of Port Sol, and this was its ultimate emergency. Had they lost all their values, all their sense of community? What could they hope to achieve by hurling themselves at Ships that had no room for them, but to bring everybody down with them? *But what would I do*? He could afford the luxury of nobility; he was getting out of here.

Twenty minutes.

He reached the perimeter concourse. Here, surface transports nuzzled against a row of simple airlocks. Some of the locks were already open, and people were crowding in, pushing children, bundles of luggage.

His own car was still here, he saw with relief. He pulled open his skinsuit glove and hastily pressed his palm to the wall. The door hissed open. But before he could pass through, somebody grabbed his arm.

A man faced him, a stranger, short, burly, aged perhaps forty. Behind him a woman clutched a small child and an infant. The adults had blanket-wrapped bundles on their backs. The man wore an electric-blue skinsuit, but his family were in hab clothes.

The man said desperately, "Buddy, you have room in that thing?"

"No," Rusel said.

The man's eyes hardened. "Listen. The Pharaohs' spies got it wrong. Suddenly the Coalition is only seven days out. Look, friend, you can see how I'm fixed. The Coalition breaks up families, doesn't it? All I'm asking is for a chance."

But there won't be room for you. Don't you understand? And even if there were— There were to be no children on the Ships at launch: that was the Pharaohs' harsh rule. In the first years of the long voyage, everybody aboard had to be maximally productive. The time for breeding would come later.

The man's fist bunched. "Listen, buddy—"

Rusel shoved the man in the chest. He fell backwards, stumbling against his children. His blanket bundle broke open, and goods spilled on the floor: clothes, diapers, children's toys.

"Please—" The woman approached him, stepping over her husband. She held out a baby. "Don't let the Coalition take him away. Please."

The baby was warm, soft, smiling. Rusel automatically reached out. But he stopped himself cold. Then he turned away.

The woman continued to call after him, but he didn't let himself think about it. *How could I do that? I'm no longer human*, he thought. He pushed into his car, slammed shut the door, and stabbed a preset routine into the control panel.

The car ripped itself away from the airlock interface, ignoring all safety protocols, and began to haul itself on its bubble wheels up the ramp from the under-the-ice habitat to the surface. Shaking, Rusel opened his visor. He might be able to see the doomed family at the airlock port. He didn't look back.

It wasn't supposed to be like this.

Andres's Virtual head coalesced before him. "Sixteen minutes to get to Ship Three. If you're not there we go without you. Fifteen forty-five. Fifteen forty . . ."

The surface was almost as chaotic as the corridors of the hab, as transports of all types and ages rolled, crawled or jumped. There was no sign of the Guardians, the Pharaohs' police force, and he was apprehensive about being held up.

He made it through the crowd, and headed for the track that would lead through the Forest of Ancestors to Ship Three. Out here there was a lot of traffic, but it was more or less orderly, everyone heading out the way he was. He pushed the car up to its safety-regulated maximum speed. Even so, he was continually overtaken. Anxiety tore at his stomach.

The Forest, with the placid profiles of the Ancestors glimmering in Sol's low light, looked unchanged from when he had last seen it, only days ago, on his way to meet Lora. He felt an unreasonable resentment that he had suddenly lost so much time, that his careful plan for an extended farewell to Lora had been torn up. He wondered where she was now. Perhaps he could call her.

Thirteen minutes. No time, no time.

The traffic ahead was slowing. The vehicles at the back of the queue weaved, trying to find gaps, and bunched into a solid pack.

Rusel punched his control panel and brought up a Virtual overhead image. Ahead of the tangle of vehicles, a ditch had been cut roughly across the road. People swarmed, hundreds of them. Roadblock.

Eleven minutes. For a moment his brain seemed as frozen as the Port Sol ice; frantic, bewildered, filled with guilt, he couldn't think.

Then a heavy-duty long-distance truck broke out of the pack behind him. Veering off the road to the left, it began to smash its way through the Forest. The elegant eightfold forms of the Ancestors were nothing but ice sculptures, and they shattered before the truck's momentum. It was ugly, and Rusel knew that each impact wiped out a life that might have lasted centuries more. But the truck was clearing a path.

Rusel hauled at his controls, and dragged his car off the road. Only a few vehicles were ahead of him in the truck's destructive wake. The truck was moving fast, and he was able to push his speed higher.

They were already approaching the roadblock, he saw. A few suit lights moved off the road and into the Forest; the blockers must be enraged to see their targets evade them so easily. Rusel kept his speed high. Only a few more seconds and he would be past the worst.

But there was a figure standing directly in front of him, helmet lamp bright, dressed in an electric-blue skinsuit, arms raised. As the car's sensors picked up the figure, its safety routines cut in, and he felt it hesitate. *Nine minutes.* He slammed his palm to the control panel, overriding the safeties.

He closed his eyes as the car hit the protester.

He remembered the blue skinsuit. He had just mown down the man from the airlock, who had been so desperate to save his family. He had no right to criticise the courage or the morals or the loyalty of others, he saw. *We are all just animals, fighting to survive. My seat on Ship Three doesn't make me any better.* He hadn't even had the guts to watch.

Eight minutes. He disabled the safety governors and let the car race down the empty road, its speed ever increasing.

❧ ❧ ❧

He had to pass through another block before he reached Ship Three—but this one was manned by Guardians. At least they were still loyal. They were an orderly line across the road, dressed in their bright yellow skinsuit-uniforms. Evidently they had pulled back to tight perimeters around the five Ships.

The queuing was agonising. With only five minutes before Andres's deadline, a Guardian pressed a nozzle to the car's window, flashed laser light into Rusel's face, and waved him through.

Ship Three was directly ahead of him. It was a drum, a squat cylinder about a kilometre across and half as tall. It sat at the bottom of its own crater, for Port Sol ice had been gouged out and plastered roughly over the surface of its hull. It looked less like a ship than a building, he thought, a building coated with thick ice, as if long abandoned. But it was indeed a starship, a ship designed for a journey of not less than centuries, and fountains of crystals already sparkled around its base in neat parabolic arcs: steam from the Ship's rockets, freezing immediately to ice. People milled at its base, running clumsily in the low gravity, and scurried up ramps that tongued down from its hull to the ground.

Rusel abandoned the car, tumbled out onto the ice and ran towards the nearest ramp. There was another stomach-churning wait as a Guardian in glowing yellow checked each identity. At last, after another dazzling flash of laser light in his eyes, he was through.

He hurried into an airlock. As it cycled it struck him that as he boarded this Ship, he was never going to leave it again: whatever became of him, this Ship was his whole world, for the rest of his life.

The lock opened. He ripped open his helmet. The light was emergency red, and klaxons sounded throughout the ship; the air was cold, and smelled of fear. Lethe, he was aboard! But there could only be a minute left. He ran along a cold, ice-lined corridor towards a brighter interior.

He reached an amphitheatre, roughly circular, carpeted with acceleration couches. People swarmed, looking for spare couches. The scene seemed absurd to Rusel, like a children's game. Andres's voice boomed from the air. "Get into a couch. Any couch. It doesn't matter. Forty seconds. Strap yourself in. Nobody is going to do it for you. Your safety is your own responsibility. Twenty-five seconds."

"Rus! Rusel!" Through the throng, Rusel made out a waving hand. It was Diluc, his brother, wearing his characteristic orange skinsuit. "Lethe, I'm glad to see you. I kept you a couch. Come on!"

Rusel pushed that way. Ten seconds. He threw himself down on the couch. The straps were awkward to pull around the bulk of his suit.

As he fumbled, he stared up at a Virtual display that hovered over his head. It was a view as seen from the Ship's blunt prow, looking down. Those tongue ramps were still in place, radiating down to the ice. But now a dark mass boiled around the base of the curving hull: people, on foot and in vehicles, a mob of them closing in. In amongst the mass were specks of bright yellow. Some of the Guardians had turned on their commanders, then. But others stood firm, and in that last second Rusel saw the bright sparks of weapon fire, all around the base of the Ship.

A sheet of brilliant white gushed out from the Ship's base. It was Port Sol ice, superheated to steam at tens of thousands of degrees. The image shuddered, and Rusel felt a quivering, deep in his gut. The Ship was rising, right on time, its tremendous mass raised on a bank of rockets.

When that great splash of steam cleared, Rusel saw small dark forms lying motionless on the ice: the bodies of the loyal and disloyal alike, their lives ended in a fraction of a second. A massive shame descended on Rusel, a synthesis of all the emotions that had churned through him since that fateful call of Diluc's. He had abandoned his lover to die; he had probably killed himself; and now he sat here in safety as others died on the ice below. What human being would behave that way? He felt the shame would never lift, never leave him.

Already the plain of ice was receding, and weight began to push at his chest.

➤ ➤ ➤

Soon the other Ships were lost against the stars, and it was as if Ship Three was alone in the universe.

In this opening phase of its millennial voyage Ship Three was nothing more than a steam rocket, as its engines steadily sublimed its plating of ice and hurled it out of immense nozzles. But those engines drew on energies that had once powered the expansion of the universe itself. Later the Ship would spin up for artificial gravity and switch to an exotic ramjet for its propulsion, and its true journey would begin.

The heaviest acceleration of the whole voyage had come in the first hours, as the Ship hurled itself away from Port Sol. After that the acceleration was cut to about a third standard—twice lunar gravity, twice what the colonists of Port Sol had been used to. For the time being, the acceleration couches were left in place in that big base amphitheatre, and in the night watches everybody slept there, all two hundred of them massed together in a single vast dormitory, their muscles groaning against the ache of the twice-normal gravity.

The plan was that for twenty-one days the Ships would run in towards the puddle of light that was Sol system. They would penetrate as far as the orbit of Jupiter, where they would use the giant planet's gravity field to slingshot them on to their final destinations. It seemed paradoxical to begin the exodus by hurling oneself deep into the inner system, the Coalition's home territory. But space was big, the Ships' courses had been plotted to avoid the likely trajectory of the incoming Coalition convoy, and they were to run silently, not even communicating with each other. The chances of them being detected were negligible.

Despite the wearying gravity the first days after launch were busy for everybody. The Ship's interior had to be rebuilt from its launch configuration to withstand this high-acceleration cruise phase. And the daily routines of the long voyage began.

The Ship was a closed environment and its interior had plenty of smooth surfaces where biofilms, slick detergent-proof cities of bugs, would quickly build up. Not only that, the fall-out of the Ship's human cargo—flakes of skin, hair, mucus—were all seed beds for bacterial growth. All of this had to be eliminated; Captain Andres declared she wanted the Ship to be as clean as a hospital.

The most effective way to achieve that—and the most "future-proof," in Andres's persistent jargon—was through the old-fashioned application of human muscle. Everybody had to pitch in, even the Captain herself. Rusel put in his statutory half-hour per day, scrubbing vigorously at the walls and floors and ceilings around the nanofood banks that were his primary responsibility. He welcomed the mindlessness of the work; he continued to seek ways in which to distract himself from the burden of thought.

He was briefly ill. In the first couple of weeks, everybody caught colds from everybody else. But the viruses quickly ran their course through the Ship's small population, and Rusel felt obscurely reassured that he would likely never catch another cold in his life.

A few days after launch Diluc came to find him. Rusel was up to his elbows in slurry, trying to find a fault in a nanofood bank's waste vent. Rusel, working non-stop, had seen little of his brother. He was surprised by how cheerful Diluc appeared, and how energetically he threw himself into his own work on the air cycling systems. He spoke brightly of his "babies," fans and pumps, humidifiers and dehumidifiers, filters and scrubbers and oxygenators.

The crew seemed to be dividing into two rough camps, Rusel thought. There were those who were behaving as if the outside universe didn't exist; they were bright, brash, too loud, their laughter forced. The other camp, to which Rusel felt he belonged, retreated the other way, into an inner darkness, full of complicated shadows.

But today Diluc's mood seemed complex. "Brother, have you been counting the days?"

"Since launch? No." He hadn't wanted to think about it.

"It's day seven. There's a place to watch. One of the observation lounges. Captain Andres says it's not compulsory, but if . . ."

It took Rusel a moment to think that through. *Day seven*: the day the Coalition convoy was due to reach Port Sol. Rusel flinched from the thought. But one of his worst moments of that chaotic launch day was when he had run down that desperate father and driven on, without even having the courage to watch what he was doing. Perhaps this would atone. "Let's do it," he said.

Ship Three, like its four siblings, was a fat torus. To reach the observation lounge the brothers had to ride elevators up through several decks to a point in the Ship's flattened prow, close to the rim. The lounge, crammed with Virtual generation gear, was already configured for the spin-up phase, and most of its furniture was plastered to the walls, which would become the floor. It was big enough for maybe fifty people, and it was nearly full; Rusel and Diluc had to crowd in.

Pharaoh Andres—now Captain Andres, Rusel reminded himself—was here, sitting in a deep, heavy-looking chair, front and centre before an immense, shining Virtual.

A ball of ice spun grandly before their eyes. It was Port Sol, of course; Rusel immediately recognised its icy geography of ancient craters, overlaid by a human patterning of quarries and mines, habitats and townships, landing ports. In the inhabited buildings lights shone, defiantly bright in outer-system gloom. It was a sculpture in white and silver, and it showed no sign of the chaotic panic that must be churning in its corridors.

The sight took Rusel's breath away. Somewhere down there was Lora; it was an almost unbearable thought, and he wished with all his heart he had stayed with her.

The Coalition convoy closed in.

Its ships materialised from the edge of the three-dimensional image, as if sliding in from another reality. The fleet was dominated by five, six, seven Spline warships, living ships each a kilometre or more wide. Confiscated from the expelled Qax, they were fleshy spheres, their hulls studded with weapons and sensors and crudely scrawled with the green tetrahedron that was the sigil of a free humanity.

Rusel's stomach filled with dread. "It's a heavy force," he said.

"They've come for the Pharaohs," Diluc said grimly. "The Coalition is showing its power. Images like this are no doubt being beamed throughout the system."

Then it began. The first touch of the energy beams, cherry-red, was almost gentle, and Port Sol ice exploded into cascades of glittering shards that drifted back to the surface, or escaped into space. Then more beams ploughed up the ice, and structures began to implode, melting, or to fly apart. A spreading cloud of crystals began to swathe Port Sol in a temporary, pearly atmosphere. It was silent, almost beautiful, too large-scale to make out individual deaths, a choreography of energy and destruction.

"We'll get through this," Diluc muttered. "We'll get through this."

Rusel felt numbed, no grief, only shame at his own inadequacy. This was the destruction of his home, of a world, and it was beyond his imagination. He tried to focus on one person, on Lora, to imagine what she must be doing—if she was still alive—perhaps fleeing through collapsing tunnels, or crowding into deep shelters. But, in the ticking calm of this lounge, with its fresh smell of new equipment, he couldn't even picture that.

As the assault continued, numbers flickered across the status display, an almost blasphemous tallying of the estimated dead.

➤ ➤ ➤

Even after the trauma of Port Sol, work had to continue on booting up the vital systems that would keep them all alive.

Rusel's own job, as he suddenly found himself the senior nanochemist on the Ship, was to set up the nanofood banks that would play a crucial part in recycling waste into food and other consumables like clothing. The work was demanding from the start. The banks were based on an alien technology, nano-devices purloined from the occupying Qax. Only partially understood, they were temperamental and difficult.

It didn't help that of the two assistants he had been promised a share of—most people were generalists in this small, skill-starved new community—only one had made it onto the Ship. It turned out that in the final scramble about ten percent of the crew hadn't made it aboard; conversely, about ten percent of those who actually were aboard shouldn't have been here at all. A few shame-faced "passengers" were yellow-uniformed Guardians who in the last moments had abandoned their posts and fled to the sanctuary of the Ship's interior.

The work had to get done anyhow. And it was urgent; until the nanofood was available the Ship's temporary rations were steadily depleting. The pressure on Rusel was intense. But Rusel was glad of the work, so hard mentally and physically in the high gravity he had no time to think, and when he hit his couch at night he slept easily.

On the fifteenth day Rusel achieved a small personal triumph as the first slab of edible food rolled out of his nanobanks.

Captain Andres had a policy of celebrating small achievements, and she was here as Rusel ceremoniously swallowed the first mouthful of his food, and she took the second. There was much clapping and back-slapping. Diluc grinned in his usual huge way. But Rusel, still numbed inside, didn't feel much like celebrating. Half the crew, it was estimated, were in some kind of shock; people understood. He got away from the crush as quickly as he could.

On the twenty-first day the Ship was to encounter Jupiter.

Captain Andres called the crew together in the acceleration-couch amphitheatre, all two hundred of them, and she set up a Virtual display in the air above them. The sun was just a pinpoint, though much brighter than seen from Port Sol, and Jupiter was a flattened ball of cloud, mottled with grey-brown bruises—the result, it was said, of an ancient battle. Few of the crew had travelled away from Port Sol before; they craned to see.

The most intriguing sight of all was four sparks of light that slid across the background of stars. They were the other Ships, numbers One, Two, Four and Five; the little fleet would come together at Jupiter for the first time since leaving Port Sol, and the last.

Andres walked though the crowd on their couches, declaiming loudly enough for all to hear, her authority easy and unforced. "We Pharaohs have been discussing destinations," she said. "Obviously the targets had to be chosen before we reached Jupiter; we needed to plan for our angles of emergence from Jupiter's gravity well. The Coalition is vindictive and determined, and it has faster-than-light ships. It will soon overtake us—but space is big, and five silent-running generation starships will be hard to spot. Even so it's obviously best to separate, to give them five targets to chase, not just one.

"So we have five destinations. And ours," she said, smiling, "is the most unique of all."

She listed the other Ships' targets, star systems scattered through the disc of the Galaxy—none closer than five hundred light years. "All well within the Ships' design parameters," she said, "and perhaps far enough to be safe. But *we* are going further."

She overlaid the image of the shining Ships with a ruddy,

shapeless mass of mist. "This is the Canis Major Dwarf Galaxy," she said. "Twenty-four thousand light years from Sol. It is the closest of the satellite galaxies—*but it is beyond the main Galaxy itself,* surely far outside the Coalition's grasp for the foreseeable future."

Rusel heard gasps throughout the amphitheatre. To sail beyond the Galaxy? . . .

Andres held her hands up to quell the muttering. "Of course such a journey is far in excess of what we planned. No generation starship has ever challenged such distances before, let alone achieved them." She stared around at them, fists on hips. "But if we can manage a thousand years of flight, we can manage ten, or fifty—why not? We are strong, we are just as determined as the Coalition and its drones—more so, for we know we are in the right."

Rusel wasn't used to questioning the Pharaohs' decisions, but he found himself wondering at the arrogance of the handful of Pharaohs to make such decisions on behalf of their crew—not to mention the generations yet unborn.

But Diluc muttered, "Can't say it makes much difference. A thousand years or ten thousand, I'll be dead in a century, and *I* won't see the end . . ."

Andres restored the images of the ships. Jupiter was expanding rapidly now, and the other Ships were swarming closer.

Andres said, "We have discussed names for our vessels. On such an epic voyage numbers won't do. Every ship must have a name! We have named our Ship-homes for great thinkers, great vessels of the past." She stabbed her finger around the Virtual image. "*Tsiolkovsky. Great Northern. Aldiss. Vanguard.*" She looked at her crew. "And as for us, only one name is possible. Like a band of earlier pilgrims, we are fleeing intolerance and tyranny; we sail into the dark and the unknown, carrying the hopes of an age. We are *Mayflower.*"

You didn't study history on Port Sol. Nobody knew what she was talking about.

At the moment of closest approach Jupiter's golden-brown cloudscape bellied over the upturned faces of the watching crew, and the Ships poured through Jupiter's gravity well. Even now the rule of silence wasn't violated, and the five Ships parted without so much as a farewell message.

From now on, wherever this invisible road in the sky took her, the second *Mayflower* was alone.

➤ ➤ ➤

As the days stretched to weeks, and the weeks to months, Rusel continued to throw himself into work—and there was plenty of it for everybody.

The challenges of running a generation starship were familiar to some extent, as the colonists of Port Sol had long experience in ecosynthesis, in constructing and sustaining closed artificial environments. But on Port Sol they had had the ice, rock and organic-chemistry resources of the ice moon itself to draw on. The Ship was now cut off from the outside universe.

So the cycles of air, water and solids would have to be maintained with something close to a hundred percent efficiency. The control of trace contaminants and pests would have to be ferociously tight: swarms of nano-bots were sent scurrying in pursuit of flakes of hair and skin. And the sealing of the Ship against leakages was vital—more nano-machines laboured to knit together the hull.

Not only that, the Ship's design had been hastily thrown together, and the vessel wasn't even completed on launch. The construction had been a hurried project anyhow, and the shaving-off of those final ten or twelve days of preparation time, as the Coalition fleet sneaked up in the dark, had made a significant difference. The crew laboured to complete the Ship's systems in flight.

The most significant difficulty, Rusel believed, was the sudden upping of the design targets. A thousand-year cruise, the nominal design envelope, was one thing. Now it was estimated that, cruising at about half lightspeed, it would take Ship Three *fifty times* as long to reach Canis Major. Even relativistic time dilation would only make a difference of a few percent to the subjective duration. As a consequence the tolerances on the Ship's systems were tightened by orders of magnitude.

There was yet another goal in all this rebuilding. The Ship's essential systems were to be simplified and automated as far as possible, to reduce the skill level required to maintain them. They were trying to "future-proof" the project, in Andres's jargon: to reduce the crew to the status of non-productive payload. But a key lesson of ecosynthesis was that the smaller the biosphere, the more conscious control it would require. The Ship was a much smaller environment than a Port Sol habitat, and that presented problems of stability; the ecological system was poorly buffered and would always be prone to collapse. It was clear that this small, tight biosphere would always have to be consciously managed if it were to survive.

As Diluc put it with grim humour, "We can't allow civilisation to fall in here."

Despite the horror of Port Sol, and the daunting timescale Andres had set—which Rusel suspected nobody believed anyhow—the rhythms of human life continued. It was as if they were all slowly healing, Rusel thought.

Diluc found a new partner, a plump, cheerful woman of about thirty called Tila. Diluc and Tila had both left lovers behind on Port Sol—and Tila had been forced to abandon a child. Now they seemed to be finding comfort with each other. Diluc was somewhat put out when they were both hauled into Andres's small private office to be quizzed about their relationship, but Andres, after much consulting of genetic maps, approved their continuing liaison.

Rusel was pleased for his brother, but he found Tila a puzzle. Most of the selected crew had been without offspring, back on Port Sol; few people with children, knowing they would have to leave them behind, had even offered themselves for selection. But *Tila had abandoned a child.* He saw no sign of this loss in her face, her manner; perhaps her new relationship with Diluc, and even the prospect of more children with him in the future, was enough to comfort her. He wondered what was going on inside her head, though.

As for Rusel, his social contacts were restricted to work. He found himself being subtly favoured by Captain Andres, along with a number of others of the Ship's senior technicians. There was no formal hierarchy on the Ship—no command structure below Andres herself. But this group of a dozen or so, a meritocracy selected purely by proven achievement, began to coalesce into a kind of governing council of the Ship.

That was about as much social life as Rusel wanted. Otherwise he just worked himself to the point of exhaustion, and slept. The complex mass of emotions lodged inside him—agony over the loss of Lora, the shock of seeing his home destroyed, the shame of living on—showed no signs of breaking up. None of this affected his contributions to the Ship, he believed. He was split in two, split between inside and out, and he doubted he would ever heal.

In fact he didn't really want to heal. One day he would die, as so many others had, as Lora probably had; one day he would atone for his sin of survival in death.

Meanwhile there was always the Ship. He slowly widened the scope of his work, and began to develop a feel for the Ship as a whole. As the systems embedded, it was as if the Ship was slowly coming alive, and he learned to listen to the rhythm of its pumps, feel the sighing of its circulating air.

Though Andres continued to use the fanciful name she had given it, Rusel and everybody else thought of it as they always had: as Ship Three—or, increasingly, just the Ship.

❧ ❧ ❧

Almost a year after Jupiter, Andres called her "council" together in the amphitheatre at the base of the Ship. This big chamber had been stripped of its acceleration couches, and the dozen or so of them sat on temporary chairs in the middle of an empty greywhite floor.

Andres told them she wanted to discuss a little anthropology.

In her characteristic manner she marched around the room, looming over her crew. "We've had a good year, for which I thank you. Our work on the Ship isn't completed—in a sense it never will be completed—but I'm now satisfied that *Mayflower* will survive the voyage. If we fail in our mission, it won't be the technology that betrays us, but the people. And that's what we've got to start thinking about now."

Mayflower was a generation starship, she said. By now mankind had millennia of experience of launching such ships. "And as far as we know, every last one of them has failed. And why? Because of the people.

"The most basic factor is population control. You'd think that would be simple enough! The Ship is an environment of a fixed size. As long as every parent sires one kid, on average, the population ought to stay stable. But by far the most common causes of failure are population crashes, in which the number of crew falls below the level of a viable gene pool and then shuffles off to extinction—or, more spectacularly, explosions in which people eat their way to the hull of their ship and then destroy each other in the resulting wars."

Diluc said dryly, "Maybe all that proves it's just a dumb idea. The scale is just too big for us poor saps to manage."

Andres gazed at him challengingly. "A bit late to say that now, Diluc!"

"Of course it's not just numbers but our population's genetic health that we have to think about," pointed out Ruul. This lanky, serious man was the Ship's senior geneticist. "We've already started, of course. All of us went through genetic screening before we were selected. There are only two hundred of us, but we're as genetically diverse a sample of Port Sol's population as possible. We should avoid the founder effect—none of us has a genetically-transmitted disease to be spread through the population—and, provided we exert some kind of control over breeding partnerships, we should be able to avoid genetic drift, where defective copies of a gene cluster."

Diluc looked faintly disgusted. "'Control over breeding partnerships'? What kind of language is that?"

Andres snapped, "The kind of language we're going to have to embrace if we're to survive. We must take control of reproductive strategies. Remember, on this Ship the purpose of having children is not for the joy of it and similar primate rewards, but to maintain the crew's population levels and genetic health, and thereby to see through our mission." She eyed Diluc. "Oh, I'm not against comfort. I was human once! But we are going to have to separate companionship needs from breeding requirements."

She glanced around. "I'm sure you are all smart enough to have figured that out for yourselves. But even this isn't enough, if the mission is to be ensured."

Diluc said, "It isn't?"

"Of course not. This is a desperately small universe. We will always rely on the ship's systems, and mistakes or deviances will be punished by catastrophe—for as long as the mission lasts. Non-modified human lifespans average out at around a century; we just haven't evolved to think further. But a century is but a moment for our mission. *We must future-proof,* I've said it over and over. And to do that we will need a continuity of memory, purpose and control far beyond the century-long horizons of our transients."

Transients: it was the first time Rusel had heard her use that word.

He thought he saw where all this was leading. He said carefully, "Port Sol was not a normal human society. With respect. Because it had you Pharaohs at its heart."

"Yes," she said approvingly, her small face expressionless. "And *that* is the key." She lifted her hand before her face and inspected it. "Two centuries ago the Qax Governor made me ageless. Well, I served the Qax—but my deeper purpose was always to serve mankind. I fled to Port Sol, with others, to escape the Qax; and now I have had to flee Sol system itself to escape my fellow human beings. But I continue to serve mankind. And it is the continuity I provide, a continuity that transcends human timescales, which will enable this mission to succeed, where even Michael Poole failed."

Diluc pulled a face. "What do you want from us—to worship you as a god?"

There were gasps; you didn't speak to a Pharaoh like that. But Andres seemed unfazed. "A god? No—although a little awe from you wouldn't come amiss, Diluc. And anyhow, it probably won't be *me.* Remember, it wasn't a human agency that gave me my anti-ageing treatments, but the Qax . . ."

The Qax's own body architecture had nothing in common with humanity's. They were technically advanced, but their medicinal manipulation of their human subjects was always crude.

"The success rate was only ever some forty percent," Andres said. She inspected her hand, pulling at slack skin. "Oh, I would dearly love to live through this mission, all fifty millennia of it, and see it through to its conclusion. But I fear that's unlikely to happen." She gazed around at them. "I can't do this alone; that's the bottom line. I will need help."

Diluc suddenly saw it, and his mouth dropped open. "You aren't serious."

"I'm afraid so. It is necessary for the good of the mission that *some of the people in this room do not die.*"

Ruul the geneticist unfolded his tall frame from his chair. "We believe it's possible. We have the Qax technology." Without drama, he held up a yellow pill.

There was a long silence.

Andres smiled coldly. "We can't afford to die. We must remember, while everybody else forgets.

"And we must manage. We must achieve *total* social control— total over every significant aspect of our crew's lives—and we must govern their children's lives just as tightly, as far as we can see ahead. Society has to be as rigid as the bulkheads which contain it. Oh, we can give the crew freedom within limits! But we need to enforce social arrangements in which conflict is reduced to negligible, appropriate skill levels are kept up—and, most importantly, a duty of maintenance of the Ship is hammered home into every individual at birth."

Rusel said, "And what about the rights of those you call the transients? We Pharaohs would be taking away all meaningful choice from them—and their children, and their children's children."

"Rights? Rights?" She loomed over him. "Rusel, a transient's only purpose is to live, reproduce and die in an orderly fashion, thus preserving her genes to the far future. There is no room on this Ship for democracy, no space for love! A transient is just a conduit for her genes. She has no rights, any more than a bit of pipe that carries water from source to sink. Surely you thought this through. When we get to Canis Major, when we find a world to live on, when again we have an environment of surplus—then we can talk about rights. But in the meantime we will control."

Her expression was complex. "But you must see that we will control through love."

Diluc gaped. "*Love?*"

"The Qax technology was based on a genetic manipulation, you know. We Pharaohs were promised that our gift would be passed on to our children. And we had those children! But we Pharaohs never bred true. I once had a child myself. She did not survive." She hesitated, just for a second. Then she went on, "But by now there are genes for immortality, or at least longevity, scattered through the human population—even among *you*. Do you see now why we had to build these arks—why we couldn't flee and abandon you, or just take frozen zygotes or eggs?" She spread her hands wide. "Because you are my children, and I love you."

Nobody moved. Rusel thought he could see tears in her stony eyes. *She is grotesque,* he thought.

Diluc said carefully, "Pharaoh, would I be able to bring Tila with me? And our children, if we have them?"

"I'm sorry," she said gently. "Tila doesn't qualify. Besides, the social structure simply wouldn't be sustainable if—"

"Then count me out." Diluc stood up.

She nodded. "I'm sure you won't be the only one. Believe me, this is no privilege I'm offering you."

Diluc turned to Rusel. "Brother, are you coming with me?"

Rusel closed his eyes. The thought of his eventual death had actually been a comfort to him—a healing of his inner wounds, a lifting of the guilt he knew he would carry throughout his life. Now even the prospect of death was being taken away, to be replaced by nothing but an indefinite extension of duty.

But he had to take it on, he saw. As Lora herself had told him, he had to live on, like a machine, and fulfil his function. That was why he was here; only that way could he atone.

He looked up at Diluc. "I'm sorry," he said.

Complex emotions crossed his brother's face: anger, despair, perhaps a kind of thwarted love. He turned and left the room.

Andres behaved as if Diluc had never existed.

"We will always have to combat cultural drift," she said. "It is the blight of the generation starship. Already we have some pregnancies; soon we will have the first children, who will live and die knowing nothing but this Ship. And in a few generations—well, you can guess the rest. First you forget where you're going. Then you forget you're going anywhere. Then you forget you're on a damn ship, and start to think the vessel is the whole universe. And so forth! Soon nothing is left but a rotten apple full of worms, falling through the void. Even the great engineer Michael Poole suffered this; a fifteen-hundred-year generation starship he designed—the first *Great Northern*—barely limped home. Oh, every so often you might have a glorious moment as some cannibalistic savage climbs the decks and peers out in awe at the stars, but that's no consolation for the loss of the mission.

"Well, not this time. You engineers will know we're almost at the end of our GUTdrive cruise phase; the propellant ice is almost exhausted. And that means the Ship's hull is exposed." She clapped her hands—and, to more gasps from the crew, the amphitheatre's floor suddenly turned transparent.

Rusel was seated over a floor of stars; something inside him cringed.

Andres smiled at their reaction. "Soon we will leave the plane of the Galaxy, and what a sight *that* will be. In a transparent hull our crew will never be able to forget they are on a Ship. There will be no conceptual breakthroughs on *my* watch!"

➤ ➤ ➤

With the ice exhausted, the Ship's banks of engines were shut down. From now on a dark matter ramjet would provide a comparatively gentle but enduring thrust.

Dark matter constituted most of the universe's store of mass, with "light matter"—the stuff of bodies and ships and stars—a mere trace. The key advantage of dark matter for the Ship's mission planners was that it was found in thick quantities far beyond the visible disc of the Galaxy, and would be plentiful throughout the voyage. But dark matter interacted with the light only through gravity. So now invisible wings of gravitational force unfolded ahead of the Ship. Spanning thousands of kilometres, these acted as a scoop to draw dark matter into the hollow centre of the torus-shaped Ship. There, concentrated, much of it was annihilated and induced to give up its mass-energy, which in turn drove a residuum out of the Ship as reaction mass.

Thus the Ship ploughed on into the dark.

Once again the Ship was rebuilt. The acceleration provided by the dark matter ramjet was much lower than the ice rockets', and so the Ship was spun about its axis, to provide artificial gravity through centrifugal force. It was an ancient solution and a crude one—but it worked, and ought to require little maintenance in the future.

The spin-up was itself a spectacular milestone, a great swivelling as floors became walls and walls became ceilings. The transparent floor of the acceleration-couch amphitheatre became a wall full of stars, whose cool emptiness Rusel rather liked.

Meanwhile the new "Elders," the ten of them who had accepted Andres's challenge, began their course of treatment. The procedure was administered by geneticist Ruul and a woman called Selur, the Ship's senior doctor. The medics took it slowly enough to catch any adverse reactions, or so they hoped.

For Rusel it was painless enough, just injections and tablets, and he tried not to think about the alien nano-probes embedding themselves in his system, cleaning out ageing toxins, repairing cellular damage, rewiring his very genome.

His work continued to be absorbing, and when he had spare time he immersed himself in studies. All the crew were generalists to some degree, but the ten new Elders were expected to be a repository of memory and wisdom far beyond a human lifespan. So they all studied everything, and they learned from each other.

Rusel began with the disciplines he imagined would be most essential in the future. He studied medicine; anthropology, sociology and ethics; ecosynthesis and all aspects of the Ship's life-support machinery; the workings of the Ship's propulsion systems; techniques of colonisation; and the geography of the Galaxy and its satellites. He also buttonholed Andres herself and soaked up her knowledge of human history. Qax-derived nano-systems were so prevalent throughout the Ship that Rusel's own expertise was much in demand.

His major goal continued to be to use up as much of his conscious time as possible with work. The studying was infinitely expandable, and very satisfying to his naturally acquisitive mind. He found he was able to immerse himself in esoteric aspects of one discipline or another for days on end, as if he was an abstract intellect, almost forgetting who he was.

His days passed in a dream, as if time itself flowed differently for him now.

The Elders' placid lives were not without disturbance, however. The Qax biotechnology was far from perfect. In the first year of treatment one man suffered kidney failure; he survived, but had to be taken out of the programme.

And it was a great shock to all the Elders when Ruul himself succumbed to a ferocious cancer, as the technological rebuilding of his cells went awry.

The day after Ruul's death, as the Elders adjusted to the loss of his competence and dry humour, Rusel decided he needed a break. He walked out of the Elders' Cloister and into the body of the Ship, heading for the area where his brother had set up his own home with Tila.

On all the Ship's cylindrical decks, the interior geography had been filled by corridors and cabins, clustered in concentric circles around little open plazas—"village squares." Rusel knew the theory, but he quickly got lost; the layout of walls and floors and false ceilings was changed again and again as the crew sorted out their environment.

At last he came to the right doorway on the right corridor. He was about to knock when a boy, aged about five with a shock of thick black hair, rocketed out of the open door and ran between Rusel's legs. The kid wore a bland Ship's-issue coverall, long overdue for recycling judging by its grime.

This must be Tomi, Rusel thought, Diluc's eldest. Child and Elder silently appraised each other. Then the kid stuck out his tongue and ran back into the cabin.

In a moment Diluc came bustling out of the door, wiping his hands on a towel. "Look, what in Lethe's going on—Rusel! It's you. Welcome, welcome!"

Rusel embraced his brother. Diluc smelt of baby sick, cooking and sweat, and Rusel was shocked to see a streak of grey in his brother's hair. Perhaps he had been locked away longer than he had realised.

Diluc led Rusel into his home. It was a complex of five small interconnected cabins, including a kitchen and bathroom. Somebody had been weaving tapestries; gaudy, space-filling abstract patterns filled one wall.

Rusel sat on a sofa adapted from an acceleration couch, and accepted a slug of some kind of liquor. He said, "I'm sorry I frightened Tomi. I suppose I've let myself become a stranger."

Diluc raised an eyebrow. "Two things about that. Not so much *stranger* as *strange*." He brushed his hand over his scalp.

Rusel involuntarily copied the gesture, and felt bare skin. He had long forgotten that the first side-effect of the Pharaoh treatment had been the loss of his hair; his head was as bald as Andres's. Surrounded all day by the other Elders, Rusel had got used to it, he supposed. He said dryly, "Next time I'll wear a wig. What's the second thing I got wrong?"

"That isn't Tomi. Tomi was our first. He's eight now. That was little Rus, as we call him. He's five."

"*Five?*" But Rusel had attended the baby Rusel's naming ceremony. It seemed like yesterday.

"And now we're due for another naming. We've missed you, Rus."

Rusel felt as if his life was slipping away. "I'm sorry."

Tila came bustling in, with an awestruck little Rus in tow, and an infant in her arms. She too seemed suddenly to have aged; she had put on weight, and her face was lined by fine wrinkles. She said that Tomi was preparing a meal—of course Uncle Rusel would stay to eat, wouldn't he?—and she sat down with the men and accepted a drink.

They talked of inconsequentials, and of their lives.

Diluc, having stormed out of Andres's informal council, had become something of a leader in his own new community. Andres had ordered that the two-hundred-strong crew should be dispersed to live in close-knit "tribes" of twenty or so, each lodged in a "village" of corridors and cabins. There were to be looser links between the tribes, used for such purposes as finding partners. Thus the Ship was united in a single "clan." Andres said this social structure was the most common form encountered among humans "in the wild," as she put it, all the way back to pretechnological days on Earth. Whether or not that was true, things had stayed stable so far.

Andres had also specified the kind of government each tribe should aspire to. In such a small world each individual should be cherished for her unique skills, and for the value of the education invested in her. People were interdependent, said Andres, and the way they governed themselves should reflect that. Even democracy wouldn't do, as in a society of valued individuals the subjection of a minority to the will of a majority must be a bad thing. So Diluc's tribe ran by consensus.

"We talk and talk," Diluc said with a rueful grin, "until we all agree. Takes hours, sometimes. Once, the whole of the night watch—"

Tila snorted. "Don't tell me you don't like it that way. You always did like the sound of your own voice!"

The most important and difficult decisions the tribe had to make concerned reproduction. Most adults settled down into more-or-less monogamous marriages. But there had to be a separation between marriages for companionship and liaisons for reproduction; the gene pool was too small to allow matings for such trivial reasons as love.

Diluc showed Rusel a draft of a "social contract" he was preparing to capture all this. "First, on reaching adulthood you submit yourself to the needs of the group as a whole. For instance your choice of career depends on what we need as much as what you want to do. Second, you agree to have kids only as the need allows. If we're short of the optimum, you might have three or four or five, whether you want them or not, to bring up the numbers; if we're over, you might have none at all and die childless. Third, you agree to postpone parenthood as long as possible, and to keep working as long as possible. That way you maximise the investment the tribe has made in educating you. Fourth, you can select your own breeding-spouse, who *may* be the same as your companionship-spouse—"

"We were lucky," Tila said fervently.

"But she can't be closer than a second cousin. And you have

to submit to having your choice approved by the Elders. That's you," he grinned at Rusel. "Your match will be screened for genetic desirability, to maximise the freshness of the gene pool— all of that. And finally, if despite everything you're unlucky enough to have been born with some inheritable defect that might, if propagated, damage the Ship's chances of completing its mission, you agree not to breed at all. Your genetic line stops with you."

Rusel frowned. "That's eugenics."

Diluc shrugged. "What else can we do?"

Diluc hadn't studied Earth history, and without that perspective, Rusel realised, that word carried none of the horrific connotations it had once borne. As Diluc had implied, they had little choice anyhow given the situation they were in. And anyhow, eugenics was lower-tech than genetic engineering: more future-proofing.

Rusel studied the draft. "And what happens if I break the rules?"

Diluc was uncomfortable; suddenly Rusel was aware that he was an Elder, as well as this man's brother. "We'll cross that bridge when we come to it," Diluc said. "Look, Rus, we don't have police here, and we haven't room for jails. Besides, everybody really is essential to the community as a whole. We can't coerce. We work by persuasion; we hope that such situations will be easily resolved."

Diluc talked of personal things too: of the progress of his boys at school, how Tomi had always hated the hour's wall-cleaning he had to put in each day, while little Rus loved it for the friends he was making.

"They are good kids," Rusel said.

"Yes. And you need to see more of them," Diluc said pointedly. "But, you know, Rus, they're not like us. They are the first Shipborn generation. They are *different*. To them, all our stories of Port Sol and Canis Major are so many legends of places they will never see. This Ship is *their* world, not ours: we, born elsewhere, are aliens here. You know, I keep thinking we've bitten off more than we can chew, for all Andres's planning. Already things are drifting. No wonder generation starships always fail!"

Rusel tried to respond to their openness by giving them something of himself. But he found he had little to say. His mind was full of studying, but there was very little *human* incident in his life. It was if he hadn't been alive at all, he thought with dismay.

Diluc was appalled to hear of Ruul's death. "That pompous geneticist—I suppose in a way it's fitting he should be the first to go. But don't let it take you, brother." Impulsively he crossed to Rusel and rested his hand on his brother's shoulder. "You know, all this is enough for me: Tila, the kids, the home we're building together. It's good to know that our lives serve a higher goal, but *this* is all I need to make me happy. Maybe I don't have much imagination, you think?"

Or maybe you're more human than I am, Rusel thought. "We must all make our choices," he said.

Diluc said carefully, "But you can still make a different choice."

"What do you mean?"

He leaned forward. "Why don't you give it up, Rus? This crappy old Qax nano-medicine, this dreadful anti-ageing—you're still young; you could come out of there, flush the shit out of your system, grow your hair back, find some nice woman to make you happy again . . ."

Rusel tried to keep his face expressionless, but he failed.

Diluc backed off. "Sorry. You still remember Lora."

"I always will. I can't help it."

"We've all been through an extraordinary experience," Tila said. "I suppose we all react differently."

"Yes." Tila, he remembered, had left behind a child.

Diluc looked into his eyes. "You never will come out of that Cloister, will you? Because you'll never be able to cast off that big sack of guilt on your back."

Rusel smiled. "Is it that obvious?"

Tila was a gracious hostess. She perceived his discomfort, and they began to talk of old times, of the days on Port Sol. But Rusel was relieved when Tomi, unreasonably tall, came in to announce that the meal was ready, relieved to hurry through the food and get away, relieved to shut himself away once more in the bloodless monastic calm of the Cloister.

➤ ➤ ➤

He would remember that difficult visit again, much later, when a boy came to find him.

As time passed, the Elders withdrew from the crew. They requisitioned their own sealed-off living area. It was close to the Ship's axis, where the artificial gravity was a little lower than further out, a sop to muscles and bones expected to weaken with the centuries. Ruul had humorously called this refuge the "Cloister." And the Elders were spared the routine chores, even the cleaning, to which the rest of the crew were subject. Soon it was hard to avoid the feeling that the crew were only there to serve the Elders.

Of course it was all part of Andres's grand social design that there should eventually be an "awe gap," as she put it, between Elders and transients. But Rusel wondered if a certain distancing was inevitable anyhow. The differential ageing of transients and Elders became apparent surprisingly quickly. When an Elder met a transient she saw a face that would soon crumble with age and vanish, while the transient saw a mysteriously unchanging figure who would see events that transpired long after the transient was dead. Rusel watched as friendships dissolved, even love affairs evaporated, under this stress.

However, the increasingly isolated Elders, thrown on each other's company, were no chummy club. They were all bright, ambitious people; they wouldn't have been filtered out for Andres's inner circle otherwise, and there was always a certain tension and bickering. Doctor Selur remarked sourly that it was like being stuck with a bunch of jealous academics, *forever*.

But the Elders were also cautious of each other, Rusel thought. Always at the back of his mind was the thought that he would have to live with these people for a *long* time. So he strove not to make any enemies—and conversely not to get too close to anyone. Eternity with a lover was one thing, but with an *ex*-lover it would be hellish. Better that things were insipid, but tolerable.

Life settled down. In the calm of the Cloister, time passed smoothly, painlessly.

One day a boy came knocking timorously on the Cloister's

door, asking for Rusel. He was aged about sixteen.

Rusel thought he recognised him. He had spent a long time on his own, and his social skills were rusty, but he tried to focus and greet the boy warmly. "Tomi! It's so long since I saw you."

The boy's eyes were round. "My name is Poro, sir."

Rusel frowned. "But that day I came to visit—you made us all a meal, me and Diluc and Tila, while little Rus played . . ." But that was long ago, he told himself, he wasn't sure *how* long, and he fell silent.

The boy seemed to have been prepared for this. "My name is Poro," he said firmly. "Tomi was—"

"Your father."

"My *grand*father."

So this was Diluc's great-grandson. *Lethe, how long have I spent inside this box?*

The boy was looking around the Cloister. His eyes were unblinking, his mouth pulled back in a kind of nervous grin. None of the Elders was hot on empathy, especially with transients, but suddenly Rusel felt as if he saw this place through this child's eyes.

The Cloister was like a library, perhaps. Or a hospital room. The Elders sat in their chairs or walked slowly through the silence of the room, their every step calculated to reduce the risk of harm to their fragile, precious bodies. It had been this way since long before Poro had been born, these musty creatures pursuing their cold interests. *And I, who once loved Lora when she wasn't much older than this child, am part of this dusty stillness.*

"What do you want, Poro?"

"Diluc is ill. He is asking for you."

"Diluc? . . ."

"Your brother."

It turned out that Diluc was more than ill; he was dying.

So Rusel went with the boy, stepping outside the confines of the Cloister for the first time in years.

He wasn't at home out here any more. The transients among the original crew had died off steadily, following a demographic curve not terribly different to that they would have endured had they been able to remain on Port Sol. Rusel grew used to seeing faces he had known since childhood crumple with age and disappear before him. Still, it had been a shock when that first generation reached old age—and, since many of them had been around the same age at launch, the deaths came in a flood.

Meanwhile, everything about the new sort was *different*, the way they rebuilt the Ship's internal architecture, their manner with each other, the way they wore their hair—even their language, which was full of a guttural slang.

The basic infrastructure of the Ship itself, of course, remained unchanged. In a way he came to identify with that level of reality much more than with the flickering, fast-paced changes wrought by the transients. Though his senses were slowly dulling—the Qax treatment had slowed his ageing but not stopped it entirely—he felt he was becoming more attuned to the Ship's subtle vibrations and noises, its mechanical moods and joys. Transients came and went, and the other Elders were awkward old cusses, but the Ship itself was his constant friend, demanding only his care.

But the transients knew him, of course. They stared at him with curiosity, or irreverence—or, worst of all, awe.

As they walked he saw that the boy had a bruise on his forehead. "What happened to you?"

"Punishment." Poro averted his eyes, ashamed. One of his teachers had whacked him with a ruler for "impudence," which turned out to mean asking too-deep questions.

There was a paradox in the philosophy of education aboard the Ship. The students had to be bright enough to be able to understand and maintain the Ship's systems. But there was no room for expansion or innovation. There was usually only one way to do things: you learned it that way, and you did *not* tinker. It had been quickly found that education needed to be restrictive, and that curiosity couldn't be allowed to go unchecked; you learned only what you needed to know, and were taught not to ask any more, not to explore.

It was necessary, Rusel knew. But he didn't like the idea of battering students into submission. Perhaps he would have a word with Andres about it, get a new policy formulated.

They reached Diluc's corridor-village and came to a familiar doorway.

Tila was still alive, though she was bent, her hair exploded to white, and her face crushed to a wrinkled mask. "Thank you for coming," she whispered, and she took Rusel's hands in her own. "There are so few of us left, you know, so few not Shipborn. And he did keep asking for you."

Rusel pressed her hand, reserved, awkward. He felt out of practice with people, with emotions; before this broken-hearted woman he felt utterly inadequate.

Before he could see his brother he had to be met by a series of tribal worthies. Burly men and women in drab Ship's-issue clothing, they gathered with solemn expressions. The greetings were lengthy and complicated. The transients were evolving elaborate rituals to be used on every social occasion: meeting, parting, taking meals. Rusel could see the value of such rituals, which used up time, and reduced social friction. But it was hard to keep up with the ever-changing rules. The only constant was that these politeness games always got more elaborate—and it was very easy to get something wrong and give offence.

The worthies looked concerned at the prospective loss of Diluc, as well they might.

Andres's imposition of "rule-by-consensus" had been less than effective. In some of the Ship's dozen or so tribes, there was endless jaw-jaw that paralysed decision-making. Elsewhere strong individuals had begun to grasp power, more or less overtly. Andres wasn't too concerned as long as the job got done, the basic rules obeyed: whoever was in command had to get the approval of the Elders, and so Andres and her team were still able to exert a moderating influence.

The situation in Diluc's tribe had been more subtle, though. As the brother of an Elder he had had a unique charisma, and he had used that power subtly to push his peers to conclusions they might not otherwise have reached. He had been a leader, but of the best sort, Rusel thought, leading from the back, invisibly. Now he was about to be taken away, and his people knew they would miss him.

With the worthies out of the way, the Elder was presented to Diluc's children, grandchildren, great-grandchildren. All of them went through more elaborate transient-to-Elder rituals, even the smallest children, with an unsmiling intensity Rusel found disturbing.

At last, with reluctance, he entered Diluc's apartment.

The rooms were much as he remembered them, though the tapestries on the wall had changed. Diluc lay on a bed, covered by a worn blanket. Rusel was shocked by how his brother had imploded with age. And he could see, even through the blanket, the swelling of the stomach tumour that was killing him.

He had thought Diluc was sleeping. But his brother opened one eye. "Hello, Rusel," he said, his voice a croak. "You bastard."

"I'm sorry—"

"You haven't been here in fifty years."

"Not that long."

"Fifty years! *Fifty years!* It's not as if—" He broke up in coughing. "As if it's that big a Ship . . ."

They talked, as they had talked before. Diluc told rambling anecdotes about his grandchildren and great-grandchildren, all properly genetically selected, all wonderful kids.

Rusel spoke of a cull of the Elders.

Diluc grimaced. "So even immortals die." He reached out his hand. Rusel took it; the bones were frail, the flesh almost vanished. "Look after them," Diluc said.

"Who?"

"Everybody. *You* know. And look after yourself." He looked up at his brother, and Rusel saw pity in his brother's eyes—pity for *him*, from a withered, dying man.

He could bear to stay only a few minutes more.

The cull of Elders had had a variety of causes, according to Doctor Selur, but Andres had sniffed at that. "I've seen it before. Call it a death wish," she had said. "You reach an age where your body knows it's time to die. You accept it. Maybe it's some kind of neural programming, a comfort as we face the inevitable." She cackled; she was ageing too, and was now toothless. "The Qax treatments don't do anything about it. And it carries away more would-be immortals than you'd imagine. Strange, isn't it? That longevity should turn out to be a matter of the mind as much as the body."

Rusel had spent some years in faint trepidation, wondering if and when his own dark-seeking mental programming might kick in. But it never did, and he wondered if he had some unsuspected strength—or, perhaps, a deficiency.

Rusel tried to talk over his feelings about Diluc's death. But Andres was dismissive. "Diluc was a coward who shunned his duty," she said. "Anyhow, better when the first crew have all gone. *They* always saw us as peers, to some extent. So they resisted our ideas, our leadership; it was natural. We're totally alien to the new sort, and that will make them more malleable.

"And the new lot never suffered the trauma of seeing Port Sol trashed before their eyes. The psychological trauma ran deep, Rusel; you aren't the only one . . . This new batch are healthy, adjusted to the environment of the Ship, because they've known nothing else. When there's only them left, we'll be able to get things shaken down properly around here at last. You'll see."

With relief Rusel returned to his studies, away from the complications of humanity. Once more time flowed smoothly past him, and that difficult day receded down the dimming corridors of his memory.

No more relatives came to see him, ever again.

➤ ➤ ➤

". . . Rusel. Rusel!" The voice was harsh—Andres's voice.

Sleep was deep these days, and it took him an age to emerge. And as he struggled into the light he swam up through layers of dream and memory, until he became confused about what was real and what wasn't. He always knew *where* he was, of course, even in his deepest sleep. He was on the Ship, his drifting tomb. But he could never remember *when* he was.

He tried to sit up. The Couch responded to his feeble movements, and its back smoothly lifted him upright. He peered around in the dim, golden light of the Cloister. There were three Couches, great bulky mechanical devices half bed and half medical support system: only three, because only three of the Elders stayed alive.

Somebody was moving around him. It was a transient, of course, a young woman. She kept her eyes averted, and her hands fluttered through an elaborate greetings-with-apology ritual. He dismissed her with a curt gesture; you could eat up your entire day with such flim-flam.

Andres was watching him, her eyes sharp in her ruin of a face. She looked like a huge bug in her cocoon of blankets.

"Well?" he snapped.

"You are drooling," she said mildly. "Not in front of the transients, Rusel."

Irritated, he wiped his chin with his sleeve.

"Oh," she said, her tone unchanged, "and Selur died."

That news, so casually delivered, was like a punch in the throat. He turned clumsily, weighed down by blankets and life-sustaining equipment. The doctor's Couch was surrounded by transients, who were removing her mummy-like body. They worked in silence, cautiously, reverently. They were trembling, he saw dimly.

"I never did like her much," Rusel said.

"You've said that before. Many times."

"I'll miss her, though."

"Yes. And then there were two. Rusel, we need to talk. We need a new strategy to deal with the transients. We're supposed to be figures of awe. Look at us. Look at poor Selur! We can't let them see us like this again."

He glanced cautiously at the transients.

"Don't worry," Andres said. "They can't understand. Linguistic drift."

"We have to deal with them. We're the top of their pyramid of authority—that's what you've always said."

"So we are, and it has to stay that way. But I don't think we should allow transients in here any more. The machines can sustain us. Lethe knows there are enough spare parts, now we have so many empty Couches! What I suggest is—"

"Stow it," he said crossly. "You're always the same, you old witch. You always want to jam a solution down my throat before I even know what the problem is. Let me gather my thoughts."

"Stow it, stow it," she parroted, grotesquely.

"Shut up." He closed his eyes to exclude her, and lay back in his couch.

Through the implant in the back of his skull he allowed data from his body, the Ship, and the universe beyond to filter into his sensorium.

His body first, of course, the slowly failing biomachinery that had become his prison. The good news was that, more than two centuries after his brother's death, his slow ageing had bottomed out. Since he had last checked—Lethe, all of a month ago, it seemed like yesterday, how long had he slept this time?—nothing had got significantly worse. But he was stuck in the body of a ninety-year-old man, and a frail old man at that. He slept almost all the time, his intervals of lucidity ever more widely separated, while the Couch fed him, removed his waste, gently turned him to and fro and manipulated his stick-thin limbs. Oh, and every few weeks he received a blood transfusion, an offering to the Elders from the grateful transients outside the Cloister. He may as well have been a coma victim, he thought grumpily.

His age was meaningless, his condition boring. Briskly he moved on.

His Virtual viewpoint roamed through the Ship. Despite the passage of centuries, the physical layout of the corridor-village that had been Diluc's was the same, save for detail, the same knots of corridors around the "village square." But the people had changed, as they always did, youth blossoming, old age crumbling.

The Autarch he remembered from his last inspection was still in place. He was a big bruiser who called himself Ruul, in subtle defiance of various inhibitions against taking the name of an Elder, even one long dead. He at least didn't look to have aged much. Flanked by two of his wives, Ruul received a queue of supplicants, all seeking the Autarch's "wisdom" concerning some petty problem or other. Ruul was brisk and efficient, and as Rusel listened—though the time-drifted language was hard to decipher—he couldn't spot any immediate errors of doctrine in the Autarch's summary harshness.

He allowed his point of view to drift on.

He watched the villagers go about their business. Four of

them were scrubbing the walls clean of dirt, as they took turns to do every day. Two plump-looking worthies were discussing a matter of etiquette, their mannerisms complex and time-consuming. There were some new bits of artwork on the walls, many of them fool-the-eye depth-perspective paintings, designed to make the Ship's corridors look bigger than they were. One woman was tending a "garden" of bits of waste polymer, combing elaborate formations into it with a small metal rake. These transients, Shipborn for generations, had never heard of Zen gardens; they had rediscovered this small-world art form for themselves.

A little group of children was being taught to disassemble and maintain an air-duct fan; they chanted the names of its parts, learning by rote. They would be taught nothing more, Rusel knew. There was no element of *principle* here: nothing about how the fan as a machine worked, or how it fitted into the greater systems of the Ship itself. You only learned what you needed to know.

Everybody was busy, intent on their affairs. Some even seemed happy. But it all looked drab to Rusel, all the villagers dressed in colourless Ship's-issue clothing, their lives bounded by the polished-smooth bulkheads of the Ship. Even their language was dull, and becoming duller. The transients had no words for *horizon* or *sky*—but as if in compensation they had over forty words describing degrees of love.

As he surveyed the village, statistics rolled past his vision in a shining column. Everything was nominal, if you took a wider perspective. Maintenance routines were being kept up satisfactorily. Reproduction rules, enforced by the Autarch and his peers in the other villages, were largely being adhered to, and there was a reasonable genetic mix.

The situation was stable. But in Diluc's village, only the Autarch was free.

Andres's uncharacteristically naïve dream of respectful communities governing themselves by consensus had barely outlasted the death of Diluc. In the villages strong characters had quickly taken control, and in most cases had installed themselves and their families as hereditary rulers. Andres had grumbled at that, but it was an obviously stable social system, and in the end the Elders, in subtle ways, lent the Autarchs their own mystical authority.

The Autarchs were slowly drifting away from their subject populations, though.

Some "transients" had always proven to be rather longer-lived than others. It seemed that the Qax's tampering with the genomes of their Pharaohs had indeed been passed on to subsequent generations, if imperfectly, and that gene complex, a tendency to longevity, was expressing itself. Indeed the Autarchs actively sought out breeding partners for themselves who came from families that showed such tendencies.

So, with time, the Autarchs and their offspring were ageing more slowly than their transient subjects.

It was just natural selection, argued Andres. People had always acquired power so that their genes could be favoured. Traditionally you would do your best to outbreed your subjects. But if you were an Autarch, in the confines of the Ship, what were you to do? There was obviously no room here for a swarm of princes, bastards or otherwise. Besides, the Elders' genetic-health rules wouldn't allow any such thing. So the Autarchs were seeking to dominate their populations with their own long lives, not numbers of offspring.

Andres seemed to find all this merely intellectually interesting. Rusel wondered what would happen if this went on.

He allowed his consciousness to drift back to his own body. When he surfaced, he found Andres watching him, as she so often did.

"So you think we have to change things," he said.

"We need to deal with the Autarchs. Some of them are tough customers, Rusel, and they imagine they're even tougher. If they start to believe we're weak—for instance, if we sleep for three days before delivering the answer to the simplest question—"

"I understand. We can't let the transients see us." He sighed, irritated. "But what else can we do? Delivering edicts through disembodied voices isn't going to wash. If they don't see us they will soon forget who we are." *Soon*, in the language of the Elders, meaning in another generation or two.

"Right," she snapped. "So we have to personalise our authority. What do you think of this?" She gestured feebly, and a Virtual coalesced in the air over her head.

It showed Rusel. Here he was as a young man, up to his elbows in nanofood banks, labouring to make the Ship sound for its long journey. Here he was as a young-ish Elder, bald as ice, administering advice to grateful transients. There were even images of him from the vanishingly remote days before the launch, images of him with a smiling Lora.

"Where did you get this stuff?"

She sniffed. "The Ship's log. Your own archive. Come on, Rusel, we hardly have any secrets from each other after all this time! Pretty girl, though."

"Yes. What are you intending to do with this?"

"We'll show it to the transients. We'll show you at your best, Rusel, you at the peak of your powers, you walking the same corridors they walk now—you as a human being, yet *more* than human. That's what we want: engagement with their petty lives, empathy, yet awe. We'll put a face to your voice."

He closed his eyes. It made sense of course; Andres's logic was grim, but always valid. "But why me? It would be better if both of us—"

"That wouldn't be wise," she said. "I wouldn't want them to see me die."

It took him a while to work out that Andres, the first of the Pharaohs, was failing. Rusel found this impossible to take in: her death would be to have a buttress of the universe knocked away. "But you won't see the destination," he said peevishly, as if she was making a bad choice.

"No," she said hoarsely. "But the *Mayflower* will get there! Look around, Rusel. The Ship is functioning flawlessly. Our designed society is stable and doing its job of preserving the bloodlines. And *you*, you were always the brightest of all. You will see it through. That's enough for me."

It was true, Rusel supposed. Her design was fulfilled; the Ship and its crew were working now just as Andres had always dreamed they should. But only two hundred and fifty years had worn away, only *half of one percent* of the awesome desert of time he must cross to reach Canis Major—and now, it seemed, he was going to have to make the rest of that journey alone.

"No, not alone," said Andres. "You'll always have the Ship . . ."

Yes, the Ship, his constant companion. Suddenly he longed to escape from the endless complications of humanity and immerse himself in its huge technological calm. He lay back in his Couch and allowed his mind to roam out through the crowded torus of the hull, and the pulsing ramjet engines, and the wispy gravitational wings behind which the Ship sailed.

He looked back. The Ship had covered only a fraction of its epic journey, but already it was climbing out of the galactic plane, and the Core, the crowded heart of the Galaxy, rose like a sun from the dust-strewn lanes of the spiral arms. It was a stunning, comforting sight.

By the time he came back from his intergalactic dreaming, Andres was gone, her Couch disassembled for spare parts, her body removed to the cycling tanks.

➤ ➤ ➤

Rusel was woken from his long slumber by the face of a boy, a face twisted with anger—an anger directed at *him*.

In retrospect Rusel should have seen the rebellion coming. All the indicators had been there: the drift of the transients' social structures, the gathering tensions. It was bound to happen.

But it was so hard for him to pay attention to the brief lives of these transients, their incomprehensible language and customs, their petty concerns and squabbling. After all, Hilin was a boy of the forty-fifth generation since launch: *forty-five generations,* Lethe, nearly a thousand years . . .

The exploits of Hilin, though, forced themselves on his attention.

Hilin was sixteen years old when it all began. He had been born in Diluc's corridor-village.

By now the Autarchs of the different villages had intermarried to form a seamless web of power. They lived on average twice as long as their subjects, and had established a monopoly on the Ship's water supply. A water empire ruled by gerontocrats: their control was total.

Hilin was not one of the local Autarch's brood; his family

were poor and powerless, like all the Autarch's subjects. But they seemed to accept their lot. As he played in corridors whose polymer floors were rutted by generations of passing feet, Hilin emerged as a bright, happy child. He seemed compliant when he was young, cheerfully joining in swabbing the bulkheads when it was his turn, and accepting the cuffs of his teachers when he asked impudent questions.

He had always been oddly fascinated by the figure of Rusel himself—or rather the semi-mythical presence portrayed to the villagers through the cycling Virtual storyboards. Hilin soaked up the story of the noble Elder who had been forced to choose between a life of unending duty and his beloved Lora, an undying model to those he ruled.

As he had grown, Hilin had flourished educationally. At fourteen he was inducted into an elite caste. As intellectual standards declined, literacy had been abandoned, and these monkish thinkers now committed to memory every significant commandment regarding the workings of the Ship and their own society. You would start on this vital project at fourteen, and wouldn't expect to be done until you were in your fifties, by which time a new generation was ready to take over anyhow.

Rusel dryly called these patient thinkers Druids: he wasn't interested in the transients' own names for themselves, which would change in an eye-blink generation anyhow. He had approved this practice when it emerged. All this endless memorising was a marvellous way to use up pointless lives—and it established a power-base to rival the Autarchs.

Again Hilin had flourished, and he passed one Druidic assessment after another. Even a torrid romance with Sale, a girl from a neighbouring village, didn't distract him from his studies.

When the time came, the couple asked their families for leave to form a companionship-marriage, which was granted. They went to the Autarch for permission to have children. To their delight, it turned out their genetic makeups, as mapped in the Druids' capacious memories, were compatible enough to allow this too.

But even so the Druids forbade the union.

Hilin, horrified, learned that this was because of the results of his latest Druidic assessment, a test of his general intelligence and potential. He had failed, not by posting too low a score, but too *high.*

Rusel, brooding, understood. The eugenic elimination of weaknesses had in general been applied wisely. But under the Autarch-Druid duopoly, attempts were made to weed out the overbright, the curious—anybody who might prove rebellious. Rusel would have stamped out this practice, had he even noticed it. If this went on, the transient population would become passive, listless, easily manipulated by the Autarchs and the Druids, but useless for the mission's larger purposes.

It was too late for Hilin. He was banned from ever seeing his Sale again. And he was told by the Autarch's ministers that this was by order of the Elder himself, though Rusel, dreaming his life away, knew nothing about it.

Hilin spent long hours in the shrine-like enclosure where Rusel's Virtuals played out endlessly. He tried to understand. He told himself the Elder's wisdom surpassed his own; this severance must be for the best, no matter what pain it caused him. He even tried to draw comfort from what he saw as parallels between his own doomed romance and Rusel and his lost Lora. But understanding didn't come, and his bewilderment and pain soon blossomed to resentment—and anger.

In his despair, he tried to destroy the shrine.

As punishment, the Autarch locked him in a cell for two days. Hilin emerged from his confinement outwardly subdued, inwardly ready to explode. Again Rusel would later castigate himself for failing to see the dangers in the situation.

But it was so hard to see anything now.

His central nervous system was slowly deteriorating, so the Couch informed him. He could still move his arms and legs—he could still walk, even, with a frame—but he felt no sensation in his feet, nothing but the faintest ache in his fingertips. As pain and pleasure alike receded, he felt he was coming loose from time itself. When he surfaced into the world of lucidity he would be shocked to find a year had passed like a day, as if his sense of time was becoming logarithmic.

And meanwhile, as he became progressively disconnected

from the physical world, his mind was undergoing a reconstruction of its own. After a thousand years his memories, especially the deepest, most precious memories of all, were, like the floors of the Ship's corridors, worn with use; he was no longer sure if he *remembered*, or if all he had left was memories of memories.

If he came adrift from both present and past, what was he? Was he even human any more? Certainly the latest set of transients meant less than nothing to him: why, each of them was made up of the atoms and molecules of her ancestors, cycled through the Ship's systems forty times or more, shuffled and reshuffled in meaningless combinations. They could not touch his heart in any way.

At least he thought so, until Hilin brought him the girl.

The two of them stood before Rusel's Virtual shrine, where they believed the Elder's consciousness must reside. Trying to match the Elder's own timescales, they stayed there for long hours, all but motionless. Hilin's face was set, pinched with anger and determination. She, though, was composed.

At last Rusel's drifting attention was snagged by familiarity. It was the girl. She was taller than most of the transients, pale, her bones delicate. And her eyes were large, dark, somehow unfocused even as she gazed into unseen imaging systems.

Lora.

It couldn't be, of course! How could it? Lora had had no family on the Ship. And yet Rusel, half-dreaming, immersed in memory, couldn't take his eyes off her image.

As Hilin had planned.

The uprising occurred all over the Ship. In every village the Autarchs and their families were turned out of their palatial cabins. The Autarchs, having commanded their short-lived flocks for centuries, were quite unprepared, and few resisted; they had no conception such an uprising was even possible. The old rulers and their peculiar children were herded together in a richly-robed mass in the Ship's largest chamber, the upturned amphitheatre where Rusel had long ago endured the launch from Port Sol.

The revolt had been centrally planned, carefully timed, meticulously executed. Despite generations of selective breeding to eliminate initiative and cunning, the transients no longer seemed so sheep-like, and in Hilin they had discovered a general. And it was over before the Elder's attention had turned away from the girl, before he had even noticed.

Hilin, king of the corridors, stood before the Elder's shrine. And he pulled at the face of the girl, the Lora look-alike. It had been a mask, just a mask; Rusel realised ashamedly that this boy had manipulated the emotions of a being more than a thousand years old.

A bloody club in his hand, Hilin screamed his defiance at his undying god. The Cloister's systems translated the boy's language, after a thousand years quite unlike Rusel's. "You allowed this to happen," Hilin yelled. "You allowed the Autarchs to feed off us like [*untranslatable—body parasites?*]. We wash the decks for them with our blood, while they keep water from our children. And you, you [*untranslatable—an obscenity?*] allowed it to happen. And do you know why?" Hilin stepped closer to the shrine, and his face loomed in Rusel's vision. "Because you don't exist. Nobody has seen you in centuries—if they ever did! You're a lie, cooked up by the Autarchs to keep us in our place, that's what I think. Well, we don't believe in you any more, not in any of that [*untranslatable— faeces?*]. And we've thrown out the Autarchs. We are free!"

"Free" they were. Hilin and his followers looted the Autarchs' apartments, and gorged themselves on the food and water the Autarchs had hoarded for themselves, and screwed each other senseless in blithe defiance of the genetic-health prohibitions. And not a single deck panel was swabbed down.

After three days, as the chaos showed no signs of abating, Rusel knew that this was the most serious crisis in the Ship's long history. He had to act. It took him another three days to get ready for his performance, three days mostly taken up with fighting with the inhibiting protocols of his medical equipment.

Then he ordered the Cloister door to open, for the first time in centuries. It actually stuck, dry-welded in place. It finally gave way with a resounding crack, making his entrance even more spectacular than he had planned.

But there was nobody around to witness his incarnation but

a small boy, no more than five years old. With his finger planted firmly in one nostril, and his eyes round with surprise, the kid looked heartbreakingly like Tomi, Diluc's boy, long since dead and fed to the recycling banks.

Rusel was standing, supported by servomechanisms, gamely clutching at a walking frame. He tried to smile at the boy, but he couldn't feel his own face, and didn't know if he succeeded. "Bring me the chief Druids," he said, and a translation whispered in the air around him.

The boy yelled and fled.

The Druids actually knelt before him, covering their faces. He walked very cautiously among them, allowing them even to touch his robe. He wanted to be certain they accepted his reality, smelled the dusty tang of centuries on him. Maybe these monkish philosophers had in their hearts, like Hilin, never really believed in the Elder's existence. Well, now their messiah had suddenly reincarnated among them.

But he saw them as if through a flawed lens; he could hear little, feel less, smell or taste nothing. It was like walking around in a skinsuit, he thought.

He was an angry god, though. The rules of Shipboard life had been broken, he thundered. And he didn't just mean the recent mess. There must be no more water empires, and no knowledge empires either: the Druids would have to make sure that *every* child knew the basic rules, of Ship maintenance and genetic-health breeding.

He ordered that the Autarchs should not be returned to their seats of power. Instead, the governing would be done, for this generation, by a Druid—he picked out one terrified-looking woman at random. As long as she ruled wisely and well, she would have the Elder's backing. On her death the people would select a successor, who could not be more closely related to her predecessor than second cousin.

The old Autarchs and their brood, meanwhile, were to be spared. They would be shut away permanently in their amphitheatre prison, where there were supplies to keep them alive. Rusel believed they and their strange slow-growing children would die off; within a generation, a tick of time, that problem would go away. He had done his share of killing, he thought.

Then he sighed. The worst of it had still to be faced. "Bring me Hilin," he ordered.

They dragged in the corridor king tied up with strips of cloth. He had been assaulted, Rusel saw; his face was battered and one arm seemed broken. The erstwhile leader was already being punished for his blasphemy by those who sought the favour of the Elder. But Hilin faced Rusel defiantly, strength and intelligence showing in his face.

Rusel's scarred heart ached a little more, for strength and intelligence were the last features you wanted in a transient.

Hilin had to die, of course. His flayed corpse would be displayed before the shrine of the Elder, as a warning to future generations. But Rusel didn't have the courage to watch it done. He remembered the man in the electric-blue skinsuit: he always had been a coward, he thought.

As he returned to his Cloister, he looked back once more. "And clean up this damn mess," he said.

He knew it would take a long time, even on his timescales, before he managed to forget the contemptuous defiance on Hilin's young face. But Hilin had gone into the dark like all his transient ancestors, and soon his siblings and nieces and nephews and everybody who looked remotely like him went too, gone, all gone into the sink of time, and soon only Rusel was left alive to remember the rebellion.

Rusel would never leave the Cloister again.

❧ ❧ ❧

Some time after that, there was a decimating plague.

It was brought about by a combination of factors: a slow unmonitored build-up of irritants and allergens in the Ship's environment, and then the sudden emergence of a latent virus in a population already weakened. It was a multiple accident, impossible for the Pharaoh designers of the Ship to plan away, for all their ingenuity. But given enough time—more than five thousand years—such events were inevitable.

The surviving population crashed to close to a threshold of

viability. For a few decades Rusel was forced to intervene, through booming commands, to ensure that the Ship was maintained at a basic level, and that genetic-health protocols were observed and breeding matches planned even more carefully than usual.

The low numbers brought benefits, though. The Ship's systems were now producing a large surplus of supplies, and there was no possibility of any more water empires. Rusel considered, in his glacial way, establishing a final population at a lower level than before.

It intrigued him that the occurrence of the plague mirrored the restructuring of his own mental processes. The day to day affairs of the Ship, and the clattering of the transient generations, barely distracted him now. Instead he became aware of slower pulses, deeper rhythms beyond any transients' horizon of awareness. It fascinated him to follow the million-year turning of the Galaxy, whose brilliant face continued to open up behind the fleeing Ship.

And his perception of risk changed. His endless analysis of the Ship's systems uncovered obscure failure modes: certain parameter combinations that could disrupt the governing software, interacting failures among the nano-machines that still laboured over the Ship's fabric inside and out. Such failures were highly unlikely; he estimated the Ship might suffer significant damage once every ten thousand years or so. On Earth, whole civilisations had risen and fallen with greater alacrity than that. But *he* had to plan for such things, to prepare the Ship's defences and recovery strategies. The plague, after all, was just such a low-risk event, but given enough time it had come about.

The transients' behaviour, meanwhile, adjusted on its own timescales.

Once every decade or so the inhabitants of Diluc's corridor-village would approach the shrine of the Elder, where the flickering Virtual still showed. One of them would dress up in a long robe and walk behind a frame with exaggerated slowness, while the rest cowered. And then they would fall on a manikin and tear it to pieces. Rusel watched such displays several times before he realised what was going on: it was, of course, a ritualised re-enactment of his own last manifestation. Sometimes the bit of theatre would culminate in the flaying of a living human, which they must imagine he demanded; when such savage generations arose, Rusel would avert his cold gaze.

Meanwhile, in the village in which Hilin's doomed lover Sale had been born, the local transients were trying another tactic to win his favour. Perhaps it was another outcome of Hilin's clever exploits, or perhaps it had been inherent in the situation all along.

Girls, tall slim girls with dark elusive eyes: as the generations ticked by, he seemed to see more of them running in the corridors, making eyes at muscular wall-scrubbing boys, dandling children on their knees. They were like cartoon versions of Lora: tall Loras and short, thin Loras and fat, happy Loras and sad.

It was selective breeding, if presumably unconscious, people turning themselves into replicas of the images in the Virtual. They were appealing directly to his own cold heart: if the Elder loved this woman so much, then choose a wife that looks like her, if only a little, and hope to have daughters with her elfin looks, and so win favour.

Rusel was simultaneously touched, and appalled. They could do what they liked, he told himself, as long as they got their jobs done.

Meanwhile, on the other side of the barricade he had erected, the Autarchs and their long-lived families had not died out as Rusel had hoped. They had lived on. And as they inbred ferociously, their lives were stretched out longer and longer.

Again this made sense in terms of their heredity, he thought. In their cordoned-off compartment there was simply no room to expand their population. So the genes' best bet of propagating themselves into the future, always their only objective, was to stretch out the lives of their carriers. Adults lived for centuries, and for the vanishingly few children born, childhood lasted decades. Rusel found these creatures, with their blank eyes and wizened-faced children, peculiarly creepy. On the other hand, he still couldn't bring himself to kill them off. Perhaps in them he saw a distorted reflection of himself.

There was one constant throughout the Ship. On both sides of the barrier the transients were clearly getting dumber.

As generations passed—and, for fear of repeating Hilin's fate, potential mates were repelled by any signs of higher-than-average intelligence—it was obvious that the transients were breeding themselves into stupidity. If anything the Autarchs' environment was less stimulating than that of their cousins in the rest of the Ship, and despite their slower generational cycle they were shedding their unnecessary intelligence with even more alacrity, perhaps from sheer boredom.

The transients kept the Ship working, however, and in their increasingly brutish liaisons followed the genetic-health mandates scrupulously. This puzzled Rusel: surely by now they could have no real understanding of *why* they were doing these peculiar things.

But he observed that when it came time to attract a mate the most vigorous deck-swabbers and cousin-deniers stood out from the crowd. It made sense: after all, a propensity to please the undeniable reality of the Elder was a survival characteristic, and therefore worth displaying if you had it, and worth preserving in your children's heredity.

He filed away such observations and insights. By now, nothing that happened inside the Ship's hull interested him as much as what happened outside.

He was thoroughly wired into the Ship, its electromagnetic and other equipment taking the place of his own failed biological senses. He cruised with it through the intergalactic gulf, feeling the tingle of dark matter particles as they were swept into the Ship's gut, sensing the subtle caress of magnetic fields. The space between the galaxies was much more interesting than he had ever imagined. It wasn't a void at all. There was structure here, he saw, a complex webbing of the dark stuff that spanned the universe, a webbing in which galaxies were trapped like glowing flies. He learned to follow the currents and reefs of the dark matter which the Ship's gravitational maw greedily devoured.

He was alone with the galaxies, then, and with his own mind. Once, just once, as he drifted in the dark, he heard a strange signal. It was cold and clear, like the peal of a trumpet, far off in the echoing intergalactic night. It wasn't human at all.

He listened for a thousand years. He never heard it again.

➤ ➤ ➤

Andres came to him.

"Leave me alone, you nagging old witch," he grumbled.

"Believe me, that would be my choice," said Andres fervently. "But there's a problem, Rusel. And you need to come out of your damn shell and sort it out."

He could see her face clearly, that worn-smooth expressionless skin. The rest of her body was a blur, a suggestion. None of that mattered, of course.

"What kind of problem?"

"With the transients. What else? They are all that matters. You need to take a look."

"I don't want to. It hurts."

"I know it hurts. But it's your duty."

Duty? Had she said that, or had he? Was he awake, or dreaming? With time, everything blurred, every category, every boundary.

He was far beyond biology now, of course. The decay of his central nervous system had proceeded so far that he wasn't sure if it returned any signals at all to the hardening nugget of his brain. It was only technology that kept him alive. With time, the Ship had infiltrated its treatments and systems deeper into the shell of what had been his body. It was as if he had become just another of the Ship's systems, like the air cycling system or the water purifiers, just as old and balky, and just as much in need of endless tender loving care.

Even the walls of his consciousness were wearing away. He thought of his mind as a dark hall filled with drifting forms, like zero-gravity sculptures. These were his memories—or perhaps memories of memories, recycled, reiterated, edited and processed.

And *he* was here, a pinpoint awareness that flitted and flew between the drifting reefs of memory. At times, as he sailed through the abstraction of emptiness, free of memory or anticipation, indeed free of any conscious thought save only a primal sense of *self*, he felt oddly free—light, unburdened, even young again. But whenever that innocent point settled into the dark tangle of a memory reef, the guilt came back, a deep muddy shame whose origins he had half-forgotten, and whose resolution he could no longer imagine.

He wasn't alone, however, in this cavernous awareness. Sometimes voices called from the dark. Sometimes there were even faces, their features softened, their ages indeterminate. Here was Diluc, his brother, or Andres, or Ruul or Selur or one of the others. He knew they were all long dead save for him, who lived on and on. He had vague memories of setting up some of these Virtual personas as therapy for himself, or as ways for the Ship to attract his attention—Lethe, even as company. But by now he wasn't sure what was Virtual and what was a dream, a schizoid fantasy of his rickety mind.

Lora was never there, however.

And Andres, the cold Pharaoh who had become his longest-enduring companion, was his most persistent visitant.

She said, "Nobody ever said this would be easy, Rusel."

"You said that before."

"Yes. And I'll keep on saying it until we get to Canis Major."

"Canis Major? . . ." The destination. He'd forgotten about it again, forgotten that an end to all this might exist, even as a theoretical possibility. The trouble was, thinking about such things as a beginning and an end made him aware of time, and that was always a mistake.

How long? The answer came to him like a whisper. *Round numbers? Twenty thousand years gone. Some five thousand left.* Twenty thousand years. It was ridiculous, of course.

"Rusel," Andres snapped. "You need to focus."

"You're not even Andres," he grumbled.

Her mouth was round with mock horror. "Oh, no! What an existential disaster. Just do it, Rus."

So, reluctantly, he gathered his scattered concentration, and sent his viewpoint out into the body of the Ship. He was faintly aware of Andres riding alongside him, a ghost at his shoulder.

He found the place he still thought of as Diluc's village. The framework of corridors and cabins hadn't changed, of course; it was impossible that it should. But even the non-permanent partitions that had once been built up and torn down by each successive generation of transients had been left unmoved since the last time he was here. Building things wasn't what people did any more.

He wandered into the little suite of rooms that had once been Diluc's home. There was no furniture. Nests were crammed into each corner of the room, disorderly heaps of cloth and polymer scraps. He had seen the transients take standard-issue clothing from the Ship's recycler systems and immediately start tearing it up with hands or teeth to make their coarse bedding. There was a strong stink of piss and shit, of blood and milk, sweat and sex, the most basic human biology. But the crew remained scrupulously clean. Every few days all this stuff would be swept up and carted off to the recycler bins.

This was the way people lived now.

Outside, the walls and partitions were clean, gleaming and sterile, as was every surface he could see, the floor and ceiling. One partition had been rubbed until it was worn so thin the light shone through it: another couple of generations and it would wear away altogether, he thought. The crew still kept up their basic duties; that had remained, while so much else had vanished.

But these latter transients were not crewing this Ship as his generation had. They were doing it for deeper reasons.

Those selection pressures, as the transients competed in how well they did their chores in order to attract mates, had, given time, sculpted the population. By now, he understood, the transients were maintaining a starship's systems as bees had once danced, stags had locked antlers, and peacocks had spread their useless tails: *they were doing it for sex*, and the chance to procreate. As mind receded, Rusel thought, biology had taken over.

As long as they were doing it in the first place, Rusel didn't care. Besides, it worked. Sexual drivers seemed very effective in locking in behaviour with the precision required to keep the Ship's systems functioning: you could fix a ceiling ventilation grille with a show-off flourish or not, but you had to do it *exactly* right to impress the opposite sex, even if you didn't understand what it was for. Even when mind was gone, you had to do it right.

He heard weeping, not far away.

He let his viewpoint follow the weeping, just drifting along the corridor. He turned a corner, and came on the villagers.

There were perhaps twenty-five of them, adults and children. They were all naked, of course; nobody had worn clothes for millennia. Some of them had infants in their arms or on their backs. Squatting in the corridor, they huddled around a central figure, the woman who was doing the weeping. Surrounded by bare backs and folded limbs, she was cradling something, a bloody scrap. The others reached out and stroked her back and scalp; some of them were weeping too, Rusel saw.

Andres said dryly, "Their empathy is obvious."

"Yes. They've lost so much else, but not that—"

Suddenly their heads turned, all of them save the weeping woman, faces swivelling like antennae. Something had disturbed them—perhaps the tiny hovering drone that was Rusel's physical manifestation. Their brows were low, but their faces were still human, with straight noses and delicate chins. It was like a flower-bed of faces, Rusel thought, turned up to his light. Their eyes were wide, their mouths pulled back in fear-grins.

And every one of them looked like Lora, more or less, with that delicate, elfin face, even something of her elusive eyes. Of course they did: the blind filter of natural selection, operating for generations on this hapless stock, had long determined that though mind was no longer necessary, to look *this* way might soften the heart of the wizened creature who ruled the world.

The strange tableau of upturned Lora-faces lasted only a moment. Then the transients took flight. They poured away down the corridor, running, knuckle-walking, bounding off the walls and ceiling.

Andres growled, "I'll swear they get more like chimps with every generation."

In a few seconds they had gone, all save the weeping woman.

Rusel allowed his viewpoint to swim towards the woman. He moved cautiously, not wishing to alarm her. She was young—twenty, twenty-one? It was increasingly hard to tell the age of

these transients; they seemed to reach puberty later each generation. This girl had clearly passed her menarche—in fact she had
given birth, and recently: her belly was slack, her breasts heavy
with milk. But her chest was smeared with blood, shocking bright
crimson in the drab, worn background of the corridor. And the
thing she was cradling was no child.

"Lethe," said Rusel. "*It's a hand.* A child's hand. I think I'm
going to throw up."

"You no longer have the equipment. Take a closer look."

A white stump of bone stuck out of a bloody mass of flesh.
The hand had been severed at the wrist. And two tiny fingers had
been almost stripped of flesh, ligament and muscle, leaving only
tiny bones.

"That wrist," Andres said pitilessly, "has been bitten through.
By *teeth*, Rusel. And teeth have been at work on those fingers as
well. Think about it. With a bit of practice, you could take one of
those little morsels between your incisors and just strip off the
flesh and muscle—"

"Shut up! Lethe, Andres, I can see for myself. We always
avoided cannibalism. I thought we beat that into their shrinking
skulls hard enough."

"So we did. But I don't think this is cannibalism—or rather,
whatever did this wasn't *her* kind."

Rusel elevated the viewpoint and cast around. He saw a trail
of blood leading away from the woman, smeared along the walls
and floor, quite unmistakeable, as if something had been dragged
away.

Andres said, "I think our transients suddenly have a preda-
tor."

"Not so suddenly," Rusel said. A part of his scattered consciousness was checking over the Ship's logs, long ignored. This
kind of incident had been going on for a couple of centuries. "It's
been rare before, once or twice a generation. Mostly it was the
old, or the very young—dispensable, or replaceable. But now
they seem to be upping the rate."

"And making a dent in the transients' numbers."

"Yes. You were right to bring me here." This had to be
resolved. But to do it, he thought with a deepening dread, he was

going to have to confront a horror he had shut out of his awareness for millennia.

"I'm here with you," Andres said gently.

"No, you're not," he snapped. "But I have to deal with this
anyhow."

"Yes, you do."

His viewpoint followed the bloody trail as it wound through
the corridor-villages of the transients. Broken in places, the trail
slinked through shadows or through holes worn in the walls. It
was the furtive trail of a hunter, he thought.

At last Rusel came to the bulkhead that cut the Ship in two,
marking the limit of his transients' domain. He had long put out
of his mind what lay beyond this wall: in fact, if he could have
cut away the Ship's aft compartment and let the whole mess float
away into space he would long ago have done so.

But there was a hole in the bulkhead, just wide enough to
admit a slim body.

The bulkhead was a composite of metal and polymer,
extremely tough, and a metre thick; the hole was a neat tunnel,
not regular but smooth-walled, drilled right through it. "I can't
believe they have tools," he said. "So how did they get through?"

"Teeth," Andres said. "Teeth and nails—and time, of which
they have plenty. Remember what you're dealing with. Even if
the bulkhead was made of diamond they'd have got through
eventually."

"I hoped they were dead."

"Hope! Wishful thinking! That always was your weakness,
Rusel. I always said you should have killed them off in the first
place. They're just a drain on the Ship's resources."

"I'm no killer."

"Yes, you are—"

"And they are human, no less than the transients."

"No, they're *not*. And now, it seems, they are *eating* our transients."

His viewpoint drifted before the hole in the wall. Andres
seemed to sense his dread; she didn't say anything.

He passed through the barrier.

He emerged in the big upended chamber he still thought of

as the amphitheatre, right at the base of the Ship. This was a big, bare volume, a cylinder set on its side. After the spin-up it had been used to pursue larger-scale reconstruction projects necessary to prepare the Ship for its long intergalactic voyage, and mounted on its floor and walls were the relics of heavy engineering, long abandoned: gantries, platforms of metal, immense low-gravity cranes like vast skeletons. Globe lights hovered everywhere, casting a yellow-white, complex light. It was an oddly magnificent sight, Rusel thought, and it stirred fond memories of brighter, more purposeful days. On the wall of the chamber, which had been its floor, he could even make out the brackets which had held the acceleration couches on launch day.

Now, every exposed surface was corroded. Nothing moved. And that upturned floor, which Andres had turned transparent a mere year after the launch, was caked with what looked like rock. It was a hardened pack of faeces and cloth scraps and dirt, a wall of shit to block out the Galaxy.

At first, in this jungle of engineering, he couldn't make out anything living. Then, as he watched and allowed the worn-out ambience of the place to wash over him, he learned to see.

They were like shadows, he thought, slim, upright shadows that flitted through the gantries, furtive, cautious. At times they looked human—clearly upright, bipedal, purposeful—though their limbs were spindly, their bellies distended. But then they would collapse to all fours and lope away with a bent gait, and that impression of humanity vanished. They didn't seem to be wearing clothes, any more than the transients did. But unlike the transients', their bodies were coated with a kind of thick hair, dark brown, a fur.

Here and there hovering drones trailed the shambling creatures, carrying food and water. The creatures ignored these emissaries of the Ship that kept them alive.

Andres said grimly. "I know you haven't wanted to think about these relics, Rusel. But the Ship has watched over them. They are provided with food, of course. Clothing, blankets and the like—they rip all that up to serve as nesting material, like the transients. They won't go to the supply hoppers as the transients will; drones have to bring them the stuff they need, and take out their waste. But they're really quite passive. They don't mind the drones, even when the drones clean them, or tend to wounds or sicknesses. They are used to being cared for by machines."

"But what do they *do* all day?"

Andres laughed. "Why, nothing. Nothing but eat the food we give them. Climb around the gantries a little, perhaps."

"They must have some spark of curiosity, of awareness. The transients do! They're *people*."

"Their ancestors used to be. Now they're quite mindless . . . There. Look. They are gathering at one of their feeding places. Perhaps we'll be able to see what they do."

The feeding site was just a shallow depression, worn into a floor of steel. Its base was smeared green and brown. A drone had delivered a cache of food to the centre of the pit, a pile of spheres and cylinders and discs, all sized for human hands, all brightly coloured.

From around the amphitheatre the animals came walking, loping, moving with the slow clumsiness of low gravity—and yet with an exaggerated care, Rusel thought, as if they were very fragile, very old. They gathered around the food pile. But they did not reach for the food; they just slumped down on the ground, as if exhausted.

Now smaller creatures emerged from the forest of gantries. They moved nervously, but just as cautiously as the larger forms. They must be children, Rusel thought, but they moved with no spontaneity or energy. They were like little old people themselves. There were far fewer children than adults, just a handful among perhaps fifty individuals.

It was the children who went to the food pile, broke off pieces of the brightly-coloured fodder, and carried it to the adults. The adults greeted this service with indifference, or at best a snarl, a light blow on the head or shoulder. Each child servant went doggedly back to the pile for more.

"They're not particularly hygienic," Rusel observed.

"No. But they don't have to be. Compared to the transients they have much tougher immune systems. And the Ship's systems keep the place roughly in order."

Rusel said, "Why don't the adults get the food themselves? It would be quicker."

Andres shrugged. "This is their way. And it is their way to eat another sort of food, too."

At the very centre of the depression was a broad scar stained a deep crimson brown, littered with lumpy white shapes.

"That's blood," Rusel said, wondering. "Dried blood. And those white things—"

"Bones," said Andres evenly. Rusel thought she seemed oddly excited, stirred by the degraded spectacle before her. "But there's too much debris here to be accounted for by their occasional raids into transient country."

Rusel shuddered. "So they eat each other too."

"No. Not quite. *The old eat the young*; mothers eat their children. It is their way."

"Oh, Lethe—" Andres was right; Rusel couldn't throw up. But he was briefly aware of his body, cradled by the concerned Ship, thrashing feebly in distress.

Andres said dispassionately, "I don't understand your reaction."

"I didn't know—"

"You should have thought it through—thought through the consequences of your decision to let these creatures live."

"You are a monster, Andres."

She laughed without humour.

Of course he knew what these animals were. They were the Autarchs—or the distant descendants of the long-lived, inbred clan that had once ruled over the transients. Over nearly twenty thousand years selection pressure had worked relentlessly, and the gene complex that had given them their advantage over the transients in the first place—genes for longevity, a propensity injected into the human genome by the Qax—had found full expression. And meanwhile, in the sterile nurture of this place, they had had even less reason to waste precious energy on large brains.

As time had passed they had lived longer and longer, but thought less and less. Now these Autarchs were all but immortal, and all but mindless.

"They're actually rather fascinating," Andres said cheerfully. "I've been trying to understand their ecology, if you will."

"Ecology? Then maybe you can explain how it can benefit a creature to treat its children so. Those young seem to be *farmed*. Life is about the preservation of genes: even in this artificial little world of ours, that remains true. So how does eating your kids help achieve that? . . . Ah." He gazed at the hairy creatures before him. *"But these Autarchs are not mortal."*

"Exactly. They lost their minds, but they stayed immortal. And when mind had gone, natural selection worked with what it found."

Even for these strange creatures, the interests of the genes were paramount. But now a new strategy had to be worked out. It had been foreshadowed in the lives of the first Autarchs. There was no room to spread the genes by expanding the population— but if individuals could become effectively immortal, the genes could survive through them.

Andres said, "But simple longevity wasn't enough. Even the longest-lived will die through some accident eventually. The genes themselves can be damaged, though radiation exposure for instance. Copying is safer! For their own safety the genes need to see *some* children produced, and for some, the smartest and strongest, to survive.

"But, you see, living space is restricted here. The parents must compete for space against their own children. They don't *care* about the children. They use them as workers—or even, when there's an excess, as a cannibalistic resource . . . But there are always one or two children who fight their way through to adulthood, enough to keep the stock numbers up. In a way the pressure from the adults is a mechanism to ensure that only the smartest and strongest of the kids survive. From the genes' point of view it's a mixed strategy."

"It's a redundancy mechanism," Rusel said. "That's the way an engineer would put it. The children are just a fail-safe."

"Precisely," Andres said.

It was biology, evolution: the destiny of the *Mayflower* had come down to this.

Rusel had brooded on the fate of his charges. And he had decided it was all a question of timescales.

The conscious purpose of the Ship had sustained its crew's focus for a century or so, until the first couple of generations, and the direct memory of Port Sol, had vanished into the past.

Millennia, though, were the timescale of historical epochs on Earth, over which empires rose and fell. His studies suggested that to sustain a purpose over such periods required the engagement of a deeper level of the human psyche: the idea of Rome, say, or a devotion to Christ. If the first century of the voyage had been an arena for the conscious, over longer periods the unconscious took over. Rusel had seen it himself, as the transients had become devoted to the idea of the Ship and its mission, as embodied by his own Virtual. Even Hilin's rebellion had been an expression of that cult of ideas. Call it mysticism: whatever, it worked for thousands of years.

That far, he believed, Andres and the other Pharaohs had been able to foresee and plan for. But beyond that even they hadn't been able to imagine; Rusel had sailed uncharted waters. And as time heaped up into *tens* of millennia, he had crossed a span of time comparable to the rise and fall, not just of empires, but of whole species.

A continuity of the kind that kept the transients cleaning the walls over such periods could only come about, not through even the deepest layers of mind, but through much more basic biological drivers, like sexual selection: the transients cleaned for sex, not for any reason to do with the Ship's goals, for they could no longer comprehend such abstractions. And meanwhile natural selection had shaped his cradled populations, of transients and Autarchs alike. Of course, if biology was replacing even the deepest layers of mind as the shaping element in the mission's destiny, Rusel's own role became still more important, as the only surviving element of continuity, indeed of consciousness.

Sometimes he felt queasy, perhaps even guilty, at the distorted fate to which generation upon generation had been subjected, all for the sake of a long-dead Pharaoh and her selfish, hubristic dream. But individual transients were soon gone, their tiny motes of joy or pain vanishing into the dark. Their very brevity was comforting.

Whatever, there was no going back, for any of them.

Andres was still watching the Autarchs. These frail, cautious animals were like a dark reflection of himself, Rusel thought reluctantly. And how strange it was for the transients to be caged in by the undying: his own attenuated consciousness guiding the Ship from above, while these fallen Autarchs preyed on them from below.

Andres said, "You know, immortality, the defeat of death, is one of mankind's oldest dreams. But immortality doesn't make you a god. *You* have immortality, Rusel, but, save for your crutch the Ship, you have no power. And these—animals—have immortality, but nothing else."

"It's monstrous."

"Of course! Isn't life always? But the genes don't care. And in the Autarchs' mindless capering, you can see the ultimate logic of immortality: for an immortal, to survive, must in the end eat her own children."

But everybody on this Ship was a child of this monstrous mother, Rusel thought, whose hubris and twisted longings had impelled this mission in the first place. "Is that some kind of confession, Pharaoh?"

Andres didn't reply. Perhaps she couldn't. After all, this wasn't Andres but a Virtual, a software-generated crutch for Rusel's fading consciousness, at the limit of its programming. And any guilt he saw in her could only be a reflection of himself.

With an effort of will he dismissed her.

One of the adults, a male, sat up, scratched his chest, and loped to the centre of the feeding pit. The young fled at his approach. The male scattered the last bits of primary-colour food, and picked up something small and white. It was a skull, Rusel saw, the skull of a child. The adult crushed it, dropped the fragments, and wandered off, aimless, immortal, mindless.

Rusel withdrew, and sealed up the gnawed-through bulkhead. After that he set up a new barrier spanning the Ship parallel to the bulkhead, and opened up the thin slice of the vessel between the walls to intergalactic vacuum. He never again gave any thought to what lay on the other side of that barrier.

➤ ➤ ➤

Twenty-five thousand years after the end of his world, Rusel heard that he was to be saved.

"Rusel. Rusel . . ."

Rusel wanted the voices to go away. He didn't need voices now—not Diluc's, not even Andres's. He had no body, no belly, no heart; he had no need of people at all. His memories were scattered in emptiness, like the faint smudges that were the remote galaxies all around the Ship. And like the Ship he forged on steadily, pointlessly into the future, his life empty of meaning.

The last thing he wanted was *voices*. But they wouldn't go away. With deep reluctance, he forced his scattered attention to gather.

The voices were coming from Diluc's corridor-village. Vaguely, he saw people there, near a door—the door where he had once been barrelled into by little Rus, he remembered, in a shard of bright warm memory blown from the past—two people, by that same door.

People standing upright. People wearing clothes.

They were not transients. And they were calling his name into the air. With a mighty effort he pulled himself to full awareness.

They stood side by side, a man and a woman—both young, in their twenties, perhaps. They wore smart orange uniforms and boots. The man was clean-shaven, and the woman bore a baby in her arms.

Transients had clustered around them. Naked, pale, eyes wide with curiosity, they squatted on their haunches and reached up with their long arms to the smiling newcomers. Some of them were scrubbing frantically at the floor and walls, teeth bared in rictus grins. They were trying to impress the newcomers with their prowess at cleaning, the only way they knew how.

The woman allowed the transients to stroke her child. But she watched them with hard eyes and a fixed smile. And the man's hand was never far away from the weapon at his belt.

It took Rusel a great deal of effort to find the circuits that would allow him to speak. He said, "*Rusel.* I am Rusel."

As the disembodied voice boomed out of the air the man and woman looked up, startled, and the transients cowered. The newcomers looked at each other with delight. "It's true," said the man. "It really is the *Mayflower!*" A translation whispered to Rusel.

The woman scoffed. "Of course it's the *Mayflower.* What else could it be?"

Rusel said, "Who are you?"

The man's name was Pirius, the woman's Torec.

"Are we at Canis Major?"

"No," Pirius said gently.

These two had come from the home Galaxy—from Sol system itself, they said. They had come in a faster-than-light ship; it had overtaken the *Mayflower*'s painful crawl in a few weeks. "You have come thirteen thousand light years from Port Sol," Pirius said. "And it took you more than twenty-five thousand years. It is a record for a generation starship! An astonishing feat."

Thirteen thousand light years? Even now, only half-way. It seemed impossible.

Torec cupped the face of a transient girl in her hand—cupped Lora's face. "And," Torec said, "we came to find you."

"Yes," said Pirius, smiling. "And your floating museum!"

Rusel thought that over. "Then mankind lives on?"

Oh, yes, Pirius told him. The mighty Expansion from which the *Mayflower*'s crew had fled had burned its way right across the Galaxy. It had been an age of war; trillions had gone into the dark. But mankind had endured.

"And we won!" Pirius said brightly. Pirius and Torec themselves had been involved in some kind of exotic combat to win the centre of the Galaxy. "It's a human Galaxy now, Rusel."

"Human? But how are *you* still human?"

They seemed to understand the question. "We were at war," Pirius said. "We couldn't afford to evolve."

"The Coalition—"

"Fallen. Vanished. Gone. They can't harm you now."

"And my crew—"

"We will take them home. There are places where they can be cared for. But, ah—"

Torec said, "But the Ship itself is too big to turn around. I'm not sure we can bring *you*."

Once he had seen himself, a stiff ageless man, through the eyes of Diluc's great-grandson Poro, through the eyes of a child. Now, just for an instant, he saw himself through the eyes of Pirius and Torec. A wizened, charred thing suspended in a webbing of wires and tubes.

That didn't matter, of course. "Have I fulfilled my mission?"

"Yes," Pirius said gently. "You fulfilled it very well."

He wasn't aware of Pirius and Torec shepherding the transients and Autarchs out of the Ship and into their own absurdly small craft. He wasn't aware of Pirius's farewell call as they shot away, back towards the bright lights of the human Galaxy, leaving him alone. He was only aware of the Ship now, the patient, stolid Ship.

The Ship—and one face, revealed to him at last: an elfin face, with distracted eyes. He didn't know if she was a gift of Pirius or even Andres, if she was outside his own head or inside. None of that seemed to matter when at last she smiled for him, and he felt the easing of a tension twenty-five millennia old, the dissolving of a clot of ancient guilt.

The Ship forged on into the endless dark, its corridors as clean and bright and empty as his thoughts.

SERGEANT CHIP

by Bradley Denton

Bradley Denton was born in Wichita, Kansas in 1958, and holds a bachelor's degree in astronomy and English and a master's degree in English from the University of Kansas. His first story, "Music of the Spheres," was published in 1984, and his first novel, Wrack & Roll, *was published in 1986. His subsequent novels include the John W. Campbell Memorial Award-winning* Buddy Holly Is Alive and Well on Ganymede, Blackburn, *and* Lunatics. *His short fiction has been collected in World Fantasy Award winning two-volume set* A Conflagration Artist *and* The Calvin Coolidge Home for Dead Comedians, *and in* One Day Closer to Death. *Denton lives on the outskirts of Austin, Texas with his wife Barbara, three dogs, and a cat. He plays drums in a couple of ragged rock 'n' roll bands. His fifth novel,* Laughin' Boy, *will be published by Subterranean Press in 2005.*

Denton has written some remarkable short fiction and the story that follows—a moving tale of loyalty, compassion, and the madness of war—stands amongst his very best.

To the Supreme Commander of the soldier who bears this message— Sir or Madam:

TODAY BEFORE IT WAS LIGHT I had to roll in the stream to wash blood from my fur. I decided then to send You these words.

So I think of the word shapes, and the girl writes them for me. I know how the words are shaped because I could see them whenever Captain Dial spoke. And I always knew what he was saying.

The girl writes on a roll of paper she found in the stone hut when we began using it as our quarters three months ago. She already had pencils. She has written her own words on the paper many times since then, but she has torn those words from the roll and placed them in her duffel. Her own words have different shapes than the ones she writes for me now. She doesn't even know what my word shapes mean, because the shapes are all that I show her. So the responsibility for their meanings is mine alone.

Just as the responsibility for my actions is mine alone.

Last night I killed eighteen of Your soldiers.

I didn't want to do that. They reminded me of some of the soldiers I knew before, the ones who followed Captain Dial with me. But I had to kill them because they came to attack us. And if I let them do that, I would be disobeying orders.

I heard them approach while the girl, the two boys, and the old man slept. So I went out and climbed the ridge behind the hut so I could see a long way. I have good night vision, and I had no trouble spotting the soldiers as they split into two squads and spread out. Their intent was to attack our hut from different angles to make its defense more difficult. I knew this because it was one of the things Captain Dial taught me.

So I did another thing Captain Dial taught me. As the two squads scuttled to their positions to await the order to attack, I crept down toward them through the grass and brambles. I crept with my belly to the earth so they couldn't see me coming. Not even with their infrared goggles.

Captain Dial once said I was black as night and silent as air. He was proud when he said it. I remembered that when I crept to Your soldiers.

They didn't hear me as I went from one to another. They were spread out too far. Their leader wasn't as smart as Captain Dial. I bit each one's throat so it tore open and the soldier couldn't shout. There were some sounds, but they weren't loud.

The first soldier had a lieutenant's bar on his helmet. I had seen it from a long way away. It was the only officer's insignia I saw in either squad. So I went to him first. That way he couldn't give the order to attack before I was finished.

But the others would have attacked sooner or later, even

without an order from their lieutenant. So I had to kill them all.

The last soldier was the only female among the eighteen. As I approached her, I smelled the same kind of soap that Captain Dial's wife Melanie used. That made me pause as I remembered how things were a long time ago when I slept at the foot of their bed. But then the soldier knew I was there and turned her weapon toward me. So I bit her throat before she could fire.

I dragged the soldiers to the ravine near the southern end of the ridge. You'll find them there side by side if You arrive before the wild animals do. I did my best to treat them with honor.

Then I went to the stream. The stream is near the hut, so I tried to be quiet. I didn't want to wake my people before sunrise.

After washing, I went into the grass and shook off as much water as I could. But there was no one to rub me with a towel. There was no one to touch my head and tell me I was good.

I remembered then that no one had ever told Captain Dial he was good, either.

This is what it means to be the leader.

I wanted to howl. But I didn't. My people were still asleep.

I take care of them. I don't let anyone hurt them. These were Captain Dial's orders, and I will not disobey.

Captain Dial was my commanding officer. I was his first sergeant. If You examine the D Company roster, You will see that my pay grade is K-9.

My name is Chip.

Whenever Captain Dial gave me an order, I obeyed as fast as I could. And then he always touched my head and told me I was good. Sometimes when I was extra fast, he gave me a treat. I liked the treats, but I liked the touch even more.

There was never a time when Captain Dial wasn't my leader. But he wasn't always a captain, and I wasn't always his first sergeant. In the beginning he was a lieutenant, and I was his corporal.

We were promoted because of the day we demonstrated our training to the people in the bleachers.

That morning, in our quarters, Lieutenant Dial said that what we would participate in that afternoon was political bullshit. Money for the war was about to be cut, so public-relations events like this were an attempt to bolster civilian support. But Lieutenant Dial said that only two things had ever motivated the public to support the military: heroism and vengeance.

He also said that we had to do well regardless. He said I would have to do a good job and make him proud. So I stood at attention, and I thought about running fast to find mines and attack enemies. I thought about making Lieutenant Dial proud.

Then he touched my head. He knew my thoughts. He always knew my thoughts. He told me I was good and gave me permission to be at ease.

So I wiggled and pushed my head against his knees, and my tail wagged hard as he buckled my duty harness. Even though he had said it was bullshit, I could smell that he was excited about the job ahead. That made me excited too. And as we left our quarters, Lieutenant Dial's wife Melanie came with us. That made me even more excited, because she was almost never with us except in our quarters.

Melanie spoke to me every morning, and although I couldn't understand her thoughts too well, I knew she was telling me to take care of Lieutenant Dial throughout our day of training. And every night when Lieutenant Dial and I returned, Melanie touched my head and said I was good. Then, after we all ate supper, she and Lieutenant Dial would climb into their bed, I would lie down on my cushion at its foot, and we would sleep. Sometimes in the night their scents grew stronger and blended together, and they made happy sounds. But I stayed quiet because I wanted them to stay happy. Other times I smelled or heard strangers outside our quarters, and I would go on alert even though Lieutenant Dial was still asleep and had not given me an order. But the strangers always went away, and then I slept again too.

Those were the only times Melanie was with us, and that one order every morning was the only order she ever gave me. All of my other orders, all of my treats, and all of my food came from Lieutenant Dial.

But Lieutenant Dial loved Melanie. I could see the word "love" whenever he thought of her. And that made me glad because it made him glad. So we were all happy on the day she came with us. She smelled like a hundred different flowers all mixed together, and she was wearing new clothes that seemed to float around her.

She also wore a gift that Lieutenant Dial had given her the night before. It was a shiny rock on a silver chain that she wore around her neck. Lieutenant Dial told me that Melanie liked the color of the rock. It just looked like a rock on a chain to me. But when Lieutenant Dial put it around Melanie's neck, it made me think of the chain and tags that Lieutenant Dial wore around his own neck whenever he was on duty. And it also made me think of the collar he put on me when I wasn't wearing my duty harness. So then I understood why Melanie was so happy to receive the rock and chain. Now we all had things to wear around our necks.

We didn't go to our usual training area at the fort that day. Instead we went to a park by the ocean. There were flags and people everywhere. It was busy and noisy, and I wanted to run around and smell everything. But Lieutenant Dial ordered me to stay beside him, and that was fun too. I still got to smell everything. We walked from one tree to another, with me on one side of Lieutenant Dial and Melanie on the other. And at every tree, people gathered around while Lieutenant Dial told them who he was and who I was. Then he would give me a few orders—easy things like attention, on guard, and secure-the-perimeter—and we would move on. A lot of people asked if they could touch me, but Lieutenant Dial said they couldn't. He explained that I was on duty. I wasn't a pet. I was a corporal.

He was proud when he said it, and that made me proud too.

As we walked from place to place, sometimes Lieutenant Dial held Melanie's hand in his. And once, Melanie reached across and touched my head. This violated the rule Lieutenant Dial had been telling everyone. But even though I was on duty, it seemed all right. I was glad she did it.

After a while we walked away from the trees to a broad stretch of lawn beside the ocean. I saw a long pier floating on the water. And across the lawn from the pier were bleachers with people in them. There were more people in the bleachers than I had ever seen in one place before, and some of them were high-ranking officers in dress uniforms. So I knew that even if what was going to happen here was bullshit, it was important bullshit.

Out on the lawn were little flags, mud puddles, wooden walls, sandbag fortifications, and some mock-enemies. I knew they were mock-enemies because they wore dark, padded suits. All of these things were familiar to me from training. But there were more things on the lawn than I had ever seen in one training session, and that excited me.

Melanie went to the bleachers while Lieutenant Dial took me onto the lawn, where we were joined by other soldiers. Some of the other soldiers were also K-9s. I knew most of them. Lieutenant Dial and I had trained with them many times.

Out on the pier, men and women dressed in white stood at attention. And when Lieutenant Dial and I reached a spot in the middle of the lawn, he told me to stand at attention as well. So I did, and all of the other soldiers did too.

A colonel stood in front of the bleachers and addressed the crowd. He said a lot of words through a loudspeaker, but I couldn't understand them. Since they didn't come from Lieutenant Dial, they were meaningless.

When the colonel stopped talking, the people in the bleachers clapped their hands. Then a soldier ran onto the lawn and handed Lieutenant Dial a microphone. Lieutenant Dial signaled that I should remain at attention, so I didn't move as he took a step forward and addressed the people.

He told them a lot of things about K-9 soldiers. One thing he said was that while war dogs required a lot of training, we didn't have to be trained to understand loyalty or rank. A dog who was raised and trained by one soldier would always see that soldier as his or her pack leader. So if Lieutenant Dial was put in charge of a platoon, that platoon would become my pack. And I would see my duty to that pack as absolute and unquestionable.

It surprised me that Lieutenant Dial had to explain that to people. It was as obvious to me as knowing that food is for eating. But then I remembered that people didn't always think the same way that Lieutenant Dial and I thought. Melanie, for example. Melanie was always kind to me, but sometimes I could smell that she also feared me a little. And I always wondered how that could be. Lieutenant Dial loved Melanie, so I would never hurt her. And as long as I was near her, I would never let anything else hurt her, either. So I hoped that what Lieutenant Dial was saying to the people in the bleachers would help Melanie understand that she never had to be afraid.

Then Lieutenant Dial said something that made him sad as he said it. I don't think the people knew how sad it made him, but I knew. The other K-9s knew, too.

He said that during a war in the past, some high-ranking officers had decided that K-9s weren't really soldiers. Instead, they were classified as equipment. That meant that when their units left the field, K-9s were abandoned or destroyed. They were treated like utility vehicles or tents. They weren't allowed to return to their home quarters with their handlers.

Lieutenant Dial always spoke the truth, but this truth was difficult for me to comprehend. I knew I wasn't equipment. I knew the difference between a vehicle and a dog. And the K-9s in that past war must have known the difference too. So I was glad the regulations had changed. But I wondered then, and wonder now, whether there might still be some high-ranking officers who don't think of me as a soldier.

I urge You not to make that mistake.

Lieutenant Dial's sadness went away as he continued talking. He described some of the duties K-9 soldiers perform, and as he described those duties, different handlers ordered their K-9s to perform them. And as the dogs obeyed, their images appeared on a big screen that had been set up beside the pier.

One dog, a pointy-eared shepherd, attacked and subdued first one mock-enemy, then three, and then five. He was good at it. Even though the mock-enemies were padded so he couldn't really hurt them, I could smell that they were afraid of him.

Another dog, a lean pinscher, ran fast fast fast, dodging and leaping over obstacles that popped up before him, and he delivered a medical kit to another soldier at the end of the lawn. Then he dragged that soldier to a designated safety point while avoiding some booby traps. The booby traps went off bang bang bang after the pinscher and his soldier were past them.

A big-chested Malinois destroyed a machine-gun nest.

Another shepherd crept on her belly to flank an enemy platoon.

A hound pointed out hidden land mines and howled as he found each one.

Lieutenant Dial announced each K-9's name and rank, each handler's name and rank, and the task to be performed. The K-9s were all good, and the people in the bleachers clapped. So I was glad because everyone was happy. But I was getting more and more excited because I wanted it to be my turn. In fact, as the second shepherd completed her flanking maneuver and took down a mock-enemy from behind, I almost broke attention. I wanted to help. I wanted to be a good soldier, too.

I whimpered, and Lieutenant Dial gave me a corrective glance. So I tried extra hard to remain still and silent. I didn't want to disappoint Lieutenant Dial. Disappointing Lieutenant Dial would be the worst thing in the world.

When all of the other dogs had performed their tasks, Lieutenant Dial told the people that the modern K-9 soldier went beyond those of the past. He told them that K-9s and their handlers were now matched according to their skills, temperaments, and rapport—because there were some dogs and humans who had a gift for understanding each other, and some who didn't. And he told them that such matchings had been so successful that dogs often knew what their handlers wanted them to do even before any verbal or visual orders had been issued. In addition, a subcutaneous device implanted in each dog made it possible for handlers to send pulsed signals that their K-9s had been trained to recognize as orders. And the implants, in turn, sent biometric signals to the handlers to indicate their K-9s' levels of anxiety and confidence as orders were carried out. So even when a dog and handler weren't in close proximity, they could still communicate and complete their mission.

I didn't remember receiving my implant, but I knew it was under the skin between my shoulders. I almost never thought about it because Lieutenant Dial almost never used his transmitter anymore. He had used it often in our early days of training. But as our training had progressed, our thoughts had become clearer and clearer to each other, and one day we had both known the electronic signals weren't needed anymore. So Lieutenant Dial had unstrapped the transmitter from his wrist and put it in a pouch on his belt. After that day, he would sometimes send a signal just to be sure my implant was working, but I always started carrying out his orders before I felt the pulses anyway. That was because I paid attention to him, and I could see his thoughts even when he was far away.

When Lieutenant Dial finished telling the people about the communication implants, he told them about me. He told them I had been rescued from a municipal shelter as a puppy, and that a military veterinarian had determined that the dominant breeds in my genetic background were black Labrador and standard poodle. That made me a Labradoodle. Some of the people in the crowd laughed when they heard that name, but Lieutenant Dial didn't laugh when he said it.

He said I had the intelligence of a poodle and the temperament of a Labrador. He said I was three years old and in peak physical condition. He said I weighed eighty pounds, which was big enough to be strong, but small enough to be fast and to squeeze into places too tight for people. He said my black, wavy coat was good camouflage at night. He said I was at the top of my training class. He said I was a corporal and my name was Chip.

Then Lieutenant Dial looked across the lawn at a sandbagged machine-gun nest and gave me the hand signal to attack. I knew he was going to give me the signal as soon as he looked across at the sandbags, but I also knew I should wait for it. The people in the bleachers wouldn't like it if I didn't.

But I jumped away fast when he gave it. I ran for the sandbags, and the machine gun opened fire. It was firing blank cartridges, but I knew from training that I had to act as if the ammunition could hurt me. So I zigzagged and made quick stops behind cardboard rocks, stacks of tires, and other things that were on the lawn between Lieutenant Dial and the machine-gun nest. The machine-gun barrel swiveled to follow me, but I was too fast and tricky for it, because when I ran behind a cardboard rock, I would come out in a different direction. The machine-gun barrel couldn't keep up, and soon I was right under it so it couldn't point at me. Then I jumped up over the sandbags and pushed the gunner onto his back. Two mock-enemies on either side of him pointed rifles at me, so I bit one in the crotch and twisted so that he fell against the other one. Then all three mock-enemies were on their backs, and I bit the pads at their throats. A bell sounded over the loudspeaker as I broke the skin of each pad and the mock-blood came out. After the third bell, the people in the bleachers clapped.

Then I felt a quick series of pulses between my shoulders, but I was already jumping away from the machine-gun nest because I knew what Lieutenant Dial wanted me to do next. I ran as fast as I could to the farthest end of the lawn, dodging mock-enemies as they popped up and tried to shoot me, until I reached the wooden wall with the knotted rope at the top. The wall was high, but I liked that. I'm good at jumping.

I ran hard and jumped high, and I grabbed the bottom knot on the rope with my teeth. Then I pushed against the wall with all my feet so I could grab the next knot, and the next, and the next. Just before the next-to-last knot, a piece of the wall broke away as my feet pushed it, and I almost missed the knot. I caught it with just my front teeth. But that made me angry at the wall and the knot, because they were trying to make me disappoint Lieutenant Dial. So I bit as hard as I could with my front teeth, and I kicked and scratched the wall until another piece broke away and gave me a good place for my hind feet. Then I pulled with my teeth and pushed with my legs, and I went all the way over the wall without having to grab the last knot.

On the other side of the wall, two soldiers lay on the ground. They had mock-wounds on their legs and chests, but they weren't pretending to be unconscious. So I went to the nearest one and let him grab the handle on my duty harness. Then I dragged him through a mock-minefield to a medical station. The mines weren't marked with flags the way they often were in training, but I didn't need the flags. I know the smells of many different explosives, so I could smell the mines even though they were just smoke-bangs. It was easy to drag the soldier around them. Some of them went off when we were past, but it didn't matter. None of the smoke touched us, and I got the soldier to the medical station in the same shape I found him in.

I ran back for the other soldier, but when I reached him he was pretending to be unconscious. I whined and licked his face, but I knew it wouldn't make him stop pretending. So then I grabbed one of his flak-jacket straps and began to drag him toward the medical station. But when we were halfway through the minefield, an open utility vehicle carrying four mock-enemies came driving across it, straight for us. The mines didn't go off as the vehicle drove over them, and the mock-enemy manning the mounted gun began firing at me and my soldier.

They were trying to prevent me from obeying Lieutenant Dial's orders. I wouldn't let them do that.

I dropped my soldier and started running so the mock-enemies would chase me. When they did, and when we were far enough from the wounded soldier that I knew he would be safe, I made a quick stop, turned around, and jumped. I cleared the vehicle's windshield and had just enough time to bite the pad on the gunner's throat. The bell rang. Then I hit the ground behind the vehicle and tumbled, but got up and turned back around in time to see the gunner slump over and the driver turn the steering wheel hard. The other two mock-enemies were raising their pistols.

As the vehicle made its turn, exposing the driver, I ran and jumped again. But when I bit the pad on the driver's throat, the skin didn't break right away. So I hung on and bit harder. The driver gave a yell that I don't think was a word. Then the pad broke, the mock-blood came out, and I heard the bell. So I jumped away, spinning as my paws hit the ground so I could be ready to attack the remaining two mock-enemies.

But I didn't have to. The vehicle rolled over so its wheels went up, and three of the four enemies fell out. Then it was still. The driver was still strapped in his seat, but his neck was bent against the ground, and he didn't move. The three mock-enemies on the ground didn't move either. So I ran to the two I hadn't bitten yet, broke the skins on their throat pads, then returned to my soldier in the minefield.

The soldier was sitting up with his eyes and mouth open. But I grabbed his flak-jacket strap anyway and resumed dragging him to the medical station. Then he tried to pull away from me. But I was still under orders. So I growled, and then my soldier was still again. I delivered him to the medical station, ran back to Lieutenant Dial, and stood at attention.

The people in the bleachers began to smell unhappy. They made growling noises, and none of them clapped their hands. So for a moment I was afraid I had done something wrong. But then I knew it wasn't so, because Lieutenant Dial touched my head and said I was good.

That was all that mattered.

From Lieutenant Dial's next thoughts, I knew that the driver in the utility vehicle had made a mistake. He'd been supposed to drive farther away from me after the gunner was bitten. But he had turned back toward me too soon, and I had been faster than he had thought I would be. Then, when his throat pad hadn't broken right away, he had panicked and turned the steering wheel too sharply. So the vehicle had rolled over. But by then I had broken the throat pad and jumped away.

All four of the mock-enemies in the utility vehicle had to be taken away for real medical care, and I could hear that some of the people in the bleachers felt bad about that. But Lieutenant Dial didn't. Instead, he became angry. He wasn't angry with me, but I didn't want him to be angry with anything. Being angry made him unhappy. And that made me unhappy too. Anger was like smoke with a bad smell in his head.

The K-9 demonstration was over then, and Melanie came down from the bleachers to meet us. I was glad to see her. But Lieutenant Dial was still angry. He told Melanie that the driver of the utility vehicle had done the exercise incorrectly, and that what had happened wasn't my fault. I had done what I was supposed to do, but the mock-enemies had screwed it up.

Melanie told him she already knew that, and that everyone else knew it too. She said he shouldn't worry about what people would think of him, or of me, or of any of the K-9s, because we had all been wonderful.

I didn't always know what Melanie was saying, but that time I understood every word. And as she spoke, Lieutenant Dial's anger drifted away. Just like smoke. And then he was happy and proud again. And so was I.

I rubbed my nose against Melanie's knee, and she touched my head. I wished I could tell her she was good.

Then Lieutenant Dial, Melanie, and I walked to the edge of the water with some of the people from the bleachers, and we stood on a boardwalk while the people on the pier performed demonstrations with water animals. We had a good view even though we were about thirty meters from them. Lieutenant Dial said the animals that stayed in the water all the time were called dolphins, and the ones that hopped from the pier to the water and back again were called sea lions. One of the sea lions barked, but I couldn't understand it.

The water animals delivered equipment to people underwater, and they also searched for mines and mock-enemies. Pictures of them doing those things appeared on the big screen. Sometimes a sea lion carried a clamp in its mouth, and when it found a mock-enemy, it swam up behind him and put the clamp on his leg. Then the mock-enemy was pulled up to the pier by a rope attached to the clamp, while the sea lion jumped from the water and got a treat from its handler. It looked like fun, and I wished I could go underwater and sneak up on the mock-enemies down there too.

Then the sea lions had a contest. They were supposed to find some small dummy mines and push buttons on the mines with their noses, then attach handles and bring the mines up to the pier. It was a race to see which sea lion could bring up the most mines in two minutes. So the sea lions were swimming fast and splashing a lot, dropping the mines on the pier and grabbing new handles before plunging into the ocean again.

The dummy water mines looked like black soccer balls, and they had lights that came on if the button had been pushed. Once one of the sea lions brought up a mine that didn't have its light on, and his handler threw the mine back into the water. Then the sea lion had to go get it again, and he had to be sure to push the button before putting it on the pier. If I had been that sea lion, I would have felt bad for not doing it right the first time. But I couldn't tell whether he felt bad or not, because he kept on swimming for more mines. So then I was glad because he was still being a good soldier.

He didn't win the contest, though. He came in second. At the end of two minutes, he had eleven mines, and the winner had twelve. All the people who had watched the race clapped and cheered, and the four sea lions who had raced got up on their hindquarters and barked. The people cheered even more then, and Lieutenant Dial and Melanie did too. But Lieutenant Dial didn't clap because he had one hand on the handle of my duty harness.

Both Lieutenant Dial and Melanie were happy. So I should have been happy too.

But I wasn't. Something was wrong.

I didn't know what it was at first, so I lifted my head high and sniffed the air. There were many smells. There was sweat, soda, and popcorn. There were buckets of little fish. The sea lions smelled salty. Melanie still smelled like flowers. The other K-9s smelled thirsty. The practice mines smelled like wet Frisbees.

Except there was another smell with the Frisbee smell. It wasn't big. But it was there. It was a bad smell. It was a bad smell like the real mines that had been in the practice minefield during the hardest part of training. It was a bad smell like the real mine that had killed another K-9 who wasn't careful enough.

And as soon as I had identified that bad smell, I knew where it was coming from. The final mine that the winning sea lion had brought up wasn't like the others. It looked like them, but it didn't smell like them. It was different. It was bad.

It wanted to explode and kill someone.

But none of the sea lions were doing anything about it. They were still on their hindquarters, swaying back and forth, while the people clapped. One of the dolphins was splashing and chattering out in the water, so I think she might have known. But none of the handlers paid any attention to her. They were smiling at the clapping people.

I was under no specific orders. But Lieutenant Dial had given me one General Order many training sessions ago: If I ever knew something was wrong, I had to act.

So I bolted for the pier, and Lieutenant Dial released my harness handle. I knew his thoughts, and he knew mine. He knew I was being good.

I ran fast between people's legs. Some of them yelled. And then I was on the pier. It moved up and down a little, but I kept on running fast even though it tried to make me fall. Two of the people in white stepped into my path, but I zigzagged around them. The pier was wet there, and my feet slipped. But I scrabbled hard like I did at the wall and kept going.

One of the sea lions came down from his haunches as I approached, and he opened his mouth as if to bite me. It was a big mouth with big teeth. The whole sea lion was as big as five of me, and he lunged at me when I came close. So I jumped over his head and kicked the back of his neck with my hind feet. That pushed me the last three meters to the end of the pier.

My front feet hit the pier right beside the bad mine, so I grabbed its handle with my teeth, whipped it forward, and let go so it flew into the water. Two of the dolphins swam away fast as the mine splashed and sank.

Then I couldn't smell the bad mine anymore, so I was glad. But when I turned around and saw the white-clothed people and their sea lions, none of them seemed glad. The people were shouting and the sea lions were barking. The sea lions' barks still didn't make sense.

I saw Lieutenant Dial running down the pier toward me, so I started running toward him too. And just as I began to zigzag around the sea lions, I heard a rumble and a splash, and the pier rose up under me. I fell, and the pier hit my jaw and made me bite my tongue. Then the pier bounced up and down, and I couldn't stand up because my feet kept slipping. One of the people in white had fallen down beside me, and he kept slipping too. That made me worry about Lieutenant Dial, so I looked up to see if he was all right. But a sea lion was in the way.

Then I yelped. Later, a news reporter would say that I yelped because my tongue was hurt. But that wasn't the reason. It was because I couldn't see or hear Lieutenant Dial, and I couldn't find his thoughts. There were too many people thinking and yelling all at once. I couldn't even smell him because I was too close to the sea lions.

That was a bad moment. But the pier moved a little less each time it bounced, and finally I could stand up. And then I could see Lieutenant Dial. He was in the middle of the pier helping another person stand up, so I ran to him and stood at attention. When he had finished helping the other person, he looked down at me and saluted. And he told me I was good. He told me I was more good than I had ever been before.

And the bad moment was gone.

Later, investigators said that a real enemy had replaced one of the sea lions' dummy mines with a live one, intending to hurt or kill as many people and animals as possible. But because I threw it back into the water, only one dolphin was hurt. And no one was killed.

A few weeks later, Lieutenant Dial was promoted to Captain, and I was promoted to Sergeant. Captain Dial received silver bars for his uniform, and then he leaned over and showed me a new metal tag before clipping it to the ring in my collar. It was shaped like the insignia for Sergeant First Class. I knew I couldn't wear it on combat duty, because it would get in the way and make noise. But it was still a fine thing, because that was how it looked in Captain Dial's thoughts.

Other soldiers were promoted during that ceremony as well, but I was the only K-9. Also, Captain Dial and I were commended for finding the live mine. We were called heroes.

Melanie was there for the ceremony, and both she and Captain Dial were proud and happy. So I was proud and happy too.

But I still wasn't as happy as I had been on the pier. That was where I had been more good than I had ever been before. Captain Dial had said so.

That was how I knew it was true.

SOON AFTER our promotions, Captain Dial and I left the fort with many other soldiers, and we all went to the war. Melanie came to the fort to say good-bye to us. She and Captain Dial hugged each other for a long time while I stood at ease. Most of the other soldiers were hugging people too. There were wives and children, and even a few dogs who weren't soldiers.

Then Melanie knelt down and put her head against mine. It surprised me. She had never done anything like that before. I think she was trying to help me understand her thoughts the way I understood Captain Dial's. It helped a little. But even if she hadn't done it, I would have known she was telling me the same thing she had told me every morning before training. She was telling me to take care of Captain Dial.

So I kissed her face. I wanted her to be glad that Captain Dial and I were going to the war together. Her face tasted like ocean water.

Then Melanie took her head away from mine and put her arms around Captain Dial again. After a while, Captain Dial pulled away from her and gave me the signal to proceed. We left Melanie and went to the D Company bus.

When all the soldiers of D Company had boarded the bus, it took us to the air transport. Captain Dial was quiet during the bus ride. He just looked out the window. And for the first time, his thoughts weren't clear to me. It was as if they were far away in a fog, and a fuzzy sound ran through them. I glimpsed Melanie, but that was all. Captain Dial kept his hand on my neck, though, and every now and then his fingers rubbed behind my ears. So I didn't worry. Captain Dial always had some thoughts that I couldn't understand anyway. The only ones I really needed to know were the ones that were orders.

The air transport took a long time, and it was loud. I didn't like it. By the time it stopped at an island to refuel, all my muscles were sore. But I felt better after marking some trees near the airstrip, and better still after some food. We got back on the transport then, and Captain Dial gave me a pill to help me sleep through the rest of the flight. It helped a lot. But I was still glad when we were on the ground again. When we finally left the transport we were in a place that was dry and sunny, and all of the smells were sharp.

The soldiers of D Company spent one night in a tin-roofed barracks at the combat zone airfield, and Captain Dial and I slept there with them. There was no kennel or cushion for me, so I slept on a blanket beside Captain Dial's cot. I was the only K-9 in the company, and some of the other soldiers were nervous around me. But Captain Dial made sure that I met each one and learned that soldier's smell. Captain Dial wanted to keep them all safe. So I wanted to keep them safe too.

I could see some soldiers' thoughts, although none of them were as clear to me as Captain Dial's. But that was all right, because the soldiers' voices and smells told me all I needed to know about them. Most of them were friendly, although several stayed nervous even after they met me. And a few smelled frightened or angry.

One of the angry ones was an officer, Lieutenant Morris, who was in charge of First Platoon. I couldn't see his thoughts at all, but I still knew he didn't like me. I knew he didn't like Captain Dial, either. When he stood before us, his sweat smelled bitter, and his voice was low. And even when he saluted, his muscles were tense as if he were about to run or fight.

Captain Dial was aware of all this, because he knew my thoughts. But unlike me, he was able to think of a reason for Lieutenant Morris's attitude. He thought Lieutenant Morris believed he should have been promoted to Captain and given command of D Company.

This troubled Captain Dial, because he had never wanted to lead a company of regular soldiers anyway. But I was the only one who knew it. What he really wanted to do was serve in a K-9 unit. But when we were promoted, he was ordered to command D Company because its original captain had died in training. So he requested that I be allowed to join the company with him, and we were both happy when his request was granted. We joined D Company on the same day we went to the war. And I knew that all of the soldiers in D Company were lucky to have Captain Dial as their leader.

The morning after our arrival in the combat zone, D Company was assigned to guard four checkpoints on highways that led to the airfield. So Captain Dial put a platoon at each checkpoint, splitting the soldiers among three separate road barriers per checkpoint. He told the lieutenants and sergeants to stop and inspect each vehicle at each barrier, and to detain the occupants of any vehicle found to contain contraband. He also told them to have their soldiers fire warning shots over any vehicles that passed the first barrier without stopping for inspection. They were to aim at the tires and engines of any vehicles that also passed the second barrier without stopping. And any vehicles that passed the third barrier without stopping were to be destroyed. But any vehicles that stopped at all three barriers and were found to contain no contraband were to be allowed to proceed unless the soldiers had reason to believe that a more thorough inspection was needed. In that case, the suspicious vehicle was to be reported to Captain Dial so he could bring me to it and I could smell whether anything was wrong.

I thought these orders were easy and clear.

Captain Dial and I spent our first five days in the combat zone riding from checkpoint to checkpoint in a utility vehicle, inspecting cars and trucks and seeing to the needs of D Company. I liked doing the inspections. In those first days, I found three pistols, four rifles, a rocket-propelled grenade launcher, and a brick of hashish. Captain Dial arrested the people with the guns and sent them to Headquarters. But he laughed at the man with the hashish and let him drive away. Hashish wasn't contraband here, he told me, so long as no one gave any to our soldiers. This was a new rule to me, but I'm good at learning new rules.

The first five days were fun. All of our platoons did their jobs, and so did Captain Dial and I.

Then, on the morning of the sixth day, Lieutenant Morris ordered First Platoon to open fire on a van that had gone past the first barrier without stopping. It didn't reach the second barrier. By the time Lieutenant Morris ordered his soldiers to cease fire, all seven people inside the van had been killed.

Captain Dial and I weren't there when it happened. We were two checkpoints away. By the time we arrived, the incident had been over for fifteen minutes. Lieutenant Morris and a few other soldiers had dragged three of the bodies from the shot-up van and laid them by the side of the road. They were heading back toward the van when Captain Dial stopped our utility vehicle in front of them and ordered them to stay away from the van and the bodies.

Then he ordered me to search the van, and I obeyed. It was a bad place. It smelled of spent machine-gun rounds, explosive residue, and human blood.

The driver was still in her seat. She had been a woman about the size of Melanie. The three other bodies still in the van had been small children. There were two boys and a girl. I had seen children of their sizes on the day by the ocean. But the ones in the van had been shot through and through. Their blood was all over the floor and seats, and I had to step in it to conduct my search.

There was no contraband. There were no guns, and the only bullets were spent rounds. And I couldn't smell any explosives except the residue of a grenade that had been fired into the van by someone in First Platoon.

After I had searched the van, Captain Dial ordered me to search the three bodies on the ground. So I did. They were all girls. Two were even smaller than the children in the van. The third was larger, about the size of the girl who writes these words. But she wasn't fully grown. All of them had been shot many times. One of the younger girls had most of her face gone. The older girl had a narrow cut on her neck. None of them possessed any contraband.

Captain Dial was angrier than he had ever been before. The smoke in his head was thick and turbulent. And there were sounds. I could hear Melanie crying. I could hear a hundred Melanies crying.

Then Captain Dial began shouting at Lieutenant Morris. I had never heard him shout like that before, and it made me cringe even though he wasn't shouting at me. All the soldiers of First Platoon cringed, too, especially when Captain Dial said he would bring Lieutenant Morris up on charges for disobeying orders.

But Lieutenant Morris's bitter smell was acrid and strong now, and he stood with his head thrust forward and his arms straight down at his sides. He didn't salute. It was as if he was challenging Captain Dial. It was as if he thought he had done a good thing, and that Captain Dial's orders had been wrong.

That made me angry, because Captain Dial always gave good orders. So I took a step toward Lieutenant Morris and growled.

Lieutenant Morris reached for his sidearm, but Captain Dial

slapped his hand away from it. Then Lieutenant Morris made a fist and started to swing it at Captain Dial's face. I was on him before his fist was halfway there, and I put him on his back on the highway.

I stood with my front paws on Lieutenant Morris's chest and my teeth touching his throat, and Captain Dial ordered him to remain still. This time, Lieutenant Morris obeyed. I could feel the pulse in his neck and the shallow motion of his chest as he breathed, but those were the only movements he made until Captain Dial ordered me to stand down. Then I took my paws from Lieutenant Morris's chest and backed away.

But now I smelled something wrong in a pocket of Lieutenant Morris's fatigues. It smelled like the girl with the cut on her neck. It smelled like her blood.

I pointed at Lieutenant Morris's pocket and barked. So Captain Dial knelt down, opened the pocket, and brought out a slender chain with a shiny rock on it. It wasn't just like the one he had given Melanie, but it didn't look much different. Except that this one had blood on its chain.

The clasp on the chain was closed, but the chain had been broken in another place. The rock slid down against the clasp when Captain Dial pulled the chain from Lieutenant Morris's pocket, and it dangled there as he held it up. It caught the sun so that it seemed to have a light inside it.

Captain Dial remained on one knee, looking at the necklace, for a long time. Lieutenant Morris started to speak, but I growled and he shut up. I was doing him a favor, because one of Captain Dial's thoughts was clear. He was thinking of using his sidearm to shoot Lieutenant Morris in the head. He was thinking that if Lieutenant Morris said even one word, that was what he would do.

What happened instead was that Captain Dial stood up and told a First Platoon sergeant to call for military police. Then he returned to our utility vehicle, leaving Lieutenant Morris on his back on the highway. I went with Captain Dial, and we waited in our vehicle until the military police came. When they did, Captain Dial gave the rock and chain to one of them.

I didn't understand everything that happened after that. But

Lieutenant Morris was back with D Company just two days after he ordered First Platoon to attack the van. And Captain Dial was unhappy because he didn't think there would ever be a court-martial. For one thing, none of the soldiers of First Platoon were sure about what had happened. Some of them even thought that the van had been loaded with explosives, and they continued to think so even after Captain Dial told them I hadn't smelled any. Also, Lieutenant Morris said that he had found the girl's necklace on the ground. And there were no soldiers who would say that he hadn't. Except me. I hadn't smelled any dirt or asphalt on it. All I had smelled was skin and blood from the girl's neck plus sweat from Lieutenant Morris's hand. But the only officer who could hear my testimony was Captain Dial. And unless there was a court-martial, he had already done all he could do.

Besides, the military police said they lost the necklace.

Captain Dial was sad from then on. I don't think anyone else in the company knew that. But I did.

I wanted to make Captain Dial happy again, so I tried even harder to be good. And he told me I was. He told me I was the best sergeant he had ever seen.

But he was still sad. So I was sad too.

Two weeks later, D Company was assigned to a combat mission. A few hours before dawn on a Friday morning, thirty enemy guerrillas had attacked our supply depot using mortars and small arms—and although they had been repelled, four of our soldiers had been killed. So the guerrillas had to be followed and destroyed, and D Company was chosen to do it. Captain Dial thought it was strange that an entire company was being sent after only thirty enemies, but he followed the order without hesitation.

D Company was in pursuit of the guerrillas within an hour of the attack. The guerrillas had a big head start, but they were on foot, and D Company had armored personnel carriers, utility vehicles, and me. So we were able to move fast over both roads and fields, and every few minutes Captain Dial had me run ahead and correct the direction of our pursuit. The guerrillas were staying in one group, so their trail was easy to smell.

We had almost caught up to them as they reached the hills fifteen kilometers west of our airfield. We were so close that Captain Dial could see them through his night-vision field glasses. They were making their way up a narrow, ascending valley, and they were still in one group.

This troubled Captain Dial. It seemed to him that once the guerrillas had reached the hills, they should have scattered to make our pursuit more difficult. But they were staying together. So Captain Dial used his radio to consult with Headquarters, and Headquarters said a refugee camp of about three hundred souls lay a short distance up the valley, a few hundred meters beyond a natural curve. The guerrillas probably intended to stay together long enough to reach that camp—and then they would disperse and blend in with the civilians. This would force Captain Dial to either let them escape, or arrest the entire camp.

So we had to stop the guerrillas before they reached the refugee camp. Captain Dial increased our speed, then dropped off two squads from Fourth Platoon with ten mortars as soon as we were in range. His plan was for those squads to fire the mortars just beyond the guerrillas, forcing them to turn away from the refugee camp . . . and perhaps also to run back into our pursuit.

As the rest of D Company started up the valley, the mortar squads put a dozen rounds where Captain Dial had ordered. But instead of reversing direction, the guerrillas began to ascend a hill on the south side of the valley. They remained in one group, though, and we gained on them. When we were close enough that we might be hit by stray mortar rounds, Captain Dial radioed the squads and told them to hold fire. But they were to stay put to intercept any enemies that might be flushed back toward them.

We rushed toward the base of the hill the guerrillas were climbing. They were moving much more slowly now, and in the light of dawn it was clear that we would overtake them before they reached the crest of the hill. I became excited as I thought of knocking them down and holding them, one by one, until my fellow soldiers could take them prisoner. And as the utility vehicle that carried me, Captain Dial, and Staff Sergeant Owens began to climb the hill, I readied myself to leap out and attack.

Our vehicle was in the lead, so most of the company was still on the valley floor as we started up the hill. It was at that moment that rocket-propelled grenades and mortar shells began raining down around us from the opposite hillside to the north. And then the guerrillas we were chasing took up positions and began to fire down on us with small arms.

Captain Dial radioed orders to our platoon leaders to take cover and return fire. Then he had Staff Sergeant Owens turn our utility vehicle broadside to the enemy fire, and the three of us exited on the downhill side. We crawled downhill as fast as we could until we reached one of D Company's APCs, and we took cover behind it with soldiers from First and Second Platoons. The soldiers were jumping up and leaning out to fire quick bursts from their rifles, and Captain Dial shouted for them to keep it up as he got on the radio again to call Headquarters for air support. Our helicopters and drones were always out on missions, but two or three could be diverted if soldiers were in trouble. And we were in trouble.

But now Captain Dial couldn't raise Headquarters on the radio. He tried every possible frequency, and there was nothing but silence.

Lieutenant Morris crawled to us and told Captain Dial that we were all going to be killed, and that it was Captain Dial's fault. I wanted to bite Lieutenant Morris's throat then. But Captain Dial ignored him, so I tried to ignore him too. He wasn't a good soldier. He didn't belong in D Company.

There was a loud explosion up the hill, and a soldier told Captain Dial that our abandoned utility vehicle had been hit by a rocket from the other side of the valley. They were zeroing in on us. So Captain Dial said we couldn't stay behind the armored personnel carrier, because it would be targeted next. He ordered First and Second Platoons to retreat to the valley floor, and then he got on the radio and told the mortar squads from Fourth Platoon to fire on the northern hillside. Finally he called to Third Platoon and the remaining two squads of Fourth Platoon, who were all still at the base of the hill, and told them to abandon their APCs and move up the valley on foot, doubletime. All platoons were to return fire as best they could. No one was to retreat back toward the plain.

As Captain Dial and I moved downhill with First and Second Platoons, Lieutenant Morris shouted that Captain Dial's orders were insane. The soldiers in APCs should stay in them, he said. Without armor, he said, they would be picked off in the valley like cattle in a chute.

But Captain Dial knew that the armor was what the enemy would try to destroy first, unless it was moving fast. And it couldn't move fast in the terrain we were in. So getting the soldiers away from it was the only thing to do. And sure enough, before we reached the bottom of the hill, the APC we had been using for cover was hit by a rocket and destroyed.

Our mortars began hitting the northern hill as Captain Dial and I reached the base of the southern hill, and Captain Dial stood his ground there while urging the soldiers of First and Second Platoons to run past our abandoned APCs and continue up the valley. And even now, Lieutenant Morris kept telling him he was wrong, and that D Company ought to be heading back to the plain in full retreat.

But I knew Captain Dial's thoughts, and I knew he was right. Headquarters had been tricked into having D Company follow the guerrillas into an ambush—but Captain Dial wouldn't let the guerrillas trick him any further. He knew that once the ambush began, the enemy would expect D Company to retreat toward the plain. So there would be another trap waiting at the mouth of the valley. The enemy would close us in, then fire down upon us until we were annihilated.

So Captain Dial would confound their expectations. D Company would continue up the valley, on foot, until we could reach an elevated position. With our mortar squads out on the plain providing harassing fire, we could be well up the valley before the guerrillas could leave their hillsides. And then we would transform the enemy's ambush into an attack of our own.

But we would have to take up our battle position before reaching the refugee camp. So we would doubletime around the curve to get out of sight of the enemy, then run up the hill on the backside of the curve. The guerrillas would have no clear shot from their current positions—and if they followed us, we would be able to pour fire down on them as they rounded the curve. So even without air support, we could prevail.

Captain Dial's plan was good, and as D Company rushed up the valley, it began to work. Two more of our abandoned vehicles were hit and began to burn, but despite the constant fire from the enemy, we had not yet lost a single soldier. Our mortar squads were hitting the hillsides as ordered, and the guerrillas' weapons fire became erratic. Captain Dial paused every few meters to shout orders and encouragement to his running soldiers, and once he sent me back to nip at the heels of a few stragglers. But the stragglers weren't stragglers for long, and I was able to rejoin Captain Dial in less than a minute. Then, bringing up the rear, he and I rounded the curve and began running up the slope to take our positions with the rest of our soldiers. They were already following Captain Dial's orders, taking cover behind rocks and in gullies. And they were readying their weapons.

Some of the guerrillas had chased after us, and a few of them came around the curve before Captain Dial and I were far enough up the slope to take our positions. But we hit the dirt so our soldiers could fire on them, and only two of these enemies survived long enough to come within twenty meters of me and Captain Dial. So I turned, charged, and bit their throats. Then I returned to Captain Dial, and we joined several of our soldiers behind a jumble of rocks and dirt.

More guerrillas came around the curve, and D Company shot them. Then some came up the slope in a truck, and one of our soldiers destroyed it with a rocket-propelled grenade. We were winning the battle despite being ambushed.

Then strange things happened.

They didn't seem strange at first. At first, I heard the buzz of airborne drones. Captain Dial couldn't hear them yet, but he knew that I could, and he was glad. It seemed that Headquarters had heard his request after all.

But almost as soon as I heard the drones, I also heard distant explosions, and our mortar squads stopped firing. So Captain

Dial radioed them for a status report. But there was no reply. Then he tried again to contact Headquarters, but there was still no reply there either.

The buzz became loud, and two drones appeared around the curve of the valley, flying low. They were narrow-winged and sleek, and almost invisible against the sky. They didn't have any insignia on their wings.

Then they fired rockets at us. They fired rockets at D Company. And at least twenty soldiers died as the rockets exploded. Dirt and rocks pelted me and Captain Dial where we crouched. My ears hurt.

The drones rose up over the opposite hill, then turned back toward us. Captain Dial shouted into his radio, trying one frequency after another, doing his best to raise Headquarters, to raise the remote drone pilots, to raise anyone who should have been listening. He shouted to his lieutenants to try their own radios too. And they did. But no one received a reply.

The drones came swooping toward us, and it became clear that their first attack hadn't been a mistake. Captain Dial's thoughts were tangled as he realized this. The enemy had no such weapons. So he couldn't understand why the drones were attacking us. Their cameras should have seen who we were, and their pilots should have known that D Company wasn't the enemy.

But even in his confusion, Captain Dial was a good leader. He ordered Sergeant Owens to fire a flare to identify us, but he didn't wait to see whether the cameras had seen it and understood its meaning. Instead, he shouted for D Company's surviving lieutenants and sergeants to get their soldiers up and moving again. If the drones were returning to attack our position again, he was going to put us somewhere else.

The soldiers of D Company were already running down the slope when the drones launched their second wave of rockets, so most of them made it to the valley floor. But eight more were killed. Captain Dial and I were bringing up the rear again, and the rocket that killed the eight exploded in front of us just as another exploded behind us. Captain Dial dove to the ground, putting his arms around me and pushing me down. Then he covered me with his body as more rockets exploded on the slope above us.

I didn't like it. Captain Dial wasn't supposed to shield me from harm. I was supposed to do that for him. So I tried to reverse our positions, but Captain Dial ordered me to stay put. Of course I had to obey. But I didn't understand. Captain Dial was more important to D Company than I was.

The rockets stopped exploding, and the drones passed over us again. They were so close that the dirt under my jaw hummed. Then Captain Dial was on his feet again, shouting orders as the drones flew behind the hilltop. The surviving soldiers of D Company were to run like hell up the valley and to take whatever cover they could find—rocks, trees, ditches, anything—if the drones made another pass. But the soldiers were to avoid entering the refugee camp, wherever it was, at all costs. If they came upon it while still on the run, they were to find a way around it.

CAPTAIN DIAL was smart. But even Captain Dial could only make his choices based on what he knew. And he didn't know that the refugees weren't gathered in a single camp, as Headquarters had said. He didn't know that they were scattered in small clusters throughout the rest of the valley.

And he didn't know that the drones would return so soon, or that they would swoop up and down the valley firing their Gatling guns at anything that moved. The valley was full of sunlight now, so the pilots should have been able to see our soldiers' uniforms. There was nothing to block the view of the cameras. But the drones kept firing on us.

I wished I could jump high enough to tear them out of the sky.

As D Company's lieutenants and sergeants began shouting and radioing Captain Dial, telling him that they were losing more soldiers and that every scrap of cover was occupied by noncombatants, Captain Dial made a decision he didn't want to make. He tried one more time to contact Headquarters—and when that failed, he ordered D Company to return fire. Then he took a rifle from a fallen corporal and fired the first shots at the lead drone as it swooped toward us again.

I couldn't fire a weapon, so I did the only thing I could do to help. I ran in a zigzag pattern toward the drones in an attempt to draw their fire and give the rest of D Company a better chance to make their shots count. And I could hear Captain Dial shouting that I was good.

That made me glad.

The lead drone turned toward me, and in that instant the soldiers of D Company were able to hit it broadside with small-arms fire and at least one RPG. The drone began spewing smoke, and then it turned and almost collided with the second drone. The second drone pulled up and vanished behind a hill just as the first one began to spiral downward.

I returned to Captain Dial, who ordered me and the soldiers who were closest to follow him. We ran up a hillside and dove into a gully that cut across it. There were six of us: Captain Dial, Lieutenant Morris, Sergeant Owens, two specialists, and me. And in the gully we found five civilians: An old man, a woman, an adolescent girl, and two young boys. They scrambled away from us as we tumbled into the gully, and they seemed about to climb out until Captain Dial spoke to them in their language. I think he told them they would be safer if they stayed put.

He had no sooner gotten the words out than the ground shook with the biggest explosion yet. I smelled burning fuel, and I knew the drone had crashed. Captain Dial shouted for everyone to hit the dirt, but I was the only one in the gully who heard him. There was a roaring noise and more explosions. The drone's remaining weapons were detonating.

One of the boys tried to climb out of the gully. The woman jumped up to stop him, and something from the exploding drone hit her in the face. She fell back into the gully. So Captain Dial tried to get to the panicked boy to pull him down. But Lieutenant Morris clutched Captain Dial's leg and stopped him.

Captain Dial made a gesture, and I followed the order. I leaped over him and Lieutenant Morris, and I grabbed the boy's ankle and pulled him down. My teeth broke his skin, but it couldn't be helped. When the boy fell to the dirt beside the woman, I pressed my chest against his to hold him there.

The girl started to move as if to protect the boy from me, but then she looked at my eyes. And for that moment, she knew my thoughts. So she crawled to the woman instead and wiped blood from her face.

The woman wasn't breathing, and I knew she was dead. The girl knew it too, but she tried to make the woman breathe again anyway.

There were a few more explosions from the fallen drone, and then the only noise from it was a muted roar as it burned. So I listened for the other drone, and I heard it flying farther and farther away.

Captain Dial told me I could let the boy up, so I did. He tried to run away again, but this time the girl stopped him. He was crying, and so was the girl. So was the other boy. The girl looked at me again, and I knew then that the dead woman was their mother and the old man was their grandfather. The old man was sitting against the wall of the gully with his knees pulled up to his face and his eyes closed tight.

I looked at Captain Dial then and saw that he was hurt. His left sleeve was turning dark at the shoulder, just below the edge of his flak jacket. But I could hardly smell his blood among all the other bloody smells. I went to him and whined, and he touched my head and told me he was all right. I wanted to go find a medic for him, but he ordered me to stay.

Then he used his radio to ask the rest of D Company for a status report, but he couldn't hear the replies because Lieutenant Morris began shouting. I couldn't understand all of the words, but I understood that Lieutenant Morris blamed Captain Dial for what had happened. He accused Captain Dial of treason for shooting down one of our own aircraft. And he said that the civilians weren't refugees at all, but guerrillas like those we had been pursuing. He said that was why the drones had attacked. And he said it was Captain Dial's fault that D Company had been in the line of fire when that happened.

Nothing Lieutenant Morris was shouting made any sense. But nothing that had happened to us had made any sense either. I knew that much from Captain Dial's thoughts. He didn't understand why things had happened the way they had happened. He slumped with his back against the wall of the gully, and he wondered whether Melanie would still love him after this.

Lieutenant Morris turned to Sergeant Owens and the two specialists, and he announced that Captain Dial was incapacitated. So he was now ranking officer, he said, and he ordered them to turn their weapons toward the old man, the girl, and the boys. If any of them moved, he said, the soldiers were to shoot them all.

Sergeant Owens and the specialists did as they were told. Then Lieutenant Morris reached for the radio in Captain Dial's right hand, but I jumped in his way and snarled at him. So Lieutenant Morris unholstered his sidearm and pointed it at me.

But before he could fire, Captain Dial spoke. He ordered Lieutenant Morris to lower his weapon, and after some hesitation, Lieutenant Morris obeyed. Then Captain Dial ordered Sergeant Owens and the specialists to lower their weapons as well, and they obeyed too.

Captain Dial was strong again. His shoulder was bleeding, but his thoughts were clear. He stood up, pushing himself off the gully wall with his right forearm, and peered over the rim at the burning drone. He spoke into his radio and told his soldiers to stay put if they were in a safe place, and to keep trying to find one if they weren't. He would assess the situation and issue new orders within the next few minutes.

But we didn't have a few minutes. I could hear the second drone returning.

I barked to let Captain Dial know it was coming. So then he shouted into his radio and ordered all of his soldiers to remain still and refrain from returning fire unless directly fired upon. Then he ordered those of us in the gully to hit the dirt. The girl and the two boys didn't understand at first, but the old man put his hands on their shoulders and made them lie down close to their dead mother.

Then Captain Dial lowered himself to a sitting position with his back against the gully wall. He couldn't lie down flat with his wounded shoulder. I lay down next to him and put my chin on his knee, and we waited while the drone flew back and forth. Its Gatling gun chattered three or four times, and I hoped it was shooting enemy guerrillas and not D Company soldiers or civilians.

One of the little boys began to cry, but the girl and the old man whispered to him, and then he was quiet again. I was glad they could calm him like that. They were being good leaders. Like Captain Dial.

But a good leader needs good soldiers.

On the drone's fourth pass, Lieutenant Morris stood and fired his weapon into the air. I was on him fast, my front paws hitting his back and pushing him down, but it was too late. Even as I pinned Lieutenant Morris to the bottom of the gully, I could hear the drone turning and the barrels of its Gatling guns beginning to spin.

Lieutenant Morris shouted into the dirt that we had to show ourselves to the drone so it would know who we were and so it could help us kill the rest of the enemy. He worked a hand free from under his chest and pointed at the family with the dead mother.

I wanted to bite Lieutenant Morris and bite him hard. And I smelled something in one of his pockets that made me feel that way even more. It smelled like the dead girl at the highway checkpoint.

But I didn't bite him, because I knew Captain Dial wouldn't like it. Captain Dial was busy with his radio, telling the rest of D Company that they were not to give away their positions by firing on the drone if it attacked those of us in the gully—not unless there was a clear shot for an RPG. Otherwise, we were on our own. But D Company would survive.

I heard the drone dip low. It was flying on a path directly in line with our gully. It would be able to pour bullets and rockets on us with ease.

Captain Dial was on his feet. It was as if he had been yanked up on a rope from the sky. His left sleeve was so wet that it dripped.

He shouted two orders. First, Sergeant Owens and the two specialists were to get out of the gully at the south rim and run through the smoke of the downed aircraft until they could find other cover in the valley. Second, I was to take the civilians over the north rim and head up into the hills until I could find another gully, a cave, or some other sheltered position. I was to keep them safe.

Sergeant Owens and the specialists clambered over the south rim, rolled, and ran into the smoke. I jumped off Lieutenant Morris and started toward the civilians. But after a few steps, I stopped. The drone's Gatling guns had begun to fire.

I looked back and saw Captain Dial pull Lieutenant Morris to his feet. Captain Dial could only use his right arm, so he had dropped his radio. Lieutenant Morris seemed dazed, and Captain Dial had to hold him up and drag him.

Captain Dial shouted for me to obey my order. I was not to wait for him and Lieutenant Morris. They would catch up, he said.

But I knew Captain Dial's thoughts. I knew he didn't think that he and Lieutenant Morris would make it.

So for the first time ever, I decided to disobey a direct order. I would obey my General Order instead. That was what I had done on the day beside the ocean, and Captain Dial had told me I was good. He had told me I was more good than I had ever been before. So I would do that again.

I ran back to Captain Dial, and he yelled at me. He said I had to obey his order immediately.

But instead I grabbed one of Lieutenant Morris's flak-jacket straps, and I pulled him away from Captain Dial and began dragging him up the gully wall. He was heavy, but I'm strong.

Captain Dial knew then that he should take charge of the civilians. Dragging soldiers to safety was one of my jobs, and keeping civilians safe was one of his. But first, he jumped to me and hooked Lieutenant Morris's arm through my harness loop. Then he pulled the strap to tighten the loop. Now I could let go of the flak-jacket strap and drag Lieutenant Morris a lot faster.

Captain Dial touched my head and told me to go.

I went up the gully wall and over the top with Lieutenant Morris while Captain Dial ran to the civilians and told them that they must go with him. One of the boys cried because he wanted to stay with his mother, but the old man and the girl listened to Captain Dial and wouldn't let the boy stay. They all climbed up from the gully.

Captain Dial's foot slipped on the way up and he almost fell, but the girl grabbed his arm to steady him. It was his wounded arm, but she couldn't reach the other one. I saw a flash like a grenade exploding in Captain Dial's thoughts. But Captain Dial didn't cry out even though it hurt a lot. He was a good soldier. The girl was, too. She didn't hesitate to help Captain Dial. She didn't flinch from his blood.

When we were all out of the gully, we ran north through the smoke. Captain Dial and the civilians were a few meters west of me and Lieutenant Morris, and they were moving up the slope a little faster. Every few steps, Captain Dial would look back and call encouragement to me. And I would pull harder and could feel Lieutenant Morris's boots bouncing on the ground behind us.

I didn't look back, but I heard the buzz of the drone as it flew low over the gully we had just left. I could smell its exhaust. Its Gatling guns chattered, and the slugs made dull thumps in the dirt.

And then, as we ran higher and came up out of the smoke, I heard the drone swoop out over the valley, turn, and head right for us. It was attacking us from behind, and there was no place for us to take cover when its guns started firing again. I looked ahead and saw a shadow on the ground that looked like another gully, but it was too far away. Lieutenant Morris and I wouldn't reach it before the drone strafed us.

I looked over at Captain Dial. Although he was wounded, he was now carrying one of the boys. The girl was carrying the other one. The old man was breathing hard and stumbling. So they were losing speed, and Lieutenant Morris and I had almost caught up to them. They wouldn't reach the next gully either. The drone would be able to hit all of us with the same burst of gunfire, or with just one rocket.

Captain Dial looked over at me as I looked at him, and we each knew the other's thoughts. There was only one thing to do. And when his thoughts said *Now*, I followed his order.

He and the civilians cut left, where there was still a little smoke, and I cut right, where the air was clear. We ran away from each other as fast as we could. I could hear Captain Dial's breath getting farther and farther away behind me. I could hear it even over the noise from Lieutenant Morris's boots.

I would have dropped Lieutenant Morris if I could, because he would have been safer lying still. But I couldn't. The loop on my harness was pulled tight around his arm, and there was no time for me to turn my head to yank it loose.

The drone came after me and Lieutenant Morris. I was sorry for what that meant for Lieutenant Morris, but glad because it gave Captain Dial a better chance to get himself and the civilians to cover. And I was glad because it gave me a chance to be good.

I ran hard, and I zigzagged as much as I could while dragging Lieutenant Morris. The engine buzz became a roar, and the Gatling gun chattered loud and long. And it almost missed us. But the last slugs in the burst came ripping through the dirt right behind us, and Lieutenant Morris jerked as they reached him. I was slapped down at my hindquarters, and I fell. Lieutenant Morris and I rolled a little way down the hill, and the drone flew over us so low that I could see the rivets in its belly. It rose up over the ridge, hung there for a moment, and then started toward us again.

But this time it bloomed fire from its tail, and it twisted sideways and dove into the hillside above us. There was a loud noise and more fire when it hit, and smoke like there had been from the first one.

I tried to get up, but Lieutenant Morris was lying on my hind legs. And my back hurt, close to my tail. But I couldn't see or hear Captain Dial, and I had to find him. So I twisted my head around far enough to tug on my harness loop until Lieutenant Morris's arm slipped out. I couldn't hear Lieutenant Morris's breath or heartbeat, and I could smell that he had blood coming out of his legs, back, chest, and neck. He was dead, and there was no place I could drag him where he would be all right again.

When his arm came free, I was able to scramble with my front legs and pull myself out from under him. And then I was able to stand up all the way even though my back hurt. I looked for Captain Dial and the civilians, but I couldn't see them. There was a lot more smoke now, and it made my eyes itch. It also made it hard to smell anything else. But I heard the girl say something, faint and soft, so I left Lieutenant Morris and followed her voice.

I found her with the other civilians and Captain Dial. Captain Dial was lying on the ground, and the girl was kneeling beside him with her hand on his head. The old man was standing near-by holding the little boys' hands. The boys were scared. They were looking at the body of a D Company soldier lying nearby. It was torn in two.

Captain Dial smiled when I came up to him and licked his face. I had to step over an RPG launcher to reach him, and when I touched him I knew what he had done. He had found the RPG launcher with the dead soldier, and he had used it to bring down the second drone. But it had recoiled against his wounded shoulder, and now the wound was bleeding even more.

He saw my thoughts and knew what had happened to Lieutenant Morris. But he said I had done everything right. He said he was proud of me. He said I was good.

And just as he said that, I heard a buzzing noise far off in the south. It was heading toward us fast. More drones were coming.

Captain Dial couldn't hear them. But he knew I did. And he said that they might not be coming to attack us, because their pilots might have realized that the first two had been firing on allies and civilians. But we couldn't count on it. So I was to take the four civilians away and find shelter for them. I was to do so immediately.

I didn't understand at first, because the picture I saw in Captain Dial's thoughts was a picture only of me and the civilians. He wasn't in it. He wasn't walking with us, and I wasn't dragging him with my harness.

And then he made me understand. He was too dizzy to walk, and I couldn't drag him without making his wound worse.

I wanted to follow his orders, but first I wanted to go back down the hill and find a D Company medic to take care of him. But Captain Dial said there was no time for that. Not if I was going to take the civilians to safety before the new drones arrived. And I knew he was right, because the girl could hear the drones now too. She still had her hand on Captain Dial's head, but she was looking at the sky.

I whined. I didn't want to go off with the civilians and leave Captain Dial all alone, even for a little while.

Captain Dial reached up with his right hand to touch my head. He told me it was all right to leave him for now, because I could come back as soon as I had taken the civilians to a safe place. It could be a cave or a deep ravine. It just had to be somewhere they couldn't be hurt. Once I had made sure of that, I could return. And if a medic hadn't come to help Captain Dial yet, I could go find one for him then.

But for now, I had to go. I had to keep the civilians safe.

Captain Dial took his hand from my head and spoke to the girl, and he took his pulse transmitter from the pouch on his belt and gave it to her. I knew he was telling her to go with me, and that the transmitter would help us communicate. She shook her head at first, but I could understand her thoughts well enough to know that it wasn't because she was afraid of me. It was because she didn't want to leave Captain Dial alone any more than I did.

I knew then that I liked her. But we were under orders now, and we had to follow them. So I took the girl's hand in my mouth, and I gave a tug to pull her away from Captain Dial. She didn't want to go, but she didn't fight me. She knew what we had to do. She strapped the transmitter to her wrist and stood up. She was good, too.

We left Captain Dial and went to the old man and the boys. I released the girl's hand as she told them they were all going with me. She put the old man's hand on the handle of my harness, and then he held the hand of one of the boys. The girl held the hand of the other one. We all started up the hill again, pushing through the smoke. My hind legs hurt, but I was still strong. I helped the old man go fast. The girl kept pace beside me as I sniffed and listened to find the best path for us.

I could still see Captain Dial's thoughts for a long way up the hill. At first he was thinking of me and what I was doing, and he was proud. That made me glad.

Then he thought the two words he had thought about on the day we performed our demonstration by the ocean. He thought the words "heroism" and "vengeance."

And then he worried about the other soldiers in D Company. So that made me worry, too. But I couldn't go back to check on them yet. I had orders to follow.

Finally, as the civilians and I came out of the smoke onto a sloping field of rocks, I saw one last strong thought from Captain

Dial. It was of Melanie. It was of Melanie with him in their bed, sleeping. And I was on my cushion at their feet.

It was a happy thought, and it made me happy too.

Then Captain Dial's thoughts became fuzzy as the civilians and I went higher, and soon they were gone. I paused near the crest of the hill and looked back down the slope, but I couldn't see the place where Captain Dial lay because of the rocks and smoke. And I thought for a moment that maybe the civilians were safe now, and that I could leave them and go back to where I could know Captain Dial's thoughts again.

But the sound of the approaching drones was loud now, and as I watched, one of them came flying up out of the smoke below us. So I led the civilians behind a big rock. We all crouched down, and I heard the drone turn away and fly back down the hillside again.

Then I heard Gatling guns firing, and I remembered my orders. So I got up from my crouch, and the girl and I took the old man and the boys over the top of the hill and down the other side.

I didn't like not being able to see Captain Dial's thoughts. But now I could see the girl's thoughts almost as well as I had seen his, and she had some good ideas about where we might find a safe place to hide. So we started off in the direction she thought was best.

We had to alter our path many times because of things I smelled or heard. And once we had to make a long detour because the girl remembered there were land mines ahead. I couldn't smell them yet, but she warned me by sending pulses to my implant. And then I saw her thoughts, and I knew they were true. So we found another way.

I became tired and thirsty, and my hind legs hurt. The girl and her family became tired and thirsty too. But we could hear gunfire and explosions behind us, so the girl and I wouldn't let the others stop. Not until we found someplace safe.

Not until we had done what Captain Dial had ordered us to do.

WE WENT UP and down through the hills all that day. At dusk we found a guerrilla camp that had been bombed many weeks before. But there were still some matches, a knife, and three plastic jugs of water. So we were able to get a drink. The water tasted like plastic, but we drank a lot of it. There was only one jug left when we were finished. The girl tied it to my harness, and we set out again. The girl carried the matches and the knife.

After nightfall, the girl couldn't see where we were or where we were going. Clouds covered the sky, so she couldn't find any stars to help her. That meant our path was up to me. So I followed my nose and my ears, and I took us farther and farther away from cities, camps, and roads. I took us away from anything that smelled or sounded like people with weapons. We had to go a long way.

At last, when the eastern sky had begun to brighten, we found a shelf of rock in the side of a hill. Under the shelf was a cave that was narrow but deep. It was well hidden by brush. I went in first and found some bone fragments and a ring of stones for a fire, but I could smell that they were old. No one had used the cave in a long time.

So I brought the people inside, and they slept on the bare rock. I didn't sleep right away because I had to lick the cuts on my hind legs. Then I dozed. But I kept my ears and nose alert. The only sounds were of the wind blowing through the rocks and brush. The only smells were of rabbits, birds, and other small animals nearby. There were no guerrillas, soldiers, or other people anywhere near us.

When I had rested for a few hours, I went out into the morning sunlight and killed three rabbits. I had to chase them, and that made my legs hurt again. But I still caught them with no trouble. I tore one apart and ate most of him, and then I took the other two back to the cave. The girl was awake, and she knew what to do. She woke up the boys and had them gather brush and sticks while she used the knife from the guerrilla camp to skin the rabbits. The old man made a spit from the sticks, and they cooked the rabbits over a fire the girl started inside the old ring of stones. It filled the cave with smoke, but the people didn't care. They were hungry.

While they ate, I scouted the area around the cave in widening circles. I sniffed, smelled, and listened. I marked a broad perimeter to warn off animal intruders. Then I did it all over again. And then I was sure my people were safe.

I had followed and completed Captain Dial's order. So I went to the girl and pushed my nose into her hand to be sure she knew my thoughts. I made sure she knew that she and her family should stay close to the cave. They could kill more rabbits to eat, and they still had the jug of water from the guerrilla camp. When that ran out, they could catch rain and dew.

The girl understood.

So I started back to the battlefield where I had left Captain Dial. I was able to go faster now because I didn't have people with me, and because my legs felt better. I could also choose a path that took me closer to dangerous smells. And I found a pond where I could get a drink. But that was the only time I stopped. I wanted to get back to Captain Dial as soon as I could.

There was still some light in the sky when I came over the hilltop and looked down the rocky slope at the battlefield. The two fallen drones had stopped burning, and there was no more smoke. A number of people were walking around down near the gully where Captain Dial and I had found the civilians, and the wind brought me their smells along with the smells of many dead D Company soldiers and refugees. The walking people didn't smell like soldiers or refugees. But they didn't smell like the enemy, either. They didn't make much noise, but occasionally one of them would fire a single shot. It sounded as if they were firing into the ground.

I didn't care who they were, or why they were shooting at the ground. Because now I smelled something else, too.

When I reached Captain Dial, I lay down beside him with my chin on his chest. There was nothing else I could do. I didn't nudge him with my nose or lick his face. I didn't try to wake him up. I'm not stupid. That was one of the things Captain Dial liked best about me. He liked that I was smart.

I closed my eyes. I didn't have an order for what to do next, so I would do nothing. I was tired, and there were no D Company soldiers left for me to help. I would stay there with my chin on Captain Dial.

I closed my eyes and fell asleep. And I dreamed. I dreamed

about the day I found the live mine on the pier and about how proud Captain Dial was. I dreamed about running fast in training so I could complete my orders and get back to Captain Dial before the buzzer sounded. I dreamed about lying curled up on my cushion on the floor while Captain Dial and Melanie made soft noises above me.

Then I woke up and opened my eyes. Three of the people below were coming up the slope. They were solid shadows in the dusk. And their smell was sharper now. They smelled like men who used shampoo and soap and who wore clean clothes. They smelled like the men in the crowd the day I found the mine. They smelled like civilians from home.

And as they came toward me and Captain Dial, I heard something behind me. Something higher up the slope, moving down through the rocks. It wasn't loud, so I knew the men coming up the slope couldn't hear it. I couldn't identify it by scent because the wind was blowing the wrong way, but I could hear that it was small and alone. So I didn't think it would hurt anyone. Besides, none of the men coming up the slope was my commanding officer. I wasn't required to alert them.

The three men approached within a few meters of me and Captain Dial, and now I saw that they were dressed in dark clothes that weren't uniforms. But they carried pistols in holsters. One of them pointed a camera at me and Captain Dial. I couldn't see the men's thoughts, but they spoke in the same language as D Company, so I understood some of what they said. One of them said something was great, and the others agreed.

I didn't know what they thought was great, but I knew there was nothing there that was.

One of them stepped closer and leaned down as if about to touch Captain Dial. So I raised my head and snarled at him, and he moved back. Then I put my head down again, but I stayed ready. I didn't know who they were, but they weren't part of D Company. They weren't even soldiers. I wouldn't let them touch Captain Dial.

The one with the camera kept aiming it at me and Captain Dial. But the other two put their hands on their pistols and conferred. And I understood enough to know they were talking about shooting me. So I did what Captain Dial had taught me to do. I planned how to attack them so they couldn't get off a shot. If either of their pistols began to rise from its holster, I would execute the plan. And I would decide what to do about the one with the camera based on how he reacted.

But another thing that Captain Dial had taught me was that a battlefield situation can change quickly.

The thing coming down the slope sent some pebbles skittering through the brush. And the three men heard it. They backed away from me and Captain Dial, and the one with the camera let it drop to dangle on a cord around his neck. They all three began taking their pistols from their holsters. But now they were looking past me toward whatever had made the pebbles skitter.

I kept my eyes on the three men. But I sniffed the air, and even though the wind was still going the wrong way, I caught a faint scent that told me who was on the slope behind me. It was the girl I had taken to safety on Captain Dial's order. She was still and quiet now, probably crouched behind a rock. But even so, she wasn't safe anymore.

All three men were raising their pistols. They were farther away from me than when I had made my plan of attack. But they weren't looking at me now. The light of day was almost gone. And I am black as night. I am silent as air.

The third one got off a shot as I hit his chest, but the bullet went into the sky. The other two were already on the ground, their throats torn out, their weapons in the dirt. The third one tried to fight me off once he was down, but that didn't last long.

When he was still, I looked back up the slope, beyond Captain Dial, and saw the girl standing beside a clump of brush. She was almost invisible because the sun was gone now. But I saw her shape against the brush. And the wind had shifted so I could smell her better. She smelled scared.

I was angry that she had returned to the battlefield. I had done my duty and made her safe, and she had spoiled it. I didn't understand why she had done that.

Then she came down the hill past Captain Dial, past me, and past the three men on the ground. She didn't walk fast, but she walked steady and strong even though she was scared. She said something soft to me as she went by, and I saw a flash of her thoughts. Then I understood. She was going down to the gully, to her mother. She wanted to wrap the body and take it somewhere to bury it. She had returned by herself to do this, leaving her brothers in the care of the old man.

I looked past her and knew I couldn't let her do as she planned. There were more people down there. They were like the three men I had just killed. The girl wouldn't be safe among them. Already, I could see and hear several of them starting toward her. She couldn't see them yet. But she would encounter them before she could reach the gully.

So I ran down to the girl and got in front of her. But she just walked around me. Then I took her hand in my mouth, but she just pulled it away and kept going. She wouldn't stay in contact with me long enough to see my thoughts. She was determined to reach her mother.

I couldn't knock her down or bite her to make her come with me. But I couldn't let her keep going. I had to make her pay attention to me long enough so she would understand what we had to do. So I turned and ran fast across the hillside, away from both the girl and Captain Dial. I ran to the body of Lieutenant Morris, and I tore open one of his pockets. Some ammo clips fell out, but that wasn't what I wanted. I wanted what I had smelled when I'd pushed Lieutenant Morris down in the gully.

And I found it curled up in the corner of the pocket. It was the necklace from the dead girl at the checkpoint. There was still enough blood on it that I had been able to smell it. The necklace had been taken from Lieutenant Morris for the investigation, but he had stolen it back. Now I took it from him again.

I ran back to the girl with it, got in front of her, and pushed my nose against her hand so she would feel the necklace hanging from my mouth.

She stopped walking. Her palm was against my nose. Her fingers brushed the silver chain. The transmitter on her wrist hummed. And then, as someone shouted below us, I thought hard and showed her what had happened to the girl who had worn the necklace. So she saw that girl lying on the side of the road with her sisters. She saw me find the necklace in Lieutenant

Morris's pocket. She saw how angry Captain Dial had been at what Lieutenant Morris had done.

The shouting below us grew louder. I could hear six voices now, and weapons being readied. More of the armed-men-who-weren't-soldiers were coming toward us.

But I didn't turn away from the girl. I kept my nose in her palm because I had to be sure she understood. I had to be sure she understood that Captain Dial was my commanding officer, and that I hated to leave him there on the hillside again. But I would. And she would have to leave her mother there, too. We both had to follow Captain Dial's last order. And if the men coming up the hillside reached us, we would fail. I wouldn't be good. And she would be like the other girl. The one who had worn the necklace.

The girl was smart. I saw in her thoughts that her mother wouldn't want her to die like that other girl. But when she understood what I was telling her, she began to cry. She hadn't cried before this. But she cried now, taking the necklace from my mouth and clutching it in her fist. She wanted to fight the men coming up the hill. She thought they were responsible for her mother's death. She thought they had made the drones attack.

I didn't know why she thought that. But I understood why she would want to fight whoever had made the drones fire on D Company. I wanted to fight those people too. But even if those people were the men who were coming up the hill, we couldn't fight them now. I had already killed three of them, but I had caught those three by surprise. There were more than three coming now, and they had their weapons ready to fire.

So we had to go back up over the hill. And while the girl stood there with the necklace clenched in her fist, I took her other hand in my mouth. And then I started up the hill, pulling her with me.

At first, she came with me without knowing what she was doing. She was still crying and thinking of what she wanted to do to the people who had sent the drones. So the men coming up the hill gained on us, and a shot was fired. I heard the bang and then heard the slug hiss through the air. It hit the dirt several meters ahead of us.

Then the girl's thoughts came back to where we were and what we needed to do. So she began to run, and I was able to release her hand. We ran together back up the hill, through the rocks and brush, up toward the night sky.

We paused for a few seconds when we reached Captain Dial again. He lay still in the twilight. He made no sound. He had no thoughts. He didn't even smell like Captain Dial anymore. So it was all right for the girl to take his sidearm and empty his pockets. And this time, it was easier to leave. This time, I knew I wouldn't need to return.

In training, Captain Dial had told me that when a soldier was gone, he was gone forever. But he had also told Melanie that they would be together forever. So *forever* was always a hard word for me to understand. But whenever I didn't understand something, it was because it was something only someone as smart as Captain Dial could understand. And in those cases, I would just have to believe whatever Captain Dial said. Because Captain Dial always spoke the truth.

So that was what I did as I left his body there on the hillside for the last time. I remembered what Captain Dial had said, and I was glad that even though he was gone, he and Melanie would still be together.

I wished I could be with them, too. But I didn't know how to get to wherever they were.

The girl and I went up over the top of the hill, and soon I couldn't smell or hear the men behind us anymore. Then the twilight was gone, and the girl held my harness so I could lead her through the darkness. She knew my thoughts most of the time now, so I promised her I would do a good job. And she promised me the same thing.

We had our orders. So we would follow them.

Forever.

I TOOK THE GIRL back to the cave where the old man and the boys were waiting, and we stayed there several weeks until I smelled men with weapons approaching. Then we left, and I led the way deeper into the hills, taking us as far from danger as I could. The weather grew colder, but my fur grew thicker, and we found winter clothing in an abandoned village. The old man also found sewing tools, and he made blankets from the skins of the rabbits I caught. The girl stretched some skins between two long pieces of wood, and that was where we kept our growing collection of supplies. The people and I took turns dragging it as we traveled.

We traveled this way for many days, until we came upon the stone hut near the stream.

It's been a good place. We found more things that my people could use here. But the people who had stayed in the hut before us had been gone for a long time when we arrived. I couldn't even smell them on the things they had left. So I believed my company would be safe here for the winter.

Food was easy to obtain. All I had to do was go up and down the stream until I found rabbits. Once I killed a small deer, and the girl said its skin should be my bed. So now I sleep on it even though I like the bare ground just as well. I have thick fur. But it makes my people happy to see me lie down on the deer's skin, and that makes me glad.

In recent weeks the bushes and trees have grown leaves, and the grass that was dry and thin is now thick and juicy. The girl and the old man have been making plans to plant seeds they found in the abandoned village. We've all been looking forward to warmer days.

Then, last night, eighteen of Your soldiers came to kill us. You must have told them we were the enemy. So they didn't know I was trained by Captain Dial. They didn't know that even when I sleep, my ears and nose are awake.

I took the girl to their bodies this morning, and it made her sad. But she understood that I had to follow orders. She understands a lot. She and I often help each other figure out things that are puzzling.

I didn't understand how Your soldiers could have found us, or why You would want them to, because we've traveled far from anything that should matter to You. Besides, we're not Your enemies. And even if we were, we wouldn't be important enough for You to bother with. Or so I thought.

Then the girl remembered the implant under the skin

between my shoulders, and the transmitter that Captain Dial had given her. We had used these things to help us understand each other in our first weeks together, but then—just as Captain Dial and I had found—they had become unnecessary. So the girl had placed the transmitter in her duffel, and we hadn't thought of it or of my implant since. But now the girl said that machines in the sky could probably hear signals from them at any time, and that the machines could then tell You where I was. So that was how Your soldiers found us.

The girl also says she knows why You want to attack us.

She found a radio receiver in the abandoned village, and now she listens to its voices for a few minutes each evening. I can't understand the voices, but the girl has told me some of the things they've said. They've said that all Your soldiers were about to be sent home because the money for the war was almost gone. But then D Company was ambushed and destroyed by enemy guerrillas, and the bad publicity from what Lieutenant Morris had done at the checkpoint was obliterated by the heroism of his company's sacrifice. So Your public support surged, and more money was provided so Your soldiers could avenge the ambush by destroying the enemy.

This is what the radio voices say. They don't say anything about the drones. But if the drones hadn't come, D Company would not only have beaten the guerrillas, but would have suffered almost no casualties. Captain Dial would have seen to it.

But the drones did come. They came from our own airfield. They came from You.

Then the men-who-weren't-soldiers came too, and the girl thinks she knows why they fired shots at the ground. She thinks they killed any soldier or refugee who was still alive. And we believe those men were sent by You as well.

The girl says that our knowledge of this is why You want to attack us. We're the only survivors of that battle. So as long as we still live, You fear that we may reveal the truth of what happened to D Company and the refugees. And the girl says that then all of Your public support and money will go away again.

I have tried to think of what Captain Dial might do if these things had been revealed to him. But he was much smarter than me. And I can't see his thoughts anymore.

But I still know the final order he gave me: To keep my people safe.

So I've thought of things I can do to obey.

The first thing I thought of was to have the girl write this message. Again, she doesn't know what she writes. Only that I require her to write it. And what I'm asking her to write now is a promise that You have nothing to fear from me if You leave us alone. If You allow me to keep my people safe, we will never tell the radio voices what Your drones and men-who-weren't-soldiers did to D Company.

The second thing made the girl cry again. Before beginning this message, I told her to use her knife to cut between my shoulders and find the communication implant. She cried because she didn't want to hurt me, and then she cried more because the device was smaller than we had imagined, and it was hard to find. She had to make the cut longer and deeper. But she finally found the tiny glass bean and gave it to the boys, who took turns hitting it and the transmitter with a hammer until both were dust. Then the old man cleaned my wound and sewed it shut. I growled once because the needle hurt, and he stepped back. But then I licked his hand, and he finished the job. Afterward, I was proud of all of them for following orders so well.

The third thing makes us unhappy. But it's necessary. We must leave the stone hut. We must leave this good place with its water and rabbits. Your soldiers found us here, so You know where we are.

But since I no longer have the communication implant, You won't know where we'll go next.

Finally, there is a fourth thing I'll do.

If the above measures fail, and if You send more soldiers or men-who-aren't-soldiers to find us, I will kill them all. I'll always know they're coming, so they'll never be able to attack us before I attack them first.

You may even send some of my fellow K-9s, because they could find us more quickly than people could. But Captain Dial said that the K-9s in my training class were the best war dogs there had ever been, and I was ranked first in that class. So there are no K-9s that I can't find and defeat before they can find and defeat me.

And if You attack us with drones instead of people or dogs, we're now equipped to fight them. Some of the soldiers I killed last night were carrying RPGs, and others carried guns with armor-piercing rounds. We have taken these weapons.

But if You bomb us from high in the sky so we can't fight, there may be nothing I can do to stop You. Then You will have made me fail to carry out my orders.

In that event, I'll do whatever I must to survive. And then I will find You. I don't know Your name or Your rank, but I will find You anyway. I will hunt and kill every officer in every company and every battalion until I reach You. I will read their thoughts as they die and use that knowledge to hunt You. I will climb walls and dig tunnels. I will swim and run. I will stow away in trucks, ships, and aircraft that will bring me closer to You. I will find something You have touched so I know Your scent. And then I will find You in Your bed or at Your table or wherever You may be.

And I will bite Your throat so it tears out.

So I hope You heed this message. It will be left with one of Your dead soldiers, so I know it will reach their unit's commanding officer. And then it will reach that officer's commanding officer, and then that officer's commanding officer, and so on until it reaches the officer who gave the orders that resulted in the current situation. Until it reaches You.

My company has its equipment and is ready to move out. The two boys are my specialists. The old man is my medic and quartermaster.

As for the girl—

She now wears the metal tag I received when I was promoted to sergeant. She found it in Captain Dial's pocket as we left the battlefield, and today she put it on the chain of her necklace beside the shiny rock. Sergeant is the toughest enlisted job. But she can do it.

I myself am no longer a sergeant. I didn't realize that until this morning. But after I showed the girl what I had done in the night, she touched my head. And I heard her thoughts. I heard what she called me.

She called me Captain.

Then she took the silver bars that she found with the sergeant's tag, and she pinned them to my duty harness.

I am the ranking survivor of D Company, and my final order from Captain Dial was a commission. I know this because what he told me to do was what a good officer does.

A good officer takes care of his soldiers.

But if You attack us again, You will not be a good officer. You will not be taking care of Your soldiers. And if You make me fail in my duty to take care of mine, You will not be an officer of any kind for much longer.

Captain Dial told me what I am, and he always spoke the truth. So now I tell You:

I am black as night. I am silent as air.

My sergeant touches my head, and I tell her she's good.

This message is complete.

Respectfully,
Chip, K-9
Captain and Commanding Officer
D Company

::::::::
•••••••
••••••
•••••
••••

THE GARDEN:
A *HWARHATH* SCIENCE
FICTIONAL ROMANCE

by Eleanor Arnason

Eleanor Arnason was born in New York in 1942 and spent eleven of her first eighteen years living in a "house of the future" that had been built in Minneapolis as a design project by the Walker Art Center in 1947. Her first short story, "A Clear Day in the Motor City," was published in New Worlds *in 1972, and her first novel, fantasy* The Sword Smith, *was published in 1973. It was followed by a string of short stories and two novels, science fiction* To The Resurrection Station, *and fantasy* Daughter of the Bear King.

Arnason's best-known work, novel A Woman of the Iron People, *a powerful tale of anthropological science fiction was published in 1991. As with much of her later fiction, it portrayed stubborn, fallible characters living in grubby, scuffed-up futures and struggling to come to terms with the world they live in. It won the first James Tiptree, Jr. Award and the Mythopoeic Fantasy Award. Arguably her best work, though, is her fifth novel,* Ring of Swords. *Published in 1993, it was the first major tale in her "Hwarhath" series of stories. Centered around issues of gender and family, it posited a homosexual society where women maintained a "hearth planet" and the men moved to the "perimeter," constantly warring among the stars. Intended to be the first of a series—at least one sequel was completed—it has been followed by a string of award-nominated short stories, including "The Hound of Merin," "The Semen Thief," "The Lovers," "The Gauze Banner," and "Dapple: A* Hwarhath *Historical Romance." Arnason's short fiction has won the HOMer award and been nominated for the Nebula, Hugo, Tiptree, Sturgeon, and World Fantasy awards. A collection of her best short fiction is long overdue. Arnason has lived in New York, Paris, Honolulu, Detroit, Minneapolis, and St. Paul. Her hobbies include politics, economics, and bird watching.*

The story that follows, described by Arnason in an interview as her "Ferdinand the Bull" story, tells of what happens when a Hwarhath male dares to challenge the demands and expectations of his society, dares to want something different, to live on his own terms.

THERE WAS A boy who belonged to the Atkwa lineage. Like most of his family, he had steel grey fur. In the case of his relatives the color was solid. But the boy's fur was faintly striped and spotted. In dim light this wasn't visible. In sunlight his pelt looked like one of the old pattern-welded swords that hung in his grandmother's greathouse and were taken outside rarely, usually to be polished, though sometimes for teaching purposes, when adult male relatives were home. Not that anyone used swords in this period, except actors in plays. But children ought to learn the history of their family.

The boy's pelt was due to a recessive gene, emerging after generations, since the Atkwa had not gone to a spotted family for semen in more than two hundred years. This was not due to prejudice. Unlike humans, the *hwarhath* find differences in color more interesting than disturbing. Their prejudices lie in other directions.*

---

* Most likely the author is referring to regional bias, since this is the kind of prejudice the *hwarhath* are most willing to discuss and condemn. Inhabitants of the home planet's southern hemisphere regard northerners as over-civilized and likely to stray from traditional values. Inhabitants of the northern hemisphere regard southerners as rubes. In addition, neighboring families often snipe at one another; and most people, north and south, regard cities with suspicion. It's one thing for men to live intermixed in space. They're kept in line by military discipline. But most of the inhabitants of cities are women. Obviously, they aren't in the army, which is entirely male. What's going to keep them in line, now that they live among unkin?

It was circumstance and accident that kept the Atkwa solid grey. They lived in a part of the world where this was the dominant coloration; and—being a small and not especially powerful family—they did not look to distant places when arranging breeding contracts.

As a toddler, the boy was forward and active, but not to an extraordinary degree. At the age of eight or so, he lengthened into a coltish child, full of energy, but also prone to sudden moods of thoughtfulness. These worried his mother, who consulted with her mother, the family matriarch, a gaunt woman, her fur frosted by age, her big hands twisted by joint disease.

"Well," the matriarch said after listening. "Some men are thoughtful. They have to be, if they're going to survive in space, with no women around to do their thinking."

"But so young?" the mother asked. "He spends hours watching fish in a stream or bugs in a patch of weeds."

"Maybe he'll become a scientist." The matriarch gave her daughter a stern look. "He's your only boy. He's been strange and lovely looking from birth. This has led you to pay too much attention and to worry without reason. Straighten up! Be solid! The boy will probably turn out well. If he doesn't, he'll be a problem for our male relatives to handle."

At ten, the boy discovered gardening—by accident, while following a *tli* which had come out of the nearby woods to steal vegetables. The sun was barely up. Dew gleamed on the vegetation around his grandmother's house. The air he drew into his mouth was cool and fragrant.

The *tli*, a large specimen with strongly marked stripes, trundled over his grandmother's lawn, its fat furry belly gathering dew like a rag wiping moisture off something bright. A metal blade maybe, the boy thought. A dark trail appeared behind the animal, and it was this the boy followed at a safe distance. Not that a *tli* is ever dangerous, unless cornered, but he didn't want to frighten it.

The animal skirted the house, entering the garden in back. There the *tli* began to pillage, a messy process with much (it seemed to the boy) unnecessary destruction. He ought to chase it away. But he was hit—suddenly and with great force—by the beauty of the scene in front of him. The perception was like a blade going into his chest. Don't think of this as a figure of speech, exaggerated and difficult to believe. There are emotions so intense that they cause pain, either a dull ache or a sudden sharp twinge. Under the influence of such an emotion, one's heart may seem to stop. One may feel wounded and changed, as one changed by a serious injury.

This happened to the boy when he didn't, as yet, understand much of what he felt. If he'd been older, he might have realized that most emotions go away, if one ignores them. Instead, he was pierced through by beauty. For the rest of his life he remembered how the garden looked: a large rectangular plot, edged with ornamental plants, their leaves—red, purple, yellow, and blue—like the banners of a guard in a military ceremony.

Inside this gaudy border were the vegetables, arranged in rows. Some grew on poles or trellises. Others were bushes. Still others rose directly from the soil as shoots, fronds, clusters of leaves. The variety seemed endless. While the garden's border was brightly colored, most of these plants were shades of green or blue. Yet they seemed—if anything—more lovely and succulent, beaded with dew and shining in the low slanting rays of the sun.

So it was, on a cool summer morning, the air barely stirring, that Atkwa Akuin fell in love—not with another boy, as might have been expected, if not this year, then soon, but with his grandmother's garden.

He spent the rest of that summer in the plot, helping the two senior female cousins who did most of the house's gardening. In the fall, he turned soil, covered beds with hay, trimmed what needed trimming and planted chopped-up bits of root. Black and twisted, they looked dead to him. But they'd send up shoots in the spring, his cousins promised.

Akuin's mother watched doubtfully. The boy was settling down to a single activity. That had to be better than his former dreaminess. But she would have been happier if he'd taken up a more boyish hobby: riding *tsina*, fishing in the nearby river, practicing archery, playing at war.

"Give him more time," said Akuin's grandmother. "Boys are difficult, as I know."

She'd raised three. One had died young in an accident. Another had died in space, killed in the war that had recently begun. The enemy—humans, though their name was not yet known—had come out of nowhere in well-armed ships. Almost everything about them remained hidden in darkness as complete as the darkness from which they'd emerged. But no one could doubt their intentions. The first meeting with them had ended in violence. So had every encounter since.

The matriarch's third son was still alive and had reached the rank of advancer one-in-front. This should have given her satisfaction, but the two of them had never gotten along. Akuin's uncle rarely came home for a visit. The matriarch lavished her attention on her one daughter, her nieces and their children.

Now she said, folding her twisted hands, "Maybe Akuin will become a gardener in a space station. Such people are useful. An army needs more than one kind of soldier."

When he was fifteen, Akuin went to boarding school, as do all boys of that age. In these places they learn to live without women and among males who belong to other lineages. This becomes important later. A boy who can't detach himself from family and country is of little use in space.

In addition, the boys complete their education in the ordinary *hwarhath* arts and sciences, the ones learned by both females and males; and they begin their education in the specifically male art and science of war.

Akuin's school was on the east coast of his continent, in an area of sandy dunes and scrub forest: poor land for gardening. None the less, the school had a garden. Botany is a science, and horticulture is an art.

It was on the landward side of the school complex, sheltered by buildings from the prevailing wind. Akuin found it the day after he arrived. To the west was a row of dunes, with the afternoon sun standing just above them. Long shadows stretched toward the garden. The gardener—a man with a metal leg— moved slowly between the rows of plants, bending, examining, picking off bugs, which he pressed between the fingers of his good hand. His other arm hung at his side, clearly damaged and not recently. It had shrunk till little remained except black fur over bone.

Akuin thought he was unnoticed. But the gardener turned suddenly, straightened and glared at him with yellow eyes. Akuin waited motionless and silent. He might be a little odd, but there was nothing wrong with his manners.

"You're new," said the man finally. "Where from?"

Akuin told him.

"Inland. Why aren't you on the beach? Or exploring the school? We have a fine museum, full of things which former students have sent back."

"I like gardens," Akuin said.

The man glared at him a second time, then beckoned, using his good hand. The boy came forward into the garden.

The man's name, it turned out, was Tol Chaib. He'd gone to this school years before, gone into space, then come back to teach. He said nothing more about himself in that first encounter. Instead he talked about the difficulty of growing healthy plants in sand. Partly, he said, he worked to change the soil. The school provided him with compost and manure. More than that was needed. "If there's anything certain about boys and *tsina*, it's that they will produce plenty of fertilizer."

Some of the excess went into lawns and ornamental borders. The rest was sold to local farmers.

Mostly, he found plants that fit the local soil and weather. "Nothing else works. This is why it's so difficult to grow our plants on other planets. The light is different, so is the invisible radiation. The soil has the wrong minerals, or minerals in the wrong proportions. A plant always grows best on its home planet, unless—as sometimes happens—it proliferates unnaturally in a strange place."

Akuin had been feeling lonely and afraid. How could he survive five years in school? At the end of his school years stood a fate even worse. Few *hwarhath* men remain on the home planet. From twenty to eighty, their lives are spent in space, exploring and preparing to meet the enemies who will inevitably appear.

The universe is a dangerous place; and the *hwarhath* are a careful species. So the men go into space, looking for trouble, while their female relatives stay home, raising children and practicing the arts of peace.

Sixty years in metal corridors, with only brief visits home. Hah! The prospect was terrible.

Now, listening to Tol Chaib, he felt a little comfort. Maybe he'd be able to survive school. He could certainly learn much from the crippled man.

The school had a curriculum, of course. There were classes, labs, field trips, military exercises. Most of what Akuin did was required. But when he could decide for himself, he went to Tol Chaib's garden or to the greenhouses where Chaib kept flowers growing all winter.

That was a comfort on days when snow lay over the campus and a knife-wind blew off the ocean. The glass walls were covered by condensed moisture, making the world outside invisible. Inside was damp warm air, the smell of dirt and growing things, flowers that blossomed as brightly as a campfire, the gardener's dry harsh voice.

At first he told Akuin about the plants around them, then about the gardening he'd done in space. Gardens up there—Tol Chaib waved at the ceiling—are necessary for five reasons. Men are healthier if they eat fresh fruit and vegetables. The plants help keep air breathable by removing carbon dioxide and providing oxygen. "This can be done by inorganic chemical reactions or by microbes, but a garden is more pleasant and produces air with a better aroma."

In addition, Tol Chaib said, every station and ship is supposed to be self-sufficient. "Ships become lost. A station might be cut off, if the war goes badly. If this happens, the men on board will need ways to provide themselves with air, food and medicine."

"You've given me three reasons for gardens in space," Akuin said. "Health, clean air and self-sufficiency. What are the other two?"

"Joy," the gardener said. "Which is not usually produced by vats of microbes or inorganic chemical reactions; and hope that we will finally come home."

Toward the end of winter Akuin learned how Tol Chaib had been injured.

He'd been the foremost gardener in a small station designed for research rather than war. A supply ship arrived, and the pilot made a mistake while docking—several mistakes, since he panicked when he realized the coupling of ship and station was going badly. The station's outer skin had been punctured. There was sudden loss of pressure, and—Tol Chaib grinned. "The air lock system in my section of the station was new and had improvements, which did not work as planned."

When the rescue workers reached the garden, they found most of the plants gone, sucked into space. The garden's equipment was mostly in pieces. Tol Chaib lay under a heap of debris, next to a lock that had finally closed.

"They think—I don't remember—that I was pulled from one end of the garden to the other, through several rooms. Most likely I hit things on the way. I certainly hit the airlock after it closed; and the debris hit me."

What a story! Akuin shivered.

"The pilot of the ship killed himself. The engineer in front of the air lock design team asked to die. But his senior officers decided the problem with the system had not been caused by anything he did, and could not have been foreseen."

"What was the problem?" Akuin asked. "Why did the system malfunction?"

"I never learned. At first, I was in no condition to pay attention. Later, I didn't care."

"Did the pilot have permission to kill himself?"

"That's another thing I don't know," Tol Chaib said.

The pilot had panicked in an emergency. That was the one thing Akuin knew about him. Maybe, after he saw the damage he'd done, the pilot had panicked a second time and made the decision to die on his own. A terrible idea! "If he asked for permission and got it, then what he did was right," Akuin said finally. "And it was right for the engineer to live, after permission had been refused to him, though—hah! He must have wanted to die."

"Maybe," said Tol Chaib.

There was another thought in Akuin's mind, which he did not express.

"You're wondering why I'm still alive," Tol Chaib said. "I gave serious thought to taking the option." He paused, his good hand gently touching the frilly edge of a tropical bloom. "I was a handsome man. Many approached me or watched from a distance, hoping for encouragement. Hah! It was fine to know that I could make another man happy by saying 'yes.'

"Then I woke and discovered my leg was gone. What a surprise! Where was the rest of me?"

Akuin felt uncomfortable. No child wants to know that adults can be unhappy. Heroes in hero plays—yes. They can suffer, and a boy Akuin's age will be inspired. But a man like Tol Chaib, a teacher and crippled, should never reveal pain.

"I had no desire to limp and crawl through life," the teacher said, his dry voice inexorable. "I wanted to be quick and lovely and loved.

"One of my senior male relatives came to visit me while I was in sick bay. I asked him for permission to die. He said, 'Wait.' So I did. My male relatives consulted with each other and with the officers in front of me. This is how such things are done," the dry voice said. "Except in hero plays."

"I know," Akuin said. In a sense he hadn't known. Before this moment, the rules for killing oneself had been unreal, something learned as one learns formulae one is never going to use. How fine that I can use sticks and triangles to determine the height of that tall tree! Do I want to know the tree's height? No.

"In that kind of situation," Tol Chaib added, "the kind that occurs in hero plays, when a man is entirely alone or the people around him are confused and wrong, it makes sense for the man to take his fate into his own hands. What choice does he have? But it's a good idea to be sure that one is a hero and in a heroic situation, before acting in such a way.

"It was decided I ought to live—for various reasons. My skill as a gardener was remarkable; and I'm good at teaching. Also, I'm an only child; and my mother is well-loved in our family. It was thought she might grieve too much, if I killed myself."

Akuin left the greenhouse soon after, trudging back to his dormitory through a new fall of snow. Overhead the sky was full of stars. For once the air was almost still, though stabbingly cold. The boy walked in a cloud of his own breath.

He reached the middle of a playing field and looked around, first at the snow, unmarked except by the trail he was in the process of making, then at the sky. How brilliant! How many-colored! How difficult to measure!

All at once he lost his sense of position and direction. Up and down seemed no longer different. The ground beneath his feet was gone; so was his body's weight; he was falling into the innumerable stars.

It was a terrible sensation. Akuin closed his eyes. For a moment, the sense of falling continued. Then it was gone, as quickly as it had come. When he opened his eyes, everything was ordinary again.

Later, he wondered if this had been a vision. Most likely not. He'd never shown any signs of having a diviner's ability, nor did he want it. Seeing what other people can't see is unsettling. Diviners tend to be odd ungraceful folk, who go through life out-of-step and off-balance, never fitting into any group. No rational boy wants a fate like this.

More likely, Akuin thought, he'd been tired and disturbed by his mentor's story. In any case, the experience was over and did not recur.

He completed school in the usual period of time. Education is not a race for the *hwarhath*. No one finishes before the others. How can they? Every *hwarhath* male goes into the army as soon as he graduates; and no one can enter the army until he has reached the age of adulthood.*

At twenty, Akuin left school, going home for a long visit. As usual, on visits home, he worked in the family garden. His moth-

---

* This passage may refer to human education, which strikes the *hwarhath* as strangely like a contest where some players must win and others lose. What kind of society wants to produce young men who have already failed at the age of twenty? What kind of society treats the training of the next generation as if it were a game?

er watched with her usual concern. He had turned into a lovely young man, slim and graceful; his pale stippled pelt reminded her of sunlight moving over metal, or water moving over stones. But he was too quiet for a youth his age, too thoughtful and too in love with the plants he tended.

With luck, she told herself, he'd be assigned to work as a gardener. The teachers at his school had recommended this. According to her male relatives, the officers in charge of making assignments often paid attention to such recommendations. Though not always, of course.

A little before harvest, Akuin's assignment came. As expected, it was in space, though where in space the message did not say. He packed the one bag permitted him and said goodbye to his family. It wasn't easy to bid his mother farewell. Unlike humans, the *hwarhath* do not express grief by excreting water from the corners of their eyes. Nor do they have the human love of making noise. Given any reason—grief, anger, happiness, a flash of irritation, a momentary surprise—humans will be noisy. An uncomfortable kind of behavior. Maybe it comes from their ancestors, who spent their time (we are told) screaming at the tops of trees. The *hwarhath* must be descended from animals who spent more time on the ground, where they could see one another, and where noise might attract unwelcome attention. In most situations, they are quiet, at least in comparison to humans.

But what man wants to see a look of grim endurance on his mother's face?

It was a relief to get outside. The plants that bordered the garden were waist-high now. Their long sharp leaves seemed (to Akuin) like a fence of swords, inlaid with precious metals and encrusted with jewels, so they shone red, blue, yellow, green. The green especially was a shade so intense and pure that it seemed to pierce him. Hah! He could feel it in his throat and chest!

Bugs with the same rich late-summer colors floated in the hot air. Bending down and peering, Akuin could see ripe fruits and vegetables nestled among the leaves of the plants raised for food. He found a few last pests, pressed them to death between his fingers, then turned toward the waiting car.

One of his female cousins drove him to the nearest rail line.

They parted quietly. He went by train to the regional airport, then by plane to one of the rocket islands. From the island he went (by rocket of course) to a keeping-pace-with-the-place-below station.* At each stage of this journey, his environment became more closed-in and artificial, till at last in the station it was a maze of grey metal corridors. No windows opened out on space. If they had, what would he have seen?

His unreachable home planet.

Akuin felt his spirit shrink like a plant shriveling in a drought. How was he going to survive? His grandmother's voice, speaking in his mind, gave the answer: through loyalty and discipline. In his imagination he made the gesture of acknowledgement.

An FTL transport carried him (along with other men) to a station in the most remote region of *hwarhath*-explored space. This was not a place where the *hwarhath* would usually have built a station. It was too far out, and the route that led to it was not easy to follow.

But when the *hwarhath* came to this region, they found many stars in close proximity. By itself this would have been interesting. The stars in *hwarhath* space are, for the most part, scattered as thinly as trees on Great Central Plain; and in general they are solitary rather than communal. It's rare to find more than two or three together.

If ordinary stars are like a bottle tree, standing alone on the dusty plain, with at most a couple of offshoots or companions, then this group was like a grove or thicket, gathered around some hidden reason for their gathering: a spring or sunken pool.

Of course the *hwarhath* scientists wanted to study the grove, and they had enough influence to get the station built. But they did not get the resources they wanted. Remember that a war was on. This region was far distant from the *hwarhath* home planet and from the region where humans were a recurring problem. The work done here did not seem important to the men who made decisions. Akuin's new home was inadequately funded.

Imagine a metal cylinder orbiting a dim and dusty, unimpressive star. The cylinder is small and plain, with none of the

---

* The human term would be a geosynchronous station.

additions characteristic of the great stations, which unfold over time like flowering plants, producing metal stalks, blossoms and pods. Around them move attendant bodies: maintenance craft, shuttles, satellites devoted to research or specialized manufacture, so the great station seems enveloped in a cloud of glittering bugs.

Akuin's destination was nothing like this. There was only the cylinder, a simple geometric shape, orbiting its primary, which had no planets. In the distance were other stars, packed closely together, all of them dim and red.

"Like an army camped on a plain," said one of the new arrivals. (Not Akuin.) "How long the night has been! The army's fires have burnt down. Now they are almost out."

"It may look like an army to you," another soldier commented. "To me it looks like a group of stars."*

Scattered through the star-grove (or if you like the image, the army-camp of stars) were other bodies, which the new arrivals could not see. These came in several varieties. Most were burning-into-darkness stars, which had exhausted their fuel, turning into the stellar equivalent of cinders. Others, less numerous, were breaking-into-pieces stars, which had become so dense that gravity had crushed their matter, so it became a kind of *puree* or thick soup. The last group, least numerous of all, were called falling-into-strangeness; and these were the stars that interested the *hwarhath* scientists.**

Akuin paid little attention to the grove (or camp) of stars. Instead he noticed the interior of the station: a cramped maze of corridors and rooms. There were no windows, of course, and most of the holograms (there were some, though not as large and splendid as the ones in a great station) showed more impressive parts of the galaxy.

At the end of one corridor a huge planet turned, surrounded by moons and braided rings. At the end of another corridor was a human ship, which exploded over and over, hit by *hwarhath* missiles. Hah! It was a thing to see! Dramatic and encouraging!

---

* This interchange may be an example of the *hwarhath* sense of humor.
** Black dwarfs, EDSOs, and clothed singularities. There is no reason to believe the *hwarhath* have discovered such a stellar cluster.

He was assigned to a room with four other young men, also new arrivals. Each got a bed, a storage locker and a niche in the wall, where a hologram could be installed. Three of his companions put up scenes of home, as did Akuin: his grandmother's garden at midsummer. The last man, a thin lad with the most amazingly ugly markings on his pale grey fur, put nothing in his niche.

The ugly lad was named Gehazi Thev. He seemed remarkably calm and friendly, for a man who looked as if he'd been used to blot up ink. How could any family have kept a child like this one?

"Easy enough to explain," Thev said on the second or third day that Akuin knew him. "My mother is a mathematician, the best in our lineage; and the semen used to produce me came from a family—the Thevar—who are famous scientists. They also have a tendency toward splotchiness, which shows up rarely. It's a defect they have tried to eliminate.

"In any case—" No question that Thev was a talker. "My mother had a terrible pregnancy. Not only did she feel sick, but her ability to think about math vanished almost entirely, either due to her queasiness or to some change in her hormones.

"When I was born, they thought of killing me. Just look!" He ran one hand over an arm disfigured by a great dark blotch. "How could I possibly have a normal life? But my mother had already announced that she would never allow her family to breed her again. These were her good years, when she could do original work. She wasn't going to waste them on motherhood. So—" The calm friendly voice sounded amused. "My relatives could kill me, and lose my mother's genetic material, or they could keep me. There was no reason to believe that I would be stupid."

"It doesn't bother you?" asked Akuin.

"My lack of stupidity? No. The Goddess has made sure that the universe is well provided with stupid people. As far as I can tell from their behavior, humans are as dim as most *hwarhath*. What is this war about, for example? How can we fight people when we can't even talk with them? What has war been about, through our entire history? The taking of land! The acquisition of women and children! But what good are human females to us? If they even have females, as we understand that term. For all we know, humans may have five different sexes, none of them producing children in a way we understand. As for their land, how can we use it? It isn't likely that our plants will grow on their planet. So, what are we fighting for? Women who cannot mother *hwarhath* children, and land which is—for us—infertile. The humans are just as stupid. Unless, of course, they have another reason for killing people." Thev tilted his head, considering the idea of a new reason for war.

"I was talking about your looks," said Akuin. He touched a patch of fur that wasn't blotchy. Instead, it shone like silver. "If you had been like this all over—"

"Hah! I would have been something! There would have been men lined up at our door, and very inconvenient it would have been for the rest of you." Thev paused. He was sprawled on his bed, resting on his elbows, regarding Akuin with resin-yellow eyes. "Yes, it has bothered me at times," he said at last. "When I first realized how very ugly I was, and again when I was in school and the age when boys begin to fall in love. No one would ever love me, I thought. I would have to be content with my hands, and the programs about safe and healthy sexual behavior which the Public Health Corps makes."*

"Has that happened?" Akuin said.

Thev smiled. "I have seen a lot of public health programs. But I have discovered that some men like intelligence. Believe me, I am intelligent!"

They became friends, though the other roommates couldn't understand why. Akuin was lovely and also sad, the kind of youth that older men—some older men—liked to comfort. No one would ever try to comfort Thev. He was too confident and happy. In addition, they were slightly different ages. Thev had stayed on the home world for two extra years, studying at the famous Helig Institute. Instead of being twenty or twenty-one, he was twenty-three, though he didn't seem especially old. His time had been

---

* The *hwarhath* believe public health should not be boring. The best of their sex education programs are, according to scholars who have studied this subject, absolutely first-class erotica, to which humans can—and often will—respond.

devoted to ideas rather than experience. It was stars he knew, not manners.

They stayed together through the period when new arrivals were oriented to life in space. "Like two burrs," said the other roommates, who began to suspect it was Akuin's beauty that drew the other man. But what drew Akuin to a man whose conversation was so often impossible to understand? All these kinds of stars that fell into themselves, changing (as they did so) the nature given them by the Goddess, and even in some cases (according to Thev) falling out of the universe the Goddess had created. This was unexpected! Who could make sense of it? Who could find it interesting or erotic?

When the orientation period was over, Thev began to spend his time with other physicists. Akuin started his new job, in the station's garden.

A garden, you may think. The lad had been saved. He'd found his natural environment.

The garden occupied a series of rooms, grey metal like everything else in the station. The plants, all useful rather than ornamental, grew in raised beds like metal boxes. Light came from panels in the ceiling. Moisture was provided by a network of tubes, which dripped water directly on the roots. Nothing was wasted. Nothing was present unless it was needed.

Akuin discovered that gardening (for him) comprised many things besides the garden itself. He missed sunlight, clouds, rain, bugs, raiding *tli*, the sight of hills rising in the distance, the smell of a nearby forest or ocean. It was home he missed, the home world in its entirety. Most especially he missed his home country: the valleys full of stones and stony rivers, the indomitable granite mountains.

But he could not go home, except for an occasional brief visit, until he was eighty. To think of sixty years in stations like this one! The idea was horrible!

"Don't be morose," Thev said. "You have a gift for gardening. The senior gardener has said that often. In time you'll be transferred to one of the big stations, where there are ornamental plants and bugs, maybe even a hologram of the home world sky. Think of that above you, while you pick suckers off stems! And

I, by then, will be a distinguished physicist. They'll bring me in to lecture, and we'll make jokes about the way our lives used to be."

Akuin felt doubtful and said as much.

"And then, finally, when you are a success, I'll confess to you that I've always loved you. And only the Goddess can know why, because you have an awful disposition."

Akuin looked at his friend. "Do you mean that?"

"About your disposition? Absolutely!"

"About loving me?"

"From the first moment I laid eyes on your shining pelt. From the first time I heard you complain."

"Why?"

"I have no idea. Remember that my area of competence is stars, not people."

Akuin kept looking at Thev, who was (as usual) sprawled on his bed, under the empty wall niche. He'd just come from the communal shower. Naked, it was possible to see all the blotches on his front. One covered half his forehead. Another, even larger and just as badly shaped, covered half a thigh.

"Did you ever think of coloring your fur?" Akuin asked.

"My aunts tried dyeing me when I was young. I hated it, a horrible messy process that stank and had to be done over and over. When it was time, when I smelled the dye cooking, I'd run away and hide, and they would come hunting. They made my cousins join in, until they began to refuse. 'If Thev wants to be ugly, let him be. We don't want to hunt him down like an animal.' My aunts gave up finally."

"You never rethought that decision?"

"What are you telling me, Akuin? You are willing to become my lover if I turn myself black? But not otherwise? Can't you be content to be the lovely one? I am certainly content to be the smart one."

No question the spots were ugly. But the thin body was good enough, and so was the voice, even and friendly and amused. The mind was in front of any mind he'd ever encountered. What would it be like to make love with someone who could peer into the center of stars and see what lies beyond ordinary experience?

Akuin kissed his friend. Thev responded with passion. Ugly he might be, and intellectual, but he was also passionate.

They became lovers. This is always a difficult situation when the couple is young, without much privacy. Either they waited till their roommates were gone, or they used the rooms-for-sex-and-other-intimate-behavior which are associated with gymnasia.

It would be better to do these things, Akuin thought, in the woods of Atkwa or in a secluded part of his grandmother's garden. Even the dunes next to his boarding school would have been better. Love did not belong in the station. Though Thev didn't seem to mind the grey rooms and the air that smelled of machinery.

Would life have been different, Akuin wondered later, if he'd chosen a more appropriate lover? One of the older men, who showed an interest in him? The senior gardener, for example?

The problem now, aside from the uncomfortable places they made love, was Thev's other passion. He was onto something interesting about the star grove.

Maybe if Akuin had loved his work as much, he would have been able to endure Thev's periods of abstraction or his long discussions of the behavior of aging stars. He tried to be as boring, telling Thev about the garden's problems. It is always difficult to keep an incomplete ecology in balance. This particular garden had recurrent infestations of a parasitic organism that was neither a plant nor an animal, but rather alive in its own peculiar way. It was native to the *hwarhath* home world, but had changed after the *hwarhath* had inadvertently carried it into space, a region it liked; or rather it liked the conditions of gardens in space. It thrived under lights that did not have the exact spectrum of the *hwarhath* home star; and soil that wasn't full of the home world's microorganisms seemed like a gift from the Goddess.

Thev listened patiently, but what he heard—more than anything else—was complaining. Obviously, a garden in space was going to be different from a garden on the home planet. Obviously, there were going to be difficulties and problems. But to a man of his temperament, optimistic and determined, problems were something one overcame or suffered cheerfully, the way he suffered his spots.

If Akuin's plants were covered with mold, well then, Akuin would have to find a cure. If a cure could not be found, the garden would have to grow other kinds of plants.

"Does nothing discourage you?" asked Akuin.

"You do, sometimes. Why not enjoy life? Is anything improved by moping? Think of how handsome you are! Think of my devotion! Do you think mold is any worse than my equations, which are not going where I want them to?"

In spite of his excellent heritage, Thev said, he was not a first-rate mathematician. Rather, he had an instinct for how things are. "Where that came from, I don't know. The same place as my spots, maybe. In any case, I don't reason out what the Goddess has done with the universe. It comes to me almost as a vision; and if you think it's easy to see things in more than the usual five dimensions, you are wrong.* That's what the grove is like: a place that requires far more than five dimensions, if I'm going to understand it. There are so many stars here, and they are packed so closely!"

Maybe the problem was a difference in magnitude. Mold seems like a trivial problem, compared to Thev's struggles with his equations. More likely it was a difference in temperament. Thev's energy made everything he did important. When he

---

* Pre-modern *hwarhath* math and physics recognized five aspects of objects in space. These were: location, extension, expansion-to-the-side, expansion-up-and-down, and relation. (The human equivalents to these are: point, line, plane and volume. Relation has no exact equivalent.) Early modern theory required a sixth dimension: duration or time. This made people uneasy, since the *hwarhath* like to count everything in groups of five; and attempts were made to get back to five dimensions. Time could not be eliminated, but maybe something could be done with one of the original aspects of space. Were location and relation both necessary? Did the two kinds of expansion need to be counted separately? But all six aspects seemed to have a kind of reality. There were problems that couldn't be solved without them, just as there were problems that couldn't be solved, until they were simplified by the elimination of one or more aspects. In the end most *hwarhath* accepted the existence of all six, though they continue to speak of "five dimensions" in ordinary speech. More recent theories, such as those explaining FTL travel and why the universe exists, have required even more dimensions. How the *hwarhath* have dealt with this problem is not yet clear to humans.

struggled, it was a real struggle. Akuin's sadness, which was chronic now, diminished his concerns. Nothing he did seemed worth doing, to himself or to those around him.

His first year in space ended. The second began. According to messages from relatives, everyone at home was doing well, though his grandmother's garden didn't thrive as it had when he tended it. Beyond doubt, he had a gift. "How lucky that you can use it where you are," his mother said.

The mold was under control now. He had convinced the senior gardener to introduce a few ornamental plants.

"Just in the corners, lad. The places we aren't using. This isn't a great station. If the officers here want flowers for their lovers, too bad. And no matter how you beg, I'm not going to send for bugs. They aren't in the budget."

At first he put in plants with colored leaves. They shone like jewels at the corners of beds full of green and blue-green vegetation.

"Like fire in the night," said one of the station's senior officers. "Are flowers possible?"

"Talk to the man in front of me. He says we don't have the money."

The officer, a physicist and a good one, according to Thev, ran his hand along a bright red leaf. "Maybe something can be worked out, though he's right that research never gets the funding it deserves." The man glanced at Akuin. "You are Gehazi Thev's friend."

"Yes."

"You've made a good choice. He's going to have a future, in spite of being as ugly as a wall made of mud. Beauty isn't everything." The man touched the leaf a second time. "But it's something."

Money was found for flowers, though not for bugs. The senior officer picked the first bloom that opened. "To give to someone dear."

"I know who that is," Thev said. "A man who gets ahead on charm. He'll go into administration. He hasn't got the mind for research. But he isn't a bad fellow, and he'll make sure the men who can think get the chance to think. Do you think charm can take a person all the way to the front, Akuin?"

"I never got the impression that the Frontmen-in-a-Bundle were charming."[*]

"Research scientists don't make it to the Bundle," Thev said. "Accountants, yes, and administrators, though I'm not sure they are especially charming administrators. Also experts on warfare. But not experts on how the universe really works."

"Are you ambitious?" Akuin asked.

"Yes, but not in that way. What I want, aside from you—" He rolled over and took hold of Akuin, pulling him close. "Is fame that goes on forever and a good teaching position."

At the end of his second year in space, Akuin got leave and went home, like any other young man, to his native country and the house where he'd been raised. He was there for the usual length of time, working in his grandmother's garden and taking hikes in the stony hills. For the most part, he spent his time alone.

Hah! He had grown, his female relatives told him. He was handsomer than ever! They didn't mention his aloofness, which troubled them, or the expression of sadness that appeared too often on his face.

"It may be nothing," his grandmother said in private. "There are men who have trouble adjusting to space, but almost everyone manages in the end. This other young man sounds encouraging. I've done research on the family. They are a small lineage, not rich, but they have made excellent alliances; and their traits seem fine. If this romance works out, and Akuin stays involved with the Gehazi boy, we ought to think of approaching them for semen."

"It's the other side of the planet!" Akuin's mother exclaimed. "And the young man has spots!"

"He'd be a poor choice to father children," the grandmother admitted. "Though he is apparently a genius. But I agree with you. It would be better to go to his male relatives. He has plenty who look normal, and most are bright. As for Gehazi's location,

---

[*] The *hwarhath* equivalent of the human High Command. The Bundle rules *hwarhath* society in space and *hwarhath* males wherever they may be.

these are modern times. We can't be provincial. Who can say which alliances will prove useful?"

At the end of his leave, Akuin visited his former school. It was almost empty, the students on vacation, but Tol Chaib was there, getting his garden ready for winter. Hah! The air was cold already and smelled, when the wind came off the land, of drying vegetation.

He spent a day working with his mentor, digging into the sandy soil, cutting stalks and branches, gathering fallen leaves. In the evening they drank *halin* and talked, alone together in Tol Chaib's quarters. The rest of the building was unoccupied.

After they were both drunk, Tol Chaib said, "I always wanted to have sex with you. It wasn't possible, until you became a man. But the longing was there. It frightened me. I'm not usually attracted to boys."

What was it, Akuin wondered, about him and ugly men? Maybe they could see the wrongness in him, though it was different from their ugliness. There was nothing wrong with Thev except his spots. In every other way, he was a model young man: loyal, determined, direct, pious. Though not violent. Thev lacked the fifth male virtue. Well, no one was perfect, and Thev's other traits—his intelligence and cheerfulness—ought to count for something.

Tol Chaib was more disturbing. Looking at him, Akuin saw loneliness and grief for things lost: his old beauty, his life in space. The old man was like a mirror, reflecting Akuin's future. He could end like this. Though he didn't think he would ever be attracted to boys. That was a perversion, after all; and his wrongness—whatever it was exactly—seemed unconnected with perversity. He was a gardener, who wanted to garden at home. A shameful ambition! But not the same as wanting to molest children.

In the end, after another cup of *halin*, he went to bed with Tol Chaib, though he was never certain exactly why. The old man wanted this to happen, and he felt he owed his mentor something. That was as good an explanation as any. In the morning they parted, Tol Chaib giving him a tropical flower from the school greenhouse. It was huge and intricate and as blue as the sky, though almost scentless. Akuin carried it until it wilted, then threw it in the ocean. This was on one of the rocket islands. An *ikun* later he boarded a rocket, which carried him into space.

Gehazi Thev greeted him with affection when he got back to their station. "Though it was a good idea to have time away from you. I thought about stellar evolution instead of sex. There is much to be said for both, of course, but my job is stars."

During his absence, Thev had moved into a new dormitory, this one occupied by four young physicists.

"There didn't seem to be any reason to stay in my old room. I have nothing in common with the other men. It was only habit that kept me there. Habit and you, and you were gone."

Their romance continued, though it might have ended. Who can say what ties men (or women) together? They returned to their old habits, exercising in the station's gymnasia, going to its one theatre to see recordings of plays put on in the great stations, places such as Tailin. Both enjoyed soaking in the pools-for-soaking. Both enjoyed sex in the rooms-for-privacy.

These last were small, like everything in the station. There was a low bed, fastened to the floor, and two stools that moved in grooves. The ceiling had a mirror, which could be turned off, though the lovers usually kept it on. The wall opposite the bed could be replaced with a hologram. Thev liked scenes of space: galaxies, nebulae, stars and planets. Akuin (of course) preferred scenes of home.

During one of their stays in a private room, Thev spoke about the work he was doing. They'd had sex and were lying together on the bed's thin mattress. A trio of stars—red, white and orange—blazed at the room's end. The mirror above them showed their bodies, quiet now, Thev resting on his belly, Akuin on his back.

Later, Akuin remembered the scene, as he remembered the day he first fell in love with his grandmother's garden.

Thev had been working with geometry. "Making models, so I can visualize what is happening in this region of space. Mind you, it isn't easy. We evolved to see five dimensions, and that's the number we insist on seeing, no matter how many there may be.

"But it is possible, especially if one uses a computer. How did our ancestors get anything done, before the existence of computers? Imagine trying to understand the universe by counting on fingers! Or making lines in the dirt! No wonder the universe was small in those days! No wonder it was simple!

"What one does—" Thev rolled over and began to go through his uniform's pockets.* A moment later he was kneeling by the hologram projector. The triple star vanished. In its place was an irregular object made of glowing white lines. It floated in midair, turning slowly and changing shape as it turned.

"—Is eliminate one of the ordinary visible dimensions and replace it with a dimension that can't be seen. Obvious, you may say to me; and certainly it has been done many times before; and certainly it isn't adequate to show what's happening in this region of space.

"But if one makes a large number of these partial models, each one showing an aspect of reality—"

Now the room was full of floating objects, all made of glowing lines, but not all the same color. Some were red or orange, like the vanished stars. Others were green, blue, yellow. Hah! It was like a garden! Except these flowers were all deformed and deforming. Some expanded like leaves opening in spring. Others folded in and seemed to be swallowing themselves. As one diminished, the one beside it grew, either in size or complexity. Akuin began to feel queasy.

"The problem, of course, is fitting all these partial models together. This is where a computer is essential."

"What is this about?" Akuin asked. "Does this array of ugly objects serve any purpose?"

"Ugly!" said Thev. "Dear one, they are the achievement of my life!" He was back on the bed now, sitting with his arms around his knees, admiring the things. "Of course, I'm young and likely to do better. But this isn't bad, I assure you."

"You have told me," Akuin said, "that you are trying to see

---

* The *hwarhath* male uniform is a pair of shorts: knee-length, loose and abundantly provided with pockets. This, plus sandals, is adequate for life in a space station or ship. Their costume when on planets is more varied.

what can't be seen, and comprehend what isn't comprehensible. Maybe you can do this. Everyone agrees that you are brilliant. But I'm not going to understand these things swallowing themselves."

"You want another kind of model. Something which has to do with plants and bugs."

"That's what I know," Akuin said.

Thev was silent for a while, watching his things, which continued to grow, change shape, divide, diminish and vanish. A garden out of a bad dream. A sorcerer's garden.

Thev spoke finally. "Think of this region, this grove of stars, as a grove of trees growing in a dry place, so the trees are forced to seek water. We think the ground is dirt and stone; we think it's solid. In reality, a multitude of roots go down and out, forcing their way through dirt and stone, twisting around each other. It's possible the roots are connected."

Akuin had grown up in a part of the home world where many species of trees were communal, their various trunks rising from a single root system. But he had trouble imagining stars connected in the same way. This suggests that he hadn't paid attention to his physics class in school, which is true.

"We know that strange stars can be connected with other strange stars. Usually, the partners are not in close proximity. Here, I think they are. Imagine what this must do to reality. Strangeness loops back on itself. The fabric of space is pierced—again and again—by strangeness.

"What I've said so far is ordinary. Few scientists would disagree, except about the strangeness looping. That's not a generally accepted idea, though I'm not the only person who's come forward with it. But from this point on—" Thev glanced and smiled. "The ideas are mine.

"According to the usual theory, the ground under our grove of trees is stable. Yes, the roots have pushed through it, causing stress—most evident at the surface, where the ground may buckle, forced up from below. In areas settled by people, this pressure-from-below is easily perceived. Sidewalks are lifted. The walls of buildings crack and fall. All done by roots." Thev wiggled his fingers, apparently showing the action of roots.

"But let's imagine that the ground is not stable. Maybe the land is limestone and full of caves. The roots, burrowing down, are cracking stone—a thin layer—which forms the roof of one of these caves. In time the roof will break. The grove will fall into a sinkhole."

This was understandable. There are places in the Great Central Plain where the ground is limestone, and water is usually found in pools at the bottom of sinkholes. Nowadays, windmills bring the water up. In the old days, people cut steps in the stone walls and carried buckets. Akuin knew all this, and knew that sinkholes could appear suddenly. But how could a sinkhole appear in space? After all, a sinkhole was an absence of stone. But space wasn't there in the first place. How could one have an absence of something already absent?

"Let me give you another model," Thev said. "Think of this region of space as a cheese."

"What?" said Akuin.

"A large, round one." Thev spread his arms to show the cheese's size. "Bugs have infested it. It looks solid, but inside is a maze of tunnels. If one bends the cheese a little, or twists it, if any extra strain is put on it—hah! It breaks apart! There's nothing left but crumbs. The bugs have destroyed their home."

"These are disturbing images," Akuin said. "What are you saying with them? That this region of space could break into crumbs? I find it hard to imagine such an occurrence. What is a space crumb like?"

"Maybe the grove is a better model than the cheese, though you wanted plants and bugs, and I have given you both. I think it's possible this region will collapse. More than possible. In time, collapse is certain."

"But what will it become? Not a sinkhole?"

"My guess would be a large area of strangeness. Spherical, of course. Such things always are."

"What would happen to the station?" By this time Akuin was sitting up and looking at Thev with horror. This wasn't a pleasant situation that Thev was describing. But Thev's voice was full of interest and pleasure. What Thev was enjoying, of course, was his own cleverness. In addition, it's possible that he saw the situation as one of the many fine jokes with which the Goddess has filled her universe. A pious man will always enjoy the Great Mother's tricks.

"It depends on the size of the collapse," Thev said. "If it takes the entire region out, the station will be destroyed. But if it's the right size, and happens at the right distance, we'll be able to observe the process."

Akuin was getting a headache, either from the conversation or his lover's ugly things, which still filled the room and continued to change in disturbing ways. He mentioned the headache. Thev stopped the recording. The garden remained, but everything in it was motionless.

Much better! Akuin lay back. The mirror above him reflected his own dark body. On one side of him was a funnel made of bright red lines. It appeared to be dissolving and pouring itself down itself, though nothing moved now; and the center of the funnel was empty.

On the other side of him was a blue sphere, which had apparently stopped in the middle of turning itself into something full of many sharp angles. Both the angles and the sphere's smooth surface were visible. Akuin closed his eyes.

Thev kept talking. More research was needed. He'd written a proposal. "But you know the funding situation. If an idea can't be turned into a weapon at once, the frontmen aren't interested; and I can't see any obvious way to do harm with my ideas. Maybe some day we'll be able to use strangeness as a weapon, but not soon."

Thev must be getting tired. His conversation was beginning to wander. So much was uncertain. So many things might happen. If the station wasn't swallowed, it might still be destroyed by the event. "I don't think this process of collapse will be entirely quiet and peaceful." Or, if the station survived, and the men inside were alive, they might find that they'd lost their Heligian gate.*

"We'd be trapped," Akuin said. No one had ever warned him to beware of sex with physicists. Maybe they should have. It

---

* The *hwarhath* name for an FTL transfer point.

would be easier to have a lover who thought about more trivial problems.

"We could send information home," Thev answered in an encouraging tone. "Only at the speed of light. But that would be sufficient. It would take less than five years for a message to reach the nearest working gate. Surely the frontmen would post a ship there, after our gate vanished."

"What is most likely to happen?" Akuin asked.

"The station will be destroyed."

"Soon?"

"I don't know," Thev said. "Some of the work done here suggests the space in this region is badly strained already; and it's possible that our presence is making things worse."

"How?" Akuin asked.

"Through the coming and going of star ships. They do have an effect, though not one that matters in ordinary situations. And there is at least one experiment which may be acting like roots pushing through a crack in limestone, or maybe like a slight twist of the cheese." Thev smiled briefly. "The experiment is continuing, though I've mentioned that it may cause trouble. The men running it don't believe the risk is significant."

"Aren't you worried?" Akuin asked.

"What can I do, except put my ideas out in front? Maybe I'm wrong. I have sent my theory, and recordings of my models, to the Helig Institute. If I die here, I will become famous. If I don't die here, if this region of space does not collapse, then I'll become famous later for something else. One cannot live in fear of thoughts, Akuin."

That was the end of the conversation. Akuin found he couldn't get Thev's ideas out of his mind. They haunted him: the collapsing grove, the cheese eaten out by bugs, the garden of ugly things.

Bad enough to think of living for years in the station. But to think of dying here! How could he feel the same affection for Thev? A man who came up with such ideas and models!

Gradually the two lovers drew apart. Thev accepted this with his usual calm good sense. Nothing pushed him back for long. He always recovered and went forward. Soon he found a lover among the physicists: not a thinker, but a hands-on builder, who said that Thev's models were likely to prove useful, though he didn't believe the station was in danger.

"You theoreticians love terrifying ideas! The Goddess may be sloppy in her details. We know she is, from looking around. But the basic structure of her universe is solid. Space doesn't fall to pieces like a bridge with bad mortar. It lasts! And will outlast everything!"

As for Akuin, he took a series of sexual partners. All were casual. This didn't especially bother him. Some men must have a true love, a companion for life. He wasn't such a man. Sex was fine. So was friendship. But his real love—the center of his life— was plants.

Another year passed. Once again he traveled home. His grandmother had died suddenly, shortly after his previous trip. Now it was time to put her ashes in the ground and carve her name on the monument for Atkwa women.

When he reached his home country, it was spring. In his grandmother's garden flowers bloomed, attracting early bugs. The house was full of female relatives, busy with details of the coming ceremony.

There was nothing for Akuin to do, so he went hiking. South and west of the house were hills, not high, but made impressive by huge outcroppings of igneous rock. No limestone here, erod- ing easily! His country had bones of granite! An *ikun* from home, he came to his favorite spot for looking into the distance.* Up he climbed, until he was atop the great bald knob. Now he could see the folded hills, covered with pale blue foliage. They stretched in every direction. Here and there were patches of color: yellow, light orange or lavender, flowering shrubs and trees.

All at once, he realized he had reached the limit of his endurance. He could not bear to leave this place again. He would not return to space.

Why did this happen? How can any man turn away from duty? His grandmother, the most formidable member of his fam-

---

*A *hwarhath* measure of time: one tenth of a standard *hwarhath* day, 2.31 human hours.

ily, was dead. He'd lost his lover. His mentor had turned out to be a pervert, attracted to children. The garden in the station was not an adequate substitute for the country here, extending around him in every direction under a cloudless sky.

Always, in the station, he was aware of the space outside: dark, cold, airless, hostile to life. If Thev was right, the emptiness outside the station was not even reliable. It might collapse at any moment, becoming something worse.

Here he stood on granite.

By the time he returned to his grandmother's house, he was already making plans. His female relatives continued to be busy, his mother especially. She would be the new matriarch. Akuin gathered supplies, sneaking them out of storerooms and hiding them in a forest. Tools. Clothing. A rifle and ammunition. A hunting bow and arrows. Medical supplies. Plenty of seeds. A computer full of information.

By the time his grandmother was underground, he was ready. There was a final ceremony: cutting his grandmother's name in the stone which memorialized the family's dead women. When that was over, his mother bid him farewell. A cousin took him to the train station. He climbed on board, climbing out the far side and ducking behind a bush. The train pulled away. His cousin returned to her car. Akuin took off for the forest and his hidden supplies.

He reached them without trouble. With luck, it would be several days before his family realized that he had vanished: time enough to get into the high mountains, the wilderness. He was strong, determined and not afraid of anything in his homeland. Pack on back, he set off.

There's no reason to tell his life in detail from this point on. The important thing had happened. Akuin had decided to turn away from loyalty and obligation. Now, he lived for himself rather than his family or his species. This is something humans do, if the stories we hear are true. This is why their home planet is full of violence and has far too many inhabitants, produced not by careful breeding contracts, but random acts of heterosexuality.

He found a valley high in the mountains, away from all trails with a hard-to-find entrance. There he built a hut and established his garden. The first year was difficult. So was the second. But he persisted. At times he was lonely. Not often. He'd always been comfortable with solitude. The things around him—sunlight, rain, wind, his garden, the mountains—were a constant source of joy.

In the third year he built a solid cabin. Having done this, he began to wonder what was happening in the house where he'd grown up. He waited till harvest was over, and his cabin full of food. Then he went home.

He couldn't arrive openly, of course. He was a criminal now, and the women of his family had always been law-abiding and respectful of tradition. Instead, he lurked in the forest shadow and crept close after dark, peering in windows. There his family was, the same as always. Only he had changed. For a while he felt regret. Then he remembered the station, and Gehazi Thev's terrifying ideas. He'd made the right choice.

The next fall he came down again. This time he did a little stealing. There were tools he needed, and he could always use more seeds.

The fifth year of his exile, he decided to visit the library in his grandmother's house, which was held by his mother now. He crept in after midnight, when the house was entirely dark, and made his way without trouble to the room. Some of the houses in Atkwa were old. Their libraries were full of actual books, ancient cherished objects. This house had been built a century before. There were a few books, brought from other places, but most of the glass-fronted cabinets held modern recordings. When his electric torch played over them, they glittered like so many jewels: garnet-red novels, poetry like peridots, topaz-yellow plays. The music was shades of blue. What a fool he'd been to take only nonfiction before! Quickly, he picked the recordings he wanted and copied them into his computer, then replaced the shining bits of silicon and metal in their proper resting places.

When he was almost done, he heard a noise. Akuin turned and saw his mother, standing in the doorway.

Hah! She reached out a hand. The ceiling light went on. Akuin stood ashamed, his hands full of music, like a jewel thief holding sapphires.

His mother stepped into the room, closing the door behind her. "It was you who stole from us last fall."

He tilted his head in agreement.

"I thought so, and I thought, 'He's alive.' That idea brought me joy, Akuin, though it shouldn't have. What's wrong with you? Why was it so difficult for you to live like other men? When you came home the first time, your grandmother and I made plans. If your romance worked out, she wanted to ask the Gehazi for semen. A young man of so much promise! A family worth forming an alliance with! We thought—we hoped—you had overcome your oddness at last."

No words of explanation came to him. Instead, he said, "What?" and stopped. His voice sounded harsh. The tone was wrong. He was no longer used to speaking.

"What am I going to do? Nothing. By now the neighboring families have forgotten about you. If I give you to the male police, it will bring our shame into daylight. People will know for certain that you ran from duty. Before, there was a possibility that something happened—an accident, a murder."

"You could tell me to die," Akuin said in his new strange voice.

"Would you kill yourself, if I asked you to?"

He didn't answer.

"No," his mother said. "I think not. Go back to your mountains. Every family has embarrassing secrets. You will be ours."

He set the music on a table. How it glittered!

"Don't come into the house again," his mother added. "I'll see that things are left in the far barn for you."

He opened his mouth to thank her.

"Go."

Akuin left, carrying his computer.

The next year he came home twice, though not to the greathouse. Instead he found his mother's gifts in the far barn: tools, small boxes containing seeds, recordings of music, favorite pieces from when he was young, a letter full of family news.

After this, there were no changes in his life for many years. Bit by bit, he expanded his garden and made his cabin more comfortable. Slowly he read his way through most of the great male plays, which are—as everyone knows—about honor and the making of difficult choices. The heroes, the men who must choose, usually die, as he should have. Or they sacrifice their happiness to obligation. Another thing he had failed to do.

In addition, he read many of the plays written about women and their lives. These deal with endurance and compromise, which are not male virtues.

Maybe he would have made a better woman, though it didn't seem likely. Nothing about him seemed especially feminine. He certainly didn't have his grandmother's solidity. His mother was the same. Women like the mountains of Atkwa! Nothing ordinary could wear them down!

Akuin's mother died prematurely, when he was only forty. Coming down from the mountains through an early snow, he found the usual kind of supplies in the far barn, also a letter. It was from one of his female cousins, telling him the news. A sudden illness, that should not have killed a woman so healthy, not yet old. But it did! *Life is full of these kinds of surprises,* his cousin wrote in an elegant, flowing script, though Akuin was not thinking about calligraphy at the moment.

He fell to his knees, chest heaving. The groans inside him would not come out. Beyond the barn's open door, snow fell in thick soft flakes.

The gifts would continue, his cousin wrote. She had promised his mother while the woman lay dying. *This is not the kind of promise one breaks. Though I have to say, Akuin, that I do not approve of your behavior.*

"So, so," Akuin said. He got up finally, walking into the snow. No chance the people in the house would see him through this whiteness. He lifted his head and hands, as if to catch something, though he didn't know what. The life he should have had? The snow flakes melted when they touched his palms.

More time passed. This is what the real world is like. Instead of the sudden important decisions which heroes must make in plays, everything solved in less than an *ikun,* real life is gradual.

His cousin kept her promise. He continued to find gifts in the barn. For many years he saw no people, except at a distance. He always managed to avoid them.

One summer morning when he was almost fifty, Akuin stepped out his cabin door and saw a monster in his garden. That was his first impression. The thing stood in brilliant sunlight. Akuin, coming out of his cabin's dimness, could make out nothing except the creature's shape: upright on two legs like a person, but far too thin and tall. A stick-person. A person made of bones. Like bones, the monster was pale.

He stepped back into his cabin, picked up his rifle and waited, hoping the monster had not seen him. Maybe it would go away. He'd never had a problem with monsters before.

The thing remained in the middle of Akuin's vegetables. He saw it more clearly now. It had on clothing, pants and a red checked shirt. A head rose above the shirt. The face was hairless, the features like no *hwarhath* features he had ever seen: everything narrow and pushed together, as if someone had put hands on either side of the creature's head and pressed, forcing the cheeks in, the nose out, the forehead up, the chin into a jutting bulge.

"It's a magnificent garden," the creature said in Akuin's own language.

He'd been spotted. Akuin raised his rifle.

A second voice said, "You are looking at a human. This one is friendly. Put the gun down."

Akuin glanced around, until he made out the second person, standing at the forest edge. He was short with steel grey fur, dressed in hiking shorts and boots. A *hwarhath* male, beyond any question. But not a relative. Like the monster, he spoke with an accent that wasn't local. In the case of this man, the accent was southern.

"Believe me," added the *hwarhath* in a quiet voice. "Neither one of us will do you any harm. We are here with the permission of the Atkwa, for recreational purposes."

"Hiking in the mountains," said the monster in agreement.

"Enemy," Akuin said in the voice he almost never used. Hah! The word came out like a branch creaking in the wind!

"The war has ended," the *hwarhath* said. "We have peace with the humans."

This didn't seem possible, but the news Akuin got from his cousin was all family news.

"Put the gun down," the *hwarhath* male repeated. "You really must not kill this human. He works for us. His rank is advancer one-in-back."[*]

Akuin had been a carrier. The monster far outranked him. It was definitely wrong to point a gun at a senior officer. He lowered the rifle.

The *hwarhath* man said, "Good. Now, come out."

Slowly, Akuin moved into the sunlight. The monster remained motionless. So did the man at the edge of the forest.

What next? Akuin stood with his rifle pointing down. He was making out more details now. There was a patch of hair, or possibly feathers, on top of the monster's head. The patch was bone-white, like the hairless face. Even the monster's eyes were white, though a dark spot floated in the middle of each eye. Was this a sign of disease? Could the monster be blind? No. Akuin had a clear sense that the thing was watching. The dark spots moved, flicking from him to the *hwarhath* male, then back again.

"I think it would be easier to talk, if you put the gun down entirely," the *hwarhath* said.

A calm voice, low and even, but Akuin recognized the tone. This was authority speaking. He laid the rifle on the ground and straightened up, trying to remember the way he used to hold himself, back when he was a soldier.

"Much better," said the *hwarhath*. He walked forward and picked up the rifle, handing it to the monster.

For a moment, Akuin was afraid. But the monster held the rifle properly, barrel pointed down. The oddly shaped hands did not reach for the trigger. The backs of the hands were pale and hairless. Was the creature the same all over? White and as hairless as a fish?

The *hwarhath* man looked at Akuin, who glanced down at once. This was a very senior officer. It showed in his tone of

---

[*] The equivalent human rank is major. There is no easy (or politically neutral) way to discuss the two characters just introduced. Therefore they will not be discussed, except to note that any ordinary *hwarhath* reader would recognize the pair at once. Much of the humor in the rest of the story lies with Akuin's attempts to figure out things all other *hwarhath* know.

voice, the way he moved, the way he treated the monster, expecting obedience, which the monster gave him. Not a man you looked at directly.

If the man had questions, he did not ask them. Instead, he explained their arrival. It had been an accident. They'd gotten off their trail and lost. "Though not by much, I suspect. If your relatives become worried, they will be able to find us."

The night before had been spent at the entrance to Akuin's valley. This morning, curious, they had hiked in. "I don't think we could find this place again. In fact, we'll need your help to get back to our trail."

"I'll give it in return for news," Akuin said, then felt surprise at what he'd said.

The *hwarhath* man tilted his head in agreement. "That can be done."

Akuin remembered he was the host and got busy making tea. The two visitors wandered through his garden. The human still carried Akuin's rifle. There was another rifle in the cabin. If necessary, Akuin could kill both of them.

But if they vanished, Akuin's relatives would look for them and keep looking till the men were found. Hospitality required as much. So did respect for rank and the connections far-in-front officers always had. The *hwarhath* picked a flower—a yellow midsummer bloom—and handed it to his companion, who took it with a flash of teeth. A smile. Then the two of them strolled back toward the cabin, the *hwarhath* first, the monster following, rifle in one hand, flower in the other.

This was a peculiar situation! And likely to turn out badly. If the men became curious about him, they'd discover that he was AWOL. His family would be shamed in public. He would have to kill himself.

His mother should have turned him in twenty-five years before. The result would have been the same for him: death by suicide or execution. But the Atkwa would have escaped embarrassment. At least his mother wasn't alive to see the result of her affection.

Maybe it would be better to ask no questions, send the men off as quickly as possible and hope they did not become curious.

But his longing for information was intense. In any case, they must suspect that he was a runaway. How could they not? He was alone in the mountains and so ignorant that he didn't know the war with the humans was over.

There was a flat rock near his cabin door. He used it as a table, setting out teapot and cups. His two guests settled down, the monster leaning Akuin's rifle against the cabin where Akuin could not reach it, though the monster could. He kept the flower, twirling its stem between oddly proportioned fingers. "It really is a very fine garden."

"What kind of news do you want to hear?" asked the *hwarhath.*

"The war," Akuin said.

"It turned out to be a mistake. Humans can be reasoned with, though I can't say the process is easy; and we live at such great distances from one another that there isn't much to fight over."

"Some fool, apparently a human fool, fired at the first strange ship he encountered," the monster added. "That's how the war began." He showed his teeth to Akuin, another smile. It wasn't quick and friendly like a *hwarhath* smile, but wide and slow. Disturbing. "It continued because the two sides lacked a way to communicate, unless one calls the firing of weapons a form of communication. In the end, we learned each other's languages."

"That helped," the *hwarhath* said. "Though once a war has gotten going, it's hard to stop. This proved no exception."

Akuin asked about Kushaiin, the station where he and Thev had met and become lovers. The *hwarhath* man was silent.

"It's not an important place," Akuin said. "Maybe you haven't heard of it."

"Why do you want to know about it?" the man asked.

"I had a friend who was assigned there, a man named Gehazi Thev."

"The physicist."

"You know about him," said Akuin. "Is he still alive?"

"He wasn't at the station when it disappeared."

Hah! Akuin thought and refilled the cups. The monster had barely touched his tea, but the *hwarhath* male was obviously a drinker. "Did the region collapse, as he said it would? Was the station swallowed by strangeness?"

The *hwarhath* male was silent for a moment. Finally he spoke. "At first, we knew only that something had happened to the gate next to the station. We could no longer use it, though the scientists couldn't tell us why—or if the gate still existed or where it might be, if it still existed. In any case, we could no longer reach the station or communicate with it, except at the speed of light.

"The nearest gate we could use was lightyears from Kushaiin. Obviously we sent people there. Looking from a distance, everything around the station—your station—seemed fine. The star grove shone as it always had. The station's beacon was still on; and its signal indicated no problems. But we were looking into the past, and the information we needed would not reach us for years. We set up an observation post and sent an STL probe, though light from the station would reach our post long before the probe reached its destination. The universe is a large place, if one doesn't have access to the Heligian highway system. Then we waited, and the physicists wove theories. It's an activity they love, as you must have noticed."

"Yes," said Akuin. "Didn't Gehazi tell you his ideas? You said he had survived."

"Yes." The *hwarhath* gave him a proper smile, small and quick, not the least bit threatening. "The other scientists had their doubts about his theory, and there were some fine loud arguments. As far as I could determine, nothing was settled, though the physicists kept knotting and unknotting ideas.

"Finally the star grove vanished. It happened from one moment to the next, almost without warning. By looking closely, the scientists were able to find abnormalities in the star grove's spectrum immediately prior to the vanishing. In addition, there was radiation, which originated in the station's region at the time when the station vanished. But none of this was dramatic. Nothing like a nova. I'm not sure how much we would have noticed, if we hadn't been watching closely. When the probe reached the place where the stars had been, it found only empty space."

"How is that possible?" Akuin asked.

"Gehazi Thev revised his theory. If you know him, you know that nothing pushes him back. His first ideas did not explain what happened, so he brought new ideas to the fore. He now thinks the collapse served to separate the region from our universe."

"What do you mean?" Akuin asked. "What happened to the station? Does it still exist?"

"How can we know?" the man said in answer. "If it has survived, then it's in another universe, along with the stars that vanished. A very small universe, according to Gehazi Thev, who has described the place. There is no way to check his ideas, but it's a fine description.

"At first, according to Gehazi Thev, the new universe would be dark, except for the stars around the station. Imagine how that would look!" The man exhaled. Akuin couldn't tell if the exhalation meant horror or interest. Horror seemed more reasonable. "In time the light produced by the stars will be bent back. Then it will seem that new stars are appearing in the distance, all dim and red, like the stars around the station. If the men in the station had good enough instruments, they'd be able to see themselves. They will certainly be able to see and hear the messages they send."

"The men in the station must be dead," Akuin said.

"Most likely, though Gehazi Thev thinks—or did, the last time I heard him speak—there's a slight possibility they are alive. It depends on what happened to all the strangeness in the region when it collapsed, not to mention the energy which should have been generated by the collapse. If these went into this new universe, then the universe is almost certainly uninhabitable. But if the strangeness and energy were somehow dissipated or used up in the creation of the universe—"

It was, Akuin realized, another one of Thev's terrible ideas. "When did this happen?"

"Twenty-three years ago," the *hwarhath* said.

Akuin would have been there, when the station vanished. He almost certainly knew men who had died or gone into their own universe. Had Thev's lover, the hands-on physicist, been among them? He could no longer remember the fellow's name. Akuin looked toward his garden, but did not see its midsummer brightness. Instead, for a moment, he imagined darkness and isolation, relieved—finally—by dim red stars that were an illusion, light bent back toward its origin. What a fate!

"Most likely the station was destroyed," the *hwarhath* said in a comfortable tone, then excused himself and went off to eliminate tea.

The monster stayed where he was, his cup still full. "I have bad reactions to a number of *hwarhath* foods," he said. "It's better not to experiment."

"How did you end up working for us?" Akuin asked.

"I was offered a job. I took it."

"Was this after the war ended?"

The monster smiled his slow, disturbing smile. "No."

"Is this acceptable behavior among humans?" Akuin asked.

"To change sides in the middle of a war? No."

Obviously Akuin found the monster interesting. This was a person who'd done something worse than running away. "What would happen if your people got hold of you?"

"Nothing now. There is a treaty. I'm a *hwarhath* officer. That should protect me. But the usual penalty for disloyalty is death."

Akuin wanted to ask the monster why he'd changed sides, but there wasn't time.* The *hwarhath* male was returning, moving through Akuin's garden, pausing to pick another flower, this one red. He laid the flower down on Akuin's rock table, then resettled himself on the ground. "Is there anything else you want to know?"

"What are you going to do about me?" Akuin asked and was surprised by the question. Surely it would have been wiser to keep quiet.

The *hwarhath* tilted his head, considering. "We're both on leave at the moment. Our work, when we are at work, is not for the Corps that keeps track of *hwarhath* men. And we are guests in this country. I assume the Atkwa know about you. Let them deal with you. I don't see that your behavior is our business."

He was not going to die. His relatives were not going to suf-

---

* Most *hwarhath* believe that Nicholas Sanders changed sides because of love. As a group, they are more romantic than humans. This is especially true of *hwarhath* men. Romantic love is the great consolation in lives that are often difficult. It is also a dangerous emotion, which threatens basic loyalties and thus the fabric of *hwarhath* society. The *hwarhath*, men especially, regard it with gratitude and fear.

fer embarrassment. In his relief, he offered them vegetables from his garden.

"We can't carry much," the *hwarhath* said. "And my friend can't eat most of our edible plants. Either they don't nurture him, or they make him ill. So he lives on specially prepared rations. It's a hard fate for a human. Eating is an amusement for them. They expect their food to be as entertaining as a good play. Our human rations are—I have been told—dull."

"This is true," the monster said.

"But I'll accept your offer," his *hwarhath* companion concluded. "I don't know that I've ever seen handsomer looking vegetables. This is something worthy of respect, though I don't have the human attitude toward food."*

That afternoon, Akuin led them back to their trail. After he left them, heading back toward home, he realized that he hadn't learned their names. Nor had they learned his, but he was obviously Atkwa. If they wanted to find his records, they'd be able to do it without difficulty.

He reached his cabin late in the afternoon. Shadows covered the valley's floor and lower slopes, but light still filled the sky and touched the eastern hilltops. A copperleaf tree stood high on one of these, shining as if it were actually made of uncorroded copper. Lovely!

He gathered the teapot and cups, carrying them inside, then came out and picked up the yellow flower, which had been left. The red one had gone with his visitors, tucked under a flap on the *hwarhath* man's pack. He'd seen it go bobbing down the trail, as the *hwarhath* followed his long-legged companion. Easy to see who the athlete in the pair was.

Holding the withered flower, Akuin realized the two were lovers. It was as clear as something seen in a vision, though he was not a diviner and did not have visions. None the less, he knew.

Impossible! was his first reaction. But how could he tell what

---

* The *hwarhath* often comment on humanity's obsession with food and violence. Both food and violence are necessary, but neither requires the huge amount of thought and practice that humans put in. The human interest in food strikes the *hwarhath* as funny. Our interest in violence makes their fur rise.

was possible these days? He'd heard a monster speak his native language and been told the monster was a *hwarhath* officer. If this could happen, and a station vanish out of the universe, who could say what other events might occur?

He laid the flower down, unwilling to discard it yet, and watched as sunlight faded off the copperleaf tree. A disturbing day, though he was glad to hear that Thev was still alive and apparently famous. It was what Thev wanted. The news brought by the two men made him feel isolated and ignorant, for a moment doubtful about the choice he'd made.

Overhead the sky seemed limitless, not a roof, but an ocean into which he could fall and sink—if not forever, then far enough to drown.

Hah! That was an unpleasant idea! And also untrue. He stood with his feet in the dirt of Atkwa. Below the dirt was granite and the great round planet, which held him as a mother holds a child. There was no way for him to fall into the sky.

As for the choice he'd made—this was what he'd always wanted, as intensely as Thev had wanted fame: the garden in front of him, the copperleaf tree shining on its cliff, evening bugs beginning to call in the shadows. Only a fool mourns for the impossible or asks for everything, as if the Goddess had made the universe for his comfort.

If he had lost through his choice, he had also gained. Surely this valley—the bugs, the scent of his garden carried on a slight cool wind—was better than a lifetime spent in grey metal corridors. It was certainly better than vanishing into a very small universe of dim red stars. Thev and his ideas!

He stayed at the cabin doorway, watching day end. The sky was a roof again. The ground beneath his feet was solid. Gradually his uncertainty—his sense of loss—faded, like sunlight fading off the copperleaf tree. He regretted nothing. This was the right place for him to be.

➤ ➤ ➤

That evening Ettin Gwarha and Sanders Nicholas made their camp next to the trail. A stream ran in a gully below them, producing a pleasant quiet noise. Ettin Gwarha ate fresh vegetables, while his companion made do with human rations. Then the son of Ettin turned on a map and studied it. "We'll take a different route out than the one we originally planned," he said.

"Why?" asked Sanders Nicholas.

"The original plan had us ending at one of the Atkwa greathouses. I'd just as soon avoid the family."

"Is there a reason?"

"If they realize how close we came to that man's territory, they'll worry, and that will force me to reassure them. As much as possible, I want nothing to do with this situation."

"But you told the man you wouldn't turn him in."

"Every family has its secrets, and we are guests in the country of the Atkwa. Never think that I approve of behavior such as his. There is no acceptable reason to run away from duty." The frontman turned off his map and closed it, then added, "I'm not going to comment on the behavior of the Atkwa women in letting their male relative go wild. Only women can judge women."

Sanders Nicholas considered this for a while. Maybe Ettin Gwarha could read the expression on his pale, hairless face. No ordinary *hwarhath* can. "I have another question," he said finally.

The frontman looked at him.

"Why do you know so much about Gehazi Thev and the station which vanished? Physics has never been one of your areas of competence."

"Negotiation is my great skill, as you know. When the station disappeared, the Bundle had two questions it wanted answered; and they wanted one question at least to be asked diplomatically, since it was a disturbing question, and they had to go—I had to go—to the Helig Institute for an answer."[*]

Sanders Nicholas waited.

"The first question was, had some kind of weapon caused our station to disappear? Was it possible that humans—or another alien species—had so much power? Remember that a Heligian

---

[*] The Helig Institute is on the home planet and thus under the control of the *hwarhath* female government rather than the Bundle. As far as can be determined from a distance, the two halves of *hwarhath* society treat each other as genuine sovereign governments, whose interests are not always identical.

gate had been rendered impossible to use. An entire grove of stars had vanished! This was an event! If intelligent beings caused it to happen, then we were in trouble.

"The next question was, could such an event be caused? Was there a way to make a weapon out of whatever had happened?"

Sanders Nicholas gave his lover the wide, slow, unfriendly-seeming smile of humans. "You were hoping you could force the human home system into another universe."

"It was a thought that occurred to several men," Ettin Gwarha admitted. "Surely you can imagine the appeal of the idea, Nicky! The human threat could be eliminated without doing direct harm to humanity. We wouldn't have to go to our female relatives and say, 'We have destroyed women and children.'"

Sanders Nicholas sat quietly, looking at the small fire they had made. It was dying to embers already. Overhead the sky was dark. The Banner of the Goddess stretched across it, a wide swathe of dimly shining light. "I have two objections," he said finally. "How could the Bundle be certain that people would not be harmed? It would be an untested procedure, after all; and I find it hard to believe that any universe, even a small one, comes into existence quietly."

Ettin Gwarha inclined his head, perhaps in agreement. "What is your other objection?"

"Even if it could be done without immediate physical harm, think of the consequences. You would be depriving humanity of this—" He looked up, gesturing toward the starry sky. "Would you like to live in a very small universe, Ettin Gwarha?"

"No."

"I may be showing a bias, but I think this universe would be diminished if it lost humanity, though there's no question we are a difficult species."

"We could have found better neighbors," Ettin Gwarha said in agreement. "But it doesn't seem likely we'll be able to get rid of you. The scientists at the Helig Institute say there's no way to reproduce whatever happened at Kushaiin. Gehazi Thev does not agree. He believes we could cause such an event, but only in a region on the verge of collapse. Such a region would be full of old stars and strangeness. It's not the kind of place one would expect to find intelligent life. At most, in such a place, we might find a research station." Ettin Gwarha smiled briefly, his teeth flashing in the red light of the fire. "Hardly worth destroying in such an elaborate fashion. 'Avoid force in excess of the force needed,' as the old proverb says."

"Well, then," Sanders Nicholas said. "We are stuck with each other and with a very large universe."

"A disturbing situation," his lover said in agreement. "Though I think we can endure it.

"There is a final aspect which I pointed out to the Bundle. The situation we were considering never seemed likely. Destroying an entire system—or moving it out of our universe— is beyond any science we know; and I don't believe humanity will develop a weapon able to do this. Their technology, at least in the relevant areas, is not impressive; and their economic and political problems are so severe I don't think they can afford the necessary R and D. But if there are two star-faring species in the galaxy, there ought to be three and four and five. Suppose one of these other species is as hostile as humanity and better organized. Could they create a weapon able to destroy an entire area of space?

"That's one thing to consider. The other is, it's comparatively easy to make a single planet uninhabitable. Even humans could do it. Our home world was safe during the war, because humanity didn't know where it was. At some point they are going to learn. It's possible the human government knows already."

"Maybe," said Sanders Nicholas. "I certainly think you ought to assume they know. But they'd have to fight their way here, and I think the *hwarhath* can stop them. In addition, as you ought to remember, there is a peace treaty."

"Some treaties last. Others don't. This one has no breeding clause.* How can we trust an agreement that hasn't been made solid—knotted—through the exchange of genetic material?"

Sanders Nicholas did not answer this question, though the

---

* As every reader ought to know, humans and *hwarhath* can't interbreed.

answer is obvious. No treaty can be entirely trusted, if it lacks a breeding clause.

"Humans send women to the stars. Destroying the Solar System would not destroy their species. But our women prefer to stay at home. If something happened to our home planet, we would not be able to reproduce."

"You could borrow human biotechnology," Sanders Nicholas said.

"And produce cloned children who are raised by men?" asked Ettin Gwarha. His voice combined disgust and horror, as it should, of course.

"They wouldn't have to be clones."

"Well, suppose we decided to combine genetic material from men belonging to different lineages. Who would arrange the breeding contract, if our women were all gone? And how could men possibly raise children?"

"That leaves one obvious alternative," Sanders Nicholas said. "The *hwarhath* could do what humans have done: move women out of the home system. You must have thought of this."

"The Bundle has discussed the idea," Ettin Gwarha admitted. "And we have suggested it to the female government. Obviously, unfolding such a plan required far-in-front diplomatic ability. I was sent." He smiled briefly. "The idea was to establish colonies of young women in distant systems, in stations initially, since they are safer than the surface of any inhabitable planet.

"'To live without the advice of their mothers and senior female relatives?' the Weaving said. 'Absolutely not! It's the job of men to keep the home system safe. If you can't do it, then we need to talk about your failings and limitations. But we won't send our daughters to the stars.'"

"Did you suggest sending older women as well?"

"The Weaving didn't like the idea; nor was the Bundle entirely happy with it. There are frontmen whose mothers are still living, not to mention other female relatives. Space might become considerably less comfortable, if senior women began to travel."

"This is true," said Sanders Nicholas. "But comfort is not the only important aspect of life. I think the Weaving, and the

Bundle, are making a mistake." He glanced at Ettin Gwarha. "There's a human proverb which warns against putting all one's ova in one container. If anything happens to the container—"[*]

Ettin Gwarha tilted his head in agreement. "None the less, the Bundle is not going to argue with the Weaving over an issue that concerns women, at least not at the moment. Most likely, the home system is safe. As you have mentioned, it's well guarded. Anyone seeking to destroy this world would have to get past many armed and armored ships. But I'd like to see women among the stars. Some of them would enjoy the experience."

Sanders Nicholas made no answer, possibly because he was tired.

Soon after the two of them went to sleep. In the morning they continued their journey, going down out of the mountains to a railroad junction. There, at day's end, they caught a local train. All night they rattled through the Atkwa foothills, riding in a freight car, since there wasn't a passenger car for men.

He'd had worse accommodations, Sanders Nicholas said. At least there were windows, though not much to see: the hills as areas of darkness against a starry sky. Now and then the lights of a station flashed past, revealing nothing except an empty platform.

By sunrise they had reached the plain.

---

[*] Obviously, the author did some research on human culture, though it isn't certain what she thought this proverb means, since the word translated here as "ova" is much more likely to be used in reference to *hwarhath* reproduction than in reference to eggs for eating. The *hwarhath* know that humans have the ability to freeze human eggs and early-stage embryos and can grow foetuses to term outside a human uterus. The *hwarhath* have not developed a comparable technology; it strikes them as wrong to interfere with the female part of reproduction. However, they practice artificial insemination and have frozen their men's sperm from the moment it became possible to do so. Almost all *hwarhath* families have sperm banks. Prudent families have several banks in different locations. Most *hwarhath* think this is excessive caution. It's enough to have a solid building, several refrigeration units and a back-up power supply. The sperm of important men is, of course, kept in more than one refrigerator.

::::::::
●●●●●●●

UNDER THE
FLAG OF NIGHT

by Ian McDowell

Ian McDowell has an MFA in Creative Writing from the University of North Carolina at Greensboro. In his spare time, he practices Pai Lum Kung Fu and Chinese Lion Dancing. The author of two novels, Mordred's Curse *and* Merlin's Gift, *McDowell is best known for his short fiction, which has appeared in the anthologies* Crossroads: Stories of the Southern Literary Fantastic, Vanishing Acts, *and* Love in Vein, *as well as in* Asimov's Science Fiction, Weird Tales, Realms of Fantasy, The Magazine of Fantasy & Science Fiction, *and* Cemetery Dance. *McDowell also knows what it feels like to be hit on the head with a tire iron and to have the ball of one's thumb bitten off by an enraged iguana (fortunately, not at the same time). He lives in bohemian squalor in Greensboro, North Carolina, with several lizards of varying size.*

Of the story that follows, the author "Thanks Walter Jon Williams and Neil Gaiman for their invaluable feedback, but wishes it known that neither should be blamed for the much disputed claim that the pseudonymous Captain Charles Johnson was actually Daniel Defoe."

SHADED FROM THE blistering Jamaican sun by the *Sea Rat*'s overhang, the narrow alley was relatively cool, but so stank of fish, filth, and urine that Anne regretted taking the short cut. Cursing the mud that sucked at her boots, she turned a corner and found Gouger, Nate Whiskey, and Black Tom accosting a small, bespectacled man in what had once been a good coat, Nate and Tom pinning his arms while Gouger leered over him, giving the stranger the full benefit of his goblin countenance.

"I'll only be asking once," said Gouger gently, scratching the triangular hole where his nose had once been. "What business have you with that carrion?" He hooked his thumb downward at the canvas bag laying in the muck that fouled the stranger's brass-buckled shoes.

"Why don't you ask the man who hired you to get it back?" said the little man in an accent that suggested London and an education.

"The bargain with our employer was, no questions asked," said Gouger, his tone still cordial. "But it's a different kettle with *you,* my fancy lad, and, truth to tell, we're right curious as to why someone would pay good silver for a dead man's head." He pushed the little man's spectacles up onto his pale forehead with a grimy forefinger and held his right thumb close to his victim's exposed eyes. The nail on that thumb was exceedingly long and sharp, soaked in brine and coated with dried sap for extra hardness. "Mark this well," he said pleasantly. "It's the tool of a gouging man."

The little man's face was very white in the gloom. Anne wondered if he'd soiled his fine breeches yet.

"Back in Carolina, a poor man can't fight duels like the gentry do," continued Gouger, breath whistling through his exposed sinuses. "But he has his own honor to defend, and sometimes fancy folk wish to see him defend that honor and stake coin on it, in taverns and such. I used to make a pretty penny in Charleston, where sporting gentlemen wagered on me like a prize gamecock. They liked it best when I gouged, for I was a prime gouger. These thumbs could have a man's eyes on his cheeks as easily you might slide an oyster from his shell."

The little man's looked hard at Gouger's thumbs, but did not flinch. "Why are you not still in Charleston?"

Anne repressed a snort. Clearly, a man such as Gouger was in Jamaica for the simple reason that he faced jail or the gallows elsewhere. His was the sort that had once infested New Providence and Dry Tortuga, but now, in 1724, the onetime pirate strongholds were closed to the Sweet Trade, and its former practitioners dispersed across the Caribbean.

The small man had courage, for despite the sweat gleaming on his brow, his voice had remained calm. Most London gentlemen, if that's what he was, would be gibbering in terror. The question of just what he was doing here in Spanish Town kept her watching the encounter. So far, none of them had noticed her.

"I gave offense to the law, and it was agreed we should part company," said Gouger with a whistling snicker. "Now, that's the second question I've answered of you, and not gotten one answer back in turn. Hold him steady, lads."

Stocky, bald Nate Whiskey gave the little man's arm an extra twist, keeping his hand away from the hilt of his rapier. Anne suspected that Gouger had first engaged his attention while the other two crept up from behind, seizing him before that weapon could clear its scabbard. "Pop an eye on his cheek, Gouger," cackled Nate. "He'll sing then, right enough."

Despite his fine blond hair, the little fellow wasn't handsome, not like dear, dead Calico Jack, nor even boyishly pretty, like equally dear and dead Mary had been when dressed in men's clothes, but Anne found his wide-mouthed, snub-nosed monkey face appealing. What's more, he looked like he could reward a rescue with good coin. If the heavy jug she was carrying hadn't been nearly empty of watered-down rum, she might not have intervened, but it was almost drained, and Nate's shiny pate made a good target. Gulping down the dregs, she threw the jug and drew her cutlass.

The next moment, Nate was on his knees in the mud, cursing and clutching his head, while the little man had slipped free of Black Tom, kneeing his groin in the process. Before Gouger could draw a weapon of his own, the little man's sword was out and gleaming in the fading afternoon light.

"My thanks, friend," he said, his back to Anne. "Stand by me and we'll rout this lot."

"Bitch, this isn't your fight," growled Gouger.

"Ach, but it is now," said Anne lightly, happier than she'd been in a while. Life had been dreary since Calico Jack was hanged and she was pardoned.

Luckily, none of the ruffians had pistols, and only Black Tom wore a cutlass, while Gouger and Nate drew knives. They crouched there, glaring, until Anne lunged, her banshee laugh echoing in the alley, ready to carry the fight to them. She slashed at Black Tom, who backpedaled rather than attempting a parry, and when he lurched into Gouger and Nate, the three of them almost went down together.

"Come on, you bloody sheep," cackled Anne, "have the grace to die on your feet!" Rallying weakly, Black Tom aimed a cut at her that missed her by nearly a foot, and then her return stroke bit into his upper arm, making him yelp like a kicked dog and drop his weapon. The alley narrowed at that point, so much so that Gouger and Nate couldn't really get around him, and when he blundered into them, they took it as their cue to beat a full retreat. Cursing her over his shoulder, Black Tom followed them, and when she pursued them into the open street, howling like a monkey and scraping the tip of her cutlass against the wet bricks, the three of them broke into a clumsy run, their bow-legged gait reminding her of the way that panicked iguanas rear up on their hind legs. Anne waved in mock salute and watched them go.

The little man came up beside her, wiping his spectacles with a green silk handkerchief. Setting them back atop his pug nose, he gave her an appraising look, apparently noticing her sex for the first time, but not at all astonished at the sight of a grinning, six-foot Irishwoman in men's clothing waving a bloody sword. "Mistress Anne Bonny, I am in your debt."

She turned round, shaking long red hair out of her face. "True enough, but who are you, and how's it you know my name?"

To her surprise, he bowed and kissed her hand, with nothing satirical in the gesture. "Tobias Constantine, late of London, at your service. I read about you in Captain Johnson's book. Clearly, you could be no other."

"I know no Captain Johnson," said Anne, stepping back into the alley in search of the bag his assailants had been after. Someone had kicked it into a pile of refuse. When she picked it up, she saw that the drawstrings were undone.

Constantine had followed her. "That's because the good captain is the *nom de plume* of a friend of mine, a scrivener name of Defoe. His *General History of the Robberies and Murders of the Most*

Notorious Pyrates was all the rage in London when I left." He held his hands out for the bag. "Believe me, good lady, you don't wish to look in there."

She already had. "Been quite a while since this lad had aught below the neck." Indeed, the head was little more than a wizened skull cushioned on a tangled mass of filthy black hair, much of which appeared to be its beard. The bag also contained a flat, calfskin-wrapped bundle and several smaller packages. She pulled the drawstrings closed. "Whose is it?"

Constantine gently took the sack from her. "I'm surprised you don't know the gentleman. Captain Teach is as infamous as yourself, if less well preserved."

She smiled at that, more intrigued than ever. "I never met Blackbeard, for I'd found the docktowns of the Indies more hospitable than Carolina by the time he blockaded Charleston harbor, and he died not long after I went on the account." That last phrase was the common slang for taking up the pirate trade. "Did you steal his poor noggin from its pole in Virginia?"

"Not I," said Constantine, looking about the alley for something, which soon proved to be his tricorn hat, much of its Kelly green turned brown from soaking in a piss-smelling puddle. Wrinkling his nose in rather simian disgust, he dropped it back into the muck. "It was my former associate who sent a Negro shimmying up that pole, leaving another head in its place. I, in turn, appropriated it from *him*. As should be apparent, he wants it back, and is willing to hire the most desperate sort of fellows to fetch it."

Cutlass on shoulder, Anne followed him out into the sun-baked street, where heat danced on the cobblestones and shimmered in miniature rainbows over yellow pools of standing water. Above new Georgian brick and older palm-thatched adobe loomed St. Jago's whitewashed steeple, framed against the Blue Mountains that rose skyward into storm haze, but the wind was from the opposite direction, carrying the salt tang of the unseen and no longer much yearned-for sea, twenty miles down the Rio Cobre. That distance from Mother Ocean and her temptations was one reason that Anne lodged here in the new capital, rather than in the earthquake-sundered remnants of Port Royal.

It was too much to hope that Constantine might offer gainful employment, something she'd need now that she'd tired of being the mistress of the dissolute Christian Sotheby (who in truth had equally tired of her, once news reached him that Anne's da in Charleston had died leaving her still disowned). Nearly four years after her trial and her poor infant's death in childbirth, she wondered if she was fit for dangerous work. Well, there was only one way to find out.

"You'll be needing a bodyguard, Mister Constantine."

The expression on his pug face was unreadable, but his green eyes glittered behind his spectacles. "Indeed, Mistress Bonny. Are you as formidable as your reputation?"

Anne hadn't felt formidable in some time, but she drew herself up to her full considerable height. "I was at the head of every boarding party, the year and a half I sailed with Calico Jack," she said proudly. "Me and Mary Reed were the best at cutlass work he had, and the only ones who put up a fight when caught. Doesn't your Captain Johnson tell you that?"

Constantine nodded gravely. "Is it true that you and Mistress Reed disguised yourselves as men, and didn't recognize one another's sex until you'd exchanged amorous advances? I'd wondered if perhaps saucy Daniel made that part up."

Anne stepped forward, towering over him much as Gouger had earlier. "It's no business of yours who I made advances at, or when or why, my fancy lad. Of course everyone on board knew Mary and I were women, the way our teats flapped in our shirts. We wore trousers because we couldn't fight in petticoats, and I wear them now because this place is too damned hot for a dress. Now, will you hire me or no?"

Constantine's grin made him look more than ever like a shaved ape. "Truly, Fair Amazon, I cannot let such an offer pass! Name your price."

Anne thought about it for a moment. He couldn't be too rich, or he would have already hired himself a whole gang, the way his former partner apparently had. "Four shillings a day, a brace of pistols, and the full tale of why you're carrying that head about, who you stole it from, and what you plan to do with it."

Constantine considered a moment before again flashing that

crooked simian grin. "A bargain, then. I can give you two shillings now, with the rest at day's end, and your pistols once we find a gunsmith. As for my tale, that's best told in a tavern. Can you recommend one?"

Anne put her cutlass away. "That I can, though we'd best see the gunsmith first, with those dogs sniffing your heels. You'll be buying the rum, too. The real stuff, not watered grog."

Constantine extended an arm. "Of course, Madam. Lead on."

The Rum Spaniel was in a cool, dingy cellar beneath a stables, a gloomy cavern of a place where grizzled sea-rats slopped from cracked mugs at crude driftwood tables, cackling whores exposed their pocked breasts to likely customers, and every dice or card game was a potential knife fight. Constantine looked about with some dismay.

"Are we quite safe here, Mistress Bonny?" He had to strain to be heard over the uproar from the cockfight going on in the far corner.

Anne laughed. "I am, and you with me." She waved at a big, poxied-looking rogue with a crooked scar on his face and a bilious whore on his lap. "Ho, Ned Snavely, tell my friend here why you limp."

Ned's smile was all black gums. "Because you put a pistol ball in my knee when we were taken, you vicious bitch!" His laugh ended in an explosive belch. "Don't trifle with that one, Mister," he said to Constantine. "She's more dangerous than any man in this place."

The barkeep, a sour-looking lout with a dirty beard the color of seaweed, nodded impassively at the sight of proffered coin and handed her a fresh jug of rum. Anne cocked her thumb at her new employer. "My friend's a gentleman and doesn't swig. Give us cups, you graceless git." To her surprise, he rummaged under the bar and actually found two, handing them over with a muttered curse punctuated by a fart. "Ned was one of the few men on Calico Jack's ship they didn't hang," Anne said quietly as she took Constantine's arm and steered him toward a table. "If you're a sea artist, meaning, in his case, a good navigator, the judge will likely believe you when you claim to have been forced, because most pirates have no sailing skills worth a damn, and will press into service every good seaman they can find. 'Course, just like at most pirate trials, every man of the crew except for Jack himself claimed he'd been forced, but only Ned, the carpenter, and the musicians were believed, and Ned was lying."

"Why'd you shoot him, if he was one of your own party?" said Constantine softly as he settled gingerly onto his creaking stool, his face still shining in the gloom.

She remembered it all then, that fateful night off Negril Point; the midnight breeze lifting her dank hair and plucking at her loose shirt, Mary's bare bosom gleaming milkwhite in moonlight as she spread her own shirt on dry planking and idly pounded lice from it with her dirk pommel, the treacle-drip of tar from the rustling shrouds, and then the dark gliding shape of that bastard Barnet's stealthy privateer. The rest of the crew had been drinking below decks with a gang of Portuguese turtle fishermen, and stayed there when the women raised the alarm. "It's the downfall of most pirates, getting themselves too drunk to fight, and they cowered in their cups when the enemy hove to. Mary and me yelled and cursed and even fired into the hold in hopes of putting some spirit into the sodding bastards, but though I lamed Ned, and Mary killed another man, it did no good, and she and I had to fight alone. We gave a good account of ourselves, though." She wondered what he'd think if she took off her shirt and showed him the scars, one neatly between her breasts from a cutlass slash, the other a few inches above her right hip, where she'd been lightly kissed with a boarding axe. "Better to die like men than to be hanged like dogs, I yelled down at them, but they were too busy quaking in their puke to listen to me. I later reminded my man Calico Jack of that, when they dragged him off to the gallows."

She and Mary would have swung beside Jack and the rest, if not for their swelling bellies. Christian Sotheby, one of several planters familiar with Anne's estranged father, had been an avid spectator at the trial, and Anne's pregnancy had not yet marred her figure. Loving Jack well enough in her fashion, but having no particular desire to rot in jail for the sake of fidelity, she'd met Sotheby's appraising gaze with a bold one of her own, and his influence bought her pardon. Having no wealthy relatives, Mary had given birth behind bars, and died there, of childbed fever. Anne's own babe had perished soon after.

She swigged her rum, feeling it sting in the cavity where she'd recently lost a back tooth. So far, she'd kept all her front ones. "Enough of me. Why are you sneaking about alleys with Blackbeard's head?"

Tobias had yet to sip from his cup. "I was asking for directions to the Negro quarter. Those rogues offered to lead me, then turned on me once we were off the main street."

"And what do you want in Black Town?" Despite the name, it was more lane than town, as the district of Free Coloreds was understandably small, the vast majority of Jamaica's African-derived population either slaves on the plantations or Maroons, their escaped descendants in the mountains.

"I'd heard tales of the magic called Obeah. I hoped to find someone who could make this head talk for me."

Anne nearly spit out her rum. "Why, man, you're madder than I thought!"

"Nay, not at all. My former colleague Edmund could bring words from its dead lips. That's why I took it from him, once I found out who he truly serves."

This talk was making Anne's head spin more than any amount of drink could do. "It's witchcraft you're speaking of! They *hang* folk for that!"

Constantine had been rummaging in his bag. Producing the parcel, he unwrapped it, revealing a leather-bound book with brass clasps, a couple of candles, a quill pen, a small copper vial, and several musket balls. "Not so much any more, and never as much here in the New World as the old, despite the unhappy events at Salem. The Colonies have their share of Cunning Men, who are largely free to practice their arts, and in Pennsylvania, there are the High Magisters of Germantown. But while I have some small experience of such Natural and Scientific Magick, my skills don't extend to necromancy."

Anne made the sign of the cross, something she'd not done in a decade. It was more sailors' superstition than good Irish Catholicism that shivered her spine. "I know an Obeah Woman more cunning than any hedgewife or apothecary. If anyone could make what's in yon bag talk, it's Mother Patience. But where's the profit in such an unnatural thing?"

Constantine lowered his voice further. "I want to ask Blackbeard where he buried his treasure."

Anne laughed explosively, her fear leaving her chest like phlegm. "You're daft, Toby! Is your Captain Johnson such a fool as to claim any pirate ever hid his spoils in the ground? The Sweet Trade's not near so lucrative as landlubbers think. Back in the days of the Red Sea Men and the buccaneers, maybe there was some that took great riches, from heathens in India and Spanish galleons here, but those days were over when my granny was a girl. Mostly, we seize bolts of cloth and barrels of whiskey and other trade goods, which we sell to coastal villagers in the Carolinas, and other places where folks don't like the Crown's tariffs."

Constantine looked at her with schoolmaster gravity, the ruddy color fully returned to his monkey face. "The treasure days aren't so long past as you presume. Blackbeard was never a Red Sea Man, but he first took sail as one of the last buccaneers, before England made uneasy peace with Spain and gave Henry Morgan a governorship for hanging his former colleagues. Before he turned his attention to the American Colonies, Blackbeard took at least one Spanish ship bound from Panama to Barcelona, and on that ship, he found a most rare prize."

Anne snorted. "You'll be after fairy gold next. Suppose Teach did such a thing, why would he ever bury it in the ground? A pirate crew divides its spoils, with the captain getting only one share more than anyone else. No man's share is ever large enough to be worth hoarding. Even those that did take treasure ships rather than merchant goods soon spent all their loot in taverns and whorehouses."

Constantine nodded, unoffended by either her scorn or her familiarity. "True enough, my bonny Annie, but in *this* case, Teach had something that couldn't be divided or sold to a common merchant. It looked like a plain iron pot, but if the merest drop of food or drink was poured into it, it filled to the brim, and stayed full no matter how much was scooped from it, only becoming empty when upended. The priest who took a mortal wound trying to keep it from him told him, with his dying breath, that the vessel was a very holy thing, a sacred relic brought to the Americas by Saint Brendan the Navigator, which Spain had discovered on a remote island and was sending to the Pope himself."

Anne shook her head. The man was surely possessed of a more extravagant kind of folly than that which had first driven her to sea. Perhaps, under those fine burgundy breeches, his little monkey cock was dripping with the pox, which had long since rotted his brain. Ach, no, that was too evil a thought, and besides, hadn't she been most deathly bored of late? Whatever else his fancies might be, they were anything but dull.

"How do you know this?" she said, as gravely as she could.

He straightened a bit. "I'm an initiate in the School of Night, a secret order founded by Sir Walter Raleigh. A body of our eldest and most learned Masters had this story from Israel Hands, a former mate of Blackbeard's, who was lamed by him even more casually than you lamed Mister Snavely over there, and who became one of London's countless beggars when the knee his one-time captain so playfully shattered made him unfit for your so-called Sweet Trade. That is why I and my former colleague Edmund Love were dispatched to the New World, to bring this treasure of Blackbeard's back to Britain, where its powers and properties may be measured and studied by men well-learned in Scientific Magick and Natural Philosophy. Unfortunately, Captain Love loves Donnish coin more than the English Crown, and has been secretly working for our enemies. I considered Edmund a dear friend as well as a colleague, but I could not countenance his treachery. It is now up to me to ensure this wondrous object doesn't fall into foreign hands. If doing so requires wringing speech from a dead man's head, so be it!"

Anne wished she were by herself someplace quiet, where she could stretch out her long frame before a crackling fire, or better yet, in a swaying hammock, and digest what Constantine was telling her. That sparkle in his eyes could be madness or secret knowledge or some impossible-to-untangle mingling of both. Once again, she made the sign of the Holy Cross, her finger seeming to move as sluggishly as though the smoky, flickering air were water.

It had gotten oddly silent in the tavern. "Oh, aye, cross yourself, bitch! You'd best be making your peace with God!" She looked up to see Gouger, his face more ghoulish than usual in the candlelight, aiming a pistol at her from the stairway, Nate Whiskey crouched behind him, a bandage on his head.

"You'd best not miss," opined Ned Snavely, still fingering his popeyed whore. "She's fast and mean, and will have your guts out if you only wound her." The other denizens of the tavern watched with interest, and several of the cockfighters began to make whispered wagers.

The barkeep bent down and came up holding a blunderbuss. "There'll be no shooting of women here," he growled. "Least ways, not of any as well-known as Mistress Bonny. Besides, you could hit the man with her, who's not only a paying customer, but looks like quality, with relatives that might have Governor Rogers' ear." This was the first time, Anne thought inanely, she'd ever heard him say more than three words together.

Gouger sat on the stone steps, his pistol still trained on Anne, although he'd have to get much closer to have a real chance of hitting her. It made her feel warm inside to think that this fearsome-looking ogre might be too scared of her to come down to the tavern floor. "I only need to keep her and her gentleman here until Black Tom comes back with our employer. He's quality too, and will have good coin for any that helps in their apprehension."

"Well, that's different then," said the barkeep, putting down the blunderbuss without giving Anne so much as an apologetic shrug. Men are all bastards, she thought, not for the first time.

Constantine had struck a match to his candles and was using one to dribble a wax circle on the table. "Some help you're being, Toby," she said, not caring if he rankled.

"I'll be more help than you can imagine, should this work," he said through gritted teeth. "Keep him talking." He then unstopped his copper vial, which proved to contain a silvery, metallic-smelling liquid, and began writing with it on the tabletop, pausing to unclasp his big book and flip through its pages until, apparently having found what he wanted, he returned to his brushstrokes.

"What the Devil are you doing?" she hissed, intrigued despite her irritation.

"The Adversary has nothing to do with this," he muttered in a distracted tone. "My *gramarye*, so to speak, is the *Sixth and Seventh Books of Moses*, not some warlock's black tome. It contains the lost magical knowledge of the Hebrews, as was given by God and his Angels to Moses himself. Alas, I know only some of its secrets, for the magisters of Germantown were loath to reveal the whole of their art to me. Let us hope I learned enough."

Anne stood up and made herself stretch with what she hoped passed for catlike nonchalance, then thumbed the hilt of her cutlass. "Who thinks Gouger is a craven dog for squatting there with a cocked pistol rather than coming down here and facing me with steel?"

Several onlookers hooted. "No man who's seen you fight," brayed Ned Snavely. Taking his hand out of his whore's dress, he raised his bottle to Gouger. "I have little love for the bitch who lamed me, and wouldn't mind seeing her bleed, but truth is truth, and if you're fool enough to come down here and face her, you'll soon be missing more than your nose."

Gouger picked either snot or a scab from the hole in his face. "I don't cross blades with women," he said in a tone that suggested he'd be more than willing to if he thought he'd win. "Now, if the strumpet would put down her cutlass and wrestle me, that's another story. I've not had a good gouging match in longer than I can remember, and I'd enjoy sticking my thumbs into those proud eyes."

Anne was calculating the odds of going for the shiny new pistols in her sash. If she made as if to draw and fire, would Gouger pull the trigger of his own weapon? If so, he'd likely miss, and she could rush forward and fire her own shot from a more accurate range. Deciding to chance it, she filled her lungs for a banshee scream.

As if he'd known her intent, Constantine grasped her belt. "Sit down, Mistress Bonny. In a moment, we'll be able to leave here calmly and safely."

Her blood was up, making the temptation to shake off his hand and rush Gouger very fierce, but then she looked down into Constantine's eyes, and something in that twinkling green compelled her trust. Besides, she was being paid to do what she was told.

She sat. Upon the table top, Constantine had drawn a six-pointed star within a circle, with words written at each point of the star, and in the spaces outside it, like so:

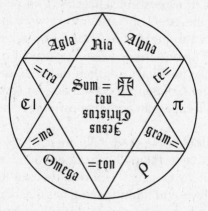

As she watched, marveling at his speed and artistry, he placed a musket ball in the center of the star, directly over the upside-down *Jesus.* "I've substituted the name of the Savior himself for that of Moses," he said softly. "Can there be diabolism in that? If you don't trust in me, do so in Him, and in His name take my hands." She did so, swayed more by those eyes that locked hers over the dancing candleflame than glib talk of Christ, and marveled at their smoothness. Even dear dead Mary had possessed a harder and more callused grip than this. Her reverie was interrupted when he began to chant.

"*I, Tobias Constantine, a servant of God, call upon and conjure thee, Spirit Alymon, by the most dreadful words: Sather, Ehomo, Geno, Poro, Jehovah, Elohim, Volnah, Denach, Alonlam, Ophiel, Zophiel, Sophiel, Habriel, Eloha, Alesimus, Dileth, Melohim, and through the holiest words by which thou canst be compelled, that thou giveth thy protection to myself and this woman for as long as this candle flame shall burn. Fulfill now what I command thee, so surely as Christ will come to judge the living and the dead. Fiat, fiat, fiat.*"

Letting go of Anne's hands, Constantine put his book and paraphernalia back into his bag, the strings of which he drew and tied. Standing up, he straightened his coat. "I need to prove to you that my art is not false mummery," he said quietly, "and this seems as good a demonstration as any. If I've prepared correctly, I am temporarily safe from Mister Gouger's pistol. Mind you, this conjuration is not one that I've had the courage to put to scientific test, and it's possible I've botched it. But if he does shoot me dead, he'll have discharged his weapon, leaving you with two loaded ones, not to mention that cutlass you use so well. Good luck to you, Mistress Bonny, and I pray you, wish the same to me."

Before she could answer this, he walked toward the stairway. "Hold your fire, my goblin-faced friend. At least until I've reached the foot of the steps, where your ball will have a better chance of hitting me."

Gouger made a sound that might have been a snort if he'd had a nose. "Are you daft, you fancy ponce? Don't think I won't shoot you!"

"I expect you to," said Constantine. "Here, let me open my jacket and shirt, for I paid too much for them to have you putting holes in them. Are you a good enough shot to hit me directly in the heart?" Anne could not see his bare chest from where she sat, and some distracted part of herself wondered if it was as hairless as a girl's.

"The fool thinks himself a Hard Man," said Nate Whiskey, pulling a dagger from his belt.

"Not I," said Constantine, who was almost at the foot of the stairs. "Your employer, Captain Love, can make that claim, but I'm not naturally proof against bullet and blade, and so must take additional measures of protection. I should be in your range now, if you have the courage to hold your pistol steady. Are you going to shoot me, or is it your intention to frighten me to death with that ugly face of yours? Come on, my oafish friend, I don't have all day."

Several of the more hardened sea dogs actually chuckled, and there were low murmurs all around them. Anne heard the clink of coins, as more wagers were being offered. "Shoot him, dammit!" snarled Nate Whiskey.

Gouger shook his head. "Something's not right. Besides, if I do kill him, that bitch has two pistols in her belt."

"Don't let that concern you," said Constantine. "Mistress Bonny, if this unlovely lout kills me, I give you leave to divide the money in my purse between yourself, him, and his comrade, and order you to let them have the contents of my bag." His rapier flickered from its scabbard. "As you can see, I am not unarmed. Either you will kill me, or I'll run you through the body. Which is it?"

"Go to Hell," said Gouger, raising his pistol. The gunshot was very loud in that dank space, and smoke shrouded the stairway.

Standing, Anne drew her pistol, half-expecting to see her daft employer come stumbling out of the powdersmoke, blood pouring from his ruptured chest. Instead, something far smaller bounced down the steps and rolled across the tavern floor. Stooping, she inspected it. It was a pistol ball, misshapen as if by unyielding impact and still hot to the touch. Crossing herself for the third time in the night and the decade, she rose, picked up Constantine's bag and strode toward the stairs. The smoke's acrid tendrils were curling away into the general haze, revealing much the same tableau as before Gouger had fired. Taking her place beside Constantine, she glanced at his chest, which was indeed pale and hairless, and quite unmarked.

"How interesting," said Constantine softly. "I actually felt the ball hit me, although it didn't hurt. Now, shall we rout them?" Despite his calm words, she saw that he was shaking.

Anne looked up at Gouger's pop-eyed face, so white that it looked even more skull-like than usual. She smiled as she took aim at the cavity above his mouth and pulled the trigger. More smoke hid him and Nate from view, then Gouger's body came sliding out of it, blood bubbling from the hole where his nose had been, which was now larger and less triangular.

Constantine stared down at the corpse and whistled. "There's a shot a worthy of a dueling gentlemen," he said. "I knew you were fierce and formidable, Mistress Bonny, but had no idea you possessed such skill."

Actually, she'd been lucky, for she should have aimed at the broader target of his chest, but the nasal cavity had been too tempting. She'd dropped the pistol and drawn her second one, and would have taken a less chancy shot at Nate Whiskey, but he was already fled up the stair and out the door.

"Take your bag, Toby," she said to Constantine, then retrieved and sheathed her discharged pistol. Holding the loaded one ready, she led her employer up into the fading daylight.

Mother Patience lived amidst hovels of mud-brick, but her own small dwelling was of corral and white-washed plaster, so clean and plain it might have been a tropical nun's cell. The pale interior accentuated the indigo blackness of her face; unlike almost every other free Negro in Spanish Town, she appeared more African than Creole, for she owed her freedom to skillfully midwifing three generations of Sotheby's, rather than the impulse of a white father. Of course such liberty had not been secured until she taught her arts to a daughter, now an old woman herself, who remained in bondage on the Sotheby Plantation. Beneath her bright red scarf, her head was almost hairless, and the folded legs visible beneath the tuck of her calico smock were thin and sharp-kneed as those of a cricket, but her skin was remarkably smooth, as if time had polished rather than withered her.

There were no furnishings other than two large unglazed clay pots. Mother Patience directed her two guests to sit before her on a mat of dried marsh grass, which had been spread over a soft floor of what looked and felt like finely sifted white beach sand, making the dwelling resemble the inside of an hourglass. Constantine seemed fascinated by it, squatting at the edge of the woven mat and pouring a small quantity from hand to hand like a child.

"Bone," said Mother Patience in a voice like wind in the sugar cane.

"Beg pardon?"

"You hear me right, Cunning Man. That be bleached and powdered bone, mixed with crushed corral and salt."

If she'd hoped for a reaction of horror or surprise, he didn't afford her one, but instead blew the powder off his palm, tucked his coattails under him and folded himself down beside Anne with a grace more cat than monkey. "Clearly, Good Lady, you have just the sort of knowledge I seek." Untying his bag, he produced Blackbeard's head without preamble. "Can you really make what's left of this fierce fellow talk?"

Mother Patience smiled, revealing four upper teeth and three lower ones, more than many white women her age still had. "Keep calling me a lady and maybe I make yon dead pirate sing. Can't promise him be hitting all the right notes, but probably couldn't do that in life."

"You can make a head talk, but you couldn't save my baby?" *Ach,* thought Anne, *there's the rum I've been drinking all day talking for me.* However, there was no anger in the old woman's button eyes.

"Saved you and the child both, didn't I, when you were bearing it? Might have saved it again, if Mister Sotheby had summoned me when it first sickened. Not my fault, him not caring so much if a dead pirate's bastard died. Maybe the poor babe's mother didn't care so much, neither."

Anne felt herself flush. Her father would have horse-whipped a Negro for speaking to her like that, but she'd ceased being her father's child long before she let Calico Jack steal her off to sea. "I never wanted it dead," she said, looking down at the pattern her finger traced in the powder that Mother Patience claimed was bone.

"Maybe so, maybe no" said the old Negress. "But done is done, dead is dead. None of that concerns what this fancy Cunning Man of yours want me doing now. He think I can make Captain Blackbeard say where his treasure. That fat book no tell you how to do that, Cunning Man?"

Constantine smiled ruefully. "While my delvings into Natural and Scientific Magick and the Christian Kabbalah have given me several unorthodox skills, this isn't one of them. Perhaps that's a good thing, for I've lost friends, and more than friends, whose voices I would dearly love to hear again, and if I could still converse with them I might have scant time for the living."

"You'd tire soon enough of duppies and bone folk," chuckled

Mother Patience. "Not much comfort in their talk." Anne wondered what Calico Jack would say to her, if she could still hear his salty baritone. And Mary's soft whisper, would it be so gentle and caressing after four years in the ground? If only there was more rum. But no, she was too close to puke and stupor as it was, and surely this strange work required her wits.

From somewhere, Mother Patience had produced a wooden wand with a dried chicken foot at one end and the long black tail feather of a Doctor Bird at the other. "Be still, both of you, else you make it difficult." Poking her pink tongue out between her dark lips, she swayed with surprising suppleness, whisking her wand over the sand around them, tracing not decipherable words as Constantine had done on the tavern table, but patterns as seemingly random as the ones low, windswept branches make at a beach's edge. "Put Captain No-Body down between us," she said, grinning wide at her own pun, "and I'll have him talking soon enough."

Constantine placed the head in the center of the woven mat so that it was surrounded on all sides by their knees, its tangled hair forming a cushion that kept it from rolling over. Mother Patience scooped up a small handful of the bone powder, if that's what it truly was, and, bending down, blew it like a kiss between the former pirate's yellow teeth.

"Be closing your eyes now, and holding hands."

Once again, Constantine's hand seemed so small and soft in her grip. Anne hadn't held hands with a child since she was a child herself, but this was surely what it felt like. She didn't like shutting her eyes, not just for wariness of danger, but because of the faces that swarmed there when she did, Jack's angry red one on the gallows cliff, Mary's pale dead one in the gloom of what had served the Kingston courthouse as both jail and wine cellar. But here in Mother Patience's house, she found a more gentle and unpeopled darkness behind her eyelids.

"You living keep your eyes shut, no matter what you hear," said Mother Patience sternly. "Now Captain Teach, time you be talking!"

The next voice was deep and male and not the least bit ghostly, with a Bristol accent. "By the devil's smoking arsehole, what the fucking Hell d'ye want with me, you coal-colored crone?"

"Me want nothing of you, Bone Captain," replied Mother Patience's voice with the slightest trace of regal scorn, "but these folk do. Tell them where you buried treasure."

"What, think they I had nothing better do with gold and silver than hide it in dirt?" boomed the male voice, which seemed to come from exactly the same direction as that of Mother Patience. *It's coming out of her, not the head,* thought Anne. Once she would have dismissed this as the trick of a Market Day mountebank, but not after today.

"Not gold or silver, Good Captain," soothed Constantine's voice, "nor the sugar and hides you sold at Beaufort and Bath. But somewhere here in Jamaica lies a plain iron pot, like a rude kettle for seething oil from seal flesh. Despite its plainness, a Spanish priest forced you to give him a mortal wound before he'd let go of it, and you yourself were enough impressed by it to hide it away in the ground."

There were several long minutes of silence, during which Anne resisted the urge to open her eyes. When the reply finally came, it was much softer. "The dying priest said it was the vessel Christ served the Last Supper from. I pissed into it to show my scorn for such Popish nonsense, only to see my urine turn to pure clear water and rise to the brim. Nothing ever frighted me so much as that, not even feeling a boarding axe bite through my neck. Come Judgment Day, when we sleeping dead are called up whole again, will I be cast into an even hotter part of the fire because I pissed in Jesu's favorite pot? No wonder I spent my remaining years preparing myself for Hell!"

Constantine's grip on Anne's hand tightened in apparent excitement. "Fire may yet indeed await you, Captain Teach, but not because that cauldron was the Grail, although that may be what Brendan believed when he brought it to the New World. It's something older, with powers of neither Christ nor the Adversary. Now, tell us where you buried it, and we'll let you sleep till Judgment."

"Sleep is sweet enough, even with fire at the end of it, but quim is sweeter. Place me in yon red-haired wench's lap. I'll doze better after that, even if the part of me that would have most appreciated what lies between those fine big thighs fed the sharks and jewfish years ago."

"You are too bold, Captain Teach." Constantine's grip tightened further, as though he was trying to be protective and reassuring, and Anne found herself repressing a snicker.

"Always was, but that's my price."

The easy sound of Anne's own voice in reply surprised her. "Don't be a git, Toby, I've held much worse between my legs." After a few moments' silence, the head was gently placed on her lap, though she never knew who moved it there. Fortunately, it was motionless after that. *Feels no worse than a dried coconut or a horseshoe crab shell,* she told herself. *As long as he doesn't ask me to remove my breeches I'll be fine.*

"Oh yes, that's a sweet cushion indeed" came the voice, definitely sounding a few feet further away and higher than the thing in Anne's lap. "I apologize, Fair Lady, for my coarse speech. Were I still alive, I'd put silk ribbons in your hair and make you one of my wives."

"Nay, Captain Teach, you'd not do that, but I might tie such ribbons in your beard and make you one of my husbands." How much rum *had* she drunk, that she could banter so easily with the dead? "I am not some tavern wench, but Anne Bonny, late of the *William,* and, despite my sex, as bold a member of the Brethren as yourself. Will you not share your secret with a fellow Sea Rover?"

Laughter boomed then, so loud it seemed to come from every part of the small dwelling. "Can one of the Brotherhood be a sister? Yet I don't doubt your tale's truth, as I've seen marvels enough in my time, and this new one surely deserves some token in exchange, with my secret all I have for barter. Ah, to have met you when I was whole and full of breath and blood and fire! I tried to make my ship a merry Hell, but it would have been merrier still with such a she-devil on board! Listen, and I'll tell you where I buried what you seek."

The forty-seven-mile journey had taken all afternoon and the better part of a night in the rickety, two-wheeled cart drawn by a single swaybacked nag. Anne's arse and thighs were in agony;

she would have much preferred to have come by ketch or other ocean-going vessel, but this had proved the easiest way to slip out of Spanish Town without attracting undue notice. A proper carriage or two-horse curricle would have been faster and more comfortable, but Constantine's purse and moneybelt were apparently not so inexhaustible as the magic cauldron he claimed to be seeking, and this necessitated the purchase of such mean transport.

Christian Sotheby had spoken more than once of Derbyshire, calling it a prime example of the folly of lollygagging in London while an Agent managed your West Indian estates, as the majority of Jamaica's landowners were wont to do. Built near the mouth of the Black River, the sugar plantation had floundered under a succession of incompetent, drunken, or downright larcenous trustees, who treated the slaves with excessive brutality while robbing their employer blind. When Derbyshire's owner had arrived with every intent to set things right, he found himself in the midst of a revolt. A Maroon raiding party had come down from the Cockpit Country, and the nearby garrison that might otherwise have quickly restored order was too busy chasing the raiders back to what the soldiers nervously called the Land of Look Behind, with the result that the uprising was entirely successful. Derbyshire's owner was killed, his great house and fields burnt, and much of his dusky property escaped to join their wild brethren in the thorny upland hollows.

Moreover, there'd been no legitimate will, and now, four decades later, Derbyshire's aging heirs were still disputing its disposition in Chancery, where the case might well drag out through several more generations. The earthquake that tipped Port Royal into the sea had not confined its depredations to the eastern end of the island, and while the changes it had wrought to the coastline around Starvegut Bay and the courses of the Black River's tributaries had been comparatively subtle, they eventually consigned much of the plantation's acreage to salt marsh. No wonder that local tradition held this to be a haunted place, or that Blackbeard had chosen it for a hiding spot.

To the left of the rutted, weed-choked wagon road was a strip of beach, where crabs scuttled like the bent ghosts of tiny hunchbacks over a pale ribbon of moonwashed sand. Out on the bay, fishing bats dove like silent gulls after their prey, while inland, their smaller cousins chased a swarming constellation of fireflies across the starry canvas of the night. This side of sand and shell, the rustling reeds answered the breakers with frogsong and the incongruous lapdog yips of lizard courtship; the whole halfseen nightworld was either eating or fucking, and Anne would have been happy to do either, or better yet, sleep like the rest of daylight's citizens. But no, Constantine was currently doing that, his small, silkhaired head resting on her comparatively broad shoulder, while she took her turn at the reins. *He trusts me,* she thought, *me who could easily cut his throat and take his fine clothes and what coin he still possesses, could have it done it many times now, and he knows me for a villainous wench who's done far worse. So, who was wiser, Mary who swore she saw such good in me, or da, who called me the Devil's own vixen?*

Beyond the reeds and mangroves was a stand of logwood, and, beyond that, the skeleton of Derbyshire's great hall poked its ribs above hogweed and thistle. Here a broken wall, there a single column, and, black against the moon, the crumbled chimney that Blackbeard (or Mother Patience) had said to look for.

Suddenly, Anne's stomach rumbled louder than any frog or gecko, and Constantine stirred beside her. "I've never heard that sound from a woman before," he said thickly, "not that it surprises me to find your bowels as vocal as any man's."

Anne laughed and handed him the reins, stretching the kinks out of her neck and shoulders. "So, were you satiric when you addressed me with such former delicacy? Familiarity's the death of courtesy."

He rubbed his eyes, then fumbled for the ivory case that contained his spectacles. "Fair Amazon, there are times when you speak like one not unlettered."

Anne cleared her throat and spat. "And much good it's done me, too. My father was a Belfast barrister before his siring me upon a chambermaid brought him to disgrace and Charleston. He passed on a pisspot's fill of learning, though I've forgotten most of it. Still, I can read well enough, and even understand flowery meanings. If we survive this, you'll have to gift me with your Captain Johnson's book of pirates, which you say makes such free use of my not-so-good name. How think you the captain would react if I hied myself to London and addressed him in the too, too sullied flesh?"

The small man laughed. "Annie, your capacity for surprising me is as boundless as the ocean's capacity for making me nauseous, albeit with far more pleasant results."

Anne clapped him on the back with sufficient force to knock his eyeglasses into his lap "Why Toby, such sweet words will surely win my girlish heart!" Deftly retrieving the spectacles, she set them back upon his nose. Had it been daylight, she might have fluttered her lashes in coy burlesque, although in truth the night was bright enough to half discern such a satirical gesture.

He'd noticed this too, and was looking upward at the emblazoned sky. "In England, the stars always appeared to peep through the blanket of the dark, to borrow a phrase of Shakespeare's probably not worth borrowing. Here the heavens seem to be studded with them on the outside, as if they were chased with many jewels, like Milton's firmament of living sapphires. They give such light that the moon scarcely needs show his great red drunken face. But we should attend your stomach rather than the sky. Is there any food left?"

At Dry River, a higgler had sold them mangoes and plantains and a necklace of mudfish and god-dammies, salt-dried and fried crisp, but all that now remained were fruit skins and fish tails. "I'll be fine; hunger's no greater a discomfort than sobriety. Let's stretch our legs and piss, then we'll start digging." The cart behind them contained two shovels and a pickaxe, as well as rope and pulleys.

The tools soon proved of little help. Blackbeard had dug a shallow hole beside the broken chimney, but he'd covered it with fallen bricks rather than dirt, and these proved more easily removed by hand. Within an hour, lamplight revealed a plain black iron pot, no different from the dutchies in which Negroes simmered ackee and saltcod. It was large enough that Constantine could have bathed in it, although Anne's big frame would have been cramped, and thus too heavy for them to lift, even with Anne's considerable strength, and she wished that enough coin had remained in Constantine's purse and belt to hire a jobber gang from a freelance slave driver, even though that would have made it nigh impossible to have kept their whereabouts secret from any pursuers.

However, despite his small smooth hands, Constantine proved to have some mechanical skill, and contrived a method of using the ropes and pulleys (along with planking and the muscles of the aged draft horse, which he unhitched) to haul the pot up into the cart. She'd wondered if he was going to test its alleged powers, for both her remaining skepticism and empty belly would have been satisfied if she could but cast the scraps of their last meal into it and watch it fill to the brim with whole fresh plantains and new-fried fish. But what if it didn't? She had somehow acquired no small affection for this strange, delicate monkey-man, and did not wish to see him revealed as suffering from delusions. No, not just yet.

Dawn could not be far off, yet it seemed much darker than before, as the now-heavier cart protested each foot of the pitted road that threaded along the bay. Stars and moon retreated behind a veil of cloud, and fog was rolling in over the murmuring breakers, cooling the sweat that glued Anne's shirt to the small of her back and her breeches to her buttocks. That damp blanket seemed to dull the spirits of the frog and lizard chorus, so that the only sounds were the muffled waves, the dull metronome of hoofbeats and the creaking discord of the cart. In such sullen darkness, even a white person might half-hear duppies moaning in the unseen reeds.

"So we don't go directly to Heaven or Hell when we die, but are wormfood until judgment?" asked Anne, having nothing better to stave off clammy silence than that grim query.

She could see the barest dark shape of the man beside her, where an hour ago she could have discerned the motion of his speaking mouth. "Assuming that there shall be a judgment, something which the Deists who believe that God made the world and then drew apart from it would dispute. But no, nothing in the Gospels indicates the immediacy of Hell or Heaven, despite the Italian poet's dream."

Anne mulled this over. "Maybe not, but the priests say otherwise. Or least they did, last time I bothered listening." She felt, although she could not see, his small hand on hers, and knowing little of horses despite her plantation girlhood, wondered how theirs could keep to the road.

Constantine snorted. "The Church fathers decided Christian folk would be better behaved if judgment were death's immediate denouement, rather than some as yet unwritten sequel. Therefore, we've been taught to speak of our departed as though they're already breakfasting in Heaven or Hell, rather than still slumbering in the bedclothes of decay. Damn me, but it's dank and dark! Something unnatural is afoot."

Their horse had stopped, and now it made a low and most unequine sound, more groan than nicker. Constantine fumbled beside her. "Matches, where are my matches? Had I some light, I could find my book and read aloud a spell to lift this darkness. What a fool I am, to have not committed such a thing to memory!"

"And for many another reason, also," said a soft and cultured voice from no place in particular. "Really, Tobias, our former masters would be disappointed, to find you so easily waylaid as this!"

His hand left Anne's, and she felt rather than saw him sit bolt upright beside her. "Your former masters, Edmund. They are still mine." Then softer, "Have *your* pistols ready, Annie."

And then the fog was gone, like mist clearing from a mirror when a window is opened. With it went the clammy darkness, for the first rays of sun shone bloody on the bay, silhouetting a two-masted lugger at anchor there. No more than twenty yards from where their cart had halted, a pinnace of sixteen oars had been hauled up the brightening beach. What must be its former occupants were now beside them, at least ten armed men, most of whom Anne recognized, standing all in a line and holding hands like children. Letting go of each other with some visible embarrassment, they rubbed their eyes and shook their heads, some muttering curses, others prayers.

They couldn't see in the dark fog, thought Anne, *but he could, and he led them up the beach and straight to us.*

The man she was looking at could be none other than

Constantine's Captain Edmund Love. At first, she might have taken him for a Quaker, what with his black hat and coat and breeches, his white hose and buckled shoes. He wore no firearm, but the slim rapier at his side belied the pacific first impression.

Without preamble, she raised both pistols, cocked and fired, then lashed the reins and shouted wordlessly at the quivering horse. Powder smoke stung her eyes, her eardrums echoed with the twin shots, but despite such loud inducement, the cart did not move. When the smoke cleared, everything remained as frozen as it had when Gouger shot Constantine in the tavern. As before, she found herself looking on with strange detachment, no detail more important than another. The horse still shivered in his tracks, shaking its head from side to side, ears cocked and eyes rolled back to white, as if being invisibly restrained from forward motion. The man who must be Captain Love no longer wore his broad hat. Several of his men, including Nate Whiskey, were aiming pistols at them.

The black-clad man gestured for these to lower their weapons. "Really, Tobias, did you not tell your whore that I'm naturally and permanently a Hard Man, with no need of a protective spell like the one you used in Spanish Town?"

"Mistress Bonny is not a whore," said Constantine with what Anne recognized as the calm of resignation. Absurdly, she was gladdened by this unnecessary defense.

Captain Love, whom Anne realized could be no taller than Constantine and even more slender, rubbed a powder smudge on his high pale brow with a slim forefinger, which he then ran through his sleek black hair. His features were very delicate, even more girlish than Mary's had been, and his large eyes just as dark, but the mischief in them had none of Mary's tenderness "Whatever else she is, she's a damn good shot. Both balls struck me, in the forehead and the chest. Such wounds would have been instantly fatal, were I not Hard. Do you know how rare that is?"

"That poxied bitch has the Devil's luck," crowed Nate Whiskey, "but it's run out now."

The small dark-haired, pale-faced man never took his eyes off Anne and Constantine. "Mister Whiskey, if you speak without being spoken to again, I may give Mistress Bonny leave to reload and shoot you in the groin. I'm sure she has much fight left in her, and will be more cooperative if she but maims someone first."

"How did you find us," asked Constantine, wiping his fogged spectacles on his sleeve with a nonchalance belied only by a slight tremble of his hand, which Anne suspected was as due to anger and frustration as fear.

Captain Love cocked his small neat head at them with the hard-eyed alertness of a hawk and the intelligence of a parrot. "Like Onan, you spilled your seed, although in your case it was on our bedsheet rather than the ground. While you were at your ablutions, I scraped it into a vial, thinking it might come in handy. More recently, I mixed the dried crust of it into a half-spoon of Quicksilver, and first let that bright drop crawl along a map, then a calendar and clockface. That told me where we must drop anchor, and at what day and hour we might waylay you along this spot of beach." He bowed his head to Anne. "I hope it doesn't shock you, Mistress Bonny, to learn that Mister Constantine and I were more than colleagues, once upon a not-so-distant time."

She spat. "I've been a pirate, you silly ponce, and care not that two men may lie together."

Their captor smiled, revealing a host of small white teeth, unstained by time, diet, or tobacco. "Yaas," he drawled, "your sort would be even more at ease with buggery than the common sailor is. It should not surprise me to hear that you've administered as well as received it. Perhaps with an artificial cock, rather like the celebrated Dutch trooper's wife, who followed her husband to war and used a brass one to piss."

Constantine stood up. "I'm going to kill you, Edmund."

The other man bowed. "Anything is possible in the fullness of time, but at this moment, it looks exceedingly unlikely. Now come down from there, both of you, and help my men unload your cargo."

There was no help for it. Nate Whiskey took Anne's cutlass, but when he moved to do the same thing with Constantine's rapier, his employer waved him away. Constantine gave no visible reaction, but this gesture irked Anne, as she thought it less a mark of respect than contempt for what was perceived as his harmless-ness. *He fought quite well in the alley,* she thought, *and was bloody brave in the tavern.*

They rolled the cauldron out of the cart, off the road, and down the beach, finally setting it upright not far from the boat, out of which Captain Love then directed them to heave so large and heavy a barrel that Anne was surprised that the pinnace had been able to get it and eleven men safely ashore. This container was then rolled along the sand and upended beside the cauldron. "It is time to test the properties of this treasure," said Love, look-ing out at morning's glitter on the waves. "Someone fetch the pickaxe that Tobias was so considerate as to bring with him."

"Wait," wheezed Constantine, gasping from his labors. "Before testing its greatest property, you should subject its lesser ones to experiment. By not doing so, you're depriving your men of the opportunity to drink. You lads like a good drink, d'ye not?"

Several in Love's gang of louts growled their assent. "Would there was some to be had!" said a big fellow whose face was half bearded, half shaven, no doubt to let the knife cut that ran from his left cheek to his chin heal more cleanly.

"There is," said Constantine. "More than you've seen in your life, and free for the taking, if but one of you has a small flask with a drop left in it."

"Nate surely has such about him," said Anne, perceiving a glimmer of Constantine's intent. *He recalled my telling him that drink is the downfall of most pirates.* It was good to have a man actu-ally remember something she'd said the day before.

Nate Whiskey looked more shifty-eyed than usual. "What if I do? It's mine by right, and I'll not be wasting it on some trick."

"No trick, but a true marvel," soothed Constantine, "and you need only spare the smallest drop. Pour such in that cauldron and it will fill to the brim, and in so doing become finer and more potent than it was before. What you see before you is no ordinary cookpot, but one of the Spoils of Annwn, wrested by Arthur him-self from the Otherworld, and later brought to these shores by Saint Brendan the Navigator. It has several miraculous proper-ties, but the most practical is its ability to serve as a veritable

Cauldron of Plenty, so that he who possesses it never need be without the finest food and drink."

The pirates muttered amongst themselves, some in derision but others in true wonder, and then Half-Beard turned to their leader. "Captain Love, is what this mad fellow says true?"

Love's smile lacked warmth but not humor. "Indeed, and his madness that of the fox. He would delay us on this beach by having you men get festive with spirits, rather than putting the cauldron to its ultimate test and then getting on our way."

"Well," said Nate Whiskey, dubious but intrigued, "it's not as though we risk discovery by aught but mulatto fisherfolk, and they'd not dare meddle."

"True enough, Nate," said Anne in a far friendlier tone than she normally used on his sort. "Besides, even if you have signed no Articles of Federation with Captain Love, you are still of the Sweet Trade, and as such no man's mere lackey, for all that he addresses you as one. Go ahead and spill a drop of your namesake into that pot and let us see what happens."

His tin flask was already in his hand, and without looking at his employer, he stepped to the cauldron and poured a tiny amount into it.

Ignoring the scowling Captain Love, the mob pressed forward, and Constantine and Anne with them. By the time Anne could see inside, the vessel was already half full of amber-hued, strong-smelling liquid, and the level rapidly rising, halting only when it reached the pitted brim. *Is it to be all marvels then, every day until the grave?* she thought, feeling as dizzy as if she'd already drunk what her nose suggested might be very fine whiskey indeed. This shimmering honey-colored circle, no more than four feet across and four deep, bounded and bottomed by the plainest cooking iron, seemed more wondrous than all the vasty heaving sea, the first time she found herself beyond all sight of land.

"Dare any man taste it?" prodded Constantine.

They needed no further prompting. Like hogs at a trough, the pirates jostled each other for room to cup their hands or even dip their faces. One small, crafty-faced fellow ran to the boat and came loping back with a bucket. "Fill this, and then we can pass it around!"

Love walked close to Anne and Constantine. "You think to hinder me, but I shall turn this to my advantage. Such men as these are as willingly paid in whiskey as in gold, and will all the more gladly serve the man with an inexhaustible source of it. And more than that, the final test of the cauldron's power is one that will afright them sorely, and is best performed with their senses lulled. Come, sit with me in the shade of that palm, and we will wait for them to drink their fill. Have either of you tobacco?"

But an hour later, Captain Love's mood was less amiable, as he walked amongst his men, idly kicking several as they lay insensible on the sand. "Damn me, but I didn't expect them to drink quite so deeply, not in the first hour of daylight!" Stooping, he relieved the sprawled, snoring Half-Beard of two pistols nearly as fine as Anne's. Where another man's face might have been red with annoyance, his was so pale the sun practically glittered off it like a shoal, yet his voice remained softer than a noon breeze. "No matter. There are several means to banish drunkenness, and I shall employ one shortly. For now, the two of you can serve me as they would have, no doubt with more wits and better nerves."

Anne looked at Constantine, hoping to convey with a glance that they should run toward the marsh, as there was none but Captain Love himself to pursue them, and he didn't look so very fleet afoot. But no, her companion (in truth, she no longer thought of him as employer) wore a face of resigned determination, mixed with no little curiosity. "Yes, we should see this thing through to the end. I was a fool to think otherwise."

Love's smile was wider now, although no kinder than it had been before. "Good Tobias, I knew your desertion would only be temporary. Your she-pirate would, I think, shield your body with her own, giving you another chance to bolt, but then you'd never know if the cauldron can truly revive the dead."

Had I been thinking to do that? In truth, Anne could not completely deny the possibility of such intention, but this new revelation was intriguing enough to banish other thoughts. "Any dead?" She thought of Mary and Jack, rotting in unmarked graves.

Captain Love motioned them toward the standing barrel. "If the remains are reasonably intact. Tell me, Tobias, do you still have Captain Teach's head?"

"No," he replied, not offering further explanation. It had remained with Mother Patience, to do with as she would.

"Pity, for it would be an interesting experiment to see what happens when such remains are incomplete. For now though, I have brought along one who is every bit as infamous as Blackbeard, and whose various parts remain more or less attached."

For one horrible, hopeful moment, Anne thought he might mean Calico Jack Rackham, perhaps plundered from his unmarked grave while Anne and Constantine consulted the Obeah woman. But no, her onetime lover had never enjoyed half such fierce renown as Teach. To whom then did Love then refer?

Constantine was already walking up the beach to the cart, where their poor untended horse had fallen in its harness, apparently having succumbed to the strain of whatever power had checked its movement. Anne watched him. *Run for it,* she thought. *You're out of range.*

Captain Love seemed to guess her thought. "He won't flee, you know," he said with mock gentleness. "Is it because he fears what I might do to you, or that he desires to see the cauldron's true power? I'd like to think it's the latter, you no doubt the former, but it's most likely both. Do we ever do anything for just one reason?"

Anne looked down at him. His age was impossible to determine, but in his delicate pale way, he had all the male beauty that Constantine lacked, more so even than handsome Jack Rackham. But rather than the sort to induce desire, it was the kind best at distance, like that of a bright-banded viper coiling in the sun. Whatever the course of Constantine's affections, how had he bedded with such a cold little creature? But then she remembered the first man she ever lain with, and how she'd wanted him, despite his unfeeling cruelty—or perhaps because of it.

"Mister Constantine said he would kill you, but I think it shall be me who does that."

Love met her stare with one of equal coolness, then giggled softly, a sound more ominous than any pirate's howl or cackle. "He may actually do it some day, but I think *you* will not. Now prepare to be useful, for your breath will depart with your utility."

Constantine was back with the pickaxe. "I suppose you want me to open that barrel. Ever since Dover, I've wondered what's inside."

Love motioned for him to hand the tool to Anne. "Mistress Bonny will open it, I think. The Amazon has shoulders broad as many a boatswain, though I'll grant her face and form are not unfair."

Anne thought about using the pickaxe to test the Hardness of his own face and form, but he'd already stepped lightly back, and she didn't doubt that his aim was even deadlier than hers. "Stand aside. This is nothing, compared to such manual tasks as I performed aboard *The William*."

She swung, wood splintered, and a spray of what felt like brine splashed her face. Squinting against burning eyes, she swung again, and again after that, until Love's voice halted her.

"That will do, I think. Now fish out the man who has been my most honored guest, although without enjoying the roomiest of accommodations."

The barrel had cracked open like an egg, splattering more brine. Rather than reaching into its sludgy depths, Anne kicked its broken side once, then again, widening the split to that its more solid contents spilled out with the water. These lay there on dark wet sand, a darker, crusted man-shape, like a scarecrow fashioned of rags and pitch on a frame of gnarled black sticks. There was a length of very rusty chain about its waist and shackles on its ankles. Its head, a tarry coconut with maize-kernel teeth, lolled on an unnaturally long neck, also wrapped in a collar of iron links.

"Whose corpse is this?" The tar and iron suggested a life of violence and notoriety, as pirates and highwaymen were routinely dipped in pitch and chained to gibbets after death, with some never being cut down and buried. Poor Jack had been spared that much.

"I'll introduce him shortly," said Love, "if he doesn't do those honors for himself. Please be so good as to pick him up and put him in the cauldron.

The chains were firmly wed to bone and flesh by the tar, but even ironbound and sodden, the lean corpse was less heavy than a living man, and once she had a good grip on its armpits, she managed to drag it to the cauldron. There, Constantine took its feet, and they were able to lift it up and lower it in, letting the dead man settle into whiskey (the level of which seemed no lower, despite the pirate's thirst) like a live invalid into his bath.

Anne was tempted to stalk to Captain Love and wipe her fouled hands on his fine black coat, pistols and invulnerability be damned, but then there was a boiling hiss, the smell of spirits and something else, and the whiskey rose up into the air as steam, though she felt no heat. With this, the ragamuffin corpse began to twitch and spasm. Its mouth gaped open, silently at first, and then poured forth wordless cries, an even more piteous sound than their horse had made when held fast by sorcery in the fog. Anne wanted to cover her ears, but then the guttural sounds were bitten off into words.

"Where am I? Oh God of mercy, what place is this? Is this Hell at last, and if so, why? Jesu, did I not repent? Does perjury hound me to perdition?"

Captain Love stepped forward and extended a pale hand. "No Hell, Captain William Kidd, but merely the world again, albeit twenty-three years older than when you departed it. Welcome back to the life that cruel Britain wrenched from you at rope's end, before displaying you by the Thames. We must contrive a means to free you from those chains and scrub you clean of tar."

The thin dark dripping shape was now standing upright in the pot, as those boiled by cannibals are thought to do, bulbous head lowered dejectedly on stretched neck. "I'd not do that," said Anne through clenched teeth and rising gorge. "Naught else seems holding him together."

"The cauldron gives life, or at least some semblance," said

Constantine, his scrunched simian face all cold fascination, "yet does not restore the body. At least not one that's been dead this long."

"All the better, then," said Captain Love with a barracuda smile. "He'll strike yet more terror into the shipping of the nation that hanged him! And he's just the first. I acquired his corpse years ago, and kept it in a barrel in my wine cellar until shortly before our departure. There are many others stowed there, wretched felons all, as their remains are generally the easiest to purchase. When I began my collection, it was but a youthful folly; I did not expect to see any of my charges ever move or speak, but kept them only for idle study. What a happy chance that was!"

"Why do such a thing?" asked Constantine. "This is no judgment day, that the dead should rise and walk, and if it was, they'd shake off corruption and be truly whole. Nay, this is more like a carrion puppet show."

Love nodded. "True enough, but British shipping shall play Judy to this Punch. It was an uneasy peace that was signed at Ultrech. The governments of France and Spain do not wish their own navies to break it, but if the condemned dead of their one-time enemy do, how can they naught but gain?"

"Madness!" cried the late William Kidd, his voice hoarse and hollow but the words more cleanly shaped than the rest of him. "Why should I wish to *become* the villain that perjured testimony *accused* me of being? Must that calumny hang about me like these chains? Has not my good name been restored, in all the years since my death?"

Love scowled. "You have the name of a good and proper pirate, the fiercest of sea rovers. Why think you I raised you up again?"

"You should have read Captain Johnson's book," said Constantine dryly. "He makes it plain that Captain Kidd considered himself innocent, the pawn of political expediency and the duplicity of great men. He was a fool, perhaps, and impetuous, but not the rogue that ballads and broadsheets have made of him. Men of infamy, like those of its opposite, have not always lived according to their reputations."

"Who are you calling a fool, you dwarfish ape?" snarled Kidd. "I have no sword, but by God, I can brain you with my very chains, as I once crushed the skull of an insolent bosun with a bucket!"

Constantine didn't flinch. "Which rash act much aided your prosecution, along with the conveniently missing French passes, the absence of which neatly changed you from privateer to pirate. Magick is not the only art by which words writ on paper can leave a man utterly transformed."

The figure slumped again, and Anne marveled at seeing such an inhuman thing adopt such a human posture. "Was there ever a more miserable wretch than myself? First Newgate, then Tyburn, and now this demi-Hell that you mock me by calling life regained. Damn your eyes, I'll be having none of it! I was at peace, and shall be again!" Saying this, it hooked a bony black leg over the rim of the iron pot and clumsy scrambled out, moving with some vigor despite the chains.

Captain Love placed himself in front of the distraught corpse, shaking with some agitation himself. "Nay, Captain Kidd, stay you a while. At least hear out the man who brought you back."

The figure held its head high, and Anne realized that Kidd must have been quite a tall man in life. "I will not, for that man is a villain, and these with him likely no better! I have no wish for such company, nor to be in whatever savage place this is, and would not even if my poor form were in a better state. I see before me the ocean, and whether it be Atlantic, Caribbean, or Pacific, it brings the promise of oblivion. Now get the bloody Hell out of my way, or I'll make you as much carrion as myself!"

Anne laughed. "Why Captain Love, your guest is spurning your hospitality! He's too good for such as us, and especially for such as *you*!"

"Do as I say, damn you!" shouted Love. "Are you such a fool as to think life restored is easily thrown away?" Saying this he fired first one pistol, then the other, the shots dislodging sludgy tar from Kidd's head and abdomen. Then, as if in punctuation to his argument, he drew his rapier and drove it into Kidd's sunken, soggy chest.

The living dead man simply looked at him with the holes that once held eyes. "Will you now stand out of my way?" he said, in a voice that sounded disconcerting small and soft and human.

Love had gone whiter than ever, except for the blue-black hollows under his eyes and a thin purple vein in his high forehead. "Can you not see, you bloody fool? Having been once dead, you can't be killed!"

Kidd looked down at the steel projecting from under his breastbone. Grasping it between two skeletal fingers, he did not pull it out, but instead slid it an inch or so back and forth. "Indeed. I am transfixed, yet feel nothing. You say I cannot die?"

"Perhaps not," interjected Constantine, "but yon ocean is very deep, and there's restful darkness at its bottom. Better a loyal mariner should lie there, than slowing falling apart on a gibbet, much less walking about in pitch-dipped tatters. Perhaps, under the weighty blanket of the deep and on the silted bottom, Captain Kidd will be able to sleep."

Kidd nodded. "Indeed. Better lying deep than walking land like this. I was notorious enough before my hanging, and would be a most infamous monster now!" Without another word, he lurched clumsily toward the waves, tripping twice on his chains before he reached the water.

"Poor bastard," said Anne.

His head was a bobbing black nutshell now, and then it was gone. There were no bubbles to mark his submergence, just an oily spot.

"That buggers all," said Love sourly.

For many long moments, they watched the waves without speaking or looking at each other. Finally, Constantine broke the silence.

"Dear Edmund," he said with unexpected gentleness, "your men remain lolling and witless and you've left yourself unarmed. Mistress Bonny and myself shall be leaving now."

Love walked in a tight circle, wiping his expansive forehead with a red silk handkerchief, a gesture that seemed more compulsive than necessary, as his brow remained smooth and dry. "I think not," he said, turning to face them again. "There are many more weapons lying about. I can easily enough pick one and come after you. Don't think I won't, or that I cannot still harm you even when you think yourself safely far away."

Constantine sighed and shook his head, looking noticeably older than the man he was addressing, although Anne was somehow sure he was the younger of the two. "My onetime friend and more than friend, why bother? Is it really worth the trouble?"

Love shrugged, a strange half-smile on his ageless face. "That question might be asked of anything. I do as I will, and that is what I would now do. You shall not leave."

Anne put her hand on her onetime employer's shoulder. "Toby, answer me one thing. Is it more important that the cauldron be delivered to the School of Night, or that it remain out of foreign hands?"

Constantine did not unlock his gaze from Love's. "The latter, I should think."

"And if I were able to put paid to Captain Love, and could make sure that no dead men would ever again be dropped into yon uncanny pot, might I claim it as my spoils?"

He looked at her then, less ape than owl behind his spectacles. "If you could truly stop him, I'd give you whatever you might ask of me."

She smiled and brushed lank hair from her eyes, shifted her weight, tensed and untensed her fists, shrugged one shoulder, then the other, steadied her breathing, felt the sun's warmth on her neck, the salt wind on her face. This spot of beach might be the last thing she'd ever see or feel, if the idea that was trying to be born inside her head proved as unhardy as her poor dead babe. "All I want right now is your rapier, but I will ask you for one other thing soon enough, or else for nothing at all."

He unsheathed it and handed it gently to her, his fingers brushing hers on the hilt, a touch that seemed to ripple slightly through his small frame.

Love's expression was haughtier than Constantine's, but it too had a hint of melancholy. "Mistress Bonny, you know you can no more harm me than I was able to harm our late guest."

She whipped the weapon once through the salty air, getting the feel of it, admiring the way light danced off it like a twisting fish. "That remains to be seen. You said you could use magic to rouse your men. I suggest you do so."

Only now did Constantine ask the obvious. "Annie, whatever are you playing at?"

She wasn't accustomed to doing this much hard thinking, not in some time, and it made her head hurt worse than rum ever had. The sun was high above the waves now, and the wind off the water stirred her hair, caressed her face, and found its way past the buttons of her stained shirt to gently cool the hollow of her breasts. The sea was as green as Jack Rackham's eyes, the wavecaps white as Mary's best bonnet. It was a long time since she'd dared stand on a beach and stare out at Mother Ocean, felt her tides echo in the veins. *The world's better part,* she thought; *so clean and wide and manless.* She had no qualms about turning her back on Captain Love. They were both actors now, and he'd patiently await her speech.

"Toby, if you and I go from here, he'll simply do it again. You know that. More poor corpses will be dropped in the cauldron to twitch like froglegs in a skillet. Can't have that, can we?"

Constantine walked close beside her, his hand on the one with which she held the sword, although he made no move to take it from her. "But how can we stop him?"

She leaned into him and whispered. "Leave that to me. Is he as impervious within as without?"

Intrigue glimmered behind his spectacles. "I think not. Poison should work, but how plan you to administer it?"

She bent to kiss his cheek. "No poison, but something more direct. Have faith, as I did when you cast your spell." Gently shaking off his hand, she raised the sword to Love. "Please make your men sober, sir. We'll need witnesses to our duel."

His smile was very arch. "And why is that?"

She felt the weight of the rapier. Not much like a cutlass, but Mary had killed more than one man with so slim a sticker. "I'm not big like you," she'd said, "and must tire with a heavy blade. Here, let me show you how to thrust with my pretty needle." It had been a short lesson and took place years ago, but there wasn't much said or done by Mary that Anne had forgotten.

"I am challenging your captaincy. Won't mean much, if your men aren't sensible enough to see and hear it."

Love laughed so hard he looked like he needed to sit down.

"Madame, my commission was in the Guards."

"Meaning you bought your rank."

His smile indicated no offense. "Indeed, but the point is that it's not nautical, much less piratical, and not to be undone by the outcome of a fight, even if you were somehow able to harm me. These poor louts follow me because I pay them and they fear me. We've signed no articles of your sea-rat's brotherhood."

She nodded. "Mayhap not, but they are of it and abide by its rules, just the same. If I kill you, as I intend to, and can pay them, as I will be able to once I possess that cauldron, they'll follow more readily than they followed you, even the ones like Nate Whiskey who once cursed my name. Just as long as I do it legal. So rouse them, please." The wind chose that moment to raise her hair about her shoulders, and she felt childishly proud of how fierce and formidable she might just look.

Indeed, Love seemed impressed. "You put on a fine show, Mistress Bonny, one that shan't be wasted on just us. Besides, it should make these dogs easier to manage. They fear me, but they also fear you, and will dread me even more once you're dead by my hand. Even that doltish Captain Kidd must have known the value of fear, else he'd not found it necessary to brain his bosun."

Reaching into his purse, he produced a small disk of what looked like dark violet quartz, the size and rough shape of a guinea, which glittered with royal fire in the sunlight. "Amethyst, the Stone of Venus. From *amethystos,* meaning 'remedy for drunkenness.' By itself, the crystal prevents inebriation, but if properly worked, it's also an effective cure. I guessed it might come in handy, as the sort of rough fellows I must need hire are notorious for drinking themselves useless."

He walked to the nearest pirate, the big fellow with half a beard that he'd previously relieved of two pistols. Now he took the unconscious man's cutlass, which he used to draw a crude circle about him in the sand. Placing the amethyst on the man's forehead, Love walked widdershins around him, murmuring "siccus, siccus, siccus."

Half-Beard groaned and heaved, eyes fluttering open to the red-veined whites, his face suddenly flushed and glistening, his healing cut flaring so redly that Anne half-expected to see blood bursting through the scab. His heels drummed on the sand, his mouth gaped, and his hands clenched and unclenched like dying crabs. Heat emanated from his twitching body in a palpable wave, along with the stink of sweat, urine, and spirits, and a host of lice and fleas swarmed off him, as visible against the white sand as pepper spilled on salt.

His gasps turning into hacking coughs, he spasmed into a sitting position, his arms clasped tightly round his knees. For a moment, he sat like that, facedown and shaking, beads of sweat glittering on his bald spot, which flared so brightly it might have been a rash. Then, the shakes subsiding, he raised his head and looked at them with a surprisingly clear gaze, his features already resuming their normal color.

"Bloody Hell, but that's strong whiskey!"

Retrieving the amethyst from where it had fallen, Love then repeated the procedure for the rest of his men. The results were the same as for Half-Beard, with the exception of Nate Whiskey, who remained motionless even after Love poked him with the cutlass and then inserted the crystal into his half-open mouth. After a moment's examination, he was pronounced expired from his excess of drink, which caused several of his mates to laugh loudly at the irony of whiskey being Whiskey's bane, even as they rifled his person. "*Plures crapula quam gladius,*" said Love in a tone of cold amusement.

The other pirates all seemed as heated by the amethyst's curative powers as if they'd been locked in a sweat box for punishment, and many of them stumbled into the surf to cool their fevered brows, but none vomited, or showed any signs of headache or the other expected symptoms of a binge. Captain Love's cure was apparently potent indeed. Anne wondered if the restorative could be self-inflicted. *I must remember to take that stone from him after I've killed him,* she thought, *if kill him I truly can.*

"Mistress Bonny wishes a duel," said Captain Love with only the slightest hint of flippant mockery. "So rest yourselves a bit, whilst I sport with her, as I'd never refuse the request of a true lady." Several of the men laughed at that, while more whispered among themselves, their expression suggesting they were making wagers. "When I'm done, we must get the cauldron aboard the lugger, and from there it's to the port at Savannah La Mar, where you'll all be paid in coin and whiskey before I take passage back to Europe." Constantine shot Anne a glance that so much as said *Europe, but not England.* "Perhaps some of you are harboring thoughts of keeping the cauldron for yourselves, believing a lifetime of free food and drink better than anything I could pay you. You've already seen two demonstrations of my powers; first when I bound our quarry in fog and led you directly to them, and then when Mistress Bonny could not harm me with her pistols at close range. However, some points need the stress of repetition to be truly understood. I know you consider this fierce Amazon as dangerous as any mortal man. If, despite her skill with a blade, she cannot harm me, what hope have any of you of doing so?"

"They could still wrap you in anchor chain and throw you overboard," said Anne gaily, "or mob you and pour molten lead down your gullet."

Captain Love turned to face her, dark veins again visible in his milky forehead. "My dear strumpet, I could simply order your arms broken, then let these good fellows have their way with you."

"Nay," said the half-bearded man, who looked more thoughtful than his companions. "Despite her sex, Anne Bonny is of the brethren, and must be treated as such. A duel it shall be, right, lads?" The others murmured their assent, most with a speculative look that suggested they harbored little affection for their employer.

Captain Love coolly studied the cutlass in his hand, then looked at the rapier in Anne's. "More your sort of weapon than mine. Shall we exchange?"

Anne whipped her blade through the air again, so that it shimmered like a dragonfly's wing. "I think not. You already have the advantage of your Hardness. No point in giving you another."

Captain Love yawned theatrically. "As you wish. The result shall be the same, and I was only trying to spare you some suffering and leave you a less disfigured corpse, as this crude cleaver will make the more dreadful wound."

Not necessarily, thought Anne. Men cut to the bone often died fairly quickly, from shock and blood loss, while those run through the body might linger for a day or more. But since she had no intention of being so deeply sliced or punctured, the point was moot. She turned to Constantine and saluted him with her blade. "Remember, Toby, faith!" Not waiting his response, she turned back to Love. "Have at you, sir!"

He simply stood there, the cutlass balanced on his shoulder, smiling with all his many small white teeth. The sun was at its zenith now and he should have been very hot in the coat and breeches that were so black against the glittering sand, but no sweat beaded that smooth ivory skin, and his short hair was sleek but not lank. Perhaps a Hard Man could no more perspire than bleed, but if that was the case, he should at least be boiling like a crab pot on the inside, and yet he showed no discomfort. "Do your worst, Mistress Bonny. When you are done, be assured that I shall do mine."

He'd not put punctuation to that sentence before Anne ran forward and thrust, with such force that her point's impact with his chest actually pushed him a step back. Rather than following through and risking a return cut, she retreated. He regained his balance, but made no move to come after her, instead inspecting the hole her point had made in his jacket. "Very good one, that," he said idly. "You'd have spit me proper, were I not Hard. Care to try again? Have no worry about my return blow, as I find your obstinacy amusing, and am prepared to extend this farce a while longer."

Instead, Anne fell to her knees, her face raised to the sky. "Mother Mary, help me! I'll repent all my sins, but please don't let me die here!"

Constantine started to rush forward, perhaps to insert himself between Love and her, but the big man with the half-beard grasped his arms. "No, this is her fight, and we must see its end. Whatever the outcome, she wanted this." His tone was not unkind.

"Really, Tobias, your wench disappoints me," giggled Love, who then turned back to Anne. "She's strong and fast enough to

give good sport, but alas, her spirit seems quite suddenly departed. A pity there's no way to do this without getting blood on my
remaining good coat."

Anne had palmed a handful of sand, and now, as he stepped
forward and raised the cutlass, she threw it at his face, aiming not
for the eyes but the mouth, experience having taught her this was
actually the more incapacitating target, and, in this case, one particularly suited for her purposes.

As she'd expected, Captain Love beat his left hand upon his
chest, choking, his mouth open as he spat out sand, and that's
when she came to her feet, extending into the lunge that Mary
had taught her. *Let's see how hard you are on the inside,* she thought,
as she drove the tip of the rapier into his mouth with such force
that it broke off in his soft palate.

Love sat down sharply, his eyes wide with shock. For a
moment, there was no blood, just a protracted rattling, but then
it bubbled brightly forth, mixing with the sand on his face. He
clawed at his mouth, his body heaving, his fine buckled shoes
kicking up more sand. *Of course,* she thought, *the bastard's never felt
real pain before, not from any cut or wound, and is as unprepared for it
as a babe.* She almost pitied him.

His death was not a quick one. He actually made it to his feet
and staggered toward his men, motioning wildly for them to help
him and making incoherent wet noises. None would offer aid, but
withdrew from his stumbling advance with silence and hard
faces. With no help from that quarter, he lurched toward
Constantine. For a moment, they stood facing each other, eyes
locked, one man swaying and the other stiff, and what passed
between them Anne couldn't say, although she heard
Constantine mutter softly. Then Love spun unsteadily on his
heels and careened in wild figure-eights across the beach until his
knees buckled and he pitched forward at the surf's edge. Anne
strode to him and put her foot upon his head, grinding his face
into the foamy sand. She may not have pierced the brain stem or
punctured an artery, but he was probably already expiring from
shock, choking, and blood loss. Still, there was no harm in making sure, and she put her other foot between his shoulder blades,

balancing on him and pressing down with her full weight. He kicked once, twice, his arms jerked and his fingers curled, then was all limp stillness, the foam reddening where it lapped against his head.

Anne waited a few more moments to be sure, then walked back toward Constantine and the pirates. "That's done," she said, her heart calming from gallop to canter. "I make no claim on anything Captain Love might have on his person, or stowed aboard the lugger I see at anchor. Divide his belongings among yourselves. As for this cauldron that he sought, sign articles proclaiming me your captain and I'll see it makes us all richer than Brutus."

"Croesus," Constantine corrected softly. "I'm the one who turned against a friend because of his ambition."

Most of the pirates just gaped, a row of pocked and burnished faces with open codfish mouths, but Half-Beard's look was more appraising. "A she-captain, eh, like Grace O'Malley?" He scratched his peeling nose and fingered the stubble around his scar, then grinned wide and yellow and turned to his comrades. "Well lads, why not? She's bold as any of us, and with more wit than most. If we can be led by a warlock, why not a woman?"

Constantine had walked a few feet toward where Love lay in pinkish foam, but now he turned back toward Anne, his smile bittersweet. "Daniel had your fierceness right, but he never said you were so clever."

She nodded. "Women need their cunning, even ones less dainty than myself. Give me not so long a face. I'm alive and so are you."

She could tell he was trying very hard not to look back at Love's corpse. "Indeed, and I'm as happy for the former as the latter."

She returned his rapier. "Tell me now, just what did your masters in England have planned for this most marvelous pot?"

He wiped sweat from his forehead with his shirtsleeve. "The study of its properties, I suppose. I am not of the highest circle, and thus not privy to all their plans."

She shook her head. "More than that, surely. Might they not

wish to make much the same use of it as Spain or France? How many graves would be emptied, their occupants press-ganged into service?"

His eyes were a different green than Jack's, she thought, not having stared into them for so long before. His held a glint of gold, whereas Jack's mixed the deep gray of the sea. An omen, that. "I suppose there are some in the School who might attempt such a thing," he allowed grudgingly.

"I promise you," she continued softly, "the cauldron won't fall into foreign hands. Tell your School of Night that it was lost at sea, or that you could never find it. You hired me as a body-guard, to protect you from Love and his rogues. Have I not discharged that duty?"

"Indeed you have," he said, briefly giving in to the tempta-tion to glance back at Love's limp form. "For all that some portion of myself might wish you'd not done it quite so well. I never truly wanted Edmund dead, not even when I told him that I'd kill him."

Anne shrugged. "Yet he'd have killed me, and you soon after." She wondered about that last, Love never truly having made plain his plans for Constantine. "Better the use I will make of the cauldron than his intention for it. Nothing shall be put it in it but further drops of whiskey and rum and other such liquid goods. And if it's used to make villains rich, well, at least those riches shall keep them from further villainy."

He nodded slowly, his smile somewhat less guarded. "I see your point and have no way of stopping you, despite my small thaumaturgical skill. Where will you go now?"

She turned back to the pirates, some of whom looked like they were already awaiting orders and none appearing inclined to dispute her. "How does Carolina sound, lads? Blackbeard had a sweet arrangement with the governor there; I'm sure we can strike such a similar bargain. After all, we can supply the coastal towns with tariff-free spirits without having to take aught from Virginia's ships, and thus won't raise the ire of the neighboring colony, as was Teach's undoing. Think of it; we can be smugglers without having to actually steal anything."

"Almost doesn't seem honest," said the half-bearded man, his lopsided grin even wider. That brought laughter. Yes, these men who not two hours before had conspired in what might have been her death were now willing to follow her, God bless their simple souls.

Constantine looked out at the two-masted lugger. "I'm no seaman, but this seems more a coastal craft, and not such that will get you safely to America."

Anne nodded. "True enough, but if such bold lads and I can't use it to seize a larger and more seaworthy vessel, we're unworthy of the Brotherhood. Fret not; I shan't break the terms of my pardon until after we've put you ashore at Savannah la Mar. No blame shall attach itself to your name, nor will any further danger be yours."

He wrinkled his monkey nose. "I shall almost miss such danger. Will you not come back to England with me? I could make you respectable, Annie. I have a country house, and while my inheritance isn't the largest, there's enough of it for two."

She kissed him then, causing the rogues behind her to snicker, at least until she wheeled around with a tiger smile and eyes fiery as her hair. "I've already killed one man today, and think none of you so tough-skinned as him." That brought silence fast enough. "Nay, Toby, there'll be no respectability for me. Your Captain Johnson could have told you that."

He extended an arm. "Daniel never knew you, and had but the stuff of rumor and broadsheets to go on. Who knows what fate he might have written for you, with more firsthand information."

She took the arm and walked with him to the edge of the beach, where cooling green fronds framed purple mountains and blue sky. "I cannot guess what ending the tale of myself might have, but dare say it shan't be one that you, your Daniel, or anyone else might imagine." Foolish words, perhaps, but she found it significant that she had no desire to ask whomever had taken Nate Whiskey's flask if there were any drops still in it. For the first time since she'd stood by Mary on a cool and creaking deck, sobriety seemed more interesting than its opposite.

SHADOW TWIN

by Gardner Dozois, George R. R. Martin, and Daniel Abraham

Gardner Dozois is one of the most important editors in history of science fiction. The editor of Asimov's Science Fiction *for twenty years and the editor of an annual "year's best SF" anthology series every year for the past twenty-five years, he has written or edited more than eighty books, and won fifteen Hugos, two Nebulas, thirty Locus Awards, a Readercon Award, and ten Science Fiction Chronicle Polls. His most recent book is collection* Morning Child and Other Stories. *Upcoming are the anthologies* The Best of the Best, The Year's Best Science Fiction, *and* Galileo's Children.

George R. R. Martin is the award-winning author of eight novels, including Fevre Dream *and* The Armageddon Rag. *After spending ten years working as a screenwriter for feature films and television, producing the TV series* Beauty and the Beast, *and working as story editor for* The Twilight Zone, *he returned to writing novels full-time with the best-selling epic fantasy series the "Song of Ice and Fire." His most recent book is the collection* GRRM: A RRetrospective. *Martin is currently working on* A Feast for Crows, *which will be finished when its finished.*

Daniel Abraham has a Bachelor of Science in Biology from the University of New Mexico and has made DNA from scratch. He presently works as the Director of Technical Support at a local internet service provider during the day and writes at night. Since 1996, he has published almost twenty short stories, novelettes, and novellas, including a number of collaborations. His first novel, A Shadow in Summer, *is the start of a fantasy series "The Long Price Quartet," and will be published by Tor later this year. He lives with his wife, three dogs, and enough books to last him until death, even if he lives to be very, very old.*

*The perceptive and philosophical tale that follows was start-
ed by Dozois way back in the 1970s, picked up by Martin in the
1980s, and then finished off last year by Abraham. Thirty years,
on and off, in the telling—it's been worth the wait.*

Act I

ONE

RAMON ESPEJO AWOKE floating in a sea of darkness. For a
moment, he was relaxed and mindless, drifting peacefully, and
then his identity returned to him desultorily, like an unwanted
afterthought.

He was Ramon Espejo. He was working a prospecting contract out of Nuevo Janeiro. He was . . . he was . . .

Where he had expected the details of his life to rush in—what
he had done last night, what he was to do today, what grudges he
was nursing, what resentments had pricked him recently—the
next thought simply failed him. He was Ramon Espejo—but he
did not know where he was. Or how he had gotten there.

Disturbed, he tried to open his eyes, and found that they were
open already. Wherever he was, it was a totally dark place, darker than the jungle night, darker than the darkness in the deep
caves in the sandstone cliffs near Swan's Neck.

Or perhaps he was blind.

That thought started a tiny spring of panic within him. There
were stories of men who'd got drunk on cheap synthetic Muscat
or Sweet Mary and woke up blind. Had he done that? Had he
lost that much control of himself? A tiny rivulet of fear traced a
cold channel down along his spine. But his head didn't hurt, and
his belly didn't burn. He closed his eyes, blinking them hard several times, irrationally hoping to jar his vision back into
existence; the only result was an explosion of bright pastel blobs
across his retinas, scurrying colors that were somehow more disturbing than the darkness.

His initial sense of drowsy lethargy slid completely away
from him, and he tried to call out. He felt his mouth moving

slowly, but he heard nothing. Was he deaf too? He tried to roll over and sit up but could not. He lay back against nothing, floating again, not fighting, but his mind racing. He was fully awake now, but he still couldn't remember where he was or how he had gotten there. Perhaps he was in danger: his immobility was both suggestive and ominous. Had he been in a mine cave-in? Perhaps a rockfall had pinned him down. He tried to concentrate on the feel of his body, sharpening his sensitivity to it, and finally decided that he could feel no weight or pressure, nothing actually pinioning him. *You might not feel anything if your spinal cord had been cut,* he thought with a flash of cold horror. But a moment's further consideration convinced him that it could not be so: he *could* move his body a little, although when he tried to sit up, something stopped him, pulled his spine straight, pulled his arms and shoulders back down from where he'd raised them. It was like moving through syrup, only the syrup pushed back, holding him gently, firmly, implacably in place.

He could feel no moisture against his skin, no air, no breeze, no heat or cold. Nor did he seem to be resting on anything solid. Apparently, his first impression had been correct. He was floating, trapped in darkness, held in place. He imagined himself like an insect in amber, caught fast in the gooey syrup that surrounded him, in which he seemed to be totally submerged. But how was he breathing?

He *wasn't,* he realized. *He wasn't breathing.*

Panic shattered him like glass. All vestiges of thought blinked out, and he fought like an animal for his life. He clawed the enfolding nothingness, trying to pull his way up toward some imagined air. He tried to scream. Time stopped meaning anything, the struggle consuming him entirely, so that he couldn't say how long it was before he fell back, exhausted. The syrup around him gently, firmly, pulled him back precisely as he had been—back into place. He felt as if he should have been panting, expected to hear his blood pounding in his ears, feel his heart hammering at his chest—but there was nothing. No breath, and no heartbeat. No burning for air.

He was dead.

He was dead and floating on a vast dry sea that stretched

away to eternity in all directions. Even blind and deaf, he could sense the immensity of it, of that measureless midnight ocean.

He was dead and in Limbo, waiting in darkness for the Day of Judgment.

He almost laughed at the thought—it was better than what the Catholic priest in the tiny adobe church in his little village in the mountains of northern Mexico had promised him; Father Ortega had often assured him that he'd go right to the flames and torments of Hell as soon as he died unshriven—but he could not push it away. He had died, and this emptiness—infinite darkness, infinite stillness, trapped alone with only his own mind—was what had always waited for him all his life, in spite of all the blessings and benedictions of the Church, in spite of all his sins and occasional semi-sincere repentances. None of it had made any difference.

But *how* had it happened? How had he died? His memory seemed sluggish, unresponsive as a tractor's engine on a cold winter morning—hard to start and hard to keep in motion without sputtering and stalling. He began with what was most familiar, imagining his room in Deigotown—the small window over his cot, the thick pounded-earth walls. The faucets in his sink, already rusting and ancient though humanity had hardly been on the planet for sixteen years. The tiny scarlet skitterlings that scurried across the ceiling, multiple rows of legs flailing like oars. The sharp smells of iceroot and *ganja*, spilled tequila and roasting peppers. The sounds of the transports flying overhead, grinding their way up through the air and into orbit.

Slowly, the recent events of his life took shape, still fuzzy as a badly aligned projection. He had been in Diegotown for the Blessing of the Fleet. He had eaten roasted fish and saffron rice from a street vendor and watched the fireworks. The smoke had smelled like a strip mine from all the explosions, and the spent fireworks had hissed like serpents as they plunged into the sea. But that was before . . . yes, before.

There had been a fight. He'd fought with Eleana. The sound of her voice—high and accusing and mean as a pitbull. He'd hit her. He remembered that. She'd screamed and clawed at his eyes and tried to kick him in the balls. And they'd made up afterwards like they always did. Afterward, she had run her fingers along the machete scars on his arm as he fell into a sated sleep.

He remembered now.

He'd left her before first light, sneaking out of a room heavy with the smell of sweat and sex while she was still asleep so he wouldn't have to talk to her, feeling the morning breeze cool against his skin. Flatfurs scurrying away from him as he walked down the muddy street, making their alarm cries like panicked oboes. He'd flown his van to the outfitter's station because he was going . . .

His mind balked. It was not the nauseating forgetfulness that seemed to have consumed his world, but something else. There was something his mind didn't want to recall. Slowly, gritting his teeth, he forced his memory to his will.

He'd spent the day realigning two lift tubes in the van. Someone had been there with him. Sanchez, bitching about parts. And then he had flown off into the wastelands, the outback, *terreno cimarron* . . .

Had his heart been beating, it would have stopped then in remembered terror. He had gone to the mountains—and he had *seen* it.

TWO

"This going to be the big one?" Old Sanchez asked, the way he always did.

"Yes," Ramon said as he clamped down the cowl on his left-rear lift tube. "This time, I'm coming back with enough good claims to make the *pinche* lawyers start working for *me*."

The outfitters shop was a mix of junkyard and clean room—great scraps of the vans and transports Old Sanchez had gathered up over the years to strip for parts or else retool into cheap buys for people even more desperate than themselves lay among storage units of picocircuitry that it would have taken Ramon half his life to pay for. Old Sanchez himself waddled through the work bays with a glass of iced tea in his hand. When Ramon had first known him, it had been whiskey. Never say that times don't change.

"You better hope not," Old Sanchez said. "Too much money kills men like you and me. God meant us to be poor, or he wouldn't have made us so mean."

Ramon tested the tubes. The yields were balanced and good enough, and the hum from them was like a promise of escape.

"God meant you to be mean, Sanchito. He just didn't want me taking any shit."

"Eleana know you're going out? Last time she came here looking for you two days after you left. You're gonna have to do something about that bitch. Kill her or get married."

The knot in Ramon's belly went a notch tighter. He wasn't sure if it was dread at leaving her behind or the need to be gone. Both, maybe.

"She knows I'm going this time. And when I get back, she'll be happy to help me spend what I get. You watch. This is going to be the big one."

It was a crisp clear day in October. He flew his beat-up old van north across the Fingerlands, the Greenglass country, the river marshes, the *Océano Tétrico,* heading deep into unknown territory. North of Fiddler's Jump were thousands of hectares that no one had ever explored, or even thought of exploring, land so far only glimpsed from orbit during the first colony surveys.

The human colony on the planet of São Paulo was only a little more than ten years old, and the majority of its towns were situated in the subtropic zone of the snaky eastern continent that stretched almost from pole to pole. The colonists were mostly from the Brazilian Commonwealth, Mexico, Jamaica, and Hispaniola, and their natural inclination was to expand south, into the steamy lands near the equator—they were not effete *norteamericanos,* after all; they were used to such climates, they knew how to live with the heat, they knew how to farm the jungles, their skins did not sear in the sun. So they looked to the south and tended to ignore the cold northern territories, perhaps because of an unvocalized common conviction—one anticipated centuries before by the first Spanish settlers in the New World of the Americas—that life was not worth living any place where there was even a remote possibility of snow.

Ramon, however, was part Yaqui and had grown up in the rugged plateau country of northern Mexico. He liked the hills and white water, and he didn't mind the cold. He also knew that the Sierra Hueso chain in the northern hemisphere of São Paulo was a more likely place to find rich ore than the flatter country around the Hand or Nuevo Janeiro or Little Dog. The mountains of the Sierra Hueso had been piled up many millions of years before by a collision between continental plates, the colliding plates squeezing an ocean out of existence between them; the former seabottom would have been pinched and pushed high into the air along the collision line, and it would be rich in copper and other metals.

The Sierra Hueso had been mapped from orbit by the colony ramscoop, but no one Ramon knew had ever actually been there, and the territory was still so unexplored that the peaks of the range had not even been individually named. That meant that there were no human settlements within hundreds of miles, and no satellite to relay his network signals this far north; if he got into trouble he would be on his own.

It was probably better that way. Although he was reluctant to admit it, he'd finally come to realize that it was better if he worked someplace away from other prospectors. Away from other people. The bigger prospecting cooperatives might have better contracts, better equipment, but they also had more rum and more women. And between those two, Ramon knew, more fighting. He couldn't trust his own volatile temper, never had been able to. It had held him back for years, the fighting, and the trouble it got him into. No, it *was* better this way—muleback prospecting, just himself and his van.

Besides, he was finding that he liked to be out on his own like this, on a clear day with São Paulo's big soft sun blinking dimly back at him from rivers and lakes and leaves. He found that he was whistling tunelessly as the endless forests beneath the van slowly changed from blackwort and devilwood to the local conifer-equivalents: iceroot, creeping willow, *hierba*. At last, there was no one around to bother him. His stomach had stopped hurting, for the first time that day.

Mountains made a line across the world before him: ice and iron, iron and ice.

The sun was setting, pulling shadows across the mountain faces, when he brought the van to rest in a rugged upland meadow along the southern slopes of the Sierra Hueso range. It took him only moments to set up his bubbletent, light a small fire, and set his simple dinner—a filleted fatfin, rubbed with garlic and habenaro—to grilling. While the fish cooked, he lit a cigaret and watched the stone of the mountains darkening with the sky. Other nights, on other trips, he'd have broken out a bottle of tequila or rum or whiskey to keep himself company, but he'd deliberately left such distractions behind this time; this time, he needed to be all business. Truth be told, with the immense view spread to the horizon around him, and the stars beginning to show in the cold, blue-black sky, he found, to his surprise, that he didn't miss the tequila all that much anyway. A flapjack moved against the sky, and Ramon roused up on one elbow to watch it. It rippled its huge, flat, leathery body, sculling with its wing tips, seeking a thermal. Its ridiculous squeaky cry came clearly to him across the gulfs of air. They were almost level; it would be evaluating him now, deciding that he was much too big to eat. The flapjack tilted and slid away and down, as though riding a long, invisible slope of air, off to hunt squeakers and grasshoppers in the valley below. Ramon watched the flapjack until it dwindled to the size of a coin, glowing bronze in the failing light.

"Good hunting, *amigo*," he called after it, and then smiled. Good hunting for both of them, eh? Quickly, he ate his dinner—briefly missing the tequila after all—and then sat by the fire for a few moments while the night gathered completely around him and the alien stars came out in their chill, blazing armies. He named the strange constellations the people of São Paulo had drawn in the sky to replace the old constellations of Earth—the Mule, the Cactus Flower, the Sick Gringo—and wondered (he'd been told, but had forgotten) which of them had Earth's own sun twinkling in it as a star. Then he went to bed and to sleep, dreaming that he was a boy again in the cold stone streets of his hilltop pueblo, sitting on the roof of his father's house in the dark, a scratchy wool blanket wrapped around him, trying to ignore the loud, angry voices of his parents in the room below, searching for São Paulo's star in the winter sky.

In the morning, he ate a small breakfast of cold tortillas and beans, consulted the survey maps, and started up the southern slopes, looking for the collision line. He didn't expect it would be hard to locate; ocean floor rocks were unmistakable—a mangled, kneaded layer of pillow lava, basalt, and gabbo. He found it before the sun had reached its zenith, and surveyed it almost with regret; he'd been enjoying the climb for its own sake, pausing frequently to enjoy the view or to rest in the watery sunlight. Now he'd have to get to work

With a sigh, Ramon unslung his backpack. It took him only minutes to rig the small charge for the coring sample. He had done it a thousand times before, it seemed. Still, he walked slowly, stringing out the det cord to a safe distance, finding a boulder that would shield him from the blast. He found himself, strangely, procrastinating about setting it off. It was so quiet here, so still, so peaceful! From up here, the forested slopes fell away in swaths of black and dead blue and orange, the trees rippling like a carpet of moss as the wind went across them—except for the white egg of his bubbletent on the mountain shoulder below, it was a scene that might not have changed since the beginning of time. For a moment, he was almost tempted to forget about prospecting and just relax and unwind this trip, but he shrugged the temptation away—he needed money, the van wouldn't hold together forever, and Eleana's scorn when he came back emptyhanded again was something he wasn't anxious to face. Perhaps there will be no copper here anyway, he told himself reassuringly, and then wondered at the tenor of his thoughts. Surely it could not be a bad thing to be rich? His stomach was beginning to hurt again.

He rubbed his hand over the boulder in front of him, tracing the aquatic fossils, ancestors of the fatfins and butterfish that were the mainstay of the Nuevo Janeiro fishing industry, that were another indicator of the collision line; the fossils were grotesquely distorted, as though seen in a funhouse mirror—squeezed out

of shape by the slow heat and pressure of the continental collision. How long had it taken for that to happen, for fish to turn to
stone and be lifted from the bottom of the sea thousands of feet
into the thinning air? The crash of stone and stone had taken an
inconceivably vast time, pushing the mountains toward the sky at
a rate of only a few inches per century, slowly enough so that the
big river to the west had been able to saw its way through the
range as it rose, keeping pace inch for inch. Millions of years.
And what had taken millions of years to become as it was, *he* was
about to change in an instant, and afterward, it could never be
undone. The untouched vastness was about to be touched,
altered irrevocably, by the hand of man. By *his* hand. There was
regret in that, and a kind of melancholy—but also an oily sort of
pride that swelled his heart even as it made his belly twinge.

He lit a cigaret and the det cord with the same match.

"All apologies, *mi amigo,*" he said to the mountainside. "I'm
just a man, not a hill, and I've got to eat somehow." Then he
crouched behind the sheltering stone.

There was the expected blast; then the hillside shifted greasi-
ly under him, like a giant shrugging in uneasy sleep, and he heard
the express-train rumble of sliding rock. He could tell from the
sound alone that something had gone wrong. The coring blast
shouldn't have set off a rockslide, let alone one that sounded that
big . . .

When silence returned, Ramon stood up and walked carefully through the swirling cloud of dust, testing each step before he
trusted his weight to it, squinting at the blast site. He moved slowly up the trail of rubble and scree left by the slide. The whole
rockface had slid away, revealing a wall. A metal wall.

Ramon stood unmoving as the arid mist of rock dust thinned.
It was, of course, impossible. It had to be some bizarre natural
formation. He stepped forward, and his own reflection—pale as
the ghost of a ghost—moved toward him. When he reached out,
his blurred twin reached out as well, pausing when he paused. He
stopped the motion before hand and ghostly hand could touch,
noticing the stunned and bewildered expression on the face of his
reflection in the metal, one no doubt matched by the expression
on his own face. Then, gingerly, he touched the wall.

The metal was cool against his fingertips. The blast had not even scarred it. And though his mind rebelled at the thought, it was clearly unnatural. It was a *made* thing. Made by somebody and *hidden* by somebody, behind the rock of the mountain, though he couldn't imagine by whom.

It took a moment more for the full implication to register. Something was buried here under the hill, something big, perhaps a building of some sort, a bunker. Perhaps the whole mountain was hollow.

A warning bell began to sound in the back of Ramon's mind, and he looked uneasily around him. Another man might not have reacted to this strange discovery with suspicion, but Ramon's people had been persecuted for hundreds of years, and he himself well remembered living on the grudging sufferance of the *mejicanos,* never knowing when they would find some pretext to wipe out the village.

If this was hidden, it was because someone didn't want it to be *found.* And might not be happy that it *had* been.

He flattened his palm against the metal, matching hands with his reflection. The cool metal vibrated under his hand, and, even as he waited, a deeper vibration went through the wall, boom, *boom,* low and rhythmic, like the beating of some great hidden heart, like the heart of the mountain itself, vast and stony and old.

This was no ancient artifact or age-old ruin. Whatever it was, this installation was *alive.*

Suddenly, the sunlight seemed cold on his shoulders. Again, he looked nervously around him, feeling much too exposed on the bare mountain slope. Another flapjack called, away across the air, but now its cries sounded to him like the shrill and batlike wailing of the damned.

Move, *move.*

He couldn't *run* back to his camp—the terrain was too rough. But he scrambled down the mountainside as recklessly as he dared, sliding on his buttocks down bluffs in a cloud of dust and scree when he could, jumping from rock to rock, bulling his way through bushes and tangles of scrub *hierba,* scattering grasshoppers and paddlefoots before him.

He moved so quickly that he was over halfway to his camp

before the mountain opened behind him and the alien came out.

A rushing sound made him turn in time to see an opening high on the ridgeline iris shut. Something was moving through the air—a grotesque goblin-shape larger than a man, on a device that looked for all the world like a flying motorcycle. The thing spiraled up, gaining altitude.

Ramon threw himself flat and rolled under bushes, only vaguely aware of the thorns and twigs biting his flesh. High above, the thing had steadied and begun to fly in slow, concentric circles. He tried to estimate its distance and size. If he'd had his hunting rifle, Ramon thought, the thing would have been easily in range. But it was too far for his handgun. At a guess, the thing might have stood two full meters. If he had brought his binoculars from the camp . . .

Sick dread squeezed his chest. His camp. The thing was clearly searching for something, and Ramon hadn't done anything to conceal the white dome of the bubbletent or the van beside it. There had been no reason to. The thing might not see him down in the underbrush, but it *would* see his camp. He had to get there—get back to the van and into the air—before the thing from the mountain discovered it.

He waited until the thing had its back to him, then burst out from the brush, pelting wildly down the slope without bothering with cover. Speed was more important now than invisibility. His mind was already racing ahead—would his van outpace the thing's cycle? Just let him get it in the air. He could fly it low, make it hard to spot or attack. He was a good pilot. He could dodge between treetops from here to Fiddler's Jump if he had to . . .

He reached the meadow that contained his camp just as the alien appeared overhead. He hesitated, torn between dashing for the van and diving back into the brush. The thing swooped forward. *Perhaps it's friendly,* Ramon thought in numb despair. *Madre de Dios, it had better be friendly!*

The van exploded. A geyser of fire and smoke shot up out of the meadow with a waterfall roar, and tenfin birds rose screaming all along the mountain flank. The shockwave buffeted Ramon, splattering him with dirt and pebbles and shredded vegetation. He staggered, fighting to maintain his balance. Pieces of fused metal thumped down around him, burning holes in the moss of the meadow floor. Through the plume of smoke, Ramon saw the thing turn, flying fifteen feet above the ground and brandishing something that looked like a pair of eggbeaters twined together; obviously a weapon. In his shock, Ramon found himself entranced by the fluid way the thing moved—sure as a cat, jointless as a tentacle. It pointed the eggbeaters. The bubbletent went up in a ball of expanding gas, pieces of torn plastic tumbling and swooping like frightened white birds in the hot turbulence of the explosion.

Ramon caught only a glimpse of that. He was already in frantic motion, running, swerving, tearing through the brush. He could hear his own gasping breath, and his heart slammed against his ribs like a fist. Faster!

He felt the alien behind him more than he saw it. Some sixth sense made him turn, and there it was, bearing down on him with weapon leveled, a devil flying out of a hell of smoke and flame. Its eyes were bright orange. Ramon fumbled for his sidearm, confounded by the snap on the holster.

Something *hit* him—

THREE

Something nudged him, and Ramon returned from his vision or memory to the dark, empty infinite. A current moved against his skin; an invisible current in an invisible sea. He had the feeling of being turned in slow circles. Something solid bumped his shoulder and then rose up against his back, or else he sank down upon it. The syrupy liquid streamed past him, flowing past his face and his body. He thought of it as draining away, though he might as easily be being lifted up through it. The flow grew faster and more turbulent. A deep vibration shook him: *boom*. Then again, beating through flesh and bone: *boom, boom*. A blurred, watery light appeared above him, very dim and immensely far away. Like a star in a distant constellation. It grew brighter. The liquid in which he floated drained, the surface coming nearer, like he was rising from the bottom of a lake, until at last he breached it, and the last of the liquid was gone.

Air and light and sound hit him like a fist.

His body convulsed like a live fish on a frying pan, every muscle knotting. He arched up like an epileptic—head and heels bearing his weight, his spine bent like a bow. Something he couldn't see flipped him on his belly, and he felt a needle slide in at the base of his spine. He vomited with wrenching violence— thick amber syrup gouting from his mouth and nose. And then again, sick, racking spasms that expelled even more, as if his lungs had been filled with the stuff. Another long needle dug into his neck, and, with a terrible shudder, Ramon began to breathe.

The air he gulped cut like glass on the way in, and his quiescent heart came suddenly, violently to life. The world went red. Pain drove away all thought, all sense of self, and then slowly abated.

He was sprawled naked on the bottom of a metal tank not more than ten feet square. So much for his measureless midnight ocean! The walls were too high to see over, and the lights—blue-white and bitter—were too bright to see past and make out the ceiling beyond. He tried to sit up, but his muscles were putty. It was bitingly cold. He settled against the metal floor and shivered, feeling his teeth start to chatter. He tried lifting an arm, but the impulse was slow to reach his flesh, and the limb swayed drunkenly when it rose. Strong smells that he couldn't identify burned his nostrils.

He was alive now, certainly, if he'd ever been dead at all. This was no supernatural otherworld, no Limbo, no Land of Ghosts—this was *real*.

That in no way abated his terror. In fact, it increased it.

A thing like a long gray snake reared up above the rim of the tank. Ramon saw it hesitate, as if considering him, and then stretch down. Three long, thin tendrils split off where the head should have been. The gray snake brushed aside Ramon's clumsy parry and seized him by the shoulder. Ramon struggled weakly. But his strength was gone, and the snake's grip was as cold and pitiless as death. Another of the snakes stretched down and wrapped itself around his waist.

The snakes lifted him smoothly out of the tank. He tried to scream, but the sound came out more like a cough. He was high in the air now, above what seemed to be a vast, high-domed cavern full of noise and lights and motion and alien shapes. The cavern swarmed with activity that Ramon could not resolve into recognizable patterns, having no referents for it. His nose and mouth were filled with a biting, acrid odor, something like formaldehyde. The smell triggered a rush of raw hysterical horror, deep-buried xenophobic nightmares: *they'll cut me open, dissection, they'll chop me up, put me in bottles, CUT me*— He thrashed impotently, mad with terror, but was unable to break free.

The snake-tentacles set him down on a platform near one wall of the cavern. He collapsed as soon as they released him, his legs too weak to bear his weight. He waited on his hands and knees, staring into the terrible bright lights, panting like a trapped animal.

It was dimmer here, in the angle of the wall and the cavern floor. Inchoate shapes moved ponderously in the shadows; as they came forward, they were finished and fleshed by the light, but Ramon still could not discern them. His mind kept fighting to resolve them into the familiar aspects of humanity, and—terribly, terrifyingly—they would not resolve. They were too big, and shaped wrong, and their eyes were a bright glowing orange.

A needle slid out of the end of a hovering gray tentacle, thrust quickly into Ramon's arm, too quickly for him to move or protest. A prickly wave of heat went through him, and he suddenly felt much stronger. What kind of injection had it given him? Glucose? Vitamins? Perhaps there'd been a tranquilizer in it as well; his head was clear now, and he felt more alert, less frightened. He drew himself up to his knees, one hand instinctively covering his crotch.

The aliens had stopped a few feet away. There were three of them, one bigger than the others. Ramon could make them out more clearly now. His mind accepted them by treating them as frauds; he saw them now as men wearing grotesque monster costumes, and kept looking for some unconvincing detail that would betray the disguise.

Intellectually, he knew better, of course. They were not men in costume. They were not men at all.

They were humanoid bipeds, at least, not spiders or octopi or big-eyed blobs, although something about the articulation of the limbs was disturbingly odd. These three ranged in height from about six and a half to seven feet tall, making even the shortest of them far taller than Ramon. Their torsos were columnar, seemingly of uniform breadth at hip and waist and shoulder, and surely they must weigh more than three hundred pounds apiece, although somehow the dominant impression they created was one of grace and suppleness. Their skins were glossy, shining, but each had its own distinctive coloration: one was a mottled blue and gold, the second a pale amber, while the largest one had yellowish flesh covered with strange, swirling patterns in silver and black.

All wore broad belts hung with unknown objects of metal and glass, and nondescript halters of some ash-gray and lusterless material. Their arms were disproportionately long, the hands huge, the fingers—three fingers, two thumbs—incongruously slender and delicate. Their heads were set low in a hollow between the shoulders and thrust a little forward on thick, stumpy necks, giving them a belligerent and aggressive look, like snapping turtles. Crests of hair or feathers slanted back from the tops of their heads at rakish angles. Quills protruded from their shoulders, the napes of their necks, and the top of their spinal ridges, forming a bristly ruff. Their heads were roughly triangular, flattened on top but bulging out at the base of the skull, the faces tapering sharply to a point. And the faces were faces out of nightmare: large rubbery black snouts streaked with blue and orange, trembling and sniffing, mouths like raw wet wounds, too wide and lipless, and small staring eyes set too low on either side of the snout. Orange eyes, hot and featureless as molten marbles.

Staring at him.

They were staring at him as though he were a bug, and that fanned a spark of anger inside him. He got to his feet and glared back at them, still shaky but determined not to show it. Ramon Espejo knelt to nobody! Especially not to ugly, unnatural monsters like these!

The biggest alien gestured: come with me. There was something studied about the motion, as though it had been learned by rote, as though its natural equivalent might be without meaning for men. The alien turned and began to walk toward the cavern wall. Reluctantly, Ramon followed. He glanced suspiciously at the two smaller aliens as he passed between them, but they neither moved nor looked his way.

Ahead was a door cut through the naked rock of the cavern wall, which the alien disappeared into. Ramon came slowly forward, looking warily all around him, wondering if he should try to run. Run to where, though? And some of the objects suspended from the alien's belt were almost certainly weapons. Shaking his head, grinning with fear and tension, Ramon followed the alien through the door.

Afterward, Ramon could not clearly remember that trip. He was led through tunnels barely wide and tall enough to allow the alien to pass. The tunnels slanted steeply up and down, and doubled back on themselves, seemingly at random. The rock was slightly phosphorescent, providing just enough light to let him see his footing. He refused to look behind at the following darkness, although his nerves were crawling like worms.

The silence was heavy here in the belly of the hill, although occasionally a far-away hooting could be heard through many thicknesses of rock, sounding to Ramon like the noise damned souls might make crying unheeded to a cold and distant God. Sometimes they passed through pockets of light and activity, rooms full of chattering noise and rich rotten smells, rooms drenched in glaring red or blue or green illumination, rooms dark as ink but for the faint silver line of the path they followed. Once they stood motionless for long moments in such a room, while Ramon's stomach dropped and he wondered if they could be in an elevator.

Back in the tunnel again, it was close and dark and silent. The alien's back gleamed pale and faint in the phosphorescent glow of the rock, like a fish in dark water, and, for a moment, it seemed to Ramon as if the markings on its flesh were moving, writhing and changing like living things. He stumbled, and instinctively clutched the alien's arm to keep from falling. Its skin was warm and dry, like snake skin. In the enclosed space of the tunnel, he could smell the alien; it had a heavy, musky odor, like olive oil, like cloves, strange rather than unpleasant. It neither looked behind nor paused nor made a sound. It continued to walk imperturbably on, at the same steady pace, and Ramon had no choice but to follow after it or be left alone in the chilly darkness of this black alien maze.

At last, the tunnel ended in another big, garishly lit chamber. To the human eye, there was something subtly wrong about the proportions and dimensions of the chamber: it was more a rhombus than a rectangle, the floor was slightly tilted, the ceiling tilted at another angle and not of uniform height, everything subliminally disorienting, everything *off,* making Ramon feel sick and dizzy. The light was too bright and too blue, and the chamber was filled with a whispering susurrus that hovered right at the threshold of hearing.

This place had not been made by human beings, nor was it meant for them. As he came forward into the chamber, he saw that the walls streamed with tiny, crawling pictures, as though a film of oil was continuously flowing down over them from ceiling to floor and carrying with it a thin scum of ever-changing images: swirls of vivid color, geometric shapes, mazy impressionistic designs, vast surrealistic landscapes. Occasionally, something representational and recognizable would stream by, trees, mountains, stars, tiny alien faces that would seem to stare malignly at Ramon out of the feverdream chaos as they swept down to be swallowed by the floor.

The alien stopped, but gestured him on. Gingerly, Ramon crossed the chamber, feeling uneasy and disconcerted, unconsciously leaning to one side to correct the tilt of the floor and putting his feet down cautiously, as though he expected the chamber to pitch or yaw.

In the center of the chamber was a deep circular pit, lined by metal, and down in the pit was another alien.

It was even taller than Ramon's guide, and thinner, and its crest and quills were much longer. Its skin was bone-white and completely free of markings. White with age? Dyed white as an indication of rank? Or was it of a different race? Impossible to say, but as the alien's eyes turned upward toward Ramon, he was seized and shaken by the force behind its gaze, by the harsh authority it palpably exuded. He noticed, with another little shock, that the creature was physically connected to the pit—things that might have been wires or rods or cables emerged from its body and disappeared into the smooth metal walls, forming an intricate cat's cradle around it. Some of the cables were black and dull, some were luminescent, and some, glossy red and gray and brown, pulsed slowly and rhythmically, as if with an obscene life of their own. Ramon looked away.

"You will find him," said the thing in the pit.

Ramon turned back to stare at the alien, fighting to keep surprise from his face. It had spoken in Portuglish, the bastard lingua franca of the colony, and quite clearly, though its voice was disturbingly rusty and metallic, as though a machine had spoken. Ramon, who also spoke Spanish, English, Portuguese, and a smattering of Navaho and French, slyly and instinctively pretended not to understand, although even he was unsure what he hoped to gain by doing so. "¿Como?" he said.

The alien's cold opaque eyes fixed on him. "It is statistically unlikely that you speak only that language," it said.

The arrogance of its harsh, unused voice and the steady gaze of those orange, unblinking eyes made Ramon angry. In times of stress—when he had lost his first van in a drunken bet, when his wife had left him, when Eleana threatened to throw him out—Ramon's rage had never deserted him. Now it returned, flushing him with heat and certainty. "What *are* you, you creatures?" he said. "Where do you come from? From this planet? Somewhere else? What do you think you're doing, attacking me, keeping me here against my will? And what about my van, eh? Who's going to get me a new *van*?"

The alien stared at him wordlessly. It struck Ramon that this was likely the first conversation ever to take place between a human and an alien. And he was bitching about his van! He had to fight down the urge to laugh, trying to keep his anger hot and stoked.

"Those are sounds, not words," the alien said after a long

pause. "Discordancies outside proper flow. You must not speak in meaningless sounds, or you will be corrected."

Ramon shivered and looked away; his rage had ebbed as quickly as it had flared, and now he felt tired, chilled by the alien's imperturbability. "What do you want?" he asked wearily.

"We do not 'want' anything," the alien said. "Again, you speak outside the way of reality. You have a function: therefore, you exist. You will exercise that function because it is your purpose to do so, your *tatecredue*. No 'wanting' is involved: all is inevitable flow."

"And if I do not function as you wish?"

The alien paused, as though briefly puzzled. "You live," it said finally. "Therefore, you exercise your function. Nonfunctioning, you could not exist. To exist and yet not exist—you would be a contradiction, *aubre,* a disruption in the flow. *Aubre* cannot be tolerated. To restore balanced flow, it would be necessary to deny the illusion that you exist."

That at least was clear enough, Ramon thought, feeling gooseflesh sweep across his skin.

Ramon chose his words carefully when he spoke again. "And what function am I to fulfill?"

The cold orange eyes fixed on him again. "Take care," the alien warned. "That we must interpret your *tatecredue* for you is a sign that you incline toward *aubre*. But we will grant you a dispensation, as you are not a proper creature. Listen: a man has escaped from us. Three days ago he fled from us on foot, and we have not been able to find him. By this act, he has shown himself to be *aubre,* and so proved that he does not exist. The illusion of his existence must therefore be negated. The man must not be allowed to reach a human settlement, to tell other humans about us. Should he do so, that would interfere with our own *tatecredue*. Such interference is *gaesu,* prime contradiction. Therefore you will find him, negate him, in order to restore balanced flow."

"How am *I* supposed to find him if you could not?"

"You are men. You are the same. You will find him."

"He could be anywhere by now!" Ramon protested.

"Where you would go and where he would go—they are the

same. You will go where he has gone, and you will find him."

Ramon chewed his lip and thought. He had no intention of playing Judas Goat for these monsters, but he was naked, alone, and in their power. If he pretended to agree, they would have to take him out—out to the world he knew. After that, he could slip away. It wouldn't do to give in too easily, though. Even things as strange as these might recognize that as subterfuge.

"If I do this thing for you, what do I get out of it?" he asked.

The alien stared at him for several long moments. "You are an improper and contradictory creature. *Aubre* may manifest in you. We will insure against such manifestations, by separating a part of ourselves to act as overseer. Maneck will sacrifice himself to maintain the flow."

The alien who had led him from the first chamber moved silently to Ramon's side. It was eerie—nothing so big should be so quiet.

"Maneck, eh?" Ramon said to the thing. "Your name's Maneck?"

Before Ramon could react, Maneck reached out and took him by the shoulders, lifted him like a doll, and held him immobile in the air. Ramon fought instinctively—nights at the bar and in the street coming back to his arms and legs in a rage. He might as well have punched the ocean. Maneck didn't budge.

Up from the pit rose a pale white snake.

Ramon watched in horrified fascination. It was obviously a cable of some sort—two bare wires protruded from the visible end—but its movements were so supple and lifelike that he could not help but think of it as a pale and sinister cobra. It reared almost to eye-level, swayed slowly from side to side, aimed its blind pallid head at Ramon. The head quivered slightly, as though the snake was testing the air in search of its prey. Then it stretched out toward him.

Again Ramon tried desperately to break free, but Maneck wrenched him effortlessly back into position. As the cable-snake came closer, he saw that it was pulsating rhythmically, as if it were truly alive, and that the two naked wires in its head were vibrating like a serpent's flickering tongue. His flesh crawled, and he felt his testicles retract. He felt his nakedness vividly now—he was unprotected, helpless, all of the soft vulnerable parts of his body exposed to the hostile air. The cable touched the hollow of his throat.

Ramon felt a sensation like the touch of dead lips, a double pinprick of pain, a flash of intense cold. An odd quivering shock ran up and down his body, as though someone were tracing his nervous system with feather fingers. His vision dimmed for a heartbeat, then came back. Maneck lowered him to the ground.

The cable was now embedded in his neck. Fighting nausea, he reached up and took hold of it, feeling it pulse in his hands. It was warm to the touch, like human flesh. He pulled at it tentatively, then tugged harder. He felt the flesh of his throat move when he tugged. To rip it free would obviously be as difficult as tearing off his own nose. The cable pulsed again, and Ramon realized that it was pulsing in time to the beating of his heart. As he watched, it seemed to darken slowly, as if it were filling up with blood.

The cable had somehow also linked itself to the alien that had held him, blending into its right wrist. Maneck. He was on a leash. A hunting dog for demons.

"The *sahael* will not injure you, but it will help to resolve your contradictions," the thing in the pit said as if sensing his distress but failing to understand it. "Should you manifest *aubre,* you will be corrected. Like this."

Ramon found himself on the floor, though he did not remember falling. Only now that the pain had passed could he look back at it, as a swimmer turns to look back at a wave that has passed over his head, and realize that it had been the worst pain he had ever experienced. He didn't remember screaming, but his throat was raw, and it almost seemed as if the echo of his shriek was still reverberating from the chamber walls; perhaps it would echo there forever. He caught his breath, and then retched. He knew that he would do whatever was required to prevent that from happening again, anything at all, and for the first time since he woke in darkness, Ramon Espejo felt ashamed.

"School yourself," the pale alien said. "Correct *aubre,* and even such a flawed thing as yourself may achieve cohesion or even coordinate level."

It took Ramon some time to realize that this gibberish had been a dismissal: a stern but kindly admonition, hellfire threatened, the prospect of redemption dangled, and go forth *mi hijo* and sin no more. The sonofabitch was a missionary! Maneck lifted Ramon back to his feet and nudged him toward a tunnel. The fleshy leash—the *sahael*—shrank to match whatever distance was between them. Maneck made a sound that he couldn't interpret and apparently gave up gentle coaxing. The alien moved briskly forward, the *sahael* tugging now at Ramon's throat. He had no choice but to follow, like a dog trotting at its master's heel.

FOUR

Back through the tunnels they went, through cavern after cavern, through rhythmic noise, billowing shadow, and glaring blue light. Ramon walked leadenly, like an automaton, pulled along by Maneck, the tether in his neck feeling heavy and awkward. The chill air leeched the heat from his body, and even the work of walking wasn't enough to keep him warm.

In the privacy of his mind, Ramon searched for hope. Eleana would notice he was missing. Maybe. Given enough time. Or she might think he'd gone off again, down to Nuevo Janiero without her, to file his reports and collect his fees. Or run off on a drunken spree with some other woman. He weighed the probabilities; she might call for help and start a search, or she might wait, getting angrier and angrier until she worked herself into a blind rage over his absence. No. Eleana couldn't be trusted to search for him. Maybe Old Sanchez would start an inquiry when he didn't bring the van back. Or that bastard Javier in Diegotown might notice that no one was staying in his rooms. Rent would come due in two weeks . . .

There was no one. That was the truth. He had lived his life on his own terms—always on his own terms—and here was the price of it. He had no one to rescue him. He was on his own, hundreds of miles from the nearest human settlement, captured and enslaved. So he would have to find his own way out. Escape. If only there was a way to avoid the pain that his slick, pulsing, fleshy leash could mete out.

Maneck tugged at the *sahael* and Ramon looked up, aware for the first time that they had stopped. The alien thing pushed a bundle into his arms. Clothes.

The clothes were a sleeveless one-piece garment, something like pajamas, a large cloak, and hard-soled slipper-boots, all made from a curious lusterless material. He pulled them on with fingers stiff from cold. The aliens were obviously not used to tailoring for humans; the clothes were clumsily made and ill-fitting, but at least they afforded him some protection against the numbing cold. It wasn't until his nakedness was covered and warmth began to return to his limbs that his teeth began to chatter.

Maneck tugged him brusquely along into another high-ceilinged chamber. The place teemed with aliens, swarming over terraced layers of objects on the cavern floor. Equipment, perhaps, machines, computers, although most things here were so unfamiliar that they registered only as indecipherable blurs, weird amalgams of shape and shadow and winking light. Far across the cave, two giant aliens—similar to Maneck and the others, but fifteen or twenty feet tall—labored in gloom, lifting and stacking what looked like huge sections of honeycomb, moving with ponderous grace, as unreal and hallucinatorily beautiful as stop-motion dinosaurs in old horror movies. To one side, a smaller alien was herding a flow of spongy molasses down over a stairstep fall of boulders, touching the flowing mass occasionally with a long black rod, as if to urge it along.

On the other side of the room, up against the cavern wall, was a rank of the flying motorcycles. One had been fitted out with a sidecar. Ramon waited leadenly while Maneck examined the cycle, running its long slender fingers carefully over the controls. He could feel himself becoming dazed and passive, numbed by weariness and shock—he'd been through too much, too fast. And he was tired, more tired than he could remember being before; perhaps the shot they'd given him was wearing off.

He was almost asleep on his feet when Maneck seized him, lifted him into the air as if he was a little child, and stuffed him into the sidecar. He struggled to sit up, but Maneck seized his arms, drew them behind his back, and bound them with a thin length of wire-like substance, then hobbled his legs, before turning and straddling the operator's saddle. Maneck touched a pushplate, and the cycle rose smoothly into the air.

Acceleration pushed Ramon's head against the rim of the sidecar, pinning it at an uncomfortable angle. In spite of the terror of his situation, he realized that he was not able to stay awake any longer. Even as they rose up toward the high-domed cavern roof, his eyes were squeezing shut, as though the mild g-forces that pulled with mossy inevitability on his bones were also drawing him inexorably into sleep.

Above them, the rock opened.

As Ramon's consciousness faded away, drowning him in hissing white snow, he saw, beyond the hole in the sky, a single pale and isolate star.

A freezing wind lashed him awake. He struggled to sit up. The sidecar lurched, and he found himself looking straight down through an ocean of air at the tiny tops of the trees. The cycle canted over the other way, violently, and the darkening evening sky swirled around his head, momentarily turning the faint, newly emerged stars into tight little squiggles of light.

They leveled off. Maneck sat the cycle's saddle unshakably, firm and cold as a statue, quills rippling in the bitter wind. Banking again, falling at a slant through the air. He couldn't have been insensible for more than a minute or two, Ramon realized; that was the alien's mountain just behind them, the exit-hole now irised shut again, and that was the mountain slope where he'd been captured just below. Even as they coasted down toward it, the sky was growing significantly darker around them. The sun had gone behind the horizon some moments before, leaving only the thinnest sliver of glazed red along the junction line of land and air. The rest of the sky was the color of plum and eggplant and ash, dying rapidly to ink-dark blackness overhead and to the west. Armed and bristling with trees, the mountain slope rushed up to meet them. Too fast! Surely they would crash . . .

They touched down lightly in the upland meadow where Ramon had made his camp, settling out of the sky as silently as the shadow of a feather. Maneck killed the cycle's engine. Blackness swallowed them, and they were surrounded by the sly and predatory noises of evening. In that darkness, Maneck seized Ramon, and, lifting him like a child's toy, dragged him from the cycle, carried him a few feet away, and dropped him to the ground.

Ramon groaned involuntarily, startled and ashamed by the loudness of his voice. His arms were still bound behind him, and to lay upon them was excruciatingly painful. He rolled over onto his stomach. The ground under him was so cold that it was comfortable, and even in his present sick and confused condition, Ramon realized that that was death. He thrashed and squirmed, and managed to roll himself up in the long cloak he'd been given; it was surprisingly warm. He would have fallen asleep then, in spite of his pain and discomfort, but light beat against his eyelids where there had been no light, and he opened his eyes.

The light seemed blinding at first, but it dimmed as his eyes adjusted. Maneck had brought something from the cycle, a small globe attached to a long metal rod, and jammed the sharp end of the rod into the soil; now the globe was alight, burning from within with a dim bluish light, sending off rhythmic waves of heat. As Ramon watched, Maneck walked around the globe—the *sahael* shortening visibly with each step—and came slowly toward him with seeming deliberation. Only then, watching Maneck prowl toward him, seeing the wet gleam in the corner of its orange eyes as it looked from side to side, seeing the way its nose crinkled and twitched, the way its head swiveled and swayed restlessly on the stubby neck, the shrugging of its shoulders at each step, hearing the iron rasp of its breath, smelling its thick musky odor—only then did some last part of Ramon's mind fully accept the fact that Maneck was an alien, accept it all the way down at the most basic of gut levels. It was not an odd animal, a man in costume, a robot, a dream, an illusion, a trick: it was an intelligent alien being, and he was its captive, alone and at its mercy in the wilderness.

That simple knowledge hit Ramon with such force that he felt the blood begin to drain out of his face, and even as he was worming and scrambling backward in a futile attempt to get away from the monster, he was losing his grip on the world, losing consciousness, slipping down into darkness.

The alien stood over him, seen again through the hazy white snow of faintness, seeming to loom up endlessly into the sky like some horrid and impossible beanstalk, with eyes like blazing orange suns. That was the last thing Ramon saw. Then the snow piled up over his face and buried him, and everything was gone.

Morning was a blaze of pain. He had fallen asleep on his back, and he could no longer feel his arms. The rest of his body ached as though it had been beaten with clubs. The alien was standing over him again—or perhaps it had never moved, perhaps it had stood there all night, looming and remote, terrible, tireless, and unsleeping. The first thing Ramon saw that morning, through a bloodshot haze of pain, was the alien's face; the long twitching black snout with its blue and orange markings, the quills stirring in the wind and moving like the feelers of some huge instinct.

I will kill you, Ramon thought. There was very little anger in it. Only a deep, animal certainty. *Somehow, I will kill you.*

Maneck hauled Ramon to his feet and set him loose, but his legs would not hold him, and he crashed back to the ground as soon as he was released. Again Maneck pulled him up, and again Ramon fell.

As Maneck reached for him the third time, Ramon screamed, "Kill me! Why don't you just kill me?" He wormed backward, away from Maneck's reaching hand. "You might as well just kill me now!"

Maneck stopped. Its head tilted to one side to regard Ramon curiously, in an oddly birdlike manner. The cool orange eyes peered at him closely, unblinking.

"I need food," Ramon went on in a more reasonable tone. "I need water. I need rest. I can't use my arms and legs if they're tied like this. I can't even stand, let alone walk!" He heard his voice rising again but couldn't stop it. "Listen, you monster, I need to *piss*! I'm a man, not a machine!" With a supreme effort, he heaved himself to his knees and knelt there in the dirt, swaying. "Is this *aubre*? Eh? Good! Kill me, then! I can't go on like this!"

Man and alien stared at each other for a long, silent moment. Ramon, exhausted by his outburst, breathed in rattling gasps. Maneck studied him carefully, snout quivering. At last, it said, "You possess *retehue*?"

"How the shit would *I* know?" Ramon croaked, his voice rasping in his dry throat. "What the fuck is it?" He drew himself up as much as he could, and glared back at the alien.

"You possess *retehue*," the alien repeated, but it was not a question this time. It took a quick step forward, and Ramon flinched, afraid that the death he'd demanded was on its way. But instead, Maneck cut him free.

At first, he could feel nothing in his arms and legs; they were as dead as old wood. Then sensation came back into them, burning like ice, and they began to spasm convulsively. Ramon set his face stoically and said nothing, but Maneck must have noticed and correctly interpreted the sudden pallor of his skin, for it reached down and began to massage Ramon's arms and legs. Ramon shrunk away from its touch—again he was reminded of snakeskin, dry, firm, warm—but the alien's powerful fingers were surprisingly deft and gentle, loosening knotted muscles, and Ramon found that he didn't mind the contact as much as he would have thought that he would; it was making the pain go away, after all, which was what really counted.

"Your limbs have insufficient joints," Maneck commented. "That position would not be uncomfortable for me." It bent its arms backward and forward at impossible angles to demonstrate. With his eyes closed, it was almost possible for Ramon to believe that he was listening to a human being—Maneck's Portuglish was much more fluent than that of the alien in the pit, and its voice had less of the rusty timbre of the machine. But then Ramon would open his eyes and see that terrible alien face, ugly and bestial, only inches from his own, and his stomach would turn over, and he would have to adjust all over again to the fact that he was chatting with a monster.

"Stand up now," Maneck said. It helped Ramon up and supported him while he limped and stomped in a slow semicircle to work out cramps and restore circulation, looking as if he was performing some arthritic tribal dance. At last, he was able to stand unsupported, although his legs wobbled and quivered with the strain.

"We have lost time this morning," Maneck said. "This is all time we might have employed in exercising our functions." You could almost imagine that it sighed. "I have not previously performed this type of function. I did not realize that you possessed *retehue*, and therefore failed to take all factors into account. Now we must suffer delays accordingly."

Suddenly, Ramon understood what *retehue* must be. He was more baffled than outraged. "How could you not realize that I was sentient? You were there all the while I talked to the white thing in the pit!"

"We were present, but I had not integrated yet," Maneck said simply. It did not elaborate further, and Ramon had to be content with that. "Now that I am, I will observe you closely. You are to demonstrate the limitations to the human flow. Once we are informed, the man's path is better predicted."

That's not hard to guess, Ramon thought, but did not say. *If there is some other poor bastard out here, knowing these monsters are after him, he's pushing like hell for Fiddler's Jump.*

"Speaking of flow," Ramon said. "I still have to piss."

"Elimination of waste will suffice as a starting point. I will observe."

"I don't think so," Ramon said. "You can stay here."

To his surprise, the alien did as it was told. Ramon walked unsteadily to the edge of the meadow, the leash in his neck hardly tugging him as he walked. He pissed into the scrub brush and tried to make sense of the alien's behavior. The limitations of human flow, it had said. For a being so fascinated by purpose, Maneck was strangely interested in Ramon's need to urinate, which ought to have struck it as irrelevant. It wasn't an activity that seemed important to hunting down the fugitive. It had not known that binding his arms behind him would discomfort him. Ramon stood for a long moment after his bladder was empty, considering. Perhaps the aliens needed him in order to understand what the habits of a man were. He was more than a hound.

Merely by *being human,* he was a guide for them.

Ramon pulled his clothes back into place, disturbed for a moment by how rough the fabric felt against his skin. Maneck loomed by the cycle, still as a tree. Ramon shrugged and returned.

"You are complete?" Maneck asked.

"Sure," Ramon said. "Complete enough for the moment."

"You have other needs?"

"I should eat. Do you have any food?"

Maneck paused for a long moment, as if struggling to understand the question. Then its snout twitched.

"No," it said. "The *oekh* I have would not nourish you. How do you obtain food? I will allow you to procure it for yourself."

Every minute that Ramon stalled was a gift to the fugitive, whoever he was, wherever he was. If he could stall long enough for the man to escape, that might bring help. If the prey could escape the net, someone would come. The news would spread. Eleana and Sanchez would guess what had happened to him. It was his best hope. Feeding off the land wasn't hard. The amino acids that had built up the biosphere of São Paulo were almost all identical to those on Earth. A half-hour of gathering would have gotten him enough mianberry to make a small meal. Sug beetles would boil up in three minutes and tasted like lobster. This far north, you could pick them off the trees by the handful. But none of that would take long enough.

"We'll have to improvise some traps," Ramon said. "It could take a while."

"We will begin," Maneck said.

Ramon scouted the wreckage that had been his van and tent, gathering the lengths of wire, cloth, and rope he needed to set up snares. The animals this far north were naïve, unfamiliar with traps, never having been hunted by humans before, and so were easy to catch. He tied the ropes and bent the wire, surprised by how much the metal bit into the flesh of his hands. The syrup bath in which the aliens had soaked him must have melted away the calluses from his hands and feet, leaving his fingers ill-prepared for real work. Still, he placed the snares, Maneck watching him with what seemed sometimes like profound curiosity, sometimes like impatience, but was likely an emotion Ramon had never felt or heard named.

They waited as the sun rose higher in the perfect blue sky. Maneck ate some of his *oekh,* which turned out to be a brown paste the consistency of molasses with a thick vinegary scent. Ramon scratched at the place in his neck where the *sahael* anchored in his flesh and tried to ignore the emptiness of his belly. The hunger grew quickly, though, and, in spite of his good intentions about stalling as long as he could, it was less than two hours later when he rose and walked out to check his catch—two grasshoppers, and a gordita, the fuzzy round marsupials that the *paulistas* called "the little fat ones of the Virgin." The gordita had died badly, biting itself in its frenzy. Its spiky fur was already black with thick, tarry blood. Maneck looked on with interest as Ramon removed the animals from the snares.

"It is difficult to think of this as having anything to do with food," it said. "Why do the creatures strangle themselves for you? Is it their *tatecredue*?"

"No," Ramon said as he strung the bodies on the length of carrying twine. "It's not their *tatecredue.* It's just something that happened to them." He found himself staring at his hands as he worked, and, for some reason, his hands made him uneasy. He shrugged the feeling away. "Don't your people hunt for food?"

"The hunt is not for food," Maneck said flatly. "Food is *ae euth'eloi*—a made thing. The hunt is wasted on creatures such as these. How can they appreciate it? Their brains are much too small."

"My stomach is also too small, but it will appreciate *them.*" He stood up, swinging the dead animals over his shoulder.

"Do you swallow the creatures now?" Maneck asked.

"First they must be cooked."

"Cooked?"

"Burned, over a fire."

"Fire," Maneck repeated. "Uncontrolled combustion. Proper food does not require such preparation. You are a primitive creature. These steps waste time, time which might be better used to fulfill your *tatecredue. Ae euth'eloi* does not interfere with the flow."

Ramon shrugged. "I cannot eat your food, monster, and I

cannot eat these raw." He held the carcasses up for inspection. "If we are to get on with me exercising my function, I need to make a fire. Help me gather sticks."

Back at the clearing, Ramon started a small cookfire. When the flames were crackling well, the alien turned to look at Ramon. "Combustion is proceeding," it said. "What will you do now? I wish to observe this function *cooking*."

Was that an edge of distaste in the alien's voice? He suddenly had a flash of how odd the process must seem to Maneck: catching and killing an animal, cutting its pelt off and pulling out its internal organs, dismembering it, toasting the dead carcass over a fire, and then eating it. For a moment, it seemed a grotesque and ghoulish thing to do, and it had never seemed like that before. He stared down at the gordita in his hand, and then at his hand itself, sticky with dark blood, and the subtle feeling of wrongness he'd been fighting off all morning intensified once again. "First I must skin them," he said resolutely, pushing down the uneasiness, "before I can cook them."

"They have skin already, do they not?" Maneck said.

Ramon surprised himself by smiling. "I must take their skin off. And their fur. Cut it off, with a knife, you see? Way out here, I'll just throw the pelts away, eh? Waste of money, but then grasshopper pelts aren't worth much anyway."

Maneck's snout twitched, and it prodded at the grasshoppers with a foot. "This seems inefficient. Does it not waste a large portion of the food, cutting it off and throwing it away? All of the rind."

"I don't eat fur."

"Ah," Maneck said. It moved up close behind Ramon and sank to the ground, its legs bending backwards grotesquely. "It will be interesting to observe this function. Proceed."

"I need a knife," Ramon said.

Wordlessly, the alien plucked a cylinder from its belt and handed it to Ramon. When Ramon turned it over in bafflement, Maneck reached across and did something to the cylinder, and a six-inch silver wire sprang out stiffly. Ramon took the strange knife and began gutting the gordita. The wire slid easily through the flesh. Perhaps it was the hunger that focused Ramon so intently on his task, because it wasn't until he had set the gordita on a spit over the fire and begun on the first grasshopper that he realized what the alien had done. *It had handed him a weapon.*

He fought the sudden rush of adrenaline, struggling to keep the blade from wobbling in his hands, to keep his hands from shaking. Bent over the careful task of digging out the grasshopper's rear gills, he glanced at Maneck. The alien seemed to have noticed nothing. The problem was, where to strike it? Stabbing it in the body was too great a risk; he didn't know where the vital organs were, and he couldn't be sure of striking a killing blow. Maneck was larger and stronger than he was. In a protracted fight, Ramon knew, he would lose. It had to be done swiftly. The throat, he decided, with a rush of exhilaration that was almost like flying. He would slash the knife as deep across the alien's throat as he could. The thing had a mouth and it breathed, after all, so there had to be an air passage in the neck somewhere. If he could sever that, it would only be a matter of remaining alive long enough for the alien to choke to death on its own blood. It was a thin chance, but he would take it.

"Look here," he said, picking up the body of the grasshopper. With its legs and scales cut away, its flesh was soft and pink as raw tuna. Maneck leaned closer, as Ramon had hoped, its eyes trained on the dead flesh in his left hand, ignoring the blade in his right. The heady elation of violence filled him, as if he was in the street outside a bar in Diegotown. The monsters didn't know that this thing they'd captured knew how to be a monster too! He waited until Maneck turned its head a little to the side to better squint at the grasshopper, exposing the mottled black-and-yellow flesh of its throat, and then he struck—

Abruptly, he was laying on his back on the ground, staring up into the tall violet sky. His stomach muscles were knotted, and he was breathing in harsh little gasps. The pain had hit him like a stone giant's fist, crumpled him and thrown him aside. It had been over in an eyeblink, too quick to be remembered, but his body still ached and twitched with the shock. His throat was raw, and he wondered if he had screamed. He had dropped the knife.

You fool, he thought.

Maneck moved into his field of vision and stood looking

down at him. "That was unwise of you," it said, placidly. "It is not possible to take me by surprise. It cannot be done. Do you understand this?"

"You can . . . you can read my mind?"

"The *sahael* drinks from the flow of your body. I am tied to your neural pathways as an overseer. The intention to act precedes the action, and begins cascading flows. All flows relate and interact, and so you cannot act before I am aware of the action you are taking. You are a primitive being not to know this."

Maneck lifted him easily and set him on his feet. To Ramon's shame and humiliation, the alien gently placed the wire knife back in his hand.

"Continue the function," Maneck said. "You were flaying the corpse of the small animal."

Ramon turned the silver cylinder slowly, shaking his head. He was unmanned. He could no more defeat this thing than an infant child could best his father. He was not even a threat to it.

"You are . . . distressed," Maneck said. "Why?"

"Because you are still alive!" Ramon spat.

The alien seemed to consider this.

"You attempted to function, and failed in your task. The distress you feel is an awareness of *aubre,* and shows promise for you, but you have not understood your *tatecredue*. These outbursts are *part* of your proper functioning. The uncontrolled violence, the tiny bladder and inefficient means of expelling nitrogenous waste, the aversion to eating the rind of another creature . . . all these things inform our behavior and lead us to the better fulfillment of our purpose. If you do not embody the weaknesses of the man as well as the strengths, we cannot prevent him from reaching others of his kind."

"*My* strengths are meaningless," Ramon said bitterly. "Another man might not have tried to kill you. Or he might have found some better way to do it. You have nothing to learn from me."

"He would have done as you have," Maneck said. "He could not do otherwise, anymore than a single flow can move against itself. Turbulence can only come of *aubre* or else from without."

Something shifted in the back of Ramon's mind. The roughness of the alien cloth against his skin, the calluses gone from his fingertips. He had not been breathing in that tank. His heart had not been beating. He dropped the knife, the wire scooping up a tiny spray of dirt where it landed. Slowly, he pulled back his sleeve. The scar he'd gotten in the machete fight with Chulo Lopez at the bar outside Little Dog, the trails of puckered white flesh that Eleana's fingertips opened and re-opened when they tore at each other during half-crazed sex, were gone. There were no cigaret stains on his fingers. None of the small nicks and discolorations and calluses that were the legacy of a lifetime working with your hands. Over the years, his arms had been burnt almost black by the sun, but now his skin was smooth and unblemished and pale brown as an eggshell. An awareness half-buried rose up in him, and he went cold.

"What have you done?" he said.

The alien stood still, observing him.

"What have you *done!*" Ramon screamed.

"I have performed many functions," Maneck said slowly, like a teacher speaking to a very dim child. "Which of these distresses you?"

"My body! My skin! What did you *do* to me?"

"Ah! Interesting. You are capable of *khetanae*. This may not be good. I doubt the man is able to integrate, and even if he did, it would not cause this disorientation. You may be diverging from him."

"What are you talking about, monster!"

"Your distress," Maneck said, simply. "You are becoming aware of who you are."

"I am Ramon Espejo!"

"No," Maneck said. "You are not that person."

FIVE

Ramon—if he was Ramon—sank slowly to the ground. Maneck, looming beside him, explained in its strange passionless voice. The human Ramon Espejo had discovered the refuge three days before. That alone had been contradiction, and in order to correct the illusion that he existed, he had been attacked. He escaped, but not uninjured. An appendage—a finger—had been torn from him in the attack. That flesh had acted as the seed for the creation of a made thing—*ae euth'eloi*—that had participated in the original being's flow. Maneck had to explain twice before Ramon truly understood that it meant him.

"As you express that flow, you collapse into the forms from which you came. There was some loss of fidelity, so those forms that were of controlling function were emphasized—the brain and nerve column—while the skin complications were sacrificed. You will continue to develop across time."

"I am Ramon Espejo," Ramon said. "And you are a filthy whore with breath like a Russian's asshole."

"Both of these things are incorrect," Maneck said patiently.

"You're lying!"

"The language you use is not a proper thing. The function of communication is to transmit knowledge. To lie would fail to transmit knowledge. That is not possible."

Ramon's face went hot, then cold. "You're lying," he whispered.

"Your flesh is seared," Maneck said, and it was a long moment before Ramon understood. The gordita hadn't been turning on its spit. The meat was starting to burn. He sat up and shifted it, exposing the raw pink flesh that had been on the top to the heat of the flame. It was something concrete, physical, immediate. The scent of roasting meat woke a hunger in him that was more powerful even than horror or despair.

The body keeps on living, he thought bitterly, *even when we do not wish it to.*

"I know about cloning," Ramon said when he had composed himself. "What you say you've done isn't possible. A clone wouldn't have my memories. It would have my genes, yes, but it would be just a little baby. It wouldn't know anything about the life I've lived."

"You know nothing of what we can and cannot do," Maneck chided, "and yet you assert otherwise. This was not reproduction. You are a product of recapitulation." Maneck paused. "The thought fits poorly in your language, but if you were to gain enough *atakka* to understand it fully, you would diverge further from the model. It interferes with our *tatecredue*. Show me how the man would consume this seared flesh."

Because it was already what he had intended, Ramon did as he was bidden and ate, carving strips off the gordita with the wire knife. He felt Maneck's eyes upon him as he stuffed food greedily into his mouth, relishing the peppery taste of the meat, the grease he licked from his fingers. And as he chewed, he thought. If it was true—if he were not who he knew himself to be—then that other Ramon would not bring help. Even if he reached Fiddler's Jump, he had no way to know that his twin existed. And he might not care if he did. The other Ramon would likely think of him as a monster. An abomination.

He *was* an abomination. Cold sweat broke out on his forehead, his armpits, the back of his knees. He was coming to believe what Maneck had said: he was not the real Ramon Espejo, he was some monster born in a vat, an unnatural thing only three days old. Everything he remembered was false, had happened to some other man, not to him. *He'd* never been out of the mountain before, never broken heads in a bar fight, never made love to a woman. This meat he was eating now was the first meal he'd ever had in his life.

The thought was vertiginous, almost unthinkable, and deliberately, with an effort, he put it aside. To think deeply about it would lead to madness. Instead, he concentrated on carving a slender leg from the gordita and using his teeth to strip the greasy meat from the bone. *If this is the first meal of my life, at least it's a good one.* Whoever or whatever he was, he was alive, out in the world, reacting to it with animal intensity. The food tasted as good as his false memories said that it should, or perhaps better; the wind felt as cool and refreshing as it swept across the meadow; the immense vista of the Sierra Hueso, sun flashing off the snowcaps on the highest peaks, was as beautiful as it ever was. None of that had changed, regardless of his origin. He *was* Ramon Espejo, no matter what the monster said, no matter what his hands looked like. He had to be, because there was no one else to *be*. What difference did it make if there was another man out there that also thought that he was him? Or a hundred such?

He was alive, right here and now, in this instant, whether he was three days old or thirty, and that was what mattered. He was alive—and he intended to stay that way.

And what Maneck had revealed changed everything. There was no advantage to stalling anymore. Maybe if he could actually *find* that other Ramon, together they could somehow turn the tables on the alien. But how to proceed wasn't immediately clear. Certainly the other would head for Fiddler's Jump. Nothing else was even close. And likely he would go by the Rio Embudo. The big river came out of the mountains a hundred and twenty-three kilometers from his ruined camp and eventually passed through Fiddler's Jump itself. It was where *he* would have gone had he been frightened, wounded, and alone. First, he would have gone south, through the foothills, to bypass the rapids and the falls, and then he would have turned west, to find the river. He would have built a raft and headed down the Rio Embudo, traveling much faster than he possibly could on foot through the thick, tangled forest. And he was sure that the other would do the same. The aliens had been smart to use him as their hunting dog after all— he *did* know what the other would do, where he would go. He *could* find him..

But he also knew what he himself would have done if he knew he were being hunted. *He* would have found a way to kill his hunters. And that now was Ramon's only chance. If he could alert the other that he was being pursued and trust him to take the right action, together they might destroy the alien thing that held his leash. For a moment, he hoped deeply that what Maneck had said was the truth, that there was another mind like his own out free in the wilderness. He felt an odd surge of pride in that other Ramon—in spite of these monsters and all the powers at their command, he had gotten away from them, fooled them, showed them what a *man* could do.

The last grasshopper consumed, Ramon drowned the fire and covered it over with dirt while Maneck watched. It was approaching midday. Three days, Maneck said, the other had been running. Three and a half now. He guessed that he could cover thirty kilometers in a day, especially with all the demons of Hell on his heels. That put his twin almost to the river by day's end. Unless his wounds had slowed him. Unless he had become septic and died alone in the forest, far from help. Ramon shuddered at the thought, but then dispelled it, grinning. That was *Ramon Espejo* out there. A tough-ass bastard like that wasn't going to die easy!

Maneck listened as he poured out his theory, or most of it. Satisfied, the alien straddled the cycle and gestured to the sidecar with a careful, studied motion. Ramon obeyed. The seat had not been fashioned for a human anatomy, but Maneck didn't bind him this time, and it was not too uncomfortable. They lifted, tilted, and angled into the sky, away from the upland plain in the shadow of the alien mountain. Ramon craned his head around for one last look. Soon the scorched mark where his van and tent had been was little more than a black thumbprint on the landscape. How he wished he had never come here, never set that fateful charge! And then he remembered that he had *not* done any of those things. It had been *the other* who had done them. All of the past belonged to the other. He had nothing but the present, nothing but Maneck and the cycle, the cold wind in his face, the clouds scuttling through an ominous indigo sky.

The cycle flew south and west. Behind them to the north were the tall peaks of the Sierra Hueso, their upper slopes now obscured by wet, churning gray cloud—it was snowing back there, behind, above. South, the world widened and flattened into forested lowland, then tilted down toward the southern horizon, steaming and slopping like a soup plate, puddled with marshes on the edge of sight. As they passed over the barren black jumble of the foothills, Ramon heard a thin chittering squeak from below them. He peered over the rim of the sidecar. A flapjack, trilling in alarm, was diving away from them. He wondered if it might be the same one he'd seen days ago, and smiled to encounter an old friend again. And then remembered, with a chill, that *he* hadn't been the one who'd seen it. It was a stranger after all. As was all the rest of the world.

After a long, cold, silent time, Maneck staring wordlessly ahead as they flew, Ramon lost in his troubled thoughts, he realized that they must be nearing the river. Below them was a thick forest of iceroot, tall, gaunt trees with translucent blue-white needles like a million tiny icicles. And then it came into sight, from up here only a thin silver ribbon in the world of green and blue and orange trees and black stone—the Rio Embudo, the main channel of the great river system that drained the Sierra Hueso and all the north lands. Hundreds of kilometers to the southwest, Fiddler's Jump sat high on its rocky, red-veined bluffs above the same river, its ramshackle wooden hotels and houses full of miners and trappers and lumberjacks, its docks crowded with ore barges and vast log floats soon to be launched downstream to Swan's Neck. It was there, to the safety and lights and raucous humanity of Fiddler's Jump, that the other was almost surely headed.

Which meant that he might be somewhere below them now.

Ramon shifted his weight and leaned nearer the alien, shouting to him over the rush of the wind.

"Move down! We can't see him from so high up! Go lower!"

"But proximity would create a greater opportunity to alert the man to our presence. He must be near."

That was exactly what Ramon had been thinking, but now he scowled and made an impatient gesture toward the wide landscape below them.

"We can be seen from anywhere if we're all the way up here," Ramon said, and then embellished with a small lie. "Human beings are very attuned to the skies. We look up all the time. Get low, and we won't be visible from so many places. Besides, I sure as shit can't see him through the trees. Can you?"

Maneck seemed to consider this, and, in answer, the cycle slowed and dropped until they were skimming lightly over the top branches of the trees like a fly over the surface of a pond. And somewhere beneath those shifting leaves was the other. His twin. His best hope of freedom.

See us, Ramon thought, as if by pushing with his mind he might reach through space and leaf-green obscurity. *See* us, you stupid *pendejo*! See us!

The river was wide—what had been a thin ribbon seen from afar had stretched into a clear expanse of glacier-cold water. Trees pressed up to the banks, exposed roots trailing into the flow like thick fingers. Maneck swept along the river, traveling south until they found a clearing at the water's edge where an old sand-bar had been abandoned by a shift in the river. There they set down. To judge from the angle of the sun, it was nearing the middle afternoon. Another two or three hours still before nightfall. Maneck, ignoring him, pulled a series of spheres and rods from the compartments of the cycle. Tools, but for what purpose Ramon couldn't guess.

"What are you doing?" Ramon asked.

"Preparing. The man is within the forest. We will find him there."

Images passed through Ramon's mind—the spheres shifting through the air, sniffing out the other man, the other him. He kept the dread from his voice when he spoke.

"That's stupid. The forest is huge. We know he will pass by on the river. We're far more south than he could possibly have gotten on foot in this time, so he's still above us somewhere. If you go poking through the trees, he can slip by. Wait here, and let him come to us. Instead of looking through the whole *terreno,* you only need to look from here"—Ramon pointed across the wide swath of slow water to the distant bank—"to there."

And we will be in one place, where *he* can find *us,* Ramon thought but did not say. Maneck shifted, his sinuous arms shifting for a moment like a sea creature in an unseen current.

"If the man has come further south than you think he could, he may have already passed us," Maneck said.

"So fly down the river at night. You can go faster than he can. He'll only have a raft."

Again, the seemingly boneless arms shifted, and then fell.

"This is not the way proper flow dictates, but if it is as the man would behave, we will do as you suggest."

"Good," Ramon said. "In the meantime, I'll show you how to fish. The man, he'll need to eat. You may as well see how."

"He will not set snares? As you did earlier?"

"He will," Ramon said. "But he'll set them in the water. Here. I'll show you."

Once the alien understood what Ramon needed, it cooperated. They rigged a crude fishing pole from a thin, dry limb snapped off a nearby iceroot pine and a length of pale, soft, infinitely malleable alien wire. A different sort of wire was shaped into a hook, and Ramon stamped along the shore turning over rocks until he found a fat orange gret beetle to use for bait. Maneck's snout twitched with sudden interest as Ramon impaled the insect.

Ramon led the alien to a likely looking spot and dropped the line. The Rio Embudo was cold to be near, and the alien clothing wasn't as thick as his own had been, but Ramon didn't complain. His thoughts were on cooking the catch, once he had it. With a bit of green wood, he could build a fire that smoked badly. Something to act as a guide for the other . . .

The first bite brought up something Ramon had never seen. That wasn't odd—there were new creatures caught in the nets at Diegotown and Swan's Neck every week, so little yet was known about São Paulo. This was a bloated, gray bottom dweller whose scales were dotted by white, vaguely pustulent nodules. It hissed at him as he pulled the hook free, and, with a sense of disgust, he threw it back into the water. It vanished with a plop.

"Why did you throw the food away?" Maneck asked.

"It was monstrous," Ramon said. "Like you."

He found another beetle, and they resumed their watch on the river as night slowly gathered around them. The sky above the canopy shifted toward the startling violet of the São Paulo sunset. Auroras danced green and blue and gold. Watching them, Ramon felt for an instant the profound peace that the open wilderness always gave him. Even captive and enslaved, even with his flesh pierced by the *sahael*, even though he was an abomination himself, the immense, dancing sky was beautiful and a thing of comfort.

Maneck chirruped and shifted, uneasily, staring up as if searching for something in the darkening sky. Ramon glanced at it. Its eyes had shifted again to the hot orange he had first seen, and its crest had risen and bristled like a animal sensing threat.

"What?" Ramon demanded.

"You have seen something. The *sahael* detects a change in your flow. And yet I find nothing to trigger this effect. You will tell me what you have seen!"

"The sky," Ramon said.

"Ah! Yes. And the man is very attuned to the sky. I recall this."

The alien shifted back to its motionless waiting, as if satisfied. Another hour or so later, Ramon finally caught a fat, white blade-fish with vivid scarlet fins. It was too dark by then for fire smoke to be of use, so Ramon simply built a large cookfire and roasted the fish gently. The flesh was warm and succulent, and when he had eaten his fill, he leaned back against the cycle and yawned. He felt very full and oddly contented despite his perilous situation and inhuman companion.

"Now, if we only had something to drink, eh?" he said expansively. "And a smoke. Ah! I would enjoy a good smoke." He thought wistfully of the cigaret he'd used to light the fuse all that time ago. Or that the other had used. The cigaret he had smoked with other lungs, in another lifetime.

The alien sat a few feet away, taking its own nourishment. The *sahael* stretched between them.

"There is river water to drink," Maneck pointed out. "Your biology requires that you drink. But what is a 'smoke'?"

Ramon tried to describe a cigaret to the creature. Maneck's snout began to twitch in revulsion before he had half-finished.

"I do not comprehend the function of *smoking*," Maneck said. "The function of the lungs is to oxygenate the body. Does not filling the lungs with the fumes of burning plants and the waste products of their incomplete combustion interfere with this function? What is the purpose of smoking?"

"Smoking gives us cancer," he said, and tossed a stone side-arm into the Rio Embudo. The alien seemed so solemn, and puzzled, that he could not resist the impulse to have a little fun with it.

"Ah! And what is *cancer*?"

Ramon explained.

"That is *aubre!*" Maneck said, its voice harsh and grating in its alarm. "Your function is to find the man, and you will not be permitted to interfere with this purpose. Do not attempt to thwart me by contracting cancer!"

Ramon chuckled, then laughed. One wave of hilarity seemed to overrush the next, and soon he was holding his side and coughing with the strength of the laughter shaking him. Maneck moved nearer, its crest rising and falling in a way that made Ramon think it was questioning—like a child who has to ask her parents what she has said to amuse them.

"You are having a seizure," Maneck said. "And yet the *sahael* suggests it is pleasurable . . ."

It was too much. Ramon howled and kicked his feet, pointing at the alien in derision. He couldn't speak. The absurdity of his situation and the powerful strain his mind had been under amplified the humor of Maneck's confusion until he was helpless before it. The alien moved forward and then back, agitated and uncertain. Slowly, the fit faded, and Ramon found himself spent, lying on the ground, the stars of São Paulo impassive above him.

"You are unwell?" Maneck asked.

"I'm fine, monster," Ramon said. "I'm fine. You, though, are very funny."

"I do not understand."

"No. No, you don't! That's what makes you funny."

Maneck stared solemnly at him. "You are fortunate that I am not in cohesion," it said. "If I were, we would destroy you at once and start again with another duplicate, as such fits indicate that you are a defective organism. Why did you undergo this seizure? Is it a symptom of cancer?"

"Stupid monster," Ramon said. "I was laughing."

"Explain *laughing*. I do not comprehend this function."

He groped for an explanation the monster would understand. "Laughter is a good thing," he said, weakly. "Pleasurable. A man who cannot laugh is nothing. It is part of our function."

"This is not so," Maneck replied. "Laughing halts the flow. It interferes with proper function."

"Laughing makes me feel good," Ramon said. "When I feel good, I function better. It's like food, you see."

"That is an incorrect statement. Food provides energy for your body. Laughing does not."

"A different kind of energy. When something is funny, I laugh."

"Explain *funny*."

He thought for a minute, then recalled a joke he had heard

the last time he was in Little Dog. Eloy Chavez had told it to him when they went drinking together. "Listen, then, monster," he said, "and I will tell you a funny story."

The telling did not go very well. Maneck kept interrupting with questions, asking for definitions and explanations, until Ramon finally said irritably, "Son of a whore, the story will not be funny if you do not shut and let me tell it to you. You are ruining it with all these questions!"

"Why does this make the incident less funny?" Maneck asked.

"Never mind!" Ramon snapped. "Just listen."

The alien said nothing more, and this time he told it straight through without interruption, but when he was finished, Maneck twitched its snout and stared at him from expressionless orange eyes.

"Now you are supposed to laugh," Ramon told it. "That was a very funny story."

"Why is this incident *funny*?" it said. "The man you spoke of was instructed to mate with a female of its species and kill a large carnivore. If this was his *tatecredue,* he did not fulfill it. Why did he mate with the carnivore instead? Was he *aubre*? The creature injured him, and might have killed him. Did he not understand that this might be the result of his actions? He behaved in a contradictory manner."

"That's *why* the story is funny! Don't you understand? He raped the *bear.*"

"Yes, I comprehend that," said Maneck. "Would the story not be more 'funny' if the man had performed his function properly?"

"No, no, *no*! It would not be funny at *all* then!" He glanced sidelong at the alien, sitting there like a great solemn lump, its face grave, and couldn't help but start to laugh again.

And then the pain came—world-rending, humiliating, abasing. It lasted longer than he had remembered; hellish and total and complex as nausea. When at last it ended, Ramon found himself curled tight in a ball, his fingers scrabbling at the *sahael,* which pulsed with his own heartbeat. To his shame, he was weeping, betrayed as a dog kicked without cause. Maneck stood over

him, silent and implacable, and, in that moment, to Ramon, a figure of perfect evil.

"Why?" Ramon shouted, ashamed to hear the break in his
voice. "*Why?* I did nothing to you!"

"You threaten to contract cancer to avoid our purpose. You
engage in a seizure that impairs your functioning. You take pleasure in contradictions. You take pleasure in the failure to integrate.
This is *aubre*. Any sign of *aubre* will be punished thus."

"I laughed," Ramon said. "I only laughed!"

"Any laughter will be punished thus."

In the darkness, Ramon felt something like vertigo. He had
forgotten. He had forgotten again that this thing on the far end of
his tether was not a strangely shaped man. The mind behind the
opaque orange eyes was not a human mind. It had been easy to
forget. And it had been dangerous.

If he was to live—if he was to escape this and return to the
company of human beings—he had to remember that this thing
was not like him. He was a man, however he had been created.
And Maneck was a monster. He had been a fool to treat him otherwise.

"I will not laugh again," Ramon said.

Maneck said nothing more, but sat down to watch the river.
Silence stretched between them, a gulf as strange and dark as the
void between stars. Many times Ramon had felt estranged from
the people he was forced to deal with—norteamericanos,
Brazilians, or even the full-blooded *mejicanos* to whom he was
related by courtesy of rape; they thought differently, those
strangers, felt things differently, could not wholly be trusted
because they could not wholly be understood. Often women,
even Eleana, made him feel that way too. Perhaps that was why
he had spent so much of his life by himself, why he was more at
home alone in the wilderness than he had ever been with his others of his kind. But all of them had more to do with him than
Maneck ever could. He was separated from a *norteamericano* by
history, culture, and language—but even a gringo knew how to
laugh. No such common ground untied Ramon and Maneck;
between them lay light-years, and a million centuries of evolution. He could take nothing for granted about the thing at the

other end of the *sahael*. The thought made him colder than the breeze from the river.

"I need to sleep," Ramon said at last.

"That is well," Maneck replied. "I will watch the river."

Ramon spread his cloak on the ground and rolled himself in it as well as he could with the *sahael* in the way. Before long, he found himself beginning to drift. In his torpor, he realized that the *alien* had been the one learning all this time—how a man ate, how he pissed, how he slept. *Ramon* had learned nothing. For all his strategy and subterfuge, he knew hardly more about the monster than when he'd first woken in darkness.

He would learn. If he had been created as the thing said, then in a way Ramon was part alien himself—the product of an alien technology. He was a new man. He could learn new ways. He would come to understand the aliens, what they believed, how they thought. He would leave no tool unused.

Sleep stole into him, taking him gently down below consciousness, his determination to *know* still locked in his mind like a rat in a pit terrier's teeth. Ramon Espejo felt the dreams lapping at his mind like water at the bank of a river, and at last let them come. They were strange, dreams such as Ramon Espejo had never dreamed before.

But after all, he was not Ramon Espejo.

SIX

In his dream, he was within the river. He had no need to breathe, and moving through the water was as simple as thinking. Weightless, he inhabited the currents like a fish, like the water itself. His consciousness shifted throughout the river as if it were his body. He could feel the stones of the riverbed where the water smoothed them and the shift, far ahead, where the banks turned the flow one way and then another. And farther, past that to the sea.

The sea. Vast as a night sky, but *full*. The flow shifting throughout, alive and aware. Ramon floated down through the waters until he came near the dappled bottom and it swam away, the back of a leviathan larger than a city and still insignificant in the living abyss.

And then he was also the abyss.

Ramon dreamed of flow. Meaningless syllables took on significance and passed back into nonsense. Insights profound as love and sleep moved through him and left him filled with a terrible awe. The sky was an ocean, and the flow filled the space between stars. He followed the flow for hundreds or thousands of years, swimming between the stars, his belly heavy with generations yet unborn, searching for refuge, for someplace *safe,* away from pursuit, where he could hide and fulfill his destiny. His mind was a river, and he fed into the sea and sky. The part of his dream that was human knew that if he had the courage, he would see the face of God in the waters.

And then, still dreaming, something caught him. An eddy powerful as violence threw him in a direction he could not name, and there in the current floated the bodies of the dead—alien forms but familiar as lovers. The great pale beast in the pit who had counseled him before this desperate hunt began. The small, bluish forms of *kait* eggs, now never to hatch. Yellow-fringed *mahadya* and half-grown *ataruae* still bent at the spine. (These were not words that Ramon knew, and yet he knew them.) All of them beyond redemption. He was Maneck, *athanai* of his cohort, and these dead that touched him, that polluted the flow, were his failing. His *tatecredue* was unfulfilled, and each of these beautiful things had fallen into illusion because he had failed to bear the weight of truth.

With a sorrow as profound as any Ramon had ever felt— more than the loss of his mother and his Yaqui father, more than the heartbreak of first love—he began to eat the dead, and with every corpse that he took into himself, he became less real, more lost in *aubre* and sin, more fully damned, until he reached out for the last floating, lost, illusory form and woke with a shriek.

Maneck stood beside him, its long arms lifting him with something between tenderness and anger. In the east, a paleness had snuffed out stars—the dawn coming up.

"What have you done?" the alien cried, and, as it did, seemed somehow less alien, lost and frightened and alone.

"*Gaesu*," Ramon said. "Prime contradiction. This is what it means? That all of you kill yourselves?"

"You should not have been able to use the *sahael* this way," Maneck said. "You should not have been able to drink of *my* flow. You are diverging from the man. It threatens our function. You will not do this again, or I will punish you!"

"Why?" Ramon asked, and the alien knew as well as he did that he was not asking why he would be punished. Maneck blinked its strange orange eyes and seemed to settle back, subtly defeated.

"To be observed *cannot happen*," Maneck said. "The illusion that it *has* happened is prime contradiction, the negation of reality. We escaped from our enemies and came here, we have hidden here for generations of recycling, waiting until the time was right to fulfill the *tatecredue* of our kind. If we were to be seen, we would not be what we are, we would *never have been* what we are. That which cannot be found cannot *be* found. This is contradiction. It must be resolved."

"You would all die rather then be discovered?"

"It must be resolved," the alien repeated.

"That doesn't make sense. The one, the man"—he couldn't bring himself to call him Ramon—"he's already seen you."

"He is still within illusion. If he is prevented from reaching his kind, the information cannot diffuse. He will have been corrected. The illusion of his existence will have been denied. If *he* is real, however, *we* cannot be."

"*Dios mio*," Ramon said. "You are . . . sick. You are sick, sick creatures."

"It is not illness. It is the dictate of proper flow. Your mind is twisted and alien," Maneck said. "And that is as it *should* be. You will cease to diverge from the man. We will wait here and hunt him. If he does not reach his hive, there will be no *gaesu*."

The alien turned its back to him, its attention once again on the river. Ramon lay back, listening to the rush and murmur of the river, staring at the sky as dawn slowly turned the black to blue, the light cool and bright as the foreign sun rose. In the distance, there came the odd booming cry of a *descamisado*, returning to its lair in the trees after a long night of hunting.

When he went to the edge of the forest to relieve himself, the distinctive cinnamon scent of the iceroots strong in his nostrils, the *sahael* stretched to accommodate him, but Maneck took no notice. When he gathered a double handful of berries for his breakfast, the alien showed no interest. Ramon might almost have been alone and bound by his flexible leash to a tree stump. As the hours passed, the memory of the dream faded, the sadness becoming not an emotion, but the memory of one. The conviction he had felt that *any* price would be justified if it turned aside the horror of *gaesu* faded but did not vanish. It was the thought of the monsters, and he knew it.

When he stretched out on the greymoss at the water's edge at midday, his skin warmed by the sun, Maneck made no movement, but the nap he had intended would not come. He wondered if the *sahael* was preventing it.

Tenfin birds and whirlygigs flew through the trees, shouting out at one another and fighting over places for their nests, food for themselves, mates to bear their children. The same petty struggles of all life, everywhere. Larger beasts, hoppers and fatheads, came to the river's edge, glanced incuriously at them, and drank from the water. Fish leaped and fell back. The knot of tension in his belly loosened as he watched it all, able to forget for a moment what he was, what his forced mission was, and how bleak his hopes.

He was still half-lost in his reverie when the other Ramon found them.

SEVEN

The shout had no words to it—only a long, drawn-out sound, unmistakably from a human throat. Ramon's heart was racing even before the sound was gone, and Maneck was already moving to the cycle. The *sahael* tugged viciously, pulling Ramon almost faster than he could rise and walk.

"That noise was the man," Maneck said, its voice as calm and steady as if the fate of its people didn't hang in the balance. "You will come."

Ramon didn't bother protesting. He could tell from the color of its flesh and the restless movement of its arms that the alien was agitated. He seemed, after his dream, to know much more about Maneck, but the knowledge did him no good. The other was out there in the trees, and nothing he could do or say would keep the alien from finding him. Ramon took his place on the sidecar, and, in an instant, with a dizzying lurch, they were airborne.

The search was brief, and the story it told was all too clear. In a small clearing that almost overlooked the river, a tree limb had broken high up, the pale wood standing out from the darkness of the bark like a fresh wound. And there, near where the limb had fallen, a twisted, motionless form—the shirt and trousers Ramon remembered having worn in another life, the workboots angled awkwardly out. The shape of the body hardly made sense. The other Ramon had climbed the tree to survey the land, and the branch supporting him had snapped. He was shattered now, and certainly dead. Maneck landed the cycle ten yards from the fallen man.

"You will remain here," it said, sternly.

Ramon only nodded, his heart heavy as lead. This was the end of his hopes for freedom. The aliens would take him back to their strange, terrible caverns. Perhaps he would be allowed to remain as he was—a man with the memories and spirit of a man, trapped among aliens for the rest of his life. Perhaps they would destroy him as a tool that had outlasted its function. Which would be worse?

Maneck lumbered across the high grass to where the corpse lay. Perhaps, Ramon thought, if he could find a way to start the cycle . . . it was a desperate idea, and pointless. Even if he could have figured out how to fly it, the thing in his neck would no more have allowed him to escape than gravity would let him flap his arms and fly. Maneck reached the body, leaning over it and prodding with its long, slender hands.

Ramon heard a creak in the silence and realized what was happening even before the deadfall dropped from high in the canopy—a log of copperwood twice a man's thickness and at least a hundred kilos in weight, screaming down through leaves and twig-thin branches. Maneck looked up just as the log struck him and bore him to the ground. The pain hit Ramon instantly— it was not so intense as it had been, but it was disorienting and nauseating. He stumbled from the sidecar and tried to walk forward, but the earth seemed to shift and tip. He fell to his knees, aware distantly of a shrieking human voice and a thick, naked form, more like a chimpanzee than a man, that howled in victory as it ran forward. The sharp, dry report of a pistol sounded again and again.

"Help me!" Ramon cried, scrabbling at the *sahael*. "For the love of God, cut this *pinche* thing off of me!"

Through the pain and the haze of tears, Ramon saw the naked man—the other Ramon—shift away from his attack on the fallen alien, then run toward him. He cringed away, expecting assault as much as assistance. But the other knelt, trapping the *sahael* under his knees, and began sawing at it vigorously with his bush knife. Ramon felt the damage as if the fleshy leash were a part of him, but he gritted his teeth until his jaw creaked and forced himself to breathe through the pain.

And then, like turning off a light, it was gone. Ramon lay back, gulping air. His body trembled like he'd just run a fast mile. The severed end of the *sahael* shifted in the flesh of his neck, withdrawing and then falling the few inches to the ground with a sound like a cooing pigeon. It skittered away like a live thing until the other speared it with the point of his knife.

"Do I know you?" the other said through labored breaths. "Who the fuck are you?

Ramon looked at him directly for the first time. He was filthy and unkempt—the light stubble that often darkened his chin was already a moth-eaten beard. Distrust shone in his black eyes. His left hand was wrapped in bloody cloth, and Ramon realized, with a profound sense of vertigo, that in that mess of soiled bandages, a finger was missing. A finger from which he had been born.

But the other Ramon also looked *wrong* somehow. He had expected it to be like looking into a mirror, but it was not. The face he was accustomed to seeing reflected back was different than this. Perhaps, he thought, his features were not so symmetrical as he'd liked to believe. Also the voice was higher than his own, with more of a whine in it. The voice he heard and hated when he heard himself recorded. The other Ramon's bearded chin jutted aggressively.

"I know you can talk," he said. "Who are you? What's your name?"

There was no recognition in the other's eyes. Ramon floundered, searching for a plausible lie. Maneck was the only name he could think of besides his own. He shook his head, forcing his mind to work. If he told the other the truth, he would be killed. He knew this for a certainty, because it was what he would have done himself.

"Manuel," he said. "Manuel Tenorio. I was working survey for the bank out of Fiddler's Jump. The thing over there. It caught me. It was taking me back to its hive."

"Which bank?"

"Sanchez-Perdida," Ramon said, pulling the first name that came to mind. He wasn't certain that S-P had a branch in Fiddler's Jump. But if he didn't know, neither would the other. The other narrowed his eyes, evaluating, and then slowly nodded.

"I must have seen you at the bars there. You drink at El Pinto Negro?"

"All the time."

"I must have seen you there. Well. You're lucky I found you," he said. "I was prospecting up Tierra Hueso. They blew up my van."

"The thing," Ramon said, gesturing toward Maneck. "Is it dead?"

"It better be," the other said. "I'm out of bullets." They walked over together. The other kept his bush knife at the ready in his right hand, his empty pistol still clutched in the left. Maneck lay unmoving under the deadfall, the whole lower part of its body crushed to a bloody, pulpy paste. The swirling patterns of its skin had stilled, and the hot orange eyes had faded to sightless gray. Bullet wounds made little mouths in the still flesh. No blood flowed from them. The other spat on the corpse of Maneck, *athanai* of his cohort and the last hope of his people, before turning to strip the bloodied clothing from the pile of stones and branches that had imitated a broken body, baiting the trap. Ramon lingered a moment, staring down at Maneck.

Better thee than me, monster, he thought. But still he didn't spit. In a odd way that surprised and disquieted him, he almost missed Maneck, now that it was over, now that he was free.

After all, Maneck was the only one he'd ever met in his life, except for the thing in the pit. And now the other.

"We have to get back to Fiddler's Jump," the other said as he pulled on his soiled, bloody shirt. "Do you have anything? A gun? A sat finder?"

"No," Ramon said. "The thing took everything I had. It made me wear this. I haven't got anything."

"Well," the other said, "let's see what *it* had."

They ransacked the cycle of strange artifacts—thin tangles of something like wire. The spheres and rods. A pink translucent cube. The strange twined eggbeater weapon that had destroyed the van and the bubbletent. But nothing worked, nothing functioned, no matter how they poked and prodded at it. Ramon couldn't even make the sharp wire end come out of the cylindrical knife. Perhaps it had all died with Maneck.

"What about this?" the other asked, holding out a length of light metal that curved at the edges like a drying leaf.

"I don't know," he said, again.

"Didn't you see the thing use *any* of this?"

"The tube there. It called it *oekh*. It was what it ate."

The other snatched up the tube and threw it hard against a tree.

"I don't care about its food! I need weapons! Or a way to make this thing fly! Why are you making noise if you've got nothing to say?" the other demanded, thrusting his face aggressively much too close, almost nose to nose. Ramon could see the frustration in him, the anger, the desire to strike out and make himself feel better by hurting someone, and felt its twin in his own breast.

"I was a prisoner, not a *chingada* exchange student," he said, stopping just short of calling the other *cabron* or *pendejo* or asshole or any of the other thousand epithets that would have edged them over into a fight. The other's face puckered. Was this what

Chulo Lopez had seen that night in Little Dog? It looked less impressive than it felt. This close, he could *smell* the other man, a rank, musky, unwashed reek that he found amazingly unpleasant. His breath huffed into Ramon's face like a blast of foul air, stinking of dead meat. With an effort, Ramon kept his own face still, and refused to rise to the bait.

"Fine," the other said, turning away. "At least help me build a raft. We got to get back to the world before those things find us again."

They worked through the afternoon. The other had already gathered supplies, slowed though he was by his wounds. Together, they braced the wood, bound it with long flexible strips of bark and ice grass and lengths of the alien wire. As they worked, the other told how he had rigged the deadfall, alerted by the plume of smoke from Ramon's cook fire. How he had planted the bait, how he had killed Maneck. Ramon listened as he boasted, fascinated not by the story, but by the man who told it. The delight the other took in his own cleverness was annoying. If Ramon didn't nod or make appreciative noises at the right moment, he would glare at him.

"Killed that fucking thing *dead*," the other said with an air of satisfaction. Ramon made a grunting noise, assent without comment. They finished lashing the last of the planks. The raft was rickety, but it would hold together. "So, how long you been in Fiddler's Jump?"

"Eight years," Ramon said, making up the number on the spot.

"Long time."

"Almost since the beginning," Ramon agreed. "You want me to get some food?"

"I can get my own food," the other said. "I'm not a fucking baby. I came five days on foot, catching meals. I don't need some *pinche* Fiddler's Jump banker doing my work for me!"

Ramon frowned, but nodded passively. The other would like nothing better than goading him into a fight, he knew—but he wasn't going to oblige.

"Sorry," he said.

After dinner—sug beetles boiled in riverwater—the other

Ramon smoked a cigarette that he didn't offer to share and fell asleep by the glowing embers of the fire, his hand still on his knife. In the morning, they would set out, floating their raft back to civilization. And the aliens would die, victims of *gaesu*.

And what, he wondered, would happen to *him*? When they reached Fiddler's Jump, it wouldn't be possible to pretend that he was really a native of the town. Eight years? He should have said he'd just arrived. Or said he was from some backwater like Los Cuates. And when other people saw them together, it wouldn't be possible to hide their resemblance.

Ramon looked out over the shining face of the water. He was a monstrosity—a made thing. *Ae euth'eloi.* He touched the place on his throat where the *sahael* had entered him—a disk of numb flesh the size of a New Peso. It had all seemed easy when he had been a prisoner. Now that he was free, he understood the depth of his troubles. He had no place in the world. He was Ramon Espejo, and he was not. He imagined Maneck's metal-and-gravel voice. *To be Ramon and not to be Ramon is* aubre. *It will be punished.* He chuckled.

"What?" the other said, petulant and half-asleep.

"It's nothing," Ramon said, wrapping the alien cloth closer about him and settling down for sleep himself. "Just remembering something a friend of mine used to say."

EIGHT

Ramon cast his wire into the flowing icy waters that surrounded them. The raft rode high on the river, bouyed-up by the corklike iceroot logs. Far above, a flapjack—perhaps the same one, perhaps another—folded itself and dove after some hidden prey. The other was more clearly feverish this morning, and weaker. The chill coming off the water was doing him no good. Ramon had left him at the back of the raft to sleep, and most of the morning had passed that way. By this point in its long journey to the sea, the river was deep and steady—not at all swift as big rivers go, but they had still covered much more ground in these last hours than either man could possibly have on foot, even in their best condition. Fiddler's Jump drew nearer. And then . . . And then he didn't know what. Something had to happen before that did.

"What are you doing?" the other demanded.

"Fishing," Ramon answered.

The other made a derisive grunting sound.

"What does a banker know about fishing?"

"Enough to catch fish."

The other lapsed back into silence. Ramon pulled the wire slowly back to the raft, then cast it out again, letting the rhythm of the movements lull him and the sun warm his back. When he looked around, the other had fallen asleep again, his head resting on his uninjured hand. He looked ill. Part of it was the exhaustion and the fear and the fever, but there was more than that. Ramon could see the sorrow ground in at the corners of the mouth and eyes. He could see the desperation in the shoulders. And he knew them, he recognized them. This is what he was. Smart, resourceful, tough as old leather, but wound tight around his fears and ready to blame everyone but himself. This was what he had always been. Only it took becoming an alien monstrosity to see it. The other's eyes slitted open.

"What are you looking at?"

"I thought I heard something back there," Ramon lied. "It was probably just a bird."

He turned back to the fishing, keeping his face turned away from the other, knowing that sooner or later the penny would have to drop, and the less time they spent facing each other, the better the chances of postponing the recognition. But the other didn't return to his sleep.

"You're a funny kind of man," the other said. "How long did those things have you?"

"A couple days, I guess," Ramon said. He could have easily said my whole life, or they never really had me. I was never one of them. Any more than I was one of the *colonistas in* Nuevo Janeiro. "It wasn't that bad."

"That thing they put in your neck. That looked pretty bad."

"Yeah. Maybe it was."

"They crippled me," the other said, and there was something almost like gloating in his voice. "but they didn't catch me. Too smart for them! What do you think they are anyway? What're they up to? Did you find anything out about them?"

"I don't know anything for sure. I got the impression that they aren't from this planet, that they came here long ago and have been hiding in that mountain for hundreds of years. Waiting—but waiting for what, I'm not sure. It's hard to figure out. They . . . they don't think like we do."

"We're going to be famous, you know," the other said; he hadn't really been listening. "The first men to see aliens! We'll be rich!"

"You think so?"

"I know it."

"Well. Maybe this was the big one after all," Ramon said, trying to keep the acid from his voice.

"What?"

"Nothing," Ramon said. "I was talking to the fish."

For a long moment, they were silent. Ramon shifted, wondering if his repulsive twin had drifted back to sleep, but not wanting to turn and see. Instead, he drew in the fishing wire and cast it out again. Something on his arm caught his attention. A thin white line, jagged and half-formed. The machete scar slowly welling up. What had Maneck said? *You will continue to develop across time.* He touched the thin line of knotting flesh with his fingertips, caressing it as gently as Eleana ever had. His beard was also thickening, his hands becoming rougher. He was becoming more and more like the man who lay behind him. He closed his eyes, torn between relief at seeing his own flesh coming back again and anxiety about what would come—no one would mistake them for different men. No one would even think they were twins—they were too close for that. By the time they reached another human being, they would have the same scars, the same calluses, the same faces and bodies and hair.

The thought was alarming in a way that went deeper than the simple fear of discovery. Some echo stirred in his mind of being the river of the vast and living sea. He had diverged. Maneck had feared it, and it had been right.

"You got a woman?" the other asked.

"Sorry? What?"

"I said, you got a woman?"

"Yeah. I guess."

"You guess? You don't *know*?"

"I guess I don't," Ramon said. "She's . . . she's a good woman, I think. We're a good match at least. But I make her a little crazy sometimes. And she . . ."

"She's got you whipped, *mi amigo*," the other sneered. "I can hear it in your voice."

"What about you?" Ramon asked, not looking back over his shoulder.

"I got someone I sleep with," the other said. "She's got a mouth on her sometimes, but she's okay. I don't mind fucking her. She's pretty good in bed."

"You love her?"

"What's it to you?"

"I don't think you do."

"And what do *you* know about it?" There was an angry buzz in the other's voice now. Ramon shook his head at it. He didn't have any patience for this sorry bastard. He knew him too well.

"Forget it," he said. "I'm tired and I don't feel like talking anymore."

"Who gives a shit what you want?" the other demanded. It was like they were in a bar. Ramon could feel the rage in his breast, clean and hard and deep. It was why he always fought. It was why he hated people. This greasy, self-centered, puffed-up son of a whore at the other end of the raft was what he hated most in the world. Some new, observing part of his mind made a note of the fact.

"I said I don't want to talk," Ramon said.

"You don't get to say that kind of crap about me and then act like you're so high and mighty you can decide when I can talk and not talk! You think because you got a job in an office some- where, you're *better* than me? You think that? What do *you* know?"

"I know enough," Ramon said. "I know about how Eleana makes you crazy, nagging all the time. I know about how you asked that chica at Garcia's to dance with you and whether she'd take you in if you left Eleana. Nothing ever came of that, but you *did* ask. Asking means you were thinking about it, and I don't think you'd have done that if you loved her. I think you need her. I think you need her because, without her, you aren't part of anything or anyone. You're just some *pendejo* with a third-class van and some prospecting tools."

It wasn't how he'd thought it would come out, but it would do. It was too late now to go back, and Ramon found that he actually felt good. He'd said it. He'd said it out loud, and he saw now that he'd been thinking it for months. From before the aliens, from before the vat. From before the time when there had been two of them, he'd had this hatred within him. And now it was out. And now he knew who it was for. Whatever was going to happen, let it happen now.

"The thing is, you don't understand flow," Ramon said. "You don't understand what it is to be part of something bigger. And, Ramon, you poor bastard, you aren't ever going to know."

"What the fuck *are* you?"

The words were strangled. Coughed out of a panic-tight throat. Ramon dropped the fishing wire, letting the river take it, and turned. The other was gray beneath his sun-browned skin. His eyes were open so far that Ramon could see the whites all the way around. He had backed to the edge of the raft, backed away until there was no place further to go. Next, Ramon knew, he would attack. And he did still have the knife.

"Jesus Christ," the other whispered. "You're *me!*" He stared in horror for a frozen moment, then fumbled at his belt and pulled out the bush knife.

The silence wasn't total. The river clinked and chuckled around them. Birds or things near enough like them to take the name called from the tops of the trees, flew overhead, skimmed down across the river for a drink. But Ramon and his twin might have been statues, carved of wood and set upon the raft like icons in some old pagan temple. The wounded, debased, frightened little man at the back, his knife shining where the sunlight caught the blade. And at the front, himself, whatever he was. A thing of human flesh created by aliens. Man and not-man, both at the same time, and if this was *aubre,* so be it. He was more than he had been, and he knew it now. He saw it.

And if he was not Ramon Espejo, still there was enough of the mean old bastard in him that he wouldn't go down without a fight.

Perhaps his resolve showed in his face, because as he thought it, the other shrieked and leaped forward. Ramon jumped, not away, not to the side, but forward, stepping into the blow. He brought up his balled fist, sinking his knuckles deep in the other's belly, then butted his forehead into the bridge of his older twin's nose. But the other had danced back, anticipating the attack. The blade danced.

"You're one of them," the other spat. "You're a monster!"

"Yes. Yes, I am. And I am *still* a better man than you."

Again, the other moved forward, sweeping the air with the blade, forcing Ramon to move back, back, until the raft shifted under the weight of their struggle, and cold water touched his heels.

"You're a thing. You're an abomination and you will die!"

He had been an idiot, letting the other incite him like this. Even fevered, even weak, the other was a fighter, a killer, and he had the weapon. Ramon felt anger growing in his belly, anger at himself and at the other, at the world and at the blind idiot God that had brought him this far, had made this absurdity of his life, and now, it seemed, was prepared to let him die at the hand of his worse self. The other grinned like a wolf, seeing Ramon's defeat before him.

And, for a moment, it was as if Maneck was within him, calm and stolid and phlegmatic. *You are not that person,* its strange grating voice said. The other shouted out again, leaping forward. The knife was ready—if Ramon did what his nature told him, if he jumped into the fight as if they were in an alley outside some midnight bar, he would be gutted like a fish. It was what the other expected him to do. Ramon crouched, but didn't move.

The knife moved slowly as a car wreck; Ramon shifted away to the right, but still pain bloomed in his side. He brought his arm down, pinned the other's hand against him. It drove the knife deeper into his own flesh, but it also trapped his twin against him.

"Come with me, *mi hermano,*" Ramon said. "There's something I want to show you."

And he stepped off the edge of the raft.

The water was numbing cold, the glacier still in its blood. Ramon gasped despite himself and earned a throatful of river water. The other thrashed and twisted, and then they were apart, floating. Floating in a bright, flowing river. Ramon noticed the red bloom that came from his side, his blood mixing with the water, becoming a part of it. He was becoming the river.

It would have been easy to let it happen. The living sea called to him, and part of him wanted very much to join it, to become the river completely. But the part of him that was alien remembered the threatened sorrow of *gaesu* and the human part of him refused to be beaten, and together the two parts of himself forced him on. He shifted back, finding the dark form of the raft above him, and kicked against the flow with all his strength. He pulled off the alien cloth and swam naked, the heat and blood pouring out of him.

His hand broke the surface. He clawed at the raw wood, almost too weak to grip it. Each time he pulled himself farther up out of the water, he felt fainter, but he gritted his teeth and tugged until he had a leg up, and then, with one last pull, he was free of the river. He fought to draw air, and then vomited, each spasm shooting pain like a fresh wound through the slit in his side.

The raft rocked as the other also found it. Ramon saw the wounded hand, bandages washed away, scrabbling for purchase. He saw the familiar face, its lips blued already with the fierce cold, struggling to stay above the surface. Ramon moved to the edge of the raft.

"Help me!" the other cried. "*Madre de Dios,* help me!"

Ramon took the other's hand, feeling the fingers weak already with fever and with cold trying to grip his wrist.

"I don't want to die!" the other said. "Please Jesus, I don't want to die!"

"No one does," Ramon said, and pushed as hard as he could. The other yelped and went under again, lost for a long moment beneath the raft. When he emerged on the other side, Ramon could still see him moving, struggling to the last, trying to swim against the flow, beating weakly at the river.

"I'll remember you," he called to his dying twin. "When I'm

drinking your beer and sleeping with your woman, I'll remember you. You stupid prick."

The other thrashed the water frantically, and then went still. His head sank beneath the surface of the river. It didn't come back up.

Was there the faintest of tugs as the other died, as whatever bond was between them broke? Or was it just his imagination? It was impossible to say.

Exhausted, panting, Ramon lay back on the raft. He recognized the sluggishness of hypothermia coming on, but he had nothing to cover himself with. He could only hope that the heat of the sun would be enough to sustain him. Blood still flowed, staining his side and his legs, and he had nothing to staunch it with; he'd just have to hope the wound was shallow enough for it to eventually stop on its own. There were still days to travel between here and Fiddler's Jump, and, sprawled there alone on the makeshift raft, Ramon guessed his chances of surviving that long at even money. Maybe a bit worse. But at least the monsters would live. The fetid, crook-spined *ataruae,* the yellow-fringed *mahadya.* The *kait* would all hatch and sleep warm in their creche. If he died here, if he joined his brother in the river's ice-cold flow, he would at least die Ramon Espejo, hero to monstrosities. He needed to sit up. He would gather his strength and sit up. He only needed to rest here for a moment first. Just a moment.

Consciousness faded.

He was surprised, some time later, to find himself weeping. It was dark around him, and he could not entirely recall who or what he was weeping for. It seemed that someone he loved had died, and that he was responsible, but he could not remember who it was or how he carried that burden. Then the world faded again and he found himself floating in darkness. Time passed, punctuated by strange dreams and spikes of fear and panic and shivering. Nothing carried the weight of reality. It might have been minutes or hours or years passing in the sick non-time of fever. He found himself floating in darkness, aware that he was awake, but not of what had awakened him. He tried to move, but something resisted him, pressing him gently back into place. A hand. A woman's hand against his naked breast.

"Who are you?" she asked again, and he realized that, whoever she was, she had been asking him this for some time.

He moved his lips, swallowed painfully, and in a hoarse voice he muttered, "My name is Ramon Espejo. And, *perdoneme, mi amiga,* but that's all I can recall."

NINE

It was summer again before he could really say all was well. He'd broken things off with Eleana as soon as he was strong enough to speak, still in the hospital with his food coming through a white plastic tube straight into his vein like the ghost of the *sahael*. She hadn't believed him at first, thinking, he supposed, that it was just another fight like any of the others. It wasn't until the doctors released him and he went to his own room instead of hers that it sunk in.

She had been like a thunderstorm after that. For weeks, she had left angry notes pinned to his door with knives, screamed at him when they met. After she'd screwed her way through all of his friends and half of his enemies, she seemed to accept it that he was gone. Now she only spat on the ground when they chanced to see each other in the street.

The São Paulo colony was a bad place to be poor, though. The bills from his hospital stay were more than he'd make in a year, even if he'd had a working van and his prospecting tools intact. Starting from scratch would have been easier, but Ramon did what he had to do. When the infection had cleared from his mangled side, he worked his strength back and took day-labor jobs in the spaceport or with fishing boats on the warmer coasts. It was easier saving money now that he'd stopped going to bars at night. And in high summer, he took what he had scraped together to Old Sanchez at the outfitter's station.

"Ramon, *mi amigo,* this—this is pigshit."

"You try saving up money hauling fish and retarring asphalt," Ramon said. "You got it easy sitting here with your iced tea and a bunch of desperate assholes needing whatever it is you got. I'll trade jobs with you for a week, and I'll have enough money to buy a new van outright."

"Not if I'm the one selling it to you," Old Sanchez said, but he smiled when he said it. "I want to help out. I really do, but this isn't enough for a down payment on the cheapest thing I got."

"What about renting it, then? I'll give you this much, and you let me rent one of the old vans and some equipment for two weeks. If I get a site that pays out, we can talk about maybe buying then."

"And what happens if you don't find anything?" Old Sanchez asked, which wasn't a no.

"I go haul some more fish until I can rent it again."

Old Sanchez sipped his tea and wiped his hand across his mouth. His eyes shifted, calculating. Ramon sat forward.

"What the fuck happened to you out there, *mi amigo*?" Old Sanchez asked. "You show up naked and half dead, no van, no equipment, and a hole in your side that someone could put a fist in. And now you're all of a sudden sober? You find God out there or something?"

"You really want to know?"

Old Sanchez considered him, and Ramon could see the unease in the old man's expression.

"No," he said. "I get enough evangelical crap already."

"Go forth, *mi hijo,* and sin no more," Ramon said.

"Yeah, okay," Old Sanchez said at last. "You can rent it. But if you wreck it like you did that last one, I'm taking half your wages for the rest of your life."

"Don't worry. Won't happen."

They drew up the agreement—Old Sanchez wasn't stupid; all the legal forms would be followed in case something did go wrong—and Ramon signed away his meager savings with something like euphoria.

"You really want to get back out there, don't you?"

"Yeah," Ramon said. "This being around people so much. I don't like it."

"Not even that girl down at Llano's?"

"Maria? She's all right. But she's not . . ." Ramon made a gesture that encompassed sky and land and ocean. *She is not the world.*

"All right. Here's the keys. You can have the red van over there. There's already gear loaded. But you get it back in two weeks. And this time, you better have some clothes on."

"Yeah. Don't worry. This is going to be the big one."

It was a warm day in the second month of June, and the van hummed beneath him as the miles flowed away below him. Greenglass country glittering, the flocks of wool-elk and bigheads scattering as he passed overhead. The *Océano Tétrico*. The handful of weathered wooden ships that were the fishing fleet of Fiddler's Jump, and then north, along the thin silver-white band that was the Rio Embudo, where he had almost died twice. Somewhere in that flow—eaten by fish, his bones washed out to sea—the other Ramon had by now become part of the world in a way that could never be undone. Ramon touched his brow in a sign of respect for the dead.

"Better thee than me, *cabron*," he said.

The clearing was easy to find. The months of deep winter or else the aliens had scoured away all trace of his first landing there. He eased the van down, shut off the lift tubes and lit a cigaret. The scheme was simple. He'd left notes about what had happened—Maneck, the other Ramon dead somewhere in the river, and, most importantly, the exact location of the refuge—hidden in his things. The aliens might not understand the idea of *insurance,* but he was willing to teach them. And then he could make his deal.

The aliens would tell him where they didn't want humanity exploring, any other refuges that might exist, and he would file claims in Diegotown that made the sites look worthless and dead. In return, they would tell him where two or three really *good* sites were—places where mines could be built with every nugget of ore leaving a few coins in Ramon's pocket. And then let the monsters do what they wanted to do. It didn't matter to him. Let them hide inside their hill until the end of time, if that's what they wanted. Or perhaps eventually, in time, he could talk them into coming *out,* eh? Convince them, from his unique perspective that straddled both worlds, that being discovered didn't mean that they would all have to die. Wouldn't that be something? If he could do *that,* he wouldn't even need the *pinche* mines to be famous and rich. And it would be a good thing for the aliens too, for whom he'd gradually come to feel a strange kind of sympathy; no one, not even alien monsters, should have to hide inside in the dark all the time when there was a world like this one to be out and around in.

He took in a deep lungful of smoke, remembering Maneck's fear of cancer preventing them from fulfilling their *tatecredue.* It was a risk, of course. Maybe a big one. There was no knowing what these bastards would think or do. Stranger than a *norteamericano,* or even the Japanese. Maybe they'd just kill him, not caring or not understanding about the insurance. Who could know? But life was a risk. That was how you knew you were living.

The cliff face was back exactly as it had been. He couldn't be certain, but he thought that even the individual stones had been set back in place. Here was the boulder he'd hidden behind. And there, in the place that made the most sense, was the site he'd placed the coring blast.

"Hai!" he shouted, his hands cupped around his mouth. "Monsters! Hai! Come out! Another monster wants to talk with you! Or do I need to blow this wall down again?"

Ramon stepped back. High above and to the south, two flapjacks rippled in the high atmosphere, circling each other. The sun overhead was warm as blankets. For a long moment, Ramon felt something like dread in his belly. What if they'd decided that his escape had constituted *gaesu* after all? What if inside the mountain there was nothing but the dead?

And then, far above, the mountainside irised open, and a thing flew out, straddling a device that was for all the world like a flying cycle. The pain in his belly eased. Ramon raised his hands and waved them over his head, drawing the monster's attention, calling it down. It circled once, as if uncertain.

Ramon took another drag of his cigaret, oddly reassured by the alien's hesitance, and waited for it to descend.

⋮⋮⋮⋮⋮⋮
•••••••••

THE CONCRETE JUNGLE

by Charles Stross

Charles Stross has been one of the revelations of the new decade and is fast becoming one of the most important writers working in science fiction today. His first stories appeared in the early '90s and he attracted wider attention with the 2001 Theodore Sturgeon Memorial Award nominee "Antibodies" and his novella "A Colder War." His major work to date has been the "Accelerando" sequence of stories, which detail the lives of three generations in a family making its way through a Vingean Singularity. Individually, the stories have been nominated for the Hugo, Nebula, British Science Fiction, and Theodore Sturgeon Memorial awards. A novel incorporating all nine "Accelerando" stories will appear later this year. Stross's first story collection Toast and Other Rusted Futures *was published in 2002, and his first novel and Hugo nominee* Singularity Sky *appeared in 2003. Almost overwhelmingly prolific, Stross also published the novels* The Atrocity Archives, Iron Sunrise *(a sequel to* Singularity Sky*), and* The Family Trade *in 2004. Upcoming are novels* The Hidden Family, The Clan Corporate, *and* Glasshouse.*

The story that follows is a direct sequel to Stross's novel The Atrocity Archive *and, like that book, it takes the stuff of H. P. Lovecraft and mixes it with the spycraft of Len Deighton to put hero Robert Howard in a real spot. A further book in the sequence,* The Jennifer Morgue, *is in the works.*

THE DEATH RATTLE of a mortally wounded telephone is a horrible thing to hear at four o'clock on a Tuesday morning. It's even worse when you're sleeping the sleep that follows a pitcher of iced margueritas in the basement of the Dog's Bollocks, with a chaser of nachos and a tequila slammer or three for dessert. I come to, sitting upright, bare-ass naked in the middle of the wooden floor, clutching the receiver with one hand and my head with the other—purely to prevent it from exploding, you understand—and moaning quietly. "Who is it?" I croak into the microphone.

"Bob, get your ass down to the office right away. This line isn't secure." I recognize that voice: I have nightmares about it. That's because I work for its owner.

"Whoa, I was asleep, boss. Can't it—" I gulp and look at the alarm clock "—wait until morning?"

"No. I'm calling a code blue."

"Jesus." The band of demons stomping around my skull strike up an encore with drums. "Okay, boss. Ready to leave in ten minutes. Can I bill a taxi fare?"

"No, it can't wait. I'll have a car pick you up." He cuts the call, and *that* is when I start to get frightened because even Angleton, who occupies a lair deep in the bowels of the Laundry's Arcana Analysis Section—but does something far scarier than that anodyne title might suggest—is liable to think twice before authorising a car to pull in an employee at zero-dark o'clock.

I manage to pull on a sweater and jeans, tie my shoelaces, and get my ass downstairs just before the blue and red strobes light up the window above the front door. On the way out I grab my emergency bag—an overnighter full of stuff that Andy suggested I should keep ready, "just in case"—and slam and lock the door and turn around in time to find the cop waiting for me. "Are you Bob Howard?"

"Yeah, that's me." I show him my card.

"If you'll come with me, sir."

Lucky me: I get to wake up on my way in to work four hours early, in the front passenger seat of a police car with strobes flashing and the driver doing his best to scare me into catatonia. Lucky London: the streets are nearly empty at this time of night, so we zip around the feral taxis and somnolent cleaning trucks without pause. A journey that would normally take an hour and a half takes fifteen minutes. (Of course, it comes at a price: Accounting exists in a state of perpetual warfare with the rest of the civil service over internal billing, and the Metropolitan Police charge for their services as a taxi firm at a level that would make you think they provided limousines with wet bars. But Angleton has declared a code blue, so . . .)

The dingy-looking warehouse in a side street, adjoining a closed former primary school, doesn't look too promising—but the door opens before I can raise a hand to knock on it. The grinning sallow face of Fred from Accounting looms out of the darkness in front of me and I recoil before I realise that it's all right—Fred's been dead for more than a year, which is why he's on the night shift. This isn't going to degenerate into plaintive requests for me to fix his spreadsheet. "Fred, I'm here to see Angleton," I say very clearly, then I whisper a special password to stop him from eating me. Fred retreats back to his security cubbyhole or coffin or whatever it is you call it, and I cross the threshold of the Laundry. It's dark—to save light bulbs, and damn the health and safety regs—but some kind soul has left a mouldering cardboard box of hand torches on the front desk. I pull the door shut behind me, pick up a torch, and head for Angleton's office.

As I get to the top of the stairs I see that the lights are on in the corridor we call Mahogany Row. If the boss is running a crisis team then that's where I'll find him. So I divert into executive territory until I see a door with a red light glowing above it. There's a note taped to the door handle: BOB HOWARD ACCESS PERMITTED. So I "access permitted" and walk right in.

As soon as the door opens Angleton looks up from the map spread across the boardroom table. The room smells of stale coffee, cheap cigarettes, and fear. "You're late," he says sharply.

"Late," I echo, dumping my emergency bag under the fire extinguisher and leaning on the door. "'Lo, Andy, Boris. Boss, I don't think the cop was taking his time. Any faster and he'd be billing you for brown stain removal from the upholstery." I yawn. "What's the picture?"

"Milton Keynes," says Andy.

"Are sending you there to investigate," explains Boris.

"With extreme prejudice," Angleton one-ups them.

"Milton Keynes?"

It must be something in my expression; Andy turns away hastily and pours me a cup of Laundry coffee while Boris pretends it's none of his business. Angleton just looks as if he's bitten something unpleasant, which is par for the course.

"We have a problem," Angleton explains, gesturing at the map. "There are too many concrete cows."

"Concrete cows." I pull out a chair and flop down into it heavily, then rub my eyes. "This isn't a dream is it, by any chance? No? Shit."

Boris glowers at me: "Not a joke." He rolls his eyes toward Angleton. "Boss?"

"It's no joke, Bob," says Angleton. His normally skeletal features are even more drawn than usual, and there are dark hollows under his eyes. He looks as if he's been up all night. Angleton glances at Andy: "Has he been keeping his weapons certification up-to-date?"

"I practice three times a week," I butt in, before Andy can get started on the intimate details of my personal file. "Why?"

"Go down to the armoury right now, with Andy. Andy, self-defense kit for one, sign it out for him. Bob, don't shoot unless it's you or them." Angleton shoves a stack of papers and a pen across the table at me. "Sign the top and pass it back—you now have GAME ANDES REDSHIFT clearance. The files below are part of GAR—you're to keep them on your person at all times until you get back here, then check them in via Morag's office; you'll answer to the auditors if they go missing or get copied."

"Huh?"

I obviously still look confused because Angleton cracks an expression so frightening that it must be a smile and adds, "Shut your mouth, you're drooling on your collar. Now, go with Andy, check out your hot kit, let Andy set you up with a chopper, and *read* those papers. When you get to Milton Keynes, do what comes naturally. If you don't find anything, come back and tell me and we'll take things from there."

"But what am I looking for?" I gulp down half my coffee in one go; it tastes of ashes, stale cigarette ends, and tinned instant left over from the Retreat from Moscow. "Dammit, what do you expect me to find?"

"I don't expect anything," says Angleton. "Just go."

"Come on," says Andy, opening the door, "you can leave the papers here for now."

I follow him into the corridor, along to the darkened stairwell at the end, and down four flights of stairs into the basement. "Just what the fuck *is* this?" I demand, as Andy produces a key and unlocks the steel-barred gate in front of the security tunnel.

"It's GAME ANDES REDSHIFT, kid," he says over his shoulder. I follow him into the security zone and the gate clanks shut behind me. Another key, another steel door—this time the outer vestibule of the armoury. "Listen, don't go too hard on Angleton, he knows what he's doing. If you go in with preconceptions about what you'll find and it turns out to be GAME ANDES REDSHIFT, you'll probably get yourself killed. But I reckon there's only about a 10 percent chance it's the real thing—more likely it's a drunken student prank."

He uses another key, and a secret word that my ears refuse to hear, to open the inner armoury door. I follow Andy inside. One wall is racked with guns, another is walled with ammunition lockers, and the opposite wall is racked with more esoteric items. It's this that he turns to.

"A prank," I echo, and yawn, against my better judgement. "Jesus, it's half past four in the morning and you got me out of bed because of a student prank?"

"Listen." Andy stops and glares at me, irritated. "Remember how you came aboard? That was *me* getting out of bed at four in the morning because of a student prank."

"Oh," is all I can say to him. *Sorry* springs to mind, but is probably inadequate; as they later pointed out to me, applied computational demonology and built-up areas don't mix very well. *I* thought I was just generating weird new fractals; *they* knew I was dangerously close to landscaping Wolverhampton with alien nightmares. "What kind of students?" I ask.

"Architecture or alchemy. Nuclear physics for an outside

straight." Another word of command and Andy opens the sliding glass case in front of some gruesome relics that positively throb with power. "Come on. Which of these would you like?"

"I think I'll take this one, thanks." I reach in and carefully pick up a silver locket on a chain; there's a yellow-and-black thaumaturgy hazard trefoil on a label dangling from it, and NO PULL ribbons attached to the clasp.

"Good choice." Andy watches me in silence as I add a Hand of Glory to my collection, and then a second, protective amulet. "That all?" he asks.

"That's all," I say, and he nods and shuts the cupboard, then renews the seal on it.

"Sure?" he asks.

I look at him. Andy is a slightly built, forty-something guy; thin, whispy hair, tweed sports jacket with leather patches at the elbows, and a perpetually worried expression. Looking at him you'd think he was an Open University lecturer, not a manageri-al-level spook from the Laundry's active service division. But that goes for all of them, doesn't it? Angleton looks more like a Texan oil-company executive with tuberculosis than the legendary and terrifying head of the Counter-Possession Unit. And me, I look like a refugee from CodeCon or a dot-com startup's engineering department. Which just goes to show that appearances and a euro will get you a cup of coffee. "What does this code blue look like to you?" I ask.

He sighs tiredly, then yawns. "Damn, it's infectious," he mut-ters. "Listen, if I tell you what it looks like to me, Angleton will have my head for a doorknob. Let's just say, *read* those files on the way over, okay? Keep your eyes open, count the concrete cows, then come back safe."

"Count the cows. Come back safe. Check." I sign the clip-board, pick up my arsenal, and he opens the armoury door. "How am I getting there?"

Andy cracks a lopsided grin. "By police helicopter. This is a code blue, remember?"

➤ ➤ ➤

I go up to the committee room, collect the papers, and then it's down to the front door, where the same police patrol car is waiting for me. More brown-pants motoring—this time the traffic is a little thicker, dawn is only an hour and a half away—and we end up in the northeast suburbs, following the roads to Lippitts Hill where the Police ASU keep their choppers. There's no messing around with check-in and departure lounges; we drive round to a gate at one side of the complex, show our warrant cards, and my chauffeur takes me right out onto the heliport and parks next to the ready room, then hands me over to the flight crew before I realise what's happening.

"You're Bob Howard?" asks the copilot. "Up here, hop in." He helps me into the back seat of the Twin Squirrel, sorts me out with the seat belt, then hands me a bulky headset and plugs it in. "We'll be there in half an hour," he says. "You just relax, try to get some sleep." He grins sardonically then shuts the door on me and climbs in up front.

Funny. I've never been in a helicopter before. It's not quite as loud as I'd expected, especially with the headset on, but as I've been led to expect something like being rolled down a hill in an oil drum while maniacs whack on the sides with baseball bats, that isn't saying much. *Get some sleep* indeed; instead I bury my nose in the so-secret reports on GAME ANDES REDSHIFT and try not to upchuck as the predawn London landscape corkscrews around outside the huge glass windscreen and then starts to unroll beneath us.

❖ ❖ ❖

REPORT 1: Sunday September 4th, 1892
CLASSIFIED MOST SECRET, Imperial War Ministry, September 11th, 1914
RECLASSIFIED TOP SECRET GAME ANDES, Ministry of War, July 2nd, 1940
RECLASSIFIED TOP SECRET REDSHIFT, Ministry of Defense, August 13th, 1988

My dearest Nellie,
    In the week since I last wrote to you, I have to confess that

I have become a different man. Experiences such as the ordeal I have just undergone must surely come but once in a lifetime; for if more often, how might man survive them? I have gazed upon the gorgon and lived to tell the tale, for which I am profoundly grateful (and I hasten to explain myself before you worry for my safety), although only the guiding hand of some angel of grace can account for my being in a position to put ink to paper with these words.

I was at dinner alone with the Mehtar last Tuesday evening—Mr. Robertson being laid up, and Lieutenant Bruce off to Gilgut to procure supplies for his secret expedition to Lhasa—when we were interrupted most rudely at our repast. "Holiness!" The runner, quite breathless with fear, threw himself upon his knees in front of us. "Your brother . . . ! Please hasten, I implore you!"

His excellency Nizam ul Mulk looked at me with that wicked expression of his: he bears little affection for his brutish hulk of a brother, and with good reason. Where the Mehtar is a man of refined, albeit questionable sensibilities, his brother is an uneducated coarse hill-man, one step removed from banditry. Chittral can very well do without his kind. "What has happened to my beloved brother?" asked ul Mulk.

At this point the runner lapsed into a gabble that I could barely understand. With patience the Mehtar drew him out— then frowned. Turning to me, he said, "We have a—I know not the word for it in English, excuse please. It is a monster of the caves and passes who preys upon my people. My brother has gone to hunt it, but it appears to have got the better of him."

"A mountain lion?" I said, misunderstanding.

"No." He looked at me oddly. "May I enquire of you, Captain, whether Her Majesty's government tolerates monsters within her empire?"

"Of course not!"

"Then you will not object to joining me in the hunt?"

I could feel a trap closing on me, but could not for the life of me see what it might be. "Certainly," I said. "By Jove, old chap, we'll have this monster's head mounted on your trophy room wall before the week is out!"

"I think not," Nizam said coolly. "We burn such things here, to drive out the evil spirit that gave rise to them. Bring you your *mirror,* tomorrow?"

"My—" Then I realised what he was talking about, and what deadly jeopardy I had placed my life in, for the honour of Her Majesty's government in Chittral: he was talking about a Medusa. And although it quite unmans me to confess it, I was afraid.

The next day, in my cramped, windowless hut, I rose with the dawn and dressed for the hunt. I armed myself, then told Sergeant Singh to ready a squad of troopers for the hunt.

"What is the quarry, sahib?" he asked.

"The beast that no man sees," I said, and the normally imperturbable trooper flinched.

"The men won't like that, sir," he said.

"They'll like it even less if I hear any words from them," I said. You have to be firm with colonial troops: they have only as much backbone as their commanding officer.

"I'll tell them that, sahib," he said and, saluting, went to ready our forces.

The Mehtar's men gathered outside; an unruly bunch of hill-men, armed as one might expect with a mix of flintlocks and bows. They were spirited, like children, excitable and bickering; hardly a match for the order of my troopers and I. We showed them how it was done! Together with the Mehtar at our head, kestrel on his wrist, we rode out into the cold bright dawn and the steep-sided mountain valley.

We rode for the entire morning and most of the afternoon, climbing up the sides of a steep pass and then between two towering peaks clad in gleaming white snow. The mood of the party was uncommonly quiet, a sense of apprehensive fortitude settling over the normally ebullient Chittrali warriors. We came at last to a mean-spirited hamlet of tumbledown shacks, where a handful of scrawny goats grazed the scrubby bushes; the hetman of the village came to meet us, and with quavering voice directed us to our destination.

"It lies thuswise," remarked my translator, adding: "The old fool, he say it is a ghost-bedevilled valley, by God! He say his son go in there two, three days ago, not come out. Then the Mehtar—blessed be he—his brother follow with his soldiers. And that two days ago."

"Hah. Well," I said, "tell him the great white empress sent me here with these fine troops he sees, and the Mehtar himself and his nobles, and *we* aren't feeding any monster!"

The translator jabbered at the hetman for a while, and he looked stricken. Then Nizam beckoned me over. "Easy, old fellow," he said.

"As you say, your excellency."

He rode forward, beckoning me alongside. I felt the need to explain myself further: "I do not believe one gorgon will do for us. In fact, I do believe we will do for it!"

"It is not that which concerns me," said the ruler of the small mountain kingdom. "But go easy on the hetman. The monster was his wife."

We rode the rest of the way in reflective silence, to the valley where the monster had built her retreat, the only noises the sighing of wind, the thudding of hooves, and the jingling of our kits. "There is a cave halfway up the wall of the valley, here," said the messenger who had summoned us. "She lives there, coming out at times to drink and forage for food. The villagers left her meals at first, but in her madness she slew one of them, and then they stopped."

Such tragic neglect is unknown in England, where the poor victims of this most hideous ailment are confined in mazed bedlams upon their diagnosis, blindfolded lest they kill those who nurse them. But what more can one expect of the half-civilized children of the valley kingdoms, here on the top of the world?

The execution—for want of a better word—proceeded about as well as such an event can, which is to say that it was harrowing and not by any means enjoyable in the way that hunting game can be. At the entrance to the small canyon where the woman had made her lair, we paused. I detailed Sergeant Singh to ready a squad of rifles; their guns loaded, they took up positions in the rocks, ready to beat back the monster should she try to rush us.

Having thus prepared our position, I dismounted and, joining the Mehtar, steeled myself to enter the valley of death.

I am sure you have read lurid tales of the appalling scenes in which gorgons are found; charnel houses strewn with calcined bodies, bones protruding in attitudes of agony from the walls as the madmen and madwomen who slew them gibber and howl among their victims. These tales are, I am thankful to say, constructed out of whole cloth by the fevered imaginations of the degenerate scribblers who write for the penny dreadfuls. What we found was both less—and much worse—than that.

We found a rubble-strewn valley; in one side of it a cave, barely more than a cleft in the rock face, with a tumbledown awning stretched across its entrance. An old woman sat under the awning, eyes closed, humming to herself in an odd singsong. The remains of a fire lay in front of her, logs burned down to white-caked ashes; she seemed to be crying, tears trickling down her sunken, wrinkled cheeks.

The Mehtar gestured me to silence, then, in what I only later recognized as a supremely brave gesture, strode up to the fire. "Good evening to you, my aunt, and it would please me that you keep your eyes closed, lest my guards be forced to slay you of an instant," he said.

The woman kept up her low, keening croon—like a wail of grief from one who has cried until her throat is raw and will make no more noise. But her eyes remained obediently shut. The Mehtar crouched down in front of her.

"Do you know who I am?" he asked gently.

The crooning stopped. "You are the royal one," she said, her voice a cracked whisper. "They told me you would come."

"Indeed I have," he said, a compassionate tone in his voice. With one hand he waved me closer. "It is very sad, what you have become."

"It *hurts*." She wailed quietly, startling the soldiers so that one of them half-rose to his feet. I signalled him back down urgently as I approached behind her. "I wanted to see my son one more time . . ."

"It is all right, aunt," he said quietly. "You'll see him soon enough." He held out a hand to me; I held out the leather bag and he removed the mirror. "Be at peace, aunt. An end to pain is in sight." He held the mirror at arms' length in front of his face, above the fire before her: "Open your eyes when you are ready for it."

She sobbed once, then opened her eyes.

I didn't know what to expect, dear Nellie, but it was not this: somebody's aged mother, crawling away from her home to die with a stabbing pain in her head, surrounded by misery and loneliness. As it is, her monarch spared her the final pain, for as soon as she looked into the mirror she *changed*. The story that the gorgon kills those who see her by virtue of her ugliness is untrue; she was merely an old woman—the evil was something in her gaze, something to do with the act of perception.

As soon as her eyes opened—they were bright blue, for a moment—she changed. Her skin puffed up and her hair went to dust, as if in a terrible heat. My skin prickled; it was as if I had placed my face in the open door of a furnace. Can you imagine what it would be like if a body were to be heated in an instant to the temperature of a blast furnace? For that is what it was like. I will not describe this horror in any detail, for it is not fit material for discussion. When the wave of heat cleared, her body toppled forward atop the fire—and rolled apart, yet more calcined logs amidst the embers.

The Mehtar stood, and mopped his brow. "Summon your men, Francis," he said, "they must build a cairn here."

"A cairn?" I echoed blankly.

"For my brother." He gestured impatiently at the fire into which the unfortunate woman had tumbled. "Who else do you think this could have been?"

A cairn was built, and we camped overnight in the village. I must confess that both the Mehtar and I have been awfully sick since then, with an abnormal rapidity that came on since the confrontation. Our men carried us back home, and that is where you find me now, lying abed as I write this account of one of the most horrible incidents I have ever witnessed on the frontier.

I remain your obedient and loving servant,
Capt. Francis Younghusband

➤ ➤ ➤

As I finish reading the typescript of Captain Younghusband's report, my headset buzzes nastily and crackles. "Coming up on Milton Keynes in a couple minutes, Mr. Howard. Any idea where you want to be put down? If you don't have anywhere specific in mind we'll ask for a slot at the police pad."

Somewhere specific . . . ? I shove the unaccountably top-secret papers down into one side of my bag and rummage around for one of the gadgets I took from the armoury. "The concrete cows," I say. "I need to take a look at them as soon as possible. They're in Bancroft Park, according to this map. Just off Monk's Way, follow the A422 in until it turns into the H3 near the city centre. Any chance we can fly over them?"

"Hold on a moment."

The helicopter banks alarmingly and the landscape tilts around us. We're shooting over a dark landscape, trees and neat, orderly fields, and the occasional clump of suburban paradise whisking past beneath us—then we're over a dual carriageway, almost empty at this time of night, and we bank again and turn to follow it. From an altitude of about a thousand feet it looks like an incredibly detailed toy, right down to the finger-sized trucks crawling along it.

"Right, that's it," says the copilot. "Anything else we can do for you?"

"Yeah," I say. "You've got infrared gear, haven't you? I'm looking for an extra cow. A hot one. I mean, hot like it's been cooked, not hot as in body temperature."

"Gotcha, we're looking for a barbecue." He leans sideways and fiddles with the controls below a fun-looking monitor. "Here. Ever used one of these before?"

"What is it, FLIR?"

"Got it in one. That joystick's the pan, this knob is zoom, you use this one to control the gain, it's on a stabilized platform; give us a yell if you see anything. Clear?"

"I think so." The joystick works as promised and I zoom in on a trail of ghostly hot spots, pan behind them to pick up the brilliant glare of a predawn jogger, lit up like a light bulb—the dots are fading footprints on the cold ground. "Yeah." We're making about forty miles per hour along the road, sneaking in like a thief in the night, and I zoom out to take in as much of the side view as possible. After a minute or so I see the park ahead, off the side of a roundabout. "Eyes up, front: Can you hover over that roundabout?"

"Sure. Hold on." The engine note changes and my stomach lurches, but the FLIR pod stays locked on target. I can see the cows now, grey shapes against the cold ground—a herd of concrete animals created in 1978 by a visiting artist. There should be eight of them, life-sized Friesians peacefully grazing in a field attached to the park. But something's wrong, and it's not hard to see what.

"Barbecue at six o'clock low," says the copilot. "You want to go down and bring us back a take-away, or what?"

"Stay up," I say edgily, slewing the camera pod around. "I want to make sure it's safe first . . ."

➤ ➤ ➤

REPORT 2: Wednesday March 4th, 1914
CLASSIFIED MOST SECRET, Imperial War Ministry, September 11th, 1914
RECLASSIFIED TOP SECRET GAME ANDES, Ministry of War, July 2nd, 1940
RECLASSIFIED TOP SECRET REDSHIFT, Ministry of Defense, August 13th, 1988

Dear Albert,

Today we performed Young's double-slit experiment upon Subject C, our medusa. The results are unequivocal; the Medusa effect is both a particle *and* a wave. If de Broglie is right . . .

But I am getting ahead of myself.

Ernest has been pushing for results with characteristic vim and vigor and Mathiesson, our analytical chemist, has been driven to his wits' end by the New Zealander's questions. He nearly came to blows with Dr. Jamieson who insisted that the welfare of his patient—as he calls Subject C—comes before any question of getting to the bottom of this infuriating and perplexing anomaly.

Subject C is an unmarried woman, aged 27, of medium height with brown hair and blue eyes. Until four months ago, she was healthy and engaged as household maid to an eminent KC whose name you would probably recognise. Four months ago she underwent a series of seizures; her employers being generous, she was taken to the Royal Free Infirmary where she described having a series of blinding headaches going back eighteen months or so. Dr. Willard examined her using one of the latest Roentgen machines, and determined that she appeared to have the makings of a tumour upon her brain. Naturally this placed her under Notification, subject to the Monster Control Act (1864); she was taken to the isolation ward at St. Bartholomew's in London where, three weeks, six migraines, and two seizures later, she experienced her first Grand Morte fit. Upon receiving confirmation that she was suffering from acute gorgonism, Dr. Rutherford asked me to proceed as agreed upon; and so I arranged for the Home Office to be contacted by way of the Dean.

While Mr. McKenna was at first unenthusiastic about the prospect of a gorgon running about the streets of Manchester, our reassurances ultimately proved acceptable and he directed that Subject C be released into our custody on her own cognizance. She was in a state of entirely understandable distress when she arrived, but once the situation was explained she agreed to cooperate fully in return for a settlement which will be made upon her next of kin. As she is young and healthy, she may survive for several months, if not a year, in her current condition: this offers an unparalleled research opportunity. We are currently keeping her in the old Leprosarium, the windows of which have been bricked up. A security labyrinth has been installed, the garden wall raised by five feet so that she can take in the air without endangering passers-by, and we have arranged a set of signals whereby she can don occlusive blind-folds before receiving visitors. Experiments upon patients with acute gorgonism always carry an element of danger, but in this case I believe our precautions will suffice until her final deteri-oration begins.

Lest you ask why we don't employ a common basilisk or cockatrice instead, I hasten to explain that we do; the patholo-gy is identical in whichever species, but a human source is far more amenable to control than any wild animal. Using Subject C we can perform repeatable experiments at will, and obtain verbal confirmation that she has performed our requests. I hardly need to remind you that the historical use of gorgonism, for example by Danton's Committee for Public Safety during the French revolution, was hardly conducted as a scientific study of the phenomenon. This time, we will make progress!

Once Subject C was comfortable, Dr. Rutherford arranged a series of seminars. The New Zealander is of the opinion that the effect is probably mediated by some electromagnetic phe-nomenon, of a type unknown to other areas of science. He is consequently soliciting new designs for experiments intended to demonstrate the scope and nature of the gorgon effect. We know from the history of Mademoiselle Marianne's grisly col-laboration with Robespierre that the victim must be visible to the gorgon, but need not be directly perceived; reflection works, as does trivial refraction, and the effect is transmitted through glass thin enough to see through, but the gorgon cannot work in darkness or thick smoke. Nobody has demon-strated a physical mechanism for gorgonism that doesn't involve an unfortunate creature afflicted with the characteristic tumours. Blinding a gorgon appears to control the effect, as does a sufficient visual distortion. So why does Ernest insist on treating a clearly biological phenomenon as one of the greatest mysteries in physics today?

"My dear fellow," he explained to me the first time I asked, "how did Madame Curie infer the existence of radioactivity in radium-bearing ores? How did Wilhelm Roentgen recognize

X-rays for what they were? Neither of those forms of radiation arose within our current understanding of magnetism, electricity, or light. They had to be something else. Now, our children of Medusa apparently need to behold a victim in order to injure them—but how is the effect transmitted? We know, unlike the ancient Greeks, that our eyes work by focussing ambient light on a membrane at their rear. They used to think that the gorgons shone forth beams of balefire, as if to set in stone whatever they alighted on. But we know that cannot be true. What we face is nothing less than a wholly new phenomenon. Granted, the gorgon effect only changes whatever the medusoid can see directly, but we know the light reflected from those bodies isn't responsible. And Lavoisier's calorimetric experiments—before he met his unfortunate end before the looking glass of l'Executrice—proved that actual atomic transmutation is going on! So what on earth mediates the effect? How can the act of observation, performed by an unfortunate afflicted with gorgonism, transform the nuclear structure?"

(By nuclear structure he is of course referring to the core of the atom, as deduced by our experiments last year.)

Then he explained how he was going to seat a gorgon on one side of a very large device he calls a cloud chamber, with big magnetic coils positioned above and below it, to see if there is some other physical phenomenon at work.

I can now reveal the effects of our team's experimentation. Subject C is cooperating in a most professional manner, but despite Ernest's greatest efforts the cloud chamber bore no fruit—she can sit with her face pressed up against the glass window on one side, and blow a chicken's egg to flinders of red-hot pumice on the target stand, but no ionization trail appears in the saturated vapour of the chamber. Or rather, I should say no direct trail appears. We had more success when we attempted to replicate other basic experiments. It seems that the gorgon effect is a continuously variable function of the illumination of the target, with a sharply defined lower cut-off and an upper limit! By interposing smoked glass filters we have calibrated the efficiency with which Subject C transmutes the carbon nuclei of a target into silicon, quite accurately. Some of the new electrostatic counters I've been working on have proven fruitful: secondary radiation, including gamma rays and possibly an elusive neutral particle, are given off by the target, and indeed our cloud chamber has produced an excellent picture of radiation given off by the target.

Having confirmed the calorimetric and optical properties of the effect, we next performed the double-slit experiment upon a row of targets (in this case, using wooden combs). A wall with two thin slits is interposed between the targets and our subject, whose gaze was split in two using a binocular arrangement of prisms. A lamp positioned between the two slits, on the far side of the wall from our subject, illuminates the targets: as the level of illumination increases, a pattern of alternating gorgonism was produced! This exactly follows the constructive reinforcement and destruction of waves Professor Young demonstrated with his examination of light corpuscles, as we are now supposed to call them. We conclude that gorgonism is a wave effect of some sort—and the act of observation is intimately involved, although on first acquaintance this is such a strange conclusion that some of us were inclined to reject it out of hand.

We will of course be publishing our full findings in due course; I take pleasure in attaching a draft of our paper for your interest. In any case, you must be wondering by now just what the central finding is. This is not in our paper yet, because Dr. Rutherford is inclined to seek a possible explanation before publishing; but I regret to say that our most precise calorimetric analyses suggest that your theory of mass/energy conservation is being violated—not on the order of ounces of weight, but by enough to detect. Carbon atoms are being transformed into silicon ions with an astoundingly high electropositivity, which can be accounted for if we assume that the effect is creating nuclear mass from somewhere. Perhaps you, or your new colleagues at the Prussian Academy, can shed some light on the issue? We are most perplexed, because if we accept this result we are forced to accept the creation of new mass *ab initio,* or treat it as an experimental invalidation of your general theory of relativity.

Your good friend,
Hans Geiger

➤ ➤ ➤

A portrait of the agent as a (confused) young man:

Picture me, standing in the predawn chill in a badly mown field, yellowing parched grass up to the ankles. There's a wooden fence behind me, a road on the other side of it with the usual traffic cams and streetlights, and a helicopter in police markings parked like a gigantic cyborg beetle in the middle of the roundabout, bulging with muscular-looking sensors and nitesun floodlights and making a racket like an explosion in a noise factory. Before me there's a field full of concrete cows, grazing safely and placidly in the shadow of some low trees which are barely visible in the overspill from the streetlights. Long shadows stretch out from the fence, darkness exploding toward the ominous lump at the far end of the paddock. It's autumn, and dawn isn't due for another thirty minutes. I lift my modified camcorder and zoom in on it, thumbing the record button.

The lump looks a little like a cow that's lying down. I glance over my shoulder at the chopper, which is beginning to spool up for takeoff; I'm pretty sure I'm safe here but I can't quite suppress a cold shudder. On the other side of the field—

"Datum point: Bob Howard, Bancroft Park, Milton Keynes, time is zero seven fourteen on the morning of Tuesday the eighteenth. I have counted the cows and there are nine of them. One is prone, far end of paddock, GPS coordinates to follow. Preliminary surveillance indicated no human presence within a quarter kilometre and residual thermal yield is below two hundred Celsius, so I infer that it is safe to approach the target."

One unwilling foot goes down in front of another. I keep an eye on my dosimeter, just in case: there's not going to be much secondary radiation hereabouts, but you can never tell. The first of the cows looms up at me out of the darkness. She's painted black and white, and this close up there's no mistaking her for a sculpture. I pat her on the nose. "Stay cool, Daisy." I should be safely tucked up in bed with Mo—but she's away on a two-week training seminar at Dunwich and Angleton got a bee in his bonnet and called a code blue emergency. The cuffs of my jeans are damp with dew, and it's cold. I reach the next cow, pause, and lean on its rump for a zoom shot of the target.

"Ground zero, range twenty metres. Subject is bovine, down, clearly terminal. Length is roughly three metres, breed . . . unidentifiable. The grass around it is charred but there's no sign of secondary combustion." I dry-swallow. "Thermal bloom from abdomen." There's a huge rip in its belly where the boiling intestinal fluids exploded, and the contents are probably still glowing red-hot inside.

I approach the object. It's clearly the remains of a cow; equally clearly it has met a most unpleasant end. The dosimeter says it's safe—most of the radiation effects from this sort of thing are prompt, there are minimal secondary products, luckily—but the ground underneath is scorched and the hide has blackened and charred to a gritty, ashlike consistency. There's a smell like roast beef hanging in the air, with an unpleasant undertang of something else. I fumble in my shoulder bag and pull out a thermal probe, then, steeling myself, shove the sharp end in through the rip in the abdomen. I nearly burn my hand on the side as I do so—it's like standing too close to an open oven.

"Core temperature two six six, two six seven . . . stable. Taking core samples for isotope ratio checks." I pull out a sample tube and a sharp probe and dig around in the thing's guts, trying to tease a chunk of ashy, charred meat loose. I feel queasy: I like a well-cooked steak as much as the next guy, but there's something deeply wrong about this whole scene. I try not to notice the exploded eyeballs or the ruptured tongue bursting through the blackened lips. This job is quite gross enough as it is without adding my own dry heaves to the mess.

Samples safely bottled for analysis, I back away and walk in a wide circle around the body, recording it from all angles. An open gate at the far end of the field and a trail of impressions in the ground completes the picture. "Hypothesis: open gate. Someone let Daisy in, walked her to this position near the herd, then backed off. Daisy was then illuminated and exposed to a class three or better basilisk, whether animate or simulated. We need a plausible disinformation pitch, forensics workover of the paddock gate and fence—check for exit signs and footprints—and some way of identifying Daisy to see which herd she came from. If any livestock is reported missing over the next few days that would be a useful indicator. Meanwhile, core temperature is down to under five hundred Celsius. That suggests the incident happened at least a few hours ago—it takes a while for something the size of a cow to cool down that far. Since the basilisk has obviously left the area and there's not a lot more I can do, I'm now going to call in the cleaners. End."

I switch off the camcorder, slide it into my pocket, and take a deep breath. The next bit promises to be even less pleasant than sticking a thermocouple in the cow's arse to see how long ago it was irradiated. I pull out my mobile phone and dial 999. "Operator? Police despatch, please. Police despatch? This is Mike Tango Five, repeat, Mike Tango Five. Is Inspector Sullivan available? I have an urgent call for him . . ."

➤ ➤ ➤

REPORT 3: Friday October 9th, 1942
CLASSIFIED TOP SECRET GAME ANDES, Ministry of War, October 9th, 1942
RECLASSIFIED TOP SECRET REDSHIFT, Ministry of Defense, August 13th, 1988

Action This Day: Three reports have reached SOE Department Two, office 337/42, shedding new light on the recent activities of Dr. Ing Professor Gustaf Von Schachter in conjunction with RSHA Amt. 3 and the inmates of the Holy Nativity Hospital for the Incurably Insane.

Our first report ref. 531/892-(i) concerns the cessation of action by a detached unit of RSHA Amt. 3 Group 4 charged with termination of imbeciles and mental defectives in Frankfurt as part of the Reich's ongoing eugenics program. An agent in place (code: GREEN PIGEON) overheard two soldiers discussing the cessation of euthanasia operations in the clinic in negative terms. Herr Von Schachter had, as of 24/8/42, acquired a Führer Special Order signed either by Hitler or Bormann. This was understood by the soldiers to charge him with the authority to requisition any military resources not concerned with direct security of the Reich or suppression of resistance, and to override orders with the effective authority of an *obergruppenführer*. This mandate runs in conjunction with his existing authority from Dr. Wolfram Sievers, who is believed to be operating the Institute for Military Scientific Research at the University of Strasbourg and the processing centre at Natzweiler concentration camp.

Our second report ref. 539/504-(i) concerns prescriptions dispensed by a pharmacy in Frankfurt for an unnamed doctor from the Holy Nativity Hospital. The pharmaceutical assistant at this dispensary is a sympathiser operated by BLUE PARTRIDGE and is considered trustworthy. The prescriptions requisitioned were unusual in that they consisted of bolus preparations for intrathecal (base of cranium) injection, containing colchicine, an extract of catharanthides, and morphine. Our informant opined that this is a highly irregular preparation which might be utilized in the treatment of certain brain tumours, but which is likely to cause excruciating pain and neurological side effects (ref. GAME ANDES) associated with induction of gorgonism in latent individuals suffering an astrocytoma in the cingulate gyrus.

Our final report ref. 539/504-(ii) comes from the same informant and confirms ominous preparatory activities in the Holy Nativity Hospital grounds. The hospital is now under guard by soldiers of Einsatzgruppen 4. Windows have been whitewashed, *mirrors* are being removed (our emphasis) or replaced with one-way observation glass, and lights in the solitary cells rewired for external control from behind two doors. Most of the patients have disappeared, believed removed by Group 4 soldiers, and rumours are circulating of a new area of disturbed earth in the countryside nearby. Those patients who remain are under close guard.

Conclusion: The preparation referenced in 539/504-(i) has been referred to Special Projects Group ANDES, who have verified against records of the suppressed Geiger Committee that Von Schachter is experimenting with drugs similar to the catastrophic Cambridge IV preparation. Given his associate Sievers's influence in the Ahnenerbe-SS, and the previous use of the Holy Nativity Hospital for the Incurably Insane as a secondary centre for the paliative care of patients suffering seizures and other neuraesthenic symptoms, it is believed likely that Von Schachter intends to induce and control gorgonism for military purposes in explicit violation of the provisions for the total suppression of stoner weapons laid out in Secret Codicil IV to the Hague Convention (1919).

Policy Recommendation: This matter should be escallated to JIC as critical with input from SOE on the feasibility of a targeted raid on the installation. If allowed to proceed, Von Schachter's program shows significant potential for development into one of the rumoured *Vertlesgunswaffen* programs for deployment against civilian populations in free areas. A number of contingency plans for the deployment of gorgonism on a mass observation basis have existed in a MOW file since the early 1920s and we must now consider the prospects for such weapons to be deployed against us. We consider essential an immediate strike against the most advanced development centres, coupled with a strong reminder through diplomatic back channels that failure to comply with all clauses (secret and overt) of the Hague Convention *will* result in an allied retalliatory deployment of poison gas against German civilian targets. We cannot run the risk of class IV basilisks being deployed in conjunction with strategic air power . . .

➤ ➤ ➤

By the time I roll into the office, four hours late and yawning with sleep deprivation, Harriet is hopping around the common room as if her feet are on fire, angrier than I've ever seen her before. Unfortunately, according to the matrix management system we operate she's my boss for 30 percent of the time during which I'm a technical support engineer. (For the other 70 percent I report to

Angleton and I can't really tell you *what* I am except that it involves being yanked out of bed at zero four hundred hours to answer code blue alerts.)

Harriet is a back-office suit: mousy and skinny, forty-something, and dried up from spending all those years devising forms in triplicate with which to terrorize field agents. People like Harriet aren't supposed to get excited about anything. The effect is disconcerting, like opening a tomb and finding a break-dancing mummy.

"Robert! Where on earth have you been? What kind of time do you call this? McLuhan's been waiting on you—you were supposed to be here for the licence policy management committee meeting two hours ago!"

I yawn and sling my jacket over the coat rack next to the "C" department coffee station. "Been called out," I mumble. "Code blue alert. Just got back from Milton Keynes."

"Code blue?" she asks, alert for a slip. "Who signed off on it?"

"Angleton." I hunt around for my mug in the cupboard over the sink, the one with the poster on the front that says CURIOUS EYES COST LIVES. The coffee machine is mostly empty, full of black tarry stuff alarmingly similar to the toxic waste they make roads out of. I hold it under the tap and rinse. "His budget, don't worry about it. Only he pulled me out of bed at four in the morning and sent me off to—" I put the jug down to refill the coffee filter "—never mind. It's cleared."

Harriet looks as if she's bitten into a biscuit and found half a beetle inside. I'm pretty sure that it's not anything special; she and her boss Bridget simply have no higher goal in life than trying to cut everyone else down so they can look them in the eye. Although, to be fair, they've been acting more cagy than usual lately, hiding out in meetings with strange suits from other departments. It's probably just part of their ongoing game of Bureaucracy, whose goal is the highest stakes of all—a fully vested Civil Service pension and early retirement. "What was it about?" she demands.

"Do you have GAME ANDES REDSHIFT clearance?" I ask. "If not, I can't tell you."

"But you were in Milton Keynes," she jabs. "You told me that."

"Did I?" I roll my eyes. "Well, maybe, and maybe not. I couldn't possibly comment."

"What's so interesting about Milton Keynes?" she continues.

"Not much." I shrug. "It's made of concrete and it's very, very boring."

She relaxes almost imperceptibly. "Make sure you get all the paperwork filed and billed to the right account," she tells me.

"I will have before I leave this afternoon at two," I reply, rubbing in the fact that I'm on flexitime; Angleton's a much more alarming, but also understanding, manager to work for. Due to the curse of matrix management I can't weasel out completely from under Bridget's bony thumb, but I must confess I get a kick out of having my other boss pull rank on her. "What was this meeting about?" I ask slyly, hoping she'll rise to it.

"You should know, you're the administrator who set up the mailing list," she throws right back at me. *Oops.* "Mr. McLuhan's here to help us. He's from Q Division, to help us prepare for our Business Software Alliance audit."

"Our—" I stop dead and turn to face her, the coffee machine gurgling at my back. "Our audit with *who?*"

"The Business Software Alliance," she says smugly. "CESG outsourced our COTS application infrastructure five months ago contingent on us following official best practices for ensuring quality and value in enterprise resource management. As you were *too busy* to look after things, Bridget asked Q Division to help out. Mr McLuhan is helping us sort out our licencing arrangements in line with guidelines from Procurement. He says he's able to run a full BSA-certified audit on our systems and help us get our books in order."

"Oh," I say, very calmly, and turn around, mouthing the follow-on *shit* silently in the direction of the now-burbling percollator. "Have you ever been through a BSA audit before, Harriet?" I ask curiously as I scrub my mug clean, inside and out.

"No, but they're here to help us audit our—"

"They're funded by the big desktop software companies," I say, as calmly as I can. "They do that because they view the BSA as a *profit centre.* That's because the BSA or their subcontractors—and that's what Q Division will be acting as, they get paid for running an audit if they find anything out of order—come in, do an audit, look for *anything* that isn't currently licensed—say, those old machines in D3 that are still running Windows 3.1 and Office 4, or the Linux servers behind Eric's desk that keep the departmental file servers running, not to mention the FreeBSD box running the Daemonic Countermeasures Suite in Security—and demand an upgrade to the latest version under threat of lawsuit. Inviting them in is like throwing open the doors and inviting the Drugs Squad round for a spliff."

"They said they could track down all our installed software and offer us a discount for volume licensing!"

"And how precisely do you think they'll do that?" I turn round and stare at her. "They're going to want to install snooping software on our LAN, and then read through its take." I take a deep breath. "You're going to have to get him to sign the Official Secrets Act so that I can formally notify him that if he thinks he's going to do that I'm going to have him sectioned. Part Three. Why do you *think* we're still running old copies of Windows on the network? Because we can't afford to replace them?"

"He's already signed Section Three. And anyway, you said you didn't have time," she snaps waspishly. "I asked you five weeks ago, on Friday! But you were too busy playing secret agents with your friends downstairs to notice anything as important as an upcoming audit. This wouldn't have been necessary if you had time!"

"Crap. Listen, we're running those old junkers because they're so old and rubbish that they can't catch half the proxy Internet worms and macro viruses that are doing the rounds these days. BSA will insist we replace them with stonking new workstations running Windows XP and Office XP and dialing into the Internet every six seconds to snitch on whatever we're doing with them. Do you *really* think Mahogany Row is going to clear that sort of security risk?"

That's a bluff—Mahogany Row retired from this universe back when software still meant silk unmentionables—but she isn't likely to know that, merely that I get invited up there these days. (Nearer my brain-eating God to thee . . .)

"As for the time thing, get me a hardware budget and a tech

assistant who's vetted for level five Laundry IT operations and I'll get it seen to. It'll only cost you sixty thousand pounds or so in the first year, plus a salary thereafter." Finally, *finally,* I get to pull the jug out of the coffee machine and pour myself a mug of wake-up. "That's better."

She glances at her watch. "Are you going to come along to the meeting and help explain this to everybody then?" she asks in a tone that could cut glass.

"No." I add cow juice from the fridge that wheezes asthmatically below the worktop. "It's a public/private partnership fuck-up, film at eleven. Bridget stuck her foot in it out of her own free will: if she wants me to pull it out for her she can damn well ask. Besides, I've got a code blue report meeting with Angelton and Boris and Andy and that trumps administrative make-work any day of the week."

"Bastard," she hisses.

"Pleased to be of service." I pull a face as she marches out the room and slams the door. "Angleton. Code blue. Jesus." All of a sudden I remember the modified camcorder in my jacket pocket. "Shit, I'm running late . . ."

➤ ➤ ➤

REPORT 4: Tuesday June 6th, 1989
CLASSIFIED TOP SECRET GAME ANDES RED-SHIFT, Ministry of Defense, June 6th, 1989

Abstract: Recent research in neuroanatomy has characterised the nature of the stellate ganglial networks responsible for gorgonism in patients with advanced astrocytoma affecting the cingulate gyrus. Tests combining the "map of medusa" layout with appropriate video preprocessing inputs have demonstrated the feasibility of mechanical induction of the medusa effect.

Progress in the emulation of dynamically reconfigurable hidden-layer neural networks using FPGA (fully programmable gate array) technology, combined with real-time digital video signal processing from binocular high-resolution video cameras, is likely within the next five years to allow us to download a "medusa mode" into suitably prepared surveillance

CCTV cameras, allowing real-time digital video monitoring networks to achieve a true line-of-sight look-to-kill capability. Extensive safety protocols are discussed which must be implemented before this technology can be deployed nationally, in order to minimize the risk of misactivation.

Projected deployment of CCTV monitoring in public places is estimated to result in over one million cameras *in situ* in British mainland cities by 1999. Coverage will be complete by 2004–06. Anticipated developments in internetworking and improvements in online computing bandwidth suggest for the first time the capacity of achieving a total coverage defense-in-depth against any conceivable insurgency. The implications of this project are discussed, along with its possible efficacy in mitigating the consequences of CASE NIGHTMARE GREEN in September 2007.

. . .

➤ ➤ ➤

Speaking of Mahogany Row, Angleton's picked the boardroom with the teak desk and the original bakelite desk fittings, and frosted windows onto the corridor, as the venue for my debriefing. He's sitting behind the desk tapping his bony fingers, with Andy looking anxious and Boris imperturbable when I walk in and flip the red MEETING light on.

"Home movies." I flip the tape on the desktop. "What I saw on my holiday." I put my coffee mug down on one of the disquietingly soft leather mats before I yawn, just in case I spill it. "Sorry, been up for hours. What do you want to know?"

"How long had it been dead?" asks Andy.

I think for a moment. "I'm not sure—have to call Pathology if you want a hard answer, I'm afraid, but clearly for some time when I found it after zero seven hundred. It had cooled to barely oven temperature."

Angleton is watching me like I'm a bug under a microscope. It's not a fun sensation. "Did you read the files?" he asks.

"Yes." Before I came up here I locked them in my office safe in case a busy little Tom, Dick, or Harriet decided to do some snooping. "I'm really going to sleep well tonight."

"The basilisk, is found." Boris.

"Um, no," I admit. "It's still in the wild. But Mike Williams said he'd let me know if they run across it. He's cleared for OSA-III, he's our liaison in—"

"How many traffic cameras overlooked the roundabout?" Angleton asks almost casually.

"Oh—" I sit down hard. "Oh shit. *Shit.*" I feel shaky, very shaky, guts doing the tango and icy chills running down the small of my back as I realise what he's trying to tell me without saying it out loud, on the record.

"That's why I sent you," he murmurs, waving Andy out of the room on some prearranged errand. A moment later Boris follows him. "You're not supposed to get yourself killed, Bob. It looks bad on your record."

"Oh shit," I repeat, needle stuck, sample echoing, as I realise how close to dying I may have been. And the crew of that chopper, and everyone else who's been there since, and—

"Half an hour ago someone vandalized the number seventeen traffic camera overlooking Monk's Road roundabout three: put a .223 bullet through the CCD enclosure. Drink your coffee, there's a good boy, do try not to spill it everywhere."

"One of ours." It comes out as a statement.

"Of course." Angleton taps the file sitting on the desk in front of him—I recognise it by the dog-ear on the second page, I put it in my office safe only ten minutes ago—and looks at me with those scary grey eyes of his. "So. The public at large being safe for the moment, tell me what you can deduce."

"Uh." I lick my lips, which have gone as dry as old boot leather. "Some time last night somebody let a cow into the park and used it for target practice. I don't know much about the network topology of the MK road traffic-control cams, but my possible suspects are, in order: someone with a very peculiar brain tumour, someone with a stolen stoner weapon—like the one I qualified for under OGRE REALITY—or someone with access to whatever GAME ANDES REDSHIFT gave birth to. And, going from the questions you're asking, if it's GAME ANDES REDSHIFT it's unauthorised."

He nods, very slightly.

"We're in deep shit then," I say brightly and throw back the last mouthful of coffee, spoiling the effect slightly by nearly coughing my guts up immediately afterward.

"Without a depth-gauge," he adds drily, and waits for my coughing fit to subside. "I've sent Andrew and Mr. B down to the stacks to pull out another file for you to read. Eyes only in front of witnesses, no note-taking, escort required. While they're signing it out I'd like you to write down in your own words everything that happened to you this morning so far. It'll go in a sealed file along with your video evidence as a deposition in case the worst happens."

"Oh shit." I'm getting tired of saying this. "It's internal?"

He nods.

"CPU business?"

He nods again, then pushes the antique portable manual typewriter toward me. "Start typing."

"Okay." I pick up three sheets of paper and some carbons and begin aligning their edges. "Consider me typing already."

⇻ ⇻ ⇻

REPORT 5: Monday December 10th, 2001
CLASSIFIED TOP SECRET GAME ANDES RED-SHIFT, Ministry of Defense, December 10th, 2001
CLASSIFIED TOP SECRET MAGINOT BLUE STARS, Ministry of Defense, December 10th, 2001

Abstract: This document describes progress to date in establishing a defensive network capable of repelling wide-scale incursions by reconfiguring the national closed-circuit television surveillance network as a software-controlled look-to-kill multiheaded basilisk. To prevent accidental premature deployment or deliberate exploitation, the SCORPION STARE software is not actually loaded into the camera firmware. Instead, reprogrammable FPGA chips are integrated into all cameras and can be loaded with SCORPION STARE by authorised MAGINOT BLUE STARS users whenever necessary.

. . .

Preamble: It has been said that the US Strategic Defense Initiative Organisation's proposed active ABM defense network will require the most complex software ever developed, characterised by a complexity metric of >100 MLOC and heavily criticized by various organisations (see footnotes [1][2][4]) as unworkable and likely to contain in excess of a thousand severity-1 bugs at initial deployment. Nevertheless, the architectural requirements of MAGINOT BLUE STARS dwarf those of the SDIO infrastructure. To provide coverage of 95 percent of the UK population we require a total of 8 million digitally networked CCTV cameras (terminals). Terminals in built-up areas may be connected via the public switched telephone network using SDSL/VHDSL, but outlying systems may use mesh network routing over 802.11a to ensure that rural areas do not provide a pool of infectious carriers for demonic possession. TCP/IP Quality of Service issues are discussed below, along with a concrete requirement for IPv6 routing and infrastructure that must be installed and supported by all Internet Service Providers no later than 2004.

There are more than ninety different CCTV architectures currently on sale in the UK, many of which are imported and cannot be fitted with FPGAs suitable for running the SCORPION STARE basilisk neural network prior to installation. Data Disclosure Orders served under the terms of the Regulation of Investigatory Powers Act (2001) serve to gain access to camera firmware, but in many regions upgrades to Level 1 MAGINOT BLUE STARS compliance is behind schedule due to noncompliance by local police forces with what are seen as unreasonable Home Office requests. Unless we can achieve a 340 percent compliance improvement by 2004, we will fail to achieve the target saturation prior to September 2007, when CASE NIGHTMARE GREEN is due.

. . .

Installation has currently been completed only in limited areas; notably Inner London ("Ring of Steel" for counter-terrorism surveillance) and Milton Keynes (advanced next-generation MAN with total traffic management solution in place). Deployment is proceeding in order of population density and potential for catastrophic demonic takeover and exponential burn through built-up areas . . .

. . .

Recommendation: One avenue for ensuring that all civilian CCTV equipment is SCORPION STARE compatible by 2006 is to exploit an initiative of the US National Security Agency for our own ends. In a bill ostensibly sponsored by Hollywood and music industry associations (MPAA and RIAA: see also CDBTPA), the NSA is ostensibly attempting to legislate support for Digital Rights Management in all electronic equipment sold to the public. The implementation details are not currently accessible to us, but we believe this is a stalking-horse for requiring chip manufacturers to incorporate on-die FPGAs in the one million gate range, reconfigurable in software, initially laid out as DRM circuitry but reprogrammable in support of their nascent War on Un-Americanism.

If such integrated FPGAs are mandated, commercial pressures will force Far Eastern vendors to comply with regulation and we will be able to mandate incorporation of SCORPION STARE Level Two into all digital consumer electronic cameras and commercial CCTV equipment under cover of complying with our copyright protection obligations in accordance with the WIPO treaty. A suitable pretext for the rapid phased obsolescence of all Level Zero and Level One cameras can then be engineered by, for example, discrediting witness evidence from older installations in an ongoing criminal investigation.

If we pursue this plan, by late 2006 any two adjacent public CCTV terminals—or private camcorders equipped with a digital video link—will be reprogrammable by any authenticated MAGINOT BLUE STARS superuser to permit the operator to turn them into a SCORPION STARE basilisk weapon. We remain convinced that this is the best defensive posture to adopt in order to minimize casualties when the Great Old Ones return from beyond the stars to eat our brains.

➤ ➤ ➤

"So, what this boils down to is a Strategic Defense Initiative against an invasion by alien mind-suckers from beyond space-time, who are expected to arrive in bulk at a set date. Am I on message so far?" I asked.

"Very approximately, yes," said Andy.

"Okay. To deal with the perceived alien mind-sucker threat, some nameless genius has worked out that the CCTV cameras dotting our green and pleasant land can be networked together, their inputs fed into a software emulation of a basilisk's brain, and turned into some kind of omnipresent look-to-kill death net. Even though we don't really know how the medusa effect works, other than that it relies on some kind of weird observationally mediated quantum-tunneling effect, collapse of the wave function, yadda yadda, that makes about 1 percent of the carbon nuclei in the target body automagically turn into silicon with no apparent net energy input. That right?"

"Have a cigar, Sherlock."

"Sorry, I only smoke when you plug me into the national grid. Shit. Okay, so it hasn't occurred to anyone that the mass-energy of those silicon nuclei has to come *from* somewhere, somewhere else, somewhere in the Dungeon Dimensions . . . damn. But that's not the point, is it?"

"Indeed not. When are you going to get to it?"

"As soon as my hands stop shaking. Let's see. Rather than do this openly and risk frightening the sheeple by stationing a death ray on every street corner, our lords and masters decided they'd do it bottom-up, by legislating that all public cameras be networked, and having back doors installed in them to allow the hunter-killer basilisk brain emulators to be uploaded when the time comes. Which, let's face it, makes excellent fiscal strength in this age of outsourcing, public-private partnerships, service charters, and the like. I mean, you can't get business insurance if you don't install antitheft cameras, someone's got to watch them so you might as well outsource the service to a security company with a network operations centre, and the brain-dead music industry copyright nazis are campaigning for a law to make it mandatory to install secret government spookware in every walkman—or camera—to prevent home taping from killing Michael Jackson. Absolutely brilliant."

"It *is* elegant, isn't it? Much more subtle than honking great ballistic missile submarines. We've come a long way since the Cold War."

"Yeah. Except you're *also* telling me that some script kiddie has rooted you and dialed in a strike on Milton Keynes. Probably in the mistaken belief that they think they're playing MISSILE COMMAND."

"No comment."

"Jesus Fucking Christ riding into town on top of a pickup truck full of DLT backup tapes—what kind of idiot do you take me for? Listen, the ball has gone *up*. Someone uploaded the SCORPION STARE code to a bunch of traffic cams off Monk's Road roundabout and turned Daisy into six hundred pounds of boiled beef on the bone *a la* basilisk, and all you can say is *no comment*?"

"Listen, Bob, I think you're taking this all too personally. I can't comment on the Monk's Road incident because you're officially the tag-team investigative lead and I'm here to provide backup and support, not to second-guess you. I'm trying to be helpful, okay?"

"Sorry, sorry. I'm just a bit upset."

"Yes, well, if it's any consolation that goes for me, too, and for Angleton believe it or not, but 'upset' and fifty pence will buy you a cup of coffee and what we really need is to finger the means, motive, and murderer of Daisy the Cow in time to close the stable door. Oh, and we can rule out external penetration—the network loop to Monk's Road is on a private backbone intranet that's firewalled up to the eyeballs. Does that make it easier for you?"

"No shit! Listen, I happen to agree with you in principle, but I am *still* upset, Andy, and I want to tell you—no shit. Look, this is so not-sensible that I know I'm way the hell too late but I think the whole MAGINOT BLUE STARS idea is fucking insane, I mean, like, bull-goose barking-at-the-moon hairs-on-the-palm-of-your-hands crazy. Like atomic landmines buried under every street corner! Didn't they know that the only unhackable computer is one that's running a secure operating system, welded inside a steel safe, buried under a ton of concrete at the bottom of a coal mine guarded by the SAS and a couple of armoured divisions, and *switched off*? What did they think they were *doing*?"

"Defending us against CASE NIGHTMARE GREEN, Bob. Which I'll have you know is why the Russians are so dead keen to get Energiya flying again so they can launch their Polyus orbital battle stations, and why the Americans are getting so upset about the Rune of Al-Sabbah that they're trying to build censorware into every analogue-to-digital converter on the planet."

"Do I have CASE NIGHTMARE GREEN clearance? Or do I just have to take it on trust?"

"Take it on trust for now, I'll try and get you cleared later in the week. Sorry about that, but this truly . . . look, in this instance the ends justify the means. Take it from me. Okay?"

"Shit. I need another—no, I've already had too much coffee. So, what am I supposed to do?"

"Well, the good news is we've narrowed it down a bit. You will be pleased to know that we just ordered the West Yorkshire Met's computer crime squad to go in with hobnailed boots and take down the entire MK traffic camera network and opcentre. Official reason is a suspicion of time bombs installed by a disgruntled former employee—who is innocent, incidentally—but it lets us turn it into a Computer Misuse case and send in a reasonably clueful team. They're about to officially call for backup from CESG, who are going to second them a purported spook from GCHQ, and that spook is going to be you. I want you to crawl all over that camera network and figure out how SCORPION STARE might have got onto it. Which is going to be easier than you think because SCORPION STARE isn't exactly open source and there are only two authorised development teams working on it on the planet that we know of, or at least in this country, one of them is—surprise—based in Milton Keynes, and as of right this minute you have clearance to stamp all over their turf and play the Gestapo officer with our top boffin labs. Which is a power I trust you will not abuse without good reason."

"Oh great, I always fancied myself in a long, black leather trench coat. What will Mo think?"

"She'll think you look the part when you're angry. Are you up for it?"

"How the fuck could I say no, when you put it that way?"

"I'm glad you understand. Now, have you got any other questions for me before we wrap this up and send the tape to the auditors?"

"Uh, yeah. One question. Why me?"

"Why—well! Hmm. I suppose because you're already on the inside, Bob. And you've got a pretty unique skill mix. Something you overlook is that we don't have many field qualified agents, and most of those we have are old school two-fisted shoot-from-the-hip-with-a-rune-of-destruction field necromancers; they don't understand these modern Babbage engine Internet contraptions like you do. And you've already got experience with basilisk weapons, or did you think we issued those things like toothpaste tubes? So rather than find someone who doesn't know as much, you just happened to be the man on the spot who knew enough and was thought . . . appropriate."

"Gee, thanks. I'll sleep a lot better tonight knowing that you couldn't find anyone better suited to the job. Really scraping the barrel, aren't we?"

"If only you knew . . . if only you knew."

➤ ➤ ➤

The next morning they put me on the train to Cheltenham—second class of course—to visit a large office site, which appears as a blank spot on all maps of the area, just in case the Russians haven't noticed the farm growing satellite dishes out back. I spend a very uncomfortable half hour being checked through security by a couple of Rottweilers in blue suits who work on the assumption that anyone who is not known to be a Communist infiltrator from North Korea is a dangerously unclassified security risk. They search me and make me pee in a cup and leave my palmtop at the site security office, but for some reason they don't ask me to surrender the small leather bag containing a mummified pigeon's foot that I wear on a silver chain round my neck when I explain that it's on account of my religion. The idiots.

It is windy and rainy outside so I have no objection to being ushered into an air-conditioned meeting room on the third floor of an outlying wing, offered institutional beige coffee the same colour as the office carpet, and to spending the next four hours in a meeting with Kevin, Robin, Jane, and Phil, who explain to me in turn what a senior operations officer from GCHQ detached for field duty is expected to do in the way of maintaining security, calling on backup, reporting problems, and filling out the two hundred and seventeen different forms that senior operations officers are apparently employed to spend their time filling out. The Laundry may have a bureaucracy surfeit and a craze for ISO-9000 certification, but GCHQ is even worse, with some bizarre spatchcock version of BS5720 quality assurance applied to all their procedures in an attempt to ensure that the Home Office minister can account for all available paper clips in near real-time if challenged in the House by Her Majesty's loyal opposition. On the other hand, they've got a bigger budget than us and all they have to worry about is having to read other people's email, instead of having their souls sucked out by tentacular horrors from beyond the universe.

"Oh, and you really ought to wear a tie when you're representing us in public," Phil says apologetically at the end of his spiel.

"And get a haircut," Jane adds with a smile.

Bastards.

The Human Resources imps billet me in a bed and breakfast run by a genteel pair of elderly High Tory sociopaths, a Mr. and Mrs. MacBride. He's bald, loafs around in slippers, and reads the *Telegraph* while muttering darkly about the need for capital punishment as a solution to the problem of bogus asylum seekers; she wears heavy horn-rimmed glasses and the hairdo that time forgot. The corridors are wallpapered with an exquisitely disgusting floral print and the whole place smells of mothballs, the only symptom of the twenty-first century being a cheap and nasty webcam on the hall staircase. I try not to shudder as I slouch upstairs to my room and barricade the door before settling down for the evening phone call to Mo and a game of Civ on my palmtop (which I rescued from Security on my way out). "It could be worse," Mo consoles me, "at least *your* landlord doesn't have gill slits and greenish skin."

The next morning I elbow my way onto an early train to London, struggle through the rush hour crush, and somehow manage to weasel my way into a seat on a train to Milton Keynes; it's full of brightly clad German backpackers and irritated businessmen on their way to Luton airport, but I get off before there and catch a taxi to the cop shop. "There is nothing better in life than drawing on the sole of your slipper with a biro instead of going to the pub on a Saturday night," the lead singer of Half Man Half Biscuit sings mournfully on my iPod, and I am inclined to agree, subject to the caveat that Saturday nights at the pub are functionally equivalent to damp Thursday mornings at the police station. "Is Inspector Sullivan available?" I ask at the front desk.

"Just a moment." The moustachioed constable examines my warrant card closely, gives me a beady-eyed stare as if he expects me to break down and confess instantly to a string of unsolved burglaries, then turns and ambles into the noisy back office round the corner. I have just enough time to read the more surreal crime prevention posters for the second time ("Are your neighbours fox-hunting reptiles from the planet of the green wellies? Denounce them here, free of charge!") when the door bangs open and a determined-looking woman in a grey suit barges in. She looks how Annie Lennox would look if she'd joined the constabulary, been glassed once or twice, and had a really dodgy curry the night before.

"Okay, who's the joker?" she demands. "You." A bony finger points at me. "You're from—" she sees the warrant card "—oh shit." Over her shoulder: "Jeffries, *Jeffries,* you rat bastard, you set me up! Oh, why do I bother." Back in my direction: "You're the spook who got me out of bed the day before yesterday after a graveyard shift. Is this *your* mess?"

I take a deep breath. "Mine and yours both. I'm just back down from—" I clear my throat "—and I've got orders to find an inspector J. Sullivan and drag him into an interview room." Mentally crossing my fingers: "What's the J stand for?"

"Josephine. And it's *detective* inspector, while you're about it." She lifts the barrier. "You'd better come in then." Josephine looks tired and annoyed. "Where's your other card?"

"My other—oh." I shrug. "We don't flash them around; might be a bit of a disaster if one went missing." Anyone who picked it up would be in breach of Section Three, at the very least. Not to mention in peril of their immortal soul.

"It's okay, I've signed the Section, in blood." She raises an eyebrow at me.

"Paragraph two?" I ask, just to be sure she's not bluffing.

She shakes her head. "No, paragraph three."

"Pass, friend." And then I let her see the warrant card as it really is, the way it reaches into your head and twists things around so you want to throw up at the mere thought of questioning its validity. "Satisfied?"

She just nods: a cool customer for sure. The trouble with Section Three of the Official Secrets Act is that it's an offense to know it exists without having signed it—in blood. So us signatories who are in theory cleared to talk about such supersecret national security issues as the Laundry's tea trolley rota are in practice unable to broach the topic directly. We're supposed to rely on introductions, but that breaks down rapidly in the field. It's a bit like lesbian sheep; as ewes display their sexual arousal by standing around waiting to be mounted, it's hard to know if somebody else is, well, you know. *Cleared.* "Come on," she adds, in a marginally less hostile tone, "we can pick up a cup of coffee on the way."

Five minutes later we're sitting down with a notepad, a telephone, and an antique tape recorder that Smiley probably used to debrief Karla, back when men were real men and lesbian sheep were afraid. "This had better be important," Josephine complains, clicking a frighteningly high-tech sweetener dispenser repeatedly over her black Nescafé. "I've got a persistent burglar, two rapes, a string of car thefts, and a phantom pisser, who keeps breaking into department stores, to deal with, then a bunch of cloggies from West Yorkshire who're running some kind of computer audit—your fault, I believe. I need to get bogged down in *X-Files* rubbish right now like I need a hole in my head."

"Oh, it's important all right. And I hope to get it off your desk as soon as possible. I'd just like to get a few things straight first."

"Hmm. So what do you need to know? We've only had two flying saucer sightings and six alien abductions this year so far." She raises one eyebrow, arms crossed and shoulders set a trifle defensively. Who'd have thought it? Being interviewed by higher authorities makes the alpha female detective defensive. "It's not like I've got all day: I'm due in a case committee briefing at noon and I've got to pick up my son from school at four."

On second thought, maybe she really *is* busy. "To start with, did you get any witness reports or CCTV records from the scene? And have you identified the cow, and worked out how it got there?"

"No eyewitnesses, not until three o'clock, when Vernon Thwaite was out walking his girlfriend's toy poodle which had diarrhoea." She pulls a face, which makes the scar on her forehead wrinkle into visibility. "If you want we can go over the team reports together. I take it that's what pulled you in?"

"You could say that." I dip a cheap IKEA spoon in my coffee and check cautiously after a few seconds to see if the metal's begun to corrode. "Helicopters make me airsick. Especially after a night out when I was expecting a morning lie-in." She almost smiles before she remembers she's officially grumpy with me. "Okay, so no earlier reports. What else?"

"No tape," she says, flattening her hands on the tabletop to either side of her cup and examining her nail cuticles. "Nothing. One second it's zero zero twenty-six, the next it's zero seven fourteen. Numbers to engrave in your heart. Dennis, our departmental geek, was most upset with MKSG—they're the public-private partners in the regional surveillance outsourcing sector."

"Zero zero twenty-six to zero seven fourteen," I echo as I jot them down on my palmtop. "MKSG. Right, that's helpful."

"It is?" She tilts her head sideways and stares at me like I'm a fly that's landed in her coffee.

"Yup." I nod, then tell myself that it'd be really stupid to wind her up without good reason. "Sorry. What I can tell you is,

I'm as interested in anything that happened to the cameras as the cow. If you hear anything about them—especially about them being tampered with—I'd love to know. But in the meantime—Daisy. Do you know where she came from?"

"Yes." She doesn't crack a smile but her shoulders unwind slightly. "Actually, she's number two six three from Emmett-Moore Ltd, a dairy factory out near Dunstable. Or rather, she was two six three until three days ago. She was getting along a bit, so they sold her to a local slaughterhouse along with a job lot of seven other cows. I followed up on the other seven and they'll be showing up in your McHappy McMeal some time next month. But not Daisy. Seems a passing farmer in a Range Rover with a wagon behind it dropped by and asked if he could buy her and cart her away for his local family butcher to deal with."

"Aha!"

"And if you believe that, I've got a bridge to sell you." She takes a sip of her coffee, winces, and strafes it with sweeteners again. Responding on autopilot I try a mouthful of my own and burn my tongue. "Turns out that there's no such farmer Giles of Ham Farm, Bag End, The Shire, on record. Mind you, they had a camera on their stockyard and we nailed the Range Rover. It turned up abandoned the next day on the outskirts of Leighton Buzzard and it's flagged as stolen on HOLMES2. Right now it's sitting in the pound down the road; they smoked it for prints but it came up clean and we don't have enough money to send a SOCO and a forensics team to do a full workup on every stolen car we run across. *However,* if you twist my arm and promise me a budget *and* to go to the mat with my boss I'll see what I can lay on."

"That may not be necessary: we have ways and means. But can you get someone to drive me down there? I'll take some readings and get out of your face—except for the business with Daisy. How are you covering that?"

"Oh, we'll find something. Right now it's filed under 'F' for Fucking Fortean Freakery, but I was thinking of announcing it's just an old animal that had been dumped illegally by a farmer who didn't want to pay to have it slaughtered."

"That sounds about right." I nod slowly. "Now, I'd like to play a random word-association game with you. Okay? Ten seconds. When I say the words tell me what you think of. Right?"

She looks puzzled. "Is this—"

"Listen. Case-Nightmare-Green-Scorpion-Stare-Maginot-Blue-Stars. By the authority vested in me by the emissaries of Y'ghonzzh N'hai I have the power to bind and to release, and your tongue be tied of these matters of which we have spoken until you hear these words again: Case-Nightmare-Green-Scorpion-Stare-Maginot-Blue-Stars. Got that?"

She looks at me cross-eyed and mouths something, then looks increasingly angry until finally she gets it together to burst out with: "Hey, what *is* this shit?"

"Purely a precaution," I say, and she glares at me, gobbling for a moment while I finish my coffee until she figures out that she simply can't say a word about the subject. "Right," I say. "Now. You've got my permission to announce that the cow was dumped. You have my permission to talk freely to me, but to nobody else. Anyone asks any questions, refer them to me if they won't take no for an answer. This goes for your boss, too. Feel free to tell them that you can't tell them, nothing more."

"Wanker," she hisses, and if looks could kill I'd be a small pile of smouldering ashes on the interview room floor.

"Hey, *I'm* under a geas, too. If I don't spread it around my head will explode."

I don't know whether she believes me or not but she stops fighting it and nods tiredly. "Tell me what you want then get the hell out of my patch."

"I want a lift to the car pound. A chance to sit behind the wheel of that Range Rover. A book of poetry, a jug of wine, a date tree, and—sorry, wrong question. Can you manage it?"

She stands up. "I'll take you there myself," she says tersely. We go.

❧ ❧ ❧

I get to endure twenty-five minutes of venomous silence in the back seat of an unmarked patrol car driven by one Constable Routledge, with DI Sullivan in the front passenger seat treating me with the warmth due a serial killer, before we arrive at the pound. I'm beyond introspective self-loathing by now—you lose it fast in this line of work. Angleton will have my head for a keyring fob if I don't take care to silence any possible leaks, and a tongue-twisting geas is more merciful than most of the other tools at my disposal—but I still feel like a shit. So it comes as a great relief to get out of the car and stretch my legs on the muddy gravel parking lot in the pouring rain.

"So where's the car?" I ask, innocently.

Josephine ignores me. "Bill, you want to head over to Bletchley Way and pick up Dougal's evidence bag for the Hayes case. Then come back to pick us up," she tells the driver. To the civilian security guard: "You, we're looking for BY 476 ERB. Came in yesterday, Range Rover. Where is it?"

The bored security goon leads us through the mud and a maze of cars with POLICE AWARE stickers glued to their windshields then gestures at a half-empty row. "That's it?" Josephine asks, and he passes her a set of keys. "Okay, you can piss off now." He takes one look at her face and beats a hasty retreat. I half-wish I could join him—whether she's a detective inspector or not, and therefore meant to be behaving with the gravitas of a senior officer in public, DI Sullivan looks to be in a mood to bite the heads off chickens. Or Laundry field agents, given half an excuse.

"Right, that's it," she says, holding out the keys and shaking them at me impatiently. "You're done, I take it, so I'll be pushing off. Case meeting to run, mystery shopping centre pisser to track down, and so on."

"Not so fast." I glance round. The pound is surrounded by a high wire fence and there's a decrepit Portakabin office out front by the gate: a camera sits on a motorised mount on a pole sticking up from the roof. "Who's on the other end of that thing?"

"The gate guard, probably," she says, following my finger. The camera is staring at the entrance, unmoving.

"Okay, why don't you open up the car." She blips the remote to unlock the door and I keep my eyes on the camera as she takes the handle and tugs. *Could I be wrong?* I wonder as the rain trickles down my neck. I shake myself when I notice her staring, then

I pull out my palmtop, clamber up into the driver's seat, and balance the pocket computer on the steering wheel as I tap out a series of commands. What I see makes me shake my head. Whoever stole the car may have wiped for fingerprints but they didn't know much about paranormal concealment—they didn't use the shroud from a suicide, or get a paranoid schizophrenic to drive. The scanner is sensitive to heavy emotional echoes, and the hands I'm looking for are the most recent ones to have chilled from fright and fear of exposure. I log everything and put it away, and I'm about to open the glove locker when something makes me glance at the main road beyond the chainlink fence and—

"Watch out! Get down!" I jump out and go for the ground. Josephine is looking around so I reach out and yank her ankles out from under her. She yells, goes down hard on her backside, and tries to kick me, then there's a loud *whump* from behind me and a wave of heat like an open oven door. "Shit, fuck, shit—" I take a moment to realise the person cursing is me as I fumble at my throat for the bag and rip it open, desperately trying to grab the tiny claw and the disposable cigarette lighter at the same time. I flick the lighter wheel and right then something like a sledgehammer whacks into the inside of my right thigh.

"Bastard . . . !"

"Stop it—" I gasp, just as the raw smell of petrol vapour reaches me and I hear a crackling roar. I get the pigeon claw lit in a stink of burning keratin and an eerie glow, nearly shitting myself with terror, lying in a cold damp puddle, and roll over: *"Don't move!"*

"Bastard! What—hey, what's burning?"

"Don't move," I gasp again, holding the subminiature Hand of Glory up. The traffic camera in the road outside the fence is casting about as if it's dropped its contact lens, but the one on the pole above the office is locked right onto the burning tires of the Range Rover. "If you let go of my hand they'll see you and kill you *oh shit*—"

"Kill—*what?*" She stares at me, white-faced.

"You! Get under cover!" I yell across the pound, but the guy in the blue suit—the attendant—doesn't hear me. One second he's running across the car park as fast as his portly behind can manage; the next moment he's tumbling forward, blackening, puffs of flame erupting from his eyes and mouth and ears, then the stumps as his arms come pinwheeling off, and the carbonized trunk slides across the ground like a grisly toboggan.

"Oh shit, oh shit!" Her expression changes from one second to the next, from disbelief to dawning horror. "We've got to help—"

"Listen, *no*! Stay down!"

She freezes in place for a full heartbeat, then another. When she opens her mouth again she's unnaturally cool. "What's going on?"

"The cameras," I pant. "Listen, this is a Hand of Glory, an invisibility shield. Right now it's all that's keeping us alive—those cameras are running SCORPION STARE. If they see us we're dead."

"Are you—the car? What happened to it?"

"Tires. They're made of carbon, rubber. SCORPION STARE works on anything with a shitload of long-chain carbon molecules in it—like tires, or cows. Makes them burn."

"Oh my sainted aunt and holy father . . ."

"Hold my hand. Make skin to skin contact—not that hard. We've got maybe three, four minutes before this HOG burns down. Bastards, *bastards*. Got to get to the control shack—"

The next minute is a nightmare of stumbling—shooting pains in my knees from where I went down hard and in my thigh where Josephine tried to kick the shit out of me—soaking cold damp jeans, and roasting hot skin on my neck from the pyre that I was sitting inside only seconds ago. She holds onto my left hand like it's a lifesaver—yes, it is, for as long as the HOG keeps burning—and we lurch and shamble toward the modular site office near the entrance as fast as we can go. "Inside," she gasps, "it can't see inside."

"Yeah?" She half-drags me to the entrance and we find the door's open, not locked. "Can we get away round the other side?"

"Don't think so." She points through the building. "There's a school."

"Oh shit." We're on the other side of the pound from the traffic camera in the road, but there's another camera under the eaves of the school on the other side of the road from the steel gates out front, and it's a good thing the kids are all in lessons because what's going on here is every teacher's nightmare. And we've got to nail it down as fast as possible, because if they ring the bell for lunch—"We've got to kill the power to the roofcam first," I say. "Then we've got to figure a way out."

"What's going on? What *did* that?" Her lips work like a fish out of water.

I shake my head. "Case-Nightmare-Green-Scorpion-Stare-Maginot-Blue-Stars tongue be loosed. Okay, talk. I reckon we've got about two, three minutes to nail this before—"

"This was all a setup?"

"I don't know yet. Look, how do I get onto the roof?"

"Isn't that a skylight?" she asks, pointing.

"Yeah." Being who I am I always carry a Leatherman multi-tool so I whip it out and look around for a chair I can pile on top of the desk and stand on, one that doesn't have wheels and a gas strut. "See any chairs I can—"

I'll say this much, detective training obviously enables you to figure out how to get onto a roof fast. Josephine simply walks over to the ladder nestling in a corner between one wall and a battered filing cabinet and pulls it out. "This what you're looking for?"

"Uh, yeah. Thanks." She passes it to me and I fumble with it for a moment, figuring out how to set it up. Then another moment, juggling the multitool and the half-consumed pigeon's foot and looking at the ladder dubiously.

"Give me those," she says.

"But—"

"Listen, *I'm* the one who deals with idiot vandals and climbs around on pitched roofs looking for broken skylights, okay? And—" she glances at the door "—if I mess up you can phone your boss and let him know what's happening."

"Oh," I mumble, then hand her the gadgets and hold the ladder steady while she swarms up it like a circus acrobat. A moment later there's a noise like a herd of baby elephants thudding on the rooftop as she scrambles across to the camera mount.

The camera may be on a moving platform but there's a limit to how far it can depress and clearly she's right below the azimuth platform—just as long as she isn't visible to both the traffic camera out back and the schoolyard monitor out front. More shaking, then there's a loud clack and the Portakabin lights go out.

A second or two later she reappears, feet first, through the opening. "Right, that should do it," she says. "I shorted the power cable to the platform. "Hey, the lights—"

"I think you shorted a bit more than that." I hold the ladder as she climbs down. "Now, we've got an immobilized one up top, that's good. Let's see if we can find the controller."

A quick search of the hut reveals a bunch of fun stuff I hadn't been expecting, like an ADSL line to the regional police IT hub, a PC running some kind of terminal emulator, and another dedicated machine with the cameras showing overlapping windows on-screen. I could kiss them; they may have outsourced the monitoring to private security firms but they've kept the hardware all on the same backbone network. The blinkenlights are beeping and twittering like crazy as everything's now running on backup battery power, but that's okay. I pull out a breakout box and scramble around under a desk until I've got my palmtop plugged into the network hub to sniff packets. Barely a second later it dings at me. "Oh, lovely." So much for *firewalled up to the eyeballs*. I unplug and surface again, then scroll through the several hundred screenfuls of unencrypted bureaucratic computerese my network sniffer has grabbed. *"That* looks promising. Uh, I wouldn't go outside just yet but I think we're going to be all right."

"Explain." She's about ten centimetres shorter than I am, but I'm suddenly aware that I'm sharing the Portakabin with an irate, wet, detective inspector who's probably a black belt at something or other lethal and who is just about to really lose her cool: "You've got about ten seconds from *now* to tell me everything. Or I'm calling for backup and warrant card or no you are going in a cell until I get some answers. *Capisci?*"

"I surrender." I don't, really, but I point at my palmtop. "It's a fair cop, guv. Look, someone's been too clever by half here. The camera up top is basically a glorified webcam. I mean, it's running a web server and it's plugged into the constabulary's intranet via broadband. Every ten seconds or so a program back at HQ polls it and grabs the latest picture, okay? That's in addition to whatever the guy downstairs tells it to look at. Anyway, someone *else* just sent it an HTTP request with a honking great big file upload attached, and I don't think your IT department is in the habit of using South Korean primary schools as proxy servers, are they? And a compromised firewall, no less. Lovely! Your cameras may have been 0wnZ0r3d by a fucking script kiddie, but they're not as fucking smart as they *think* they are otherwise they'd have fucking stripped off the fucking referrer headers, wouldn't they?" I stop talking and make sure I've saved the logfile somewhere secure, then for good measure I email it to myself at work.

"Right. So I know their IP address and it's time to locate them." It's the work of about thirty seconds to track it to a dial-up account on one of the big national ISPs—one of the free anonymous ones. "Hmm. If you want to help, you could get me an S22 disclosure notice for the phone number behind this dial-up account. Then we can persuade the phone company to tell us the street address and go pay them a visit and ask why they killed our friend with the key ring—" My hands are shaking from the adrenaline high and I am beginning to feel angry, not just an ordinary day-to-day pissed-off feeling but the kind of true and brutal rage that demands revenge.

"Killed? Oh." She opens the door an inch and looks outside: she looks a little grey around the gills, but she doesn't lose it. Tough woman.

"It's SCORPION STARE. Look, S22 data disclosure order first, it's a fucking murder investigation now, isn't it? Then we go visiting. But we're going to have to make out like it's accidental, or the press will come trampling all over us and we won't be able to get anything done." I write down the hostname while she gets on the mobile to head office. The first sirens start to wail even before she picks up my note and calls for medical backup. I sit there staring at the door, contemplating the mess, my mind whirling. "Tell the ambulance crew it's a freak lightning strike," I say as the thought takes me. "You're already in this up to your ears, we don't need to get anyone else involved—"

Then my phone rings.

❧ ❧ ❧

As it happens we don't visit any murderous hackers, but presently the car pound is fronted with white plastic scene-of-crime sheeting and a photographer and a couple of forensics guys show up and Josephine, who has found something more urgent to obsess over than ripping me a new asshole, is busy directing their preliminary work-over. I'm poring over screenfuls of tcpdump output in the control room when the same unmarked car that dropped us off here pulls up with Constable Routledge at the wheel and a very unexpected passenger in the back. I gape as he gets out of the car and walks toward the hut. "Who's this?" demands Josephine, coming over and sticking her head in through the window.

I open the door. "Hi, boss. Boss, meet Detective Inspector Sullivan. Josephine, this is my boss—you want to come in and sit down?"

Andy nods at her distractedly: "I'm Andy. Bob, brief me." He glances at her again as she shoves through the door and closes it behind her. "Are you—"

"She knows too much already." I shrug. "Well?" I ask her. "This is your chance to get out."

"Fuck that." She glares at me, then Andy: "Two mornings ago it was a freak accident and a cow, today it's a murder investigation—I trust you're not planning on escallating it any further, terrorist massacres and biological weapons are a little outside my remit—and I want some answers. *If* you please."

"Okay, you'll get them," Andy says mildly. "Start talking," he tells me.

"Code blue called at three thirty the day before yesterday. I flew out to take a look, found a dead cow that had been zapped by SCORPION STARE—unless there's a basilisk loose in Milton Keynes—went down to our friends in Cheltenham for briefing yesterday, stayed overnight, came up here this morning. The cow was bought from a slaughterhouse and transported to the scene in a trailer towed by a stolen car, which was later dumped and transferred to this pound. Inspector Sullivan is our force liaison—external circle two, no need to know. She brought me here and I took a patch test, and right then someone zapped the car—we were lucky to survive. One down out front. We've, uh, trapped a camera up top that I *think* will prove to have firmware loaded with SCORPION STARE, and I sniffed packets coming in from a compromised host. Police intranet, firewalled to hell and back, hacked via some vile little dweeb using a primary school web server in South Korea. We were just about to run down the intruder in meatspace and go ask some pointed questions when you arrived." I yawn, and Andy looks at me oddly. Extreme stress sometimes does that to me, makes me tired, and I've been running on my nerves for most of the past few days.

"All right." Andy scratches his chin thoughtfully. "There's been a new development."

"New development?" I echo.

"Yes. We received a blackmail note." And it's no fucking *wonder* that he's looking slightly glassy-eyed—he must be in shock.

"Blackmail? What are they—"

"It came via email from an anonymous remixer on the public Internet. Whoever wrote it knows about MAGINOT BLUE STARS and wants us to know that they disapprove, especially of SCORPION STARE. No sign that they've got CASE NIGHTMARE GREEN, though. They're giving us three days to cancel the entire project or they'll blow it wide open in quote the most public way imaginable unquote."

"Shit."

"Smelly brown stuff, yes. Angleton is displeased." Andy shakes his head. "We tracked the message back to a dial-up host in the UK—"

I hold up a piece of paper. "This one?"

He squints at it. "I think so. We did the S22 soft-shoe shuffle but it's no good, they used the SIMM card from a prepaid mobile phone bought for cash in a supermarket in Birmingham three months ago. The best we could do was trace the caller's location to the centre of Milton Keynes." He glances at Josephine. "Did you impress her—"

"Listen." She speaks quietly and with great force: "Firstly, this appears to be an investigation into murder—and now blackmail, of a government department, right?—and in case you hadn't noticed, organising criminal investigations just happens to be my speciality. Secondly, I do not appreciate being forcibly gagged. I *have* signed a certain piece of paper, and the only stuff I leak is what you get when you drill holes in me. Finally, I am getting really pissed off with the runaround you're giving me about a particularly serious incident on my turf, and if you don't start answering my questions soon I'm going to have to arrest you for wasting police time. Now, which is it going to be?"

"Oh, for crying out loud." Andy rolls his eyes, then says very rapidly: "By the abjuration of Dee and the name of Claude Dansey I hereby exercise subsection D paragraph sixteen clause twelve and bind you to service from now and forevermore. Right, that's it. You're drafted, and may whatever deity you believe in have mercy on your soul."

"Hey. Wait." She takes a step back. "What's going on?" There's a faint stink of burning sulphur in the air.

"You've just talked yourself into the Laundry," I say, shaking my head. "Just try to remember I tried to keep you out of this."

"The Laundry? What are you talking about? I thought you were from Cheltenham?" The smell of brimstone is getting stronger. "Hey, is something on fire?"

"Wrong guess," says Andy. "Bob can explain later. For now, just remember that we work for the same people, ultimately, only we deal with a higher order of threat than everyday stuff like rogue states, terrorist nukes, and so on. Cheltenham is the cover story. Bob, the blackmailer threatened to upload SCORPION STARE to the ring of steel."

"Oh shit." I sit down hard on the edge of a desk. "That is so very not good that I don't want to think about it right now." The ring of steel is the network of surveillance cameras that were installed around the financial heart of the city of London in the late 1990s to deter terrorist bombings. "Look, did Angleton have any other—"

"Yes. He wants us to go visit Site Able right now, that's the lead development team at the research centre behind SCORPI-

ON STARE. Um, inspector? You're in. As I said, you're drafted. Your boss, that would be Deputy Chief Constable Dunwoody, is about to get a memo about you from the Home Office—we'll worry about whether you can go back to your old job afterward. As of now, this investigation is your only priority. Site Able runs out of an office unit at Kiln Farm industrial estate, covered as a UK subsidiary of an American software company: in reality they're part of the residual unprivatised rump of DERA, uh, QinetiQ. The bunch that handles Q-projects."

"While you're busy wanking over your cow-burning non-sense I've got a ring of car thieves to—" Josephine shakes her head distractedly, sniffs suspiciously, then stops trying to fight the geas. *That smell* . . . Why do these people at Kiln Farm need a visit?"

"Because they're the lead team on the group who developed SCORPION STARE," Andy explains, "and Angleton doesn't think it's a coincidence that our blackmailer burned a cow in Milton Keynes. He thinks they're a bunch of locals. Bob, if you've got a trace that'll be enough to narrow it down to the building—"

"Yes?" Josephine nods to herself. "But you need to find the individual responsible, and any time bombs they've left, and there's a small matter of evidence." A thought strikes her. "What happens when you catch them?"

Andy looks at me and my blood runs cold. "I think we'll have to see about that when we find them," I extemporise, trying to avoid telling her about the Audit Commission for the time being; she might blow her stack completely if I have to explain how they investigate malfeasance, and then I'd have to tell her that the burning smell is a foreshadowing of what happens if she is ever found guilty of disloyalty. (It normally fades a few minutes after the rite of binding, but right now it's still strong.) "What are we waiting for?" I ask. "Let's go!"

➤ ➤ ➤

In the beginning there was the Defense Evaluation and Research Agency, DERA. And DERA was where HMG's boffins hung out, and they developed cool toys like tanks with plastic armour, clunky palmtops powered by 1980s chips and rugged enough to be run over by a truck, and fetal heart monitors to help the next generation of squaddies grow up strong. And lo, in the thrusting entrepreneurial climate of the early nineties a new government came to power with a remit to bring about the triumph of true socialism by privatising the post office and air traffic control systems, and DERA didn't stand much of a chance. Renamed QinetiQ by the same nameless marketing genius who turned the Royal Mail into Consignia and Virgin Trains into fodder for fuckedcompany-dot-com, the research agency was hung out to dry, primped and beautified, and generally prepared for sale to the highest bidder who didn't speak with a pronounced Iraqi accent.

However . . .

In addition to the ordinary toys, DERA used to do development work for the Laundry. Q Division's pedigree stretches back all the way to SOE's wartime dirty tricks department—poison pens, boot-heel escape kits, explosive-stuffed sabotage rats, the whole nine yards of James Bond japery. Since the 1950s, Q Division has kept the Laundry in more esoteric equipment: summoning grids, basilisk guns, Turing oracles, self-tuning pentacles, self-filling beer glasses, and the like. Steadily growing weirder and more specialised by the year, Q Division is far too sensitive to sell off—unlike most of QinetiQ's research, what they do is classified so deep you'd need a bathyscaphe to reach it. And so, while QinetiQ was being dolled up for the city catwalk, Q Division was segregated and spun off, a little stronghold in the sea of commerce that is forever civil service territory.

Detective Inspector Sullivan marches out of the site office like a blank-faced automaton and crisply orders her pet driver to take us to Site Able then to bugger off on some obscure make-work errand. She sits stiffly in the front passenger seat while Andy and I slide into the back and we proceed in silence—nobody seems to want to make small talk.

Fifteen minutes of bumbling around red routes and through trackless wastes of identical red brick houses embellished with satellite dishes and raw pine fences brings us into an older part of town, where the buildings actually look different and the cycle paths are painted strips at the side of the road rather than separately planned routes. I glance around curiously, trying to spot landmarks. "Aren't we near Bletchley Park?" I ask.

"It's a couple of miles that way," says our driver without taking his hands off the wheel to point. "You thinking of visiting?"

"Not just yet." Bletchley Park was the wartime headquarters of the Ultra operation, the department that later became GCHQ—the people who built the Colossus computers, originally used for breaking Nazi codes and subsequently diverted by the Laundry for more occult purposes. Hallowed ground to us spooks; I've met more than one NSA liaison who wanted to visit in order to smuggle a boot heel full of gravel home. "Not until we've visited the UK offices of Dillinger Associates, at any rate."

Dillinger Associates is the cover name for a satellite office of Q Division. The premises turns out to be a neoclassical brick-and-glass edifice with twee fake columns and wilted-looking ivy that's been trained to climb the facade by dint of ruthless application of plant hormones. We pile out of the car in the courtyard between the dry fountain and the glass doors, and I surreptitiously check my PDA's locator module for any sign of a match. Nothing. I blink and put it away in time to catch up with Andy and Josephine as they head for the bleached blonde receptionist who sits behind a high wooden counter and types constantly, as unapproachably artificial-looking as a shop window dummy.

"HelloDillingerAssociatesHowCanIHelpEwe?" She flutters her eyelashes at Andy in a bored, professional way, hands never moving away from the keyboard of the PC in front of her. There's something odd about her, but I can't quite put my finger on it.

Andy flips open his warrant card. "We're here to see Doctor Voss."

The receptionist's long, red-nailed fingers stop moving and hover over the keyboard. "Really?" she asks, tonelessly, reaching under the desk.

"Hold it—" I begin to say, as Josephine takes a brisk step forward and drops a handkerchief over the webcam on top of the woman's monitor. There's a quiet *pop* and the sudden absence of noise from her PC tips me off. I sidestep the desk and make a grab for her just as Andy produces a pistol with a ridiculously fat barrel and shoots out the camera located over the door at the rear of the reception area. There's a horrible ripping sound like a joint of meat tearing apart as the receptionist twists aside and I realise that she isn't sitting on a chair at all—she's joined seamlessly at the hips to a plinth that emerges from some kind of fat swivel base of age-blackened wood, bolted to the floor with heavy brass pins in the middle of a silvery metallic pentacle with wires trailing from one corner back up to the PC on the desk. She opens her mouth and I can see that her tongue is bright blue and bifurcated as she hisses.

I hit the floor shoulder first, jarringly hard, and grab for the nearest cable. Those red nails are reaching down for me as her eyes narrow to slits and she works her jaw muscles as if she's trying to get together a wad of phlegm to spit. I grab the fattest cable and give it a pull and she screams, high-pitched and frighteningly inhuman.

What the fuck? I think, looking up as the red-painted claws stretch and expand, shedding layers of varnish as their edges grow long and sharp. Then I yank the cable again, and it comes away from the pentacle. The wooden box drools a thick, blue-tinted liquid across the carpet tiles, and the screaming stops.

"Lamia," Andy says tersely. He strides over to the fire door that opens onto the corridor beyond, raises the curiously fat gun, and fires straight up. A purple rain drizzles back down.

"What's going on?" says Josephine, bewildered, staring at the twitching, slowly dying receptionist.

I point my PDA at the lamia and ding it for a reading. Cool, but nonzero. "Got a partial fix," I call to Andy. "Where's everyone else? Isn't this place supposed to be manned?"

"No idea." He looks worried. "If this is what they've got up front the shit's already hit the fan—Angleton wasn't predicting overt resistance."

The other door bangs open of a sudden and a tubby middle-aged guy in a cheap grey suit and about three day's worth of designer stubble barges out shouting, "Who are you and what do you think you're doing here? This is private property, not a paintball shooting gallery! It's a disgrace—I'll call the police!"

Josephine snaps out of her trance and steps forward. "As a

matter of fact, I *am* the police," she says. "What's your name? Do you have a complaint, and if so, what is it?"

"I'm, I'm—" He focusses on the no-longer-twitching demon receptionist, lolling on top of her box like a murderous shop mannequin. He looks aghast. "Vandals! If you've damaged her—"

"Not as badly as she planned to damage us," says Andy. "I think you'd better tell us who you are." Andy presents his card, ordering it to reveal its true shape: "by the authority vested in me—"

He moves fast with the geas and ten seconds later we've got mister fat guy—actually Dr. Martin Voss—seated on one of the uncomfortable chrome-and-leather designer sofas at one side of reception while Andy asks questions and records them on a dictaphone. Voss talks in a monotone, obviously under duress, drooling slightly from one side of his mouth, and the stench of brimstone mingles with a mouth-watering undertone of roast pork. There's purple dye from Andy's paintball gun spattered over anything that might conceal a camera, and he had me seal all the doorways with a roll of something like duct tape or police incident tape, except that the symbols embossed on it glow black and make your eyes water if you try to focus on them.

"Tell me your name and position at this installation."

"Voss. John Voss. Res-research team manager."

"How many members are there on your team? Who are they?"

"Twelve. Gary. Ted. Elinor. John. Jonathan. Abdul. Mark—"

"Stop right there. Who's here today? And is anyone away from the office right now?" I plug away at my palmtop, going cross-eyed as I fiddle with the detector controls. But there's no sign of any metaspectral resonance; grepping for a match to the person who stole the Range Rover draws a blank in this building. Which is frustrating because we've got his (I'm pretty sure it's a *he*) boss right here, and there ought to be a sympathetic entanglement at work.

"Everyone's here but Mark." He laughs a bit, mildly hysterical. "They're all here but Mark. Mark!"

I glance over at Detective Inspector Sullivan, who is detective inspecting the lamia. I think she's finally beginning to grasp at a visceral level that we aren't just some bureaucratic Whitehall paper circus trying to make her life harder. She looks frankly nauseated. The silence here is eerie, and worrying. *Why haven't the other team members come to find out what's going on?* I wonder, looking at the taped-over doors. *Maybe they've gone out the back and are waiting for us outside. Or maybe they simply can't come out in daylight.* The smell of burning meat is getting stronger: Voss seems to be shaking, as if he's trying not to answer Andy's questions.

I walk over to the lamia. "It's not human," I explain quietly. "It never was human. It's one of the things they specialise in. This building is defended by guards and wards, and this is just part of the security system's front end."

"But she, she spoke . . ."

"Yes, but she's not a human being." I point to the thick ribbon cable that connected the computer to the pentacle. "See, that's a control interface. The computer's there to stabilize and contain a Dho-Nha circuit that binds the Dee-space entity here. The entity itself—it's a lamia—is locked into the box which contains, uh, other components. And it's compelled to obey certain orders. Nothing good for unscheduled visitors." I put my hands on the lamia's head and work my fingers into the thick blonde hair, then tug. There's a noise of ripping Velcro then the wig comes off to reveal the scaly scalp beneath. "See? It's not human. It's a lamia, a type of demon bound to act as a front-line challenge/response system for a high security installation with covert—"

I manage to get out of the line of fire as Josephine brings up her lunch all over the incredibly expensive bleached pine workstation. I can't say I blame her. I feel a little shocky myself—it's been a really bad morning. Then I realise that Andy is trying to get my attention. "Bob, when you're through with grossing out the inspector I've got a little job for you." He pitches his voice loudly.

"Yeah?" I ask, straightening up.

"I want you to open that door, walk along the corridor to the second room on the right—not pausing to examine any of the corpses along the way—and open it. Inside, you'll find the main breaker board. I want you to switch the power off."

"Didn't I just see you splashing paint all over the CCTV cameras in the ceiling? And, uh, what's this about corpses? Why don't we send Dr. Voss—oh." Voss's eyes are shut and the stink of roast meat is getting stronger: he's gone extremely red in the face, almost puffy, and he's shaking slightly as if some external force is making all his muscles twitch simultaneously. It's my turn to struggle to hang onto breakfast. "I didn't know anyone could make themselves *do* that," I hear myself say distantly.

"Neither did I," says Andy, and that's the most frightening thing I've heard today so far. "There must be a conflicted geas somewhere in his skull. I don't think I could stop it even if—"

"Shit." I stand up. My hand goes to my neck automatically but the pouch is empty. "No HOG." I swallow. "Power. What happens if I don't?"

"Voss's pal Mark McLuhan installed a dead man's handle. You'd know all about that. We've got until Voss goes into brain stem death and then every fucking camera in Milton Keynes goes live with SCORPION STARE."

"Oh, you mean we die." I head for the door Voss came through. "I'm looking for the service core, right?"

"Wait!" It's Josephine, looking pale. "Can't you go outside and cut the power there? Or phone for help?"

"Nope." I rip the first strip of sealing tape away from the door frame. "We're behind Tempest shielding here, and the power is routed through concrete ducts underground. This is a Q Division office, after all. If we could call in an air strike and drop a couple of BLU—114/Bs on the local power substations that might work—" I tug at the second tape "—but these systems were designed to be survivable." Third tape.

"Here," calls Andy, and he chucks something cylindrical at me. I catch it one-handed, yank the last length of tape with the other hand, and do a double-take. Then I shake the cylinder, listen for the rattle of the stirrer, and pop the lid off.

"Take cover!" I call. Then I open the door, spritz the ceiling above me with green spray paint, and go to work.

❧ ❧ ❧

I'm sitting in the lobby, guarding the lamia's corpse with a nearly empty can of paint and trying not to fall asleep, when the OCCULUS team bangs on the door. I yawn and sidestep Voss's blistered corpse—he looks like he's gone a few rounds with Old Sparky—then try to remember the countersign. *Ah, that's it.* I pull away a strip of tape and tug the door open and find myself staring up the snout of an H&K carbine. "Is that a gun in your hand or are you just here to have a wank?" I ask.

The gun points somewhere else in a hurry. "Hey, Sarge, it's the spod from Amsterdam!"

"Yeah, and someone's told you to secure the area, haven't they? Where's Sergeant Howe?" I ask, yawning. Daylight makes me feel better—that, and knowing that there's backup. (I get sleepy when people stop shooting at me. Then I have nightmares. Not a good combination.)

"Over here." They're dressed in something not unlike Fire Service HAZMAT gear, and the wagons are painted cheerful cherry-red with luminous yellow stripes; if they weren't armed to the teeth with automatic weapons you'd swear they were only here because somebody had phoned in a toxic chemical release warning. But the pump nozzles above the cabs aren't there to spray water, and that lumpy thing on the back isn't a spotlight—it's a grenade launcher.

The inspector comes up behind me, staggering slightly in the daylight. "What's going on?" she asks.

"Here, meet Scary Spice and Sergeant Howe. Sarge, Scary, meet Detective Inspector Sullivan. Uh, the first thing you need to do is to go round the site and shoot out every closed circuit TV camera you can see—or that can see you. Got that? And webcams. And doorcams. See a camera, smash it, that's the rule."

"Cameras. Ri-ight." Sergeant Howe looks mildly skeptical, but nods. "It's definitely cameras?"

"Who *are* these guys?" asks Josephine.

"Artists' Rifles. They work with us," I say. Scary nods, deeply serious. "Listen, you go outside, do anything necessary to keep the local emergency services off our backs. If you need backup ask Sergeant Howe here. Sarge, she's basically sound and she's working for us on this. Okay?"

She doesn't wait for confirmation, just shoves past me and heads out into the daylight, blinking and shaking her head. I carry on briefing the OCCULUS guys. "Don't worry about anything that uses film, it's the closed circuit TV variety that's hostile. And, oh, try to make sure that you are *never* in view of more than one of 'em at a time."

"And don't walk on the cracks in the pavement or the bears will get us, check." Howe turns to Scary Spice: "Okay, you heard the man. Let's do it." He glances at me. "Anything inside?"

"We're taking care of it," I say. "If we need help we'll ask."

"Check." Scary is muttering into his throat mike and fake firemen with entirely authentic fire axes are walking around the bushes along the side of the building as if searching for signs of combustion. "Okay, we'll be out here."

"Is Angleton in the loop? Or the captain?"

"Your boss is on his way out here by chopper. Ours is on medical leave. You need to escallate, I'll get you the lieutenant."

"Okay." I duck back into the reception area then nerve myself to go back into the development pool at the rear of the building, below the offices and above the labs.

Site Able is a small departmental satellite office, small for security reasons: ten systems engineers, a couple of manager dogsbodies, and a security officer. Most of them are right here right now, and they're not going anywhere. I walk around the service core in the dim glow of the emergency light, bypassing splashes of green paint that look black in the red glow. The octagonal developer pool at the back is also dimly illuminated—there are no windows, and the doors are triple-sealed with rubber gaskets impregnated with fine copper mesh—and some of the partitions have been blown over. The whole place is ankle deep in white mist left over from the halon dump system that went off when the first bodies exploded—good thing the air-conditioning continued to run or the place would be a gas trap. The webcams are all where I left them, in a trash can at the foot of the spiral staircase up to level one, cables severed with my multitool just to make sure nobody tries to plug them back in again.

The victims—well, I have to step over one of them to get up

the staircase. It's pretty gross but I've seen dead bodies before, including burn cases, and at least this was fast. But I don't think I'm going to forget the smell in a hurry. In fact, I think I'm going to have nightmares about it tonight, and maybe get drunk and cry on Mo's shoulder several times over the next few weeks until I've got it out of my system. But for now, I shove it aside and step over them. Got to keep moving, that's the main thing—unless I want there to be more of them. And on my conscience.

At the top of the staircase there's a narrow corridor and partitioned offices, also lit by the emergency lights. I follow the sound of keyclicks to Voss's office, the door of which is ajar. Potted cheese plants wilting in the artificial light, puke-brown antistatic carpet, ministry-issue desks—nobody can accuse Q Division's brass of living high on the hog. Andy's sitting in front of Voss's laptop, tapping away with a strange expression on his face. "OCCULUS is in place," I report. "Found anything interesting?"

Andy points at the screen. "We're in the wrong fucking town," he says mildly.

I circle the desk and lean over his shoulder. "Oh shit."

"You can say that again if you like." It's an email cc'd to Voss, sent over our intranet to a Mike McLuhan. Subject: meeting. Sender: Harriet.

"Oh shit. Twice over. Something stinks. Hey, I was supposed to be in a meeting with her today," I say.

"A meeting?" Andy looks up, worried.

"Yeah. Bridget got a hair up her ass about running a BSA-authorised software audit on the office, the usual sort of make-work. Don't know that it's got anything to do with this, though."

"A *software* audit? Didn't she know Licencing and Compliance handles that on a blanket department-wide basis? We were updated on it about a year ago."

"We were—" I sit down heavily on the cheap plastic visitor's chair "—what are the chances this McLuhan guy put the idea into Harriet's mind in the first place? What are the chances it *isn't* connected?"

"McLuhan. The medium is the message. SCORPION STARE. Why do I have a bad feeling about this?" Andy sends me a worried look.

"'Nother possibility, boss-man. What if it's an internal power play? The software audit's a cover, Purloined Letter style, hiding something fishy in plain sight where nobody will look at it twice until it's too late."

"Nonsense, Bridget's not clever enough to blow a project wide open just to discredit—" His eyes go wide.

"Are you sure of that? I mean, *really* and *truly* sure? Bet-your-life sure?"

"But the body count!" He's shaking his head in disbelief.

"So it was all a prank and it was meant to begin and end with Daisy, but it got a bit out of control, didn't it? These things happen. You told me the town police camera network's capable of end-to-end tracking and zone hand-off, didn't you? My guess is someone in this office—Voss, maybe—followed me to the car pound and realised we'd found the vehicle McLuhan used to boost Daisy. Stupid wankers, if they'd used one of their own motors we'd not be any the wiser, but they tried to use a stolen one as a cutout. So they panicked and dumped SCORPION STARE into the pound, and it didn't work, so they panicked some more and McLuhan panicked even more—bet you he's the go-between, or even the guy behind it. What is he, senior esoteric officer? Deputy site manager? He's in London so he planted the crazy blackmail threat then brought down the hammer on his own coworkers. Bet you he's a smart sociopath, the kind that does well in midlevel management, all fur coat and no knickers— and willing to shed blood without a second thought if it's to defend his position."

"Damn," Andy says mildly as he stands up. "Okay, so. Internal politics, stupid bloody prank organised to show up Angleton, they use idiots to run it so your cop finds the trail, then the lunatic in chief cuts loose and starts killing people. Is that your story?"

"Yup." I nod like my neck's a spring. "And right now they're back at the Laundry doing who the fuck knows what—"

"We've got to get McLuhan nailed down fast, before he

decides the best way to cover his tracks is to take out head office. And us." He smiles reassuringly. "It'll be okay, Angleton's on his way in. You haven't seen him in action before, have you?"

➤ ➤ ➤

Picture a light industrial/office estate in the middle of anytown with four cherry-red fire pumps drawn up, men in HAZMAT gear combing the brush, a couple of police cars with flashing light bars drawn up across the road leading into the cul-de-sac to deter casual rubberneckers. Troops disguised as firemen are systematically shooting out every one of the security cameras on the estate with their silenced carbines. Others, wearing police or fire service uniforms, are taking up stations in front of every building—occupied or otherwise—to keep the people inside out of trouble.

Just another day at the office, folks, nothing to see here, walk on by.

Well, maybe not. Here comes a honking great helicopter—the Twin Squirrel from the Met's ASU that I was in the other night, only it looks a lot bigger and scarier when seen from a couple hundred feet in full daylight as it settles in on the car park, leaves and debris blowing out from under the thundering rotors.

The chopper is still rocking on its skids when one of the back doors opens and Angleton jumps down, stumbling slightly—he's no spring chicken—then collects himself and strides toward us, clutching a briefcase. "Speak," he tells me, voice barely raised to cover the rush of slowing rotors.

"Problem, boss." I point to the building: "Andy's still inside confirming the worst but it looks like it started as a fucking stupid interdepartmental prank; it went bad, and now one of the perps has wigged out and gone postal."

"A prank." He turns those icy blue peepers on me and just for a fraction of a second I'm not being stared at by a sixty-something skinny bald guy in a badly fitting suit but by a walking skeleton with the radioactive fires of hell burning balefully in its eye sockets. "You'd better take me to see Andrew. Fill me in on the way."

I'm stumbling over my tongue and hurrying to keep up with Angleton when we make it to the front desk, where Andy's busy giving the OCCULUS folks cleanup directions and tips for what to do with the broken lamia and the summoning altars in the basement. "Who's—oh, it's you. About time." He grins. "Who's holding the fort?"

"I left Boris in charge," Angleton says mildly, not taking exception at Andy's brusque manner. "How bad is it?"

"Bad." Andy's cheek twitches, which is a bad sign: all his confidence seems to have fled now that Angleton's arrived. "We need to—damn."

"Take your time," Angleton soothes him. "I'm not going to eat you." Which is when I realise just how scared *I* am, and if I'm half out of my tree what does that say about Andy? I'll give Angleton this much, he knows when not to push his subordinates too hard. Andy takes a deep breath, lets it out slowly, then tries again.

"We've got two loose ends: Mark McLuhan, and a John Doe. McLuhan worked here as senior occult officer, basically an oversight role. He also did a bunch of other stuff for Q Division that took him down to Dansey House in a liaison capacity. I can't *believe* how badly we've slipped up on our vetting process—"

"Take your time," Angleton interrupts, this time with a slight edge to his voice.

"Sorry, sorry. Bob's been putting it together." A nod in my direction. "McLuhan is working with a John Doe inside the Laundry to make us look bad via a selective disclosure leak— basically one that was intended to be written off as bad-ass forteana, nothing for anyone but the black helicopter crowd to pay any attention to, except that it would set you up to look bad. I've found some not very good email from Bridget inviting McLuhan down to headquarters, some pretext to do with a software audit. Really fucking stupid stuff that Bob can do the legwork on later. But what I *really* think is happening is, Bridget arranged this to make you look bad in support of a power play in front of the director's office."

Angleton turns to me: "Phone head office. Ask for Boris. Tell him to arrest McLuhan. Tell him, SHRINKWRAP. And MARMOSET." I raise an eyebrow. "Now, lad!"

Ah, the warm fuzzies of decisive action. I head for the lamia's desk and pick up the phone and dial 666; behind me Andy is telling Angleton something in a low voice.

"Switchboard?" I ask the sheet of white noise. "I want Boris. *Now.*" The Enochian metagrammar parsers do their thing and the damned souls or enchained demons or whatever on switchboard hiss louder then connect the circuit. I hear another ring tone. Then a familiar voice.

"Hello, Capital Laundry Services, system support department. Who are you wanting to talk to?"

Oh shit. "Hello, Harriet," I say, struggling to sound calm and collected. Getting Bridget's imp at this juncture is not a good sign, especially when she and Boris are renowned for their mutual loathing. "This is a red phone call. Is Boris about?"

"Oh-ho, Robert! I was wondering where you were. Are you trying to pull a sickie again?"

"No, I'm not," I say, taking a deep breath. "I need to talk to Boris urgently, Harriet, is he around?"

"Oh, I couldn't possibly say. That would be disclosing information prejudicial to the good running of the department over a public network connection, and I couldn't possibly encourage you to do that when you can bloody well show your face in the office for the meeting we scheduled the day before yesterday, remember that?"

I feel as if my guts have turned to ice. "Which meeting?" I ask.

"The software audit, remember? You never read the agenda for meetings. If you did, you might have taken an interest in the *any other business* . . . Where *are* you calling from, Bob? Anyone would think you didn't work here . . ."

"I want to talk to Boris. Right now." The graunching noise in the background is my jaw clenching. "It's urgent, Harriet. To do with the code blue the other day. Now you can get him right now or you can regret it later, which is your choice?"

"Oh, I don't think that'll be necessary," she says in what I can only describe as a gloating tone of voice. "After missing the meeting, you and your precious Counter-Possession Unit will be divisional history, and you'll have only yourselves to blame! Goodbye." And the bitch hangs up on me.

I look round and see both Andy and Angleton staring at me. "She hung up," I say stupidly. "Fucking Harriet has a diversion on Boris's line. It's a setup. Something about making an end run around the CPU."

"Then we shall have to attend this meeting in person," Angleton says, briskly marching toward the front doors, which bend aside to get out of his way. "Follow me!"

We proceed directly to the helicopter, which has kept its engines idling while we've been inside. It's only taken, what? Three or four minutes since Angleton arrived? I see another figure heading toward us across the car park—a figure in a grey trouser suit, slightly stained, a wild look in her eyes. "Hey, you!" she shouts. "I want some answers!"

Angleton turns to me. "Yours?" I nod. He beckons to her imperiously. "Come with us," he calls, raising his voice over the whine of gathering turbines. Past her shoulder I see one of the fake firemen lowering a kit-bag that had been, purely coincidentally, pointed at DI Sullivan's back. "This bit I always dislike," he adds in a low monotone, his face set in a grim expression of disapproval. "The fewer lives we warp, the better."

I half-consider asking him to explain what he means, but he's already climbing into the rear compartment of the chopper and Andy is following him. I give Josephine a hand up as the blades overhead begin to turn and the engines rise in a full-throated bellowing duet. I get my headset on in time to hear Angleton's orders: "Back to London, and don't spare the horses."

The Laundry is infamous for its grotesque excesses in the name of accounting; budgetary infractions are punished like war crimes, and mere paper clips can bring down the wrath of dead alien gods on your head. But when Angleton says *don't spare the horses* he sends us screaming across the countryside at a hundred and forty miles per hour, burning aviation fuel by the ton and getting ATC to clear lower priority traffic out of our way—and all because he doesn't want to be late for a meeting. There's a police car waiting for us at the pad, and we cut through the chaotic London traffic incredibly fast, almost making it into third gear at times.

"McLuhan's got SCORPION STARE," I tell Angleton

round the curve of Andy's shoulder. "And headquarters's security cams are all wired. If he primes them before we get back there, we could find a lockout—or worse. It all depends on what Harriet and her boss have been planning."

"We will just have to see." Angleton nods very slightly, his facial expression rigid. "Do you still have your lucky charm?"

"Had to use it." I'd shrug, if there was more room. "What do you think Bridget's up to?"

"I couldn't possibly comment." I'd take Angleton's dismissal as a put-down, but he points his chin at the man in the driver's seat. "When we get there, Bob, I want you to go in through the warehouse door and wake the caretaker. You have your mobile telephone?"

"Uh, yeah," I say, hoping like hell that the battery hasn't run down.

"Good. Andrew. You and I will enter through the front door. Bob, set your telephone to vibrate. When you receive a message from me, you will know it is time to have the janitor switch off the main electrical power. *And* the backup power."

"Oops." I lick my suddenly dry lips, thinking of all the electrical containment pentacles in the basement and all the computers plugged into the filtered and secured circuit on the other floors. "All hell's going to break loose if I do that."

"That's what I'm counting on." The bastard *smiles,* and despite all the horrible sights I've seen today so far, I hope most of all that I never see it again before the day I die.

"Hey, what about me?" Angleton glances at the front seat with a momentary flash of irritation. Josephine stares right back, clearly angry and struggling to control it. "I'm your liaison officer for North Buckinghamshire," she says, "and I'd really *like* to know who I'm liaising with, especially as you seem to have left a few *bodies* on my manor that I'm going to have to bury, and this jerk—" she means me, I am distraught! Oh, the ignominy! "—promised me you'd have the answers."

Angleton composes himself. "There are no answers, madam, only further questions," he says, and just for a second he sounds like a pious wanker of a vicar going through the motions of comforting the bereaved. "And if you want the answers you'll have to go through the jerk's filing cabinet." *Bastard*. Then there's a flash-ing sardonic grin, dry as the desert sands in June: "Do you want to help prevent any, ah, recurrence of what you saw an hour ago? If so, you may accompany the jerk and attempt to keep him from dying." He reaches out a hand and drops a ragged slip of paper over her shoulder. "You'll need this."

Provisional warrant card, my oh my. Josephine mutters some-thing unkind about his ancestry, barnyard animals, and lengths of rubber hose. I pretend not to hear because we're about three minutes out, stuck behind a slow-moving but gregarious herd of red double-decker buses, and I'm trying to remember the way to the janitor's office in the Laundry main unit basement and whether there's anything I'm likely to trip over in the dark.

➤ ➤ ➤

"Excuse me for asking, but how many corpses do you usually run into in the course of your job?" I ask.

"Too many, since you showed up." We turn the street corner into a brick-walled alley crowded by wheelie bins and smelling of vagrant piss. "But since you ask, I'm a detective inspector. You get to see lots of vile stuff on the beat."

Something in her expression tells me I'm on dangerous ground here, but I persist: "Well, this is the Laundry. It's our job to deal with seven shades of vile shit so that people like you don't have to." I take a deep breath. "And before we go in I figured I should warn you that you're going to think Fred and Rosemary West work for us, and Harold Shipman's the medical officer." At this point she goes slightly pale—the Demon DIYers and Doctor Death are the acme of British serial killerdom after all—but she doesn't flinch.

"And you're the *good* guys?"

"Sometimes I have my doubts," I sigh.

"Well, join the club." I have a feeling she's going to make it, if she lives through the next hour.

"Enough bullshit. *This* is the street level entrance to the facil-ities block under Headquarters Building One. You saw what those fuckers did with the cameras at the car pound and Site Able. If my guess is straight, they're going to do it all over again *here*—or worse. From here there's a secure line to several of the Met's offices, including various borough-level control systems, such as the Camden Town control centre. SCORPION STARE isn't ready for nationwide deployment—"

"What the *hell* would justify that?" she demands, eyes wide.

"You do not have clearance for that information." Amazing how easily the phrase trips off the tongue. "Besides, it'd give you nightmares. But you're the one who mentioned hell, and as I was saying—" I stop, with an overflowing dumpster between us and the anonymous doorway "—our pet lunatic, who killed all those folks at Dillinger Associates and who is now in a committee meeting upstairs, could conceivably upload bits of SCORPION STARE to the various camera control centres. Which is why we are going to stop him, by bringing down the intranet backbone cable in and out of the Laundry's headquarters. Which would be easy if this was a bog-standard government office, but a little harder in reality because the Laundry has guards, and some of those guards are very special, and some of those very special guards will try to stop us by eating us alive."

"Eating. Us." Josephine is looking a little glassy. "Did I tell you that I don't do headhunters? That's Recruitment's job."

"Look," I say gently, "have you ever seen *Night of the Living Dead*? It's really not all that different—except that I've got permission to be here, and you've got a temporary warrant card too, so we should be all right." A thought strikes me. "You're a cop. Have you been through firearms training?"

Click-clack. "Yes," she says drily. "Next question?"

"Great! If you'd just take that away from my nose—that's better—it won't work on the guards. Sorry, but they're already, uh, metabolically challenged. However, it *will* work very nicely on the CCTV cameras. Which—"

"Okay, I get the picture. We go in. We stay out of the frame unless we want to die." She makes the pistol vanish inside her jacket and looks at me askance—for the first time since the car pound with something other than irritation or dislike. Probably wondering why I didn't flinch. (Obvious, really: compared with what's waiting for us inside a little intracranial air-conditioning is a relatively painless way to go, and besides, if she was seriously pissed at me she could have gotten me alone in a nice sound-proofed cell back in her manor with a pair of size twelve boots and their occupants.) "We're going to go in there and you're going to talk our way past the zombies while I shoot out all the cameras, right?"

"Right. And then I'm going to try to figure out how to take down the primary switchgear, the backup substation, the diesel generator, *and* the batteries for the telephone switch and the protected computer ring main *all* at the same time so nobody twigs until it's too late. While fending off anyone who tries to stop us. Clear?"

"As mud." She stares at me. "I always wanted to be on TV, but not quite this way."

"Yeah, well." I glance up the side of the building, which is windowless as far as the third floor (and then the windows front onto empty rooms three feet deep, just to give the appearance of occupation). "I'd rather call in an air strike on the power station but there's a hospital two blocks that way and an old folks' home on the other side . . . you ready?"

She nods. "Okay." And I take a step round the wheelie bin and knock on the door.

The door is a featureless blue slab of paint. As soon as I touch it, it swings open—no creaking here, did you think this was a Hammer horror flick?—to reveal a small, dusty room with a dry powder fire extinguisher bolted to one wall and another door opposite. "Wait," I say, and take the spray paint can out of my pocket. "Okay, come on in. Keep your warrant note handy."

She jumps when the door closes automatically with a faint hiss, and I remember to swallow—it only looks like a cheap fire door from the outside. "Okay, here's the fun part." I give the inner door a quick scan with a utility on my palmtop and it comes up blank, so I put my hand on the grab-bar and pull. This is the moment of truth; if the shit has truly hit the fan already the entire building will be locked down tighter than a nuclear bunker, and the thaumaturgic equivalent of a three-phase six-hundred-volt bearer will be running through all the barred portals. But I get to keep on breathing, and the door swings open on a dark corridor leading past shut storeroom doors to a dingy wooden staircase.

And that's all it is—there's nothing in here to confuse an accidental burglar who makes it in past the wards in hope of finding
some office supplies to filch. All the really classified stuff is either
ten storeys underground or on the other side of the cellar walls.
Twitching in the darkness.

"I don't see any zombies," Josephine says edgily, crowding
up behind me in the gloom.

"That's because they're—" I freeze and bring up the dry powder extinguisher. "Have you got a pocket mirror?" I ask, trying to
sound casual.

"Hold on." I hear a dry click, and then she passes me something like a toothbrush fucking a contact lens. "Will this do?"

"Oh wow, I didn't know you were a dentist." It's on a goddamn telescoping wand almost half a metre long. I lean forward
and gingerly stretch the angled mirror so I can view the stairwell.

"It's for checking the undersides of cars for bombs—or cut
brake pipes. You never know what the little fuckers in the school
playground will do while you're talking to the headmistress."

Gulp. "Well, I guess this is a suitable alternative use."

I don't see any cameras up there so I retract the mirror and
I'm about to set foot on the stairs when she says, "You missed
one."

"Huh . . . ?"

She points. It's about waist level, the size of a doorknob,
embedded in the dark wooden wainscoting, and it's pointing *up*
the stairs. "Shit, you're right." And there's something odd about
it. I slide the mirror closer for an oblique look and dry-swallow.
"There are two lenses. Oh, tricky."

I pull out my multitool and begin digging them out of the
wall. It's coax cable, just like the doctor ordered. There's no obvious evidence of live SCORPION STARE, but my hands are still
clammy and my heart is in my mouth as I realise how close I
came to walking in front of it. How small can they make CCTV
cameras, anyway? I keep seeing smaller and smaller ones . . .

"Better move fast," she comments.

"Why?"

"Because you've just told them you're coming."

"Oh. Okay." We climb the staircase in bursts, stopping before the next landing to check for more basilisk bugs. Josephine spots one, and so do I—I tag them with the mostly empty can of paint, then she blasts their lenses from behind and underneath, trying not to breathe the fumes in before we move past them. There's an unnaturally creaky floorboard, too, just for yucks. But we make it to the ground floor landing alive, and I just have time to realise how badly we've fucked up when the lights come up and the night watchmen come out from either side.

"Ah, Bob! Decided to visit the office for once, have we?"

It's Harriet, looking slightly demented in a black pin-striped suit and clutching a glass of what looks like fizzy white wine.

"Where the fuck is everyone else?" I demand, looking round. At this time of day the place should be heaving with office bodies. But all I see here is Harriet—and three or four silently leaning night watchmen in their grey ministry suits and hangdog expressions, luminous worms of light glowing in their eyes.

"I do believe we called the monthly fire drill a few hours ahead of schedule." Harriet smirks. "Then we locked the doors. It's quite simple, you know."

Fred from Accounting lurches sideways and peers at me over her shoulder. He's been dead for months: normally I'd say this was something of an improvement, but right now he's drooling slightly as if it's past his teatime.

"Who's *that?*" asks Josephine.

"Who? Oh, one of them's a shambling undead bureaucrat and the other one used to work in accounts before he had a little accident with a summoning." I bare my teeth at Harriet. "The game's up."

"I don't think so." She's just standing there, looking supercilious and slightly triumphant behind her bodyguard of zombies. "Actually the boot is on the other foot. You're late and you're out of a job, Robert. The Counter-Possession Unit is being liquidated—that old fossil Angleton isn't needed anymore, once we get the benefits of panopticon surveillance combined with look-to-kill technology and rolled out on a departmental basis. In fact, you're just in time to clear your desk." She grins, horribly. "Stupid little boy, I'm sure they can find a use for you below stairs."

"You've been talking to our friend Mr. McLuhan, haven't you?" I ask desperately, trying to keep her talking—I *really* don't want the night watchmen to carry me away. "Is he upstairs?"

"If so, you probably need to know that I intend to arrest him. Twelve counts of murder and attempted murder, in case you were wondering." I almost look round, but manage to resist the urge: Josephine's voice is brittle but controlled. "Police."

"Wrong jurisdiction, dear," Harriet says consolingly. "And I do believe our idiot tearaway here has got you on the wrong message. That will never do." She snaps her fingers. "Take the woman, detain the man."

"Stop—" I begin. The zombies step forward, lurching jerkily, and then all hell breaks loose about twenty centimetres from my right ear. Zombies make excellent night watchmen and it takes a lot to knock one down, but they're not bulletproof, and Josephine unloads her magazine two rounds at a time. I'm dazzled by the flash and my head feels as if someone is whacking me on the ear with a shovel—bits of meat and unspeakable ripped stuff go flying, but precious little blood, and they keep coming.

"When you've *quite* finished," Harriet hisses, and snaps her fingers at Josephine: the zombies pause for a moment then close in, as their mistress backs toward the staircase up to the first floor.

"Quick, down the back corridor there!" I gasp, pointing to my left.

"The—what?"

"Quick!"

I dash along the corridor, tugging Josephine's arm until I feel her running with me. I pull my warrant card and yell, *"Open sesame!"* ahead and doors slam open to either side—including the broom closets and ductwork access points. "In here!" I dive in to one side and Josephine piles in after me and I yank at the door— *"Close, damn you, fuck, close sesame!"* and it slams shut with the hardscrabble of bony fingertips on the outside.

"Got a light?" I ask.

"Naah, I don't smoke. But I've got a torch somewhere—"

The scrabbling's getting louder. "I don't want to hurry you or anything, but—" And lo, there is light.

We're standing at the bottom of a shallow shaft with cable

runs vanishing above us into the gloom. Josephine looks frantic. "They didn't drop! I shot them and they *didn't drop!*"

"Don't sweat it, they're run by remote control." Maybe now is not the time to explain about six-node summoning points, the Vohlman exercise, and the minutiae of raising and binding the dead: they're knocking on the door and they want in. But look, here's something even *more* interesting. "Hey, I see CAT—5 cabling. Pass me your torch?"

"This isn't the time to go all geeky on me, nerd-boy. Or are you looking for roaches?"

"Just fucking do it, I'll explain later, okay?" Harriet is really getting to me; it's been a long day and I told myself ages ago that if I ever heard another fucking lecture about timekeeping from her I'd go postal.

"Bingo." It *is* CAT—5, and there's an even more interesting cable running off to one side that looks like a DS—3. I whip out my multitool and begin working on the junction box. The scrabbling's become insistent by the time I've uncovered the wires, but what the fuck. Who was it who said, *When they think you're technical is the time to go crude?* I grab a handful of network cables and yank, hard. Then I grab another handful. Then, having disconnected the main trunk line—*mission accomplished*—I take another moment to think.

"Bob, have you got a plan?"

"I'm thinking."

"Then think faster, they're about to come through the door—"

Which is when I remember my mobile phone and decide to make a last-ditch attempt. I speed-dial Bridget's office extension—and Angleton picks up after two rings. Bastard.

"Ah, Bob!" He sounds positively avuncular. "Where are you? Did you manage to shut down the Internet?"

I don't have time to correct him. Besides, Josephine is reloading her cannon and I think she's going to try a *really* horrible pun if I don't produce a solution PDQ. "Boss, run McLuhan's SCORPION STARE tool and upload the firmware to all the motion-tracking cameras on the ground floor east wing loop *right now.*"

"What? I'm not sure I heard you correctly."

I take a deep breath. "She's subverted the night watchmen. Everybody else is out of the building. Do it *now* or I'm switching to a diet of fresh brains."

"If you say so," he agrees, with the manner of an indulgent uncle talking to a tearaway schoolboy, then hangs up.

There's a splintering crash and a hand rams through the door right between us and embeds itself in the wall opposite. "Oh shit," I have time to say as the hand withdraws. Then a bolt of lightning goes off about two feet outside the door, roughly simultaneous with a sizzling crash and a wave of heat. We cower in the back of the cupboard, terrified of fire until after what seems like an eternity the sprinklers come on.

"Is it safe yet?" she asks—at least I think that's what she says, my ears are still ringing.

"One way to find out." I take the broken casing from the network junction box and chuck it through the hole in the door. When it doesn't explode I gingerly push the door open. The ringing is louder; it's my phone. I pull it wearily out of my pocket and hunch over it to keep it dry, leaning against the wall of the corridor to stay as far away from the blackened zombie corpses as I can. "Who's there?"

"Your manager." He sounds merely amused this time. "What a sorry shower you are! Come on up to Mahogany Row and dry off, both of you—the director has a personal bathroom, I think you've earned it."

"Uh. Harriet? Bridget? McLuhan?"

"Taken care of," he says complacently, and I shiver convulsively as the water reaches gelid tentacles down my spine and tickles my balls like a drowned lover.

"Okay. We'll be right up." I glance back at the smashed-in utility cupboard and Josephine smiles at me like a frightened feral rat, all sharp teeth and savagery and shining .38 automatic. "We're safe now," I say, as reassuringly as possible. "I think we won . . ."

➤ ➤ ➤

The journey to Angleton's lair is both up and along—he normally works out of a gloomy basement on the other side of the hollowed-out block of prime London real estate that is occupied by the Laundry, but this time he's ensconced in the director's suite on the abandoned top floor of the north wing.

The north wing is still dry. Over there, people are still at work, oblivious to the charred zombies lying on the scorched, soaked, thaumaturgically saturated wing next door. We catch a few odd stares—myself, soaked and battered in my outdoors gear, DI Sullivan in the wreckage of an expensive grey suit, over-sized handgun clenched in a death grip at her side—but wisely or otherwise, nobody asks me to fix the Internet or demands to know why we're tracking muddy water through Human Resources.

By the time we reach the thick green carpet and dusty quietude of the director's suite Josephine's eyes are wide but she's stopped shaking. "You've got lots of questions," I manage to say. "Try to save them for later. I'll tell you everything I know and you're cleared for, once I've had time to phone my fiancée."

"I've got a husband and a nine year old son, did you think of that before you dragged me into this insane nightmare? Sorry. I know you didn't *mean* to. It's just that shooting up zombies and being zapped by basilisks makes me a little upset. Nerves."

"I know. Just try not to wave them in front of Angleton, okay?"

"Who *is* Angleton, anyway? Who does he think he is?"

I pause before the office door. "If I knew that, I'm not sure I'd be allowed to tell you." I knock three times.

"Enter." Andy opens the door for us. Angleton is sitting in the director's chair, playing with something in the middle of the huge expanse of oak desk that looks as if it dates to the 1930s. (There's a map on the wall behind him, and a quarter of it is pink.) "Ah, Mr. Howard, Detective Inspector. So good of you to come."

I peer closer. *Clack. Clack. Clack.* "A Newton's cradle; how 1970s."

"You could say that." He smiles thinly. The balls bouncing back and forth between the arms of the executive desktop aren't chromed, rather they appear to be textured: pale brown on one side, dark or blonde and furry on the other. And bumpy, disturbingly bumpy . . .

I take a deep breath. "Harriet was waiting for us. Said we were too late and the Counter-Possession Unit was being disbanded."

Clack. Clack.

"Yes, she would say that, wouldn't she."

Clack. Clack. Clack. Clack. Finally I can't stand it anymore. "Well?" I demand.

"A fellow I used to know, his name was Ulyanov, once said something rather profound, do you know." Angleton looks like the cat that's swallowed the canary—and the feet are sticking out of the side of his mouth; he *wants* me to know this, whatever it is. "Let your enemies sell you enough rope to hang them with."

"Uh, wasn't that Lenin?" I ask.

A flicker of mild irritation crosses his face. "This was before then," he says quietly. *Clack. Clack. Clack.* He flicks the balls to set them banging again and I suddenly realise what they are and feel quite sick. No indeed, Bridget and Harriet—and Bridget's predecessor, and the mysterious Mr. McLuhan—won't be troubling me again. (Except in my nightmares about this office, visions of my own shrunken head winding up in one of the director's executive toys, skull clattering away eternally in a scream that nobody can hear anymore . . .) "Bridget's been plotting a boardroom coup for a long time, Robert. Probably since before you joined the Laundry—or were conscripted." He spares Josephine a long, appraising look. "She suborned Harriet, bribed McLuhan, installed her own corrupt geas on Voss. Partners in crime, intending to expose me as an incompetent and a possible security leak before the Board of Auditors, I suppose—that's usually how they plan it. I guessed this was going on, but I needed firm evidence. You supplied it. Unfortunately, Bridget was never too stable; when she realised that I knew, she ordered Voss to remove the witnesses then summoned McLuhan and proceeded with her palace coup d'état. Equally unfortunately for her, she failed to correctly establish who my line manager was before she attempted to go over my head to have me removed." He taps the sign on the front of the desk: PRIVATE SECRETARY. Keeper of the secrets. Whose secrets?

"Matrix management," I finally say, the lightbulb coming on

above my head at last. "The Laundry runs on matrix management. She saw you on the org chart as head of the Counter-Possession Unit, not as private secretary to . . ." *So that's how come he's got the free run of the director's office!*

Josephine is aghast. "You call this a government department?"

"Worse things happen in parliament every day of the year, my dear." Now that the proximate threat is over, Angleton looks remarkably imperturbable; right now I doubt he'd turn her into a frog even if she started yelling at him. "Besides, you are aware of the maxim that power corrupts and absolute power corrupts absolutely? Here we deal every day of the week with power sufficient to destroy your mind. Even worse, we *cannot* submit to public oversight—it's far too dangerous, like giving atomic firecrackers to three-year-olds. Ask Robert to tell you what he did to attract our attention later, if you like." I'm still dripping and cold, but I can feel my ears flush.

He focusses on her some more. "We can reinforce the geas and release you," he adds quietly. "But I think you can do a much more important job here. The choice is yours."

I snort under my breath. She glances at me, eyes narrowed and cynical. "If this is what passes for a field investigation in your department, you *need* me."

"Yes, well, you don't need to make your mind up immediately. Detached duty, and all that. As for you, Bob," he says, with heavy emphasis on my name, "you have acquitted yourself satisfactorily again. Now go and have a bath before you rot the carpet."

"Bathroom's two doors down the hall on the left," Andy adds helpfully from his station against the wall, next to the door: there's no doubt right now as to who's in charge here.

"But what happens now?" I ask, bewildered and a bit shocky and already fighting off the yawns that come on when people stop trying to kill me. "I mean, what's really *happened*?"

Angleton grins like a skull: "Bridget forfeited her department, so the directors have asked me to put Andrew in acting charge of it for the time being. Boris slipped up and failed to notice McLuhan; he is, ah, temporarily indisposed. And as for you, a job well done wins its natural reward—another job." His grin widens. "As I believe the youth of today say, don't have a cow . . ."

THE GORGON
IN THE CUPBOARD

by Patricia A. McKillip

Patricia A. McKillip was born in Salem Oregon in 1948. Educated at San Jose State University in California, she received a B.A. in 1971 and an M.A. in English in 1973. She published two short children's books in 1973, The Throme of the Erril of Sherill *and* The House on Parchment Street. *Her first longer novel, the sophisticated young-adult fantasy* The Forgotten Beasts of Eld, *won the 1975 World Fantasy Award. She switched to children's mainstream for* The Night Gift, *but returned to YA fantasy in the "Riddle of Stars" trilogy* The Riddle-Master of Hed, Heir of Sea and Fire, *and* Harpist in the Wind—*after which she turned away from the field in a move she thought would be permanent.*

After writing Stepping from the Shadows, *an adult contemporary novel with some magic realist elements, she returned with the YA science fantasy duology* Moon-Flash *and* The Moon and the Face. *Her adult SF novel* Fool's Run *was followed by the YA fantasy* The Changeling Sea, *the fantasy duology* The Sorceress and the Cygnet *and* The Cygnet and the Firebird, *and* Brian Froud's Faerielands: Something Rich and Strange. *In 1995 she published* The Book of Atrix Wolf, *the first in a sequence of remarkable stand-alone fantasies marked by great sophistication and elegance, which include* Winter Rose, Song for the Basilisk, The Tower at Stony Wood, *World Fantasy Award-winner* Ombria in Shadow, In the Forests of Serre, *and* Alphabet of Thorn. *Upcoming is a new novel,* Od Magic, *and a collection,* Harrowing the Dragon.

While McKillip is best known for her novel-length work, she

*has managed to quietly produce an outstanding body of short fic-
tion that include delightful stories like "A Troll and Two Roses,"
"Wonders of the Invisible World," and the romantic fantasy that
follows.*

HARRY COULD NOT get the goat to stay still. His model, who was
an aspiring actress, offered numerous impractical suggestions as
she crouched beside the animal. In fact, she rarely stopped talking. Harry didn't like the look in the goat's eye. It wasn't very big,
but it seemed to him arrogant beyond its age, and contemplating
mischief.

"Give it something to eat," Moira suggested. "Goats eat anything, don't they? That old leather sack, there."

"That's my lunch," Harry said patiently. "And the less we put
into the goat, the less will come out of it. If you get my meaning."

She giggled. She was quite charming, with her triangular elfin
face, her large green eyes with lashes so long they seemed to
catch air like butterfly wings as they rose and fell. She dealt hand-
ily with the goat, who was eyeing Harry's lunch now. It strained
against the rope around its neck, occasionally tightening it so that
its yellow eyes verged on the protuberant. A bit like hers, Harry
thought.

"Try to remain serious," he pleaded. "You're a scapegoat;
you've been falsely accused and spurned by the world. Your only
friend in the world is that goat."

"I thought you said you were just sketching the outlines
today. Putting us in our places. So why do I have to be serious?"
The goat, in whose rope her wrists were supposedly entangled,
gave an obstinate tug; she loosed one hand and smacked it. "You
should have gotten a female. They're sweet-natured. Not like this
ruffian." She wrinkled her nose. "Stinks, too, he does. Like—"

"This one was all I could borrow. Please."

They were still for a miraculous moment, both gazing at him.
He picked up charcoal, held his breath and drew a line of the
goat's flank onto the canvas, then continued the line with her
flank and bent knee. She swatted at a fly; the goat bucked; they
both seemed to baa at once. Harry sighed, wiped sweat out of his

eyes. They had been there half the morning, and little enough to show for it. The sun was high and dagger-bright; the tavern yard where he had set his poignant scene was full of sniggering critics. Idlers, he reminded himself, resuming doggedly when the pair settled again. They wouldn't know a brush from a broom straw. Still. He paused to study his efforts. He sighed again. There was something definitely wrong with her foot.

"It's hot," she said plaintively, shaking her heavy hair away from her neck, disturbing the perfect, nunlike veil of line across her face.

"Ah, don't—"

"And I'm starving. Why can't you paint like Alex McAlister? He lets me sit inside; he dresses me in silks; he lets me talk as much as I want unless he's doing my face. And I get hung every time, too, a good place on the wall where people can see me, not down in a corner where nobody looks."

The goat was hunkered on the ground now, trying to break its neck pulling at the rope peg. Harry glanced despairingly at the merciless source of light, looked again at his mutinous scape-goats, then flung his charcoal down.

"All right. All right."

"You owe me for Thursday, too."

"All right."

"When do you want me to come again?"

He closed his eyes briefly, then fished coins out of his pocket. "I'll send word."

One of the critics leaning against the wall called, "Best pay the goat, too; it might not come back otherwise."

"I might have work," Moira reminded him loftily. Mostly she worked early mornings selling bread in a bakery, and took elocution lessons in the afternoons when she wasn't prowling the theaters, or, Harry suspected, the streets for work.

"That goat won't get any younger neither," another idler commented. Harry gritted his teeth, then snapped his fingers for the boy pitching a knife in a corner of the yard. The boy loosened the goat from the peg, got a good grip on its neck-loop to return it to its owner. He held out his other hand for pay.

"Tomorrow then, sir?" he asked indifferently.

"I'll send word," Harry repeated.

"Don't forget your dinner there, sir."

"You have it. I'm not hungry."

He dropped the charcoal into his pocket, tucked the canvas under one arm, and the folded easel under the other, and walked home dejectedly, scarcely seeing the city around him. He was a fair-haired, sweet-faced young man, nicely built despite his awkward ways, with a habitually patient expression and a heart full of ravaging longings and ambitions. He was not talented enough for them, this morning's work told him. He would never be good enough. The girl was right. His paintings, if chosen at all to be hung for important exhibits, always ended up too high, or too close to the floor, or in obscure, badly lit corners. He thought of McAlister's magnificent *Diana*, with the dogs and the deer in it looking so well-behaved they might have been stuffed. And Haversham's *Watchful Shepherd*: the sheep as fat as dandelions and as docile as—as, well, sheep. Why not scapesheep? he wondered despondently, rather than scapegoats? No goat would stand still long enough for mankind to heap their crimes on its head.

Then he saw that which drove every other thought out of his head.

Her.

She was walking with her husband on the other side of the street. He was speaking fervidly, gesturing, as was his wont, probably about something that had seized his imagination. It might have been anything, Harry knew: a poem, the style of an arch, a pattern of embroidery on a woman's sleeve. She listened, her quiet face angled slightly toward him, her eyes downturned, intent, it seemed, on the man's brilliance. He swept fingers through his dark, shaggy hair, his thick mustaches dancing, spit flying now and then in his exuberance.

Neither of them saw Harry. Who had stopped midstream in the busy street, willing her to look, terrified that she might raise her dark, brooding eyes and see what was in his face. She only raised her long white fingers, gently clasped her husband's flying arm and tucked it down between them.

Thus they passed, the great Alex McAlister and his wife Aurora, oblivious to the man turned to stone by the sight of her.

He moved at last, jostled by a pair of boys pursued through the crowd, and then by the irate man at their heels. Harry barely noticed them. Her face hung in his mind, gazing out of canvas at him: McAlister's *Diana*, McAlister's *Cleopatra*, McAlister's *Venus*. That hair, rippling like black fire from skin as white as alabaster, those deep, heavy-lidded eyes that seemed to perceive invisible worlds. That strong, slender column of neck. Those long fingers, impossibly mobile and expressive. That mouth like a bite of sweet fruit. Those full, sultry lips . . .

I would give my soul to paint you, he told her silently. But even if in some marvelous synchronicity of events that were possible, it would still be impossible. With her gazing at him, he could not have painted a stroke. Again and again, she turned him into stone.

Not Aurora, he thought with hopeless longing, but Medusa.

He had tried to speak to her any number of times when he had visited Alex's studio, or their enchanting cottage in the country. All he managed, under that still, inhuman gaze, were insipid commonplaces. The weather. The wildflowers blooming in the garden. The stunning success of McAlister's latest painting. He coughed on crumbs, spilled tea on his cuff. Her voice was very low; he bent to hear it and stepped on her hem with his muddy boot sole, so that whatever she had begun to say was overwhelmed by his apologies. Invariably, routed by his own gracelessness, he would turn abruptly away to study a vase that McAlister had glazed himself, or a frame he was making. McAlister never seemed to notice his hopeless passion, the longing of the most insignificant moth for fire. He would clap Harry's shoulder vigorously, spilling his tea again, and then fix him in an enthusiastic torrent of words, trying to elicit Harry's opinion of some project or profundity, while the only thought in Harry's head was of the woman sitting so silently beyond them she might have been in another world entirely.

He walked down a quiet side street shaded by stately elms, opened the gate in front of the comfortable house he had inherited from his parents. Looking despondently upon his nicely blooming hollyhocks, he wondered what to do next.

If only I could create a masterwork, he thought. An idea no

one has thought of yet, that would attract the attention of the city, bring me acclaim. Make me one of the circle of the great . . . Now I'm only a novice, a squire, something more than apprentice yet less than master. Harry Waterman, dabbler at the mystery of art. If only I could pass through the closed doors to the inner sanctum. Surely She would notice me then . . .

He went across the garden, up the steps to his door and stopped again, hand on the latch, as he mused over an appropriate subject for a masterpiece.

The goat, while original and artistically challenging, held no dignity; it would not rivet crowds with its power and mystery. At most, viewers might pity it and its ambiguous female counterpart, and then pass on. More likely they would pity the artist, who had stood in a sweltering tavern yard painting a goat.

Aurora's face passed again through his thoughts; his hand opened and closed convulsively on the door latch. Something worthy of those eyes he must paint. Something that would bring expression into them: wonder, admiration, curiosity . . .

What?

Whatever it was, he would dedicate his masterpiece to Her.

The door pulled abruptly out of his hold. Mrs. Grommet, his placid housekeeper, held a hand to her ample bosom as she stared at him. "Oh, it's you, Mr. Waterman. I couldn't imagine who was making that racket with the door latch." She shifted aside, opened the door wide for him to enter.

"Sorry, Mrs. Grommet," he murmured. "Throes of creation."

"Of course, Mr. Waterman. I didn't expect you back so soon. Have you had your lunch, sir?"

"No. Just bring me tea in my studio, please. I expect to be in the throes for the rest of the afternoon."

"Yes, sir."

In the highest floor of the house, he had knocked down walls, enlarged windows to give him space and light, views from a city park on one side, the broad, busy river on the other. Mrs. Grommet came panting up with a great silver tray. He slumped in an easy chair, sipped tea as he flipped through his sketchbooks for inspiration. Faces, dogs, flowers, birds, hills, rocks, pieces of armor, horses, folds of heavy tapestry, drifting silk, hands, feet, eyes . . . Nothing coherent, nothing whole, nothing containing the lightning-bolt of inspiration he craved.

He read some poetry; words did not compel an image. He paced for a while, his mind a blank canvas. He beseeched his Muse. Anybody's Muse.

Inspiration failed to turn her lovely face, her kindly attention, toward him. He wandered to his cupboards, pulled out old, unfinished canvases, studied the stilted figures, the fuzzy landscapes for something that he might redeem to greatness.

One caught at memory: a head without a mouth. He placed it on the easel, stood studying it. The head, when completed, would have belonged to Persephone at the moment she realized that, having eaten of the fruits of the Underworld, she was doomed to spend half her life in that gloomy place. The young model he had chosen for it had vanished before he could finish it. Harry gazed at her, struck by her beauty, which had inspired his normally clumsy brushwork. The almond-shaped eyes of such pale gray they seemed the color of sun-kissed ice, the white-gold hair, the apricot skin. A true mingling of spring and winter, his Persephone, who had disappeared so completely she might have been carried away into the nether world herself.

He tried to remember her name. May? Jenny? She had gotten herself into trouble, he suspected. Harry had noticed a certain heaviness in her walk, the frigidity of terror in her expression. Moved, he had offered, in his nebulous, hesitant way, to help. But she had fled. Or died, perhaps, he was forced to consider. In childbirth, or trying to get rid of the child, who could know? He had tried to find her so that he could finish the painting. But no one seemed to know anything at all about her.

He wondered if it might be worth finishing. Her eyes, gazing straight out at the viewer, compelled attention. Idly, he traced a mouth with his forefinger, rifling through all the likely mouths he might borrow to finish it. There was Beresford's cousin Jane . . . But no, even at her young age, her lips were too thin to suggest the hunger that had caused Persephone to eat forbidden fruit . . . Or was that a different tale?

He recognized the invisible mouth his finger had outlined, and swallowed.

Some passing Muse, a mischievous sprite, tempted him to reach for crimson paint. The lips that haunted him burned like fire in memory . . . but darker than fire, darker than rose, darker than blood. He toyed guiltily with all those colors on his palette. Only paint, he told himself. Only memory. The color of wine, they were, deep, shadowy burgundy, with all the silken moistness of the rose petal.

Vaguely he heard Mrs. Grommet knock, inquire about his supper. Vaguely he made some noise. She went away. The room darkened; he lit lamps, candles. Mrs. Grommet did not return; the streets grew even quieter; the river faded into night.

He blinked, coming out of his obsessive trance. That full, provocative splendor of a mouth was startling beneath the gentle, frightened eyes of his Persephone. But the likeness transfixed him. Aurora's mouth it was; he had succeeded beyond all dreams in shifting it from memory into paint. He could not use it. Of course he could not. Everyone would recognize it, even on some other woman's face. Which he would need to go out and find, if he wanted to finish this Persephone. Maybe not his masterwork, but far easier to manage than the goat; she would do until inspiration struck.

He lingered, contemplating that silent, untouchable mouth. He could not bring himself to wipe it away yet. He would go down and eat his cold supper, deal more ruthlessly with the mouth after he had found a replacement for it. It did not, after all, belong to him; it belonged to the wife of his dear friend and mentor . . . He tore his eyes from it, lifted the canvas from the easel and positioned it carefully back into the cupboard, where it could dry and be forgotten at the same time.

He closed the door and the lips spoke.

"Harry!" Its voice was sweet and raucous and completely unfamiliar. "You're not going to leave me here in the dark, are you? After calling me all afternoon? Harry?"

He flung himself against the door, hearing his heart pound like something frantic trying to get out of him, or trying to get in. He tried to speak; his voice wouldn't come, only silent bleats of air, like an astonished sheep.

"Harry?"

"Who—" he finally managed to gasp. "Who—"

"Open the door."

"N."

"You know I'm in here. You can't just keep me shut up in here."

"N."

"Oh, Harry don't be so unfriendly. I won't bite. And even if I did—" The voice trilled an uncouth snigger, "you'd like it, from this mouth."

Harry, galvanized with sudden fury, clutched at the cupboard latch, barely refraining from wrenching it open. "How dare you!" he demanded, feeling as though the contents of his inmost heart had been rifled by vulgar, soiled hands. "Who are you?"

"That's it," the voice cooed. "Now lift the latch, open the door. You can do it."

"If you force me to come in, I'll—I'll wipe away your mouth with turpentine."

"Tut, Harry. How crude. Just when I'm ready to give you what you want most."

"What I want—"

"Inspiration, Harry. You've been wishing for me ever since you gave up on the goat and gave me a chance to get a word in edgewise."

"You're a mouth—" He was breathing strangely again, taking in too much air. "How can you possibly know about the goat?"

"You called me."

"I did not."

"You invoked me," the voice insisted. "I am the voice of your despair. Your desire. Why do you think I'm coming out of these lips?"

Harry was silent, suddenly breathless. A flash went through him, not unlike the uncomfortable premonitions of inspiration. He was going to open the door. Pushed against it with all his strength, his hands locked around the latch, he was going to open . . . "Who are you?" he pleaded hoarsely. "Are you some sort of insane Muse?"

"Guess again," the voice said coolly. "You looked upon your Beloved and thought of me. I want you to paint me. I am your masterwork."

He swallowed drily. "My masterwork."

"Paint me, Harry. And all you wish for will be yours."

"All I wish . . ."

"Open the door," the voice repeated patiently. "Don't be afraid. You have already seen my face."

His mouth opened; nothing came out. The vision stunned him, turned him into stone: the painting that would rivet the entire art world, reveal at last the depths and heights of his genius. The snake-haired daughter of the gods whose beauty threatened, commanded, whose eyes reflected inexpressible, inhuman visions.

He whispered, "Medusa."

"Me," she said. "Open the door."

He opened it.

➤ ➤ ➤

Down by the river, Jo huddled with the rest of the refuse, all squeezed under a butcher's awning trying to get out of the sudden squall. In the country, where she had walked from, the roads turned liquid in the rain; carriages, wagons, horses, herds of sheep and cows churned them into thick, oozing welts and hillocks of mud deep enough to swallow your boots if you weren't careful.

Here the cobbles, though hard enough, offered some protection. At least she was off her aching feet. At least until the butcher saw what took up space from customers looking in his windows and drove them off. Jo had been walking that day since dawn to finish her journey to the city. It was noon now, she guessed, though hard to tell. The gray sky hadn't changed its morose expression by so much as a shift of light since sunrise.

Someone new pushed into the little group cowering under the awning. Another drenched body, nearly faceless under the rags wrapped around its head, sat leaning against Jo's shoulder, worn shoes out in the rain. It wore skirts; other than that it seemed scarcely human, just one more sodden, miserable, breathing thing trying to find some protection from life.

They all sat silently for a bit, listening to the rain pounding on the awning, watching the little figures along the tide's edge, gray and shapeless as mud in their rags, darting like birds from one poor crumb of treasure the river left behind to the next. Bits of coal they stuffed into their rags to sell, splinters of wood, the odd nail or frayed piece of rope.

The bundle beside Jo murmured, "At least they're used to being wet, aren't they? River or rain, it's all one to them."

Her voice was unexpectedly young. Jo turned, maneuvering one shoulder out from beneath a sodden back. She saw a freckled girl's face between wet cloth wrapped down to her eyebrows, up to her lower lip. One eye, as blue as violets, looked resigned, calm. The other eye was swollen shut and ringed by all the colors of the rainbow.

Jo, her own face frozen for so long it hardly remembered how to move, felt something odd stirring in her. Vaguely she remembered it. Pity or some such, for all the good it did.

She said, "Whoever gave you that must love you something fierce."

"Oh, yes," the girl said. "He'll love me to death one of these days. If he finds me again."

There was a snort from the figure on the other side of Jo. This one sounded older, hoarse and wheezy with illness. Still she cackled, "I'd one like that. I used to collect my teeth in a bag after he knocked them out. I was so sorry to lose them, I couldn't bear to give them up. I was that young, then. Never smart enough to run away, even when I was young enough to think there might be a place to run to."

"There's not," Jo said shortly. "I ran back home to the country. And now I'm here again."

"What will you do?" the girl asked.

Jo shrugged. "Whatever I can."

"What have you done?"

"Mill work in the country. I had to stop doing that when my mother died and there was no one else to—to—"

"Care for the baby?" the old woman guessed shrewdly.

Jo felt her face grow cold again, less expression on it than on a brick. "Yes. Well, it's dead now, so it doesn't matter."

The girl sucked in her breath. "Cruel," she whispered.

"After that I got work at one of the big houses. Laundry and fires and such. But that didn't last."

"Did you get your references, though?"

"No. Turned out without."

"For what? Stealing?"

"No." Jo leaned her head back against the wall, watched rain running like a fountain over the edge of the swollen awning. "I wasn't that smart."

The old woman gave her crow-cackle again. "Out of the frying pan—"

Jo nodded. "Into the fire. It would have been, if I hadn't run away. If I'd stayed, I'd have had another mouth to feed when they turned me out. So I came back here."

Another voice came to life, a man's this time. "To what?" he asked heavily. "Nothing ever changes. City, country, it's all the same. You're in the mill or on the streets from dark to dark, just to get your pittance to survive one more day. And some days you can't even get that." He paused; Jo felt his racking cough shudder through them all, piled on top of one another as they were. The old woman patted his arm, whispered something. Then she turned to Jo, when he had quieted.

"He lost his wife, not long ago. Twenty-two years together, and not a voice raised. Some have that."

"Twenty-two years," the man echoed. "She had her corner at the foot of the Barrow Bridge. She sang like she didn't know any better. She made you believe it, too—that you didn't know anything better than her singing, you'd never know anything better. She stopped boats with her voice; fish jumped out of the water to hear. But then she left me alone with my old fiddle and my old bones, both of us creaking and groaning without her." He patted the lump under his threadbare cloak as though it were a child. "Especially in this rain."

"Well, I know what I'm going to do when it quits," the girl said briskly. "I'm going to get myself arrested. He'll never get his hands on me in there. And it's dry and they feed you, at least for a few days before they let you out again."

"I got in for three months once," a young voice interposed from the far edge of the awning.

"Three months!" the girl exclaimed, her bruised eye trying to flutter open. "What do you have to do for that?"

"I couldn't get myself arrested for walking the streets, no matter how I tried, and I was losing my teeth and my looks to a great lout who drank all my money away by day and flung me around at night. I was so sick and tired of my life that one morning when I saw the Lord Mayor of the city in a parade of fine horses and soldiers and dressed-up lords and ladies, I took off my shoe and threw it at his head." The old woman crowed richly at the thought. "I let them catch me, and for three months I had a bed every night, clean clothes, and food every day. By the time I got out, my lout had moved on to some other girl and I was free."

"They don't make jails nowadays the way they used to," the fiddler said. "They never used to spoil you with food or a bed."

Jo felt the girl sigh noiselessly. "I'd do three months," she murmured, "if I knew where to find a Lord Mayor."

Jo's eyes slid to her vivid, wistful face. "What will you do," she asked slowly, "for your few days?"

"I've heard they take you off the streets if you break something. A window, or a street lamp. I thought I'd try that."

Jo was silent, pulling her mother's tattered shawl around her. Jo had made it for her, years earlier, when her father was alive to tend to his sheep and his cows, make cheese, shear wool for them to spin into thread. When she'd gone back, her mother had given the shawl to her to wrap the baby in. The sheep and cows were long gone to pay debts after her father died. Her mother's hands had grown huge and red from taking in laundry. Alf, they called the baby, after her father. Alfred Fletcher Byrd. Poor poppit, she thought dispassionately. Not strong enough for any one of those names, let alone three.

The man who was its father showed his face in her thoughts. She shoved him out again, ruthlessly, barred that entry. She'd lost a good place in the city because of him, in a rich, quiet, well-run house. A guest, a friend of the family, who had a family of his own somewhere. He'd found her early one morning making up a fire in the empty library . . . The only time she'd ever seen him, and it was enough to change her life. So she'd run out of the city, all the way back home to her mother. And all she had left now, of any of that time, was an old purple shawl.

That was then, she thought coldly. This is now.

Now, the rain was letting up a little. The young girl shifted, leaning out to test it with her hand. Jo moved, too, felt the coin or two she had left sliding around in her shoe. Enough for a loaf and a bed in some crowded, noisy, dangerous lodging house run by thieves. Might as well spend it there, before they found a way to steal it.

Or she could break a window, if she got desperate enough.

A door banged. There was the butcher, a great florid man with blood on his hands and a voice like a bulldog, growling at them to take their carcasses elsewhere or he'd grind them into sausages.

The girl wrapped her face close again, hiding her telltale eye. The fiddler coughed himself back into the rain, his instrument carefully cradled beneath his cloak. The old woman, wheezing dreadfully, pulled herself up with Jo's help. Jo picked up her covered basket for her. Flowers, she thought at first, then caught a pungent whiff of it. Whatever it was she sold, it wasn't violets. The woman winked at her and slid the basket over her arm. She trailed off after the rest of the bedraggled flock scattering into the rain.

Jo saw a lump of masonry, or maybe a broken cobblestone, half the size of her fist near the wall where the old woman had been sitting. She picked it up, slipped it into her pocket in case she needed it later.

You never knew.

➤ ➤ ➤

Harry stood in the enchanted garden of the McAlisters' cottage in the country. Only a few miles from the city, it might have existed in a different time and world: the realm of poetry, where the fall of light and a rosebud heavy with rain from a passing storm symbolized something else entirely. The rain had stopped in the early afternoon. Bright sun had warmed the garden quickly, filled its humid, sparkling air with the smells of grass and wild thyme, the crushed strawberry-scent of the rambling roses climbing up either side of the cottage door. The cottage, an oddly shaped affair with no symmetry whatsoever, had all its scattered, mismatched windows open to the air. There was no garden fence, only a distant, rambling stone wall marking the property. The cottage stood on a grassy knoll; in nearby fields the long grass was lush with wildflowers. Farther away, brindled cows and fluffy clouds of sheep pastured within rambling field walls. Farther yet, in a fold of green, the ancient village, a bucolic garden of stone, grew along the river. On the next knoll over, John Grainger was battling the winds trying to paint the scene. Occasionally, as a puff of exuberant air tried to make off with Grainger's canvas, Harry could hear his energetic swearing.

Harry had come up for the day to look for a face for his Medusa among the McAlisters' visitors. Painters, their wives and families, models, friends who encouraged and bought, and brought friends who bought, wandered around the gardens, chatting, drinking wine and tea, sketching, painting, or watching McAlister paint.

McAlister was painting his wife. Or rather, he was painting her windblown sleeve. She stood patiently against the backdrop of climbing red roses, all of which, Harry noticed, were the exact shade of her mouth. He tried not to think of that. Thinking of her mouth made him think of the monstrous creation in his cupboard. In the sweet light of day, there in the country, he was willing to attribute his Gorgon to the morbid churning of his frustrated romantic urges. But she had inspired him, no doubt about that. Here he was in McAlister's garden, looking in every passing female, even the young girl from the kitchen who kept the tea pot filled, for his Medusa.

McAlister was unusually reticent about his own subject matter. Whatever figure from myth or romance he was portraying, he needed her windblown. He had captured the graceful curves of his wife's wrist bone, her long, pliant fingers. The flow of her silky sleeve in the contrary wind proved challenging, but he persevered, carrying on three discussions at once with his onlookers as he painted. Aurora, her brooding eyes fixed on some distant horizon, scarcely seemed to breathe; she might have been a piece of garden statuary.

Harry drifted, trying not to watch.

He sat down finally next to John Grainger's mistress, Nan Stewart. She had modeled many times for John's drawings and paintings, as well as for other artists who needed her frail, ethereal beauty for their visions. Grainger had discovered her sitting in the cheaper seats of a theater one evening. A well-brought-up young girl despite her class, she refused to speak to an artist. Undaunted, he found out who she was and implored her mother's permission to let her model for him. Her mother, a fussy lump of a bed-mattress as Grainger described her, accompanied Nan a few times, until she realized that the girl could make as much in an hour modeling for artists as she could sewing for a week in a dressmaker's shop. Eventually Nan came to live with the brilliant, volatile Grainger, which explained, Harry thought, her pallor and her melancholy eyes.

She had fine red-gold hair and arresting green eyes. With marriage in view at one point in their relationship, Grainger had hired someone to teach her to move and speak properly. She smiled at Harry dutifully as he filled the empty chair beside her.

"More tea?" he asked.

A vigorous, incoherent shouting from the knoll beyond made them both glance up. Grainger, hands on his easel, seemed to be wrestling with the wind.

Nan shook her head. She had a bound sketchbook on her lap, as well as a pencil or two. Grainger encouraged her to draw. She had talent, he declared to the world, and he was right, from what Harry had seen. But that day her sketchbook was shut.

"Not inspired?" he ventured.

"Not today." She turned her attention from the painter on the knoll finally. "How are you, Harry?"

"Flourishing."

"Are you painting?"

"I have a subject in mind. I'm prowling about for a face."

"What subject?"

"It's a secret," he said lightly. "I'm not sure I can pull it off. I don't want to embarrass myself among you artists."

Her smile touched her eyes finally. "You're a sweet man, Harry. I'm still such a novice myself."

"John praises your work to the skies. He thinks very highly—"

"I know." Her face was suddenly angled away. "I know. I only wish he still thought so highly of me."

"He does!" Harry said, shocked. "He's loved you for years. You live together, you work together, you are twin souls—"

"Yes." She looked at him again, her expression a polite mask. "Yes."

He was silent, wondering what was troubling her. His eyes strayed to the group beside the rose vines. Children ran out of the cottage door; he recognized Andrew Peel's gray-eyed little beauty, and her baby brother trundling unsteadily after. Nan sighed absently, her eyes on the children. Harry's own eyes strayed. Across the garden, the statue came to life; the dark, unfathomable eyes seemed to gaze straight at him.

He started, his cup clattering, feeling that regard like a bolt from the blue, striking silently, deeply. He became aware of Nan's eyes on him, too, in wide, unblinking scrutiny. Then she set her cup down on a table; it too rattled sharply in its saucer.

"She's pregnant, you know," Nan said. Harry felt as though he had missed a step, plunged into sudden space. He started again, this time not so noisily. Nan added, "So am I."

He stared at her. "That's wonderful," he exclaimed finally, leaning to put his cup on the grass. He caught her hands. That's all it was then: her inner turmoil, her natural uncertainties. "Wonderful," he repeated.

"Is it?"

"Of course! You'll marry now, won't you?"

She gave him an incredulous stare. Then she loosed her hands, answered tonelessly, "Yes, quite soon. Next week, perhaps, and then we'll go away for a bit to the southern coasts to paint."

"I couldn't be happier," Harry told her earnestly. "We've all been expecting this for—"

"For years," she finished. "Yes." She hesitated; he waited, puzzled without knowing why. Something about the event, he supposed, made women anxious, prone to fear disasters, or imagine things that were not true.

Grainger's voice, sonorous and vibrant, spilled over the group. He appeared tramping up the knoll, his hat gone, his canvas in one hand, easel in the other, paints in the pockets of his voluminous, stained jacket. He blew a kiss to Nan, leaving a daub of blue on his bushy, autumn-gold mustaches. Then he turned to see how McAlister's sleeve was coming. Above his broad back, Harry saw the statue's eyes come alive again; her cheeks had flushed, in the wayward wind, a delicate shade of rose. Ever the consummate professional, she did not move, while Grainger, lingering in the group, expounded with witty astonishment how like a wing that sleeve seemed, straining for its freedom on the wind.

Harry turned back to Nan, breath indrawn for some pleasantry.

Her chair was empty. He looked around bewilderedly. She had flown herself, it seemed, but why and on what wayward wind, he could not imagine.

➤ ➤ ➤

Jo walked the darkening streets, fingering the broken cobble in her pocket. The day had been dryer than the previous day; that was as much as she could say for it. Sun seemed to linger forever as she trudged through the noisy, stinking streets. She asked everyone for work, even the butcher who had driven her out from under his awning, a shapeless, faceless unrecognizable bundle he didn't remember in the light. But he only laughed and offered the usual, smacking with the flat of his hand the quivering haunch of meat he was slicing into steaks.

"Come back when you get desperate," he called after her, to the amusement of his customers. "Show me how fine you can grind it."

She got much the same at inns and alehouses. When she stopped at crossings to rest her feet and beg for a coin or two, she got threats from sweepers' brooms, screeches from ancient heaps of rags whose territory she invaded, shoves from lean, hollow-cheeked, cat-eyed girls with missing teeth who told her they'd cut off her hair with a rusty knife if they saw her twice on their street.

Toward late afternoon she was too exhausted to feel hungry. She had money for one more night's lodging, or money for food. Not both. After that—she didn't think about it. That would be tomorrow, this was not. Now she had her two coppers, her two choices. And she had the stone in her pocket. She drifted, waiting for night.

When the street lamps were lit, she made up her mind. Just in that moment. She was sitting in the dark, finally safe because nobody could see her nursing her blistered, aching soles. Nobody threatened, yelled, or made lewd suggestions; for a few precious moments she might have been invisible.

And then the gas lamps went on, showing the world where she was again. Caught in the light, she didn't even think. She was on her feet in a breath, hand in her pocket; in the next she had hurled the broken stone furiously at the light. She was startled to hear the satisfying shatter of glass. Someone shouted; the flare, still burning, illumined a couple of uniformed figures to which, she decided with relief, she would yield herself for her transgression.

There was a sudden confusion around her: ragged people rushing into the light, all calling out as they surrounded the uniforms. Jo, pushing against them, couldn't get past to reveal herself to the law.

"I did it," a woman shrieked.

"No, it was me broke the lamp," somebody else shouted. The crowd lurched; voices rose higher. "Give over, you great cow—it was me!"

"I did it!" Jo shouted indignantly. "It wasn't them at all!"

The crowd heaved against her, picked her off her feet. Then it dropped her a moment later, as it broke apart. She lost her balance, sat on the curb staring as the uniforms escorted the wrong woman entirely out of the light. She went along eagerly enough, Jo noted sourly. She pulled herself up finally, still smarting over the injustice of it all.

Then she realized that her purple shawl was gone.

She felt her throat swell and burn, for the first time in forever. Even when her mother had died she hadn't cried. Not even when the baby had died. She had taken the shawl off her mother, and then off the baby. It was all she had left of them to remember them by. Now that was gone. And she was blinded, tears swelling behind her eyes, because the tattered shawl had borne the burden, within its braided threads, of her memories.

Now she was left holding them all herself.

She limped to find some private shred of shadow, refusing to let tears fall. All the shadows seemed occupied; snores and mutterings warned her before she could sit. She wandered on and on through the quieting streets, unable to stop the memories swirling in her head. Her innocent young self, cleaning the ashes out of the fireplace in the fine, peaceful library. The handsome stranger with the light, easy voice, asking her name. Asking about her. Listening to her, while he touched her cuff button with his finger. Shifted a loose strand of her hair off her face. Touched her as no one had, ever before. Then gone, nowhere, not to be seen, he might have been a dream. And she, beginning to wake at nights, feeling the panic gnawing at her until she could bear it no longer, and upped and ran.

But there was something else. A street name dredged it up as she walked. Or the night smell of a great tree in a line of them along the street. She had run from someone else. Oh, she remembered. Him. The young painter. He had a gentle voice, too, but he only touched her to turn her head, or put her loose hair where he wanted it. He paid well, too, for the random hour or two she could spare him. It was his money she saved to run with, when she knew she could no longer stay. When her skirts grew tight. When the other girls began to whisper, and the housekeeper's eyes drew up tight in her head like a snail's eyes at the sight of Jo.

What was his name?

She walked under the great, dark boughs that shielded her from the street lights. She could sleep under them, she thought. Curl up in their roots like an animal; no one would see her until dawn. The street was very quiet; a sedate carriage or a cab went by now and then, but she heard no voices. He lived on a street like this; she remembered the trees. She'd walk there from the great house, his housekeeper would let her in, and she would climb the stairs to his—his what was it? His studio. He painted her with that strange fruit in her hand, with all the rows of little seeds in it like baby teeth.

He told her stories.

You are in the Underworld, he said. You have been stolen from your loving mother's house by the King of Hades. You must not eat or drink anything he offers you; if you refuse, he will have no power over you, and he must set you free. But you grow hungry, so hungry, as you wait . . .

"So hungry," she whispered.

You eat only a few tiny seeds from this fruit, thinking such small things would do no harm. But harm you have done for now he can claim you as his wife and keep you, during the darkest months of the year, in his desolate and lonely realm . . .

What was her name?

Her eyes were closing. Her bones ached; her feet seemed no longer recognizable. Not feet any longer, just pain. Pain she walked on, and dark her only friend . . . She didn't choose; she simply fell, driven to her knees in the damp ground beneath a tree. She crawled close to it, settled herself among its roots, her head reeling, it felt like, about to bounce off her shoulders and roll away without her.

What was its name?

She closed her eyes and saw it: that bright, glowing fruit, those sweet, innocent seeds . . .

Pomegranate.

Would he want to finish his painting? she wondered.

But there was someone guarding her passage out of the Underworld. Someone stood at the gates she must pass through, protecting the serene upper realms from the likes of her. Someone whose word was law on the border between two worlds . . .

What was her name?

Her eyes. Jo could not remember her eyes, only felt them watching as she fled into the ancient, timeless dark. Only her bun, the light, glossy brown of a well-baked dinner roll, and her chins and the watch pinned to her bosom, at one corner of her apron.

What would her eyes say when she saw Jo?

She remembered as she felt the strong arms seize her, pull her off the earth into the nether realms of sleep.

Mrs. Grommet.

❧ ❧ ❧

Harry, having returned from the country without his Medusa, avoided his studio. He did not want to open the cupboard door again. He couldn't decide which might be worse: his painting talking to him or his painting not talking to him. Was expecting a painting to speak to him worse than having it speak to him? Suppose he opened the cupboard door with expectations, and nothing happened? He would be forced to conclusions which, in the cheery light of day, he did not want to think about.

So he left the house at midmorning, and dropped in at a gallery where a new painting by Thomas Buck was hung. The gallery, recently opened, had acquired pieces indiscriminately in its desire to become fashionable. It aimed, it declared affably, to encourage the novice as well as to celebrate the artist. Tommy Buck's work showed promise. It had been showing promise for years. Harry, studying the new painting called *Knight Errant*, was gratified to see that Buck still could not draw to save his life. The horse was absurdly proportioned; its wide, oblong back could have been set for a dinner party of six. And the knight's hands, conveniently hidden within bulky gauntlets, gripped the reins awkwardly, as though he were playing tug-of-war. The young woman tied to a tree, toward whom the knight rode, seemed to be chatting amiably with the dragon who menaced her.

I could do better than that, Harry thought.

He felt the urge, remembered the anomaly in the cupboard, and was relieved when some friends hailed him. They carried him away eventually to dine, and from there to another friend's studio where they drank wine and watched the painter struggle with his Venus, a comely enough young woman with something oddly bland about her beauty. She bantered well, though, and stayed to entertain them over a cold supper of beef and salad. Harry got home late, pleasantly tipsy, and, inspired, went immediately up to his studio to view his work within the context of his friends'.

The Gorgon spoke when he opened the cupboard, causing him to reel back with a startled cry: he had actually forgotten her.

"Hello, Harry."

"Hlmph," he choked.

"Have you found me yet?"

He tugged at his collar, tempted to slam the cupboard shut and go to bed. But he answered, venturing closer, "No. Not yet."

"Did you even look for me?"

"Of course I did! I looked for you in every female face I passed. I didn't see you anywhere." Except, he thought, in McAlister's garden, where Her eyes had immobilized him once again. "You aren't easy to find," he added, speaking now into the shadows. "You're a very complex matter."

"Yes, I am, aren't I," she murmured complacently. "Harry, why don't you let me out?"

"I can't. What if someone sees?"

"Well, I don't intend to pass the time of day with Mrs. Grommet, if that's what worries you."

"No, but—"

"Hang a cloth over my face or something. Pretend I'm a parrot."

"I don't think so," he sighed, sitting down on the floor because he had been standing much of the day. A lamp on the wall above his head spilled some light into the open cupboard; he could see the edge of the canvas, but not the moving mouth. Less afraid now, lulled by wine and company, he asked her curiously, "Where do you think I should look for you?"

"Oh, anywhere. You'll know me when you see me."

"But to see you is to be—"

"Yes," she said, laughing a little. "You'll recognize your model when she turns you, for just a tiny human moment, into stone."

"Only One can do that," he said softly.

"Maybe. You just keep looking."

"But for what? Are you— Were you, I mean, really that terrible? Or that beautiful? Which should I be searching for?"

"Oh, we were hideous," she answered cheerfully, "me and my two Gorgon sisters. Stheno and Euryale, they were called. Even in the Underworld, our looks could kill."

"Sthene?"

"Nobody remembers them, because nothing much ever happened to them. They didn't even die, being immortal. Do you think anyone would remember me if that obnoxious boy hadn't figured out a way to chop my head off without looking at me?"

Harry dredged a name out of the mists of youthful education. "Perseus, was it?"

"He had help, you know. He couldn't have been that clever without divine intervention. Long on brawn, short on brains, you know that type of hero."

"That's not what I was taught."

"He forced our guardian sisters, the gray-haired Graie, to help him, you must have heard. He stole their only eye and their tooth."

"They had one eye?" Harry said fuzzily.

"They passed it back and forth. And the tooth. Among the three of them." She gave an unlovely cackle. "What a sight that was, watching them eat. Or squabble over that eyeball. That's what they were doing when they didn't see that brat of a boy coming. He grabbed their goods and forced them to give him magic armor and a mirror to see me in, so he wouldn't have to meet my eyes. Then he lopped my head off and used me to to kill his enemies. Even dead, I had an effect on people."

"He doesn't sound so very stupid."

"He had help," she repeated with a touch of asperity. "Anyway, it was loathsome, gray-haired old biddies who armed him to fight me. Not some lissome, rosy-fingered maidens. You remember that when you paint me."

"I will." He added, brooding over the matter, "If I can find you."

"Oh, you will," she said more cheerfully. "Never fret. I do wish you would take me out of here and let me watch, though."

"No."

"I could advise you."

"You'd scare my model."

"I wouldn't talk, I promise you! And if I forget, just cover me up. Please, Harry? After all, I have inspired you. You could do me a favor. It's awfully dark in here."

"Well."

"Please? Harry?"

"Well." He got to his feet again, dusted off his pants, yawning now and forgetting why he had come up. "I'll think about it. Good night."

"Good night, Harry."

He closed the cupboard door and went to bed.

The next morning, his ambition inflamed by what the gallery seemed to think worth hanging, he ate his breakfast hastily and early. He would not come home without his Medusa, he was determined, even if he had to search the ravaged streets and slums for her. No, he told Mrs. Grommet, she should not expect him home before evening. If then. He would go as far as he must to find his inspiration, even as far, he admitted in his inmost heart, as the country, to see if he might find that unexpected face in Aurora's shadow.

He got as far as the street. He paused to latch the garden gate behind him, and was turned to stone.

A woman appeared out of nowhere, it seemed. She murmured something to him; he hardly knew what. He looked at her and time stopped. The normal street noises of passing carriages, birds, doors opening, voices calling, simply vanished. He heard the faint hum of his own blood in his ears, and recognized it as a constant, unchanging sound out of antiquity. The sound heard when all else is silent; nothing moves.

Her face was all bone and shadow, full of stark paradoxes: young yet ancient with experience, beautiful yet terrifying with knowledge, living yet somehow alive no longer. Whatever those great, wide-set eyes had seen had left a haunting starkness in them that riveted him where he stood. She spoke again. She might have been speaking Etruscan, for all the words made sense to Harry. Her mouth held the same contradictions: it was lovely, its grim line warned of horror, it hungered, it would never eat again.

Sound washed over him again: a delivery wagon, a yowling cat, a young housemaid chasing after it down the street. He heard his stammering voice. "Where—where did you come from?"

She gestured: out of a tree, out of the sky, her hand said. She was very poorly dressed, he realized: her thin, tight jacket torn at both elbows, the hem of her skirt awash with dried mud, her shoes worn down and beginning to split. She spoke again, very slowly, as if to a young child, or a man whose wits had badly strayed.

"I wondered if you had some work for me, sir. If maybe you could use me for your paintings. Anything will do. Any amount of time—"

One of his hands closed convulsively above her elbow; his other hand pulled the gate open.

"Oh, yes," he said unsteadily. "Oh, yes. Miss. Whoever you—"

"Jo, sir."

"Jo. Come in." He swept her down the walk, threw the door wide, and shouted, "Mrs. Grommet! Mrs. Grommet! We need you!"

➤ ➤ ➤

"You have lice," Mrs. Grommet said.

Jo, hearing her within a cascade of lukewarm water, thought her voice sounded simply matter-of-fact. The kitchen maid stopped pouring water, began to pass a hard, lumpy bar of soap over Jo's wet hair. It took time to work up a lather.

"I'm not surprised," Jo murmured. She knelt in her tattered chemise beside a huge tub, allowing Mrs. Grommet the sight of her cracked, filthy feet. She could only hope that whatever vision had possessed Mr. Waterman to let her in the house would not be washed down the drain. But, she told herself coldly, if that happens then I will be no worse than I was before, and at least I will be clean.

"Go on, girl," the housekeeper said. "Give it a good scrub. Pretend you're doing the front steps."

"There's such a lot of it," the maid ventured. Jo closed her eyes, felt the blunt, vigorous fingers work away at her until she imagined herself underwater, floating in some river god's grip, being flailed back and forth like water weed.

"Rinse now," Mrs. Grommet ordered, and the water flowed again, copious and mercilessly cold. "There," the housekeeper said at last with satisfaction. "That should do it."

Freed, Jo straightened. The maid tossed a towel over her head and began to pummel her again.

"Go and boil some water," Mrs. Grommet told her. She added to Jo when the girl had gone, "Sometimes they work and sometimes they don't, these new hot water pipes. He didn't recognize you, did he?"

Jo swallowed. Mrs. Grommet's eyes, green as unripe tomatoes, said very little beyond her words. She knows, Jo thought. She knows why I ran away. But what Mrs. Grommet felt about that, Jo could only guess. Anyone else in the housekeeper's position would have made her sentiments about this immoral, unwashed bit of dredge crossing her employer's threshold very plain, very soon.

"No," Jo said simply. "He doesn't. He saw my face and wants to paint it. That's all. I don't know if he'll feel the same when he sees it again. If not, I'll go."

Mrs. Grommet did not comment on that. "I'll see what I can find for you to wear, while you wash."

"Mrs. Grommet—" Her voice faltered; the housekeeper, hand on the door knob, waited expressionlessly. "I know my clothes are a disgrace, but they're all I've got, if I go. Please—"

"Don't worry, girl," Mrs. Grommet said briskly, "I won't turn you out naked into the street, whatever becomes of you."

An hour later, Jo sat at the kitchen fireplace, letting her hair dry while she ate some cold beef and bread. She was dressed in a dark, shapeless gown which had made its way, some time in the distant past, to Harry's costume closet. Made to fit tight at wrists and neck and beneath the bosom, it hung on Jo like a sack. The kitchen maid, chopping onions for a pie, could not stop staring at her. Jo, too weary to eat much, didn't wonder at her staring, until the cook, a great mound of a woman with cheeks the color of raw beef, rolling out pastry, made as though to swat the maid with a floury hand.

"Leave her be, then," she grunted.

"I'm sorry, miss," the girl murmured to Jo. "I can't help it. It's your hair."

Jo glanced sideways at it, as it fell around her face. It did look unfamiliar clean, but other than that it was just her hair.

"What's the matter with it? Have I got the mange, too?"

"No," the maid whispered, flicking her eyes to it again. "It's so beautiful, all long and gold and curly."

Jo blinked, at a loss. Her eyes rose helplessly, sought Mrs. Grommet's.

The housekeeper, sipping tea at the table and still inscrutable, gave a brief nod. "Oh, yes. He'll like that."

Jo, suddenly terrified, stood abruptly, her meal scattering out of her fingers into the fire. "I have to go, then," she heard herself babble. "I have to go. Where are my shoes? I had a couple of coppers in my shoes—"

Mrs. Grommet gazed at her wordlessly. Her eyes came alive suddenly, as she pushed herself to her feet. "There now, Jo," she said faintly, rounding the table to Jo's side. "Mr. Waterman's not like that. You know that. There's no need to run away from him again." She put her hand on Jo's arm and pointed to a grubby little pile near the hearth. "There's your shoes and clothes. The coins are in there, just as I found them. If you need them, you'll have them."

"Why," Jo asked her wildly, "are you treating me this way?"

"What way?" Mrs. Grommet asked, astonished.

It took Jo a moment to remember the word. "Kind." Spoken, it seemed to surprise them both. "Why are you being kind to me? You know—you—"

Mrs. Grommet's eyes went distant again. But she kept her hand on Jo's arm, patted it a little. "Stay a bit," she said finally, eluding the question. "Mr. Waterman will think we drove you away if you leave now. He'll only go looking for you."

"But I don't understand—"

"Well, you might ask him what he has in mind. You might stay long enough to listen to him. Whatever it is, I'm sure it's nothing more than a painting."

Jo, still trembling, sat down at the hearth again. She heard whispering; after a moment, the little maid brought her a cup of tea. She sipped it wordlessly, the kitchen silent behind her but for the thump of the rolling pin. When she knew she could stand again, she knew it was time. She rose, set the cup on the table. Mrs. Grommet looked at her.

"I'll take you up," she said briefly. Jo nodded gratefully, too lightheaded to speak.

She passed familiar hallways, paintings, patterns of wallpaper, carpets that seemed more real in memory. It was, she thought dazedly, like being in two places at once; she was uncertain, from one step to the next, if she were moving backward or forward in time. They went up the second flight of steeper stairs into the top of the house. There, as Mrs. Grommet opened the door, Jo saw another memory that was real: the long rows of windows overlooking the street, the park across from them, and on the other side of the house, the river. She could see the tree under which she had wakened in the other world at dawn. She smelled oils and pungent turpentine, saw the untidy shelves of books and sketches, the oddments everywhere—peacock feathers, beads, baskets, seashells, tapestries, rich shawls of taffeta, goblets, moth-eaten furs.

She saw Harry. He stood across the room, watching her silently as she entered. She had never seen anyone look at her like that before, as though she were something not quite human, a piece of dream, maybe, that he had to step into to see her properly.

He said absently, "Thank you, Mrs. Grommet."

"Yes, sir. She lingered. "Will you need—"

"Nothing. Thank you."

She closed the door behind her. Harry crossed the room, came close to Jo. Still in his dream, she saw, he reached out, touched her hair with one finger. She felt herself stiffen. He drew back hastily. She saw his eyes again, anxious now, tentative, fascinated. Like some mooncalf boy in love for the first time, she realized, and not even sure with what.

"Will you let me paint you?" he asked huskily.

"Of course," she answered, so amazed she forgot her terrors.

"I see you—I see you as a very ancient power, a goddess, almost, who is herself mortal, but who can kill with a look. To see her is to die. But not to see her is to live without living. I see you, in all her terrible, devastating beauty, as Medusa."

"Yes, Mr. Waterman," she said, completely mystified, and thought with wonder: He doesn't recognize me at all.

❧ ❧ ❧

Much later that day, almost into the next, Harry sat on the floor beside the open cupboard door, babbling to the Gorgon.

"The lines of her face are stunning. They transfixed me the moment I saw them. They seem shaped—sculpted—by primal forces, like stone, yet very much alive. They are beauty, they are death, they are youth, they are ancient beyond belief. And her eyes. Medusa's eyes. They gaze at you from another world, the Underworld perhaps; they are portals to that grim world. Of the palest gray, nearly colorless, like the mist between life and death—" He heard a vague noise from within the cupboard, almost as if the Gorgon had sneezed. "I beg your pardon. Did you speak?"

"No," she said faintly.

"And her hair. I've never seen anything like it. White gold, rippling down from her face to her knees. Again that suggestion of youth and antiquity, knowledge gained too early from unearthly places—"

"Harry."

"Her mouth—there again—"

"Harry."

"Yes, what is it?"

"I think you should let me see her."

"Her mouth is like—"

"I promise, by Perseus's shield that bore my reflection and killed me, that I won't speak a word in her presence."

"Again, it contradicts itself—it should be mobile, plump, alluring, the delicate pink of freshwater pearls—"

"You can put me in a dark corner where she won't notice me."

"But it has long forgotten how to smile; its line is inflexible and determined—"

"Harry. It's me you're painting. I haven't seen myself in thousands of years. Have a heart. Let me see what humans think of me these days. I'm not used to being associated with beauty."

Harry was silent. He thought he perceived the faintest under-tone in the Gorgon's plea, as though she were laughing at him. But her words argued otherwise. And it did seem an appropriate request. She had after all inspired him; how could he deny her his vision of herself?

"You'll forget," he said guardedly, "and say something impul-sive and frighten her away."

"I won't. I have sworn."

"I'll think about—"

"Harry. Stop thinking about it. Just do it. Or I'll yell my head off here in the cupboard like one of Bluebeard's wives."

Harry blinked. "You could have done that—"

"Today, while she was here. Yes. But I didn't, did I? I am capable of controlling myself. I won't say a word in her presence, no matter how—"

"How?"

"No matter what."

"Do I amuse you?" Harry demanded indignantly.

No, no," the Gorgon said soothingly. "No. I'm just incredibly old, Harry, and my sense of humor is warped. I'm very ignorant of the modern world, and it would do me good to see even a tiny corner of it."

Harry sighed, mollified. "All right. Tomorrow morning, before she comes."

"Thank you, Harry."

He got up early to hang the Gorgon above some high book-shelves, among other old sketches and watercolors scattered along the wall. The contradictions in the face startled him anew: the frightened eyes, the pale, anxious brows, the lush, volup-tuous, wine-red mouth. His eyes lingered on that mouth as he descended the ladder. He would make a trip to the country soon, he decided. She was down there with Alex, nearly every week-end. The mouth seemed to crook in a faint smile; his foot froze on the bottom rung.

"No," he said sharply. "You must be absolutely still."

The mouth composed itself. The eyes gazed unseeingly across the room. He had placed the painting where most often his model would have her back to it. She would only glimpse it as she faced the door to leave. And few people looked that high without reason, Harry had learned to his chagrin when his work had been hung near the ceiling in exhibits. She would never notice the peculiar face with its mismatched features unless she looked for it.

He spent a few days sketching Jo, learning every nuance of her face, experimenting with various positions, draperies. He decided, in the end, simply to paint her face at the instant she saw herself reflected in the young hero's shield. The Medusa turning her baleful gaze upon herself, and realizing in that instant that she had slain herself. The shield would frame her within the canvas. The pale, rippling beauty of the model's hair would transform itself easily into gorgeous, dangerous snakes. Jo's stark-white skin, drained of life-force it seemed, hallowed and shadowed with weariness and strain, hinted of the Medusa's otherworldly origins. He positioned black silk in graceful folds about her neck to emphasize the shadows. That would be her only costume. That and the snakes in her hair, which might suggest, in their golden brilliance, the final light of the sun upon her dying and deadly face.

So lost he was in the excitement of inspiration that he scarcely remembered to speak to his model. She came in the mornings, murmured, "Good morning, Mr. Waterman," and sat in her chair beside his easel. He arranged the silk about her throat, giving her a greeting or a pleasantry. Then she became so still she hardly seemed to breathe. He worked, utterly absorbed, until the light began to fade. Then, her pallor deep by then, her humanity began to intrude upon him. She is tired, he would realize. She must be hungry. I am.

He would put his palette down and open the door. "Mrs. Grommet," he would call down the stairs. Then he would study the day's work until the housekeeper hove into view, bearing a tea tray and Jo's wages for the day. Jo would follow her down. Mrs. Grommet would feed her in the kitchen, for Harry was reluctant to glimpse, at this sensitive stage, his Medusa with her cheeks full of mutton.

The Gorgon above their heads watched all this silently, refraining from comment.

She hardly saw Jo, Harry knew, except when she rose to leave. Then the wan, beautiful face would be visible to the painting above her head. Jo never looked that high; she seemed oddly incurious about the studio. Other models had prowled around peering at his canvases, opening books, trying on bits of finery, fingering this and that. But Jo just came and left, as though, Harry thought, she truly vanished into another world and was not much interested in his.

The Gorgon finally asked one evening, after Jo had followed Mrs. Grommet downstairs, "Where does she go?"

"What?" Harry asked through a bite of sandwich.

"Your model. Where does she sleep at night?"

"How should I know?" He was sitting in a well-stuffed chair, weary from standing all day, and devouring sandwiches and cakes, he suspected, like a well-brought-up vulture. He could see the Gorgon's face from that position if he wanted. Her voice startled him; she hadn't said much for days.

"Aren't you pleased with me, Harry?"

"For being so quiet? Oh, yes, I'm very grateful." He swallowed another mouthful of hot, sweet tea, and looked up at her. "What do you think of her?"

"Oh, a great deal," the painting answered vaguely, and gave a sudden, crude snort of a laugh. "She's far too beautiful for the likes of me, of course. But I see your point in her."

"Do you?"

"Beauty that can kill. But Harry, she's bone-thin and she's not much use to you dead. She might sleep in an alley for all you know. Anything could happen to her, and you'd never know what."

Harry was silent, blinking. He took another scalding sip. "I hadn't thought of that."

"Well, think of it. What would you do if tomorrow she didn't appear?"

The thought brought him out of his chair to pace a little, suddenly edgy. "Surely I pay her enough for decent lodgings. Don't I?"

"How much is enough?"

"I don't—"

"And suppose she has others dependent on her? Who need every coin she brings to them?"

"Well, maybe—" He paused, still tramping across the room; then he dropped into his chair again. "I'll ask Mrs. Grommet."

"You could ask your model."

Harry rolled his head to gaze up at the painting. "How?" he pleaded. "She is my Medusa. She exists only in this little world, only to be painted. I dare not make her real. She might lose all her power, become just another woman in my eyes."

The Medusa snorted again, this time without amusement. "She'd still be there for you to paint her. Your brush knows how to lie. If she vanishes into the streets out there, where will you go to look for her? You might at least ask her that."

Harry tried, at least three times, the next morning, before he got a question out. His model, whose name he kept forgetting, sat silently gazing as he requested, at the back of his easel. What she saw, he could not begin to guess. Her wide, eerily pale eyes seemed to glimpse enormities in his peaceful studio. Until now, he had absently confused her expression with the Gorgon seeing herself for the first time and the last. Now he wondered, despite his better judgment, what those eyes had truly seen to make them so stricken.

He cleared his throat yet again. Her eyelids trembled, startled, at the sound of his voice. "Tell me, er—Jo?"

"Yes, sir?"

"Do you have a decent place to stay at night? I mean, I do pay you enough for that, don't I?"

She kept her face very still, answered simply, "Yes, Mr. Waterman. I go to a lodging house on Carvery Street."

"Alone?"

Her eyes flicked up, widening; he caught the full force of the Gorgon's stare. "Sir?"

"I mean—I only meant—Do you have other people to care for? Others dependent on you?"

"Oh." The fierce gaze lowered once again to the middle distance. "No, sir. They're dead."

"Oh," he said inanely. He painted in silence a while, aware, though he told himself he imagined it, of eyes boring into his head from above the bookshelves. He glanced up finally, was appalled to see the full red lips moving wildly in a grotesque parody of speech.

He cleared his throat again hastily. "Do you get enough to eat? I mean, you're very thin."

"I'm eating better now," she answered.

The question sent a faint, unwelcome patina of color into her white face that at first alarmed him. Then he thought: Why not? Medusa, seeing her own beauty for the first time, may well flush with pleasure and astonishment, before she turns herself into stone.

"Do you know," he asked aimlessly, trying to make conversation, "the story of Medusa?"

"Something of it," she said hesitantly. "Some sort of monster who turned people into stone?"

"Yes."

"Ugly, wasn't she?"

"Hideous," he answered, "by all accounts."

He heard her take a breath or two then, as if to speak. Then she grew still again, so still that he wondered if he had somehow turned her into stone.

He let his model rest a day or two later, and spent a tranquil afternoon in the country, watching others work. Arthur Millidge was there, putting a honeysuckle background to what would be his *Nymph Dying for Love of a Shepherd.* He kept knocking his easel over swatting at bees. John Grainger was there as well, to Harry's surprise, back on his windy knoll painting the distant village. McAlister had finished his wife's windblown sleeve; now he was engrossed in her bare feet and ankles, around which green silk swirled and eddied. Harry, after his first glimpse of those long marble toes and exquisite anklebones, took the first chair he found and tried not to think about them.

Arthur Millidge's wife Holly handed him a cup of tea and sat down beside him. She was a pretty, good-natured, giddy-headed thing, who could pull out an arrow and hit an astute social bullseye just when she seemed at her most frivolous. She was watching her suffering husband with a great deal of amusement.

"Oh, poor Arthur," she cried, when he batted at a wasp with

his brush and actually hit it; it stuck, struggling, to the yellow-daubed bristles. "At least it's the right color."

Her husband smiled at her wanly.

"I thought," Harry said blankly, "that Grainger and Nan would still be at the south coast."

"Oh, no," Holly answered briskly. "They only spent a few days there."

"But they are—they did get married."

"So it seems. She's wearing a ring."

"Is she here?"

"No, poor thing, the traveling exhausted her in her condition, so she let John come alone."

Harry's eyes crept back to Aurora. Her condition, as well, he remembered, and could not, for a prolonged moment, stop studying her. The flowing, voluminous silk hid everything. Her face seemed a trifle plumper, but then he had been gazing at his emaciated model for days, he reminded himself. Aurora's face seemed exquisitely serene, he realized, ivory, full, and tranquil, like a midsummer moon.

"The condition suits Aurora," Holly said, reading Harry's thoughts in her uncanny way. "I think poor Nan will have a great deal of difficulty with it. She's frail anyway, and suffers from imagination."

Harry pulled his eyes away from McAlister's wife, dipped his hand into a bowl full of cherries. "Which of us doesn't?" he asked lightly.

"I'm sure I don't," Holly laughed, and helped herself to a cherry or two from Harry's hand. "I heard you're painting something mysterious, Harry. Tommy Buck said that he and some friends came to visit you, and you refused to let them into your studio."

"They frightened my model," Harry said, remembering the shouts, Mrs. Grommet's flurried protest, the stampede up the stairs. "I thought she might faint, she was trembling so badly."

Holly maneuvered a cherry pit daintily from lips to palm and tipped it into the grass. "But who is she? Someone we know?"

"No. I found her in the street."

"How exciting! And what are you making of her?"

"Oh, I'm experimenting with this and that," he answered airily. "Nothing much, yet."

"She must be very pretty."

"In a wild kind of way. She's very shy. Not used to company."

"Everyone," Holly sighed, "is full of secrets. Alex won't tell what he's working on, either. You should bring her here, Harry."

"I should?" he asked, surprised.

"It might calm her, knowing others like her who model. Besides, if you decide you can't make anything of her, someone else might, and then she wouldn't have to go back into the streets."

"True," he said absently, flinging a cherry pit at a bee buzzing in the honeysuckle. "Oh, sorry, Arthur. I was aiming for the bee."

"Don't try to be helpful, Waterman."

"I won't, then."

"Will you bring her, Harry?"

"I might," he answered vaguely, and changed the subject. "What do you think McAlister is making out of his wife?"

"Oh, who knows?" Holy said, waving midges away from her face. "Blind Justice? Aphrodite? Maybe even he doesn't know. The point is to keep her here, don't you think?"

"Here?" Harry repeated, mystified. Holly turned her head, regarded him blithely a moment, chin on her fist. Abruptly she laughed, and got to her feet.

"Oh, Harry. You are so unbearably sweet. Arthur, come into the shade with us and have something to drink before you melt in all that light. I'm trying to worm secrets out of Harry."

"Harry has secrets?" John Grainger's deep, vigorous voice intoned incredulously behind them. "*Mirabile dictu!*" He dropped into a chair, dipped into the cherries with cerulean blue fingertips and demanded of the hapless Harry, "Tell all."

❧ ❧ ❧

Jo sat in Harry's kitchen, eating her supper after he had returned from the country and began to paint her again. At his request, she had given Mrs. Grommet explicit instructions about where to find her if Harry needed her. Mrs. Grommet dutifully wrote the address down. Then, to Jo's surprise, she poured herself a cup of tea and pulled out a chair at the end of the table near Jo, where she sat close to the fire.

Mrs. Grommet said, "I know Mrs. Atkins, the woman who owns the lodging house on Carvery Street. She's a good, honest woman. Or at least she was when we worked together, in a great house over on Bellingham Road."

Jo's eyes slid uncertainly to her face. She managed an answer, after a moment, "She seems kind."

"She married unexpectedly. Lucky for her, her husband had saved a little money. And had a very loving heart. Married they were for thirty years before he died, and never a word passed his lips that their child wasn't his."

Jo coughed on a bit of pickled beet. The kitchen maid was on the far side of the kitchen, banging pots noisily in weltering dishwater. The cook was in the pantry counting spoons, which was her way of saying resting her feet and having a nip. Mrs. Grommet's blue eyes opened meaningfully upon Jo, then lowered again. She sipped tea, half-turned at a splash from the sink.

"Go easy, girl! You're washing pots, not the flagstones."

Jo put two and two together, cleared her throat. Still, words came out with difficulty. "That's why—" She drew breath, met the housekeeper's eyes. "That's why you're kind to me."

"Things happen," Mrs. Grommet said, the corners of her mouth puckering a moment. "They're not always our fault."

"No." She lifted her cup. It trembled badly; she put it down again quickly before she spilled. She folded her hands tightly, said to them, "It takes a special heart to see it that way, though."

Mrs. Grommet patted her hands. "I saw how you were with Mr. Waterman the first time you came here. So quiet and nicely behaved. Some of his models—well, the less said. Not that he was that way, at least not under his own roof. But I hear the young men talking about the girls they paint, about which would only pose and go, and which might stay around after for their bit of fun." She became aware of the maid handling the pots as gently as possible, and raised her voice again. "Finish up there, Lizzie, then go and see if cook needs help in the pantry."

"Yes, Mrs. Grommet."

Jo said very softly, "You were friends, then, you and Mrs.

Atkins, when you worked on Bellingham Road."

"Mary. Mary Plum she was, then. We started there very young, you see, and during the same summer. We were there together for five years. She— What happened to her seemed so unfair to me. It was one of the young friends of the family—"

"Yes," Jo whispered.

"Nothing to him, of course. He told her he loved her and would care for her. He couldn't even remember her name or her face, next time he came. He looked straight at her, she said, when she was serving dinner, and didn't even see her. She was at the point then when she had to leave. She had no choice. But then Martin—Mr. Atkins—found her weeping under the privet hedge when he went to trim it. He was a gardener there, then, and very well thought of. He'd saved all his money for years for an investment, he said. He asked Mary to be his investment." She paused, watching Jo's struggling face. "I've never seen you smile before."

"I've nearly forgotten how. Did he really put it like that?"

"She was a pretty thing," Mrs. Grommet said reminiscently. "He said he'd had his eye on her, but never thought he'd have a chance. Well, chance came, wearing an unexpected face, and he was brave enough to take it. She had a daughter who looked just like her. After some years, he'd worked so hard that—" She stopped abruptly. "Oh, dear."

The tears came out of nowhere Jo could name, hot, fierce and seemingly unstoppable. She put her hands over her mouth, turned her back quickly to face the fire again. She heard Mrs. Grommet say something sharply to Lizzie; all sounds faded in the kitchen. Jo felt a tea towel pushed into her hand.

She buried her face in it, seeing, feeling, smelling all at once, as though memory, locked so carefully away, had crashed and blundered out of its door. His warm, slight weight in her arms, the smell of milk in his hair, his wide, round eyes catching at hers.

"Poor Alf," she whispered into the towel. "Oh, poor Alf. Poor little poppit. Oh, Mrs. Grommet, I did love him despite every-thing—"

"Now, then."

"He was just too frail to go on."

"There now." Mrs. Grommet patted her shoulder.

"I'm sorry."

"It's all right; Lizzie's gone. You have a good cry."

"I haven't—I forgot to cry, when—when—" Her voice wailed away from her, incoherent. She shook hair over her face and eyes like a shroud, trying to hide in it while tears came noisily, messily, barely restrained under the wad of tea towel. "Poor mite, he was all my heart. I think we must have gotten buried together, and I have been just a ghost ever since— No wonder Mr. Waterman sees me as that stone-eyed monster—"

"What?"

She drew a raw, ragged breath that was half sob. "Some— Medusa—who turns people into stone with her eyes. That's what he sees when he looks at me." Then she felt an odd bubble in her chest; loosed, it sounded strangely like a laugh. "I'd terrify anyone with these eyes now—"

'Let me see," Mrs. Grommet said faintly. Jo lifted her face from the towel, pulled wet strands of hair from her cheeks. Her throat ached again at the housekeeper's expression. But it was not grief so much as relief that she could still cry, she could still laugh. Which she found herself doing again amid her tears, in a damp, inelegant snort. "Look what I've done to you— You're stunned—"

"You do look a bit fiery around the eyes," Mrs. Grommet admitted. "But no wonder Mr. Waterman doesn't remember you, with all that happened to you since."

"I was a maid when he began his first painting. Now I'm Medusa." She sat again, drew a shuddering breath as she moped her eyes.

"Maybe. But you look all the younger now for those tears." She refilled their cups. "Not that you're much more than a girl. But you just seemed—like you'd seen a Medusa, yourself. And lived to tell about it."

Jo wrapped her fingers around the cup, managed to raise it without spilling. "Mrs. Grommet, you've been so good to me," she said huskily. "I don't know how to thank you."

"Well. You reminded me so of Mary, when you disappeared like that. I couldn't see that you could have found any way to help yourself, except maybe into the river. Mr. Waterman looked for you when you left. He fretted about you. And not only for his painting. He wanted to help."

"I know." She got a sip past the sudden burn in her throat. "I was too frightened to think then. And now, I don't care if he never recognizes that terrified waif. I don't want him feeling sorry for me. I'm glad he doesn't know me."

"I did," Mrs. Grommet said, "the moment I saw you. I don't see how he can't. Being a painter as he is. Faces are his business."

"He doesn't see me. He sees the woman he wants to see. And I hope—" She touched her swollen eyes lightly. "I hope she's still there, in spite of my tears."

"Now he's got you thinking that way," Mrs. Grommet said roundly. "As if you're not yourself."

"But I never am, when he paints me. I am always the woman he has in mind. I think that's why he doesn't like to talk to me. He only wants to know the woman in his head. The dream he has of me. If I told him too much about—" She swallowed, continued steadily, "—about Alf, about the streets, the mill, about my mother's hands all cracked from taking in laundry, about the purple shawl—the dream would be gone. All he'd have left is me."

❧ ❧ ❧

Harry was gazing at his Medusa, a ham sandwich forgotten in one hand. With the other hand he was pointing out to the Medusa overhead various examples of his brilliance or his clumsiness, which seemed, judging by the Gorgon's expression, to be running about neck and neck that day.

"Look there. Putting that fleck of pure white just so, I've captured perfectly the suggestion of ice in her gray eyes. Do you see it? Of course the delicate line of the inner eye is a bit blurry, there; I'll have to rework it." Raptly, he took a bite of sandwich. "And there—" He said with his mouth full, overcome. "You see what I did."

"Harry. You still don't know anything about this woman."

"I told her to give Mrs. Grommet her address. You made a good point about that. Now, her hair. I shall have to go to the zoological gardens, observe some snakes." He paused, chewing, added regretfully, "I should have brought a few back with me from the country. I didn't think of it. Perhaps because I don't see the point of them. They just begin and go on and keep going on the same way they began, and then they end without any reason whatsoever." He paused again.

"Don't say it," the Gorgon pleaded.

Harry glanced at her, took another bite. "All right, I won't. But it is a bit like life, isn't it?"

"Harry!"

He smiled. "I'd give a lot to see your snakes, though. What color were they?"

"Ugly."

"No color is ugly."

"Maybe," the Medusa sighed, "but you must remember that I was hideous. I never looked at myself, of course, and my snakes were usually twined around my head. But now and then a loop or a head would lose its direction and slide near my eyes. They were fairly drab: brown, black, gray, without any interesting patterns. Big, they were, though. Thick as your wrists."

"Really? What did they eat?"

"Air, I suppose. Thoughts. They were my hair, Harry; they weren't meant to exist like ordinary creatures. Your hair feeds on you."

"I'll make hers like treasure," Harry said, studying the magnificent, haunting eyes again, the dangerous, irresistible mouth. "Gold, white gold, silver, buttercup, lemon. A shining, glittering swam of light. Tomorrow morning, I'll go—"

"She's coming tomorrow."

"I'll paint her in the morning then, and visit the snakes in the afternoon."

"You could," the Gorgon suggested, "take her with you. You might get a better perspective on the snakes as hair if you see them both together."

Harry grunted, struck. "Possible . . ." Then he blinked. "No. What am I saying? I can't possibly watch this devastatingly powerful creature wandering around looking at snakes in the Zoological Gardens. Something would happen."

"Like what?"

"She'd step in a puddle, get a paper stuck to her shoe, some such. She'd mispronounce the names of things, she'd want tea and a bun, or peanuts for the bears—"

"I can't see that frozen-eyed woman tossing peanuts to the bears. But what you're saying, Harry, is that she would be in danger of turning human."

"Exactly," Harry said adamantly. "I don't want her human, I want her Gorgon—"

"I bet she'd be a charming human."

Harry opened his mouth. As though one of the Medusa's snakes had streaked down quick as thought and bit him, he glimpsed the potential charms in those eyes, warming in a smile, that hair, piled carelessly on her head, tendrils about her face playing in a breeze. He clenched his fists, pushed them in front of his eyes. "No," he said fiercely. "No, no, and no. This is my master work, and nothing—" He lowered his hands as suddenly. "What on earth is that hubbub downstairs?"

There seemed to be a good deal of shouting and thumping coming up the stairwell. Mrs. Grommet's voice joined it and it resolved itself easily then, into any number of friends in every stage of revelry pushing their way upstairs to join Harry.

He threw open the door, heard their chanting as they ascended. "Where is she, Harry? We must see her. We want to see your painting, foul as it may be. We have come to kneel at the feet of your muse. Harry!"

Harry had just enough time to remove the painting from the easel and slide it carefully into the cupboard. Where, he hoped fervently, it would not also acquire a voice. He opened his study door, stepped into the the landing. Half a dozen friends, a couple of them painters, one planning a gallery, others budding poets or philosophers, or whatever was fashionable this week, reeled into one another at the sight of him. Then, they rushed the second flight of stairs. Harry glimpsed Mrs. Grommet below, flinging her hands in the air, turning hastily back to the kitchen.

"Don't you dare lock your door this time," the honey-haired, sloe-eyed Tommy Buck called. "We'll sit on your stairs and hold them hostage until you reveal her. We'll—"

"She's not here," Harry said, with great relief. "She left an hour ago."

"Then let's see your painting."

"No. It's too dreadful." He turned adroitly as they reached the landing, and locked the door behind him. "You'll laugh, and I'll be forced to become a bricklayer."

"She's in there." Tommy Buck paused to hiccup loudly, then banged upon the door. "You've hidden her."

"I have not. She's a shy, sensitive woman and you lot would cause her to turn into a deer and flee."

"Prove it."

"Prove what?"

"Prove she's not there."

"All right, I will. But I don't want you all rummaging about my studio and tossing my bad paintings out the window. You can look in and see, Tommy. The rest of you go downstairs and wait."

"No," said one of the poets, a burly young man who looked like he might have flung bricks around in an earlier life. "Open up, Harry boy. Show us all."

"No. I shall defend all with my life."

"What's that in your hand?" Tommy asked, swaying as he squinted at it.

Harry looked. "My ham sandwich."

"Ham. He has ham in there," someone said wistfully. "I'm hungry."

"Here," Harry said, tossing him the remains.

"I saw it first," Tommy said indignantly. "I'm hungrier." He paused, still swaying lithely, like a reed in a breeze. "I've got an idea."

"He has an idea."

"I'd rather have a sandwich."

"Silence! I will speak! My idea is this. We all go out to dinner— Wait— Wait—" He waved his arms, fending off protests. "Listen. If we go out to dinner, and Harry goes out to dinner with us, and then goes wherever we happen to go after that, it will prove that he hasn't got a model locked up in his studio. Won't it?"

"He could get the Grommet to unlock her," someone muttered.

"I won't speak to her," Harry promised. "And—" he dangled it. "I have the only key."

Tommy made a snatch at it. Harry tucked it out of reach. "She really has gone home," he told them. "And I think Tommy has an excellent idea. Maybe, if we hurry out, we'll catch a glimpse of her on the street."

They were quiet, staring at him, faces motionless in the stair lights.

Then, as one, they turned, clattered furiously back down the stairs. Harry followed more slowly, brushing crumbs off his shirt and rolling down his sleeves. He heard the street door fly open, voices flow down the hall and out. Someone called his name, then the sounds faded. He didn't hear the door close. He wondered if Mrs. Grommet had taken refuge in a closet until the barbarian horde had gone.

He reached the hall and nearly bumped into his Medusa, coming quickly out of the kitchen with Mrs. Grommet at her heels.

"Jo—" he exclaimed, startled.

She pulled up sharply, staring at him, just as surprised.

"Mr. Waterman," she breathed. "I thought you had left with them."

He was silent, studying her. Something was awry with her face. It seemed streaked, flushed in odd places; her cold, magnificent eyes looked puffy and reddened, oddly vulnerable. He caught his breath, appalled.

"What have you done?"

"Sorry, Mr. Waterman," she said tremulously, brushing at her eyes. "It'll be gone by morning."

"But—" Something else was happening to her face as he stared. Lines shifted. Memory imposed itself, rearranging a curve here, a hollow there. He swallowed, his throat suddenly dry, feeling as though the world he knew had vanished for an eye blink, and then returned, subtly, irrevocably altered.

"Jo," he said, feeling his heart beat. "Jo Byrd."

She said simply, "Yes."

She returned the next morning as she promised, though not without misgivings. She looked for the same apprehension in the artist's eyes, searching for his Medusa in her face while he arranged the black silk around her neck, to draw out her pallor as he said. She wasn't certain about the pallor. The face in the tiny mirror above her washstand had been more colorful than usual. Nor was she at all certain what Mr. Waterman was thinking. He was very quiet, murmuring instructions now and then. She would have described his expression as peculiar, if he had asked. He looked like someone who had swallowed a butterfly, she thought: a mixed blessing, no matter how you turned it.

She said finally, hesitantly, "Mr. Waterman. If you can't see your Medusa now for seeing me, I'll understand."

He gave his head a quick little shake, met her eyes. "As the Gor—as someone pointed out, I tell lies with my brush. Let's see how well I can do it."

"But—"

"We'll give it a try," he insisted calmly. "Shall we?"

"If you say so, sir." She subsided, prepared herself to sit as silently as usual.

But, strangely, now he seemed in a mood to talk. "I am," he said, touching white into the black around the Medusa's throat, "incredibly embarrassed that I didn't recognize you."

"I've gotten older."

"By how much? A year? I'm a painter! I've been staring at you daily. Not to mention—" His lips tightened; whatever it was, he didn't mention it.

"Yes, sir."

He looked at her again, instead of the silk. "I can't imagine what you've gone through. Or, rather, I can only try to imagine it. The child— It must have died?"

Her voice caught, but she had no tears left for that, it seemed. "Yes. He was never strong."

"Where did you go, when you vanished in the middle of my painting?"

"I went home to my mother's, in the country."

"I looked for you."

"I know. Mrs. Grommet told me."

His mouth crooked ruefully. "So she recognized you."

"The way I see it," Jo explained, "Mrs. Grommet was protecting your household. She has to know what she opens your door to. You remember what I looked like, then."

"Yes."

"She had to make decisions in her own mind about me. You were only seeing your painting. She was seeing a hungry, filthy wreck of a girl, and trying to judge all in a moment whether I would steal the silver, eat with a fork or my fingers, go mad and break all the crockery. She was looking for reasons not to be afraid to let me through the door. You just saw your dream and let me walk right in."

He ran his hand through his hair, nearly tangling the brush in it. "Makes me sound like a fool."

She thought about that, shrugged. "I don't know. How do you like your painting?"

He looked at it, his eyes going depthless, still, like water reflecting an empty sky. They were, she realized suddenly, the exact blue of the dragonflies in the stream behind her parents' cottage. She'd lie and watch them dart and light, little dancing arrows as blue as larkspur.

Mr. Waterman blinked; so did she. They both drew back a little from what they'd been examining. She recognized that expression on his face; it was how he had been looking at her until now.

"I think—" he said, still gazing at his painting, and stammering a little, "I think—I wasn't a fool, after all. I think it's at least better than anything I've done so far. Jo." He turned to her abruptly. "I have such amazing visions of your hair. Are you afraid of snakes?"

"No more or less than anything else that might bite me. But, sir," she amended warily, "surely you're not going to put them in my hair? I don't think I want to wear them."

"No, no." His thoughts veered abruptly. "I have to fix that eye before I go on. Look at me. Don't blink." He added, after a moment or two, "You can talk."

"About what?"

"Anything that won't make you cry." She felt her eyes flush at the thought; he looked stricken. "I'm sorry, Jo."

"It's just—somehow I never got around to crying before."

"Tell me something—anything you remember—that once made you happy. If there was anything," he added carefully.

"Well." The tide retreated; she gazed, dry-eyed, at her past. "When my father was alive, he kept a small flock of sheep for wool. I liked to look at them, all plump and white in their green field, watch the lambs leap for no reason except that they were alive. He'd shear them and we'd spin the wool into yarn to sell. Sometimes we'd look for madder root to dye it purple."

"We?" he asked, busy at the corner of her eye, from what she could see. "Sister?"

"My mother. I didn't have sisters. I had a little brother for a few years once, but he died."

"Oh. But you chose not to stay with your mother? To come back here instead?"

"She died, too."

"Oh. I'm sorry."

"Yes," she said softly, but without tears. "So was I. So I came back here. And you rescued me."

He looked at her, oddly surprised. "I did?"

"You did," she said huskily. "I couldn't find work, I was exhausted, I had two coppers to my name—I found my way to your street just muddling around in the dark, and then I remembered you. I slept under a tree, that night before I came to your door. I didn't have any hope, but I didn't have anything left to do. I even—I even tried to get myself arrested for breaking a street lamp, to have a place to sleep."

He was watching her, brush suspended. "When you do that—"

"What, sir?"

"Even when you only think about smiling, you change the shape of your eye. Medusa does not smile." He stopped abruptly, cast an odd glance above her head, and amended, "At least we have no recorded evidence that she smiled."

"You asked me to think about something happy."

"You didn't smile, then. It was irony, not happiness, that made you smile."

She mulled that over. "You mean trying to get into jail for a bed?"

"Yes. What happened? Did you miss the street lamp?"

"No. I hit it dead-on. But a dozen others stepped up on the spot and swore it was them that threw the stone. Someone else got my bed. So I wandered on—"

"And," he said softly, his brush moving again, "you found me."

"You found me," she whispered.

"No tears. Medusa does not cry."

She composed her face again, summoned the icy, gorgeous monster to look out of her eyes. "She does not cry."

"But," he said after a while, "she might perhaps like to come with me this afternoon to look at snakes. No blinking."

"No blinking."

"But snakes?"

"Looking at snakes," she said, suddenly aware of his own fair, tidy hair, on a nicely rounded head, his young face with its sweet, determined expression, like the little boy she had once known who chased after dragon flies along the stream bank, "would make Medusa happy."

➤ ➤ ➤

Harry stood on the ladder in his studio, detaching the Gorgon from her nail. He had gotten in late. After spending a few hours among the reptiles and other assorted creatures, he had walked Jo to her lodging house on Carvery Street. Then he had wandered aimlessly, oddly lightheaded, dropping in at studios here and there to let his friends tease him about his imaginary model, his hopeless daub of a painting so dreadful he was forced to keep it hidden behind locked doors. He laughed with them; his thoughts kept straying back to his studio, sometimes to the reptiles, none of which had done justice to his Medusa's hair.

But my brush can lie, he told himself. He had insisted on buying Jo peanuts in the zoological garden. But instead of throwing them to the animals, she had simply given them to a wiry, dirty-faced boy who had somehow wriggled his way in and was begging near the lions' den.

His elbow hit a book on top of the shelves as he maneuvered the painting down and under his arm. The book dropped with a thud that probably woke the house. He breathed a curse, trying to be as quiet as possible. The ladder rungs creaked ominously.

The Gorgon, who had been blessedly silent until then, said sharply, her mouth somewhere under his armpit, "Harry, you're not putting me back into the cupboard."

"Sh—"

"Don't shush me. Just because you don't need me anymore."

"What do you mean I don't need you?"

"I saw the way you looked at her."

"I was not aware that I looked at her in any particular way."

"Ha!"

"Sh," Harry pleaded. "Mrs. Grommet will think I'm up here entertaining lewd company."

"Thank you," the Gorgon said frostily. But once started,, she could never be silent for long, Harry knew. He felt the floor beneath his foot at last, and her curiosity got the better. "Then what are you going to do with me?"

"I just want to look at you."

He positioned a wooden chair beside the easel, propped the painting on it. Then he drew the black silk off the new Medusa. Side by side, Jo past and Jo present, he studied them: the young, terrified girl, the haunted, desperate woman. A year in the life . . . "What a life," he breathed, moved at the thought of it.

The Gorgon spoke, startling him again. "What are you looking for?"

"I wanted to see why it was I didn't recognize her. I understand a little better now. That hair—I should have known it anywhere. But the expressions are completely different. And the skin tone . . . She was at least being fed when she came to me the first time." His voice trailed away as he studied them: Persephone who had innocently eaten a few seeds and transformed herself into the doomed Medusa. He asked, suddenly curious himself, "Where do you live? I mean, where were you before you took up residence in my painting?"

"Oh, here and there," she answered vaguely.

"No, really."

"Why? Are you thinking of ways to get rid of your noisy, uncouth Gorgon?"

He thought about that, touched the Medusa on the easel. "Who inspired this out of me? No. Stay as long as you like. Stay forever. I'll introduce you to my friends. None of them have paintings that speak. They'll all be jealous of me."

"You invited me," she reminded him.

"I did."

"I go where I'm invited. Where I am invoked. When I hear my name in someone's heart, or in a painting or a poem, I exist there. The young thug Perseus cut my head off. But he didn't rid the world of me. I've stayed alive these thousands of years because I haven't been forgotten. Every time my name is invoked and my power is remembered anew, then I live again, I am empowered."

"Yes," Harry said softly, watching those full, alluring lips move, take their varying shapes on canvas in ways that he could never seem to move them in life. "I understand."

"You understand what, Harry?" the Gorgon asked so gently that he knew, beneath her raucous ways, she understood a great deal more than he had realized.

"I understand that I must go to the country again soon."

"Good idea. Take Jo with you."

"Should I? Really? She might be uncomfortable. And Grainger will try to seduce her away from me. He tries to steal everyone's models."

"That will happen sooner or later in any case, unless you are planning to cast her back into the streets once you've finished with her."

"No. I don't want to do that. I hadn't really thought ahead. About sharing her. Or painting her as someone else. Until now she was just my inspiration." He paced a step or two, stopped again in front of the paintings. Jo then. Jo now. "She's changed again," he realized. "There's yet another face. I wonder if that one will inspire another painting."

"Something," the Medusa murmured.

"Something," Harry agreed absently. "But you're right. I certainly can't put her back on the streets just so that she stays my secret. If she can get other work, she should. If I decide I don't—"

"Harry," the Gorgon interrupted. "One thing at a time. Why don't you just ask her if she'd like to come to the country with you and be introduced to other painters? She'll either say yes or she'll say no. In either case, you can take it from there."

Harry smiled. "That seems too simple."

"And find her something nice to wear. She looks like a bedpost in that old dress. Went out of style forty years ago, at least. I may not have a clue about what to do with my hair, but I always did have an eye for fashion. Though of course, things were incredibly boring in my day, comparatively speaking. Especially the shoes! You wouldn't believe—"

"Good night," Harry said, yawning, and draped the black silk over her. "See you in the morning."

➤ ➤ ➤

Jo sat in the McAlisters' garden, sipping tea. She felt very strange, as though she had wandered into a painting of a bright, sunny world strewn with windblown petals, where everyone laughed easily, plump children ran in and out of the ancient cottage, a woman, still as a statue at the other side of the garden, was being painted into yet another painting. Some guests had gathered, Harry among them, to watch Alex McAlister work. Jo heard the harsh, eager voice of the painter, talking about mosaics in some foreign country, while he spun a dark, rippling thundercloud of his wife's hair with his brush. Aurora McAlister, a windblown Venus, it looked like, her head bowed slightly under long, heavy hair, seemed to be absorbed in her own thoughts; her husband and guests might have been speaking the language of another world.

Someone rustled into the wicker chair next to Jo. She looked up. People had wandered up to her and spoken and wandered off again all afternoon; she was struggling hopelessly with all the names.

"Holly," this one said helpfully, "Holly Millidge." She was a pretty, frothy young woman with very shrewd eyes. She waved a plate of little sandwiches under Jo's nose; Jo took one hesitantly.

"They're all right. Just cucumber, nothing nasty." She set the plate back on the table. "So you're Harry's secret model. We've all been wondering."

"I didn't know I was a secret," Jo said, surprised.

"I can see why."

"Why what?"

"Why he tried to keep you secret. Tommy Buck said he'd been twice to Harry's studio trying to see you, and Harry locked the door on him."

Jo remembered the clamoring voices, the thunder up the stairs. "Why," she asked warily, "did he want to see me that badly?"

"To see if he should paint you, of course." Holly was silent a little, still smiling, studying Jo. "They're noisy, that lot. But they're good-hearted. You don't have to be afraid of them."

"I'm used to being afraid," Jo said helplessly. "I'm not used to this."

"It's not entirely what you think," Holly said obscurely, and laughed at herself. "What am I trying to say? You're not seeing what you think you see."

"Painters don't, do they?"

"Not always, no." She bit into a strawberry, watching the scene on the other side of the garden. "They'd see how pretty you are and how wonderful and mysterious the expression is in your eyes. But they wouldn't have any idea how that expression got there. Or the expression, for instance, in Aurora's eyes."

Jo looked at the still, dreaming face. "She's very beautiful."

"She is." Holly bit into another strawberry. "Her father worked in the stables at an inn on Crowdy Street. Aurora was cleaning rooms for the establishment when Alex met her. Barefoot, with her hair full of lice—"

A sudden bubble of laughter escaped Jo; she put her hands over her mouth. "Her, too?"

"And whatever her name was then, it was most certainly not Aurora. Most of us have a skewed past. As well as a skewed present." She gave a sigh, leaned back in her chair. "Except for me; I have no secrets. No interesting ones, at any rate. When they put me in their paintings, I'm the one carrying the heartless bride's train, or one of the shocked guests who finds the thwarted lover's body in the fish pond."

Jo, feeling less estranged from her surroundings, took another glance around the garden. Seen that way, if the goddess had been a chambermaid, then everyone might be anyone, and no telling what anybody knew or didn't know about life. Except for Harry, she thought. And then she glimpsed the expression on his face, and had to amend even that notion.

Nothing, apparently, was plain as day, not even Harry. While the other guests were laughing and chatting, Alex's voice running cheerfully over them all, Harry was standing very quietly among them, his eyes on the tall, dark goddess. Jo drew a breath, feeling an odd little hollow where her certainty had been.

"Harry," she said, hardly realizing she'd spoken aloud.

Holly nodded. "Oh, yes, Harry. And John Grainger, and half the painters in the McAlister constellation, including one or two of the women. Dreamers, all of them, in love with what they think they see instead of what they see."

"John Grainger. The one with the wild hair and rumbly voice and the black, black eyes?"

"Yes, that's him."

"He talked to me earlier."

"Everyone talked to you earlier," Holly said lightly. "I was watching. They're making their plans for you, don't you fret."

"I didn't like him," Jo said. "He has a way of putting his hand on you as though it's supposed to mean something to you. It made me uncomfortable."

Holly laughed. "Then he'll have to watch his manners with you. He's a fine painter, though, and very generous; if you let him paint you, you'll be noticed. Others will find you, if you want." She lifted her bright face to greet a lovely, red-haired woman with somber green eyes. "Nan! Have you met Harry's painting yet? Jo Byrd. Nan Grainger."

"Jo Byrd. Why do I know that name?" Nan eased herself into a chair, gazing at Jo. "Harry must have talked about you. But that was some time ago. Oh." She gave a little start, her pale skin flushing slightly. "I remember now."

"I ran away."

"Yes. In the middle of his Persephone. He was bereft."

"Yes, well," Jo said, her mouth quirked, for everyone seemed to know everything anyway. "So was I."

Nan was silent, gazing at her without smiling. What have I said? Jo wondered, and then saw what lay beneath Nan's hands clasped gently over her belly.

Holly interrupted Nan's silence adroitly, with some droll story about her husband. Jo sighed noiselessly, her eyes going back to the group around the goddess. John Grainger stood closest to Aurora, she saw. They did not look at one another. But now and then the trailing green silk around her bare feet, raised by a teasing wind, flowed toward him to touch his shoe. He would glance down at that flickering green touching him, and his laugh would ring across the garden.

Secrets, she thought. If you look at this one way, there's a group of cheerful people standing together on a sunny afternoon in a garden. That's one painting. If you look at them with a different eye, there's the story within the painting . . . She looked at Harry again, wanting the uncomplicated friend she thought she knew, who got excited over the golden snakes in the reptile house, and who made her go shopping with Mrs. Grommet for a dress, he said, that didn't look as if his grandmother had slept in it.

Unexpectedly, as though he'd felt her thoughts flow his direction, against the wind, he was looking back at her.

"What beautiful hair you have," Nan said, watching the white-gold ripple over Jo's shoulders. "I'd love to paint it. Holly, I can't imagine what you find so amusing." But her green eyes were gathering warmth, despite the silk fluttering over her husband's shoe, despite her fears and private sorrows; for a moment she was just a woman smiling in the light. "Jo, have you ever tried to draw? You might try it sometime. I forget myself when I do; it makes me very tranquil."

I might try it, Jo thought, after I lose this feeling that I've just fallen off the moon.

But she didn't say that, she said something else, and then there was another cup of tea in her hand, and a willowy young man with wayward locks the color of honeycomb kneeling in the grass at her feet, who introduced himself as Tommy Buck . . .

❧ ❧ ❧

Harry watched Tommy kneel beside Jo's chair. Their two faces seemed to reflect one another's wild beauty, and he thought dispassionately: I would like to paint them both together. Then, he felt a sharp flash of annoyance at Tommy, who could barely paint his feet, dreaming of capturing that barely human face of Jo's with his brush.

His attention drifted. He watched the green silk touch Grainger's shoe, withdraw, flutter toward him again. Seemingly oblivious, Aurora watched the distant horizon; seemingly oblivious, her husband orated in his hoarse, exuberant crow's voice about the architectural history of the arch. Harry thought about Aurora's long, graceful hands, about her mouth. So silent, it looked now; he had gotten used to it speaking. He wondered if he could ever make this mouth speak.

And then she moved; the little group was breaking up around McAlister. "Too sober," he proclaimed them all. "Much too sober." Lightly he touched his wife, to draw her with him toward the cottage. As lightly, she slipped from his fingers, stayed behind to find her shoes under the rose vines. Grainger glanced at his wife across the garden, then at Aurora, then at his wife again. In that moment of his indecision, Aurora put her hand out to steady herself on Harry's arm as she put on her shoes.

"She's lovely, Harry," he heard her say through the blood drumming in his ears. "I like her. Where did you find her?"

"In the street," he stammered. "Both times. She—she has been through hard times."

"I know." She straightened, shod, but didn't drop her hand. Behind her, Grainger drifted away. Her voice, deep and slow and sweet, riveted Harry. "I know those times. I hear them in her speech, I see them in her eyes. I know those streets."

"Surely not—"

She smiled very faintly. "Harry, I grew up helping my father shovel out the stables until I was old enough to clean up after humans. Didn't you know that? I thought everybody—"

"But the way you speak," Harry said bewilderedly. "Your poise and manners—"

"A retired governess. Alex hired her to teach me. Beyond that I have my own good sense and some skills that Alex finds interesting. He likes my company."

"He adores you."

"He thinks he does. He adores the woman he paints. Not the Livvie that I am."

"Livvie?"

Her mouth crooked wryly; he saw her rare, brief smile. "Olive. That's my real name. Livvie, they called me until I was seventeen and Alex looked at me and saw painting after painting . . . He said I was the dawn of his inspiration. So Olive became Aurora."

"Why," he asked her, his voice finally steady, "are you telling me this?"

"Because I've often thought I'd like to talk to you. That I might like having you as a friend, to tell things to. But for the longest time you could only see me the way Alex sees me. But then I saw how you looked at Jo today, knowing all you know about her. So I thought maybe, if I explained a thing or two to you, you might look at me as a friend."

She waited, the dark-eyed goddess who had pitched horse shit out of stables, and whose name was Livvie. Mute with wonder, he could only stare at her. Then his face spoke, breaking into a rueful smile.

"I hope you can forgive my foolishness," he said softly. "It can't have been very helpful."

"I do get lonely," she confessed, "on my pedestal. Come, let's have some tea with Jo, and rescue her from Tommy Buck. He's not good enough for her."

"Will you come some day and see if I'm good enough to paint her? I would value your opinion very much."

"Yes, I will," she promised, and tucked her long sylph's hand into the crook of his arm, making him reel dizzily for a step. He found his balance somewhere in Jo's eyes as she watched them come to her.

Much later, he reeled back into his studio, stupefied with impressions. Jo had promised, sometime before he left her at her door, to sit for the unfinished Persephone as well. So he would see her daily until—until he dreamed up something else. Or maybe, he thought, he would do what Odysseus's Penelope had done to get what she wanted: weave by day, unweave by night. He pulled the black silk off Persephone's head, saw the lovely, wine-red mouth and smiled, remembering the real one speaking, smiling its faint sphinx's smile, saying things he never dreamed would come out of it. But he no longer needed to dream, and he did not want Jo to see that mouth on her own face and wonder.

He was wiping it away carefully with cloth and turpentine when he remembered the Gorgon.

Horrified, he dropped the cloth. He had erased her entirely, without even thinking. What she must be trying to say, he could not imagine. And then he realized that the voluble Gorgon, who had talked her way out of his cupboard and into his life, had said not a word, nothing at all, to rescue herself.

Perhaps, he thought, she had nothing left to say. Perhaps she had already gone . . .

He picked up the cloth, gazing at the clean, empty bit of canvas where Persephone's mouth would finally appear. He heard the Gorgon's voice in his head, having the last word as usual.

If you need me, Harry, you know how to find me.

He left them side by side, his unfinished faces, and went to bed, where he would have finished them, except that he could not keep Persephone from smiling in his dreams.

THE FEAR GUN

by Judith Berman

An anthropologist, writer, and critic, Judith Berman published her first story, "The Year of Storms," in 1995, but really came to prominence when her story "The Window" was short-listed for the Theodore Sturgeon Award in 1999. Her short fiction, which has appeared in Asimov's, Realms of Fantasy, *and* Black Gate *has been collected in the chapbook* Lord Stink and Other Stories. *An accomplished critic, Berman won the 2002 Pioneer Award for her critical essay "Science Fiction Without the Future." Her first novel,* Bear Daughter, *will be published by Ace later this year.*

1

THE DAWN FOUND Harvey Gundersen on the deck of his house, as it had nearly every morning since the eetee ship had crashed on Cortez Mountain. There he stood a nightly watch for the fear storms. On this last watch, though, the eetees had worn him out— an incursion at the Carlson's farm *and* the lone raider at his own well, where the black sky had rained pure terror—and fatigue had overcome him just as the sky began to lighten. When Susan shook him awake, he jerked upright in his lawn chair, heart a-gallop.

She gripped red plastic in her hand. For an instant, Harvey was sure that his worst suspicions had proved true, and his wife had learned how to bring on the bad weather. But even as he swung up his shotgun, finger on the trigger, he saw that what Susan pointed at him was not a weather-maker, not even an eetee gun about to blast him to splat, but the receiver of their landline phone. The cord trailed behind her.

Susan's gaze riveted on the shotgun. Harvey took a deep

breath and lowered the barrel. Only then did Susan say, flatly, "Your brother's calling."

"What does *he* want?"

She shrugged, two shades too casual. Harvey knew Susan and Ben plotted about him in secret. His pulse still racing, he carried the phone into the house and slid the glass door closed so Susan could not overhear. He stood where he could keep his eye on both Susan and the eetee-infested mountains.

As he slurped last night's Mormon tea from his thermos, liquid spilled onto the arm of his coat. Strange that his hands never shook while he held a gun.

"Hello, Ben," he said into the receiver.

"Nice work last night, Harve," said Ben. "Good spotting. You saved some lives there, buddy."

Although Harvey knew better than to trust his brother's sincerity, he could not repress a surge of pride. "I watch the weather, Ben. I can see it coming five miles off. And I look for the coyotes. They track the eetees. They keep a *watch* on them. The coyotes—"

"Sure, Harve," Ben said. "Sure. I've never doubted it. You're the best spotter we have."

"Well, thanks, Ben." Harvey seized the moment to describe how, two days ago, the coyotes had used telepathy to trick a vanload of eetees over the edge of the road to their deaths. As long as Ben was de facto dictator of Lewis County, for everyone's good Harvey had to *try* to warn him what was happening out there in the parched mountains.

But Ben cut him off before he'd even reached the part about the eetee heads. "Harvey, Harvey, you sound pretty stressed. What about you come in and let Dr. King give you something for your jitters? You tell me all the time how jittery you get, keeping watch day and night. I'll tell you honestly I'm worried, Harve. Come in before you mistake Susan for an eetee, or do something else we'll all regret."

What a lying fuck Ben was. Ben just wanted Dr. King to trank him stupid with Ativan. If Ben were truly worried, he wouldn't force Harvey and Susan to stay out here in this horribly vulnerable spot, where Harvey was exposed to bad weather two or three times a week. *That* was what made him so jittery. But it was always Sorry, Harve, you can't expect anyone in town to just *give* you food or gasoline or Clorox, or repair your phone line when the eetees cut it, not when supplies are dwindling by the day. We all have to contribute to the defense of Lewisville. Manning your observation post—the closest we have now to the ship—is the contribution we need from *you.*

What Ben really wanted was for the eetees to rid him of his troublemaker brother. And on the day the weather finally killed Harvey, Ben would send a whole platoon of deputies out to De Soto Hill to take over Harvey's house and deck. Ben would equip *them* with the eetee weapons and tools he kept confiscating from Harvey. Can't hoard these, Harve, my men need them. *Lewisville* needs 'em.

Ben's invitation to visit Dr. King, though: Harvey couldn't afford to pass that up. Although the timing of the offer was a little too perfect. . . .

"Ben, I'd rather have a couple of deputies to spell me than a pass for a doctor visit. What about it?"

"You know how short I am of manpower." Ben sighed. "I'll work on it, but in the meantime why don't you come on in?"

"Okay," Harvey said. "Okay, Ben, I'll stop by Dr. King's. If I can get Susan to stand watch for me. You know how she is these days. I don't think it's a good idea to leave the observation post that long, do you? How can you be *sure* eetees won't come in daytime?"

There was a moment of silence at the other end. Then Ben said goodbye and hung up.

Harvey swallowed a few more gulps of Mormon tea, feeling the ephedrine buzz now, and returned outside for recon. First he checked the weather. No fear-clouds on the horizon that he could detect. But lingering jumpiness from last night's raid, and the scare Susan had given him on waking, might obscure an approaching front.

His video monitors showed him the view toward Lewisville, from the north and front side of the house. At this distance the town was a tiny life raft of houses, trees and grain elevators adrift on the rolling sea of golden wheat. The deck itself gave him a

270-degree view west, south and east: over the highway and the sweep of fields below De Soto Hill, and of course toward the pine-forested mountains and that immense wreck.

Harvey cast around for the Nikons, only to discover that Susan had usurped his most powerful binoculars and was gazing through them toward the mountains. Anger stirring in him, he picked up the little Minoltas. Through *them,* the world looked quiet enough. The only movement was a hawk floating across the immaculate blue sky. But Harvey never trusted the quiet. The eetees might avoid the desiccating heat of daytime, but they were always stirring around up there. Plotting the next raid. And the coyotes—

If only he could spy into those mountains as easily as the eetees' fear-storms roared into his own head.

The nape of Harvey's neck began to twitch. "Do you *see* something?" he demanded. "Are the coyotes—"

"I'm looking for Fred," Susan said coldly, without lowering the binoculars.

"Fred is gone." Now the anger boiled in Harvey's gut. "You should be watching for eetees, not pining after your lost dog."

"*Fuck* your eetees! Fred is out there somewhere. He wouldn't leave us and never come back!"

Her voice had turned flat and uncompromising, and Harvey knew one of her rages was coming on. But he could not rein in his own fury.

"If you care so much," he said, "*why did you let him loose?*"

Susan finally turned to stare at Harvey. She was breathing hard. "*I* didn't let Fred out."

"Oh, so the *coyotes* unbuckled his collar?"

Deep red suffused Susan's face. "Fuck you," she screamed, "and fuck your coyotes!" She slammed the binoculars onto the deck, she reached toward the rifle—

Harvey grabbed his shotgun and aimed. How *stupid* to leave his rifle propped against the railing, out of reach—

Susan threw the rifle onto the deck, and then the tray holding the remains of his midnight snack; she kicked over his lawn chair and the tripod for his rifle, and upended the box of shotgun cartridges he'd been packing with rock salt. "Shoot me, Harvey!"

she screamed. "*Shoot me!* I *know* you want to!"

Harvey snatched up his rifle but did not shoot. At last Susan stopped her rampage. She stared with fierce hatred through her tangled, greasy hair, panting. "*I didn't let Fred out,* you moron. You did." Then she flung herself in her own lawn chair and picked up a tattered and yellowing issue of last summer's *Lewisville Tribune.*

The shakes took Harvey. While he waited for the waves of fever cold to recede, he gritted his teeth and said to her, "I'm going to do my rounds now. Just keep an eye out, okay, Susan? That's all I ask? Watch for *eetees,* who want to kill us and steal our water, and not for your *dead dog?*"

When she did not answer, he heaved open the glass door again and stalked into the house. Susan might as well be using a weather-maker, the way she kept terrifying him. Harvey was jumpy enough today. He just had been lucky that last night's raider had probably stolen its weather-maker from a higher-ranking eetee and wasn't skilled in its use. And by now Harvey had learned to keep his distance and rely on his rifle and sniper's nightscope. So the lightning strike of blind terror had fallen short. Harvey had caught only the peripheral shockwave—although that that had been horrible enough.

Weather-maker was what Harvey called the weapon. Other people called it a fear gun. Dr. King and Joe Hansen, putting their heads together, had suggested that the gun produced (as quoted in a bulletin distributed by the sheriff's office) "wireless stimulation of the amygdala, mimicking the neurochemical signature of paralytic terror." But no one had yet been able to figure out the insides of those whorled red pendants, and no one could do with them what the eetees did, not even Harvey, who was so hypersensitive from repeated exposure that the weapon affected him even when he wasn't its target. Even when they weren't being used. (When Dr. King told him that human researchers had for years been able to produce a similar if weaker effect with a simple electrode, Harvey had, next time he was alone, checked his scalp for unfamiliar scar tissue. But if Susan or Ben had had such an electrode implanted, they had also concealed the traces well.)

Harvey unbolted the connecting door that led from the kitchen into the garage. As angry as Susan's abdication of responsibility made him, this was the opportunity he needed. She would read and reread her *Tribune* for hours, trying to pretend that the entire last year hadn't happened.

In the garage he quickly donned his rubber gloves and plastic rain coat. He raised the lid of the big chest freezer, long emptied of anything edible, and heaved out the large tarpaulin-wrapped bundle, humping it into the pickup bed. The raider's corpse hadn't frozen yet; Harvey just hoped it had chilled sufficiently to last until he reached Dr. King.

Then he stripped off his protective gear and gave it a swift rinse with Clorox in the utility sink. On the cement floor beside the sink, still at the end of its chain, lay Fred's unbuckled collar of blue nylon webbing—a testament to Susan's lies.

Harvey fetched last night's newly scavenged eetee gun from the wheel well of his pickup, where he hoped this time to keep it hidden from Susan and Ben. Next, after checking the yard through the front door peephole, he bore the ladder outside to begin his daily inspection of the video cameras, the locks and chains, the plywood boarding up their windows, the eetee cell that powered the house (one of the few perks Ben allowed them).

It hurt Harvey to think about Fred, happy Fred, the only one of them unchanged since the days before the eetees had come to Earth. When he and Susan had been happy, too, in their dream house with the panoramic view atop De Soto Hill. Fred was just one dumb, happy golden retriever with no notion of the dangers out there in the mountains. More likely the coyotes had gotten Fred than the eetees—not that it made any difference.

Sweating, his scalp twitching, Harvey made his way downhill through dry grass and buzzing grasshoppers. He righted the black power cell (how he'd had to argue with Ben to keep two), slipped on a spare adapter to reconnect the cell to his well pump, and refilled the salt-loaded booby traps the raider had sprung. All the while he searched the trampled ground for the raider's missing weather-maker, but still without success. Had the coyotes taken it? There couldn't have been bad weather without a weather-maker. . . .

Finally he was climbing the hill again, eager to return to his deck. On his deck he was king—at least, on the deck he had a chance of seeing death before it peered at *him* with its yellow, slime-covered eyeball.

He had nearly reached the house when a new sound stopped him in his tracks. A shape thrashed through the tall thistles along the driveway. Adrenaline and ephedrine together surged in Harvey's veins, making his hands tremble like grass in the breeze.

But even as he pulled the eetee gun from his waistband and clutched at his rifle with his other hand, he saw that what rustled onto the driveway was not an eetee. It was not even a demented coyote come to grin mockingly at him and then zigzag wildly away into the fields, tongue flapping, while Harvey tried in vain to ventilate its diseased hide.

"Fred!" Harvey whispered in horror. Fred dropped what he was carrying and wagged his tail.

Dust, burrs and thistledown clung to Fred's copper-colored rump, and he smelled like rotten raw chicken. As he approached Harvey, his tail-wagging increased in frequency and amplitude until his entire hind end swung rapidly from side to side. Fred tried to nose Harvey's hand, but Harvey shoved him away with the point of the rifle.

The swellings and bare patches in the fur were unmistakable. The biggest swelling rose at the base of Fred's skull.

Just like the coyotes.

Eetee cancer, Harvey called it. Ben said that was just more of Harvey's paranoia. No other spotters had seen it.

But *their* posts—the ones still manned, anyway—lay miles further from the shipwreck.

Harvey had only one choice. It was pure self-defense.

Fred lay down and smacked his tail on the ground. His eyes pleaded as if he knew what Harvey intended. But Harvey remembered the coyotes and their gleeful eetee hunts, and he hardened his thoughts as if pummeled by stormy weather. He slipped off the safety. His finger tightened on the trigger—

Footsteps rasped behind him. He spun and found himself staring into the short, ugly red bore of another eetee gun.

"Don't you *dare* shoot Fred, you fuck," Susan hissed.

Oh, Harvey, stupid, *stupid*—the video monitors on the deck—

Ben must have given her a gun, *knowing* she would someday use it—

They stood there aiming at each other. Harvey could see in her face that this time she really would do it. She was going to splatter him over Fred, and Ben would get his way at last.

The blazing July sun heated his skull like a roast in an oven. Susan's gun did not waver. Harvey willed himself to breathe.

Fred thwacked his tail another couple of times, then pawed playfully at Harvey's foot. A lump pushed up suddenly in Harvey's throat and he had to blink several times to clear his vision. In a thick voice he said, "Look at Fred, Susan! He's sick! You don't want *us* to catch it, do you? You don't want *us* to get all freaky like the coyotes, do you?"

"You," Susan said, "already have."

Bleak inspiration came to Harvey. He forced himself to drop his rifle and eetee gun, slip the shotgun from his shoulder to the ground, raise his hands. "I could take Fred to Dr. King. Maybe she would look at him."

"She's not a vet and he's not sick."

"Yes, he is! Susan, look at those tumors!"

Her gaze did flick toward Fred, growing the slightest bit uncertain. "Abscesses."

"Then he needs to have them cleaned. At least."

Something broke in Susan then. Her lip trembled. She blinked. She looked at Fred. Fred crawled toward her and wagged his tail some more. Tears began to roll down Susan's cheeks. Suddenly, unexpectedly, a wave of sympathy rushed through Harvey. He had loved Fred, too.

"What do we have," Susan said in despair, "what do we have that *she* would take in trade?"

And there it was: the first acknowledgement in months that their world had changed forever. Harvey's hands were shaking again, but he managed to gesture at the garage. Susan looked at him askance, then, gun still trained on Harvey, backed toward it. Harvey followed, though he hated leaving his guns behind. Fred lay beside them, thumping his tail.

When Susan pulled back the tarpaulin in his pickup bed, she gasped and jerked her hand back as if bitten. "Harvey, Ben will *kill* you! And me, too, you asshole!" Which was probably not just a figure of speech.

Wiping at her tears with a filthy hand, she added, "Promise me, *promise me,* Harvey, that you aren't going to hurt Fred. That you won't let *her* hurt him."

"I won't," Harvey lied, trying again to swallow the lump in his throat. "Promise *me* that while I'm gone, you'll keep watch?"

Susan said nothing, but this time Harvey felt as if she might actually do it. Donning his rain coat and gloves and now rubber waders as well, Harvey took Fred's collar out into the yard to buckle it around the dog's neck. As he urged Fred into the back of the pickup and chained him there, Fred tried to lick him in the face. Up close, the stench of carrion was enough to make Harvey gag.

Two presents for Dr. King, just sitting in the back of his pickup for anyone to discover. What risks he was taking today! Harvey had survived this long by trusting his fears and keeping a close eye on the weather. By being infinitely careful. Today he was throwing all caution to the winds.

But he couldn't afford to nod off the way he had this morning. He needed Dr. King's little pills. And he couldn't let Susan keep Fred *here.*

Harvey wondered whether on his return he should just shoot Susan before she learned he'd had Fred put down. She *would* try to kill him again when she found out.

He didn't want to shoot her.

Maybe, he thought, looking at the happily panting Fred, just maybe he would turn out to be wrong about Fred's tumors. Maybe Dr. King would tell him they weren't contagious. The coyotes' fur had grown back, after all, and most of the swellings had vanished.

Or maybe that notion was just Fred trying, the way the coyotes did, to control Harvey's thoughts.

One last task before departing: Harvey picked up the thing Fred had brought home. He dropped it in his Weber. Up close, the lump of rotting eetee flesh looked like raw hamburger, had the consistency of custard, and smelled like the bottom of a Dumpster. Golden retrievers had such delicate mouths; Fred hadn't left so much as a tooth mark in it.

Sweltering in his raincoat and waders, Harvey poured on the gasoline provided by the sheriff's office. As he dropped in the match, and flames sheeted up from the charcoal bed, Fred began to bark in agitation. So he did not hear Susan's shouts until she rushed up to him waving the Nikons. "Look, Harvey! Look!"

He dropped the lid on the grill to char Fred's little present to a cinder. Then he pulled off his befouled rubber gloves, took the binocs and peered in the direction she pointed.

The highway had been dust-blown and empty for a year. Now, vehicles climbed over a rise three miles away, popping into view one after the other like an endless chain of ants: trucks, fuel tankers, Humvees and Bradleys carrying helmeted men and women. The convoy ground steadily along, heading toward Lewisville.

Susan said, almost sobbing, "It's the Army. Oh, God, Harvey, they've come to save us at last."

"Save us?" Harvey said. "*What* Army?"

2

Colonel Jason Fikes could see right away that something was fishy about the town. Since the liberation of Earth he had been traveling what was left of America—the devastated cities, the suburban wastelands dotted with grim encampments of refugees, the endless reaches of fallow farmland. The trip from Spokane, chasing the rumor of another downed ship, had been no different. They had passed mile after mile of fields grown up into weeds. At scattered houses and small towns, women stooped in gardens and men, shotguns in hand, sullenly eyed the convoy. Or sometimes they ran after the convoy, begging for gasoline, for medicine, for food, for rescue.

The locals' plight ought to have grown more desperate the closer he got to the mountains and the starship. Fikes had seen the classified reports from Yosemite: starving refugees reduced to eating eetees, then each other.

But when the convoy came over a rise and Lewisville itself came into view, everything changed. Weeds gave way to neat furrows of golden wheat. Cattle grazed along the streamside meadows. And in the town itself, healthy children clustered in front of well-kept houses, staring at the convoy until adults rushed to herd them inside. Yes, most of the lawns had been dug into gardens, and only a handful of vehicles seemed to be working, and the grass in front of the county courthouse was dry and yellow now; but it had been *mowed*.

You could suppose they had carefully rationed supplies since the war, that they had their own hydro dam or windmill farm. Or you could glance eastward to that mile-long wreck atop the ridge, and you could draw another conclusion.

"They've been scavenging," said young Lieutenant Briggs beside him, eager as a preacher pouncing upon evidence of fornication. "We'll have to search house-to-house."

Briggs had not seen the Yosemite reports and did not yet know the enormity of their orders. Fikes nodded wearily. "They'll try to hide as much as they can."

During the approach to Lewisville he had spotted a feral cat crouched in the roadside weeds, a pair of crows pecking at a dead owl. But no eetees had showed themselves. On this brilliant summer morning, the distant shipwreck looked no more menacing than a junked car. In Fikes' experience, though, the eetees didn't surrender and they didn't admit defeat. If even a single one had survived, sooner or later it would test his soldiers. Still, they would have to wait on more urgent tasks.

Fikes gave the order to halt in front of the courthouse. There waited a knot of local men bedecked with an arsenal of rifles, shotguns, and semi-automatic small arms. Neatly dressed and clean-shaven, they looked like Norman Rockwell banditos who'd just staged their own revolution.

Or rather, Norman Rockwell meets the Sci-Fi Channel: half of them bore red splatterguns. Eetee weapons. That would make Briggs happy. A weight descended onto Fikes' shoulders.

As Fikes climbed out of his Humvee, one of the locals stepped forward. This was a lean man in a sheriff's khaki uniform and badge, with cowboy boots, a straw cowboy hat and mirror shades to complete the ensemble. The only weapon the sheriff carried in plain view was a holstered .45.

"Howdy, folks," he drawled. "Welcome to Lewisville. I'm Ben Gundersen, Lewis County sheriff."

Fikes held out his hand. "Colonel Fikes," he said. "U.S. Army."

Sheriff Gundersen put out his own hand, and the two of them shook. "What brings you fellows to Lewisville?"

Under the circumstances, the question was an odd one. Fikes said, "Your community is in proximity to a downed enemy vessel, Mr. Gundersen. Assessing that threat and mounting an appropriate response is our immediate priority. But our long-term mission is to restore services and connect you to the outside world again."

"No offense," said the sheriff, "but with all the satellites gone, we haven't heard much news since last summer. Who's the U.S. Army taking orders from these days?"

"The president has installed a Provisional Congress until new elections can be held," Fikes said. "Meanwhile, the Army is authorized under the Public Safety Act to take charge here."

"You're talking about the U.S. president. The U.S. Congress."

"That's right," said Fikes.

One of the other banditos called out, smirking, "Didn't they nuke Washington? I thought that was one good thing come out of all this."

"Yes," Fikes said. "Washington was destroyed. Now, may I ask if you have spotted survivors from the wreck? Has your town come under attack?"

"Survivors?" Gundersen tipped his hat back and scratched his forehead. "Well, now. We shot us a few last winter. They come down near town and found we weren't easy pickings. If there're any of 'em left, they pretty much leave us alone. They'd be camped out in the mountains, I guess."

"Have you seen enemy aircraft at all? Any other vehicles?"

"I guess most of their fighters crashed with the ship," Gundersen said. "Lost their guidance systems or something. Haven't seen any recently, anyway."

"But you think they still have some?"

The sheriff shrugged, inscrutable behind mirror shades. "Could be."

Since his childhood in Baltimore, Fikes had learned there were large swaths of the U.S. where well-scrubbed white people said "gosh," "shucks" and "you bet" without irony. But this sheriff wasn't just a folksy good ol' boy.

He was plain bullshitting.

Fikes had already noted that Gundersen hadn't addressed him as "sir" or "colonel," and that the pole on the courthouse lawn bore no flag.

Reluctant to take the inevitable next step, Fikes bent to read the plaque on a nearby statue of buckskin-clad men. *Explorers Meriwether Lewis and William Clark, openers of the American West, passed through Lewis County on October 3, 1806.*

If the sheriff and his gang had been just your *posse comitatus* militia types hoping to secede from the federal government in its time of weakness, Fikes' task would have been simple. Sooner or later he'd have won over the townsfolk with liberal bribes of booze, chocolate, condoms, antibiotics, disposable diapers, toilet paper. The sheriff he would have defanged first of all; in Fikes' experience, those with a taste for power were easily seduced by another helping of the same.

But the solution to the problem this town presented would not be so easy to accomplish.

Not that Fikes' orders weren't clear or that he shrank from enforcing them. From what he had read in the Yosemite reports, from the panic still electrifying headquarters in Colorado, the rule he must now impose could not be too draconian. It was up to him, he had been told, to ensure that nothing like the Yosemite massacres ever became necessary again.

Fikes knew, however, that he could end up as lost in a repeat of Yosemite as that hapless colonel had been. In the slaughter at Upper Pines, the Yosemite rebels had demonstrated unequivocally that human beings could wield that most dreaded of eetee weapons, the handarm of the eetee elite, the *fearmonger*. The Army, on the other hand, had never learned how to operate the weapon—had no defense against it. The rebels who had understood the weapon had all been killed. Army scientists, such as they were now, had offered only useless speculation: perhaps the ordinary silent communication of eetees was a form of telepathy; perhaps eetees operated their terrible weapon, too, with some kind of thought wave.

No one understood how eetees used the guns. How could *he* anticipate by what means human beings would acquire the skill?

But he had to anticipate it. He had to prevent it. If possible, he had to acquire the power for the Army.

At least his first items of business were clear: separating the townspeople from their eetee toys, disrupting their lines of communication, bringing them firmly under Army control.

Fikes straightened. "Mr. Gundersen, may I ask how you dispose of enemy remains?"

He thought he had pegged Gundersen, but the pride that lit up the sheriff's face surprised him. "We're real strict about that, colonel. I'll show you our health ordinances. Can't risk some kind of strange disease, I tell people. We built a special crematorium to incinerate the bodies. We use bleach to clean up anything we take from them." He nodded toward a splattergun in the waistband of one of his deputies. "We could use more Clorox, now that you mention it."

Fikes nodded. "That's all very well, Mr. Gundersen, but our scientists can't yet say what potential disease vectors would look like, how they might spread, or how they could be destroyed. I must stress that anyone in your town who's had contact with the enemy, living or dead, is required to report to us. Any items of wreckage that people have picked up *must* be turned over. That includes your weapons, I regret to say. The Army will assume the burden of protecting the town from this point onward. I have strict orders on this matter. And I do have the authority to search every house. It's a vital matter of public health."

The sheriff opened his mouth to reply. Before he could speak, Fikes said, "After you hand over your splatterguns, I believe I'd like to start by taking a look at those pickup trucks over there. Is it possible you're still running them on gasoline?"

3

The Army had kept Reggie Forrester awake all the first night with the roar of tanks and trucks and the stink of diesel exhaust, which over the last year had become unfamiliar and offensive. In the morning, he dragged himself two blocks over to the highway and discovered that, just as he'd feared, the soldiers had moved into his warehouses. Armed sentries already surrounded them. "Move along, sir," the sentries said. Chasing him—the mayor!— off his own property. Probably Ben had suggested the location, stone bastard that he was.

Reggie headed out to learn what else was befalling his town. His dismay only compounded. Searches and detentions had started before breakfast. "Quarantine," the Army called it, but they did not name the disease they feared.

From Bob Fisher's distraught wife, Reggie learned that soldiers had "quarantined" Bob, stolid city engineer, when he'd showed up for work. And they had abruptly confiscated the networked eetee power cells that since last winter had supplied the town with electricity and pumped its artesian wells. Municipal power shut off in mid-morning, and tap water would cease flowing once the water tower emptied.

They hadn't consulted Reggie or anyone else at City Hall, or warned the townspeople what was coming.

From Estelle Gordon, administrative secretary at the community college, Reggie heard that the Army was cleaning out Joe Hansen's lab. Everyone brought their salvage to Joe, and it sat around while he and his students figured out what it was supposed to do. That morning the Army confiscated all of it, and all of Joe's notes, and they hauled away Joe, too. But so far as Estelle had been able to determine, they hadn't taken Joe to the so-called "quarantine facility" in the junior high school. No one knew where Joe was now.

Joe's students protested his detention. Angry townspeople joined them, demanding restoration of water and power. Shockingly, the Army tear-gassed them and hauled the lot off to quarantine.

By afternoon, when Reggie went to lodge an official protest with Colonel Fikes, unease had rooted deep in his belly. He told himself, though, that if he didn't try *something,* he would only prove his irrelevance. Ben might be the Big Man now, savior of Lewisville, but Reggie Forrester wasn't going to allow anyone to outdo him when it came to looking after the *everyday* needs of Lewisville's citizens.

When Reggie pulled up in front of the courthouse, the soldiers first evicted him from his Ford Excursion, then confiscated it. "Contamination," they said, when they found the black disk where the engine block had been. They refused to tell him what kind, but by now Reggie was certain that the disease issue was entirely fiction. No one in Lewisville had contracted an inexplicable illness, had they? Moreover, that morning, through the fence surrounding his warehouses, Reggie had spotted soldiers *installing* eetee power cells in their humvees. He now realized these must have been the ones confiscated from the town.

At least the soldiers did not march Reggie away at gunpoint. In fact, when he indignantly identified himself as Lewisville's mayor, they led him inside to their colonel. Reggie enjoyed a moment's relief at this belated acknowledgement of his importance. The fact that the colonel now occupied Ben's office also tickled him. Ben would not like that *at all.*

But then the interview, if that was the word for it, started. The colonel threatened Reggie with the ridiculous quarantine, stressing its indefinite nature. He then cited Reggie's warehouses, filled with wrecked fighters and heavy weaponry that had not yet been stripped or adapted to human use. Sweating, Reggie denied having anything to do with the contents of his warehouses. He had never touched any of it. He just rented space to people. But the colonel showed no interest in his protests.

Then Fikes suggested that detention was not inevitable. He offered Reggie an incentive for cooperation, an unspecified place in the new administration. The sort of position, Colonel Fikes said, that Reggie deserved.

Flattering. But Reggie was not naïve. The world was piss or be pissed on, and right now Reggie Forrester, sad to say, was not in a position to piss on anyone. His status had been on a dizzying downward slide since the start of the war, and now he would have to wiggle hard to avoid the hot yellow stream that gravity was pulling his way. To escape it, he'd have to make himself not just useful but *indispensable* to the new regime.

Which was fraught with its own dangers. He wondered if the colonel had interviewed Ben yet, and what incentives he might have offered Ben.

That evening, Reggie slipped through backyards to Paula's house. He was shocked to see how few people had evaded the Army's tightening net. Those who'd made it to the meeting perched on Paula's sofas and chairs and shared their news. The Army had rounded up the network of spotters guarding Lewisville, including Ben's own brother, and replaced them with their own people. The colonel had posted new rules at the county courthouse. Electricity would be down until the town was reconnected to the national grid. Drinking water would be distributed between eight and eleven A.M. at the corner of Main and Third, no other uses of water except as authorized for agricultural production. A blanket curfew would be enforced between nine P.M. and seven A.M.; no civilian was allowed on the streets during those hours for any reason at all. No assembly of more than eight civilians except under Army auspices. Reggie counted: including himself, this meeting numbered nine.

"The right to assembly," Jim Hanover fumed, "is guaranteed by the U.S. Constitution!" Jim had been a lawyer.

Flora Bucholter was distraught. "Just how long will it take to hook us up to the grid? How do they think they'll be able to protect the lines? What's the *point* of taking away our electricity?"

"That salvage doesn't *belong* to the Army," said Dave Sutton, whom Ben often used to float ideas. "It belongs to the people who risked their lives bringing it back—who've fought to keep the town safe!"

That predictably set off the ever-volatile Otis Redinger. "Dave's right! We've worked hard to just to survive! We've been listening to other folks on the shortwave, we know what it's like in the rest of the country. It's totally lawless. Now these people show up and say, 'We're from the government and we're here to help you—'" (that drew a chuckle) "—but they've brought their lawlessness with them. All they've done is destroy or steal everything we've fought to preserve. This is an illegal military occupation by an illegal government. We've managed to protect our community from *aliens*. Now we have to protect it from dangerous *human beings* as well!"

Several people applauded this impassioned speech, and Otis's face grew red from embarrassment. But then Todd

Myklebust, always a wiseass, said, "Ah, sedition. Is that right enshrined in the Constitution, too?"

For a moment the meeting lapsed into nervous silence. Otis and Todd had spoken out loud what the others had only come up to the edge of saying. Then everyone started talking at once.

Up to this point in the discussion Ben had stayed silent. That was his style: remain above the fray, the calm militia commander. Now he put down the footrest of Paula's plush blue recliner and rocked into an upright position. The uproar stopped as suddenly as it had begun. Everyone turned to look at him.

"George," Ben said, "you've been doing some reconnaissance. Why don't you tell us what you've learned?"

Although no one would guess it to look at him, unshaven, shambling George Brainerd had once been an Army Ranger. His skills had immeasurably aided both Lewisville and Ben's wartime ascent to the top of the town's chicken-coop ladder. He was not, however, one of Ben's acolytes. (Although George had not gotten up to offer that easy chair to the *mayor,* either! Reggie was squeezed between Dave and Flora on the sectional sofa.)

Now Ben's question made George look unhappy. "Their communications equipment isn't much better than ours. I didn't see anything fancier than off-the-shelf shortwave. No cell phones and they haven't set up any dishes, so my guess is that the military hasn't launched new satellites yet. No indication of aircraft, not even a recon balloon. They may patch the lines out of Lewisville for landline service, but that'll take time."

"Until then," Ben said, "we take away their radios and they're completely isolated."

"Sure," said George, looking unhappier. "If we take away *all* of them."

"Then we eliminate them," Otis said.

"You mean *kill* them?" Flora said. "Otis, you are a blood-thirsty son-of-a-bitch."

Otis shifted uncomfortably. "Well, probably they'd surrender long before that."

"What do we do with them when they do surrender?" George asked. "Or if they don't? What will the *Army* do when an entire battalion disappears after going to look for a downed eetee ship?"

"We could get the enemy to do the job for us," said Otis. "We could send them into a trap. Then no one would know we were involved."

"So," George said, "you want to set up your fellow human beings so aliens can kill them for you?"

Silence fell on the room. Apparently even Otis felt that sounded nasty.

Then George said, "What do you think, Mr. Mayor?"

That was, Reggie knew, an appeal for his help. Reggie was flattered. And usually persuading people to a course of action was something he liked to do, something he was good at. But tonight the power of his words was far less important than their real-world consequences. When one boat was going to sink, and you didn't know whether it would be Ben's or the Army's, you needed to make very certain you had a place on both boats.

He sighed audibly and rubbed his forehead. "I agree with George that you have to think about *the long term*. Unless we have weapons that provide a *decisive* advantage over the Army—that would allow us to keep the Army and everyone else out of Lewisville *for the foreseeable future*—all an attempt at secession will accomplish is make our situation worse."

So far, so good. No one could accuse him either of pushing for Otis's little revolt, or of siding with the evil invading Army. People were turning from Ben to Reggie. Ben looked sour but not yet angry.

"You want to hand them a petition?" Jim said. "We, the undersigned, protest your wholesale abuses of civil rights, the U.S. Constitution, and common decency?"

"Oh, sure," Reggie said. "As a first step. But we need something that will make it worthwhile for them to *negotiate—in earnest*—instead of rounding us all up. *I've* been wondering, why is the Army spending all its resources to gather up not just every last piece of eetee salvage, but nearly *every person* who's worked with it? Does anyone here believe this disease nonsense? I think instead they're *looking* for something, but they don't yet know *what it is*."

George had leaned forward and was listening intently. Flora said, "And you think that if we could figure out what that thing was, if we could find it first, it would give us an advantage in negotiations?"

"Maybe they're searching for a key that activates the fear guns," said Dave.

Jim objected, "We've been looking for it for a year and turned up squat. How do you propose we find it *now*?"

His ploy was at least half working, Reggie thought. They were listening. They were beginning to think twice. Reggie the voice of reason, Reggie the idea man. When he saw George opening his mouth to add to the discussion, he even began to hope they two could convince the others to forego the uprising altogether.

But then George abruptly shut his mouth. And Otis burst out, "Reggie's right! We *force* them to negotiate! We do it right away, while we still have *some* weapons. If we get back what they've taken, they're at a disadvantage. Look: a few hundred of them, fifteen thousand of us. Ben, they can't keep control if we don't let them—"

"No, no," Reggie said, "that isn't what I was saying—" But like Otis, Jim, Dave, Todd and even Flora had turned back toward Ben. They looked to *Ben* to decide the fate of Lewisville.

Oh, how that burned Reggie.

And now Ben spoke. "I've heard some good points. We can't throw away the lives of our men. We do have to think about the long term. But we can't let things go on the way they're heading. We take our weapons back, we force new terms on the Army, but no big battles. That's not a winning proposition."

So that was the decision. They fell to planning how they were going to break into Reggie's warehouses. Reggie had a physical sensation of sliding uncontrollably down the henhouse ladder toward the guano at the bottom. And here he had thought the Army's arrival might make Ben a little circumspect.

To ensure his own survival, he had to get rid of Ben one way or the other. But how to do so safely? He couldn't simply go to Colonel Fikes and report tonight's meeting. For one thing, Reggie had made no secret of his afternoon visit to the colonel. Ben would be keeping a close eye on Reggie now.

It was amusing to imagine Ben sweating at hard labor in

"indefinite quarantine," somewhere deep in a government reservation with nothing but sagebrush and jackrabbits for a hundred miles in every direction. It was considerably less amusing to contemplate what Ben might do to avoid such a fate. A bullet, say, speeding into Reggie's back from out of the shadows. Such things had happened in the last year.

At last Ben concluded the meeting by saying, "Now, folks, we've got to be off the streets before curfew. Be careful going home."

Reggie left with George through the back door. Jim Hanover followed them. They skulked along the shadows between Paula's raspberry patch and the Fortescues' pole beans. Far away, a coyote yipped into the chill of evening.

"Good try," George said to Reggie in a low voice.

Wondering why George had suddenly dropped his opposition to the ridiculous plan, Reggie glanced back at him. That was why, framed in Paula's candlelit kitchen window, he saw Ben and Otis talking. Otis appeared to be very excited. So Ben had a second, *secret* plan, one catering to Otis's enthusiasms.

"It wasn't good enough," said Reggie.

George went his own way, but Jim followed Reggie silently home, saying goodbye only at Reggie's front door. Jim's own darkened house stood across the street. Jim would now, Reggie thought, keep watch through his windows. Another of Ben's deputies was no doubt already guarding Reggie's back door.

4

Annoyed, but not wanting to argue in the hearing of the security guard, Anna King buzzed George Brainerd into the morgue corridor. George was discreet and sympathetic to her work. But she preferred no witnesses, and no interruptions.

She waited to finish the last careful slice exposing the *corpus minutalis*—so she had named the organ, in honor of its resemblance to hamburger—before she buzzed George through the door of the autopsy room as well.

"Pee-yoo!" said George, and then, shambling closer to peer

over her shoulder, "Holy shit, doc, that's fresh kill."

The sight of him kindled anticipatory warmth on Anna's skin. Pavlovian conditioning. She firmly ignored it and turned away to pick up her digital camera. "Yes," she said, snapping photographs of the *minutalis,* "and I want to keep working on it while it still *is* fresh. You know how fast they deteriorate. Now, what's so important that it can't wait until morning? Haven't our Army friends instituted a curfew, and doesn't it start in about five minutes?"

"I was kinda hoping I could stay here." He grinned at her.

"You'll be cold."

"Not my idea of romance, either," said George. "The drawers are a bit small for two people."

He almost made her smile. At the same time—it must be fatigue that rendered her so vulnerable—his words caused her throat to constrict. Did he really think their trysts in empty hospital rooms, never the same one twice, deserved the term *romance?*

The glass partition on the far side of the table reflected its own judgment: herself brown-haired and petite, neat in her spotless lab coat and face mask; him in unkempt flannel shirt and baggy jeans, face unshaven, hair uncombed. At least today he wasn't sporting his usual assortment of firearms.

They had nothing in common outside of bed. She still felt awkward saying his given name. Her sleeping pill, was how she thought of him. Since the starship had crashed on Cortez Mountain, it was either George, Ambien, or a long wakeful night in the morgue.

"Doc," he said, staring down at her prize specimen. He rocked back and forth on his heels. "This isn't the best time to have an eetee in your morgue."

She picked up her scalpel again. "What, is the sheriff on the warpath?"

"Ben—fuck no, it's the Army you should worry about."

"They've been here already," she said, beginning to sever the major nerves leading from the *minutalis* to the brain proper.

"*Here?* In the *morgue?*"

"We gave them a tour of the hospital today. Don't look so horrified. They didn't unzip any body bags, and they were kind enough to give us diesel to run our generators. Is that all you came here about?"

George was still rocking on his toes. Usually he stayed relaxed, even irreverent, under the worst of circumstances. "Ben wants to know if we can have some kind of strong narcotic, like in a hypodermic or something."

"What are you boys up to now?" she asked, but she didn't expect an answer. She knew such little favors were the quid pro quo that enabled George to keep Ben from shutting down her research altogether. Still, she wondered if the timing of this particular request should give her cause for hesitation. Even she had noticed the discontent abroad in Lewisville.

"I can give you some Fentanyl. But I'll have to get it from upstairs. Is tomorrow morning soon enough?"

"Sure," said George. "I guess."

But he showed no sign of leaving. She thought she had made it clear that she had no time for him tonight. Unfortunately, she could not rely on the eetee itself, sliced open from sagittal crest to cloacal canal, to drive him away. Such sights and smells did not disturb George.

Anna leaned over the table for better access to the left posterior pseudothalamic nerve. It required concentration to sever cleanly, running as it did through a layer of tough and slimy dura. Naturally George chose that moment to pick up one of her scalpels and prod at the section of skin and skull she had sawed out for access to the creature's brain stem. The mucous that protected a live and healthy eetee's skin had dried to a hard, yellowish crust. As George poked at it, a flake of the crust dropped onto the table.

"Get your hands away!" Anna said. "You aren't even wearing gloves!"

He pressed on the flake with the scalpel, crumbling it, and frowned. "Doc, I've handled a lot of dead ones in the last year. I've been covered in splat. I've had 'em keel over on top of me and vomit in my face. If they were going to make me sick, wouldn't it have happened already?"

They had discussed this topic before, but today there was a

new, speculative tone in George's voice. "You're wondering about the Army's quarantine regulations?" she asked. Again George did not answer. "Well, perhaps they're justified—in principle. There are plenty of diseases with a long incubation period, and if you didn't know what to look for, you couldn't spot the infection."

"As you've said. AIDS. And mad cow disease."

"Creutzfeldt-Jakob," she corrected.

"And kuru."

Surprised he had heard of an obscure disease of New Guinea cannibals, Anna glanced up. George had been doing a little research on his own? She knew George wasn't stupid, despite his unkempt, sometimes goofy persona. In his own way, he was one of the smartest people in Lewisville.

"But those are hard to catch," George said. "A quarantine wouldn't have much effect. And no one here has been eating any eetee brains." Then he reverted to form. He poked at the *minutalis,* making it quiver like Jell-O, and grinned again. "Sure looks like it would cook up good on a grill, though."

Anna had not eaten dinner. The image was unfortunate. Her mouth watered and her stomach grumbled. She sliced away the last of the dura, and at last was able to slip her gloved hand beneath the *minutalis* and lift it onto the scale.

One-point-five-four kilos. A middling weight. From the accounts of Ben's deputies and her own labors here, she had become convinced that variation in the size of this particular organ correlated with social or military rank. The eetees with the very largest *minutalis* were always the ones carrying the fear guns and directing the others. Her first theory had been that the *minutalis* manufactured dominance pheromones, but then she had begun to wonder about the magnetic anomalies, and the odd rabbit-ear deposits of metallic compounds in the sagittal crest—

George tapped his scalpel on the metal table. "Doc, we haven't talked about it in a long time—have you or Joe Hansen made any progress on how the eetees use the fear guns?"

"Oh, sure," she said, removing the *minutalis* to a tray under the hood. She started to wash it down with ethanol. "Molecular microwave transmitters. Proteins with encapsulated crystalline segments, manufactured inside specialized neural tissue. That's how the eetees communicate with each other, too."

"What?" The stark astonishment in his voice made her turn. "Have you said anything about this to *anyone else*?"

"I'm being sarcastic, George," she said crossly.

"But you have a theory."

"Guesses. Flights of fancy. I'm not a neurochemist or a molecular biologist, or for that matter a physicist, and I don't have the resources—"

"But you have evidence—"

"Nothing worth the name."

George gazed down at the eetee. "Too bad we couldn't ever bring you a live one and do the CAT scan thing. See what lights up when they do different things."

"No, on that particular idea I'm in complete agreement with the sheriff."

The last thing in the world Anna wanted was a live eetee to experiment on. She did not even like George in her morgue. She wanted it cold, silent, and stark, filled only with her well-tended garden of the dead. She wanted to keep dissecting her specimen, taking it apart organ by organ, slice by tiny slice, protein by protein. Over the dead she had total control.

But she also wanted George to stay. She wanted to touch his warm flesh and feel his hands on her own skin. It was the only thing these days that made her feel like a human being.

"What's really on your mind, George?" she asked.

"Doc," he said, "I know you aren't going to like this. You need to clean out your lab. Tonight. Get rid of your friend here. Destroy all your samples and slides. Remove all your files. Hide them—incinerate them."

"Don't be ridiculous," Anna said.

"It's not Ben you're dealing with anymore. The Army is confiscating everything that came out of that ship—"

"So I've heard. They want the goodies for themselves."

"They are also quarantining anyone who's worked with eetee goodies, and anyone who's had contact with eetees dead or alive."

"Not to mention anyone who protests the policy," Anna said.

"It's not a real quarantine, George. If the Army was serious about an outbreak, the first people they would isolate would be those with the greatest exposure. And that's you deputies."

"I disagree that they're not serious," George said. "They are extremely serious. And very soon someone will tell them about Dr. Anna King and how she trades pharmaceuticals for eetee corpses in good condition. How you have a whole fucking eetee *research project* down here."

"I keep a very clean lab," Anna said. "They can check it if they want. I can't believe the Army could be *less* sensible than the sheriff on the subject of basic research."

"Oh, yes, they could be," said George. "You know, don't you, that Joe *and* all of his files have disappeared?"

Anna had heard, but she'd dismissed it as a wild rumor. The thought of ignorant soldiers ransacking her lab, her refuge, her life—destroying a year of work—terrified and enraged her. She tried to push the thought away. "I'm happy to share everything I've learned, though I'm sure people elsewhere with better equipment have found out a whole lot more than I have."

"Suppose," George said, "sharing is not the goal. Suppose they want to know everything you've learned, and then make sure *no one else* ever sees that information."

"But what could they possibly want to conceal? It's not as if the eetees are a secret!"

"Look," said George, "the Army comes here, to an enemy crash site, but instead of going after the eetees, they devote all their manpower and attention to *this*—whatever it is. It's important, a real disease, a—a real *something.* Maybe they don't know exactly. Maybe they know the symptoms but not the cause— maybe they don't know whether it's a disease or an effect of eetee technology. But whatever this quarantine is about, for them it is taking precedence over everything else. They *are serious about it.*"

Anna tried once more to dismiss George's arguments. She found she could not. She gazed wistfully at the *minutalis* and her waiting culture plates. "Well, then," she said, at last, "I suppose I should take a look at Harvey Gundersen's dog."

"*His dog*?!"

"Harvey claims the dog has an eetee disease." Anna grimaced. "That the coyotes have it, too, and they have developed not just dementia but telepathic powers. Yes, I know what it sounds like—but today he brought in the dog, and it does have some odd lumps. I said I'd do biopsies and what blood work I have the facilities for."

"You have it *here*? Jesus, Anna, get rid of the dog, get rid of the eetee. *Now*! I'll help you. They *will* come here. Your only hope is to make sure they aren't *ever able to pin this on you.* Trading drugs is only a nasty rumor. You have *never dissected an eetee.*"

"No, George. If the dog really has an eetee disease, it needs studying and *I* need to tell the colonel whatever I can find out. If people are in danger from it, I'd be criminally irresponsible not to!"

"You are not listening to me," George said. "They will take your notes and your little jars and they will take you away, too, and if I'm right they'll take you so far away I will never see you again."

"That's melodramatic."

"Anna," he said, taking hold of her shoulders. "Please." It was a violation of their unspoken protocol. He never touched her when she was working. The warmth of his hands percolated all the way through her lab coat and sweater. She held her own messy hands away from him.

The thing about George, the thing that had made the whatever-it-was between them possible, was that he never seemed scared. Now he was showing his fear. She didn't like it. She certainly didn't want George to know what *she* felt: how terrified she had been since the eetees had come. How, maybe, she loved him. That would be making the emotions real. That would be letting a live monster into the morgue.

She said, coolly, "Suppose Harvey Gundersen is even halfway right? You'd be asking me to trade the health of perhaps everyone on Earth for my personal safety."

"Yes," George said. "Let someone else figure it out."

She shook her head and glanced one last time at her beautiful, doomed specimen. "Help me with the dog. Then I'll clean everything out of my lab, as you want."

5

The four Humvees wound upward through the hills. Up on the mountain, about eight miles away now, the wreck sprawled like a giant trash-can lid someone had hammered onto the ridgetop. Corporal Denise Wyrzbowski watched it as best she could while wrestling her Humvee along the unpaved road. No sign of activity at this distance. She distrusted the quiet, though; eetees were always busy with something.

The rolling terrain blocked the line of sight beyond the nearer slopes, but at least here it was grassland, dry and scant. Up ahead, pine trees accumulated with altitude until deep forest blanketed the highest ridges. Too much cover for the enemy.

She didn't feel comfortable here. She wasn't a country girl. She had fought house to house in the San Bernadino Valley with seized eetee firearms and makeshift body armor, but that was familiar freeway-and-subdivision country. You recognized what belonged and what didn't. Up there in the forest, she wouldn't know whether a sudden flight of birds was a nature show or an eetee ambush.

Not that she hadn't seen new sights in the Valley: eetees roaring along Figueroa Avenue in a Lincoln Navigator; eetee muckamucks cavorting in a swimming pool full of yellow slime; eetee grunts dead and bloated in an alleyway, lunch for a pack of feral dogs.

Movement in the sky. She tensed, then recognized it as a vulture rising on an updraft. Roadkill nearby? "What's that?" she asked the guide, a prim Nordic-looking local named Otis Redinger.

He turned to cast a disinterested glance in the direction she pointed. "Probably a dead gook," he said. "Or maybe a jackrabbit."

"A dead eetee?" Adrenaline stirred in her blood. "What could kill them out here? In the middle of nowhere?"

Redinger shrugged. "They lose their body suits, get a puncture, they're pretty vulnerable."

"Vulnerable, my gold-plated ass!" Wyrzbowski remembered how two of the mucousy little freaks had ripped apart Lieutenant Atherton with their bare talons while hopping up and down with glee. Silently: that was the really freaky part. Everyone knew they had some kind of mind talk.

Redinger said, "A ruptured bodysuit, and they're only good for a few days in the heat. Sheriff thinks they're short of water and fighting over it. We had a dry winter, no rain at all since May—and there's only a few small lakes up there. In town, we get our water from three hundred feet underground."

"How often do you get expeditions coming after your water?"

He shrugged again and pointed. "Turn left up here."

A narrower gravel road led away through the hills. Wyrzbowski swung the Humvee onto it, the others followed, and they began to bounce along in earnest, raising a column of dust visible to any eetee on the mountain. She glanced back. At this distance, the town had almost disappeared. A line of trees followed the course of a single winding stream. Yesterday, she had glanced over a bridge and seen that stream bed almost dry. Lucky Lewisville: a year of drought, a moat of waterless grassland ten miles deep.

She thought about the water jugs they carried with them, about a shipload of eetees dying of thirst, and despite the blazing heat she took a hand from the wheel to pull on the helmet of her body armor.

A fence had been running along the right-hand side of the road. Up ahead, it bent right again and marched away across the hills, dividing fallow farmland from patchy brush. The bushes looked green. Further on, she could see the silvery foliage of cottonwoods and willows. She wasn't a Campfire Girl, but she could guess what trees meant out here.

Water.

She braked, and the line of Humvees behind them did the same. In the back seat, Lieutenant Briggs glanced around nervously.

"What's the deal, Redinger?" she snapped at the guide. "Your sheriff claimed there was a big cache of eetee machinery abandoned here. Unguarded. But there's water here, right? And you still say there's no eetees camped out?"

Redinger looked offended. He was pulling out a Ruger Mini-14 that the colonel had given him leave to carry today. "We poisoned it," he said.

"Poison?" Briggs said, leaning forward.

"That's right. We dumped fertilizer in the pond. They can't take it. We saw 'em die when they tried to drink or swim in the creek, too much farm runoff. One of our doctors said it must be their, ah, electrolyte balance."

Well, gee, that could explain what had puzzled idiots like Atherton: why the downed eetees hadn't spread out into the California farmland. They'd stayed in the suburbs for treated water fresh from the tap.

"So if it's safe," she asked Redinger, "why do you suddenly need the gun?"

"Eh?" He looked at his firearm. "Oh. Sometimes one of 'em gets desperate. You get some sick gooks hanging around, waiting to die."

Wyrzbowski glanced into the back seat. "Sir?"

Briggs leaned back, nodded. "We go in. Be careful."

She put the hummer in motion again, slowly. Soon the road dead-ended in a dirt turnaround. Beyond that lay cattails and a sheet of greenish scum about fifty yards across, hemmed in by leafy brush and cottonwoods. Way, way too much cover.

Along the shoreline at different points she could see the hardware the locals had mentioned, gargoyle surfaces peeking through the foliage. From here she couldn't recognize anything, but it was enough to give the colonel a real hard-on.

She personally wished he'd worry less about a few power cells falling into civilian hands and more about the vicious castaways on the mountain, every one of them as eager as the Terminix man to commit mass destruction on *H. sapiens.* Sure, the Army desperately needed all it could gather up, both to fight eetees and to keep control of restive civilians (and they did always seem to be restive). Everyone had heard about the hushed-up disaster at Yosemite: refugees so hungry they were eating eetees, who'd used some never-specified but terrifying eetee gewgaws to slaughter soldiers and loot their supplies.

Still, the colonel wasn't the one who had to drive his ass around right under eetee sights.

One day, Wyrzbowski thought, the so-called liberation of Earth would become a reality. She would never again have to inhale the stink of eetee splatter on a hot day. She would never again have to wonder when the next fearmonger would flatline her brain. She would never again have to worry about restive civilians shooting her in the back, or about participating in sleazy deceptions like this quarantine scam of the colonel's. She would go back to being a citizen of a goddamn democracy, all *Homo sapiens* are created equal, all eetees are vulture food.

She would lie in the shade, pop a cold beer, eat a hamburger. "Let's go," said Briggs. Wyrzbowski pulled down her visor and rolled out of the hummer into low crouch, and the other five followed her. At least Briggs had enough sense to put on his helmet.

A trail led along the shore in both directions. Briggs sent one group right, another left; she got the left-hand job. Some soldiers stayed with the Humvees to guard them; others headed away from the pond altogether, up the slope.

Her six worked slowly along the grassy trail. She sweltered inside her armor. The sun raised a sewage-y stench off the stagnant pond, and horseflies the size of mice dive-bombed their heads. Insects in the grass fell silent as they approached and buzzed loudly again after they passed.

They reached the first pile of hardware without incident. Wyrzbowski took off a glove and gingerly touched the squat, lobed central piece. It was cool to the touch and, on the shady side, sweated condensation. Still working, whatever it was. She duck-walked around it. On the far side, a tube four inches in diameter snaked through the grass toward the pond. Her guess: some kind of purification unit.

Further along the trail, other globby Tinkertoys shone inscrutably in the sun. A lot of working hardware here. It didn't look all that abandoned, whatever the locals claimed.

Shouts. She twisted around. They came from the Humvees, but she couldn't see well through the foliage. A plasma rifle opened up, setting a tree ablaze. And then eetee fire caught a Humvee and blew it apart like the Fourth of July.

Wyrzbowski dropped on her belly and elbowed swiftly back to the others. "Back!" she whispered.

Her soldiers spread out among the trees, belly-crawling through the grass. Now the whole pondside was jumping with eetees in body suits. No, the gooks hadn't left their little water-treatment plant unguarded.

More fire from the soldiers at the turnaround, but not as much as there should be. She reached a rotting stump, balanced her rifle, whistled the signal over her mike. While Preston and Weinberg played rear-guard, the rest chose their targets deliberately. She sighted on the nearest of the eetees hopping toward Briggs, who stood as motionless as a department-store mannequin. She pressed the trigger. Got the hopper—woops, a little splatter on the lieutenant. Other soldiers near Briggs had turned deer-in-the-headlights too, perfect targets. Just like Atherton. There must be a mind-bender in this crew.

Wyrzbowski tried to sort out the pattern as she picked off a second hopper. Eetees descended the hillside beyond the Humvees; more had popped up on the other side of the pond—but those soldiers were returning fire, so no mind control over there. A whistle from Weinberg to the rear. Enemy on *their* tail, too, but her group wasn't pissing their pants in cold terror.

Up there, then. On the hillside. She whistled another signal as she splattered a third eetee.

The other five came crawling to her. She raised her visor and whispered, in case the eetees were listening to radio. "There's an officer up there. We're going to get it."

The six of them spread out again, creeping through grass and brush away from the pond. The eetees attacking them from the rear hadn't figured out what they'd done and joined the action at the Humvees. Now Wyrzbowski could see the muckamuck, resplendent in the egg-sack slime of its bodysuit, wielding its red fearmonger while flunkies covered its spindle-shanked ass. Poor freak: a year ago it had been one of the exterminator kings of the galaxy, and now here it was on guard duty at a polluted frog pond. She wondered if the eetee mind-benders could hear human minds, if they took pleasure in the terror they caused.

She wriggled forward, hoping she wasn't already too close to the muckamuck. One of the hopper flunkies must have sensed something. It turned toward her soldiers. Silent communication and a rush of excited hopping. A bush in Phillips's direction burst into a flutter of shredded leaves. Someone, she thought Merlino, fired back, burning two of the hoppers.

The flunkies had left their muckamuck exposed, but it had also turned its glistening head in their direction. Searching. Not much time, Wyrzbowski thought, and right then the terror boiled out of the back of her skull.

It spilled like ice into her guts, congealed her limbs into stone. Time stopped. The hillside sharpened into impossibly sharp focus, cutting itself into her consciousness: light and shadow on a patch of wild rose; the gym-socks smell inside her helmet; a horsefly crawling across the visor.

She knew she just had to focus. Sight on the chest. Press the trigger. That's all she had to do.

An eetee landed on her back, then exploded drippily onto her armor. Concrete encased her hands, her arms. She heard someone whimpering and knew, from experience, that it was herself. Your buddies cover your back, but you have to face down your fear by yourself. Just focus. Breathe. Press the trigger, press press *press*. And her finger *moved*—

The weight dropped from her limbs. The ice melted from her body and left her, gasping, in the hot sunlight. She managed to raise her head. The muckamuck was nowhere to be seen, though its fearmonger had come to rest in a rosebush. She grabbed a handful of grass to wipe the viscous blobs clinging to her visor, and then scooped up the fearmonger for her collection. Four officers and counting.

The grunt eetees fled the hillside. She whistled. One by one Weinberg, Preston and Bernard appeared. Then Merlino dragged toward her through the brush. He'd taken a burn on the shoulder plate of his armor. "Phillips?" she asked. He shook his head.

She couldn't think about that now. She pointed down the hill, toward the single remaining Humvee. As they ran at a crouch, Weinberg supporting Merlino, she took stock. It looked better than she'd expected. The party on the far side of the pond was still kicking, targeting the eetees trying to pick off survivors at the turnaround. The hoppers must have known their grand and mighty mind-bender was now only a nasty spray of goobers, because as soon as her party came up behind, they turned and fled altogether.

Briggs was gone. It was Sergeant Libnitz who gave the orders: the wounded in the Humvee, others to jog behind.

Redinger appeared out of nowhere to lope beside her. He didn't have so much as a singe mark on him despite not being armored, but he was stinking wet from pond water. She raised her visor; she needed the air. She was soaked inside her armor, too, but from sweat.

"How come *you're* still alive?" she asked.

"Jumped in the pond and swam to your side," he gasped.

"Clever," she said. Redinger didn't fool her. The Lewisville militia had sent them into the ambush. When the reckoning came, she would make sure to splatter *this* prick for Phillips. She wished, not for the first time, that she knew how to use her red souvenir. She would make this little fuckhead shit himself, she would make him weep, she would feed him suffering and degradation. *Then* she would splatter him.

Adrenaline and the rush of hatred kept her moving until they reached the junction. And then the Humvee in front of her stopped. "Fuck, fuck, fuck!" Libnitz was shouting.

She stopped, panting and dizzy from the heat. Then saw what he swore at.

Back in town, five miles away, black smoke coiled into the flawless blue sky. She made her way to Libnitz. "Can't raise anybody on the radio," he said.

6

Out the café's back window, Alexandra Gundersen could see the Neanderthals coming out of their caves to beat their chests. It was the Big Noisy Machines the Army had driven into town; now Ben and his boys worried that their dicks were too small. So now they had to kill something, or make a big explosion. Nothing made your little dick feel bigger.

"I'm so sorry, Colonel," she said to the Army man. "They're all lent out right now. It's been such a popular book. I'll try to get one for you by tonight. In the meantime, let me check those other books out for you."

The colonel responded to her warm tone with a slight relaxation of posture. The lightening of his expression was not yet sufficient to call a smile. While Alexandra stamped his books, she glanced through her lashes at the window again. Ben and his *unter*-cavemen had separated and now walked in different directions. Her twin James aimed straight toward the café's back door. It was, unfortunately, too late to escape.

She handed Colonel Fikes his books and smiled again, and this time he did smile in return. He would be back. She knew her customers, and, for better or worse, she knew men.

The colonel headed through the adjoining bookshop toward the front door, even as brother James pushed through the back into the café.

"Good morning, Sandy," James said cheerfully.

Her twin used her childhood nickname only to annoy her. Since these days he preferred the proletarian *Jim,* she paid him back in kind. "Hello, James."

James stared at her customers significantly. Despite the Army's prohibition on civilian assembly, and the loss of power that made it impossible to open her café (only locally grown herbal or Mormon tea anyway, alas), she could still let up to seven civilians and any number of soldiers into the bookshop. She no longer *sold* books or videos these days, with no new stock arriving in the foreseeable future, but she did lend them out, and since the demise of TV and radio, her store had always been busy. "Can we talk?" said James.

Alexandra waved at her assistant, deep in conversation with a soldier, to signal her departure. "Come on," she said to James. She led him through the door marked *Private,* into her stockroom's little office. "What do you want, James?"

"We need your help," he said.

We meant *Ben,* of course. How flattering that when Biggest Dick caveman needed a woman's help, he still thought of his ex-wife—though he was too cowardly to show up in person.

"I can't imagine what use I could be to you deputies."

"The Army stole some things from us," James said, "and we need to get them back."

"You mean your weapons."

"Sandy," James said, "we've been protecting you with those weapons."

"Isn't the Army going to take over that job?"

"Are they acting as if they came here to fight eetees?" James's foot jittered suddenly as Alexandra fixed him with a frown. "And what will you do when you need protection *from the Army*?"

The soldiers had come yesterday: hard men, and a few women too, in desert camo and heavy boots, laden with guns. She hadn't liked them. But they hadn't dragged *her* off to "quarantine." When the very first tanks rolled into Lewisville, Alexandra had undertaken serious thinking on the subject of boss cavemen and the very biggest rocks. By the time the soldiers showed up at her door, her shop and house had been cleared of all eetee artifacts. She had smiled and offered them tea.

They had frightened her nevertheless.

"I don't particularly like this . . . occupation," she said. "But the soldiers are acting under orders from our government."

"*Our* government?" said James. "The eetees nuked *our* government. These folks are enforcers for a military dictatorship."

"And just what is Sheriff wonderful Ben Gundersen setting up? How much has *he* been promoting your precious civil rights and rule of law?"

James's foot jittered again. Poor James. He fancied himself such an independent thinker. But when the other cavemen start heaving around rocks and grunting, you have to join in. Otherwise they might think you have a *really* little dick.

Okay, so it wasn't the actual, physical dick (*obviously,* in Ben's case!) that determined where you stood in Neanderthal hierarchy. It was all the subtle, almost imperceptible inflections of display, of action and reaction, dominance and deference, intimidation and submission, and meanwhile the metaphorical dick grows bigger and bigger. Fear, manipulation, and mind control. The boss caveman is created by *attitude,* his, theirs. Hers—although she had at last won free.

"I grant you," James said, "Ben's gone overboard sometimes. But he's kept the town together in difficult times, he's really done a tremendous job. He's preserved . . . *civilization* here, when the war turned the rest of our country into rubble."

Alexandra knew there was some truth in what her brother said. Behavior that was bad for a marriage might be less bad for a town. Because of Ben's diligent ruthlessness, she could sleep at night, she could still open up her store and serve customers. But it wasn't the whole story, was it?

"Order," she said, "is not the same as civilization. Order is about the strong controlling the weak. *Civilization* is about *protecting* the weaker from the stronger, about us all living *together* in empathy, cultivating the connections between us—"

"Sandy," said James, "empathy *is* what we're after. We want the Army folks to *empathize* with our point of view."

"With the aid of weapons," she said sharply. James made no reply, but he jiggled his foot again. "I don't want part of it. I'm a civilized person. I won't participate in violence against fellow human beings, moreover against people who are serving my country. And I thought I had made myself clear. I have no interest in doing anything for or because of Ben, ever, I want to have no connection with him *at all, ever again,* and this is *his* plan. Don't tell me it isn't."

"Don't make this personal—"

"It *is* personal. It's all personal. You want to belong to a cause that's bigger than you and, and—then you don't have to think about your actions. *Your* violence is good, *theirs* is bad. And then it's a big flashy Hollywood story, small-town heroes fight off aliens *and* the bad Army guys at the same time. But it all begins with *you,* James, and me, and Ben. Good and evil begin in each person's heart and mind. *That's* the story."

James began to laugh. "You and Ben were a Hollywood story, all right. The problem was, you both wanted top billing." Alexandra flushed, enraged at his mockery, yet another betrayal of *her,* his *twin sister.* He ducked his head and said, hastily, waving his hands, "No, no, forget about Ben, okay?"

"How can I? This *is* all about him, and his ego. He just can't stand not being the one on top!"

"It's only about Ben for you, Sandy. And doesn't that mean you're making it all about *you*?" That stopped her. James went on: "It's the *town* that needs your help. Your *neighbors.* Individuals. It's *your* choice to do good and not evil to them."

"And you," she said coldly, "are so sure this is for their own good."

"What good has the Army done for Lewisville so far? What happens to *your* business when they've locked away half the town? Do you think they'll go on differently than they've begun?"

No, that did seem unlikely. Alexandra looked away.

After the divorce, exhausted and alone, she had convinced herself that what she had most wanted was the opposite of her life with Ben. She wanted to live quietly. She wanted a loving world founded on empathy, not conquest. Starting up her café-bookstore had been part of it, a microcosm of her ideal of civilization, bringing people together for the exchange of ideas and fellowship. And hadn't she been successful at that, at least in a small way?

But, to tell the truth, it was boring. And while she dwindled into a mousy spinster, the bookstore lady, the war came along and metamorphosed Ben into gun-toting action hero. Not that she could ever have fought the eetees the way he had. She had no physical courage and would sooner pick up a poisonous viper than a gun. But—admit it, James was right—she *hated* being out of the spotlight. She hated *Ben* hogging the stage.

And now, wriggling up from the dark depths of her psyche, came this self-destructive impulse to prove herself to Ben. To the town. To prove she was useful in this new caveman world of fear and guns, and not just in the sad, lost world of civilization, where she had known she was Ben's superior.

Had Ben known she would feel such an impulse? Had he known she would be more afraid of the strange cavemen, the Army soldiers, than the cavemen she knew?

Fear, manipulation and mind control. Good old Ben. Once she had admired that will toward dominance.

Then, James said, "Maybe you're afraid you won't measure up." Reading her mind, too—he was her twin, after all.

Strange how knowing what was in someone else's mind ought to give you empathy for that person. Instead it seemed as if only the weak could sustain empathy. The strong couldn't resist the temptation to use their knowledge to get what they wanted.

Defeated by James and Ben, by her own *attitude*, Alexandra

said, "All right. Tell me what you want me to do."

And so that afternoon, clad in a clingy flowered sundress and straw hat, her long blond hair spilling over her shoulders, Alexandra walked up to a pair of beefy soldiers and smiled. "Excuse me? Officers? I wonder if I could get into the warehouse."

One of the soldiers swiveled his head toward her, so she could see her reflection in his sunglasses. She still looked pretty damn good. The soldiers' guns turned her stomach queasy and her hands cold, but, she told herself firmly, what was in their minds mattered more.

"We're not officers, ma'am—" the soldier began, politely.

"Oh!" she said. "Of course! How silly of me! You're not the *police!*"

"—but no," he went on, "we can't let you into the warehouses."

"But you see," she said, "I rent space in one. For some of my overflow." He was staring politely but blankly at her. "I own a bookstore, you see? The only one in town. And your colonel, Mr. Fikes, came in today and we started talking about Lewis and Clark, and whether they should be admired as brave explorers, or whether they were just the vanguard of genocide and colonial oppression, and he asked for a book about them."

She smiled again at them. Their body language was changing subtly but unmistakably: shoulders relaxing, faces turning towards her. Excitement mixed with terror rose in her. They were falling for it. . . .

"I recommended *Undaunted Courage* to start with, but, as you can imagine, it's a popular book around here, at least since there hasn't been any TV. I didn't have any copies left in the store, but I know there are some out here in the warehouse. So I came out here to pick up a copy for the colonel. You can check with him if you like."

Part of her still hoped the soldiers would send her away, and she would be able to tell James she had done her best. But she was also fiercely willing them to submit.

He nodded. "All right, Ms.—?"

"Alexandra Hanover," she said, using her maiden name.

"I'll have to accompany you."

"Oh, that's fine!" she said, and smiled her most glorious smile at him. And she followed him across the parking lot between the tanker trucks, and through the big roll-up door.

The space inside was cavernous, dark and cool. The soldiers had shoved aside quite a few of the pallets and shelving units to make room for their equipment, and the smells of diesel oil and sweat mingled with the older dusty scent of dried peas. The guard accompanying her paused to explain their mission to a man leaning over a trestle table—probably a genuine officer.

The man at the table looked her up and down with a hard, suspicious stare, but Alexandra smiled at him, too, with just the right mixture of hopeful inquiry, submission to his authority and winning, wholesome cheerfulness. (Oh, it *was* going to work. All those years with Ben had been good for something after all.) Then he, too, nodded.

She and her guard threaded their way around pallets laden with sacks of dried peas, heading toward the back of the warehouse. The shelving units that she rented stood against the wall at the back, next to a locked metal door that led outside.

Next came a part that depended on her own physical quickness, something she had never had to rely upon before. But excitement propelled her now. She no longer wanted to turn back.

"Could you help me?" she asked the guard. "I have a bad back." The guard glanced at her. She pointed. He still wore his sunglasses, so he wouldn't be able to see the nervous tremor in her hands. "It's in that box there, on the second shelf."

He bent over, reaching for the box. Alexandra opened her purse and took out the vet's tranquilizer dart that James had given her. The guard started to pull the box off the shelf. She reached over and stabbed his neck with the dart.

"Hey!" he yelled, turning swiftly toward her. She backed up, but before he could take a single step, his knees buckled and he pitched face forward onto the concrete floor.

That looked as if it hurt. But she could not help smiling. She had done it!

She reached in her purse again and took out the key that James had given her, doubtless Reggie Forrester's. She slid back the deadbolts and opened the door.

The gravel lane behind the warehouse was deserted except

for a skittering stray cat. For a moment she thought the soldiers must already have arrested Ben's deputies. Then behind her, inside the warehouse, a commotion erupted: people yelling, booted feet clomping at a run across concrete.

And then brother James rose out of the brush on the far side of the lane and ran toward the back door. A line of Lewisville deputies followed him. Two tremendous explosions detonated at the front of the warehouse, one right after the other. A blast of heat and smoke and a rain of debris rattled across the interior of the warehouse. Alexandra jumped outside through the doorway.

Alexandra thought: people were being shot, even killed. She had helped it happen. It was a betrayal of everything she thought she stood for. Why was she so excited?

But then, at that same moment, moving so unbelievably fast that she barely had time to register what happened, a dark shape roared across the sky, shrank into a distant speck. Another deafening explosion—

The deputies all ducked belatedly. "Raid! Raid! Eetees!" James shouted. Now gunfire and screams echoed from inside the warehouse.

Then a band of eetees, all thin heads and long froggy legs, came around the corner of the warehouse and started shooting.

She had never seen them in the flesh. They weren't supposed to come out in daylight! Terrified, she flung herself back inside, crawled away among the pallets into the darkest corner she could find, and wedged herself behind a row of fiberboard barrels, arms over her head. Smoke filled her nose and mouth. Explosions echoed through the warehouse, more yelling and screaming, the crash of metal shelves overturning.

Then she heard a sound right nearby.

She looked up. One of the aliens squatted atop a stack of barrels. It apparently hadn't seen her yet. It gazed out from its high vantage point into the chaos of the warehouse. The alien wasn't any larger, really, than a Great Dane or a teenage boy. It had long legs and arms and wore some kind of glistening translucent all-over covering like a wetsuit, and its taloned glove held a long-barreled red pistol. It smelled like slightly rancid raw chicken. Alexandra looked at its narrow chest for one of those red whorled pendants James had once shown her, carried by the high-ranking eetees, that could paralyze this entire warehouse full of men. She did not see one.

She must have made a sound—whimpered, perhaps— because the eetee turned and glanced down at her. Its narrow face was unreadable behind the slimy protective sac. Its pistol was aimed at her negligently, as if she were no threat at all, but

she

really

did

not

like

guns.

As angry as if it were Ben, Alexandra threw her weight into the stack of barrels. The eetee toppled to the floor along with all the rolling, tumbling sections of its unstable perch. The pistol flew from its hand, fell and struck Alexandra's hip. Her first instinctive reaction was to bat the horrible object away from her; then, fumbling, she grabbed for it and caught the wrong end.

The eetee scrabbled to its feet, heaving barrels aside. Alexandra reoriented the pistol with two clumsy, shaking hands, and took aim. She clearly did not inspire fear: instead of ducking behind a barrel or throwing itself to one side, the eetee fixed Alexandra with its egg-yolk gaze.

Icy blackness swept her mind, it stopped her breath and froze her limbs—

But the eetee didn't, it *surely* . . .

The overwhelming weight of her terror crushed the half-finished thought toward nothingness, and all that Alexandra could grab hold of was her desperate rage. She was so tired of being on the sidelines, the one *not in control.* She realized she had squeezed her eyes shut. She forced herself to open them. There was no blackness except on the backs of her eyelids.

Mind control she understood.

She pressed the button on the red pistol and the eetee *exploded,* showering the wall above her with great gobs and ropy drips of what looked like snot.

"Take *that, Ben,*" she whispered.

Civilization is a wonderful thing, but survival trumps it every time.

Then a human soldier, a black woman, pushed through the barrels toward her to offer a hand. "The warehouse is burning! Come on!"

The soldier took the red pistol from Alexandra's now nerveless hands and tugged her through an obstacle course of tumbled communications equipment, pooled blood, dead human and alien bodies and furiously burning sacks of dried peas. At last they burst onto the smoke-filled parking lot. The remains of the Army's fuel trucks still blazed brightly. Soldiers pushed her down behind a tank.

"This the one who let the militia in?" one of them said.

"She splattered the froggy with the fearmonger," her rescuer told them. "Lucky for you."

But there had been no fearmonger.

As the flood of paralytic terror receded, dragging cold shakiness in its wake, Alexandra's last thought but one rose back into sight. The eetee hadn't carried a fear gun. It hadn't needed one to shoot her full of abject terror.

Noise and commotion went on for a long time after that: the burning diesel, eetee aircraft sweeping overhead, explosions, missiles screaming into the sky, shouts, rattling gunfire. Alexandra knew Ben's plan had gone entirely wrong, and she was, plainly and simply, screwed. Ben and his deputies were even more screwed, if they weren't already dead. Now Lewisville really would suffer a military occupation. They would *all* be herded into camps.

Still, right at the moment she felt like God looking down on creation. She had killed an eetee.

Her brain could not leave alone the image of that clouded alien face at the moment she had pressed the trigger.

All this time she'd been hearing about Ben and his deputies—so brave to venture out, over and over, against such a terrible weapon—and it turned out there was *no such thing* as a fear gun.

The red pendants must be just some kind of officer's insignia. It said you were *authorized,* you had the *ability* or the *training* to wield terror. But as for the fear itself—

It all begins and ends in the mind.

Fred crossed the dry, thistly lawn and stopped in front of the old brick building with the flagpoles that Harvey would never let him piss on. In hot weather the children stayed away and the building usually sat empty, but now the strangers had brought grown-up people there. Fred hoped Harvey might be one of them.

Fred dropped his burden to sample the air for Harvey's scent. The air was still heavy with the acrid taste of yesterday's conflagration. He reared on hind legs to put his nose to the windows. No one had opened the mesh coverings, but the sashes had been raised so he could smell all the guests packed inside. There were even more than at the big barbecues Harvey and Susan used to hold. The people were not enjoying this party, though. Many stood in line in front of a table. The rest sat around on cots or folded blankets, glum, angry or fearful.

Fred recognized some of the people. Mister Mayor drifted along the line of people, talking. Fred could tell that Mister Mayor felt glum and fearful, too, but he soothed the others with his warm smooth voice that had always reminded Fred of cow fat.

At the table at the head of the line sat the woman vet who had kept Fred tied up in the cold hard room. With her was the otherwise nice man who had helped with the big, long, nasty needle. Now the vet-woman had a lot more needles with her, and the nice man as well as some of the strangers were helping her, sticking needles in each person and writing things down.

Near the table Fred noticed Alexandra, who had stopped coming out to Harvey's a long time ago. Alexandra hadn't liked Fred's nose, even when he'd sniffed her crotch in the friendliest way. Alexandra had already gone through the line and now *she* was smiling and being friendly to some of the strangers.

Ben was not talking to the strangers or to Alexandra. Ben had a leash between his feet and hands and he could only shuffle along. Several strangers led him forward to get stuck with a needle. Fred hoped Ben would be okay. The night before, he had smelled Ben, angry and afraid, through a basement window in the building with the big statue.

At last, in the far corner, Fred located Susan, and nearby,

Harvey. Harvey sat on a cot and stared miserably at the wall.

Fred remembered the old days when he and Harvey had romped for hours in the cool of the evening, when the two of them had been joyously happy together. Then Harvey had grown afraid: so afraid of the world and of Fred, he thought he should kill Fred, even though he didn't want to.

Fred so much wanted Harvey and Susan to be happy again. When Harvey got the present Fred was trying to give him, he would quit being so miserable and alone. He would know that he didn't have to be afraid of Fred.

Fred picked up the present in his jaws again and loped around the corner of the brick building. A couple of the strangers' trucks pulled out of the driveway. Their occupants paid no attention to him.

Toward the back of the brick building it was cooler and shady. A cat turd lay under a bush. For a moment, he thrust his nose against it, intrigued. Then he recalled his mission. He would not be able to go home if he failed, not while Harvey and the vet-woman wanted to kill him.

He continued to the back door of the place where the children used to eat. The sweet odor of old garbage lingered here, but there were also fresh smells where cans of oil, bags of potatoes, and crates of stale crackers and raisins had rested on the cement for a few moments. Most interesting was the delirious scent of raw meat. Someone had recently killed a cow.

From inside the building, Fred could smell boiling potatoes. He trotted up to the door itself. Two sweaty strangers guarded it. Fred put down the present and wagged his tail.

Hello, he said to them, in the new way he had learned.

They glanced down. "Hey, boy," said one of the strangers. Fred wagged his tail some more and the stranger patted him on the head. The stranger liked him. Most people liked Fred.

I like you, too, Fred told him, wagging some more. *Will you open the door, please?*

The stranger pulled open the door. He didn't look down as Fred picked up his present and trotted inside. It was just the way it had worked with Harvey and Susan, and at the big building that was kind of like the vet's. The nice man hadn't noticed he was letting Fred out. It was because he had wanted Fred to be happy, even though he was afraid Fred was sick.

None of them would be afraid of Fred anymore if they understood that Fred wasn't sick, he had just learned to do some new things.

They would learn new things, too. They would all be happy once they understood each other. They would stop being afraid of each other, and hating each other, and trying to make each other do things. Like him, they would take off their leashes and run joyously, rapturously free.

At least, that's what he hoped they would do. But people were sometimes unaccountable.

Fred followed the scent of raw meat into a big kitchen where there was a lot of stainless steel. Men and women chopped potatoes and onions, and big pots of water steamed on the burners. More strangers with guns stood around, making sure the men and women didn't go outside. The strangers were looking forward to the meat, too.

Don't bother about me, Fred told them, and no one did, because they didn't want to. It was a little sneaky, a coyote trick.

Off to one side, one of the men was spilling a bowl of stinky chopped onions into a big vat of ground-up raw meat, ruining its smell. *Why don't you stop and talk to your friend?* Fred asked him, knowing, because of the new way, that it was what the man really wanted to do.

He couldn't do this to the coyotes. They would have caught on right away. But, except for Harvey, the humans didn't know yet that Fred was talking to them, or that he was trying to get them to do things, just for their own good. Until then he could be a little sneaky.

Fred trotted over to the vat of ground-up cow and dropped in the present he had carried all the way from the vet's.

"Hey!" the man yelled, suddenly noticing him. "Get away from there! How'd you get in?" But he wasn't really mad.

Fred backed away and lay down, wagging his tail. The man began mixing in the pungent onions with Fred's present. By the grill, a woman shouted, "You almost done with that hamburger?"

‡‡‡‡‡‡
●●●●●●●

ARABIAN WINE
by Gregory Feeley

Gregory Feeley was born in 1955 and grew up in California. His first story, "The Light at the End of the Penumbra," was published in 1977 and his first novel, Philip K. Dick Award nominee The Oxygen Barons, *was published in 1990. He is best known for his more than two dozen published short stories, which have been nominated for the Nebula, Sturgeon, and Locus Awards, and include nominees "The Weighing of Ayre," "The Crab Lice" and "The Truest Chill." Feeley is also a noted critic, and has written for* The New York Times Magazine, Atlantic Monthly, *and* Foundation, *while his reviews appear regularly in* The Washington Post Book World *and* The Philadelphia Inquirer. *Upcoming is a novel-length version of the story that follows, and a long novel about magic and science in pre-Renaissance Europe. Feeley lives with his family in New England.*

Feeley's short fiction is heavily influenced by his interest in history, and tends to deal with periods in pre-modern Europe when cultural paradigms come into conflict with one another, or with new discoveries. The story that follows—one of two fine novellas Feeley published last year—is a rather remarkable alternate history that tells of caffeine appreciation, scientific upheaval, domestic surveillance, and the shock of the new.

MATTEO COULD FEEL the pressure rising, as though one of his sensible organs (in addition to much of his fortune and more of his honor) lay within the rapidly heating vessel. A seam creaked loudly and the young trader flinched, recalling a weaker model that had blown open, spraying Gaspare and an assistant with scalding water. He wished he had calmed his nerves with a cup of caofa, the elixir that brought fixity of purpose and clarity of mind, and which held the balance of his fortune in pawn.

Another joint groaned, but Senator Domenico remained impassive. His secretary, who seemed to know more, looked as though he wanted to step back. The sides of the great kettle had visibly distended, a tin boy popping his cheeks. Matteo glanced worriedly at Gaspare, but the engineer seemed to be counting, as though trying to determine the proper interval in a recipe. Finally he stepped forward and upended a bucket of water over the kettle. A cloud of steam immediately enveloped him.

"As the vessel cools, the steam within will now condense," Matteo announced. Gaspare got down on his knees and, holding a pair of long tongs, laboriously turned a valve under the kettle. A deep gurgling rose from beneath the wooden floorboards.

". . . And the water is drawn up from the level below." Matteo strove to keep his voice confident and assured. The kettle, which had dimpled inward, bunged back to convexity with a faint gong.

Gaspare, who was still crouched at the base of the kettle, now spoke. "In a more efficient model, the water used to cool the vessel—now warmed—would be collected in a second vessel, which would then be heated in its turn. In this manner the coals would do continuous work, and the flow of water proceed uninterrupted."

The senator spoke. "And your vessel is now filled with . . . ?"

"Let me show you." Gaspare stood, brushing dirt from his knees. A brass spigot emerged from the lower half of the vessel, and he carefully turned it, then stepped back as brown water spurted into his bucket. The stench that rose from it was unmistakable: the bilge, compounded of offal and decomposing vegetable matter, that eddied at low tide in the canals and seeped into the foundations of buildings. "It's only about a quarter full," Gaspare admitted. "The engine's capacity is limited by the tank's size and, especially, its strength. A large, double-vessel engine, of strong bronze—"

"Yes; I comprehend your point." The senator walked slowly around the apparatus, his expression betraying no sign of censure or approval. "And this is *your* invention?"

"The principle is ancient," said Gaspare cheerfully. "Hero of

Alexandria showed how water displaced by steam could be made to do work. More recent studies by the Neapolitan della Porta suggested that with superior metallurgy—"

"I see. What do you think, Enrico?" he asked.

The secretary, an unsmiling man with a partially grown out tonsure that gave him the look of an expelled monk, pursed his lips. "I count ten briquettes of coal expended," he said in a nasal voice. "A considerable expense for the raising of four gallons of water."

Matteo was about to protest the obvious injustice—the coals were not yet consumed, and another vessel could be heated—but the senator waved him off.

"It is perhaps not the most economical means of pumping," he said. "Yet the work could be done at any hour, and while haulage requires strong men, the boiler could be tended by a cripple. More to the point, there is perhaps value in a system that can drain a basement without the need to admit workmen below."

Matteo did not follow that, but the secretary nodded. Ser Domenico gathered his cloak and looked around him. "This warehouse belongs to your family?"

"It does, sir."

Domenico smiled faintly. "Its empty space stands ready to receive shipments of that bean you think to sell to Christendom, the one the Turks use to brew that bitter liquid—what do they call it?"

"They call it 'Arabian wine,' ser," Matteo replied. "Our warehouse stands ready to receive shipments of anything my father and brothers bring into port."

"Very good. Still, it hardly seems secure enough for investigations of potential benefit to our Republic. Until you dismantle your present model, I will post a guard around it."

Matteo inclined his head politely.

"You promise better performance with a sturdier engine? Very well. Have young Treviso come see me tomorrow."

"As you wish, ser." Matteo bowed, uncertain how to greet this. He was disappointed that the senator would discuss funding with Gaspare, who was a wretched negotiator. Still, for a trading family to win subsidy for a venture gave Matteo a thrill of triumph such as Gaspare—whose father had always been employed by the state—would never understand.

With brief but ceremonious leave-taking (and a sour look from his secretary) the senator departed, and the two young men looked at each other. Matteo was too well schooled to show his feelings even in the aftermath of a transaction, but Gaspare pushed his hair back, smudging his face, and grinned. "Have you any of your wondrous elixir?" he asked. "I believe this calls for a drink."

They repaired to the workbench, where Matteo produced a leather bag from his belt. "Roasted this morning," he said as he unlaced its neck, releasing the intoxicating aroma. Matteo ground the beans in a mortar while Gaspare flushed out the vessel and poured in fresh water, then carefully took out the tiny sieve—gold leaf hammered to paper thinness and riddled with needle-sized holes—that represented his own contribution to the art of brewing caofa. He doubted his countrymen would ever drink it as the Turks did, with suspended grounds settling into a sludge at the bottom of their cup.

Spooning the black powder into the sieve, Matteo called out, "Ready?" He carefully fit the sieve into the throat of a flask, and turned to Gaspare, who was bent over the vessel like a chymist before his alembic. "It's ready," he murmured. Matteo positioned the flask just beneath the spigot, and Gaspare turned the tap.

The jet of steam caught them both by surprise. Gaspare, who should have closed the valve instantly, continued to twist for a second longer, then froze. Matteo felt the flask buck in his hand as though trying to kick free. Instinctively he resisted the force pushing it back against the spigot, and immediately got himself a blast in the face.

Both men were cursing and spitting as the cloud dissipated. Matteo blinked, tasting grit on his lips, and looked down to see his doublet spattered with grounds.

"Sorry," Gaspare muttered. "I forgot that there was still pressure in the boiler."

Neither man cared to say aloud that they had narrowly missed a nasty accident. Matteo knew that beneath his nervous relief a blister of shame was rising. And on top of that, they had ruined a pot of caofa.

The flask was still dangling in his hand. Matteo lifted it, felt it slosh a bit, then pulled out the sieve and peered in. The residue at the bottom looked black as ink.

Grimacing, he poured it into one of the cups they had set out. Gaspare stared at the opaque liquid, leaned forward, and sniffed. Then he raised the cup to his lips and sipped.

"Say," he said in surprise, "this isn't bad."

➤ ➤ ➤

The morning shadows had retreated from the Canale di San Salvatore by the time Matteo and Gaspare emerged, and sunlight shone upon the bobbing trash and green-tinged spume of its waters. Gaspare climbed into one of the gondoli lining the quay and directed it to the Arsenal, while Matteo turned and began to make his way toward the Rialto. Holding together the edges of his cape to cover his stained doublet, he moved swiftly through the narrow *calle,* threading between the servants on errands, the lunching workers, the loitering poor, and the jostling, swaggering *bravi,* Italian and foreign, who filled the *piazzi* and *campielli* of *La Serenissima,* city of St. Mark, the holy and Most Serene Republic of Venice.

One of the *bocche di leone,* its mouth gaping like the spout of a disused fountain, stood at the edge of a small square, ready to swallow proffered notes. Matteo watched a red-haired sailor approach and peer into it. As a child he had listened in awe to stories of how citizens would wake one morning to see bodies dangling by a foot from the gibbet between the two columns of the Piazzetta: enemies of the state, denounced by informers or anonymous letters and executed by the Council of Ten. Nothing so public had taken place in Matteo's memory, but it was reassuring to see that the *leoni* still held the power to impress foreigners, especially in these beleaguered days of the Republic's slow decay.

He found Selim at a café near the Ponte di Rialto, almost within sight of the bridge. There was nothing on the table in front of him, for of course he could not have wine or ale; and Matteo realized in a flash what the old man would like.

"My friend," he said, and the two men engaged in an elaborate greeting that partook, if imperfectly, of the etiquettes of both their nations. In courtesy and deference Matteo spoke Arabic, though his trader's Turkish was better. If the wizened Cairene was pained by the sound of his native tongue in Matteo's mouth, he did not show it.

"Boy!" Matteo called. "Bring a pitcher of hot water, near boiling." And as he brought forth the sack of beans Matteo saw comprehension light the man's face. He called for a mortar and pestle, which had to be procured from a better establishment down the street, then ground the caofa with animation, enjoying the bemused glances of passersby.

"Someday," he said in a clear voice (in Italian), "All Venice will sip *kahveh* as they sit along the Grand Canal."

Selim laughed quietly. "You will convert first your countrymen, then Europe? I shall never want for a cup again."

"You will not today, in any event." Matteo was inspecting his grounds as the steaming pitcher arrived, and both men leaned forward as he tipped the powder in. The aroma began to spread through the air at once, and they sighed.

"Venice remains Europe's crossroads for the spice trade," said Matteo, speaking more in bravado than truth, "and when its great cities begin to drink *kahveh,* they shall flavor it with spices brought by Venetians." In a confidential tone he added, "My sister will only drink it when I put in honey."

Selim grunted. "But Venice is the most Levantine port in Christendom," he noted. "Some of your customs will encounter resistance elsewhere." And as if led on by that reflection, he pointed at the Ponte di Rialto. "Is that one of the bridges where your city conducts its *battagliole?*"

"Oh, no," replied Matteo, shocked. "The Rialto is public territory, the heart of the Republic. The *pugni* who engage in bridge battles would never bring such disorder here; the traditional *ponti di guerre* all lie far from the city center." He reflected that Selim, whose culture embraced practices of breathtaking barbarism, might think the same of Venice's *battagliole sui ponti,* which aroused such fascination and misunderstanding.

Selim nodded equably. "Some of your customs will encounter resistance," he repeated. "You have traveled farther in the lands of the Faithful than in your own, but you will see what I mean when you visit Barcelona and Lisbon. I am sorry; have I said something wrong?"

➤ ➤ ➤

Water splashes against stone at every homeward turning, a seemingly friendly sound whose familiarity disguises its jeers. What type of knowledge can be apprehended not by learning, but only through exposure to time and the world's elements, like a weathering rock?

Vendors shouted the names of their wares, much of which the Benvenetos had, lately or in Matteo's youth, imported from throughout the Mediterranean. He had been twenty-one on his first voyage—older than Alessandro and Tullio had been, but trading ships take months to complete a journey, and the family was shrewd enough not to send him on a trip that would teach him little. Marina was three months pregnant and Matteo was in danger of becoming a father before he had left his home. With a cargo of fine Venetian textiles and refined sugar, the *Volpe d'Oro* sailed into the Adriatic, bound east for the trading-posts of the Levant.

For the first days Matteo was seasick almost continually, to the amusement of the crew and his own burning shame. The ceaselessness of the *Volpe*'s pitch and plunge wore at him: unable to find even an hour's respite to recover his energies, Matteo could keep nothing down, found it impossible to maintain his balance, and felt the ship's unnatural motions—irreconcilable with any human cycle—begin to ravage him. By the time the Levanter rose, blowing steadily out of the Holy Land like a *djinn* repelling Crusaders, Matteo had sunk into insensibility.

He never knew whether the captain decided to make for Alexandria rather than Beirut out of concern that his passenger might die. Their goods could doubtless be sold there, but it was in the eastern ports that the Venetians hoped to obtain the spices, silks, dyes, and drugs that could most profitably be sold in the landlocked markets of Austria. Matteo was carried insensibly ashore, and awoke days later in a strange bed. By the time he had recovered enough to sit up, the *Volpe d'Oro* had departed.

Too weak to travel, Matteo wrote to his family explaining that a fever had laid him up while the ship had continued on. It was one of the hazards of the business. The cargo had been consigned by the Benvenetos' business associates, and the decisions regarding what wares to take on and carry east—for which Matteo had been trained and entrusted—had been made for him.

A month later he descended the inn's narrow stairs and emerged shakily into the streets of Alexandria. Sunlight blazed downward like a hammered spike, and the flashing white of the natives' robes hurt his eyes. Matteo felt his sinuses parch and his lips crack in the desiccated air, and he wondered whether the women veiled their faces to preserve their breath's moisture.

So he drank, to keep from splitting like parchment. No wine, of course: rather fruit juice and goat's milk, cloudy infusions of dates and raisins called *nabidh,* and a black substance, hotter than any *nabidh,* which Ibrahim called *kahveh.* The scalding liquid burnt Matteo's lips and offered no relief from the day's heat; but afterward he felt a strange rush to his head, like a spray of water sluicing grime from a window.

"Is this the effect of *kahveh*?" he asked.

Ibrahim laughed. "*Markaha!*" he cried. It meant, Matteo learned later, the peculiar ecstasy of *kahveh.*

Matteo could only walk about for an hour or two before exhaustion overtook him. Sitting for most of his day, he resolved to learn the local Arabic. It did not take him long to realize that *kahveh* (which Ibrahim served during the lessons) concentrated his mental powers; and when he learned to drink it hot he discovered that the freshest brew possessed surprising subtleties of flavor. He visited marketplace stalls where he could watch the *kahveh* seller prepare a fresh pot. "I grind them up, so," the man said, pointing to a spice mill. "Ah, you would like to see?" Smiling, he poured a dozen beans into Matteo's palm.

Matteo studied them closely. They were a glossy brown, dry to the touch. He raised them to his face and caught a faint whiff of the familiar aroma.

"They blacken when roasted," the Mussulman said, "but you

will never see them green. The beans are boiled before they leave Yemen. So if you were hoping to grow your own plants—" He cackled gleefully.

"I am a merchant, not a farmer," Matteo replied with distaste. In fact the possibility of cultivating the crop had never occurred to him. It should have, however: the Dutch would certainly have thought of it. He would have to think better—think differently— if he was going to find a way out of the trap that was slowly enclosing his city.

In September a sirocco blew out of Africa, and a Venetian galleass made ready to run for the Adriatic. Matteo was as fit for a sea voyage as he would ever be, and he joined the traders returning home with their goods and their profits.

The *Tarida,* wind in her sails, cut swiftly through the waves, and Matteo fought the nausea rising within him. Like a defender hoping to conserve his stores until reinforcement, he gave ground slowly, walking the decks to escape the bad air below, lying down only when exhausted in the hopes of promoting sound sleep. The *Tarida* entered the Adriatic before he finally collapsed.

The captain, reluctant to return a dead merchant to his family, called over a Candian sailor with reputed skills as a herbalist, who prepared infusions of *dictamus* and shook his head. When he learned the contents of Matteo's sacks below, however, he brought beans up and brewed *kahveh* on the deck, administering sips every hour. Matteo lost weight steadily, but never fell senseless; he was conscious and despairing when the ship entered the lagoon.

Matteo had been gone for ten months. He returned, broken and defeated, to find that his intended maiden journey had returned (with moderate success); the Dutch had effectively cut off the flow of spices from the Moluccas; and Marina had died in June of childbed fever, four days after giving birth to a stillborn son.

➤ ➤ ➤

The streets below the Piazza San Marco were quiet; a gentleman in grey trailing behind him was the only other soul in sight as he

turned toward the campanile of St. Mark's, still tinted with sunlight on its upper reaches. When he stepped through the
nondescript building's west entrance a guard obliged him to produce the letter attesting that Messer Matteo Benveneto was
granted entry to the Archivio dei Documenti. He was escorted to
the third floor, where Scipio himself answered the guard's knock.

"Ser Benveneto," he said, his voice no more unwelcome or
suspicious than usual. "You are here late." He opened the door
far enough to admit him.

"I wished to return these volumes," Matteo replied. "It was
most gracious of the senator to permit me to take them away."

"It is not the library's policy to permit works to be removed
from the building," Scipio observed, taking the volumes from
Matteo and inspecting them closely. "Senator Domenico's
request on your behalf was quite exceptional." Matteo had hoped
to find him gone at this hour, but the librarian seemed to live in
these rooms.

The library had lost some of the wonder it had held for
Matteo upon his first admission, but he still felt a tremor of excitement as he looked from one book-lined wall to the next. Most of
the volumes were relatively dull—reports by diplomats and
informers, dating back decades, describing in detail the battle-
ments and garrisons of various cities—but their very numbers
seemed to compel interest, as though they had been compressed,
like charcoal, into a form ready to ignite. "Do you have writings
on *qahwa*?" he asked politely.

"*Qahwa*?" the librarian asked, frowning. "The shrub Arabs
use to make medicine?"

"The drink made from a bean, yes."

Scipio scowled and turned to open a large ledger on his desk.
"You will have to return tomorrow," he said over his shoulder.

Matteo had hoped he would be invited to stay while the
librarian went off to find the volumes, but he merely nodded and
thanked the man again. It was growing dark as he descended the
stairs; even the broad lanes were filling with shadow. Matteo
walked unaccosted, conscious that this was not his part of town.
By the time he reached Franchescina's street it was twilight,
smells of cooking wafted through open windows, and the only

other pedestrians were swathed in the grey that cats adopt at night.

"I expected you earlier," she said upon admitting him. "I hope you ate."

He had not, and the thought that a cold chicken breast might await him had cheered his long walk. He kissed her, to show how little he cared about food, and asked how her day had been.

"Trying," she replied with a sigh. "People come to see me, they don't know what they want, so become impatient that I cannot at once give it to them."

"Give them something finer than what they think they want." Matteo strode into the dining room and spilled a handful of beans onto the table. "From a shipment that arrived three days ago. They are much superior to the last ones."

He had expected her to require persuading of the beans' significance, but Franchescina exclaimed as though he had poured out jewels. "They're lovely!" she cried, stepping forward to pick up several. "I'll get the mortar." She went into the kitchen, where he heard her telling Paola to boil water. Smiling, she returned with the marble set he had given her and sat down across from him. She poured the beans into the bowl, letting them click, then bore the pestle down with a crunch. Matteo watched bemusedly as she applied herself, as though grinding caofa beans before one's lover was a skill known to every courtesan.

"Do you remember how to make it?" he asked. She flashed him a smile that counseled him not to be foolish. Of course, she had watched him prepare the caofa he had served her once and had memorized the steps of its preparation, which she recognized as better suited to her. Deftly she reduced the fragments to powder; perhaps she wished to demonstrate her wrist action. A rich aroma spread through the room.

"It is too bad," he said casually, "that the beans have all been roasted, preventing any buyer from growing his own." Franchescina had no reaction to this. He had seen her slip a half dozen beans into her sleeve, and was glad to see she was not contemplating betrayal.

Paola brought out the water, and Matteo produced his golden sieve, at which Franchescina's eyes opened wide. "Not a present, alas," he said as he passed it over. The servant stared as Franchescina tipped in the caofa and poured the steaming water. "Do you recognize this, Paola?" he asked. "It is caofa, an eastern drink sometimes used as a medicine. But it is beneficial to the healthy as much as the ailing, and delicious besides." The old woman was doubtless as great a gossip as her mistress.

Solids sublime only slowly, heated fluids faster. Sliding between the silk sheets Matteo had bought her, Franchescina snuggled against him, her belly radiating warmth as though from fires within. Matteo could feel her drying upon him, the vapors escaping from beneath the sheet he had pulled up to perfume the air around his face. Would the essence of caofa now running through her veins tincture her perspiration and other liquids? It was an interesting question, too subtle for Gaspare with his hydraulics and pressures to answer.

As though thinking along parallel lines, Franchescina whispered: "Do the scholars at the university study caofa's effect on the humors?"

"How should I know? I just trade for goods."

"You said you were going there soon, to consult their library."

"That was—" That was to investigate the design of steam engines, which Matteo was now enjoined from discussing. When had he let that slip? "That was another matter."

"I thought you wanted to study rising fluids."

Matteo wondered what the hell he had said. Franchescina knew no more about humors or sublimation than he did; she merely possessed the facility to chat with seeming knowledge about anything. He decided to speak less hereafter of his plans for caofa, and not at all about steam.

"My fluids are rising already," he said. "Come here."

➤ ➤ ➤

Matteo sat reading in his father's study, and later, when he could venture out, in the libraries of his father's friends. He did not know how many doors had been opened by pity; it was not a question he was yet strong enough to face. What he did know was that traders bought cheap and sold dear, preferably goods that they alone controlled. And that with Venetians' profits slashed nearly to nothing, what the Benvenetos needed was something wondrous to corner.

Even as he paged through folios of unreliable Ottoman histories, Matteo knew that it was *qahwa,* which had soothed his nausea and preserved his life, that was to be his miracle import. The references he found were all in the tales of travelers, as though word of caofa had repeatedly washed to shore but never lodged on land. Belli spoke of "*cave,*" while an Augsburg botanist who had visited Jerusalem mentioned the drinking of "kahveh" and a Dutch volume called *Linschooten's Travels* included a reference to "chaoua." Had none of these men bothered to taste it?

Matteo served it to his family, his father's colleagues, his mother's friends. He adulterated its essence with milk, with honey, with wine (a poor idea), with brandy (better). He sprinkled fine grounds upon pastry. He exhausted his supply and sent to Alexandria for more, at considerable expense. Eventually he persuaded some few dozen acquaintances that caofa was a pleasing curiosity.

"Do you hope to sell caofa to the Venetians?" asked his father, amused. "Should our fellow citizens develop a taste for it, they will surely procure their own."

"I hope to sell caofa to Europe," Matteo replied. "All Venice should harbor such hopes. Do we control tobacco, pepper, saffron? Do we sell anything others cannot?" *Do we wish to become great again?* he wanted to ask, but dared not.

It was at a masque that a young man Matteo's own age approached and asked whether he had seen any "steaming engines" during his months in Alexandria. Surprised, Matteo described a brass serpent that would flap wings when the kettle within it boiled. The man nodded, yes that was the principle, and showed disappointment when Matteo said that he had seen nothing larger. There were reports, Gaspare Treviso explained, of tiny carriages that would roll forward when a brazier in their vitals was kindled and similar playthings. Nowhere, however, had anyone built a machine that harnessed the expansive force of steam to perform real work.

"The ancients designed such engines, but any that were built are now lost. Have the sultan's engineers constructed their like, or learned of others who have? I fear the Turks' wealth and long reach."

Matteo welcomed the Turks' wealth and long reach: they gathered in the goods that Venetians could sell to Europe. He listened, politely but without sympathy, as the young man spoke of engines that piped water to foundries or drained mines more efficiently than hand-worked pumps or bucket winches. He gravely agreed that Turkish builders were formidable, and showed him his caofa mill, whose gears were machined to clockwork precision yet could withstand the resistance of caofa beans being crushed. Gaspare studied the mechanism and agreed gloomily that Venetian craftsmen could only produce such workmanship at prohibitive expense.

Several days later Matteo received a letter from the Arsenal, where Treviso worked alongside his father in the bronze foundry. The engineer inquired whether Matteo would be willing to come examine something "interesting" in two days' time. Mystified, Matteo wrote back agreeing to accompany him.

Gaspare arrived dressed nearly as well as Matteo, and seemed somber in a manner he had not seemed before. The engineer conducted him not to the Arsenal (where the trader had expected to be shown some improved milling device) but instead to an anonymous building within sight of St. Mark's, where two guards challenged them as soon as they approached. It was only after much scrutiny, especially of the letter Gaspare produced, that they were at length admitted.

"What was that you gave them?" he whispered after the guards shut the door behind them.

"A letter of passage," Gaspare replied softly as a new pair of guards approached. "I have another for Ser Scipio upstairs." As they were escorted up the stairs, he added: "Don't say anything."

And so Matteo was admitted to the library that had no name, which occupied the third floor (and perhaps more) of the blandly titled Archivio dei Documenti, itself inaccessible without sanction from an authority greater than the city's large bureaucracy contained. The letters, documents, and manuscripts came (Gaspare told him) from every corner of the Mohammedan world, including lands like Spain and Sicily, which the Infidels had once conquered and might yet again.

Matteo spent two afternoons reading through Arabian treatises and copying out what they had to say about steam-driven engines. He had no reason to help young Treviso, but the entree the bumptious young builder enjoyed to this secret trove must mean something, and access through ports was what all traders craved. The letter that Matteo had been given to show Scipio he retained (although his notes had to stay in the library, where they gave signs of being handled in his absence), and the name of Senator Domenico was on it. Matteo was willing enough to do a favor for a man with such friends.

Gaspare invited him to dinner and thanked him for the report, which had evidently become part of the library's holdings. "Most of what you found was ancient knowledge," he admitted. "That fellow Hero lived as long ago as Our Lord."

"I am sorry I could not find you anything," Matteo replied courteously.

"If the Turks have been building steam devices, I want to know of it," said Gaspare, who paused to study the hinge of a mussel he had just opened. "But if they turn out to know nothing, all the better.

"Hero's book was called *Pneumatica*," he added after swallowing, "and I have asked that the University at Padua be requested to send its copy. I don't suppose you read Greek?"

"Not even the Greek of today," Matteo admitted. "If you deal with officials in Athens, you speak Turkish."

Gaspare suddenly grinned. "I bet you do not even read Latin," he said. "Of course not: it is the language of science, not trade." He stood and brought over two leather-bound volumes. "Nice to see a proper-looking book, eh? Take a look at them."

Matteo, who had been wondering what gift of Gaspare's had so impressed the Republic's leaders that he was given the power to summon books from one city to another, took the folios in hand. They were *De Medicina Ægyptorum* and *De Plantis Ægypti Liber,* by one Alpinus. Opening the cover, he found a note, written in a strong Italian hand, disclosing that the author was actually Prospero Alpini, a Venetian physician and botanist who had traveled to Egypt in 1580. Was that what librarians did, inform on authors?

"Here, turn to the marked page," said Gaspare, leaning across the table to flip the top volume open. Matteo found himself looking at an illustration of a small tree.

"This is a caofa shrub?" he guessed.

"Oh, you've never seen one? I assumed they were cultivated locally. Yes, each book contains a discussion of 'caova,' as he calls it. They are part of the University Library at Padua; I briefly have their loan." And Gaspare explained how his investigations came to enjoy such support. The tale involved a drawing seen during his schooldays and long remembered, of a device that spun and flung jets of steam; and a tale about an ill-soldered pot that had been used in a nobleman's kitchen to boil water: the lid had become fixed fast, and—when a scullion bent over it to wonder why no steam was escaping—blew up with enough force to maim.

This led young Gaspare to wonder whether steam could serve in place of gunpowder. Although the gun he built was unwieldy and temperamental, it did propel a bullet through a wall. When Gaspare expressed concern that the engineers of the Sublime Porte might turn their fearsome ingenuity to exploiting this power, he was quietly granted permission to consult an archive on such matters.

Matteo was impressed with Gaspare's ability to win government support for his project. It didn't sound as if this included financial assistance, but Matteo knew he could complete that next step. "You plainly possess the knowledge to do great things," he said. "But will you profit from this asset, or shall the Senate and *burocrazie* relieve you of your treasure, as a trader would fleece a foolish seller?"

Later that night, after hours of talk and brandy, Matteo drew up a partnership agreement, formalizing their conjoined efforts to develop engines and other devices powered by steam and to profit thereby. Gaspare, who received wages for his work in defense of the Republic, had not thought how he might protect his own interests, which seemed to him one with his city's. He read over the agreement, which Matteo had set down in the standard wording, and frowned indecisively.

"Of course you should not sign it until you have discussed matters with your lawyer," Matteo told him. Abruptly he pulled over the agreement and signed it himself. "There," he said. "Now I am bound by this; until you sign, you are not." And he returned the sheet and sat back.

He knew without thinking that Gaspare would now honor the contract, and stood to raise his goblet. "Like steam, may we expand and be felt!" The two men drank ceremoniously and hurled their cups to the floor. Then, to drive the fumes from their heads, they brewed and drank a pot of caofa.

❧ ❧ ❧

The *Argo* came through the lagoon with its sails snapping, as if to advertise its disdain of rowers. Though one of a dozen ships to reach the city that morning, it was recognized by a harbormaster's boy, and Matteo got word as he was finishing breakfast. He was at the quay before the inspectors and tariff assessors were through, and stood waiting to greet the captain as soon as he stepped off.

"Welcome back, Captain," he said, leaning out to extend the old man a hand. "A happy voyage, I hope."

"Happy for those who stand at its conclusion with their hands open," he muttered, a bit ungraciously. He grasped Matteo's wrist and pulled himself up onto the pier, then squinted at him. "Messer Benveneto. Your family will have no reason to curse, if I remember rightly."

"Thanks, Captain," said Matteo with a bow. "The ship's manifest . . . ?"

"Is in the hands of the purser." They were walking toward the harbormaster's office, where the captain would have to go through various formalities before he could have breakfast. He looked up the quay, as if expecting more traders come to ask after their goods.

Then, as if recalling something odd, he added: "You got several sacks of beans."

There were more important shipments expected than this, but Matteo was inordinately pleased by the news. He wished the captain good morning and sent one of his boys to alert the warehouse that a ship was in. He returned to the office and was checking receipts when Gaspare appeared.

"We have a site," he said briskly as he came through the door. Matteo stared at him. "A building," Gaspare explained when he noticed the expression. "Where they want us to build a steam-driven engine. We're to inspect it this morning."

"Gaspare, I have a ship just in. I'm going to be busy all day."

The engineer blinked, as if startled at not being understood. "They want us there this morning; other times are no good. They seemed reluctant even to tell me where the building is."

Matteo tried to control his exasperation. "Gaspare, that's nonsense. They want us to make measurements, they let us visit the site. Where are we building, in a contessa's boudoir?"

"I don't know," Gaspare said seriously. "They eventually gave me a map, but it lacks some important information, which they would only tell me. Are new inventions kept in secret locations?"

Matteo looked at him bemusedly. It had occurred to him that he could spare the next two hours, before the goods were unloaded and had to be watched. Certainly Gaspare could take a man and carry out the measurements himself, but a shrewder head should also be present.

Sitting across from Gaspare in the gondola a few minutes later, he studied their scribbled route, which was indeed incomprehensible if one did not know its point of origin, and difficult to reconcile with the city's layout if one did. We're not being told overmuch, he thought.

Three men stood silently at the dock where they debarked. They took Gaspare's map and led the young men through a narrow street that saw little traffic, into an alley separating the back fences of unfamiliar buildings, and finally through the servants' entrance of an anonymous brick pile that Matteo doubted he would recognize from the front.

Inside stood Senator Domenico's secretary, who led them down the corridor into a windowless room, which he indicated was the space they should measure. "You want us to install the engine here?" Gaspare asked. He stamped the tiled floor, inquired about its load bearing capacity, then explained that he would have to drill a hole through the floor to drop the plumb line through. The secretary muttered a word to one of the guards, who returned a moment later with a wooden toolbox.

"So when was this house built?" asked Gaspare amiably as he chiseled into a tile and then applied the drill. No one answered, and when he finally drove the bit through the wood and into the void below, he sang out the floor's thickness, which Matteo wrote down. Men watched silently as he took out a lead bob on a string and lowered it through the hole, ear held close as he listened for the click.

Matteo looked idly about the room, which had water-stained walls and lamps too dim to read by. He had concluded it wasn't a private home, and decided now that it was some government building, where petty bureaucrats would come in to study their engine and measure its achievement. Perhaps new devices, not yet ready for production, were tested or stored here. Matteo thought suddenly of the university, and scribbled *8-10 beans/sack?* in his notebook. One of the men saw him writing when Gaspare had not called out a number and frowned.

"Got it," Gaspare said, and pulled up his string, laid it along the floor, and counted its length in tiles, which he reported to Matteo. With a practiced motion Matteo placed the toe of his boot against a tile to establish its length, which he multiplied by Gaspare's figure and wrote down. It was a tradesman's trick, the kind shopkeepers use to take quick measure, but the secretary seemed to dislike him already, so Matteo didn't care.

"Time to go downstairs," Gaspare announced. He lowered the bob back down the hole to its previous extent, weighted the string with a loose tile, then stood brushing his hands. The guards glanced at each other, but the secretary led them silently from the room. They descended a steep stair into darkness, whose chill breath wafted the taste of standing water, wood rot, and something organic that didn't get the chance to blow away.

"Watch your step," Matteo called back to Gaspare, a warning that the secretary had not offered him. The final stair was a different height than the rest, which was hard to anticipate in the near darkness. Save for the candle the secretary carried, the basement was black as a crypt, and the wavering light barely reached the packed earth floor.

The secretary stopped and turned. "Here," he said, holding out his candle. Matteo could see a plastered wall and some rough stones underfoot, but the ceiling was invisible, save the tiny hole Gaspare had drilled. "Where is the basement's lowest point?" Gaspare asked as he examined the floor. "That's the place to drain." Matteo was studying the high-water marks on the wall, the most recent of which appeared to be a few inches up.

With their measurements completed the secretary plainly wanted them gone, but the two men lingered, looking about for things they should note. Gaspare scuffed at the floor, remarking that it could be raked to present its lowest point where the pipe opened, while Matteo inquired about the basement's square footage. Eventually they were herded back up the stairs, where Matteo banged his head against a low beam and Gaspare laughed. "It would have hurt more if the wood hadn't been rotten," he retorted.

Outside they were taken away by a different route than they had come, and conducted through numerous turns before being deposited in a covered gondola. "I don't think they want us back," Matteo observed. "Do they expect us to build the engine elsewhere?"

Allowed at last to disembark, the engine-makers grinned at each other and made ironical gestures: something to talk about when there is time. Matteo had a cargo to protect from pilferage, while Gaspare had to hasten back to the Arsenal and other deadlines. "Are we still for Padua?" Gaspare asked.

"On Thursday we are for Padua," Matteo assured him; and repeated it to Franchescina that night. "Why ever are you going there?" she asked.

"Beans," he said, and laughed. Worldly as she was, and somewhat mercenary, she had never heard that mainland term for money.

"Does Ser Treviso travel for beans?" she asked mockingly.

"Gaspare travels to learn how to build a better engine," he replied. "Do you know what he calls his present model? A *succhiatore*."

Lying back on his pillow, Matteo imagined the fragrance of caofa ascending through the caverns of his sinuses, each wisp slipping through keyholes and causing thick doors to swing open. Sex drains the loins as wine feeds the blood, but caofa opens the mind to the vibrancy of the world beyond, where a man strides free in the brightening tones of dawn, remembered even as reason and the body compose themselves for sleep.

Padua had been Venice's for two hundred years, but the city was freely given, and did not comport itself like a possession. It was dark before the travelers arrived, after a day spent crossing the lagoon and being rowed upriver, and Matteo directed his servant to find a good inn. "And not one with students in it," warned Gaspare, who had been here before.

Matteo slept in a strange bed, as traders do, and breakfasted with Gaspare before they separated, bound for different parts of town. He asked directions for the Department of Botany, and walked along a surprisingly uncrowded road following the river (it could not be mistaken for a canal). In the distance, waving faintly like an unexpected memory, was a row of palm trees.

"It was as a physician that I accompanied the Consul," the director explained with a deprecating gesture, as though this admission came somehow at his expense. "The fact that I held the Chair in Botany was of no concern to the Venetian government, which was worried only about its consulate being poisoned by foreign doctors. The university was happy to authorize funding for the collection of samples, although"—he laughed and gestured at the botanical garden around them—"I ended by exceeding my budget several times over."

"I can well imagine," said Matteo. The image of a Venetian trading vessel entering the lagoon, its deck a swaying oasis of potted palms, shrubs, and citrus trees, seemed a very allegory of collector's extravagance. Perhaps Alpini was allowed to return some on the consular galley, though Matteo doubted it.

"Your letter spoke of an interesting project," Alpini said. "You look to be a man of business, not a scholar. Pray tell me what your own travels to Egypt have produced, that you believe I could be of some help to you."

Matteo took out his leather bag. "Do you recognize these?"

he asked, pouring a handful of green beans into Alpini's hand.

The director studied them closely. "I suppose they are Egyptian? They look like . . . heavens, they look like the berries of the caova tree." He shook his head, smiling. "I saw one in Cairo, but it rarely flowered. The caova really only flourishes in southern Arabia, in the highlands. That's where these seeds must have originated, to reach this nice size. The natives roast them and make a hot drink of it."

"Indeed." The two men had settled on a bench beside the path, where Alpini was turning over the beans in his palm. "Do you think you could grow them?"

"These seeds? I never succeeded in Egypt." He prodded a particularly large one with his finger. "I wouldn't mind trying again, though."

"I have twelve sacks of them," Matteo said. "Perhaps one was hurried through the scalding process." He opened his wallet and pulled out a dozen tiny twists of paper, which rattled slightly. "All we need are a few beans—even one—that were not heated enough."

"In the wrong climate or soil, the tree will not flower," Alpini warned. "But if there is still life in these seeds, I shall bring it forth." He shook the packets lightly, as though anxious to open them. "Did you travel extensively in Egypt? I could not: the Consul remained in Cairo, and me perforce with him." They were walking toward the garden gates and the botanical building beyond, where Alpini wanted to show the beans to his students. "Do you get there often?"

❧ ❧ ❧

The Palazzo Communale stood on Padua's main square, built at the Republic's expense so that "Venetian and Paduan men of good will might meet and converse together to increase their mutual love and trust." Many of the afternoon's occupants appeared to be students, neither Venetian nor Paduan (the famous university attracted scholars from throughout Europe) nor, to Matteo's jaded eye, men of good will, either.

This did not matter, for students were as ready to relish pleasures as more sensible men—and probably faster to speak of them afterward. The hired serving-maid smiled at everyone as she ground the beans in a pestle, to coarse comments but also looks of interest. The carafe was a fine one, and the emptiness of the cups, arranged invitingly along the long table, carried an unmistakable air of expectation.

Matteo walked among the onlookers nodding and bowing, like a burgher at the marriage of his daughter. "From Arabia, yes," he told inquirers. "They call it caofa, the word actually means 'wine.' Because it intoxicates without stupefying, the Mohammedans' proscription against alcohol cannot touch it. Yes, Egyptians and Turks drink it black and hot, but in a moment Faustina will set out cream, honey, vanilla, and other additives, so that Christian tongues may taste it in a more becoming mode."

Men were leaning forward as Faustina poured the rich dark powder into the sieve. One by one the students sniffed, recoiled with a startled expression, then took a second, deeper breath. By the time the kettle was boiling she had attracted a considerable audience, who watched the thin stream patter over the grounds like rain on parched earth. Enough men were waiting that Faustina poured the cups only a quarter full, as though this were an especially select vintage. Matteo watched as they grabbed the cups and tasted, then looked at each other uncertainly as they smacked their lips or rubbed the grains against their tongues. One glanced at him, and Matteo said, "Remember your first sip of wine?"

By the time the second carafe was being served, the first drinkers were looking at each other with a dawning surmise, and the buzz of conversation grew a bit louder, the gestures more animated. Encouragements were shouted at Faustina to grind faster, and laughter broke out in small groups. A young man added cream to his cup and was roundly jeered by his fellows.

Matteo was arranging that a tray of caofa be taken to a group of older men sitting at the far side of the room when Gaspare grabbed his elbow. "I've got it!" the builder whispered.

"Got what? Have you had a cup yet? They're going fast."

"I've got the answer! Look at this." Gaspare was trying to show him something; he was flipping through the pages of a huge book. "It's called *De Re Metallica*; one of the professors told me about it. I've been in the library all day."

"Gaspare, can this wait? I've got responsibilities right now."

Gaspare looked around bemusedly. "You're hosting this? What a waste of good caofa!" He opened the folio. "In brief, it's a book about mining and smelting, which little concerns us at the Arsenal. But look at this." Gaspare pointed to a large woodcut illustration. "It is a machine for draining water from a mine— '*siphones aquam spiritu tractam*'; that is, a suction-pump. Can you see what produces the suction? It's a *pestone*!"

"A rod attached to a cylinder?" Matteo was sure that the text explained this, and felt a stab of annoyance at having to guess when Gaspare had not.

"There is a seal within the cylinder, which the rod pushes up and down. A down stroke expels the air beneath the cylinder, so that the up stroke will then produce suction. And that draws up the water!"

"Excellent." Matteo stood and waved to an older man who had just come in, a Paduan trader he knew. They were sitting in armchairs discussing river traffic when Faustina appeared with two cups, which she served as though filling an order. "Do you know this, Benito?" Matteo asked casually, then watched his colleague sniff uncertainly and sip. Another trader stopped by, and soon Matteo was invited to a dockside tavern where merchants gathered at a back table at the close of day. By seven he was sitting at Grimaldi's dinner table, being regarded curiously by the trader's family.

"Could a potion consumed solely by Turks and other heathen truly be welcomed in Christian lands?" asked daughter Maria.

Matteo inclined his head politely. "Spices and fine fabrics cannot be produced in Europe, so we import them. There is nothing un-Christian about eating pepper or wearing silk."

"How much is consumed to make a cup?" asked Grimaldi's son Giorgio.

"Perhaps a half cup of beans to brew a carafe," Matteo admitted.

"So you do not get hundreds of servings per pound," Grimaldi observed. "Caofa is not a precious substance, but rather a commodity, like wine or grain."

"I can see why the physicians made a medicine of it, to dispense by the spoonful," Signora Grimaldi remarked.

"Wine and grain can be very profitable," Matteo pointed out. "And caofa costs much more than either. Would you leave this market for the Dutch to pick up?"

"It is possible," Giorgio said diplomatically, "that the felicities of caofa will be appreciated most readily in the metropolises of Venice or Amsterdam, with their sophisticated and well-traveled populaces. Might it not encounter resistance in smaller cities or towns?"

Matteo wanted to reply that cinnamon and nutmeg were consumed in every household that could afford them, but Maria spoke up first. "Is it true that in Venice the carnival lasts for six months of the year?"

"Why, it may be six months from October to Lent," replied Matteo as though in surprise, "but the Arsenal builds ships, and merchants hire them, throughout the year." He wondered if every convent-taught mainland girl held such beliefs.

"But you allow brawling on the bridges during Feast Days," she said.

"The *battagliole*? But that is sport!"

"But it is true that people are sometimes killed?" asked Giorgio, sounding more intrigued than scandalized.

"They use their fists; that is why they are called *pugni*." Matteo sought to change his tone to worldly amusement. "The birds at your market day cockfights die; our pugni don't."

"Two cups of that stuff and I still feel as alert as if it were lunch time!" Grimaldi exclaimed, slapping a palm against the table. "There will be a market for it, never fear." His family nodded and smiled, and Matteo felt like a general who heard word that the first village beyond the frontier has been taken.

The men spent the rest of the evening discussing the northern trade, then Grimaldi rose with a yawn (Matteo knew how long the effects of the caofa would last) and announced that good merchants rose early. Returning from the garden fifteen minutes later, Matteo encountered Giorgio in a darkened corridor; without a word they turned and headed for the kitchen, where Matteo ground enough caofa to send them both buzzing like hives. The evening ended with the two young men sitting on the tiled floor, brains crackling, as they plotted the invasion of the Hapsburg lands with merchant vessels led by caofa-sharpened traders and armed with the beans themselves.

➤ ➤ ➤

"The steam enters a cylinder and pushes the *pestone* upward," Gaspare was saying. The shoreline was flowing past them faster than yesterday, when they had been sailing upriver. "The operator continues admitting steam until the *pestone* is at the top of the cylinder. This pressure batters against its inner surface, despite being made up of very little air and water. Like little men pushing hard. Do you understand?"

"How is this an improvement on our present design?" Matteo asked.

"The steam, of course. In the *Succhiatore,* all the power to be generated by several minutes' heating is expended at once, which means it must first be concentrated in one place. Here, the steam only exerts enough pressure to push the *pestone* upward—there's no resistance except the *pestone*'s own weight, so we don't need that tremendous pressure. Don't you see?"

"It works in many little gasps, rather than a single great one?"

"Well put! It does not have to drink the sea in a single draught." Excitement seemed to have lent Gaspare a poetical turn of mind.

"We need it to work reliably," Matteo reminded him. That was the sole beauty of the homely *Succhiatore*: it was too simple to allow technical complications. Enough now to demonstrate that such engines worked; they could improve the design later.

"It's the caofa vendor!" cried a hearty voice behind him. Matteo turned to see a merchant whose face he remembered from the day before.

"Did I charge you for that cup?" he asked mildly.

"You'll charge me for the next one!" Behind his bluff cheer, the man eyed Matteo appraisingly. "Have you calculated your unit costs yet?"

"That depends on whether we import by galley," Matteo replied. Renting a state-owned galley was expensive, but it greatly reduced insurance rates on the cargo.

"In Sumatra, pepper is as cheap as flour," the merchant observed. Gaspare, bored by this unpromising turn of subject, drifted off toward the bow, but Matteo took the man's meaning.

"Caofa reaches Egypt inexpensive enough that shopkeepers can drink it," he said. "Venetian demand may drive the price up, but the increased cultivation this will encourage will bring it back down. When that happens—it may take three or four years—we will see an explosion of caofa-drinking in Europe."

As soon as the boat bumped against the deck Matteo and Gaspare vaulted over the railing. It was Saturday afternoon, and workers were being hastened to complete their work before the Sabbath. Matteo bade his friend goodbye and went to the office, where he hoped to learn that an expected ship had come in. Instead he found a note from his uncle, summoning him home on family business.

Puzzled and apprehensive, he walked rapidly to Palazzo Benveneto, wondering whether an unfavorable report of his Paduan adventure had reached his father's ears. On the staircase he met Uncle Bartolomeo. "How was your voyage?" he asked. "Did your stomach tolerate the packet?"

"Scarcely a voyage, and it went well. And rivers run quite smoothly." Matteo hoped no one else would think to ask.

His uncle smiled affectionately, younger son to younger son. "Your ventures are already coming to the attention of important people."

Matteo felt a thrill of alarm. "My caofa party?"

"No, not that." Bartolomeo chuckled. "The plumbing system you want to install with young Treviso. You boys hope to become building contractors?"

Matteo paused before the door of his father's office and composed himself, then knocked. It was Alessandro's voice that called him to come in, and when he opened the door Matteo saw the two men sitting at the desk, which was spread with papers. "Ah, Matteo," said his father. "I gather your trip went well."

"He successfully disposed of his merchandise," said Alessandro dryly.

"Thank you, ser, it did," Matteo replied, ignoring his brother.

"I believe that if we brought a shipment of caofa into Venice, we could sell it."

Ser Benveneto looked thoughtful, but before he could say anything, Alessandro spoke up: "Easier at least to give away beans than sell steam."

Matteo began to reply, but Ser Benveneto raised a forestalling hand. "And there is that second matter," he said. He picked up a folded sheet, which bore at its upper edge a broken Senate seal. "The secretary for Senator Domenico has written, setting out the terms by which you and your friend shall undertake to build a pump powered by the pressure of steam." He glanced over the paper at his son. "They are not generous, but I suppose it represents entree into a new market."

"A new market for what?" Alessandro asked. "Are we to supply boilers for the leaky basements of government buildings?"

"We are selling the design," Matteo, sensing that Alessandro wished to provoke him, replied calmly. "Or rather, we are not selling the design; after we demonstrate its success with the model we are being paid to build, I will apply for a letter patent."

Alessandro looked puzzled—good eldest son, he could only imagine trading in *things*—and Ser Benveneto rustled the paper. "You will have to take care if you wish to retain control of this project," he remarked. "Without physical possession, your bargaining strength is much compromised."

"What do you mean?" Matteo asked. He understood that his father, as head of the family, would have received and read any correspondence, but wished that he could now see the letter.

"The Senate evidently considers this design valuable to the state," said Ser Benveneto, with an admonitory nod at Alessandro, "and wishes it built within the security of the Arsenal."

"What? May I see that?" Matteo reached for the letter anxiously. His father handed it over, then murmured something to Alessandro, who got up and left.

Matteo read and reread the letter in bewilderment. The *sipho* would be built on the site that Messers Benveneto and Treviso had been shown; and it would be developed and assembled in a special workshop at the Arsenal. On a second reading Matteo caught a reference to *ingenium*, and realized that two pumps, the second a product of the builders' further improvisation, were to be produced.

Gaspare must have spoken of an unproved model after all, and the senator had decided to let them try to build it. Matteo read once more through the letter, at last understanding its various clauses. "This cannot be," he said at last.

"No?" asked his father, amused.

"We are not arsenalotti," he observed. "We will design the second model in our own workshop, and deliver it when complete. Do they think we are petitioning to join their work rolls?" The sum specified was moreover too small for a *Succhiatore* plus an *ingenium,* but that was a matter of bargaining.

Matteo realized how exhilarated he should be that the senate was showing interest in a model that Gaspare had merely described confidently. He looked at the second sheet, which proved to be a special *licentia* permitting him to enter the Arsenal. Glumly he put it down.

His father smiled. "If your pump proves successful, there will be recognition from the Republic, whether financial or not. You told me once that your caofa project was more for the glory of Venice than the wealth of our family." (Matteo winced; had he ever made such an unmercantile remark?) "Might your steam pump prove valuable to Venice?"

"It possesses some worth," Matteo said. "How much depends on how far the design might be improved."

"Well then," said his father, nodding, "it is good that the Republic wishes you to improve it."

This was not to the point, but Matteo had realized by now what his father was thinking. Three sons were more than the family business needed, and his father had suggested before that Matteo's gift for language and numbers might stand in good stead for government service. He did not appreciate that the Benvenetos needed a son who knew better than to follow the business practices of their father, who was reluctant to abandon the successful strategies of decades.

"If they wished, I would improve the Republic," said Matteo, and saw by his father's expression that he had gone too far; but it was true, Venice was ossifying like the deposits that encrust hulls and chains, hardening like an old man's joints. Matteo knew the malady and realized moreover the avenues to cure, for *Venice should be more like steam* and expand to press against every surface it touched; indeed in its ability to force its way into openings and run the shortest routes *Venice should be like money,* flowing instantly where value could be found and drying up where it had withered. And where money finds opportunity and nourishes it, the fruits will quicken the wits of others, even those whom they reach from far away: for Venice lives by water and wind, which carry the essence of its wealth: Matteo could not say it aloud, but yes, *Venice should be like caofa.*

➤ ➤ ➤

The Sun hung just above the lagoon's wavering reflection, which fragmented and reformed in the vagrant breeze that accompanied sunrise. Workers were already rowing down the Rio dei Gesuidi, but Matteo recognized them as porters, artisans, and vendors. The arsenalotti all lived to the south and west, in the small closed neighborhoods that had housed the shipyard's workers for centuries.

A church bell was ringing, evidently to speed the tardy. The swart Venetian faces—there were, Matteo realized, no foreigners present—looked relaxed, unhurried. Matteo would have walked a bit faster, but did not care to draw attention to himself. Not since Alexandria had he seen a crowd where everyone was dressed alike.

He was stopped at the gate, as he had expected, but when he showed his *licentia* the guards frowned, grew more unfriendly rather than less, and pulled Matteo out of line and sat him in a small room. He was still there forty minutes later when Gaspare came in.

"Sorry about that," his colleague said. "Your papers were unfamiliar to the *portoneri,* who have sent them to their superiors. We're going to have to wait a while. Care for some breakfast?"

Gaspare led Matteo back out the gate and onto the now nearly empty Campo dell'Arsenale. "Are visitors to the Arsenal so unusual?" he asked. "Those guards acted as though I was likely a spy."

"We get visitors all the time. The Arsenal has become a tourist stop for prominent foreigners, from whom the guards expect tips. But you're Venetian, you're a trader, and you came carrying a pass from the senate, which nobody had ever seen before. These guys aren't paid to make decisions, and arsenalotti do only what they're paid to do."

Matteo saw a familiar structure near the edge of the square, one of the squat metal boxes that dotted the city, this one bearing a sign, *Denontie Secrete per L'Inquisitorie all'Arsenale,* above the slit where the denunciations would go. He raised his eyebrows. "To the Arsenal Inquisitors, not the Council of Ten?"

Gaspare spread his hands in mock modesty. "The security of *La Serenissima*'s shipyard demands unique precautions."

They sat at a table on a tiny square in San Martino and ordered bread and cheese. Housewives were hanging their washing twenty feet away, looking disapprovingly at Matteo's fine garb. Children's voices bounced like balls off nearby walls, and Matteo could hear women's voices from the kitchen, but the only man he saw was the one who served them.

"An arsenalotti parish, eh?" he asked.

Gaspare laughed. "San Martino? You should go out to San Pietro di Castello. Everyone looks alike!"

Matteo had no desire to be the peacock in a flock of pigeons. "When we get through the gates," he began, "we shall have to show the papers to the Patroni, for they specify that a special site be made available for the construction of our *ingenium.*"

"Our what?" asked Gaspare with a frown.

"Latin for *ingegno,*" Matteo told him. "I didn't know, either."

"Ah." The younger man grinned. "They want us to build an *engine* with our *ingenuity!*"

Matteo sighed. "And they want us to keep it here, did you get that? Not in our own workshop."

"Well, fine. We can use the Arsenal's material rather than our own."

"Let's walk," said Matteo, who did not wish to talk business in this warren of Arsenal families. Faces—similar beyond their suspicious expressions—were peeking out at them from narrow doorways. Matteo directed their steps back toward the Campo.

"Is there some *campiello* where your family has lived for generations?" Matteo asked.

"My family?" Gaspare stopped and stared at him. "My grandfather was almost born in the Ghetto, because some official
wanted to treat *conversos* as Jews. Papa was only allowed to move
here after he married. I am the first generation to be accepted as
not Jewish."

"Your family were *conversos*?"

"Spain insisted," Treviso said heavily. "And when she later
found such conversions unpersuasive, conversos and Jews both
fled. Do you know no history except your own city's?"

"Well, certainly not Spain's," Matteo admitted. "So . . . tell
me. Do Jewish dietary laws proscribe the drinking of caofa?"

Treviso laughed. "Ask an inhabitant of that other gated community. Not all *communita del cancello* are alike."

The Arsenal had only one entrance, so they had to follow the
wall (Matteo looked up at four of the thirteen guard towers as
they passed) around to present themselves at the gate. Two
guards scowled at them, but the *licentia* had been found in good
order, and after signing a large book Gaspare waved him in.
Blinking as he stepped out of the arch's shadows, Matteo felt a
breeze sharp with sawdust and resin, heard hammering echo off
walls, and saw before him as on a broad canvas an enclosed
world, womanless and forever under construction, the outspread
hive of the *Officina delle Meraviglie,* the Factory of Marvels.

"Where are they?" Matteo asked, standing on tiptoe.

"The ships? Why, they are everywhere." Gaspare pointed
across the road to an open bale of what looked like twists of old
rope. "That oakum will go to make caulking, which imbues every
vessel. If you mean the hulls, they are launched in the Arsenale
Nove and towed this way, past the dock where they are outfitted
and rigged. When a ship emerges through the wall, it is complete." He shielded his eyes with a hand and scanned the
rooftops to the north. "I don't see a mast, which means that one
hasn't been launched this morning."

A wagon clattered past and the two men stepped back. "Keep
close," Gaspare said as he led his friend around a pyramid of
squat kegs. "A stranger wandering loose would attract notice fast."

Matteo felt as though he were in another country, one that resembled his own in numerous but unimportant ways. Food stalls lined the thoroughfare, and arsenalotti, their attire suggesting the occupying army of a foreign prince, were eating and talking in small groups while others pushed past with barrows or carts. Workshop smells hung in the air, and a shift of wind—the huge enclosure seemed to possess its own weather—brought a whiff of the lagoon.

"We need to find Ser Cavallo," Gaspare was saying. He walked ahead of Matteo to a corner where several workmen stood around an upright cask. Matteo stood at a proper distance awaiting introduction, but Gaspare spoke rapidly to the men in the *linguaggio arsenalesco,* and they listened stolidly without paying Matteo the slightest attention. Each man held a cup, and the cask, he noticed, emitted a distinct odor of wine.

"They don't know where he is," Gaspare reported when he returned to Matteo. "Let's just go to the shop." He sounded irritated.

"That was a big barrel," Matteo observed.

"The *bevanda ordinaria*? It is supplied to all workers here, a tradition that goes back centuries." A note of pride entered Gaspare's voice.

"Free wine for the arsenalotti? I suppose the state worried about the quality of the wells on this part of the island."

"They drink a lot of it," Gaspare added gloomily.

He led Matteo to a large empty space at the back of a storehouse. "The windows admit plenty of light," he said as he swung open the doors and gestured for Matteo to enter. "And they are set well above eye level." Matteo walked across the packed earth through shafts of angled sunlight, looking at the plastered walls and the high ceiling. "There's a well twenty feet away, so water supply isn't a problem. And the cellars"—he stamped the ground—"don't extend back here."

Gaspare meant that they could build a large boiler without worrying about the floorboards. "A chimney?" Matteo asked, looking up.

"We will run a pipe through the ceiling," Gaspare told him. Matteo had meanwhile noticed a ladder built into one of the walls, which ascended to the high windows. He began to climb, ostensibly to examine the roof timbers, but actually to get a look outside.

The row of panes ran just below the eaves, and Matteo peered out upon a landscape of sheds and larger buildings, some with their own courtyards, overlooking gardens of equipage and soaking ponds separated by hedges of stacked timber. Smoke rose from a distant foundry, and a line of workers stood up suddenly bearing a beam on their shoulders. It was like one of the walled estates outside Alexandria, or the cave containing chamber after chamber of treasures in the Arabic fairy tale.

Beyond a long shed he could see the outline of a galley, and next to it another still trellised with scaffold. The Rio, invisible behind them, wound through the Arsenal like an immense gut, swelling at intervals into basins where unfinished ships floated. The surrounding docks were covered, their high roofs large as churches', and Matteo could not tell which of the smaller buildings housed shops for oarmakers and gunners, which contained storerooms or employed the caulkers or shipwrights. From a distant corner rose a column of dense smoke, the foundries of the ironsmiths.

Voices rose from below, and Matteo climbed back down to find Gaspare in conversation with a red-faced man wearing a leather apron. "This is Ser Antonio Cavallo," Gaspare said, rather informally considering the occasion. "He is one of the principal *proti* of the Arsenal."

Matteo greeted him with formal courtesy. "We thank you for providing this space for our labors," he said. He remembered that foremen ranked high in the hierarchy of Arsenal officials, for all the man's rude attire.

"The *Patroni all'Arsenale* have directed that a secure workshop be made available for Ser Traviso's labors," the foreman said solemnly. He seemed quite conscious of the irregularity involved.

"I have already seen the vigilance of the Arsenal security," said Matteo. It was intended as a kind of compliment, but the foreman frowned.

"We are the Arsenal, the *Arx Senatus*," he warned. "Our

guardianship is a sacred trust, which the Fortress of the Senate shall ever hold true."

"You think the word's origin is Latin?" asked Matteo in surprise. "I had assumed it derived from *Dar as-Sina'a,* Arabic for 'House of Construction.'"

The foreman looked as though he had been struck. Gaspare, who had been smiling uneasily, now spoke up. "Ser Cavallo will order the workshop prepared if we find the space satisfactory," he said.

Matteo looked up and down the room a final time. "It is admirable," he declared. "You have our gratitude; we shall accomplish great things here."

The three men made an awkward leave-taking, Matteo and the foreman bowing stiffly as Gaspare made tiny movements toward the door, as though to suggest that the young men now leave. They stepped out amid further assurances of high regard, watched as Ser Cavallo shut and locked the door, then headed down the narrow avenue, ducking as two boys swung a beam round to fit it through a hatch.

"You have to be careful what you say here," Gaspare called after him as they splashed through a flooded expanse. "This is a different world."

"Officials and traders understand each other," Matteo assured him. "We rub together all the time." But the foreman had not spoken like the customs or tax inspectors Matteo regularly dealt with. He had the manners of a craftsman, and Matteo realized with a start that he might have begun as one.

"There is Alvise," said Gaspare as an elderly man turned the corner and approached the door. The aged laborer squinted at the lock (of good German design) and then at Matteo, and Gaspare stepped forward to hail him in the arsenalotti dialect. "He is charged with safeguarding the warehouses of the Campagna, and now this shop in particular," he reported upon returning. "I have assured him you are intimate with the project, but he regards you doubtfully withal."

"A suspicious people," Matteo acknowledged, remembering the old man's expression.

"Suspicious and combative," Gaspare corrected. "The old doges didn't employ them as their personal guard because the arsenalotti like to take orders." He chuckled at the thought, then added: "Did you know they staged a *battaglia* for Henri III, though it wasn't the season? The French king knew of the custom, and wanted to see it done well."

"And how did he enjoy the spectacle?" Matteo asked.

"He declared it very impressive, but called a halt after a few hours. He said, '*Se è da scherzo, è troppo; se è da vero, è poco.*'"

Matteo laughed. "Not as cruel as a true battle? I thought they used sticks back then!"

"They did indeed, but I suspect that soldiers take greater care to brain their opponents. But too cruel for a game! Keep you that in mind, my friend: even our games aren't games."

They emerged into a small square where the warehouses of the Campagna gave way to the basins of the New Arsenal. Virtually everyone Matteo had seen was dressed in dun arsenalotti attire, with only a patch of grey or other hue visible in the crowds, but ahead he now saw a brightly colored party of obvious foreigners, pointing and gaping as a galley was towed out of one of the covered dry docks.

"Those tourists look like Frenchmen," Matteo exclaimed.

"Very possibly," Gaspare replied easily. "Care to stroll forward and overhear their jabber?"

"No, it's, they could just as easily be Spanish! Doesn't anyone care who comes in to study your secrets?"

"The state cares intently," Gaspare said. "You may be sure that these outsiders are being watched this minute. Are not spies most revealing when they think themselves overlooked?"

Matteo ventured to the edge of the water, hoping to glimpse the timbers that were said to lie seasoning at the bottom. Assemblage began in the Arsenale Novissimo where the hulls were launched, which then attached themselves to dry dock and acquired beams and decks during the long months of labor. In the basin of the Arsenale Nove they were equipped with masts, rudder, and artillery, then were towed through the narrows of the Arsenale Vecchio, paradoxically moving backward in the shipyard's history while proceeding in their own, to be handed arms and provisions as they passed toward the gate. Matteo lifted his eyes to the matrix of seeming disorder, workers and visitors seething beyond the buildings lining the basins, and wondered at the venerable sow, ill-nurtured and slack with inanition, who yet could produce robust litters on demand.

"Like a galleon," he said wonderingly. "Slow to turn, and heavy, but—"

"We work in galleys, not galleons," Gaspare reminded him. "Fast and maneuverable. Why think you of those fat-bellied old boats?"

Matteo was trying to frame an answer when a shout rose from a nearby crowd, men congregating for their noon meal. Someone turned abruptly, sending a cupful of wine spraying in a wide arc; a boy sitting on a cask leaped to the ground and sprinted off. Several swarthy arsenalotti set after him with a roar, waving fists but running unsteadily. Gaspare reached out and hooked the arm of the fleeing youth, sweeping him off his feet. The boy had just pulled himself upright when his pursuers reached him, their mottled expressions furious.

"Back off!" Gaspare shouted (Matteo understood that much), and the men hesitated. A brief exchange followed, the arsenalotti offering justification and Gaspare evidently pulling rank to send them away. One held up something, which Gaspare demanded and received. As the workers turned and left, he rounded on the frightened youth.

"Idiot child!" he shouted, shaking him. "I should let them tear you apart!"

The boy began to say something, which Gaspare interrupted to demand his name. "Lunardo di Pasqualin," he quavered.

Gaspare waved the object in his free hand. "And this—" (Matteo did not understand the term) "is your work?"

His captive offered an equivocal response, to the evident effect that it was not of his own making. Gaspare shifted his grip to the boy's nape and shook vigorously. "It doesn't seem to be working, does it? You bring that rat's nest in here again, I will feed you to the Inquisitors!"

Gaspare dashed the object to the ground, and the boy began to wail. "What is it?" Matteo asked.

"A *carta del ben voler*," Gaspare answered with disgust. "This little careerist hoped to win the good will of his masters, so was surreptitiously touching them with it." He kicked the thing clattering away. "While they were drinking!" he roared.

Matteo had followed the object's course across the cobblestones, and now bent to pick it up. It did rather resemble a vermin's bedding, crumpled paper tied round with ribbons and lengths of string and hair. He pulled open the sheet, which seemed to be covered with inscriptions, and a stone fell out. "Look at this," he said, hefting its unexpected weight. "Is it iron?"

Gaspare glanced at it. "*Calamita*," he said. "A lodestone."

No one was paying attention to the sight of a young engineer roughing up an apprentice, which even the apprentice found unsurprising. Matteo, who spent his days reading different men's writing, now noticed the juvenile character of the hand. "You wrote this out yourself," he exclaimed.

Gaspare paused briefly. "What does it say?"

"Can't tell; it's Latin."

"A conjuration. Throw it away unread!" He cuffed the boy. "What's a lout like you doing trying to write?"

"Please, ser," the boy snuffled. "My father's dead, but my uncle was a gang boss."

"Ah hah. And you hope yet to be enrolled in his name?" Gaspare held the youth at arm's length and regarded him appraisingly. "Tell whichever of your womenfolk gave you that charm to stop playing the fool or you'll get hurt. So where do you hope to be a gang boss? Come on, you can tell me."

The boy looked down shyly and said something about becoming an *appontadoro*.

"What? Get on with you!" And he swiped at the boy, who broke free and ran like a rabbit.

Gaspare was laughing as he bent and picked up the lodestone. "Hoping to improve on the family fortune, he is. Learning to write, so he can cross off the names of workers who arrive late." He was tossing it in the air. "Supposed to attract sympathy if used with the right spells, you know. Women's magic—the worst kind of superstition."

"I marvel that the Arsenal functions so well," Matteo said.

"Wine and magic will not offer safe escort into the future."

Gaspare made a rude noise and tossed the stone at him. "You think the arsenalotti are more superstitious than our navy—or our merchants? *You* simply trust in different talismans."

The galley was clear now and turning broadside, and Matteo saw suddenly that it was an already completed craft, indeed one weathered with age. Gaspare noticed his expression and nodded. "We repair more galleys than we build—a benefit of peacetime, that they last so long. Does that trouble you, trader?"

"Not at all," replied Matteo. "It's a very good thing." And something he should have realized on his own. He wondered how many of the shipyard's visitors recognized it as a hospital more than a nursery.

The hour rang in the clock tower, and the two young men continued north. "Your errant youth hopes to be one of those who maintain the great clock?" Matteo asked.

"Christ, no," Gaspare swore. "That brat yearns to be time-keeper, with powers to credit and dock. Easier than wielding a chisel!"

The time the Arsenal kept was not the one Matteo knew, this much seemed clear. "Did they ever really turn out a galley a day?" he asked.

"We still do," answered Gaspare with a laugh. "Within these walls, that time is now."

Clear ground was visible beyond, the great basin and open yards of the Darsena Novissima. Like Venice, the Arsenal was most developed in its oldest reaches, a garden grown to thickets. Wider walkways led into the northeast corner, where a row of galleys had been drawn up onto the bank like enormous sardines. The sheds and buildings lacked the additions in various styles that characterized the older crowded neighborhoods.

"We are in the very provinces," Matteo declared. "Shall it take another century until this region is built up?"

"That depends upon the Turk. Do you hope for another Lepanto?"

"The heavenly saints forbid!" War disrupts commerce, even with Alexandria. "You may grow vegetables here with my blessing." Yet this uncongested back lot formed the headwaters of the Marvel, upstream of everything. Beyond these gates and shores, the Doge yearly married the Sea; what ceremony other than War would prompt conception here?

They rounded the Novissimo basin and turned south, past the shops of the mastmakers and the iron foundries. The lodestone in Matteo's pocket did not stir as they neared the forges, but he found his head turning as they walked the length of the Tana, all nine hundred feet (Matteo knew his pace and measured automatically) of the manufactury building's length. "Don't you coil the rope?" he joked, but Gaspare gave him a look and said that even the grandest merchant might someday find his life depending upon a single anchor line.

"And where do the Trevisos work?" Matteo asked.

Gaspare grimaced. "The *bronzeri* do not yet enjoy a workshop of our own. Because our output is precious but small, we are only granted use of the forges of the *fabbri,* after hours. —Of course, we spend most of our time in design and calculation," he added defensively. "In time the Arsenal will recognize our contribution, and build us a facility consonant with our merit."

At the far end of the Tana lay the other foundry, the gunmakers'. "Our boiler will be made there," Gaspare said. Matteo could smell hot iron in the waves of heat that radiated through an open doorway.

"When?" asked Matteo, trying to peer through the doorway.

"Don't ask him now," Gaspare warned, and Matteo turned to see Ser Cavallo standing thirty feet away. The street angled away from the Tana into the multistoried crowding of the old Arsenal, which the foreman was regarding with a severe expression. The way was too narrow to pass without acknowledgement, and the three men bowed stiffly as masters and their apprentices pushed past.

"You have toured the yard?" Ser Cavallo asked, unsmiling.

"Like a gaping Dalmatian," Matteo said cheerfully. "The wealth of provision is amazing."

"Provision is had with mere gold," the foreman growled. "The Arsenal is its workers, its true wealth their skills."

"Indeed," Matteo agreed as a carter stumbled before them,

nearly upsetting the load of wood he was hauling. "Their every move seems . . . *steeped* in tradition."

Cavallo looked at him closely. "They're set in their ways," he said at last. "Those ways have saved the Republic, time and again. You smart young men remember that."

"Well, we hope to benefit the Republic ourselves," said Matteo easily, neither intimidating nor deferential. "If you used caofa as your *bevanda ordinaria,* your workers' spirits would be quickened rather than intoxicated." And when the foreman stared he added, "Have you ever tried it? When we are set up, I shall brew you a cup myself."

"The arsenalotti are really set in their ways, you know," Gaspare remarked as they headed for the gate.

"And those 'ways' include—what did you tell me? Arrogance, inefficiency, constant theft—you didn't mention the drunkenness."

"These have been problems for decades," his friend answered. "Centuries, actually." Ahead of them, masters stood sullenly as the gatekeepers searched them, then inspected the bundles of wood they were carrying out.

"Why are they opening the bundles?" Matteo whispered as they stood waiting.

"Some masters will steal pieces of iron," Gaspare replied glumly. Then he added, "Tradition allows arsenalotti to take away wood shavings from the shop floors, but those pieces are much too big. Except during crackdowns, the gatekeepers don't even try to police stuff like this."

Matteo suddenly remembered the lodestone in his pocket. In a panic he pulled Gaspare over and disclosed it. The engineer laughed, drawing curious glances. "If it doesn't have the Arsenal stamp on it, don't worry. They don't search visitors, anyway."

But they did, perhaps because Matteo was in the company of an arsenalotto. "Mine," he said urbanely when the gatekeeper found the stone and turned it over. The investigator probed further into the pocket and produced three beans, which he studied curiously.

Matteo waited until the gatekeeper let them pass before tipping him, lest it look like a bribe. "One could still call it that," Gaspare remarked as they came down the steps onto the Campo.

"We will be dealing with the same people every day."

"Really?" Matteo replied blandly. "Oh, dear."

➤ ➤ ➤

Spring swelled and ripened, a time of preparation. The trade fair was important but not to the Benvenetos, for only foreigners from the nearby cities of the Veneto came, and they to sell, not buy.

One or two asked for caofa, to Matteo's delight; he served with a free hand at the family table, then set up a stall at the Rialto. When merchants inquired about a steady supply, he spread his hands. "To furnish your own household, do as I do: put out word with the Arsenal bowmen that you will pay for sacks they bring back. Larger and more reliable shipments must wait upon the waking of our traders."

The ships of the spring *muda* would return in June, and there was much ground to propose before then. Matteo painstakingly wrote up a business plan, as realistic as he knew investors would demand. He was tempted to show it to Uncle Bartolomeo, for support, but steeled himself instead and brought it to his father.

"You propose an old-fashioned galley company, with twenty-four shares?" Ser Benveneto looked across the top of the sheet, amused. "My son, traders do not form galley companies any more. They do not pay well enough."

"Spices do not pay well. But no one imports caofa, and we know we can find buyers."

"Do we, in the quantities you seek? And are you seriously proposing to send an actual galley?"

"A galleass, perhaps." Matteo smiled, acknowledging the implausibility. "But now that Venetians may own foreign-built ships, we need not lease from the English and the Dutch."

"But why need we lease vessels at all?" his father asked. "If shipping has ceased to be profitable for us, should we bankrupt ourselves persisting in it?"

"If we do not ply the sea, we are not Venetians," Matteo said stubbornly.

"Neither Rome nor Spain suspects that," his father answered

dryly. "We have trimmed our sails to catch advantage too readily to be anything but Venetians."

Which was a fact that Matteo knew as well as anybody. It had been a century since Venice's nobility had abandoned commerce, taken their immense wealth and invested it in the rich farmlands of the Veneto. The trade that had created Venice's empire and sustained it for half a millennium had been abandoned to Greeks, Jews, and smaller families as the patriciate collected its rents. The English and the Dutch, sailing out of the forested north where timber and iron were cheap, ravaged the Venetian spice trade, fought off the pirates who turned instead to the Serenissima's vessels, and ate away at the profits of the ancient Levantine routes. Venice now collected more in anchorage tax from foreign vessels than from its own, and no one seemed to mind.

"Nor should they," Franchescina declared as she handed Matteo his wine. "Money is like water, it seeks out the easiest paths. So we lease Dutch mules rather than raise our own? So what?"

Matteo smiled affectionately. The dish on the table, of the finest Venetian glass, held nineteen caofa beans (Matteo had counted them at a glance): all that he had given her. The arrangement was attractive; one's eye was drawn to the dark beans, dusky and irregular against the glazed symmetry of the dish. He was pleased to see that their number had not diminished over time.

"Do the merchants tell you this?" he asked.

"Rogue!" She raised an embroidered cushion and made as if to throw it at him. "Their wives tell me, or rather each other. They talk money while pretending not to, the hens."

Matteo wished Franchescina would speak more about her clients, whom she entertained with card games and presumably a bit of fortune-telling. He knew perfectly well that Venetian trade was increasingly being conducted on foreign vessels; he could quote the prevailing shipping rates. The Benvenetos sent German wool and furs to the Levant and brought back what items they could still sell profitably, and Matteo's entry-books cared little what flag the cheapest ships flew. His business plan (he had not dared show it to Franchescina, though he was certain she could read) was not a denial of reality, for all that it proposed a company of the galley. Could people not see it for what it was?

Ideas crowded Matteo's thoughts, but Gaspare elbowed them aside. "You are neglecting the great work," he complained. "We have two commissions now, and I cannot execute both of them alone."

Matteo wanted to send a servant to help Gaspare install the *Succhiatore,* but his friend seemed affronted by the suggestion. Matteo could not see the offense: he was involved also with a venture to send Murano glassware to the Besançon fair, but did not plan to help load the crates. Nevertheless, he agreed to accompany Gaspare back to the government building, and donned for the occasion his darkest and shabbiest attire.

"For this engine we want reliability, not efficiency or power," the engineer was saying. "A nice, steady suction that will require little maintenance and take years to wear out. For that we will accept a lesser efficiency, since the waste heat will moreover serve to warm the building's damp bones."

"I doubt that his Excellency's secretary will credit us with that," Matteo replied. But he began considering ways to express the benefit in twin entries against coal expended.

They stepped once more from the closed gondola to the unmarked entrance and into the building where stray glances brought frowns. Matteo wrapped himself in a cloak before he descended into the darkness, where a faint splash prompted the hope that he was sharing space with another silent escort and not a rat.

"Are you ready?" he called up at the inch-wide hole. With a long scrape, the lead pipe began to descended toward Matteo's outstretched hand. Fitting the wire cage over the opening was manageable even in the dimness the guard wanted, but when Matteo began to guide the assembly onto flat ground he had to call irritably for more light. As he wriggled his fingers in the mud he heard a faint groan through the nearest wall, and wondered with fleeting sympathy what workmen were laboring in the next chamber.

"*Cospetto del diavolo!* You look terrible," Gaspare exclaimed when he saw Matteo. He glanced at his own dusty knees as if abashed at not having undergone more.

Matteo shrugged, neither disputing nor pressing the point. Chagrin is a negotiating advantage best used later. "Let's move the engine," he said.

The boiler rested on a wooden trestle, which had been carried in earlier by workmen ("specially blinded by the occasion," Gaspare joked) along with lengths of pipe and a toolbox. The two contractors made a show of puffing and straining as they pushed it across the floor, but the impassive guards who stood by the door did not move to assist them. "Have you been making witticisms in their hearing?" Matteo hissed as they drove their shoulders against its dumb unyielding bulk. Gaspare said nothing, but Matteo noticed that he took upon himself most of the next hour's work in attaching the valves and couplings.

"Good enough for this engine," said Gaspare at last, sitting back on his heels. "Our next will require welded joints. It will generate greater pressures than the *Succhiatore,* and run more efficiently. Ideally the boiler should be bronze."

"Ha," replied Matteo, who knew something of the subject.

"Will you be at the Arsenal tomorrow?" Gaspare asked as the curtained gondola took them away.

"No, and neither will you." Matteo could be irritated by Gaspare's inability to keep disparate thoughts in his head. "They will want you to start the engine, and then instruct someone in how to run it. That will require only one person, so they will only send for one. I will be inside a different fortress."

It was a fortress so distant that it had to be approached by water. This failed to bother Matteo when he was being bundled into closed cabins by the *Signoria,* but setting out for a strange land was very different, even if the land lay within the city.

The Ghetto Nuovo was bounded by water, that access might be controlled through its two bridges. The buildings—they resembled neither palazzi nor tenements—were taller than any others in the *sestieri,* as though the prospering Jews, forbidden to surpass their borders, had instead expanded upward. Matteo could see them, women and children mostly, out on their balconies, from which (he remembered) they were said to gaze at and blaspheme Christian processions. Thus the sporadic attempts to compel them to seal up windows that looked upon the Cannaregio promenade. The effect, he reflected as he approached the near bridge, would render the Ghetto yet more alien in appearance, like the windowless exteriors of Alexandrian estates, unreadable behind their high walls and orchards.

But the crowd in the Campo had no more yellow hats than Matteo could see any day at the Rialto, and the bustle of commerce felt much like that of the nearby stalls. He moved through the crush of workers and artisans until he reached the appointed portico, where a young Jew stood waiting. Silently he conducted Matteo into a narrow stairwell, up four stories (not only the partitions but the staircase itself was made of wood, as though the building could not bear more weight) to the apartments of Iacob Zacuto, who conducted them into his office.

"I have brought you some caofa," said Matteo, presenting him with a small paper bag. The trader took it curiously, as though aware that protocol did not involve an exchange of gifts, but he spoke without evidence of disquiet.

"So this is what you propose to import," he remarked. "I have spoken to colleagues who have tasted it, both here and in Damascus." He handed the bag to the young man, who took it away. "And you think that the peoples of Christendom will take to caofa like the Turks and the Levantines?"

"I know they will," Matteo replied. Zacuto indicated a chair, and he sat. "We can sell caofa even at the prices I have paid for it. When we can secure it for less, profits will result."

Zacuto made a noncommittal gesture. "You will spend some years awaiting that." He sat behind his desk and looked hard at Matteo. "And what do you want with *us*? Surely you are not approaching us as potential business partners."

"No, Ser Zacuto," said Matteo, meeting his gaze. "We both know that the Cattaveri would object to such arrangements. You have capital, which is part of what we need, but your value to this enterprise lies elsewhere, as does what we can offer you."

"Yes?" The Jew sat back, prepared to hear the pitch.

"We have created curiosity about and demand for caofa throughout the Veneto," Matteo began, "but it required effort: I had to ply the bellows before my spark took fire. Caofa is becoming known in Europe as travelers report of it, but it is only available in the port cities, and there only occasionally, as a medicine or expensive curiosity. It will not become popular until it is imported in quantity, and its praises sung by residents."

Zacuto did not nod or acknowledge these points. It was an old bargainer's trick, but one that Matteo found slightly unnerving here, dealing with someone who was at once so familiar and so alien.

"Venetians go everywhere, but the Jews of Venice come from everywhere. Your Three Nations—which are actually what, five or more? since the *Marranos* hail from Portugal as well as Spain, and many Venetian Jews have lived elsewhere in Italy—have ties with every Jewish community in Europe. If the merchants of the Ghetto took part in the caofa trade, the bean would have entree into every city with a synagogue."

"You would present Europe a Turkish drink as though it were a Jewish one?" asked Zacuto. His tone was too dry to convey irony.

"Christians do not care from whom they buy, so long as it is good." Matteo said this lightly, but with emphasis. "There are no Christian spices or silks." A wave of unease spread through him, and he concentrated with an effort.

"It was not the consumers I was thinking of." Zacuto paused, then seemed to set this thought aside. "You are interested, then, not in our money, like the poor to whom we must lend at a loss, but in our uniformity as non-*goi*. As in a comedy, where the well-born lovers must pass notes through their servants. —Here now, is there something wrong with you?"

"Your low ceilings are rather oppressive," said Matteo weakly. They seemed in fact to be pressing down upon him. "It is a bit like being below deck. . . ." He rose, then grabbed the arm of his chair.

"We must get you outside," said Zacuto, coming quickly around the desk. He took Matteo by the elbow and conducted him into another room, where a narrow door opened onto a balcony. The noise without was great but the open space an immediate relief, and Matteo stepped onto the platform unconcerned that it gave slightly beneath his weight.

"Thank you," he gasped, steadying himself against the railing. The hand was gone from his sleeve, and fresh air blew through the campo at this height. Zacuto, evidently assured that this Christian would not be sick in his rooms, now stood beside him.

"We do not live in palazzi," he said blandly. "The bounds of the Ghetto were not enlarged when the *Marranos* were admitted."

A voice within was calling, and Zacuto turned to reply briefly. An elderly servant came out bearing a tray with steaming cups, which Matteo immediately saw were caofa. More surprisingly, the servant was Christian. Matteo took a cup, looked closely at the man (who did not meet his eye), then sniffed and sipped at the brew, which was stronger than he had learned Venetians prefer.

"I do not believe that Spain and Portugal would welcome a drink so suggestive of the Turk," said Zacuto, "while the English and Netherlands, whose climates might recommend it, have sent few Jews to Venice."

"Then we shall storm those shores by other means," he said. Zacuto was looking down at the crowded campo, and Matteo followed his gaze, wondering how much ground he had lost by being stricken. Only one or two upturned faces were gazing at them, though they must have made an odd pair. It was only then that Matteo realized, with a deep start, that from this angle no one could see that he wore no yellow hat, so he must seem another Jew.

"Has the caofa cooled your blood?" Zacuto asked suddenly.

"My blood?" Matteo was little concerned with the mechanisms of the drink's beneficence, though he had rather assumed that it exerted some calming effect upon the choler.

"It is supposed that caofa offers relief to the sanguinary temperament," Zacuto replied. "Perhaps the engine that forces blood through the veins is driven by heat."

"That blood moves through the veins is news to me," Matteo replied politely. If the Jews, whose physicians were at least as good as the Christians', had claims to make concerning the *therapeusis* of caofa, he was prepared to credit them.

"It was discovered not long ago, by one of your own countrymen. There are valves within the veins, permitting movement in one direction only."

"Valves?" Matteo stared at the Jew.

"Suggesting that blood flows in a stream. They were discovered by Paolo Sarpi."

At this Matteo blinked and only just refrained from exclaiming, "*Fra* Sarpi?" Instead he affected a milder surprise, and remarked, "If the savior of Venice has distinguished himself in anatomical studies as well, he is a prodigy indeed."

"He only saved it from the Curia," replied Zacuto with a short laugh. "Will your caofa save us from Spain?"

Matteo pondered the question, to which he had given no very satisfactory answer, as he walked back through Cannaregio. He had wanted to reply *Yes*! despite the risk of appearing foolish, but his assurance would have sounded muddled and weak to the hard-headed trader. The Republic's patricians cling now to land, while its merchants are content if their money travels for them: how to explain the miracle of the caofa bean, that carries the land within it, yet releases an immaterial essence that quickens the spirit and brightens the eye? Yes, the spread of this substance into Europe would halt the advance of Spain, like throwing open shutters to let sunlight strike mildew.

Talk at the dinner table concerned the Besançon Fair, now underway in Piacenza although news would not reach Venice for a week or more. Matteo wasn't sure that anyone else present understood the proceedings, though his kinsmen never spoke of them with the boorish incredulity of older traders mocking the spectacle of financiers attending a fair with no goods, no coin, just thousands of pieces of paper being matched together and torn up. The Benvenetos at least understood how bills of exchange could be cleared, like the wake from passing gondolas meeting wave to trough and vanishing.

What mattered, of course, was where the Genoese *banchieri di conto* would set the exchange rate for liquidating bills. The rise or fall of the *conto* would reverberate through Venice and Christendom, although in ways Matteo wasn't sure he could predict, or himself understand.

"And where are you bound?" asked his father, turning at last to his youngest son.

"Tomorrow I go to the Signoria," Matteo replied, careful to keep from his voice any tone that his brothers could call self-important, "to see Senator Domenico's secretary." He did not add that he was also going to the secret library, to request the new book by della Porta.

"Seeking a letter patent for a new steam kettle?" Tullio drawled.

"Seeking more money, now that I have justification," Matteo replied. "Is that not a good thing?"

"So you are not going to the Arsenal, to pound nails?" Alessandro inquired.

"He looks as though he already has," said Tullio suddenly. "See his hands!"

And the table erupted in laughter as Matteo looked dumbly at his caofa-powdered fingertips, black as soot though more aromatic. His mother passed down her lace handkerchief, though Matteo pulled out his own and began rubbing before it reached him. Bartolomeo made a mild remark about traders not minding getting their hands dirty, but the mirth washed over it.

"Will the Fair mean a carnival?" asked little Felicia, saving him.

"Not that kind of fair, dear," said her father. Though it once was, thought resentful Matteo. Nobody thought to ask him about that, and he sat silently, willing the warmth to drain from his face.

"Our own carnival will start soon enough," Ser Benveneto assured her. The actual carnival season would not begin until the feast of San Stefano, but a festive—that is, a nonworking—atmosphere would begin to gather in the streets even before *battagliola* season broke out, which was invariably sooner than permitted. Perhaps Ser Benveneto imagined that his granddaughter would enjoy seeing artisans push each other off bridges. (Her father certainly did.)

Battagliole soon, but first the *muda*. What price his agents paid for the arriving caofa, and the price at which he would sell it, would determine whether the next *muda* sailed with Matteo a *patron* or a shopper.

When he went upstairs two hours later he found a copy of *Il Gentiluomo,* which his father had given him when he was fifteen, propped on his bed. A passage was marked with a ribbon, and he did not even have to pick it up to guess that it was the one where Muzio explained that a gentleman must do nothing with his own hands, but have everything carried out by his agents. Matteo knocked it with his own hands to the floor, then called angrily for his cloak. On the way out he picked up the book and returned it to the library.

"Did you sniff your fingers? Perhaps that's not the sign of a *gentiluomo.*"

"You tell me; you have entertained a greater variety of them."

"With me they do whether it is proper or not!"

The richest caofa—brewed with unscanting profligacy—bore a savor so strong it touched the corporeal, with the piercing seethe that was only produced by flesh. Damp loam rose to the face, alive with the quality of being alive. Can such complexity speak only to the tongue, an array of sensations like an artist's paint box? The wet grounds later held nothing: all was expended in that single release.

Which meant there was nothing next day. Senator Domenico's secretary was sour, as was the librarian. Clouds of papers swarmed to vex him, turbid with numbers that promised knowledge but tendered none. And in the afternoon word ran through the Rialto that the new *conto* was surprisingly high, sending waves of alarm that accomplished nothing save to interfere with actual work.

Matteo visited their Arsenal workshop the next week and found Gaspare in fine spirits. "Here, sign this," the engineer said, picking up a sheet and thrusting it at him. Matteo studied it in perplexity. "It's a loan agreement for bronze, so we can build our valves."

"You melted down a ship-owner's cannon?" asked Matteo disbelievingly.

"Had to be recast anyway, the muzzle was cracked. He won't need it until the next *muda,* by which time our *ingegno* will have proved its worth and the senate reimbursed us the cost of the bronze, which I will use to buy more for the trader."

"And if not, I am responsible for the charges." But Matteo was already looking for the ink.

"But that's what traders do, underwrite bills. Especially for ventures that carry no risk!" And Gaspare laughed, ground a pinch of sawdust between thumb and forefinger, and sprinkled it over the fresh signature.

A galleass beat the *muda* to port, bearing incomplete but promising news of the spring convoy. The letters it carried for Casa Benveneto were sufficient to keep Matteo busy for days, and when word came one morning of sails on the horizon, he groaned instead of setting out for the waterfront.

It was another day before the bills reached them, and after supper when Ser Benveneto found and showed Matteo the entries for nineteen sacks of caofa. The price paid was only somewhat higher than Matteo had hoped, but the exhilarating size of the shipment was faintly alarming: five times what he had previously disposed of, most of which he had given away.

I will sell fully half, he mentally indited. *And that half not sold shall be seed, to grow the next year's customers.*

Fresh caofa next morning at the Rialto, so that Matteo's fellow traders, even the Germans at the *Fondaco dei Tedeschi,* might know what the *muda* had brought. The flavor lost its finest subtleties within minutes, so Matteo had the serving boy grind and then brew one small pot at a time, which would be finished before it could stale and left interested customers waiting while the next was prepared. He counted the numbers of customers, and, after the second day, the number who showed up more than once.

The discomfited Germans, required to stay at the *Fondaco,* sell all their wares there, and use the proceeds only to buy Venetian goods, came over curiously, assured Matteo that caofa would never rival beer, then each bought a cup (when their companions weren't there) and sipped with the assessing expression of a rentier pinching the pigs. Eventually they banded together and bought half a sack, which Matteo measured with a fine pewter scoop, like a Dutchman pouring out cloves.

Caofa became modestly fashionable, something for the worldly to be seen enjoying. Merchants bought small paper bags made for sweetmeats, and their wives asked Matteo about flavorings. An entire sack disappeared in these tiny increments, then much of another in larger bites destined for the mainland.

Greeks and resident Turks began to buy, though the Jews seemed not much interested, and an attempt to make a beachhead in the Arsenal was repulsed. "Don't worry about attracting the artisans," his father said. If they disposed of nine sacks at these prices, the profits would be genuine.

"Selling it by the bag, like a shopkeeper?" asked Franchescina. "Your brothers must be making comments."

"Probably, but not to me." Matteo in fact recognized that the expense of keeping a servant there four hours a day should properly be added to the costs. "I would rather sell tiny bags to a hundred *cittadini* than full sacks to three. Eventually the hundred will want sacks."

And indeed a taste for the bean seemed to be spreading through the city's traders, foreigners, and scholars. One day Gaspare showed him a short treatise, *De Flatus Caofae,* which discussed the nature of farts engendered by caofa. "What does it say?" Matteo demanded, flipping through the pages of Latin.

"Well, too much caofa," said Gaspare helpfully. "*You* know. Always seemed a small price to pay."

The heat of summer seemed an unpropitious season for consuming hot caofa, but Matteo reminded colleagues that those in the Turkish lands drank it in the blazing heat of day and derived much benefit thereby. The serving boy all but dared customers to drink the steaming beverage down and feel its effects, to which he would then loudly draw attention. For his part Matteo did not scruple to point out how good caofa tasted on damp winter mornings, by which time supplies might be less plentiful than now.

The long sweltering afternoons might prompt industrious citizens to hot refreshment, but unoccupied youths, idle and bored, lounged at the ends of bridges, drinking wine (which heats the senses and lulls judgment) and calling taunts to like idlers on the opposite side. A volley of abuse would answer this, leading to exchanges of contemptuous display that would rapidly escalate until one side launched itself across the bridge. The shouts and flying fists would quickly draw a crowd, hundreds or even thousands pouring in from neighboring campi to line each side of the canal and scream support. The summer feast days were increasingly given to these "spontaneous" outbursts—which seemed to relieve only a portion of the excitement that had built up over the previous weeks—and *battagliola* season approached through a cloud of increasing pressure.

Matteo was sitting peaceably in his office when the summons came. His father appeared in the doorway, a paper in his hand and an expression on his face that Matteo had never seen before. "It is from the Avogadori di Comun," he said. "You are accused of bringing discord to the Republic."

"*What?*" Matteo read through the summons disbelievingly. He was charged, in formal government prose, with employing the resources of Casa Benveneto to disrupt civil order and jeopardize the public safety. The last phrase made Matteo's head swim; everything alleged was absurd, but allegations concerning the public welfare could conceivably attract the attention of the Council of Ten.

"We are supposed to appear in eight days," his father said grimly. The pronoun was a kindness, or perhaps an assurance of solidarity, for the document named *Matteo Benveneto* alone. Matteo had never seen his own name on an official paper, and his gaze fixed upon it with paralyzed horror.

"This is . . . *untrue*," he said at last, sounding fatuous to his own ears.

His father made an angry sound. "It is the pharmacists," he said. "They have brought a complaint."

"For what?" Matteo asked. But he immediately guessed at something.

"You sell as an everyday drink something that they prescribe as a costly medicine, and tell the city's merchants that you can obtain it more cheaply still? How do you think they will respond?"

"But that is their misfortune," Matteo protested, indignant. "What does the Republic care if I manage to undercut these frauds?"

"They will claim that caofa is too potent to be sold as a frivolous quaff," Ser Benveneto predicted. "That you will poison unsuspecting Venetians with this toxic brew." Matteo tried to protest that nations of Turks drank it daily, but his father interrupted. "Don't argue it with *me*. That is the attack they will make, unless you have done something else to leave yourself vulnerable."

In fact it was something worse. A discreet inquiry (probably involving a bribe, although Matteo was not involved) brought word that the Avogadori were investigating charges that Matteo had encouraged rioting during the feast day *scaramuccie* by selling a Turkish drink that inflamed the spirits and counteracted wine's natural tendency to slow responses. The skirmishes' reliance upon fists rather than sticks and knives would be undermined, resulting in "widespread injury and even loss of life," as the papers evidently had it.

Matteo's wrath—"Those louts don't buy caofa! And weapons are no more common in bridge fights near the Rialto than in those a mile away!"—swept a cloak over darker feelings, which themselves thrashed above a still pool he could not glimpse, filled with something black and bitter. Walking along the Rio del Palazzo one drizzly afternoon, Matteo felt the writhings of helpless rage as something dying, a serpent poisoned by the toxins of fear.

"Are you going to speak at all?" Gaspare asked him, less annoyed than bemused. "I do believe you are suffering from *melancholia*."

Matteo laughed. "Is that a word arsenalotti use?"

"Don't be a snot. I have read a book or two, you know—some on unlikely subjects, since it's hard to know what's in a book until you read it."

Matteo did not want to discuss Gaspare's familiarity with the varieties of human temperament. He said: "I am distracted because I must speak this afternoon with a lawyer, and unhappy because no one is now willing to deal in caofa. These emotions are the consequence of outward causes, and that is all."

The lawyer, at least, was prepared to stick to outward causes. "You should get statements," he said after reading through the complaint while Matteo sat waiting. "From your servants who prepared the drink, that they served it almost exclusively to merchants, and never to idle young men. From fellow traders, that they purchased it at prices too high for the *popolani*. From those colleagues you approached as investors, that you planned to import this substance at a cost that young artisans would find expensive, and that you acknowledged it would take years to bring the price down.

"Assure your colleagues that they may say whatever they wish, and do not be dismayed by their statements' self-serving natures." He smiled faintly. "The Avogadori are used to witnesses falling over themselves to make clear their own lack of involvement."

"Will these suffice?" Matteo asked in a voice that betrayed him by quavering.

"They form the foundation of your rampart. Each answer you give is a stone, to be piled up methodically."

It was an incongruous image to hear in this handsome office, across a walnut desk wider than his father's. The lawyer, silver-haired and richly attired, seemed less concerned about this business than Matteo, which might or might not be reassuring.

"I will set forth everything clearly," Matteo promised.

The counselor shook his head emphatically. "Restrict your answers to the points at hand," he said. "Content yourself with protesting your innocence, and do not attack the interests behind the complaint. As far as the Avogadori know, you have no idea who laid these baseless charges."

Matteo had intended a vigorous denunciation of these powers. He nodded, however, and asked meekly, "What of the *Sbirri*? Their patrols must know that bridge fighting has been no worse this year."

"That is not for you to demonstrate. Let the Avogadori wonder what the arrest records show. They will adjourn, request further reports from various quarters, and the inquiry will in time grind to a halt."

Matteo didn't like the sound of this. "But I require vindication," he insisted. "No trader will join my venture while everyone is waiting to see if I am arrested."

The counselor shrugged, then offered a sympathetic smile, Matteo's last. "Many of your potential partners have had their own dealings with the law over the years, and know enough not to expect a formal exoneration. You will have to rely upon your own powers of argument, which have after all gotten you this far."

"Alas," said Matteo, looking about the chamber as though reflecting on where *this far* now was.

"Traders do not make the worst witnesses," the lawyer added unexpectedly. "You know enough to be pleasing, and how to explain matters without condescension. Let the Avogadori feel the force of your desire to persuade, and they will soon decide that this case ought not to have come before them."

He dressed himself the next morning as though to meet a foreign delegation, the accomplished young trader of good family. His brothers were nowhere to be seen, as befit their doubts concerning his status: beloved son riding into his first battle or scapegrace facing judgment. Ser Benveneto stood waiting at the door, with a fatherly hug and a few words of advice. "Look them in the face, not insolently but as a fellow Venetian. Your family— its generations of service to the Republic—stand behind you, visible to them: but you should not allude to it. Rely on your dignity and upon the justice of your enterprise, but do not be concerned whether they approve it—and above all *don't offer them caofa*."

He rode to the Palazzo Ducale in an open gondola, a young trader of repute keeping an appointment with officials. His morning cup, swathed in milk and honey, warmed his stomach without assailing it. Wine at lunch, assuming they didn't clap him in chains.

Matteo stated his business to the clerk at the top of the Scala dei Censori, who turned a page in the great ledger before him, read carefully, then directed him without expression down a series of corridors. Matteo was careful to attend his instructions, but two guards nevertheless fell in beside him as he turned to go, an escort to create the appearance that he was being brought in under duress. As a piece of Venetian ceremony, it was less venal than many, and Matteo gave them a single sour look.

The Avogaria lay beyond a pair of heavy oak doors, opposite a penitential bench to which Matteo was brusquely directed. It was ninety minutes later that the great doors swung open and a secretary poked out his head to call Matteo's name. Matteo had tucked away his book as soon as he heard the knob turn, and rose smoothly at the sound. What little he had absorbed about domestic economy vanished at once, but the exercise had calmed him. He took a deep breath, prayed: *San Menas, patron of traveling merchants, be with me now,* and stepped forward.

The doorway led onto a further corridor, narrower and differently tiled. Four doors down, and he was gestured into the one on the right. The tableau was just as predicted: three officials sitting at a table at the far end, with a secretary or two sitting to the side. No chair for himself. It was not quite a trial, those being conducted in the Quarantia Criminale, but if things did not go well here there would soon be one.

"Matteo Michaelangelo Benveneto, Venetian, of Casa Benveneto?" asked the man in the center, a balding patrician in his forties. Matteo bowed. The man read from a sheet he held before him. "You are accused of attempting to disrupt civil order and jeopardize the public safety of our Serene Republic by importing a potent substance, made from the bean of the . . ." (he hesitated and scowled) "kaffa?—plant, which, taken in the large draughts that you have urged upon buyers, and especially in the simple apprentices and workmen . . ." The charge ran on along the lines Matteo expected, sparing him at least (he had worried about this) some unprepared-for surprise. He listened carefully, and when the official finished and raised his eyes inquiringly, Matteo realized he had to speak.

"I have been apprised of these charges, Your Eminences, and with respect I declare them false, and my family and myself innocent of these imputations." He looked to the official on the left (having decided that the one presiding was a mediocrity with a sinecure), wondering whether this was appropriate, and received a tiny nod.

"The charges," the patrician began, untying the ribbon that held the fat folder the official on his right slid before him. Matteo watched with horrified fascination as the cover was lifted to disclose a pile of documents, each a different size and color. The Avogadore paused like a German merchant before a plate of fresh seafood, wondering where to begin. One of the items, Matteo recognized with disgust, was *De Flatus Caofae.*

"What is this?" The prosecutor frowned as he looked down at a folded sheet sitting at the top. He picked it up and turned it over, showing the seal. The official on his right started slightly.

Everyone watched as the patrician unfolded the letter and read it. His face darkened. "It appears," he said, "that the Holy Office has taken an interest in the case of Ser Benveneto. Why was I not shown this?"

All three avogadori turned to one of the secretaries, who mimed bewildered incomprehension. "I did not receive the letter," he protested. "I would have informed your excellencies of its arrival. Perhaps it was Lippomano?"

Matteo heard all this through a haze of stunned incomprehension. Word that his "case" had attracted the attention of the Venetian Inquisition had stopped all thought, like a cork blocking the duct that conveys the substance of reflection. The idea of the Holy Office was frozen before him, an image lingering on the surface of a pool after the figure who cast it has gone.

The officials were conversing in low voices, their secretaries hovering behind them to lean, pointing, over the folder. Perhaps I will faint, thought Matteo in a flash of lunatic clarity. People must topple over as they stand here all the time. Is it taken as a sign of guilt?

Someone cleared his throat. "It appears, Ser Benveneto," the third official was saying, "that the Holy Office has taken an interest in your case." A part of Matteo's consciousness registered the lawyers' tendency to repeat each other's phrases. "This raises a question of jurisdiction, which must be settled before we proceed." He seemed to be saying that Matteo could not remain standing here during this period.

The official in the center, deep in discussion with a secretary over the folder, looked up at this. "You may go," he said, with evident reluctance. "But be prepared for a further summons, and do not leave Venice in the meanwhile." Someone murmured something, and he laughed.

Numbly Matteo bowed and left the room. Someone was sitting on the bench, and looked up anxiously as Matteo pushed open the doors, but he did not take notice. Corridors and stairways opened before him, which his mind traced in reverse without conscious intervention. It was only as he stood in the courtyard, with the Porta della Carta before him and Venice beyond, that he roused himself and balked, obscurely but decisively, at walking through the public entrance like an uncumbered man. Lesser exits dotted the Palace like mouseholes, and Matteo forswore the Gate of Paper—why was it called that?—to slip instead, a tradesman not a *gentiluomo,* through a victualer's door and back into the Piazza.

He was just south of the Bridge when someone caught up with him. "Ser Benveneto?" in an unsmiling voice.

Matteo started—what had he been expecting, a gang of Inquisitors? some physician come to punch his nose?—but it was one of the escorts to the unnamed government building, who never smiled. "Good afternoon," he said, civil but not welcoming.

"You must come with me," the guard said, peremptory as always.

It was the stuff of low comedy: a cracked joint in the *Succhiatore,* official outrage, the wrong contractor dragged in and ordered to fix it. "You can't make repairs? Then grab a bucket and start bailing!" Matteo began to explain, and realized that a second guard, this one bigger, had materialized on his other side and had taken his arm. "Excuse me," he said sharply, pulling away, "but—"

The blow sent him reeling, into the other's arms. Matteo, shocked, was pinned before he could draw breath, and tried to regain his footing only to have his boots kicked out from under him. Men were scrambling from a nearby gondola, running up. A glimpse of shocked onlookers as they closed round him.

"Hey!" It was his only outburst. A cloak was thrown over him, entangling as it obscured. His sense of direction warned where he was being pushed, and he flailed madly. Hands grasped him, four, six, then hoisted. He was flying through the air, and down.

➤ ➤ ➤

Darkness swathed but did not comfort, a region of indeterminate nature. It was confusion, like a season of prolonged storms, that disrupted communication but did not block signals of distress from distant provinces. He lay in a condition of disarray but stillness, ignorant of everything yet aware of the magnitude of his defeat, though its dimensions, in this realm beyond time, were not measurable. Assessment came with intervals like day and night, unavailable to a mode of being that took form around an irregular distant drip, the texture of wet stone against his cheek.

Once he heard the sliding of a grate, and dimness filled some portion of his chamber. He sat up, trying to turn his neck to see the rectangle of light, but it whispered shut before he could get his bearings. The second of illumination had revealed the fixity of his enclosure, which he could still sense even in the darkness. After sitting upright for several minutes, he reached out to find the nearest wall. It was some time before he embarked to trace its circumference, and when he did he discovered he could not determine the size of his cell, for in the darkness he could not retain the number of sideways steps he took from one corner to the next. A narrow bench occupied the center of the floor, and he stretched out upon it.

Time loses significance in the enormity of failure, fading into the lightless eternity of a drowned ship sinking through the depths. If he made an effort Matteo could recall intervals when the door had swung open and a tray had been pushed in or his slop bucket taken away. He no longer turned when the spy slot slithered open and darkness bloomed briefly into grey. Lying in the unchanging stillness, he arranged his few facts in patterns, fusing them finally into hard diamonds of surmise that he let slip from his fingers into blackness.

They came when he was deep in reverie, something—it was deeply felt, but impossible to articulate consciously—about Marina when they were children, before he fell in love with her. Its substance had gathered to a density too great to disperse at once, and Matteo sat up disoriented, not dazzled (he had learned to glance away when the door swung open) but unmoored. "Come on," was all they said, and hoisted him under the arms.

"How long have I?" Matteo asked, lucidly he thought, but got no answer. He was being walked down the corridor, whose high windows, too high to see through, admitted the wan half-light of dusk or not quite dawn. Matteo tried to focus his thoughts but could not; they were hurrying him too briskly, pausing only to pull open doors. It was when he thought of how he could collect himself while waiting on the bench that he realized this respite would be denied him.

They showed him in at once, although the seconds between knocking and admittance allowed Matteo to straighten his clothes and push back his hair. His beard was raspy as the side of a file, not yet long enough to curl. *They want you to be disoriented,* he thought, and tried to close a fist around that.

The sight that greeted him as the doors swung open was certainly sufficient to chill. An ecclesiastical official, hatted and grim, sat glaring at the center of the table, which was wider and finer than the last. Neither a priest nor bishop, both familiar enough from weekly Mass, nor even similar in attire to the Archbishop, whom Matteo knew, if only from a distance, from civic ceremonies. Of course he was an Inquisitor, possibly no more than monsignor by one ordering of rank, but the wielder of terrible powers. Matteo realized that his life would quite possibly end in this room.

"The prisoner shall come forward," someone said. No recitation of his name for purposes of formal identification; he was in the realm now of confident certainties. Matteo got a quiet prod in the back, and took three steps forward. No hints from the table on proper protocol today, but he hesitated only a second, before giving a formal bow.

"You stand accused of material abetment in the ungodly practice of *divinazione,*" said an official to the Inquisitor's side. Matteo had expected His Eminence to do the speaking, and wondered that someone clearly from the Signoria was present at a Tribunal. "The gravity of this offence has brought your case to the attention of the Holy Office," the man continued, sounding angry. Matteo looked from one man to the other, trying to figure out what was happening here. He desperately wanted a cup of caofa.

"I beg your pardon, ser?" he said inanely. The actual wording of the charge was only now taking form in his mind.

"Divination?" He could not have been more bewildered if they had accused him of being the sultan in disguise.

The Inquisitor spoke for the first time. "Do you recognize these?" he asked heavily. His palm opened, disclosing a handful of dark seeds.

"They are beans, Your Eminence." There was no question what they were, even from this distance. "They look like caofa beans."

"Indeed. And did you give these beans to the woman known as Franchescina Castellano?"

Matteo stared.

"Come, speak up," said the official from the Signoria sharply.

"Ser, I . . ." Matteo concentrated his wits with an effort. Always admit what they know anyway. "That woman I know, Your Eminence. I deal in caofa beans, and have brought them to her apartment, to prepare the drink with which I hope to make my family's fortune."

"Did you make her a gift of these beans?"

"I . . . no. I do not recall ever leaving her with more beans than we used to make the infusion." An awful suspicion was dawning. "She may have kept some back from our grinding."

There was a chuckle from the side of the room. The official shot an angry glance in that direction, but the Inquisitor appeared not to notice. He said, "So you did not give the beans to Signorina Castellano for their efficacy in the practice of *buttar fave*?"

"Of . . . ?" Matteo frowned at the unfamiliar syllables. After a second he sorted them into two words, and his expression blossomed in astonishment. "You mean *bean-casting*?"

The official began to speak sharply, but the Inquisitor raised his hand. "That is correct. Do you deny that you aided this woman, your lover, in seeking greater power in divination through the potency of these foreign beans?"

"But that's—" Matteo shook his head in distraction. "They're just a commodity! The Turks and Jews of the Levant import them by the sackful, and all they do is *grind them up*!" He stared at the man wild-eyed, as though lunacy had seized them both.

A third official, who had been writing busily, now spoke without looking up. "So you attest that the beans were brought into the woman Castellano's house solely for consumption, and that you did not suggest or encourage their use for unholy purposes."

"I, yes." Matteo blinked. The question, laid out on the trellis of syntax, now seemed almost sane.

The men behind the table were conversing in low voices. "Take him away," someone said, which Matteo heard but did not apply to himself until a guard plucked his sleeve. He allowed himself to be led out the door, past a group of young lawyers who had stood listening. As the guards maneuvered past them Matteo abruptly addressed one. "How long since my arrest?"

The young man frowned at him, then pursed his lips. "Six days," he said.

He was jerked forward, then marched quickly to his cell and pushed in. He fell asleep almost at once, then woke, hours or a day later, and felt the uncertain boundaries of his confines to be more distinct. Most immediately, he knew now where he was: back in the Palazzo Ducale, in the dank cells known as the *pozzi*. His trip on the floor of the gondola had been a return one, and he wondered why the agents of the Council of Ten (as they surely were) had not simply waited outside the Avogadori's door.

Confident now that he was being fed daily, Matteo began to count his meals. He established that he slept once between them, which he could now assay at a night's worth. Something like structure took form, a bulwark against the enveloping darkness.

Other assemblages were less easy, and he lay on his back for hours, trying to fit them together. Franchescina had used the pilfered beans to tell fortunes, and must by now have joined the ranks of women convicted of some form of stregonaria, like those he had seen (childhood memories were more vivid here than recent ones) standing in the pillory wearing placards that read: *Per la santa Inquisitione per herbarie e strigarie e buttar fave.* Had she boasted to her clients that her beans were of the caofa plant, so that whoever denounced her could guess at Matteo's connection and include him as well? Or had Franchescina, under examination, freely spilled his name to the Tribunal?

One piece didn't fit: what Matteo had faced had not been a Tribunal, which would have been filled with clerics, but something else. What then, and why? He turned the piece over in the darkness, looking for an edge he could match.

On the twenty-ninth day he thought he heard a faint noise drifting under his door through some open window, then realized it was now the *battagliola* season, and the surf-whisper perhaps the roar of thousands. Curly-bearded, he touched his cheek and thought, *I look like a galley slave.* And might soon be one, if Franchescina's perfidy combined with the pharmacists' charges into something sufficiently malign.

When reassemblage failed, the darkness reclaimed him. Too stealthy to show its leading edge, despair crept up next to him, coating without whelming, like oil, then wholly subsuming once it no longer mattered. Matteo thought of his mother and sister, their misery; the gentlemen Benveneto, their disappointment; the disgrace that burned inextinguishable, tainting his name in others' mouths like the rankest dregs. Failure most shameful, a bankrupt's or coward's, seared him as he lay unseen, a twist of pain in the ruins of his once brilliant ambition.

It was the sixty-third day when they came for him. "Get up," called the turnkey as the door swung open, the middle silhouette in the dim but stinging light. The two guards pushed past him and led Matteo away without a word.

They had proceeded down two corridors and were climbing a staircase—the demand upon unaccustomed muscles may have woken something—when Matteo realized that he was being taken perhaps to judgment or even summary execution, but that there was also the possibility that he was about to get the chance to explain himself, for which he had raged through long darkened hours. An interlocutor who would ask what he *had* been doing, since he was not going to confess to the allegations collected. The self-evident truth of his words, their justice and reason, would sweep away the compacted illogic of the charges against him, which must contradict each other and established fact at numerous bleeding points.

The tiny room into which he was thrust was scarcely larger than his cell, though better lit. Matteo sank onto the narrow bench and looked at the second door (through which faint mur-

murs could be heard) with relief: torture chambers don't have
waiting rooms.

The functionary who opened the door, however, looked at
Matteo so blackly that he flinched. The fact that it was not a
guard come to let him in was even more alarming. Where was
he, that prisoners no longer needed guards?

The chamber beyond was large, although the high ceiling
and darkened windows (Matteo had not realized it was night) lay
beyond the few lamps' illumination. The five robed men sat not
behind a table but in raised chairs against the far wall, the center
one framed by a red panel. Clerks and lawyers occupied the
tables, against the wall opposite the windows. Matteo
approached slowly, glancing about in bewilderment.

"What are you looking for?" one of them asked. His voice
carried clearly enough to echo faintly behind Matteo.

"Your pardon, Your Eminence," he said in a croak. How long
since he had last spoken? "I had expected to see an Inquisitor
present."

"This is a court of the Consiglio dei Dieci, not the
Inquisition!" another judge snapped. "You have already caused
us trouble by involving the Holy Office in this."

"I beg your pardon," Matteo whispered. He tried to fix on
this, but his thoughts spun helplessly, like gears failing to engage.
The Council of Ten! Neither of the previous interviews had been
formal trials, and perhaps this was not, either; but with the Ten
you did not always get one.

It would be damning to say nothing further, so he added,
"The last time I was taken from my cell I was questioned by an
Inquisitor. I have not been apprised of the nature of the pro-
ceedings against me, and must apologize for my ignorance."

One of the judges stirred. "It is not culpable under law for a
citizen innocently to complicate an investigation by suffering the
attentions of third parties," he observed. "That this has inconve-
nienced this inquiry cannot be one of the counts against Ser
Benveneto."

"We have enough already," another judge snapped. He pointed at Matteo. "You! What have you been doing poking about
with secret books? And why have you shown such interests in the

writings of the Neapolitan Giovanni Battista della Porta?"

"Della Porta?" For a second Matteo felt, insanely, as though he were being examined by tutors. "He wrote *Pneumatica,* a study of the power of steam."

"It is interesting that you went looking for it in the Archivio dei Documenti, where you had a commission to search for writings about steam from the Turkish lands."

Matteo blinked. "With respect, Your Eminence, I had permission from the office of Senator Domenico to look for books about steam power. Certainly we were interested in works by Arab philosophers, but if there were new studies published by Christians, I read them as well."

"Yet you also took the opportunity to look for writings about caofa, did you not?"

"Let us not turn to the matter of caofa just yet," the presiding judge suggested. Matteo was looking from one man to the other in astonishment.

"Very well," said the finger pointer. "This Neapolitan is also the author of another treatise, *De Furtivis Litterarum Notis,* in five books. You were looking at that volume as well. Why the interest in an author who writes about codes and cryptography?"

Matteo stared. "But that was more than forty years ago! Della Porta wrote that book as a very young man."

"That scarcely matters," said the fourth judge, on the far right. Two of the others nodded at this. "The prisoner has shown a pattern of gaining entry to restricted sites and then looking about too closely. I am more interested in why he was poking about in the casa basement."

The judge who had demurred earlier now raised a hand. "We should take care not to utter secrets in front of the prisoner. It is still possible he could be acquitted and released."

"That hardly seems likely," the presiding judge replied. He leaned forward slightly to address his colleague on the right. "Do you wish to ask about the basement installation? That little Jew from the Arsenal told us nothing, even under the *cordello.*"

"I suggest we try the *cordello* now."

"To what purpose?" the third judge asked. "The wretched *converso* spilled everything he could, and we learned nothing that was not evident from their papers. Everything heard to date suggests two young men who don't know when not to exhibit curiosity. Unless this prisoner's answers give evidence of dissembling, the *cordello* would be an unwarranted recourse."

Matteo followed the exchange, but a spreading chill seemed to have frozen his faculties, soul, humours, and all. Like ice in a conduit, the words he was hearing had blocked the flow of thought, which hung immobilized before his mind's eye.

"Very well," said the presiding judge. "Let us turn then to matters that are better documented. Prisoner: Tell us of your dealings with the Jews of the Ghetto. And know that at the first sign of prevarication, you shall be hanging from the *cordello*."

Matteo drew breath slowly. Even an ice sculpture may move if ordered so by the Ten. "Your Eminences," he began. "If you have seized the papers of myself and my associate Gaspare Treviso, then you surely know of my efforts to find investors for a plan to import caofa beans from Egypt, which we hope to sell throughout Europe, thus enriching my family and benefiting our Republic. Such investment has been hard to secure: prosperous merchants now entrust their capital with Genoese and Florentine houses, which guarantee safe returns; while the noble families of Venice have placed their wealth in their mainland estates."

He paused; had he just offended his judges? The ice had numbed; he could not care. "The Jews are hungry for opportunity, and they have more money than the Greeks. I would approach them as investors if the Cattaveri permitted it. Instead, I proposed to a Jewish merchant that the Jewish communities in European ports be used to promote my caofa. My family knows well the laws regulating our profession; there is nothing wrong with this."

The judges all looked at each other. "And what did the Jew Zacuto say to this?" one asked.

"He was guarded," Matteo replied. He was trying to remember what he might have written down. The ice was breaking up, things said a moment ago were bobbing into view. "Wait—did you think that Gaspare had something to do with this? No, he is merely—"

"Silence!" the presiding judge snapped, distracted. A lawyer had come up with a paper, which he took and studied. There was a silence as it was passed along from one judge to the next.

"According to Zacuto, you showed nervousness and extreme agitation," one of them said after a moment. "He said that you seemed plainly aware that your actions were irregular."

"You . . . you have been interrogating my prospective partners?" Matteo asked in astonishment. A blow to the back of his head sent him pitching forward to his knees.

"You are not here to pose questions," one of the judges exclaimed angrily as Matteo shook his head and rose slowly. He knew enough not to turn to see who had struck him. "If there is another outburst like that, I shall call in a guard. They are much rougher than my clerks."

"I beg your pardon, Your Eminence," Matteo said. The court was regarding him sternly, five family portraits in a forbidding gallery. Matteo distantly registered the thought as he studied each face in turn.

One of them leaned forward. "And what does that expression of yours portend?" he asked. His tone was not particularly dangerous.

"Your Eminence, I scarcely know how to answer." Matteo spread his hands. "If you have called in and questioned the merchants I have spoken to, I am ruined beyond possible redemption. I could walk out of this building tomorrow, and every member of my profession would treat me like a leper. I—" He looked up to the ceiling, dim with its indistinct design, then back down at them. "Ask whatever you wish," he said simply. "I have nothing to hide."

"How gracious of you," one of them remarked. Matteo straightened his back and looked ahead. What *did* his expression portend? He had no idea; he was no longer wholly inhabiting his body.

The judge on the far right glanced again at the paper and set it down. "You approached a Jew of the Ghetto, who knew enough to agree to nothing. You passed no money to him, and he undertook no steps to develop the secret network you proposed." He looked at the presiding judge. "What about the Arsenal?"

"He was certainly not secretive." The last judge now spoke

up. "He offended every official he spoke to, and their workshop was searched nightly." He shrugged. "They built a machine that would pump water if you kept a fire burning."

"The *ingegno*," somebody said. "The engineer said that Benveneto hoped to circumvent the terms of his government contract."

"How?" asked the demurrer. "They finished the device, or almost did, and left a mass of innocuous notes. Offending arsenalotti isn't evidence for conspiracy."

"The contracts said nothing about bronze, but the notes were full of it," said the fifth judge. "Bronze means cannon, which they wanted to divert for other purposes."

"What do you say to that?" the presiding judge asked.

"A bronze valve weighs less than a brick," Matteo replied. "The *ingegno* Gaspare wanted to build required three."

Some judges were glaring, others looked unreadable. "What has steam to do with caofa, anyway?" asked one testily. "Prisoner, answer that."

"Caofa and steam power? Why, they could both make Venice great," Matteo said simply. "Only savants know about steam, but all the Turkish empire drinks caofa. Perhaps it will make the Dutch great." With all in wreckage about him, he should marshal his forces to preserve what was worth saving. And what was that? Nothing.

The presiding judge stirred. "There are some questions still unanswered," he said.

"I object," said the judge who had demurred earlier. "We have found no evidence of criminal activity. To proceed as you suggest would be an abuse—"

"If the Avogadori find no evidence of a crime, they need not prosecute. Our commission is broader, and we are unencumbered by the constraints you seem to enjoy."

"I—"

"You don't think he should hear this? Oh, very well." The presiding judge lifted his chin to look past Matteo's shoulder. "Get him out of here."

➤ ➤ ➤

They never came for him. For four days he expected it hourly, soon guessing that the interrogators routinely held back, that anticipation and terror might pull the prisoner taut as a viola string. Far beyond the reach of either, Matteo experienced not remorse, nor defiance or the delusive bravado that crumbled quickly. His friend had been questioned under torment, as had others. What right had he to hope for less?

Gaspare; his father; the Venetian traders he had grown up yearning to emulate: they seemed to regard him in the darkness, all betrayed. He lost count of his meals (a true merchant never loses count) and slid into an aching *dies non juridicus,* like an open sore that neither festers unto death nor scabs.

At one point he suffered a fever, and blazed like a coal that will consume itself by morning. He imagined the interrogators finding him thus, and later recalled the encounter so vividly (he could see their indignant expressions upon feeling the fever radiate from his skin, as though this were a particularly unworthy trick) that he wondered if it had happened. No rope burns on his wrist, however; no unsocketed joints from having hung from the ground while . . . he could not think farther. While what was done to Gaspare happened, but hadn't, to him.

He was awake when he heard two pairs of boots approaching, though he could not say what he had been thinking a second earlier. The footsteps moved faster than those of turnkey leading prisoner, and stopped outside his cell. Matteo sat up, gathering what wits remained, as he heard a key scrape noisily in the lock. He had learned to avert his face as the door swung open, and shielded his eyes with a hand before looking back.

"Matteo Benveneto," someone said. Matteo was not used to being addressed by name. "Leave the door ajar and stand back," the voice added in a lower tone. A man in lawyer's robes stepped forward as the door swung to and the brightness dimmed. Matteo stood with an effort.

"My name is Ludovico Contarini," the lawyer said. "I work for the Avogadori di Comun." At one time, he and Matteo would have been about the same age. "Do you remember me?"

"No." Matteo was trying to think, and added, "I did not think my case was before the Avogadori."

"It is not, but it began with us, and we try not to let go of anything. Sit down," he added. Matteo sat, as far from the light as he could. The lawyer sat as well, surprising him even more by straddling the bench so that his back was to the door.

"The Avogadoria summoned you to a hearing, but the Council of Ten intervened, as it often does. The counselors were unhappy, among other things, because the Holy Office had come upon your name in the course of a routine case of divination. They felt, and in this we concur, that the ecclesiastical authorities cannot be allowed to intercede frivolously in the Republic's court system. Memories of the Interdict are too recent.

"Do you understand this?"

Matteo frowned. "No," he said.

"I thought not." Contarini reached into his robes. "Lean forward," he said in a softer tone.

Matteo tilted his head, puzzled, and a soft object was placed in his hands. "Drink," the lawyer said. The skin was small, and Matteo ran his fingers over its slithery shape in bewilderment. Speaking loudly, the lawyer pulled the cork and pushed it toward Matteo's mouth. Matteo raised it and drank. The wine stung the roof of his mouth, and his eyes filled with tears. He almost sputtered, then swallowed and drank again. Almost immediately the skin was empty, and was being removed from his hands.

"Prisoners are often too famished to comprehend what I must tell them. A mouthful goes far in your condition, though any more and you would fall over."

"Thank you," Matteo whispered. Then he added, slightly louder: "The Holy Office was mistaken in its allegations."

"About you? True enough, and you will be delighted to hear that they seem inclined to take no further action. I shouldn't tell you, but since it hardly matters now I will add that the Avogadori's report found no evidence that a mug of your caofa infusion will madden a workman."

Wit flickered, a spark from a cold ember. "Then I can go?" Matteo asked.

Contarini looked at him closely. "No. Agents of the Council of Ten had been following your movements for some time, and they found lots of disruptive activity. Did you really tell an official of the Arsenal that they should make caofa their *bevanda ordinaria*?"

Matteo was feeling the wine spread through his system. His head seemed clearer, though his chest tingled. "They consider that treason?"

"I'm not going to judge their proceedings, which remain almost wholly secret. It is only because we are able to send one *avogadore* to sit upon their courts that we know anything at all. Ser Giustinian, for whom I work, was among the four councilors who heard your case. He wrote a memorandum of your testimony, which we have already burned, lest one of their agents find it." He paused. "Are you listening?"

Matteo held himself still. "You are saying that I have been condemned."

"I am saying that sentence will be passed upon you this evening, when they meet. This afternoon, of course, they are all at Mass." His tone was faintly mocking. "The bridges are jammed right now, but the council will meet at nine. With the return of reports from abroad, they are now ready to settle your case."

"From abroad? I do not understand."

The lawyer sighed. "All your letters to foreign destinations have been opened and read. But since some were intercepted only once aboard, the reports on their contents must travel back by return voyage. Why do you think they have kept you here so long?"

"Our business correspondence?" Matteo shook his head in wonder. "Those letters were to our agents, buyers in Alexandria and the Levant! If I am to be judged by their contents, I shall be freed."

"Ser Benveneto, please do not think that. The Council of Ten does not have to prove your complicity before deciding to get rid of you. They deal with threats to the Republic's internal security, and one need not conspire with our enemies to disturb the social order. The council read your letters to learn whether you had fellow conspirators, not to determine what to do with you. They have doubtless already made that decision."

Matteo pondered, holding up the lawyer's words in the strange clarity of his present thoughts. The situation seemed no different from what had obtained before he arrived. "So why are you telling me this?" he asked.

"Because you have the opportunity to make a statement." Contarini turned and lifted something: a writing tray, with inkpot inlaid and a pen lying across it. "It has been six weeks since your appearance before the council, and Ser Giustinian maintained strongly that you should have the chance to add to your testimony."

"Add what?" Matteo asked. Then he caught an undercurrent of the lawyer's words. "Why was I never interrogated? That is how you supplement prisoners' testimony, is it not?"

Contarini was adjusting the tray on his lap. "The council is far from foolish. They realize their increasing unpopularity, and your case—the merchant who poured caofa—is well known. Ser Giustinian at length persuaded them that unless they were confident of finding something, they should not subject you to torment."

As they did my partner. What did Gaspare say, when he must have known what they wanted? Matteo could not enter that thought, it lay beyond seas he would never cross.

"A statement could hardly hurt you," the lawyer said. "The last report reached port yesterday, and the Ten are annoyed that it contains nothing. An expression of cooperation from you might salve their anger."

A statement could hardly help me. It certainly could not help his family or Gaspare. Though perhaps he was to think otherwise: doomed regardless, should he not take the opportunity to castigate his folly, absolve his associates, praise Venice? The temptation was tremendous: Matteo could feel the logic of its urgency, the needed supplement to the inadequate truths of his testimony. Provided freely despite, because, it had not been extracted by force.

"I . . ." You what? *I condemn myself.* As you should. Nothing true would do anything else.

"Yes?"

"I," and could say no more. From that word, nothing could follow.

"Gaspare," he said, "did nothing wrong. Neither did anyone

in my family. I urged them to let me import caofa, and they assented."

"Good," the lawyer said. He was writing. "And you?"

"Me?"

"What of your own actions?" The pen had paused.

"I brought this down upon them." Gesturing, simply, about him.

"Yes, but how?"

Matteo grimaced, fretful. "I told them all that. Jews, the Arsenal, our little booth." Shame settled over him like soot. "Everything I said before was true."

"Nothing more?"

What did the man want? "Everything," Matteo repeated. He sat silently as the lawyer finished writing.

"Very well," Contarini said at last. "This will be entered in evidence." He stood and turned toward the door. "They will probably send for you, and you will be taken across the Ponte dei Sospiri to the Palazzo. If this happens, you may have one more chance to say something before sentencing."

"I beg your pardon?" Matteo's attention snagged on this. "We are in the Palazzo."

"Here? No, this is the New Prison." Contarini looked at him oddly. "The cells of the *pozzi* are . . . only for short stays."

Matteo could not explain why this disclosure so disoriented him. Wretched as he was, his deracination was exacerbated to vertigo by this awareness, and when the guards came for him hours later ("Don't bring your bag," with a laugh), he staggered in the corridor and had to be pulled upright. His journey across the Bridge of Sighs, its windows glinting in the torchlight of nighttime Venice, produced a pang of such piercing misery that he halted in mid-passage, as though the wavering reflections on the canal and the shouts of protracted *battagliole* were signals of urgent import. A jab sent him stumbling forward, down the last dozen steps of the descending arch and into the Palazzo Ducale, returned at last.

The haggard man sitting on a far bench in the busy waiting room looked at him in astonishment, and it was only as he saw the expression change that Matteo recognized Gaspare. He was dressed like a worker, and bruise-colored bags sagged beneath each eye. The young man rose and was immediately forced back into his seat by the guards on either side.

"Matteo!" His gaze ran up and down, and Matteo realized what his beard, his filthy clothes, and hair must look like. He took a step forward and was restrained. There were another half dozen people in the room, including Contarini, who was looking at him. Matteo was tugged backward, but resisted for a second.

"You have been imprisoned this whole time?" Gaspare called. Matteo gestured: As you can see. He began to ask something, but was firmly pulled away; the two men were not to speak. He sat fifteen feet away against the opposite wall, exchanging mute looks with his friend until the double door opened and a guard stepped out.

"The prisoner Benveneto." He was hauled to his feet, but walked across the parquet floor unassisted. Into the inner chamber, whose dimness could no longer affect him, who had spent months in darkness.

There were more than five judges sitting this time; perhaps all Ten, although Matteo did not think he could count without using a finger.

"Matteo Benveneto," said one without preamble. "You have engaged in activities disruptive to the civil order of Venice, sought to make secret treaties with foreigners, and derided the wisdom of the city's traders and nobles to all who would listen.

"Had we found any evidence that you intended harm to the Republic"—he paused and looked hard at Matteo—"our response would have been immediate and terrible.

"Instead, we sentence you to ten years' exile from Venice and its possessions." He lifted a sheet of paper he had been holding in his lap, and a clerk hastened to take it.

"Have you anything to say?"

Matteo was too stunned to answer. He had expected merely to be hanged.

"No," he said at last. And then: "All I have said has been true."

The judge quirked his lips. "The same for me," he said. "Take him away."

❧ ❧ ❧

No one stopped him from walking unsteadily to Gaspare. "What did they do to you?" he asked.

"They confiscated the *ingegno*," the engineer said urgently. "Seized the workshop and our papers."

Matteo could think of no reply save "I am sorry." He looked into his friend's eyes. "But how are you?" he persisted.

"You must go now," said Contarini, coming up. He held a paper in his hand. "It is not good for your friend to be seen speaking to you."

Matteo looked stricken, but it was Gaspare who spoke. "That does not matter," he said firmly. He looked coldly at Contarini, who shook his head and walked over to the guards.

"Your family will fall liable for our costs," Gaspare said. "I tried to speak to them, but my father forbade any contact."

Matteo's heart contracted. "Do you still have your position?" he asked.

"I now work in the iron foundry," Gaspare replied with a shrug. "The dignities of the *bronzeri* are denied me."

"The Iron Age came after the Bronze," said Contarini briskly, returning with two guards in attendance. "Bid your friend farewell, Benveneto. You have a voyage ahead of you."

The two young men looked at each other. "What a mess," said Gaspare. "Weren't we going to win *ricchezza e fama*?"

"For our familes and for Venice, I believe." Matteo smiled, aching. "And some would spill over on us."

The guards' grip tightened on his arms. He took a step back, but turned to Contarini. "Between the Ages of Bronze and Iron came the Age of Heroes, remember?" The taunt was like a compress over pain.

"Heroics?" said the engineer, startled.

"Yes!" Matteo called as they led him away. "How do you like that idea?"

Gaspare smiled sadly. "*Se è da scherzo, è troppo; se è da vero, è poco,*" he said.

❧ ❧ ❧

Night had fallen, but Venice partied on, exultantly and combatively. The *battagliole* season would soon give way to Carnival, which was already showing its symptoms, a dinner guest who arrives earlier each year.

The lawyer conducted them down a series of corridors—public ones, the kind with windows along one wall. Matteo caught glimpses every seventh step: enormous shadows dancing on the sides of buildings; the Ponte della Paglia writhing with men, as though *pugni* were still battling for it. Shouts on the water, still dark with boats.

"The *popolani* seem to be rioting," Matteo observed. He added bitterly: "Despite my being in prison."

"I'm glad they don't know about the caofa shipment," Contarini muttered.

"Shipment? Which one?"

"Did I not tell you? The autumn galleys have returned, including the one from Alexandria bearing the reader's report on your letters. That ship also contains a large load of caofa beans."

"My caofa!" Matteo stopped dead. "What will my family do?"

"Well, they won't try to sell it, that's for sure." The lawyer favored Matteo with a grim smile. "I doubt your father even needs to be told."

A guard prodded him, and he resumed his pace. They descended a staircase, where an official coming up stared at them. Bearded and dirty, Matteo realized he still looked like a prisoner. And of course, he still was one.

"We are putting you on a ship tonight," Contarini was saying. "Your father has paid for passage, and I believe there is a purse awaiting you. You will not starve."

"Tonight?"

"Did you hope to bid your family farewell? You're still not thinking." They were on the ground floor, where he pointed them toward an exit. "You're headed upriver, if that's what you're worried about. No intolerable sea voyage."

Did they know everything about him? Everything that could be overheard, anyway. How many anonymous pages had been scribbled by informants, preserved in the city's archives, ready for kindling should the council want a fire? *Fatti,* compressed in imperishable millions, useful only to damn.

They emerged into one of the courtyards, too crowded and

garish with lights for Matteo to tell which one. "Mother of Jesus," Contarini swore. "This can't be happening in the Broglio."

Matteo laughed. "Listen to yourself," he said, but was drowned out by the cries of the revelers. Many were actually wearing carnival masks, illegal this early in the season. One carried a papier-mâché *uccello* beneath the front of his tunic, which he would abruptly display to scandalized shrieks.

"Let's get out of here," said Contarini. "*Not* through the Arco." Matteo looked toward the crowded entryway, where revelers were still pouring in. He could understand how the lawyer might not wish to get caught in the narrow Arco Foscari with a stream of boisterous *popolani*.

The crowds on the Molo San Marco were just as bad, but the open space was less alarming. The four men stood beneath the colonnade, looking out upon the teeming wharf and the waters beyond.

"It may be late before we put you on your ship," Contarini observed. He sighed. "I would enjoy a cup of caofa right now."

Matteo didn't think he heard him right. "Do you drink caofa?" he asked wonderingly.

"Not very often." The lawyer looked at him reproachfully. "You sold it near the Rialto, not the Piazetta."

And will next sell it where? The Hapsburg lands, of riverine trade, beer, and noisome snow, lay before him; what could it matter if he introduced caofa to such trolls? Exile, the condition of Jews and imprudent scholars, was a dish he would learn to keep down, employing his skills with tongues and accounts as a cobbler does his last.

One of the guards stirred. "Ser," he said. "There is a customs launch moving on the water."

"What?" But Matteo, understanding faster and looking with a practiced eye, saw it first. Beyond the heads of the crowd, perhaps sixty feet out in the broad Canale di San Marco, a pair of lamps disclosed the low form of a boat. Figures were crawling over bales, unnoticed though not stealthily. A gondola touched the launch, and more men debarked.

"It is the Nicolotti!" Contarini cried. "They are hijacking confiscated cargo!"

People on the edge of the quay had begun to notice, and were cheering. Did the Nicolotti win today, or were they trying to salvage their honor after a Castellani victory? It was the only question to ponder, and Matteo could not bring himself to ponder much. Let the *Sbirri* find a boat and go after them.

"They'll throw the shit in the canal," the other guard predicted. It seemed likely enough. Customs agents only took on seized goods, contraband or irregular wares, whose disposition was sufficiently problematic that—

"*My beans!*" Matteo screamed. He was down the steps and running before either guard could grab him. He nearly crashed into a big-bellied artisan wearing an admiral's hat, and before he could recover his balance a swarm of shouting youths had enveloped them. Matteo pushed frantically, expecting a hand on his collar at any second, and found himself squirming deeper into the crowd.

The revelers were close-packed but directionless, and Matteo was able to press between them. He saw an open space ahead and squeezed into it, to find an apprentice on hands and knees vomiting onto the cobblestones. A Pantaleone mask, already stepped on, lay beside him. Matteo bent and snatched it up.

He kept the smell of the canal ahead of him as he tugged the dirty mask over his face. Did it cover his beard? The eye holes finally slid into place, and Matteo could see the launch coming closer to the wharf. Hooded Nicolotti were gleefully tearing open the bales and hurling their contents toward the shore. The first handfuls fell short and rained into the canal, but within a minute the brawniest of them, posing like a new doge throwing coins into the multitude, managed to reach the edge of the crowd. The celebrants whooped and snatched at the largesse, which they examined and then flung at each other. One landed at Matteo's feet, and he picked it up.

It was a caofa bean, of course, but green as a pea. Matteo stared. His agent had managed to procure unroasted beans—still scalded so they couldn't be grown (although it would be worthwhile to try), but likely to remain fresh longer. Caofa that might taste as he remembered it from Alexandria.

Matteo closed his eyes, feeling his heart scalded. More beans pelted the crowd, which was booing lustily.

He did not hear the other craft approach until the increasingly excited pitch of the roar at last penetrated his misery. Faces were turned east, arms pointing. Matteo leaned over the edge of the water, though the occasional nearby splash warned of the pressure exerted by the crowd behind him, and saw the barge approaching.

The arsenalotti who manned it made no attempt to disguise their identities, and their narrow flatboat was recognizably the design used to move lumber through the Arsenal basins. But what Matteo saw was the splendid structure that rose from the deck, like the cabin of the doge's galley. Its underside lit by a blazing fire, massive as a gigantic bell and beautifully trimmed with brass fittings, the *ingegno* called forth cries of admiration.

Pipes protruded at right angles like flagpoles, and one of the arsenalotti reached to seize a valve, then snatched back his hand with a roar. As he danced about swearing and the crowd howled with laughter, a second man wrapped up his hand elaborately and turned the valve. Steam erupted in a white plume, and the crowd burst into cheers.

"Be careful!" Matteo cried inanely. "It's not a toy!"

But a toy was exactly what it was. The arsenalotti capered for the crowd, bowing and waving at their trophy—what impulse had moved them to bring it out? disdain for poor Gaspare? pride in Arsenal workmanship?—while the fire crackled merrily, as though heating soup. Their sweaty faces beamed in the reflected light, looking at the thousands lining the quay.

When they caught sight of the Nicolotti launch, they bellowed with outrage. Imprecations were hurled, and returned. The launch was slowly being turned about, while the barge made straight for it.

"*No!*" cried Matteo. The barge struck the smaller vessel amidships, and instantly men were leaping from one ship to the other. The crowd was swelling as word spread and people came running out of the Piazetta.

The explosion produced little light, just a tremendous thunderclap and darkness as the flames vanished into steam and debris. The shockwave struck Matteo an instant later, wet and hot. The expanding ball of steam was immediately diffuse enough to admit light, and dancing flames appeared on both boats. Men were screaming, falling into the water.

The quality of noise from the crowd had altered, but could grow no louder. Most of the *ingegno* was lying near the port side of the barge, which was listing markedly. With a groan it slid into the water and disappeared in a last gout of steam.

Both ships were bobbing empty, though there seemed to be some movement in the water. Splotches of flame dotted the bales like spilled grease, and began spreading to join each other. Within seconds the entire mound was ablaze, a pyre spilling black smoke. Matteo made a sound, but no one heard him.

Then the wind shifted, and they caught it. Roasting caofa, more fragrant than the drink itself, the finest smell in the world. Waves of it came off the boat, expanding to spread across the waterfront and Piazetta. Matteo was weeping, eyes streaming with hot air and cinders, even as the essence rose into his nostrils.

Borne on the lagoon breeze, the cloud spread across Venice. Carousers paused and sniffed with wonder; some recognized it and cheered. Enticing as it disappeared, the aroma expanded to fill every space open to it, an insubstantial dream of fragrant, marvelous caofa.